THE SILENCER SERIES

BOOKS 5-8

MIKE RYAN

WWW.MIKERYANBOOKS.COM

POINT BLANK

1

Recker was sitting on an oversized chair in a dark corner of the living room, waiting for his target to come home. The lack of light disguised his presence. Now that he knew the man's wife and two young kids would not be home, Recker no longer had to wait for the right opportunity to come along. After a brief stay in the hospital, the wife texted her husband she was taking the kids to her parents' house for a couple of days. It would take a little longer, though, for the bruises to go away.

Teresa Golden had been abused by her husband for at least a year from what Jones could figure out. It wasn't until this last time she had to go to the hospital for treatment. Though she told everyone she fell down the stairs, it was quite obvious it wasn't the case. Jones first got wind of her problem several weeks earlier when his software program picked up a text from Golden to her sister, saying her husband had hit her. With his target having children at the ages of nine and six, Recker wanted to take Richard Golden out permanently, fearful the abuse he unleashed on his wife would eventually spill over to their children. Jones, though, successfully debated that the loss of their father at such a young age would be devastating to them and made Recker reluctantly agree to his partner's plans. Jones argued he could continue to monitor the situation to make sure the kids were never harmed. Recker wasn't so sure Jones would be able to tell and the kids' case wouldn't get lost eventually under the sea of assignments they were likely to get in the coming months. Plus, Jones had convinced his partner he had to change his ways of handling things or else they'd always have to wind up moving after a few years. They had to start working towards handling killing as a final option and not the first choice.

Recker wasn't very fond of their newfound way of doing things, but he was willing to try it for a while. At least until he proved to Jones it wasn't working, which he suspected would be relatively soon. In the case of Teresa Golden, Jones hoped just working her husband over would be enough to scare him by letting him know he was being watched. Recker didn't believe it would work though. He feared giving Richard Golden some bruises of his own, would only make the man angrier and worse, thinking his wife had something to do with it and told someone about him.

Recker didn't particularly care for this less violent and friendlier, at least in his mind, version of himself. It'd been a long time since he pulled the trigger with a target standing in front of him, and while he still didn't enjoy it, he still believed it was as necessary as ever with some people. No matter what Jones said, or how he explained it, or how it benefited them by keeping their profile lower, Recker would never be convinced some people could be rehabilitated or scared into better behavior. Some people just had to be dealt with by violence. It's just the way it was.

Regardless of his own personal views, Recker was playing Jones' game for the moment. He'd been waiting in the Golden home for about an hour in anticipation of Richard Golden getting home from the bar, his usual stop every Friday after work. Recker was staring against the far wall at a big bow window, looking into the dark night air through an open slit of the brown curtains. He'd just taken his phone out to look at the time when he noticed a bright flash before a pair of steady car lights shone through the windows. He slowly put the phone back in his pocket as he calmly waited for his victim to walk through the door.

Recker heard the metal juggling of keys as they clanged against each other as Golden tried to steady his hand to unlock the front door. He could already tell Golden wouldn't be much of a problem. Judging by how long it took the man to open the door, Recker felt confident his target already had too much to drink. He was soon proven right as he watched Golden stumble his way into the house. Golden staggered his way into the living room and flicked on the lights via the switch on the wall. He did a double take and took a step backward, not sure if he was seeing correctly or if he was more under the influence of alcohol than he thought. He shook his head to shake off the effects of the booze as if it would suddenly make the man sitting in his living room go away. Once Golden realized his vision wasn't going away, he wiped the sweat from his hands off on his shirt, then his pants. He moved slightly to his right as he steadied himself on the back of a nearby chair, looking uncomfortable in the presence of a stranger in his home.

"Who the hell are you?"

"I'm uh, just a concerned citizen," Recker said.

"Get out of my house before I call the police."

"I think that would be a mistake on your part. Or if you'd like, we can wait until they get here and we can exchange stories. You can tell them how I broke into your house, I can tell them how much you've beaten up on your wife over the past few months, including her hospital trip yesterday."

Golden looked stunned that his visitor knew about his misdeeds.

"So, who are you and what do you want?"

"I told you, I'm just a concerned third party," Recker said.

"Did my wife put you up to this?"

"No, I come from an organization that oversees matters like this. We watch from a distance," Recker said, standing up.

As Golden watched his visitor get up from his chair, a lump went down his throat in anticipation of what the man might do to him. Recker never had a pleasant look on his face when he was on an assignment and he looked even more intimidating to someone whose mind was in a haze. Recker took a few steps toward his impending victim, causing Golden to panic. He ran back into the hallway, racing up the steps to get to his son's room, though in his condition it was more like stumbling up the stairs. Recker followed his target, though in no apparent hurry to inflict the damage he was about to unleash. He slowly and methodically walked up the stairs, knowing Golden wasn't in a state where he could easily slip away from him. And Recker wouldn't have even feared him if Golden's mind was clear, let alone in the alcohol infested haze he was in. But even though Recker didn't fear the man, it didn't mean he wasn't alert. Anybody could get in a lucky shot if he wasn't being careful or took his opponent for granted.

As Recker reached the top step, he was bracing himself for a surprise attack. As soon as both feet were on the second floor, he looked in both directions, not sure which way Golden went. As he looked to his right, he saw movement out of the corner of his eye. It was almost like a blur coming toward him, though Recker ducked just in time as he saw the baseball bat swinging at him. The bat shattered pieces of the corner of the drywall, plaster falling onto the floor. Once Recker rose up after the bat whiffed past him, he countered Golden's assault with a thunderous left hand across the cheek of the drunken man's face. Hurt from the blow, Golden staggered into the wall, unable to counter with an offensive of his own. With his target seemingly stuck to the wall, Recker moved in and alternated between his right and left hand across both sides of Golden's face in a furious fashion. Once Golden put his hands up to guard the onslaught across his face, Recker turned his attention a little lower. He gave Golden a few shots to his midsection, knocking the wind out of him and causing him to hunch over. As his victim crossed his arms and clutched at his stomach, Recker looked down and saw the baseball bat lying there. He picked up the wooden weapon with his left hand then cocked his right hand in order to deliver a vicious uppercut to Golden's jaw. The back of Golden's head smacked into the wall, putting a slight indentation into the drywall, and giving him an even bigger headache. As he put his hands against his chin, Recker grabbed the handle of the bat with both hands and swung at Golden's stomach. The man instantly fell to his knees as he struggled to breathe, feeling his ribs crushed by the blow. As Golden was on the ground on all fours, he began spitting out blood as he gasped for air.

In the heat of the moment, Recker's first inclination was to keep the punishment raining down onto Golden's body. He took a firm handle of the bat once more and waved it over his head, ready to deliver at least one more blow to the back of Golden's head, possibly a fatal one. But before he swung down, Recker thought of Jones' words to him, about trying to turn over a new leaf. As he looked down at his victim, unsure what to do, some of the rage inside Recker's body slowly evaporated. He took a deep breath and tried to compose himself. He slowly brought the bat down and held it with one hand at his side before he let it slip away from his fingers as it knocked around on the laminate flooring.

Figuring his time there was done, Recker delivered a final message by kicking Golden once more in the midsection. The blow caused him to crumple to the ground in agony. As he lay there on the floor, writhing in pain, moaning amongst the coughing and blood-spitting, Recker squatted to give him some lasting words to remember him by.

"This was just a little warm-up," Recker said. "In the coming weeks and months, I'll be keeping an eye on things. You'll never see me or know when I'm near. But if I hear you have laid another hand on your wife or kids, I'll be back. And I guarantee I won't be nearly as friendly as I've been tonight."

Recker stood back up and adjusted his clothes before taking a final look at his victim on the ground. He calmly walked back down the steps as if nothing had ever happened, without a care in the world. He continued right out the front door and into his car, driving away with the satisfaction from successfully completing another assignment, even if it wasn't quite to the level he would have liked.

Six months had gone by since Recker and Jones had relocated to Michigan. Instead of living inside the city limits of Detroit, they set up shop in the suburbs, just as they had done in Philadelphia. Dearborn was the city Jones had chosen. Located in Wayne County and part of the Detroit metropolitan area, Dearborn was one of the larger cities in the state and also the home of Ford headquarters. Their operation worked so well in Philly that Jones sought to replicate everything almost entirely in their new home, right down to the office setup. The only difference for the professor was, instead of getting his own apartment, he lived right there in the office. This one was a little larger than their previous one, with an extra room off of the main quarters. It was supposed to be for another small office but Jones turned it into a bedroom with a foldout couch which turned into a bed. Considering he spent most of his time in the office anyway, it didn't seem worthwhile to him to get his own place. With the couch, a TV, and a small table, it was all he needed. The bathroom had a small shower, and they kept a large refrigerator in the main office, so it contained all the comforts of home for him.

Recker, on the other hand, made a few minor changes from how he approached things in Philadelphia. Though he did get another small apartment as he did before, that was it. He didn't attempt to get to know any other players in town like he did with Vincent and Jeremiah, didn't try to establish any contacts the way he did with Tyrell, and he didn't make friends with anyone like Mia. He felt the risks outweighed the benefits in trying to do the same in Detroit. Plus, he just wasn't interested in complicating relationships the way they once were. Recker had just finished an assignment and walked into the office, finding Jones on the computer as he usually was. He plopped down on the couch and intentionally let out a sigh, loud enough for Jones to hear.

"Something wrong?" Jones said.

"No, not really."

"Then what was the sigh for?"

"Oh, nothing I guess," Recker said.

"I think I know you better than that. What are you not happy with? Did you not like the conclusion of your spousal abuse case?"

"No, it turned out fine. I did like you asked and just roughed him up some."

"You preferred taking him out permanently?"

"Well after his ribs heal, there's a good chance we'll wind up dealing with him again. You know I don't like to handle the same people more than once."

"Well, it's all in the interest of trying to keep a lower profile," Jones said. "We're trying to prevent what happened at the end of our last stop, remember?"

"Yeah, I understand your reasons for it, but it doesn't mean I have to like it. It also doesn't mean it's going to change anything. Might not kill anybody for the next year and we could still wind up in the same boat."

"Yes, I'm aware. But can we just try it my way for a little longer before you break out your artillery?"

"I guess," Recker said, letting out another sigh to indicate his displeasure.

"What else is bothering you? Is it just the fact you haven't killed anybody in six months and you're getting an itchy trigger finger?"

"That's part of it."

"Is killing really so much ingrained into your soul you can't find another way to settle things?" Jones said.

"We seem to go over this every couple of months since we've known each other. It's not the killing per se, it's that sometimes it's the only way to handle things. Why postpone the inevitable?"

"Because I don't believe it is inevitable."

"That's the fundamental difference between us," Recker said. "You believe people can change and I don't."

"You just don't want to believe people can change."

"David, out of all the people I've killed since we started this, which one of those do you honestly believe would have never committed another crime if I had let them live?"

"Well...," Jones said, struggling to come up with a name.

"Exactly."

"Part of it is self-preservation. I'm trying to prevent another ending like the one in Philadelphia."

"All the planning in the world won't change that."

"Well I disagree."

"You know my philosophy. You're just as likely to run into trouble as you are to walk. You're just getting there faster. Historically, Detroit's been one of the most violent cities in the country with some of the highest murder rates. Sometimes you gotta fight fire with fire. If I bump a few criminals off, is it really going to put me on the radar?"

"So, if I give you the thumbs up to kill the next ten people you come across, will it make you happier?"

"Eh," Recker said with a shrug of the shoulder.

Jones threw his hands up in frustration. "What is it you're looking for then?"

"I dunno."

Jones could see in Recker's mannerisms and body language, he was troubled by something. It couldn't have just been his unhappiness about the way they were now working. There must have been something else on his mind. After a few minutes of silence, Jones thought he might have come up with a solution. Recker hadn't spoken of Mia in about three months. Jones figured his friend might have been missing her.

"Is it Mia?"

"What?" Recker said.

"When was the last time you spoke with her?"

"A few months I guess."

"Is that why you're unhappy?"

"I didn't say I was unhappy."

"You didn't have to. It's written on your face," Jones said.

"Oh."

"So?"

In prior years, Recker might not have been so forthcoming and honest in his answers. But with the relationship and rapport he and Jones had built up, they no longer seemed to keep things to themselves anymore. They were even becoming comfortable in talking about their unpleasant thoughts they used to keep private. Recker briefly thought about not talking about it any further but eventually relented and came clean.

"I dunno. It's a bunch of things I guess."

"Such as?" Jones said.

"Our work here, our life here, Mia, Philly... all of it."

"It's not just the killing thing bothering you, is it? You're just unhappy about being here in general."

Recker took a deep breath before answering. "Yeah," he said. "I thought with time I'd be better with this."

"Well six months isn't exactly a lot of time."

"I know. But it's just... I dunno, I guess I just felt like Philly was my home. I never really had one before. I felt at ease there, comfortable. Moved all over ever since I was eighteen. Sticking in one spot always felt like a dream to me. Something unattainable. I guess since I finally got a taste of what amounted to one, it's been hard to let go."

"I can understand. But maybe it's because you haven't really tried to fit in here," Jones said. "I've noticed you haven't done the same things you did there."

"Trying to do what you suggested and keep a lower profile. Fewer contacts and people who know me."

"You know we can't go back, right?"

Recker didn't reply and just shrugged his shoulders.

"Mike, if we ever go back there, the CIA will latch onto you again in a heartbeat. You somehow dodged a bullet the last time. But you're not Houdini. The next time you most likely won't be so lucky."

"Maybe so."

"Is it because you miss Mia?"

"Well, I do miss her. But as far as I know she's still with whats-his-name."

"Josh."

"Yeah."

"So why haven't you established contacts here like you did in Philadelphia?"

"To try and avoid the personal entanglements," Recker said.

"Well I can understand such an approach in terms of pretty

female friends, but what about people like Tyrell, Vincent, Jeremiah? You haven't met any of those types here."

"I don't know. Just didn't care as much this time I guess."

"I wonder how Tyrell is," Jones said. "He grew on me."

"I talked to him about a month ago. He said he's doing all right."

"Did you tell him where we were?"

"No. He asked, and he wondered when we'd be back, but I didn't say."

As Recker sat there, Jones could tell his mind started drifting away to other things. The professor kept talking but Recker wasn't responding. It was clear to him Recker wasn't ignoring him, as the blank stare on his face was an indication his thoughts were elsewhere.

"Mike? What is it?"

Recker snapped out of his stare and looked over at his partner without saying a word. He just looked at him for a few moments as if he was still thinking.

"You said we couldn't go back to Philly because of the CIA," Recker said.

"Yes?"

"What if we could?"

"I'm sure there's a point in there somewhere though I can't seem to find it."

"If we could be assured the CIA isn't on my trail anymore, would you consider going back?"

"I suppose, theoretically, I would think about it," Jones said. "I don't know how you would go about getting such an assurance though."

"Only way I know of is to ask."

"Now you're just talking crazy."

"Lawson. If I could talk to her again, I could find out."

"And how do you propose on doing that?"

"If I can get a message to her, I can find out whether I'm still in the CIA crosshairs."

"Seems risky," Jones said.

"I think I can trust her. She easily could've killed me before."

"What makes you think she wouldn't try it the second time?"

"Faith."

"Faith? Since when was faith a word you employed?" Jones said.

"Gotta start sometime, right?"

"I'm not sure I'm on board with this plan of yours. We've successfully gotten away from the CIA, away from the police pressure in Philadelphia, we've started over, and you want to ignore it all and go back to it. There's just no logic to it."

"I never said I was logical."

Knowing he wasn't likely to talk his friend out of whatever was floating around inside his mind, Jones threw his hands up in defeat. "Do as you wish. I know you're probably not going to change your mind."

"I don't think it'll hurt just to have a conversation with her," Recker said.

"And like I said, I think you're just talking crazy."

2

It'd been a couple days since Recker had talked about reconnecting with Michelle Lawson and Jones had hoped he'd given up on the idea. The professor was mistaken, though, and disappointed when one morning Recker came into the office looking for one of his burner phones. Recker rifled through one of the desk drawers until he pulled one out.

"This one good?" Recker asked.

"They're all good, Michael."

"Well, not traceable, right?"

Jones stopped typing and looked at his partner with a strange face, not believing he actually asked the question. "Do you really believe I would have a traceable phone?"

"I'm just making sure."

"Can I ask what you're planning on doing with it?"

"I think you already know the answer," Recker said.

"That's what I was afraid of. You're really planning on calling her?"

"Why not? Don't you think it's worth knowing if they're going to keep on pursuing me or whether they've got other fish to fry? The worst she can say is I'm still on their radar."

"Assuming she's going to tell you the truth," Jones said.

"I think she will."

"And how do you plan on getting in touch with her? Do you have her number in your little black book?"

"Don't be ridiculous. You know I don't have a little black book. I'll find her the easiest way possible. I'll call up the agency and ask for her."

Recker immediately called the agency's main number, and while he knew it was unlikely he'd be connected to her right away, he left a message for her.

"Just tell her John Smith would like to speak with her. She'll know who I am."

Recker left a callback number and tossed the phone down on the desk.

"When do you think you'll hear back from her?" Jones said. "Assuming you do?"

"She'll call back. Even if it's just out of curiosity. I'd expect it to be pretty quick."

The call came even quicker than Recker expected. His phone rang about thirty minutes after leaving the message for Lawson. Recker and Jones looked at each other as they heard the ringer go off, neither expecting it to be quite so soon. Jones didn't appear to be pleased the call was being returned at all and began squirming in his seat as he anticipated the contents of the conversation. Recker walked over to the phone, and after the fourth ring, finally picked up.

"You're faster than I anticipated," Recker said. "I wasn't expecting you to call for a little while yet."

"Well, when a rogue super-agent who's missing for several years leaves me a message, I usually assume it's urgent," Lawson said.

"Fair enough. I was hoping to have another discussion with you."

"Seems like we are, doesn't it?"

"How about we do it in person? Phones have more ways of being traced than most people realize."

"Where and when?"

"How about tomorrow, say noon?"

"I think I can manage that. Where?"

"Are you still in New York?"

"Yes."

"There's a pizza joint on eighth called Anthony's. I'll be inside in one of the booths waiting for you," Recker said.

"Can't make it at a park or something?"

"Too public. I wouldn't want to meet another of those treacherous darts you used like last time in case I've misjudged you."

"I guess I could go for a slice, anyway."

"I'll see you then."

Recker put the phone down on the desk and kept his hand on it as he looked at the wall, deep in thought. Jones watched him for a few moments, waiting for him to reveal his plans in more detail. Though Jones overheard the parts of the conversation he most needed, he still assumed there was more to it. After several minutes ticked by, he tired of waiting,

"Are you going to share the gist of the conversation with me?"

"Weren't you listening?" Recker said.

"Yes, but all I got out of it was that you're meeting her in New York tomorrow at noon at a pizza place called Anthony's."

"That's all there was."

"How do you know this is a good spot to meet?"

"I've been there before. When I worked in Centurion, I visited the place a few times for business purposes. It's a busy place, people going in and out all the time. Plus, there's a back door."

"That doesn't really make it any better than meeting out in the open," Jones said. "All that means is that after your meeting is over, that there could be people waiting for you outside. It doesn't really change anything."

"You're right. But don't you think it'd be nice to know if I still have to look over my shoulder?"

"Yes, it would be. But I don't know if the risks outweigh the potential rewards."

"David, I just don't want to keep staying here, wondering if they're coming in another six months. I want to know. And if it means they take me for good this time... well, I guess it's better to just get it over with."

A peculiar look came over Jones' face, worried about his friend's mental condition. Considering Recker was the ultimate survivor, a fighter, someone who never quit, to hear him talk about getting it over with was somewhat alarming. Recker walked over to a computer and started figuring out his itinerary. It was over six hundred miles to go along with a nine-hour drive to head back to New York. It'd be the first time Recker set foot in New York since his time at Centurion ended. He thought back to a few of the meetings he'd previously had at Anthony's Pizza, where he gleaned information for an upcoming assignment from confidential sources. Though he knew Jones had a valid point about walking into trouble once he left the restaurant, it wasn't totally accurate. One of the reasons Recker picked Anthony's was because of his history there. Recker got to know the owner of the joint and knew that through the kitchen was a door leading to an upstairs office. From the office was a fire escape leading to the roof, and the businesses attached to it. He'd gotten in trouble there once before with some people who weren't what they appeared to be and had to use the route as an escape path. It was one of the reasons Recker befriended the owner, though he led him to believe he was an undercover FBI agent, since CIA operatives were not supposed to conduct operations within United States borders. It was always a good idea to make friends in places you might have to make a quick and unexpected exit out of.

"When do you plan to start this trek of yours?" Jones asked.

"Well, if I leave by one, then I should get there about ten or so. Should be enough time if I don't hit traffic."

"Do you not plan on sleeping?"

"I figured I'd knock off a little early tonight. If I go to bed around eight or nine, it'll give me three or four hours. That's enough," Recker said. "Think you can hold down the fort for a day until I get back?"

Jones faked a smile. "I'm sure I can manage."

The rest of their day went by without incident or any issues needing immediate attention. That enabled Recker to enact his plan by leaving the office at eight o'clock to get a few hours of sleep before his big meeting. Right on time, he woke up after a three-hour sleep and left at 1am. Jones didn't get much sleep either, spending most of the night tossing and turning as he worried whether Recker was making a mistake and walking into another trap. He probably wouldn't feel at ease until his partner texted or called to let him know the meeting was over, or what was more likely, when Recker was back in Michigan.

Recker arrived in New York a few minutes after ten and spent an hour driving around the city. Just being back there after such a long time away felt soothing to him. Until he made his way to Philadelphia, he'd always considered New York home, though for different reasons than how he considered Philly. It's where the Centurion offices were and he often stayed there between missions, at least before he met Carrie. Cruising around the streets, it almost felt like he'd never left. He remembered the street names, the buildings, the businesses scattered throughout the city, it actually seemed therapeutic for him. After reminiscing to his satisfaction for a while, Recker finally wound up at Anthony's at 11:30. One of his personal rules was to always be first at a meeting, just in case shenanigans were about to happen. Sometimes it couldn't be helped when he arrived at a conference later than whoever he was meeting, but when he was able to, he liked to scout around ahead of time. Walking into Anthony's, the place hadn't changed in the time he'd been gone. The tables, the counters, the menus, even the pictures on the wall. Everything was exactly the same as he remembered them. The place was starting to fill up, but Recker saw an open booth near the back of the establishment against the far wall. He'd no sooner sat down when he heard someone shout his name. Well, his former name anyway.

"John!" a man shouted.

Recker took a sharp look to his left and saw Anthony, the shop's owner, with a big smile on his face and walking toward his table. The two shook hands as Recker greeted his acquaintance, who sat down across from him.

"I was sure I'd never see you again," Anthony said, almost in disbelief now Smith was there again in his restaurant.

"It's been a long time."

"Yeah, it's been what, three, four years?"

"Yeah, about that."

"Well you're looking good. Where you been all this time?"

"I've been all over. Overseas, Philly, Michigan, spent some time in Ohio, they're running me ragged."

"What are you doing back in town? Here to stay?"

"Got a meeting here in a little bit. Figured I'd do it in the best pizza shop in town," Recker said, smiling.

"Hey, you know it. You want a slice and a Coke?"

"That's an offer I couldn't refuse."

"My man, I'll be right back."

A minute later, Anthony brought back two slices of pizza and a soda for his guest. The owner sat down so they could continue their conversation as his guest ate. Recker nodded his head, looking satisfied as he quickly downed the first piece of pizza.

"I've missed this," Recker said.

"How could you not miss the best pizza in town?" Anthony asked, laughing.

"You still have the office upstairs?"

"Yeah. Why? You gonna be needing it?"

"Ahh, you never know. I don't think so, but it's good to know it's there if the need arises."

"Some things never change, huh? I'll make sure the entrance by the kitchen's unlocked for you just in case."

"I appreciate it."

The two talked for a few more minutes before Anthony left, attending to other customers. The counter was starting to get busy. Recker finished his last remaining slice as he waited for his counterpart to arrive. He didn't have long to wait. He pulled out his phone to look at the time. It was 11:55. He took a quick look around the restaurant and saw a familiar face coming through the front doors. Lawson also liked to arrive ahead of schedule, just not as early as Recker. She stood near the counter as she looked around, not yet seeing Recker near the back. He took a deep sigh before revealing himself, just in case it was his last taste of freedom for a while. After a few more seconds, Recker stood up in front of his table in order for Lawson to see him. Once they locked eyes, she hesitated and looked away for a moment. She ordered a slice before walking over. Recker remained standing until she found her way to his table, not sitting down until she did as well. Lawson put a file folder down on the table as she nestled into the booth.

"Thanks for coming," Recker said.

"I haven't had a good piece of pizza in a while," she said, smiling. "So, what's this about?"

"A few things I guess. How'd you make out with the mess we left back in Philly?"

"Davenport's been fired and will never hold a government position again."

"And Agent 17?"

"It was wrapped up to everyone's satisfaction."

"And John Smith?"

"His case was closed since he's living a quiet life in Detroit."

Recker's mouth dropped open as he looked at her, surprised she knew where he was.

"Yes, we know where you are," Lawson said.

"How?"

"A good secret intelligence agency doesn't divulge their secrets."

Recker snickered as he took a sip of his soda.

"Is that what you're worried about?" Lawson asked.

"What makes you think I'm worried about anything?"

"Well I assume it's not because you decided to take me up on my job offer. You wouldn't have requested this meeting if you were."

"You're smart."

"Thank you. It's nice to hear it sometimes."

"I guess I just wanted to know if I was still on the radar."

"Why? Figuring on blowing something up in Detroit?"

"Not yet. I guess I'm just getting tired of looking over my shoulder and wondering what's coming," Recker said.

"If you're in the tunnel and seeing the light of an oncoming train, it isn't gonna be us. You're clear. Your case is closed, you're not deemed a threat in any way to this agency or any other."

"Is that only when you're around?"

"No," Lawson said, opening up the folder. She removed some documents and slid them across the table for Recker to look at.

The papers consisted of memos and reports about Recker. It had different communications from Lawson, Director Roberts, as well as a few others talking about their findings in regard to Recker. They all seemed to agree their time and efforts were better spent elsewhere. He was no longer deemed a security risk, or a threat. Lawson assumed he would have trouble believing it just coming from her mouth and figured bringing some proof would help soothe his mind a little.

"You're free. You can go and do whatever you want without looking for us," Lawson said.

"Even back to Philly?"

"Even back to Philly. If we really wanted you, we would've picked you back up again when you set foot in Detroit six months ago."

"Are you really not going to tell me how you managed to figure out where I was?"

Lawson looked around, then leaned forward before spilling her secret. "You probably should've gotten a new car after our last encounter."

Recker leaned back, with a peculiar look on his face, getting the hint. "No, I checked the car inside and out before I left."

"You probably should've checked the license plate."

"There's nothing on the license plate, I looked."

"You know the square little registration sticker in the corner? We replaced it with one which doubles as a GPS tracker," Lawson said.

Recker smiled, realizing she got one over on him. "I must be slowing down in my old age."

"We can be pretty clever sometimes. You know how it is. So, are you ever gonna tell me about the guy you're working with?"

"Who?" Recker asked, feigning ignorance.

"You know, the smaller guy you work with. Kind of looks like a nerd."

"I don't know who you're talking about."

Lawson smiled, impressed he was going the distance with his story, not that she really expected anything less. She probably would have been more surprised if he'd actually admitted he had a partner. Not one to give up herself, she opened her folder up again and pulled out some pictures and slid them across the table. Recker hesitantly picked up the 4x6 photos and went through them one at a time. He peered up over the pictures at Lawson, wondering how he could have been so sloppy. Every picture was one of him, or Jones, or of the both of them together since they moved to Detroit.

"So, what are you going to do with these?" Recker said.

"Nothing. I didn't bring them to blackmail you or warn you of anything. Just to let you know we're aware of your whereabouts. If we wanted you, we'd have picked you up already. I figured the pictures would be more proof for you to trust me. I recall you saying something to me about not trusting people. I figured it still applied."

"You can't put a name to the face?"

"No. We've run him through all the databases we have and we can't seem to come up with anything. Who is he?"

"Who's asking? Michelle Lawson the person? Or Michelle Lawson the CIA agent?"

"Does it make a difference?"

"Maybe."

"Let's say Michelle Lawson the person then."

Recker nodded, then looked away at the bustling crowd, trying to figure out how he'd phrase the answer. "His name is David. His situation is a little different from mine."

"David what?"

"Doesn't really matter. Neither name I'd give you is his real identity anyway and it wouldn't come up in your computers, regardless."

"So why him? What made you throw in with him?" Lawson said.

"He actually sought me out," Recker said, remembering their first meeting at the airport. "He gave me an interesting proposition, and I decided to take him up on it."

"Doing what? Playing hero?"

"He wanted to make a difference somewhere. Help good people who needed help. Plus, I needed a job and a reason to keep going after London."

"I'm guessing he's pretty good with computers."

"Yeah, you could say."

"He'd have to be to hide his identity even from us, not to mention get the information you guys need to do what you're doing," Lawson said. "So, is he on the run too?"

"Uh, not from you. Why all the interest in him? Wondering if he's a former agent too?"

"No. It's more of a personal curiosity. Just wondering how and why you got into what you're doing now. So, what makes you wanna go back to Philly?"

"I dunno. I guess I just felt a connection there. Like I belonged."

"Well, you won't hear from us again, unless you decide you want to join up again."

"Not likely."

"The police now know you there, though, so you'll have to deal with them on your own. But according to Commissioner Boyle, half the force wants to shake your hand, though the other half probably wants to shoot you on sight. But you know we can't do much about it. Your problem."

"I know," Recker said. "What about you? Eventually they're gonna realize I'm back. Are they gonna give you a hard time about not taking me in?"

"Eh, not really my concern. I don't answer to them. If they ask, I'll just say you escaped."

"And if they ask for your help again?"

"We're not in that business anymore. We have other, more pressing matters to attend to."

Satisfied with her answers so far, Recker started turning the questions around. "So, what do they have you working on these days? Besides keeping tabs on me obviously. You hunting down a new rogue agent?"

"No, not at the moment. Right now, they have me on special assignment. For the past few months I've been helping to run Centurion since they're down a director. As soon as they appoint a new head, they'll switch me to something else."

"I hope you've eliminated the program where they terminate good agents for no apparent reason."

"Yeah, it's being run a little differently these days. Hopefully, for the better."

"If you're involved, I'm sure it is."

Recker was still fumbling with the pictures, periodically looking at them, but eventually stopped and attempted to slide them back over to his guest. Lawson, though, returned the favor and slid them back to him.

"You can keep them if you like," Lawson said. "I don't think we really have need for them anymore."

Recker smiled, appreciative of the gesture. "If you're not careful, I might actually end up liking you."

"Now that'd be a catastrophe."

"This little meeting of ours almost seems like it's going too well. You don't happen to have a few men waiting outside, ready to pump some lead into me, do you?"

"Now where would you get such a crazy idea?"

"It might've been mentioned to me somewhere along the drive here."

"Your partner thought it was a bad idea, huh?"

"Something like that," Recker said. "He's not as trusting as I am."

"Well you can take those pictures back to him and let him know neither of you have anything to fear from us. You don't have to look over your shoulder anymore."

3

Recker's meeting with Lawson took much longer than he had anticipated as they didn't wrap things up until two o'clock. They enjoyed talking to each other openly and honestly, without the need for secrecy as so often summed up meetings with people in their line of work. By the time they finished, Recker was convinced he had nothing to fear from her. He also knew he didn't have to worry about being shot once he left the restaurant, as Jones had suggested. When Recker did finally leave the restaurant, he drove around the city for another hour, soaking in the sights of The Big Apple before he returned to Michigan.

He got back to the Detroit area around midnight and immediately went to his apartment to catch up on some much-needed sleep. Before doing so, he let Jones know everything went OK at the meeting and he'd fill him in when he got to the office in the morning. Recker didn't provide any other details. He figured if he dropped the bombshell that the CIA still knew where they were, and had the pictures to prove it, neither of them would wind up sleeping. With the way Jones' mind worked, Recker knew he'd stay up all night peppering him with questions on how it was possible and trying to think of a way to get out from underneath their grasps.

Once Recker arrived in the office in the morning, he was armed with some breakfast sandwiches, along with the photos Lawson had given him. He figured it was about to be a long day. He just hoped Jones didn't freak out as much as he thought he would. After both sat down to start eating, Recker reached into his pocket to remove the pictures. He placed them face down in front of Jones.

"What's this?" Jones asked, putting the remaining half of his sandwich down.

"A gift from my meeting."

Jones wiped his hands and looked at his partner, sure he was not going to like what he was about to see as he picked them up. There were ten pictures in all, and with each one he passed, Jones' face became even more flabbergasted. He didn't glance up at Recker one time as he perused the pictures. Recker was trying to analyze his friend's face as he looked through the photos and could obviously see Jones had become uncomfortable with what he was seeing, though he didn't voice any concerns yet. Maybe he was just too surprised for him to vocalize anything. After looking through the set of pictures three times, Jones finally was able to take his eyes off them as he set them back down on the table.

"These were from Ms. Lawson?"

"Yep," Recker said.

"She knows where we are. She knows who I am."

"Well, not quite. They now know you're involved and have a picture of you. Fortunately for you, your face isn't recognized in any of their databases. They haven't actually put a name to you yet."

"I guess that's something," Jones said, only looking slightly relieved. "So, what does all this mean? Should we be reinforcing the doors today?"

Recker let out a small laugh. "No. We're in the clear. They're not coming for us, or more specifically, me. They've known where we were since the day we got here. If they wanted us, they would've gotten us long before now."

"So, what now then? What are their plans?"

"They have none. Lawson said I've been taken off their to-do-list. I don't have to look over my shoulder anymore. No one's coming."

Jones looked at him incredulously with the revelation. "Are you sure you can believe her?"

"Well, she's had the chance to take me out twice. There's no logical reason to let me walk away twice."

"I see," Jones said, seemingly having a hard time processing everything. "And uh... what of me? Am I included in that?"

"They're not after you. She wondered who you were more out of a personal curiosity than professional interest. She gave me those pictures so I'd believe that they weren't after us. It's proof that they could've taken us out at any time since we've been here. They know this office and where we are at this exact minute. They don't care."

"Startling."

"The man who originally put the kill order on me is no longer in control of Centurion," Recker said.

"This is... a lot to take in right now."

"I know. But it's also grounds for us to go back to Philly, right? Admit it, you don't like it here as much as back there, do you?"

"I will admit a certain fondness for there that I have not yet acquired here. But that may also be that I don't get out as much here, with having the bedroom off the main office," Jones said.

"We established something there. A name, an identity, an

intimidation factor... we haven't gotten that here. And maybe in time we will, but we already invested ourselves there."

"And the police? Did Ms. Lawson give you assurances about them as well?"

"No, of course not. The police are our concern. But that's the way it's gonna be no matter where we go. We can handle them, though. Besides, Lawson told me half the police force there is on our side, anyway."

Jones took another bite of his sandwich before leaning back in his chair, arms crossed, giving the matter more thought. He wasn't against the move back to Philadelphia, and he'd probably enjoy it more than he'd let on, but part of him felt that by moving again so soon, they just wasted the last six months. But he did miss the city streets, the vibe of the place, the few relationships he did have, such as Mia, and even the few times he'd met or talked with Tyrell. He still owned the office and laundromat, so it'd be easier moving back there than it was setting up shop in Detroit. Recker had moved to another computer to work on things, giving Jones some time to himself to collect his thoughts on the subject. After thirty minutes, Jones was ready to announce his opinion.

"If I do agree to go back, we cannot just pick up and leave. We have a few things to finish here, people who need help. I don't want to just abandon them."

"Agreed," Recker said.

"But I can start the process by unplugging the software program, so to speak, so we don't get additional cases."

"How many do we have now?"

"Four. I would think as soon as they're done, we can head back."

They talked a little while longer about the ramifications of moving back, with Recker wanting to make sure Jones was completely on board and not just giving him lip service. The longer they discussed it, the more comfortable Jones became with it, and sounded just as excited as Recker was to be about going back. He did miss it too; he was just more convincing with putting up a front to disguise it. Recker immediately started working on their remaining cases, wanting to wrap things up as quickly as possible. He hoped to be back in Philadelphia within a week, which was probably a bit of a reach.

Once Recker latched onto an idea and really got behind something, it would be wise for everyone to get out of his way. Though Jones had doubts he'd be able to finish the four cases within a week, Recker worked overtime and sacrificed a few hours of sleep every night in order to accomplish it. Eight days after they agreed to return to Philadelphia, they wrapped up all their remaining cases in Detroit. Except for one last hiccup. Jones had a moving van outside the office and most of their things had already been removed from the office. But he left one computer running until the very last minute, just in case of an emergency. He had a fear how the moment they left, something major would go down and somebody would get hurt or killed. Something which could've been prevented if they were still around. Jones was standing by the computer, getting ready to shut it off and pull the plug, when he got one final alert. It was a familiar name and phone number. Recker just finished putting the last of the boxes in the van when he walked into the office and saw Jones standing in front of the computer.

"What's up?" Recker asked.

Jones turned to him without saying a word. His face did all the talking Recker needed though.

"Don't even tell me," Recker said. "David, we're ready to go."

Jones didn't reply and turned back to the computer, looking at the screen. Recker, slightly agitated Jones was considering another case when they were just about to leave, walked over to him. His first inclination was to not look at anything and turn everything off for Jones, then they wouldn't have to bother with anything. But, like Jones, Recker couldn't just turn his back on someone who legitimately needed help. After all, it was what he did, what he lived for. Reluctantly, Recker stood beside his partner and looked at the screen. After quickly scanning the monitor, Recker looked a little more closely at the information. His face turned from annoyed to concern, then to anger. He had a feeling this would happen. Some people just couldn't change their spots. The two men stood there silently, both knowing what was about to happen. Jones looked over at Recker, and sighed, feeling like this might've been his fault. If he'd have let Recker do what he wanted to do in the first place, Teresa Golden might not have been suffering from the new batch of bruises at the hands of her husband. Jones picked up another text message sent from Teresa to her sister, detailing the latest attack. Though her sister implored her to go to the authorities, and the hospital, Teresa refused both requests, not wanting to get anyone else involved. Richard Golden blamed his wife for him getting beat up, believing she must have gabbed about his infractions to somebody.

"I guess he didn't get the message," Recker said.

"I should've let you do what you wanted from the start."

"You can't blame yourself for other people's actions."

"But you predicted this would happen. I should've listened," Jones said.

"Yeah, but you can't take responsibility for it. It's on them. Not on you."

"Should we take care of this before we go?"

Recker reached inside his coat and removed a gun, double checking to make sure it was loaded. "Absolutely. But we'll take care of it my way."

"Understood."

"Why don't you finish up here and start heading back? I'll do what I have to do then meet up with you somewhere along the road."

Recker immediately left the office and got in his truck to meet Golden before he got to work. Recker wasn't going to be able to catch him before he left his house and he wasn't sure if his wife and kids would still be there, anyway. And Recker wasn't going to do what he had to in front of them. Golden worked in downtown Detroit at an office building with a parking garage. Recker would be there waiting for him. From their initial investigation of Golden, before Recker dusted him up inside his home, they knew Golden got to work at nine o'clock every day. Recker got to the garage at 8:30. He parked near the entrance inside so once he saw Golden arrive, he could follow him to his spot. At 8:55, Recker spotted Golden's car enter the garage. He gave Golden a short lead of a few seconds before tailing him. Once Golden pulled into a spot against the wall, Recker pulled up behind the rear bumper of the car, blocking it from reversing. Golden was consumed with getting some of his things together and didn't even noticed the impending danger looming. Recker noticed there were no security cameras near the entrance, so he didn't have to worry about being spotted. It wouldn't have concerned him if there were since he was leaving the city right after this, anyway.

Recker got out of his car and walked around the hood until he stood just outside of the driver's side window. Golden was leaning over toward the passenger side seat where he was looking through some papers, still oblivious to the dangerous man who was only inches away on the other side of the glass. Recker figured he'd make a grand entrance and took the handle of his gun and smashed the window. Golden jumped in his seat, surprised at the falling glass. He put his arms up over his head to try to protect himself. Once he put his arms down and looked at the man on the other side of his window, he started to shake. It was partly out of fear, knowing what his attacker was capable of, remembering what he did to him before. The other half of him was shaking because he was injured, as small pieces of glass lodged into his face and arm. Recker turned the gun around and pointed it at the frightened man.

"Guess you didn't get the message from our last meeting," Recker said.

"Go to hell. What I do with my family is my business."

"Wrong answer."

Recker didn't wish to continue the conversation any longer or put off the inevitable. He simply pulled the trigger and fired two rounds into Golden's chest. Recker's victim slumped over across the middle console, perishing immediately upon the bullets entering his body. Recker stood there for a moment, analyzing his work, and shook his head.

"Some people just don't get it," Recker whispered. "Give them all the chances in the world and they just don't get it."

Recker then put his gun away and went back to his car. He peeled out of the garage and made his way to the highway to trek back to Philadelphia. He sent a text message to Jones to let him know his work was done and how he'd meet him back in the office when they arrived back in town. With Jones getting a head start on him, he was already moving some of the boxes into the office by the time Recker got there nine hours later. Jones didn't bother asking him any questions about how things turned out with Golden. He knew what had been done. They finished unpacking and moving all their equipment back into the office, getting finished around midnight. Considering neither had bothered to get a new apartment yet, they each wound up taking separate couches to sleep for the night.

When they awoke in the morning, Jones wasted no time in getting his computers up and running. He had hooked everything up the night before, but running his programs and getting them to coordinate the way he wanted, took some time. As he did it, Recker restocked his gun cabinet with the weapons he'd just stashed in the corner before going to bed.

"How long you gonna take?" Recker asked.

"Not too much longer. Everything should be ready to go in an hour or so," Jones said. "It will take a little longer until we start getting cases again. The program will have to start over again and go through mountains of data before it starts spitting things out."

"Oh."

"Itching to get back to work already?"

"Just wondering what I'll do until then."

"Why don't you get out, see the city. I'll let you know when it's time."

"Maybe I will."

"Maybe let Mia and Tyrell know we've returned. Maybe look for a new apartment."

"That reminds me, what are you gonna do for a new place?" Recker asked.

"I hadn't really given it much thought. The place in Detroit seemed to work well, so I thought I may just stay here."

"But there's no extra room here."

"No, but I don't really need much," Jones said. "I can sleep on the couch. We've got a bathroom, a TV, I don't really require much else. Besides, there's nobody else coming in here except you and me so I don't have to worry about any unwelcome visitors."

"You want me to just stay here too?"

"No, of course not. Don't be foolish. Go get a new place, enjoy your apparent newfound freedom. You don't appear to have to hide from the CIA any longer, so you shouldn't stay cooped up in here. But don't forget, one of us is still a government fugitive, so staying in here will be fine for me. I have no complaints," Jones said, forging a smile.

"OK, well, let me know when everything's ready."

"You'll be the first to know."

Recker thought about his living arrangements and figured his last apartment worked fine for him. It was in a nice area and relatively close to everything. When he went back to see if anything was still available, his old apartment had been rented out, but there was another unit almost identical to his, the difference being this one had a small balcony off the living room. When he left for Detroit, he left most of his furniture behind. The only thing he took with him was the TV. He signed the papers for the apartment, but the unit wouldn't be ready until the following day, which gave him some time to order some furniture so he wouldn't be sitting on the floor for too long.

With his living situation taken care of, Recker started driving around the city again. Though he wasn't going anywhere in particular, and didn't have a specific destination in mind, he somehow found himself at the hospital where Mia worked. Outside of Jones, she was his closest friend, so maybe it was just instinctual when he wound up there. Once he parked, Recker sat in his car for a few minutes, wondering if he really wanted to go in. Not that he didn't want to see her, but it had been three months since they'd talked. He wasn't sure what type of reception he'd get. He never wound up telling Mia where he was going and she was the last one to try to communicate. She left a text message along with a voicemail Recker just never bothered returning. He wanted to, but something kept nagging at him to just let her go. For her own sake. He figured if he was gone, unlikely to ever return, she'd have been better off putting him out of her memory. And she couldn't if they continued talking. Part of him wondered if he would be better off driving away, not even telling her he was back. But he knew, somehow, someway, she'd find out he'd returned, and it'd probably be worse if she found out than if he told her himself.

After ten more minutes, and a lot of thought and reflection, Recker decided to go in. He asked at the front desk whether Mia was working, and once it was confirmed, he went over to the cafeteria, their usual meeting spot. Though he didn't know her exact schedule, going from memory, when she worked day shift, he figured he had an hour or two to wait until she came down for lunch. It gave him more time to reflect on their relationship. It was additional time to think he really didn't need as he was already beating himself up over how he handled things with her. He sat at the back table and fiddled around with his fingers as he stared at his hands, wondering what he was going to say to her when he saw her. This was probably the most nervous he'd ever been.

And he was right. It was a long wait. Two hours that felt like it was two days. Mia walked into the cafeteria and got some food, not initially seeing her visitor. She didn't see him until she was looking for a seat in the crowded room. Recker was still fumbling with his hands and looking down at the table and never even saw her come in. When Mia's eyes finally did locate him, she couldn't believe what she was seeing at first. She looked away, hoping it was just a vision that would somehow go away. Maybe she'd been working too hard. It was no vision, though, no mind trick. She locked eyes on him once again, and instead of being happy he was there, anger started flowing through her veins. For the last three months, she tried to get him out of her system. Without hearing a word from him, she could only assume the worst, he was dead. On the nights when she convinced herself he was still alive, she could only assume he just didn't want anything to do with her anymore.

As she stood there, holding her tray, she struggled with whether she wanted to go sit with him and see what he wanted. She debated whether she'd be better off sitting by herself and pretending he wasn't even there. He didn't appear to be paying much attention anyway, she could quickly eat and be gone before he knew she was there. But she quickly dismissed the idea since Recker knew where she lived. He could always show up at her door. Or he could just come back another day. Even if she wanted to avoid him, she knew she couldn't do it for long. She eventually figured it would be better to see what he was doing there and walked over to his table. Recker was so fixated on his hands and his own thoughts he never even noticed someone standing across from him. It wasn't until Mia forcefully slammed her tray down on the table that he took his eyes off his hands. He looked up at her, licked his lips to remove the dryness, and gave a nervous-looking smile.

"What are you doing here?" Mia asked, still standing.

"You uh, gonna sit and eat?"

"I don't know if I'm gonna be here long enough."

Recker put his hand out, imploring her to sit. "Please."

Mia let out a sigh, thinking she shouldn't comply with his request, but reluctantly agreed and sat at the table.

"Thank you," Recker said.

Mia wasn't feeling too hospitable though. "So, what is it you want?" she asked bluntly, devoid of almost any feeling.

"David and I are back in town."

"For good?"

"Yeah. Umm, I had another encounter with the CIA last week and they informed me I'm clear now. They're not looking for me anymore."

"Oh. So, what does that mean exactly?" Mia asked, several months of anger showing in her voice. "You just come back here six months after you left like nothing happened?"

"I know I didn't um..."

"Mike, I haven't heard from you in three months. I didn't know where you were, I didn't know what happened to you, I didn't even know if you were alive or dead."

"I know. I'm sorry."

"For the last three months, not one word from you. I just assumed you were dead. And now, suddenly, out of the blue, you're sitting here at my work for some reason."

"You have every right to be angry."

"You're damn right I'm angry. How else would you expect me to feel?"

Recker shrugged. "Nothing else."

"So why are you here? Just to say you're back? Injured? Have a gunshot wound you need me to look at?"

"No. I guess I deserve that though. To be honest, I really don't know what I'm doing here. I was just out driving around and suddenly I found myself here."

"When'd you get back?"

"Late last night."

"So where were you all this time?"

"We went to Detroit."

"Why? What was there?"

"People who needed help."

"I just don't understand what you want from me. You tell me you're leaving, you show up at my door shot again, then you're gone. You leave for six months, I don't hear from you for the last three of them then you just appear and say you're back."

"I dunno. I guess I just came here to say hi," Recker said, struggling to find something that would soothe her. "I missed you."

"You missed me?"

"Yeah. I don't know what else you want me to say."

"You know, there was a time when you could've said anything to me and I would've believed it," Mia said. "I would've followed you anywhere, done anything. But not now. Not anymore."

Recker nodded his head, feeling a sense of sadness, realizing he may have made a mistake in coming. "Are you still with uh, whatshisname?"

"Josh. And yes, we're still together," Mia said, a little perturbed that he still wouldn't say her boyfriend's name.

"Happy? He treating you well and all?"

"Yeah, basically. Sorry, there's nothing for you to beat him up over or kill him or anything."

Recker forced a smile, not taking offense at her harsh words, realizing her feelings had been hurt.

"Are you going to try and explain why you basically ignored me for the last three months?"

"I would but I don't know if anything I say will be good enough to satisfy you. Or satisfy me either."

"You can try."

"The only thing I can really say is I thought you'd be better off without me in your life. I wasn't sure if I was ever coming back. You found someone new, it seemed like you were moving on," Recker said. "I thought by continuing to talk to me, you would still be living in the past, instead of the future."

"And what do you think coming here now is doing?" Mia asked, still not cooling off.

Recker could see, no matter what he said, it wasn't going to make a difference. She had her mind made up. She was going to be angry, and there was no changing that. But he still couldn't blame her for it. She'd had three months to build up to this point. Three long months of hostility and she wasn't letting up. Right then, he figured maybe the best thing he could do was leave. He could see he wasn't doing anybody any good by being there.

"Well, I guess I've taken up enough of your time. Enjoy the rest of your lunch," Recker said.

"I still don't understand what it is you really want. You pull me in, then push me away, draw me close, then say we can't be together, then we kiss, then you leave, then you want to be friends, then you move away, then we're friends, then we don't talk, then you show up. You constantly tell me one thing, then do another. Over and over again."

"I guess I can't really dispute it, can I?"

"You could. You'd be wrong if you tried though. You just confuse me and I can't take it anymore. I won't. I deserve better."

"You're right. You do deserve better," Recker said, standing up.

"Leaving again? It seems it's what you do best. Push people

away, run off, leave people behind. You only get involved with anybody if it suits whatever angle you're working at the time."

Recker still didn't take offense to anything she said. He seemed like a defeated man. Quite unlike himself. "I've never worked an angle with you. You take care of yourself."

He started to walk away but was stopped by Mia, who grabbed his forearm. She looked up at him, not wanting to end their conversation by being mad at each other, even if she was really the only one who seemed indignant.

"Mike, eventually you have to figure out what it is you really want. You have to admit to yourself that it's OK to let go of whatever it is that holds you back. But until you do, you'll never be at peace with yourself."

Recker gave her one last smile before walking away, thinking it might be the last time he ever saw her. He would have hoped their last meeting would be a more pleasant one, but he knew she had every right to bitch him out the way she did. Mia turned around to catch a final glimpse of him before he left, seeing him just in time to exit the cafeteria. She turned back toward her food and used her fork to play around with it, still steaming from their conversation. She shook her head, a flood of emotions overtaking her.

Recker left the hospital and had returned to his truck. He sat there for a few minutes, reflecting on his conversation with Mia. After getting her out of his mind, his phone rang just as he turned on the engine.

"I hope you have someone for me to shoot," Recker said, indicating his mood.

"Uh, no," Jones said. "But I did want to let you know everything is up and running."

"Great. Let me know when you have something. Preferably dangerous. And with people armed. The more dangerous the better."

Jones didn't quite know how to respond. "Umm, are you encountering some problems out there?"

"No, why would you think that?"

"Oh, no reason. What have you been doing?"

"I dunno. Just thought I'd try and fix a mistake."

"What kind of mistake?"

"It's nothing."

"I guess it didn't go so well."

"No, it didn't."

"Well, the good thing about mistakes is they can sometimes be erased," Jones said, offering some hope.

"Yeah, I don't know about this one. I think this might be one mistake that can't be fixed."

4

ecker had just gotten back to the office after his outing at the hospital.

"Nice to see you return in one piece," Jones said.

"Huh?" Recker replied.

Recker wasn't sure if he'd missed something. Maybe he was in a battle he wasn't aware of. He noticed Jones had set the Keurig up and went over to the counter to get a cup of coffee.

"Well there's no holes in me," Recker said, patting his chest and legs. "Did you have doubts about me coming back in one piece?"

"Well, after our conversation earlier, it sounded as if you'd just escaped from a confrontation."

"I did. Not of the physical variety though. Still, it was lethal nonetheless."

"Am I to assume you had a little chat with Mia?" Jones asked.

"Chat's not quite the word for it. Chat indicates a level of respect and calmness between the two parties. There wasn't much of that going on."

"I take it she wasn't pleased to see you."

"No, not at all. It was more like she chewed me up, spit me out, then stomped on whatever was on the ground."

"You certainly are a glutton for punishment," Jones said. "Our first day back and you're already the worse for wear."

"I don't know what I was doing there. Trying to make things right I guess."

"You really do know how to put your foot in it, don't you? Well you can't say you don't deserve whatever tongue lashing she dished out. You've put Mia through the ringer."

Recker sighed, not wanting to hear about his shortcomings all over again. "Listen David, getting verbally ripped apart once a day is enough, OK? I don't really need it coming from you too."

"You're right. I'm sorry, I wasn't trying to pile it on."

"I know. Let's just not talk about Mia, OK?"

"As you wish."

"Anything on the horizon yet?" Recker asked, hoping for a case to take his mind off things.

"Sadly, no. Don't you have something else to keep you busy?"

"Well, I already got my apartment back. Well, not back. Different unit, same building."

"I guess everything's not so glum then."

"Easy for you to say. Maybe I'll check with Tyrell to see if anything's been brewing while we've been gone."

"Excellent idea."

Jones mostly just wanted to get Recker out of the office. Since they didn't have any cases at the moment, he worried in case Mia's verbal assault would have an adverse effect on Recker. Jones knew whenever Recker had personal problems, which wasn't often since they didn't have many friends, and they usually revolved around Mia, he usually stewed over it for most of the day. Jones didn't really want to play psychiatrist the first day they were back in town, no matter how much he cared for the both of them. He just had too much to do to get the systems back up and running properly.

While Recker was bothered by the events at the hospital, he didn't think she was wrong, and he didn't want to dwell on it either. Her feelings were what they were, and he wasn't going to be able to change it. The best thing he figured he could do was to get a beat on what was happening around town. Tyrell was usually the best person to get that information out of, so Recker pulled out his phone and gave him a call.

"Tyrell, what's going on?"

"Not much, man, how you doin'?"

"Good. I just wanted to let you know I was back in town."

"Really? We'll have to get together. You back for good or just to visit?"

"For good."

"Sweet, man, we can use you around here," Tyrell said.

"Why? Something wrong?"

"Ahh, you know, just the usual."

"That's one of the reasons I called. I just wanted to see what was happening out there and if there was anything I should know about."

"What, you mean like Vincent and Jeremiah going to war with each other? Stuff like that?"

"Yeah, that would qualify."

"Then nah, nothing big. Not yet, anyway."

"Do me a favor," Recker said. "Can you start spreading the word? I'm back in town."

"Why? You don't wanna make a grand entrance somewhere?"

"Not this time."

"Yeah, I can do that."

"Thanks. So, what's the word been since I've been gone? People been breathing easier?"

"Yeah, you ain't kidding. Lot of people not as worried about doing things because they knew they didn't have to deal with you once word got out you were gone."

"It's why I want word to get out that I'm back. Time to put a healthy dose of fear back into people," Recker said.

"I'll tell you what though, for as much damage as you inflict, I think the city missed you."

"Is that so?"

"Yeah. Like I said, you put fear into the underhanded folks, and the regular people, they feel like they got a guardian angel watching over their backs if someone starts messing with them."

"Well I don't know about the angel part."

"Plus, I think you help keep the peace, especially between men like Vincent and Jeremiah. They were too afraid to make a move on anyone out of fear you'd show up on the other side of them," Tyrell said. "Nobody wants to go up against you and make you an enemy. You know Vincent and Jeremiah are gonna wonder and worry why you're back, right? They're gonna worry the other brought you back to help them take the other out. They might wanna have a word."

"No, I'm not doing that again. I did it once before when I first got here. I'm not explaining myself or my intentions again. If they ask, tell them I haven't changed."

After his call with Tyrell concluded, Recker left the office and drove around for a while to pass the time. He didn't get back to the office until later in the day, bringing dinner back for him and Jones. The professor was armed with some information he might find useful, though not quite what Recker was hoping for.

"Figured you could use some food," Recker said, placing a sandwich and fries on the desk.

"Yes, I could. You know, I found out some interesting information while you were gone."

"We got a case?"

"No, but it's still interesting, anyway."

"I'd still prefer a case."

"I know, but listen to this," Jones said, looking at his computer screen after taking a bite of his sandwich. "I started digging into the crime statistics in the time we were away."

"You're right, it is interesting," Recker said, not really interested at all.

"No, since we've been gone, crime's gone up across the board."

"So?"

"So, it proves what we were doing before was effective. You were a deterrent."

"I'd rather have a case."

"Yes, I know. But that should make you feel good."

"I'll feel good when I have a case."

"It's coming," Jones said, getting more exasperated.

"If crime's up across the board, how come we don't have anything yet?"

"Mike, we just got here. Give it some time."

"Yeah, yeah. So, everything's been up since we've been gone?"

"Surprising to say, but yes. Small crimes up, major crimes up, violent crimes up, murders up."

"I think it's a little premature to say we were the difference," Recker said.

"Perhaps so. But the numbers are the numbers. I'm especially surprised by the murders being up."

"So, what's that say to you?"

"Maybe by you killing people, it prevented others from doing the same."

"And if that's the case, then maybe it throws a wrench into your idea of me handling things a different way."

"Possibly. But you know the saying, violence begets violence."

"I don't care what anybody says, being intimidating and violent will scare some people. The people who are violent and ruthless will still be, no matter what. I'm just taking them out of the equation."

"I don't suppose you'd be interested in handling things the way we did in Detroit, would you?" Jones asked.

"I'll handle things the way I think they need to be. No more, no less. If a gun's required, I'll use it. If it's not, I won't. I'm not going out of my way like I've done the last six months. It really didn't get us anywhere. Ask Teresa Golden."

"Mike, she was one example out of hundreds."

"That we know of. How do you know how many others are going to happen in the next few weeks or months?"

It was a familiar discussion between the two of them, one they seemed to have every few months, or after something extreme happened. It was likely to be a thorn of contention between them for as long as they would work together. Jones always advocated for handling things as diplomatically as possible with the least amount of violence. Recker usually opted for whatever would get the job done, as long as he wouldn't have to come back to the same situation at a later time. No matter how many times they discussed it, though, they both knew they weren't changing the other one's mind on it. They were both locked in to their positions and Recker didn't really care to talk about it anymore and changed the subject.

"You think you could still monitor the CIA like you did before?" Recker asked.

"For what purpose?"

"For the purpose of being safe and not taking chances."

"If you said you're not on the list anymore, I don't see what the point would be," Jones said.

"Like I said, just as a precaution. I believe Lawson at her word when she says I'm off the radar. But what if someone new comes along and decides to open my case up again for some reason?"

Jones nodded, seeing his position. "It will take a couple days but I can get the same program as before running."

"Even if nothing ever comes of it, I'd rather know what's coming instead of getting a surprise party."

It wasn't until the following day Jones found their first case to work on since they'd been back. Recker was at his new apartment getting the furniture delivery he'd ordered the previous day. He actually furnished it like a normal person this time instead of the bare bones approach he used before. He bought a sofa, recliner, dining room set, a bed, along with some tables. It was a new style for him, but he figured if they were making it home, maybe he should dress it up a little. Jones told him not to bother coming back to the office until he had something for him to work on since there was no reason for both of them to be there with nothing to do. As soon as Jones called, Recker left his swanky new place to head back to the office.

"So, what do we got?" Recker said, asking the moment he set foot in the office.

"We've got what may pass for our most difficult case yet."

"What? We've handled some tough stuff before."

"Yes, but none of those situations involved police officers," Jones said.

"Police?"

"Yes. It looks like our subject is one of Philadelphia's finest."

"Well that is a new one. What's the story?"

"The story is, apparently Officer Eduardo Perez has found himself on the hit list of a dangerous man," Jones said.

"How's that?"

"It seems that several years ago Officer Perez was responsible for arresting a man named Adrian Bernal. Mr. Bernal just got out of prison about a month ago and is already plotting his revenge."

"I take it Bernal is not someone to be taken lightly?"

"Very violent past and criminal record."

47

"I assume the police and Perez aren't aware he's coming?" Recker asked.

"No. He's made no apparent threats."

"Then how'd you pick up on it?"

"Because Mr. Bernal sent a text message to his girlfriend saying he was, 'going to get the stinking cop' who arrested him."

"Could be just talk," Recker said. "Criminals make threats all the time. They very rarely act on them. Especially on a cop."

"Well, it will be our job to ascertain the severity of the threat. That is, assuming you want to look into this."

"Why wouldn't we?"

"As I mentioned before, we've never had a police officer as someone who needed our protection. Things could get... hairy, as some would say."

"I don't think it really makes a difference, do you?"

"Well now that you're as known as you are, interacting with the police on any level is more dangerous than it's ever been. If this came up two years ago, it wouldn't be much of an issue since they had no idea who you were. Now they know your face. If you happen to come into contact with Officer Perez, even in the interest of helping him, and he recognizes you, he may arrest you before you can help him."

"Doesn't matter. The police aren't our enemy. We're on the same side."

"I agree," Jones said.

"We may have different methods, but we both want the same thing. To clean up the streets. They just have more rules than I do."

"It doesn't change the fact that you must tread carefully."

"I will. But we can't pass on this one. Even if it puts me on the hot seat. We can't sit still for someone killing a cop. Does Perez seem like he's on the up and up?"

"In what way? Like he's not dirty or something?" Jones asked.

"Yeah."

"From what I can gather, nothing seems out of the ordinary. No complaints on file. He appears to be a good cop trying to do a good job."

"Then he is good enough for our help. There's too many police officers in this country getting ambushed or killed when all they're doing is trying to do the job they were hired for," Recker said. "You agree?"

"I've already said as much. As long as it doesn't end up with you in the back of a squad car."

"What district's Perez in?"

"He's assigned to the twenty-sixth," Jones said.

"Any idea how or when Bernal's going to enact this plan of his?"

"Not as of yet. I've still got some more digging to do though. I didn't want to get knee deep in research only for you to say to let the police handle it on their own."

"You know as well as I do I wouldn't have."

"Perhaps not."

"So how long's it gonna take you to get into the rest of it?" Recker asked.

"Probably a good part of the day. I've got to dig into Bernal's background, his girlfriend, friends or relatives they might turn to, pore over their phone records, text messages, it all takes time."

"I know. I know the process, you don't have to explain it to me. I was just wondering when."

"Well if you want to help, then it will make everything go quicker."

With nothing else on the agenda, Recker was all too willing to jump in and help. Though Jones was usually faster at digging up the required information, Recker needed anything to keep him busy. Plus, with a police officer's life at stake, Recker wanted to get started on it as soon as possible. Even though he was wanted by them, he really did admire the work and dedication most of them displayed. But Jones was right, this was probably the most delicate case they'd had. Sometimes Recker had to interact with the people he was assigned to help, there was just no way around it. But sometimes the people he was helping had no idea they had a guardian angel watching over them. This would have to be one of those times. The fact the person he was helping was also danger-ous, carried a gun, and had the ability to lock him up only compli-cated things somewhat.

They worked straight through dinner to get the information they needed. Jones tracked down as many friends and relatives of Bernal's he could find, though most of them appeared to be of no use. Outside of his girlfriend, Bernal only disclosed his intentions to one other person, a cousin of his. Through their text messages, Jones concluded that whatever was being planned, it was going to happen quickly. The problem was, Bernal didn't give an exact date or time for when he was going to execute his plan. The other problem was, Bernal didn't have a known address. Though Recker and Jones assumed Bernal might have been staying with his girl-friend, they couldn't say for sure. It would require Recker staking out her place. But if Bernal was staying elsewhere, such as a motel, Recker could be wasting his time at the girlfriend's residence and Bernal might enact his plan without Recker even being in the picture. The only other option was to follow Perez around, and that was deemed too dangerous. If Perez got the slightest hint he was being followed, who knows what might've happened, not to mention following a police patrol car for half the day wasn't exactly an ideal situation. Jones couldn't find any digital traces of Bernal anywhere, such as credit cards being used, or through online social media websites, so he assumed his subject was sticking with cash transactions and deliberately keeping a low profile. It would make finding him much more difficult.

5

Recker had been staking out the row home of Bernal's girlfriend for two days without seeing a single sign of the man he was looking for. He'd seen the girlfriend come and go multiple times, but unless Bernal was hiding inside the house, Recker had to assume that he wasn't coming and they had to come up with a new strategy.

Recker pulled out his phone to call his partner. "I dunno, David, this seems like a waste of time."

"Well, right now, the only other options are sitting on the cousin or tailing Perez and I'm not sure how viable either of those are either."

"Yeah, well, I gotta do something. Just sitting here watching the wind blow isn't accomplishing anything."

"I understand but right now it's all we have. Bernal's kept an extremely low profile since being let out of jail," Jones said.

As Recker sat there watching the house, listening to Jones, he was also thinking of alternatives. Suddenly a new idea came to him. It might be considered risky, but without knowing what time frame Bernal was working on, he didn't want to waste more time than he already had.

"David, I'll call you back. I'm gonna try something."

"That sounds extremely vague," Jones said. "Would you like to share before doing something we might regret?"

"I'm gonna talk to the girlfriend."

"Are you sure that's wise?"

"No. But maybe she can tell us something."

"I don't know if it's such a good idea. If he thinks someone's on to him, he might speed things up before we're ready to deal with him."

"Could also scare him away too."

"I would prefer getting more information before confronting anyone," Jones said.

"That's why I'm not gonna ask her anything. I'm gonna have Detective Scarborough do it."

"Oh, dear."

"Keep close tabs on her phone after I'm done."

Recker figured his alter ego might have more luck in getting some kind of useful information out of the girlfriend than if he just approached her on his own as a random citizen. Posing as a police officer was a tactic he'd used successfully several times before. He didn't necessarily expect Maria Guerrero to say anything which would really help him, but hopefully she'd panic at him asking pointed questions and would lead them to Bernal's location. As Recker approached the house, he noticed curtains move on the bow window in the living room. He didn't see a face but assumed someone inside had seen him coming. Guerrero was supposed to be living in the house along with her two kids, but no other adults. Bernal was not the father of the children. As Recker took a few steps up the concrete walkway, he heard a few young kids screaming and playing inside. He knocked on the door and almost immediately the playful screams of the children inside came to a halt. Recker knocked another three times, more force-fully than he did the first time. Knowing they were inside, he patiently waited for someone to answer the door. He knocked a few more times, determined to stand there until he talked to Guer-rero. Sensing their visitor wasn't going away, Guerrero finally came to the door.

"Can I help you?" she asked, clearly annoyed in her tone.

Recker took out his badge from his pocket and showed it to her. "Mike Scarborough, Detective Division."

She took a quick glance at the badge, hardly paying much attention to it. "What do you want?"

"I'm looking for Adrian Bernal."

"He's not here."

"Mind if I come in and check?"

"Not without a warrant you're not."

"Do you know where he may be at?"

"No, I have no idea."

"Aren't you his girlfriend?" Recker asked.

"Yeah, so?"

"And you don't know where he's at? Where he's living? Work-ing? Anything?"

"Adrian comes and goes as he pleases. It's his own business, not yours. And he's not working right now. Nobody's exactly beating down his door to offer him a job. One of the perks of our penal system."

"He's been out for, what, a month now?"

"Yeah, and your point?"

"In the time he's been out you haven't seen him, talked to him, nothing?"

"I've met him at a couple bars or whatever," Guerrero said.

"Which ones?"

"I forget the names. He picked me up. Never been to any of them before."

"What kind of car's he driving?"

"Beats me. What I know about cars you could stick in your hat."

Recker let out a smile, amused by the runaround. "Well I need to talk to him and I'd appreciate your help in locating him."

"What do you want him for?" she asked.

"Just some routine questions. There's an investigation we have going on involving some people we think he might have known before, maybe had dealings with," Recker said.

"You're wasting your time. After what he's been through, if you think he's gonna help you guys with anything, you got another thing coming."

"Well, that may be, but I still need to locate and talk to him."

"Good luck with it."

"Did you know him before he was sent up this last time?" Recker asked.

"Yeah, why?"

"So, you remember the arresting officer?"

Guerrero looked at him kind of funny, wondering why he would ask such a question. She hesitated before answering. "No. I don't remember. Why?"

"Well we received an anonymous tip that Officer Perez, the officer who arrested Adrian, may be the subject of some sort of retaliation because of the arrest."

"I wouldn't know anything about that," Guerrero said, shaking her head violently.

"So where would Adrian be right now?"

"I told you I don't know."

"Are you aware, if something happens to Officer Perez, and it's found out you knew something about this before it happens, you can be charged as an accessory to murder? Did you know that?"

"Yes. I know," she said defiantly.

"Be a shame for your kids to grow up without a mother,"

Recker said, hoping to scare her into some type of admission. "Kids visiting a parent in prison, especially a mother, is never a pretty sight. You might wanna think about it."

"I don't have to think about anything. Are we done?" Guerrero asked, putting a hand on the edge of the door.

"For now. I might be back though. This was more of a courtesy. Maybe next time I'll have a search warrant."

"Great. Thanks."

Guerrero then slammed the door as Recker turned to leave. Though she stuck to her guns and didn't reveal anything which would lead to Bernal directly, Recker felt like his trick worked. He thought she seemed rattled and flustered and there was no doubt in his mind, within minutes she would be calling her boyfriend to inform him the police were just there. Recker walked back to his car and just sat in it for a few minutes, just in case Bernal was actually inside the house. He called Jones to let him know his impersonation was over.

"How did your acting go?" Jones asked.

"Fabulous. Maybe after London I should've gone to Hollywood."

"Let's not get carried away."

"Anyway, keep tabs on Guerrero's phone. If I'm right, she'll be contacting Bernal any minute now," Recker said.

"Why? What did you do?"

"Just tried to step up the pressure."

"Did she tell you anything?"

"No, she clammed up like nobody's business. But she seemed nervous and eager to get rid of me."

"Who wouldn't be?" Jones joked.

While Jones was doing his thing, Recker started the car and began driving, though he didn't leave the area. He just drove down the street to get a different view of Guerrero's house and make it appear like he was leaving the area. If Bernal was inside, which

Recker didn't believe he was, he suspected he might bolt out of the house relatively quickly. The more likely scenario was, Guerrero would call her boyfriend to alert him of Recker's presence and questions. But just in case they had some other system in place, Recker stood by in case Guerrero left the house to tell Bernal in person now the police were on to him. Recker wound up waiting in his spot for another hour without any sign of movement from the house. Nobody was coming or going. He knew nothing was going to come from him sitting there any longer. If they were going to have face-to-face contact, they would've done it by now. The best Recker could hope for now was if Jones was able to track something on his end. Before leaving, Recker gave his partner another call before making the decision to flee the scene.

"I'm about to wrap things up here, there's nothing happening," Recker said. "If Guerrero was going to meet him or warn him, she would've done it by now. You come up with anything?"

"I have, though I can't say it's the break we've been looking for either. Not just yet."

"Well what'd you get?"

"You were right. You spooked Guerrero. Right after you left she called a phone number which I cannot establish a name to, but I can only assume it's Bernal's."

"Burner phone?"

"Most likely. And it's a different number than she's called before so it's likely he has several of them. Or he keeps switching phones. Both of which are entirely plausible," Jones said.

"Smart. Not like the usual dumbbell we come into contact with. Can you still get a trace on it?"

"Well, as you know, most burner phones can still be traced in some way. Though I don't know if I'll be able to get an exact location, I should be able to trace it to the nearest cell tower."

"Lot of good that'll do," Recker said.

"I know. Tracing burners takes a lot more work, and it's not as precise. By the time I can triangulate his general position and figure out where he may be, it's likely he'll be long gone."

"Well, do it anyway. At the very least it's more than we've got now. Maybe if we can figure out where he's been we can figure out where he's going."

"Let's just hope we can figure it out before he enacts his plot on Officer Perez."

"Maybe we should just phone in a tip about Bernal's plans. At least Perez would be aware of it and can keep his head up."

"We can, but you know as well as I do the police get threats all the time," Jones said. "It doesn't mean they can or will do anything. Especially if there's no evidence."

"They don't need evidence. They just need to know the possibility is out there. What about his parole?"

"What about it?"

"He had to put an address down upon release," Recker said.

"It's a dead end. I've already looked into it. He used his girlfriend's address as his residence and he should've already checked in with a parole officer in the last couple of weeks."

"I guess it's checked out?"

"Well there hasn't been an arrest warrant issued so I imagine everything turned up fine on those fronts. Another dead end I'm afraid. Unless he really is living at his girlfriend's house."

"I really don't think so. If he is, he hasn't come up for air in two days. Plus, I doubt she would've made a call after I visited. He would've known if he was stashed in a different room. Who would she have called?"

"Maybe he is living there and was just out when you knocked," Jones said.

"No, no way. I've been sitting here day and night for two days. I would've noticed him coming or going at some point. Or another car at least."

"Unless he snuck out the back."

"The only reason to do that is if you think you're being watched," Recker said.

"And maybe he knows you're there."

"No. I'd stake my reputation on it."

Though Recker wanted to head back to the office, Jones convinced him to stay put for a little longer. There wasn't much he could do at the office and Jones figured he was better served where he was, just in case Bernal made an appearance, even if it was unlikely. After a couple more hours of watching and waiting, without anything to show for it, Jones finally called him with a lead.

"What's up?" Recker asked, hopeful of good news.

"I've tracked him down as far as I can."

"Great. Where is he?"

"Well, his call from Guerrero was bounced off a cell phone tower that is right next to the Cedar Motel," Jones said. "I'm fairly confident that he's likely to be in one of those rooms. Well, I should say confident that's where he was. Whether he's still there is an entirely different matter."

"I'm on my way there now," Recker said, driving away from Guerrero's house.

"I'll let you know if I pick up anything else."

"By the way, how many rooms does the motel have?"

Recker listened while Jones clicked around his keyboard. "Looks like twenty."

"Shouldn't make it too difficult for Detective Scarborough," Recker said.

The Cedar Motel wasn't too far away from Guerrero's house. Recker got there in under twenty minutes. Once he got there his first stop was the management's office. When Recker walked in, he saw a balding, older man sitting behind the desk doing a crossword puzzle.

"Help ya?" the man asked.

Recker took out his badge and showed it to him. "Looking for a man. We believe he's been staying here and wondering if you can confirm it."

"Oh. Got a picture?"

"Sure do," Recker said, taking out his phone to show Bernal's photo.

The man grunted as he looked it over. "Yeah. He's been here."

"Have any problems with him or anything?"

"Nope."

"He still here?"

"As far as I know. He hasn't officially checked out yet."

"What room's he in?" Recker asked.

"Fourteen."

"Thanks."

"Wait," the man said, getting nervous about what was to happen.

"Yeah?"

"You're not gonna break the door down or anything or get in a gunfight are you?"

"I dunno. Why?"

"Well I just don't want the room to get messed up. Getting repairs done is a pain in the you know what."

"I'll do my best," Recker said, not the least bit concerned.

"Wait, wait, wait... here's a spare key to the room. At least don't kick the door in, huh?"

Recker couldn't help but smile and let out a laugh. "Fine. The door will stay intact. Can't guarantee about bullet holes in the wall though."

"Great. Of all the cops who could come through here, I gotta get Wyatt Earp," the man whispered.

"Stay here in case there's shooting," Recker said, exiting the office.

There were only a few cars in the parking lot, and all the

rooms weren't currently rented, so Recker couldn't be sure whether Bernal was there or not. Even if he was, Recker had no idea what kind of car he was driving. He quickly walked past each room, clinging to the brick wall lining the building, until he got to room fourteen. Recker tried looking through the window into the room, but the curtains weren't pulled back and he couldn't even get the tiniest view in there. He squatted and walked underneath the window to avoid his shadow from being seen crossing it from inside the room. If Bernal was in there, Recker knew it was likely he was going to be drawing gunfire the moment he opened the door.

With the key still in his hand, he put it in the hole of the handle and unlocked the door. He tried to do it as slowly and quietly as possible, but he thought it was unlikely that someone on the inside wouldn't have heard him coming. To give himself better odds of surviving an initial flurry of bullets, Recker squatted again, figuring his best chance at eluding gunfire was to dive into the room. He thought it best to dive in quickly before Bernal got impatient and started blasting at the door before it opened. He turned the handle of the door and violently pushed it open so it slammed against the wall. With his gun drawn, he dove into the room, quickly looking for a target. Everything was quiet. There were no guns firing, no bullets piercing through walls, no commotion of any kind.

Recker got up and took a look around the room, even checking under the bed. These motel rooms were pretty small, and there weren't many places someone could hide, even if they wanted to. There was a small kitchen area off the main space and the only other room was a bathroom. Recker took a look in there as well, but like the rest of the place, came up empty. At least the manager would be pleased his room didn't get shot up. Recker then searched through the room, looking for the smallest of clues to help to tell him where Bernal was headed, or where else he might have been. Anything at all. A piece of paper with a name or address written on it, a crumpled up paper in the trash bin, something he might have forgotten or left behind in a drawer, anything. But it was no use. The room was spotless. Recker even looked in the refrigerator, but there wasn't a single thing in there. It was a lost cause. There was nothing to be learned there. He called Jones to inform him of his findings.

"Looks like Bernal's already gone," Recker said.

"Well I can't say I'm shocked. I was afraid this would be the result."

"I've looked through this room several times for some kind of lead but there's nothing here."

"Mr. Bernal does appear to be good at hiding his tracks," Jones said. "I have to say I'm a little surprised he's been this difficult to find. Nothing in his background suggests he moves in the shadows or that he's capable of being this deceptive."

"People can surprise you with what they can pull off when they have something major like murder at stake."

6

Recker and Jones were in the office, trying everything within reason to try to find out where Bernal may have been hiding. Beyond what they were doing with the computer, which wasn't turning up much, Recker knew he had to put everything at his disposal in play. It would mean calling in some favors.

"I think it's time to get Tyrell involved," Recker said.

"You think he can help?"

"When has Tyrell not been able to help? He knows these streets far better than you and I do. He might know a friend of a friend of a friend or something."

"It surely wouldn't hurt."

Recker immediately dialed Tyrell's number, who picked up on the second ring. "You got anything going on right now?" Recker asked.

"At this exact minute?"

"Well, relatively soon."

"Depends. Whatcha need?"

"Information. I'm looking for a guy."

"I might be able to help you," Tyrell said.

"Guy I'm looking for is named Adrian Bernal."

"Adrian Bernal," Tyrell said, racking his brain. "Bernal. Bernal."

Recker hoped by the silence it meant Tyrell could remember him. "Know him?"

"Nah, I don't think I know the cat."

"You think you can put the word out or find out about him?"

"Depends on what you want. Depends if you're looking to find him and have a talk or you're looking to find him and take him out. You want one of those hush-hush deals?"

"Yeah. He can't know I'm coming or else it'll scare him off," Recker said.

"All right, I gotcha. What's he wanted for? He dangerous?"

"He's looking to kill a cop, Tyrell. I'd say he's pretty dangerous."

"Oh, man, that's bad news. All right, I'll put my minions on it and let you know if I find out anything. How soon's all this going down?"

"To be honest, I have no idea. The quicker you can get something, the better off we'll be."

"You know it. I'll get back to you."

Recker hung up, putting the phone back in his pants pocket. "Hopefully it pays off," Jones said.

"You think he can pull this off by himself?" Recker said.

"Who? Tyrell?"

"No. Bernal. I mean, taking out a cop requires precision planning, not to mention acquiring weapons."

"Why not? You could."

"Comparing a street thug to me isn't exactly a fair comparison."

"True. You also may be putting too much thought into it. Your level of planning into something like this might not be equal to his. If you do a hit, you're looking at exit strategies, plans, the environment, onlookers, etc. He may not be interested in any of that. He may only be looking at killing Perez without worrying about how he's getting away, if he is at all," Jones said. "Plus, I'm sure he's well aware of who he can go to for a weapon."

It didn't take long for Tyrell to find something that would be useful. About three hours after getting the nod from Recker, he called back with his findings.

"Hey, you're in luck," Tyrell said.

"What'd you find out?" Recker asked.

"Looks like your man's got himself a few guns."

"How do you know?"

"Who's the major gun supplier in this city?"

"Jeremiah."

"Exactly. I got word to Jeremiah to see if he knew who this cat was and they said they did business with the dude."

"Did you find out what the exact transaction was?" Recker asked.

"Nah, they wasn't talking too much about specifics. From what I could tell it was more than one though."

"Find out anything else?"

"No, not yet. But Jeremiah might have more info for you if you're of a mind."

"Why?"

"Well they wanted to know why I was asking about Bernal," Tyrell said. "So, I told them I was asking on your behalf."

"That was kind of you."

"Hey, you know, when you start asking someone like Jeremiah about his business, you better be prepared to have some answers for him as to why you're asking," Tyrell said with a laugh. "And the only thing I had was, you wanted to know."

"Don't worry about it, it's fine."

"Well anyway, Jeremiah's willing to talk to you about it."

"He's got something else on his mind, I take it," Recker said.

"Yeah, sounded like it."

"Know what it is?"

"No, but, I dunno, he seems different lately," Tyrell said.

"Different how?"

"I don't know how to explain it. He just seems jumpier. Like he's restless or something."

"That doesn't sound very encouraging."

"Maybe he's getting ready for a war with Vincent."

"What makes you think that? Hear something about it?"

"Nothing specific. Just, Jeremiah's been recruiting hard. Usually when men like him start looking for more soldiers, they got something specific in mind. Like taking more territory or something."

"Or maybe he just fears Vincent's getting too big and he'll make a move on him first," Recker said.

"Could be. Anyway, if you wanna meet with him, I'll let him know you're coming."

"What time?"

"He said one hour."

"Usual spot?"

"Same spot as always."

"I'll be there."

"Good news?" Jones asked, overhearing part of the conversation.

"Could be. Looks like Bernal went to Jeremiah for some guns."

"I take it you're meeting with him to see if he has anything else to offer?"

"Yeah."

"What was that stuff about Jeremiah and Vincent?"

"I don't know. Tyrell said Jeremiah seemed jumpy lately.

Maybe he's getting worried about Vincent getting too big a stake of the city."

"Possible."

"Yeah, well, doesn't really matter to me. I'll be back."

Recker immediately left the office to head to the meeting with Jeremiah. It'd been a while since they had one. The last time was after Recker killed Bellomi, and Jeremiah wondered if The Silencer was working with Vincent, after the mob boss publicly displayed the dead body of Mancini to announce he was taking on more territory. By the time Recker got to the area of the meeting house, he was a half hour early, but he didn't mind sitting for a while. He parked down the street as it wasn't wise to sit in front of a place Jeremiah owns for too long if you're not conducting business at the time. It'd give the impression he was running surveillance on them. And if it was the case, then whoever's sitting there might as well get their gun out, because Jeremiah's men would be, and they'd come out shooting. It gave Recker time to think and look around. It'd been a year since he'd been to the house, or the area in general, but it didn't look like anything had changed. Once the time came near, Recker pulled down the street, parking in front of the house. He saw the same burly man standing by the front door as usual.

"Good to see you're still kicking around," Recker said as he walked past him. "Don't bother to show me in, I know my way around."

The man stood pat, not really appreciating Recker's sense of humor. If he had his way, he probably would've tried working Recker's face over a couple of times. But those weren't Jeremiah's wishes, so his desires would have to go unfulfilled. As Recker walked into the living room of the boarded-up house, he saw his host sitting in the chair in the middle of the room. Recker sat down across from him and looked around, seeing that they were alone.

"When you gonna get around to decorating this place?" Recker said.

"You know, I think you say the same thing every time you come here," Jeremiah said.

"Well, I guess I figure one of these times you'll start listening."

"Still crazy as ever I see."

"Don't wanna ruin my reputation."

"I heard you left town for a while. Too much heat on you?"

"No, nothing I couldn't handle. Just had to take care of some business elsewhere for a while. I'm back for good now."

"Glad to hear it."

"Are you?"

"Yeah. Why wouldn't I be?" Jeremiah asked.

"I dunno. Just checking. Not everybody's so happy to see me."

"I can understand how it is. Enough of the pleasantries though. I hear you wanna know about this guy I sold some guns to."

"Yeah. Adrian Bernal."

"Why? What's it to you?"

"I just have an interest in it. What'd you sell him?"

"Handgun and an assault rifle."

"You know what he wants them for?" Recker asked, not sure how involved he was.

"Yeah. He wants to kill a cop. At least that's what he told me. Why you looking for him?"

"I've been hired to stop him."

"What would you wanna do that for? As far as I'm concerned, one less cop is good for everybody."

"Well, my employer thinks otherwise."

"I'd have thought this would be a case you'd turn down," Jeremiah said. "Since when'd you get so chummy with the cops? I'd think you'd be happy about one less cop hunting you."

"Nah. Not my thing. I just go where the money is."

"Yeah, I bet."

"So you know where Bernal's heading or when he's planning on doing this thing?"

"Maybe I do. It's nothing I can talk to you about though."

"Why not?"

"It'd be bad for business."

"How you figure?" Recker said.

"People come to me 'cause they know I'll have the merchandise they're looking for. They know they can trust me once they get it," Jeremiah said. "Now, how would it look if I sold people out after I sell them the goods? My reputation takes a hit and I start to lose business."

"You're assuming someone would find out about it. You know I'm certainly not gonna spill the beans. After I kill him, who's gonna know?"

"And you're assuming you live and he doesn't. What happens if it's reversed, or he finds out about it?"

"You really think some small-time hood's gonna get one over on me?"

"What, you think you're gonna live forever?" Jeremiah asked, smiling. "Time's gonna come for all of us. You and me both. We're not any different."

"Probably true," Recker said, confused by his host's intentions. "If you're not willing to help me find this guy, I have to wonder what I'm doing here then. I mean, what was the point of this? The only thing you told me was what weapons you sold him. Not really much of a revelation, I could've guessed as much."

"Because I got some other things to discuss with you. Wasn't sure you'd come otherwise."

Intrigued, Recker sat up a little straighter in his chair. "And just what might those other things be?"

"Where your allegiances lie."

"My allegiances? They lie at the same place they always have. With myself."

"Nah, you're gonna have a dog in this fight. You have to," Jeremiah said.

"You know, I'm sure we both have things we need to get done so why don't you stop talking in circles and tell me what it is you really want," Recker said.

"Things seem to be heating up between me and Vincent."

"Really? I haven't heard anything about it."

"Mostly low-key stuff right now."

"Is that why you've been recruiting?"

Jeremiah smiled, impressed his visitor seemed on top of his game. "That's what I like about you. Whether you're here or not, you always know what's going on, always got one ear on the street."

"So, what's been happening?"

"Like I said, just small stuff, but it's adding up. Some of Vincent's men have been seen in my territory from time to time. I can only assume it means they're scouting things out."

"Could mean anything," Recker said, not jumping to any conclusions. "Doesn't necessarily means he wants to start a war."

"You know what his intentions are?"

"Haven't the foggiest."

"If things happen, I wanna know which side you're on," Jeremiah said.

"I'm not on anybody's side. I've done business with you. I've done business with him. I'm on even terms with both of you. I don't have a dog in this fight."

"A man like you can really tip the scales, tip the balance as to who's got the upper hand, who has the most power."

"Not taking sides," Recker said.

"Maybe I can persuade you."

"Before you get all hot and bothered with what you think is

going on, why don't you actually request a meeting with Vincent and talk? Then you can get everything out in the open."

"You think he's really gonna tell me if he's trying to move in? All it'd do is give him a better target."

"I think you're worrying about nothing."

Jeremiah leaned forward in his chair as he was about to drop his next bombshell. "I need to know you're with me."

"I don't know how many times I can tell you I'm not. I'm not with anybody. The only person I'm with is me. If you and Vincent go to war, it's on you guys. I won't get involved."

Jeremiah's eyebrows dropped as a scowl came over his face. He looked at Recker with mean intent, not pleased at The Silencer's stance. He was hoping to convince Recker to join his side before trying to blackmail him into it. But a man like Recker could give either side the edge in an upcoming war between the two parties, and Jeremiah wasn't about to let Vincent swing him over to his.

"I was hoping you wouldn't take such an adversarial tone," Jeremiah said.

"There's nothing adversarial about it. I'm just not taking sides."

"I was hoping you'd fall in with me on your own and I wouldn't have to do this, but it seems you're not giving me much choice. I can't afford to let you walk out of here without knowing you're with me. If you fall into Vincent's hands, then that's on me."

"You're not listening to me," Recker said.

"I think I am."

Recker was starting to get a little antsy at the way the conversation was going. It seemed to be going in the wrong direction. The manner in which Jeremiah was talking was making Recker feel uneasy, like he had to start looking around for some unwelcome guests to come into the room who might take some shots at him. Luckily, he was armed and Jeremiah didn't have him frisked for weapons when he got there. Of course, he might not have been as willing to hand over his guns to Jeremiah's crew as he was to

Vincent's. For whatever reason, he was always more trusting of Vincent than he was of Jeremiah. Though they were both equally as dangerous, Recker always considered Jeremiah more of a loose cannon, someone who was more likely to double cross him than Vincent was. His suspicions were about to be proven correct.

"I'm not waiting around anymore for Vincent to make the next move," Jeremiah said. "We both know he's eventually gonna make a play for what I got. Maybe it's today, maybe it's next month, maybe it's not for another year. But we both know it's gonna happen. I figure it's better to go on the offensive and hit him before he does it to me."

"No concern of mine," Recker said.

"I want your help."

"You're not getting it."

"I think I will."

Jeremiah reached into his pocket, causing Recker to squirm in his seat in anticipation of a gun being pointed at him. Recker reached into his coat and put his hand on the handle of his gun in case he needed to react quickly. Jeremiah pulled out a piece of paper and looked at it for a minute, causing Recker to relax his hand away from his weapon.

"I understand you know her," Jeremiah said, holding the paper out in front of him.

With a concerned look on his face, Recker glared at his host, before grabbing the piece of paper. He let his eyes drop down to it, horrified at what he saw. It was a picture of Mia taped to the sheet of paper, with her name and address written underneath her photo. Recker, not wanting to admit he knew her, tried to play it off. He shrugged and handed the paper back to Jeremiah.

"So? Who is she?" Recker asked.

"You're saying you don't know her?"

"Not to my knowledge. Why? What's this about?"

A sinister smile overtook Jeremiah's face as he took out

another piece of paper, this one having nine more pictures stapled to it. Once again, he handed it over to his surprised guest. Recker quickly looked the pictures over and saw several pictures of him and Mia sitting together at the hospital cafeteria. It looked to him like the photos had been taken several months ago, probably just before Recker left for Detroit. His blood started boiling. Recker took his eyes off the pictures and peered up at Jeremiah, wanting to extract his revenge on him by filling him full of holes.

"Now that's the face of a man I need," Jeremiah said.

"What is this about?"

"So you admit now you know her?"

"Met her at the hospital when I was having some work done," Recker said. "Talked to her for a little bit, nothing came of it."

"Looked a little cozier than a chat."

Tired of the conversation, Recker wasn't handing the pictures back and put them in his pocket as he started to get up.

"That's all right. You can keep those," Jeremiah said. "I got copies made."

Recker sat back in his seat, anger clearly visible on his face. "What do you want?"

Jeremiah threw his hands up, looking like he hadn't a care in the world. "I keep telling you. I want you working for me."

"Are you trying to blackmail me?"

"You can call it whatever you want. I know where this girl works. I know where she lives. I got people tailing her. If you care anything at all about her, you'll play ball."

"Or else?"

"Or else she's fish food, man."

"You really think this is a good idea? Making an enemy out of me?" Recker asked angrily.

"The thing is, it's not what I'm doing. We're gonna be partners. You help me out. I'll help you out."

"I don't need any help from you."

"You help me get rid of Vincent and the girl lives. It's as simple as that," Jeremiah said, confident in his actions.

"Until you want something else from me and you take someone else hostage to try to get my assistance."

"All I want is Vincent. If you'd just said yes to begin with, I wouldn't have to go through these extreme and drastic measures. And if you have any thoughts to putting a bullet in my head before you leave here, just know this; if my man's watching her doesn't hear from me, he's got instructions to put two in her chest."

"And just how do you propose doing this takeover of yours?" Recker asked.

"You set up a meeting with him. I don't care what you tell him, say whatever you want, just get him and his top guys together. Then take them out."

"Just like that, huh? Just get them together and kill them all?"

"You set it up, you tell us where it's gonna be, I'll have men already waiting there inside the building. Then I'll have more guys swoop in and surround the place," Jeremiah said. "There'll be nowhere for him to escape."

"And the odds of me escaping this crossfire exchange?"

"That's why you should hurry up and get it done so you can get to ducking."

"And your time frame for all this?" Recker said.

"Let's make it within the next week or so. I don't like long setups. Too many things can change, people start to get stupid ideas in their heads, like maybe there's other ways around doing what needs to be done. The quicker the better. This will also be the last time we meet face to face until the job is done. Just in case there's ideas about taking me out and rescuing her before the job is completed."

Recker reached back into his coat and pulled out the pictures of him and Mia, looking them over. "How'd you come across these?"

"Just dumb luck really. I had some acquaintances of mine who happened to be at the hospital," Jeremiah said. "They just happened to be in the cafeteria when they recognized you. They saw you sitting with a pretty girl who looked like she worked there and started snapping some pictures. They showed them to me and I thought I needed to find out who this girl was. She your girlfriend?"

"No. Just a friend."

"But an important friend. I can dig it, man. I got some pretty friends like her too."

"So, what, you've just been sitting on these for a few months, waiting for the right time to spring them on me?"

"Something like that."

"So, are you on board?"

"Guess I don't have much choice, do I?"

Jeremiah smiled, knowing he had his dangerous friend over a barrel. With their business concluded, Recker stood up to leave. Jeremiah extended his hand to cement their deal, which Recker spurned, instead choosing to ignore his new business partner as he left the premises. Jeremiah followed him to the door and watched Recker get into his car and drive away.

"Is he playing ball?" one of Jeremiah's men asked.

"Oh yeah."

"You really think we can trust him?"

"As long as we got the leverage. Put a couple more men on his lady friend, just in case he gets any funny ideas."

As Recker was driving, he tried to think of how he was getting out of his predicament. Nobody was going to blackmail him and get away with it. He certainly wasn't getting involved in Vincent and Jeremiah's feud and he definitely wasn't going to kill anyone for them, or do their dirty work. But he was kicking himself for getting Mia involved. Even though it wasn't his doing, she was in danger because of her relationship to him. He just had to figure out how he was going to get her out of it. He was going to have to figure out a way to protect her while also permanently getting rid of the problem. And the problem was Jeremiah. If he threatened her once, he'd do it again. In order to protect Mia, he was not only going to have to shield her from whoever was tailing her, Recker was going to have to kill Jeremiah.

7

By the slamming of the office door, Jones could tell Recker wasn't in the best of moods. He assumed the meeting with Jeremiah didn't produce the results they were looking for. Little did he know Recker was about to spring a new problem on him. Recker was so consumed with rage, and stewing over his problems, he didn't even bother to let Jones know what was going on. And with the news Jeremiah had sprung on him, Recker had almost completely forgotten about why he went there to begin with. Ever since he was told Mia was being used as a bargaining chip, Recker hadn't had a single thought about Adrian Bernal. Jones greeted him as he came in, though Recker didn't acknowledge him. Jones assumed he didn't hear him, as was sometimes the case when Recker was deep in thought. Usually Jones either kept pestering him until he responded or he just left Recker alone until he came around. Considering Recker kept pacing around the room, causing Jones to lose his concentration, he began pestering his partner until he snapped out of whatever funk he was in.

"Didn't go well, I take it?" Jones asked.

"Huh?"

"No answers?"

"What?" Recker said, not really comprehending what was being said to him.

"Did you find out anything?"

"What?" Recker asked, still pacing, hearing something, but not concentrating on the words.

Finally, Jones figured he had to go to extremes to get his friend's attention. He stood up and started waving his arms around, eventually succeeding in catching Recker's attention.

Recker stopped and looked at Jones curiously. "What are you doing?"

"Well, considering I've been talking to you for five minutes without a reply, I was starting to get desperate."

"Oh. Sorry."

"Good thing you responded. If you didn't notice then I was beginning to think the only thing you'd notice was if I stripped down to my boxers."

"Uh, yeah, don't do that."

"Desperate times call for desperate measures."

"Right. So what were you trying to talk to me about?"

"I was asking how your meeting with Jeremiah went," Jones said.

"Oh. Horrible. Couldn't have gone worse."

"Didn't have anything on Bernal?"

"No, not really. Just told me he sold him a couple guns. Nothing more."

"Didn't know more or just didn't want to reveal more?" Jones asked.

"Said it was bad for business to inform on his clients."

Recker looked away as he thought about Mia. Jones could tell something else was on his mind. He didn't think Recker would look so despondent just because he came away from a meeting without any new information. Not unless it was something personal. Whatever it was, it didn't seem like something that Recker was too interested in sharing.

"Mike, what is it?"

"Huh?" Recker asked, hearing Jones' voice, but not his words.

"Something else is bothering you. I can tell. It's not just about Bernal, is it?"

"No."

"Something from your meeting with Jeremiah or something else entirely?"

Knowing that a picture was worth a thousand words, Recker dug into his pocket and took out the photos he took from Jeremiah. As he looked them over, Jones could tell he was troubled by whatever it was. Recker briefly looked at them, then handed them to Jones. As the professor browsed through the pictures, he now understood what Recker's problem was, though he hadn't yet learned of how big the issue actually was.

"So, Jeremiah knows about you and Mia?"

"Worse," Recker said.

"You're holding something back. What else aren't you saying?"

"Jeremiah's using Mia as a bargaining chip. He's got people tailing her."

"Oh," Jones said, realizing the severity of the situation. "For what purpose? What does he want?"

"He's using her to get me to work for him."

"To do what?"

"He wants me to take out Vincent for him," Recker said, drawing a surprised look from his friend.

"That's uh... I don't understand why he needs you involved."

"He thinks that at some point, whether soon or not, Vincent's going to try and take over his territory. Instead of waiting and being on the defensive, he wants to get out in front and take Vincent by surprise."

"I still don't see how that involves you."

"Because he knows I've dealt with Vincent before. He thinks I have Vincent's trust and can get a meeting with him, where he wouldn't suspect anything," Recker said. "And then I take him out."

"And why does he need to involve Mia?"

"Because I told him I wouldn't do it. I said whatever they do is between them. Then he showed me those," Recker said, nodding at the pictures. "He said he's got men on her all day. That if I don't take Vincent out, that Mia would be killed."

"Well that certainly is troubling, isn't it?"

"Troubling is hardly the word for it."

"So, what are you going to do?" Jones said.

"Well I'm not killing anybody for Jeremiah and definitely not Vincent. I don't have anything against him and nobody's gonna blackmail me into doing something like that for them."

"Just don't do it then. You can get to Mia before Jeremiah realizes it."

"The problem would then be what do I do with her? She has a boyfriend, she works, I can't just stuff her someplace for who knows how long. And I can't just sit there with her indefinitely either."

"I see what you mean. When does he expect you to do this?"

"Within the week," Recker said.

"Doesn't give us much time."

"No, it doesn't. Especially when we still have another pressing matter to attend to."

"Bernal. I almost forgot how urgent that was."

"I can't protect Mia and look for Bernal at the same time. Because if I take Mia off the grid, even for a couple weeks, and don't take out Vincent, I've declared war on Jeremiah and his men."

"Well, he'd have taken the first shot."

"Doesn't really matter, does it? In his mind, I'd be going back on the deal."

"Or you continue after Bernal until you find him. While you're doing that, I'll stay with Mia," Jones said.

"It's a nice gesture, David, but I don't think it'll work. If they see someone staying with her, like a bodyguard, they'll know something's up. And they'll come after you. You won't be able to defend either one of you against Jeremiah's crew."

"What about Tyrell? Or even Vincent? No doubt he'd be thankful for the news of the impending assassination. I'm sure he'd be willing to supply protection for Mia as a measure of thanks."

"I don't think Tyrell can be of help on this one," Recker said. "Every time he's helped us on something, he didn't have ties to who we were looking for. He does with Jeremiah. He's one of his biggest customers. As friendly as we are with Tyrell, I don't think he'll want to mess with where his bread is buttered."

"You forget, money is not an issue for us. I can give him enough money to last him for years. Even send his brother to college. The least we can do is ask."

"I still don't know. Even if he's willing to help, he's a major resource for us," Recker said, resisting the idea. "He's got connections, he knows people, if others found out he went against Jeremiah, they may turn against him. He may wind up being not as valuable to us. He might even end up dead."

"I would say Mia's life trumps any possible future connections Tyrell may have in store for us. If he's a well of information that dries up then so be it. This is an all hands on deck situation."

"I know. There's just... there's gotta be another way."

"I'm assuming the only way this ends is with Jeremiah being dead, correct?" Jones asked.

"Has to. Otherwise Mia will always be a target."

"I know. I'm not railing against it or anything. I understand this is the only way. What if you take out Jeremiah, and as you're doing it, I'll make sure Mia's safe? We'd have to time it precisely."

"No, won't work. Jeremiah won't meet with me again until Vincent's dead. He's afraid of something bad happening."

"OK. What about my suggestion of having Vincent help?"

"Up to now Vincent and I have been on good terms," Recker said. "But it may not always be the case. Up to now, Jeremiah and I were on good terms. Things can change in a heartbeat. I don't want to get her out from Jeremiah's grasps just to put her in Vincent's."

"He already knows about her though. We both know it."

"You were the one way back when who told me we should be cautious in dealing with him and asking for favors. We've already done it one too many times. Eventually he's gonna ask for a receipt on those."

"What if we don't tell Vincent anything? We just ask for his support in taking out Jeremiah. He obviously wouldn't be opposed to that."

Recker let out a laugh, amused at the prospect of taking out Vincent's competition yet again. "Kind of funny, isn't it?"

"What is?" Jones asked, not seeing the humor.

"When we first started this, I said I wasn't going to help any criminals. Wasn't gonna help them, wasn't gonna save them."

"Things happen we always can't envision."

"Just weird how things work out sometimes. If I take out Jeremiah, it means I'd have eliminated two major criminal organizations in this city. When I arrived, there were three main players here. Once Jeremiah's gone, there will only be one."

"Well the other two only have themselves to blame for their downfalls."

"Yeah," Recker said, shaking his head. "It's just hard to fathom how much I helped shake things out here. Vincent had two enemies when I got here. I already took out one. Now I'm about to take out the other. Both gone without him having to lift a finger."

"Well if it makes you feel any better, you probably helped avoid more bloodshed."

"How'd you figure?"

"Well it's true you helped shrink things down, but it was always going to happen, anyway. It was inevitable. We both know it. You taking out Vincent's competition isn't something that wouldn't have occurred if you hadn't been here. Those three factions would have had their war for more power at some point. You just sped things up. And you did it without the war. If those three factions had erupted, who knows how many innocent people would have gotten caught up in their dealings?"

"Yeah, I guess so."

"Why don't you just tell Vincent that Jeremiah wants you to kill him then let things take their course? Let them deal with each other," Jones said.

"Nice in theory but it doesn't exactly help Mia," Recker said. "Vincent's not just gonna find Jeremiah in a matter of minutes. And don't forget how Vincent likes to meticulously plan things out. He likes to play the slow game. As soon as Jeremiah gets wind of Vincent planning action against him, and that I helped him, or that I didn't kill him myself, he'll put a bullet in Mia's head."

"You're right."

"No, what I gotta do is protect Mia, kill Jeremiah, and find Bernal. And I gotta do it all at the same time."

"It's a good thing we came back," Jones said. "Who else would've been able to handle all this?"

"Yeah, nothing like coming back with a bang."

"Not to complicate matters even more, but based upon your last conversation with Mia, how do you propose to protect her considering she probably doesn't even want to see you?"

"You sure like to pile on, huh?"

"Well it is something of a quandary, is it not?"

"Umm, well," Recker said, stuttering as he tried to think of a solution. "I guess I've got two choices."

"Which are?"

"I either protect her covertly so she doesn't know I'm there. Or... I sneak up behind her, throw her in my car and kidnap her, taking her to a secure location until this matter's settled."

"Hmm," Jones said. "I have to think the second way may not go over so well."

"Yeah."

"You also have another problem?"

"You really are a bearer of bad news, aren't you?"

"Well, since you said it, it reminds me of the fact we don't have a secure location. We've never protected somebody this way before, by hiding them somewhere. We've always done it lurking in the shadows. Without their knowledge until the last possible second."

"I know. Any suggestions or ideas?" Recker asked, ready to listen to just about anything.

Jones thought for a few seconds, but nothing came to him. "Not at the moment."

Recker continued thinking, and after a couple minutes of silence between them, finally came up with what he thought was a good solution. He was positive Jones wouldn't like it though. The professor could tell Recker had thought of something by the little grin on his face and the way he was staring into nothingness. It was a sure indication he'd come up with something.

"I almost hate to ask," Jones said, observing his partner's face. "What are you scheming in that head of yours?"

"You really wanna know?"

Jones closed his eyes and sighed, knowing there was no good answer to the question. "I do, though I have a feeling I may not like the answer."

"Well, you're wrong about us not having a secure location," Recker said. "We do have one. We use it all the time."

Jones tilted his head as he tried to wrap his head around what Recker was talking about. Then, after a few seconds, his eyes almost bulged out of his head and his mouth fell open as he realized what his friend was talking about.

"Please tell me you're not suggesting what I think you are?"

"Can you think of a more secure location than here?" Recker asked.

"Mike, the only people who know about this place are you and I."

"I know. It's perfect."

"But... there's a reason we decided to have a place of business to operate out of which nobody else knew about," Jones said. "If someone else outside of our circle knows of it, then it's no longer effective."

"Mia's not really out of our circle. I mean, she's the closest friend either one of us has."

"Yes, I know, and I know she's trustworthy—"

Recker interrupted. "She could've given us up a long time ago."

"I'm not debating her character."

"Then what are you debating?"

Jones put his hands on his face and rubbed his eyes as he tried to formulate his thoughts into something cogent. "Though I do not believe Mia would ever intentionally give us or our location up, we've now seen several times, whether through her own means or ours, she is a target because of her relationship to us."

"You're worried that six months from now, if she knows our

location, she'll show up and lead someone to us who she's not aware of?"

"That is my fear."

"Then we find a new office after this is over. We move somewhere else," Recker said. "I'm sure you can find another spot within the city, or in the suburbs which would work just as well."

Jones turned away from his partner for a minute, instead choosing to concentrate on the computer screen in front of him as he contemplated Recker's request. Knowing it was a lot to ask, Recker kept himself busy for a few minutes by attending to his guns in the cabinet. Though he believed it was the only solution for the time being, he knew it threw Jones for a loop, springing something of that magnitude on him suddenly. After briefly considering the pros and cons of the situation, and realizing they were losing time on all fronts, Jones finally rendered his decision.

"I guess there really is no other decision to make right now, is there?" Jones said.

Recker closed the gun cabinet and shook his head. "No, not really."

"We got into this business to help people. And no one is more important than Mia," Jones said, looking around the room. "And as you said, this is just an office, nothing more really."

"I know this place holds sentimental value for you since this is where we started everything. But in the end, it's just a building."

"I suppose you're right. The bigger question is how you intend to get Mia here without Jeremiah's men knowing about it."

"Oh, I have a few ideas," Recker said.

"Why does that not surprise me?"

"Do these ideas involve killing anyone or just losing them?"

"Well, if they're dead then they'd be considered lost, wouldn't they?"

"Yes, I suppose they would in some sort of logic."

"I'm not as concerned about the men watching her. I'm more

concerned about her," Recker said. "I'm not exactly her favorite person right now."

"Well if you explain the situation, I'm sure she would understand."

"Getting my foot in the door to explain it might be the tricky part. Maybe you might have better luck."

Jones looked at him strangely, hardly believing his ears. "Are you afraid to talk to her?"

"What? Pffft. Don't be ridiculous. Of course I'm not afraid to talk to her."

Recker may have insisted he wasn't apprehensive about talking to Mia, but his body language said otherwise. He was shifting in his stance and his eyes were dancing about the room, not wanting to look at Jones as they talked about it. The longer the professor looked at him, the more amazed he was. Recker would rather face ten guys with guns in a locked room than face one woman who rightfully chewed him out. Jones couldn't believe it. He never thought he'd see the day when Recker actually appeared afraid to do something, especially something as trivial as talking to someone who he had feelings for.

"You are," Jones said again. "You're afraid of her giving you the business again."

Recker put his hand up to debate the point but quickly put it down, seeing as he really didn't have a leg to stand on. Jones was right. Not necessarily about being afraid to talk to Mia, but him not wanting to get verbally dressed down again. He couldn't recall a time when anybody talked to him like that. And what bothered him the most, wasn't what she said, or how she said it, but the fact she was right. He was always pushing her away, regardless of his feelings for her, and always seemed like he was giving her mixed signals. Maybe now he knew the CIA wasn't chasing after him anymore, he could have the life he once sought. The one he thought he would have with Carrie. The one Mia, at one time, wanted with him. It didn't seem likely at the moment he'd ever get a life with her now, seeing as how she had a boyfriend she appeared to be happy with. But maybe it was the missing piece inside him and why he always seemed drawn to her, even though he always convinced himself to leave. Maybe secretly he still yearned for that life, and until he fully admitted it to himself, he would never be free of the pain which always tormented him.

8

Recker tried calling Mia several times, though she never picked up. He wasn't sure of her work schedule these days, so it was possible she couldn't get to her phone. It was also equally possible she saw him calling and chose to ignore him. He sat down and put his elbows on his knees as he rubbed his eyes, not sure what to do next. Jones could see he was frustrated he couldn't get through to Mia and wondered what else was going through his mind. Though Recker wasn't showing any other outward signs of debate, Jones was sure he must've been having a lively conversation within himself, probably beating himself up over how he's handled things with her. Jones started to feel bad for his friend and tried to make things easier for him.

"Fine. I'll call her," Jones said.

"Well if she picks up right away I guess we'll know what's what."

Jones took out his phone and dialed Mia's number. Much to his surprise, she picked up barely after the second ring. It wasn't too surprising to Recker, however, as it merely confirmed what he suspected. She was in fact ignoring him.

"Mia. Hi."

"David. Hi," Mia said, mimicking his tone.

Jones coughed, trying to figure out the best way to begin. "So, um..."

Mia could tell right away by Jones' stammering he was uncomfortable with whatever he had to say and attempted to snuff out what she suspected it might be. "David, if you're calling to plead Mike's case, please don't bother. I know he's tried to call me a couple times, but right now I'm just not interested in talking to him. I said everything I had to say back at the hospital and nothing's changed since then."

Jones cleared his throat as he attempted to proceed. He might have been worse at relationships than Recker was. And he didn't even have a romantic interest in her. After all, telling someone their life is in danger isn't exactly a pleasant conversation.

"No, Mia, I'm not calling to talk about Michael."

"Then what? Is everything OK?" Mia asked, sounding concerned.

Though she had her issues with Recker at the moment, she didn't have those same problems with Jones. They'd always had a pleasant relationship, and probably because neither had romantic feelings for the other, always seemed to respect each other and their positions. So if Jones was calling to discuss something other than her relationship with Recker, she knew something was amiss.

"What is it?" she asked again, knowing something was wrong.

"Well..."

"David, you always dance around the subject when you have bad news or you don't really wanna talk about what you need to talk about."

"I do?" Jones asked, not realizing he did.

"Yes. You do. Now spill it."

"Fine. The reason Mike's been calling you is not because he's trying to make up, well, he is, but that's not it right now."

"David," Mia said sternly.

"The reason we're both calling is, we're concerned for your safety right now," Jones said finally.

"My safety? What are you talking about? I'm fine."

"I only wish that was the case."

"David, just say it," Mia said, clearly getting worried.

"Several months ago, you and Mike were spotted in the hospital cafeteria by a very dangerous person who runs a rather large criminal enterprise in the city."

"And?"

"The man just gave Mike an ultimatum and is planning on using you for leverage," Jones said.

"Leverage? How? What would he want with me?"

"He doesn't want you per se. He wants Mike to kill Vincent for him so he can take control of the criminal enterprise of the city."

"I still don't get what this has to do with me."

"Because Mike doesn't want to do it."

"You mean there's someone out there Mike doesn't want to kill?" she asked sarcastically.

"Mia."

"I know. I'm sorry. Unfair."

"It's OK. Anyway, that's the gist of it, so we need you to lay low for a few days until we get things sorted out."

"Wait, wait, wait, wait, wait. That's it? There's gotta be more to it. What you told me doesn't seem to have anything to do with my laying low. Why would I have to do that? What are you not telling me?"

Jones sighed, knowing she was too smart to pull the wool over her eyes. "As I said, Mike doesn't want to kill Vincent, certainly not for someone else. This man, Jeremiah, has threatened to hurt you if Mike doesn't do it though."

"Why? What do I have to do with it?"

"Because he knows you're important to Mike, and he needs to use you as leverage to get Mike to do what he needs him to do."

"Yeah, well, if this guy really knew us he'd know I'm not important to him," Mia said.

"Mia, you know that's not the case."

"I'm not gonna hide somewhere, David. Just tell Mike to take care of it."

"It's not quite so simple."

Mia sighed loudly into the phone, fearing there was yet another shoe to drop. "Is there something else you're not saying?"

"Well, that's pretty much it," Jones said.

"David, if you don't spit out the rest of it, all of it, I'm hanging up this phone right now and never talking to either one of you again."

"Jeremiah's got men watching your every move."

"What?"

"If Mike doesn't kill Vincent within the week, then Jeremiah will have you dealt with."

"Dealt with? Are you trying to say he's planning on killing me?"

"Well, I was trying to say it a little more diplomatically, but that's basically the gist of it."

"Why do these things keep happening to me? You may not believe this but I never had my life threatened before I met you guys. Seems to be an annual occurrence now."

"I know. I'm sorry. I wish there was something else I could say."

"So what are we gonna do?" Mia asked.

"Until Jeremiah's been dealt with, we're going to have to keep you here for your safety."

"Here? Where? You mean your office?" she asked, clearly surprised.

"Unfortunately, yes. It's the safest place we know. We can't take you somewhere else and fight this threat effectively, so here it is."

Knowing there was nothing else to say and no use in fighting it, Mia resigned herself to her fate. At least for the moment. "So, should I just come there now or what? How are we doing this?"

"No. As I said, there are men watching you wherever you are. Where are you at right now?"

"At home."

"In order to bring you here safely, Mike's going to have to deal with the men watching you."

"Can't you just do it?"

"Mia, I understand your feelings right now, but for the moment, let's put all that aside for the betterment of the situation."

"OK. You're right. When's he gonna get here?"

"Good question. Uh, hold on, I'll get right back to you."

"You mean you haven't figured it out yet?"

"Well, no. We figured the toughest part was you agreeing to come with us," Jones said. "Let me talk to Mike and come up with a game plan and I'll call you right back."

Jones put the phone on the desk and turned toward Recker, wondering what their next move would be. Getting Mia on board was the first step, now, they had to figure out how to lose her watch dogs. Or kill them. Whichever would be easier.

"Well, we've got her in the loop, now how are we going to bring her in?" Jones said. "It's a cinch you can't just go over to her apartment, put her in the car, and drive over here."

"I'll have to meet her somewhere. A neutral location."

"Hospital's too dangerous," Jones said.

"Somewhere they haven't seen her go before, but a place we both know," Recker said, thinking of a location. "Somewhere I can take out whoever's behind her without a crowd or alerting anyone who's nearby."

"Sounds like Jeremiah's meeting house."

"Yeah, someplace like that," Recker said, still thinking. "Wait. I've got it."

"Where?"

"Haddix Apartments. She knows it, I know it, and they've never seen her go there. If I get there first, I can see how many people follow her in."

"And if any shooting starts?"

"They'll be used to it. And it's not if... it's when. We'll do it tonight, use the cloak of darkness so we're not easily spotted by anyone."

Though they'd continue talking it over and come up with the exact specifics later, Jones called Mia back to let her know the general plan. She expressed disdain at going back to the Haddix Apartments after the last time she went there, but she reluctantly agreed to do it. She was told Recker would call her later with a more detailed plan, but for now just to stay put and get some time off from the hospital since they didn't know how long she'd be gone. With things settled for the time being, Jones would leave Recker to figure out how he was gonna save Mia. His chore was to get back to Bernal and find him.

Even though Jones was knee deep in trying to locate their target, and was a little behind due to the Mia situation, he still found some time to start running a new program. It was actually something Recker said to him before they left for Detroit, but it had been ruminating inside his head for a while as he considered the merits of it. Over the past year, they'd increasingly seen tougher and more dangerous assignments, and at times seemed like they had more work than they could handle. Now, Jones was finally ready to bring someone else aboard, if he could find someone who met his qualifications. Someone like Recker would be ideal, with his values, with his work ethic, with his skills, but maybe with slightly fewer violent tendencies. Jones didn't particularly care if it was a man or a woman, as long as they had the required prerequisites. It wasn't something he was ready to pour himself into totally yet, not with the other issues they had at the moment, but he could at least get the algorithms working.

When he ran his first program, it took Jones several months until he found Recker. He assumed if he constructed his software in a similar manner, the results would probably take around the same amount of time. Of course, with the experience of the first search, he could eliminate a few mistakes he made previously. He hadn't yet let Recker know he really was considering bringing someone new into the fold. He figured he would do that once the Mia situation was resolved and Bernal had been taken down. Since Recker was the one who originally mentioned it, Jones assumed he'd be relieved he was commencing the search. With Recker's input, it might even take less time than he anticipated, but it was something to worry about for another day. His chief concern at the moment was just bypassing the CIA's infrastructure without being noticed, which was no small task. Once he did that, he could start extracting the desired information a little at a time.

Recker saw Jones was feverishly working on the computer, splitting his time between several at once, though he didn't question what his partner was doing. He just assumed it was all in the effort of finding Bernal. But his main worry at the moment was protecting Mia. For the next several hours he went over various plans and ideas, tweaking a few things, abandoning other components entirely until he finally came up with something he was comfortable with. And something he legitimately thought would work. With Jones wrapped up in his own work, Recker didn't bother to share the details. All Jones needed to know was if it would work. Hopefully, it would. Any more issues might be too much for them to handle.

As the sun was setting, Recker grabbed his gear and left the office, only letting Jones know he'd be back later, with Mia of course. His plan was to survey the area of the Haddix Apartments, and even though he was already remotely familiar with it, he still preferred to stake it out for a while first to cement his getaway plan, just in case the police came in hot and heavy. Once he pulled into the parking lot of the apartments, he gave Mia a call to inform her of his plans. Though he was relatively sure she was going to answer his call this time, there was still part of him expecting a hostile response. Much to his surprise, the phone never got to a second ring.

"Hey," Mia said solemnly.

"Hey. So, I'm at the Haddix Apartments now. At eleven o'clock, I want you to leave your place and head over here."

"Why do I have to wait so long? Why can't I just come over now?"

"It's gonna take me a little time to set some things up," Recker said.

"Set what up?"

"Well, I can't say yet. I wanna make sure it's viable first."

"OK."

Recker could hear in her voice that she seemed depressed and sought to reassure her. "Don't worry, I won't let anything happen to you."

"I know. I trust you completely," Mia said. "If there was anybody I had to do this with, you'd be the person I'd call."

"I guess this is the one thing I'm good at."

"Not the only thing."

"Yeah, well, I guess I'll see you when you get here."

"Wait. What do you want me to do when I arrive?"

"Go inside. When I figure out which apartment, I'll text you the number."

Recker went inside, and as Detective Scarborough, knocked on a few doors until he came across an empty apartment. It was just what he was looking for. He jimmied the lock of the apartment he was intending to use and looked around inside, just to make sure there would be no surprises later. Satisfied it would suit his purposes just fine, he texted the number to Mia. Then he went back outside to his car and drove out of the lot. Next to the apartments was a shopping center which Recker drove into and parked. The shopping center and apartments were separated by grass and a clumping of trees and bushes. There was a dirt path which led from the apartments to the center, but it was further down from where Recker was setting up. The foliage was thick and would allow Recker to stand beside the trees without being spotted from either the shopping center or the apartments. He could stay there and watch anybody coming into the apartments. Besides the trees and bushes, the spot he was standing was not well lit and nobody would be able to see him unless they already knew he was there, and even then it would be a stretch.

Recker was eager to see how many people would be following Mia. He estimated it would be three, though he had nothing to base that off of and was just a guess. He hoped it would be less since it would be less work for him. His plan was to pick off her guards, hopefully by splitting them up if possible. He didn't want Mia to get caught up in any crossfire, which is why he hoped to kill everyone before they knew he was there. As he waited amongst the trees and bushes for all the players to arrive, he mentally went over how he envisioned the events playing out. He also predicted any problems and how he would handle them if they arose.

As eleven o'clock hit, Recker noticed Mia's car pull in, right on time. He watched as she parked the car, then got out and entered the apartments. As directed, she went right to apartment 108. Recker left the door unlocked so she could go right in and wait for him. She felt uneasy being there, especially after what happened the last time she visited the place. It didn't help matters that it was so late at night. It was bad enough being there in the daytime, the night just made it seem worse. She also didn't like waiting in the apartment alone. But when Recker texted her the apartment number, he also gave her advance warning she'd be in there by herself for a few minutes until he arrived. It didn't really help her anxiety though.

Recker didn't especially like Mia being in the apartment by herself either, but he needed to see who was following her. About a minute after she arrived, a black SUV pulled into the lot. The vehicle stopped by the curb near the entrance and two rough looking characters got out of the back seat of the car and headed inside. Then the truck pulled into a parking spot, the driver staying inside and waiting for his friends to return. Though the rear of the truck was now facing Recker, he noticed as it pulled in there was also someone in the passenger side of the front seat. He emerged from the darkness of the trees and headed straight for the truck. He removed his police badge from his pocket and held it in his left hand, then gripped his gun in his right. His biggest fear then, was one of the men inside the car recognizing him and jumping out of the vehicle blasting away at him. After a minute of cautiously walking toward the car, Recker reached it without incident. He walked up to the driver side window and tapped on the glass, surprising the men inside. Recker showed his badge, and the driver sighed, thinking their plans had just gone down the drain, and reluctantly rolled down the window.

"What are you guys doing here tonight?" Recker asked.

"Nothing. Just waiting for a friend to come out."

"You guys carrying guns or anything?"

"No, sir."

"You guys work for Jeremiah, don't you?" Recker asked, ready to come up firing.

The two men inside the car looked at each other, wondering how he knew, and whether they should reveal the truth. The man in the passenger seat leaned forward and looked more closely at the man outside their window and thought he looked familiar. Before Jeremiah met with Recker to reveal his plans for Mia and

Vincent, he had distributed Recker's picture to most of his men so they could be sure what he looked like in case they ran into him. The man in the car remembered the photo as he looked at the police officer questioning them.

"Wait a minute," the man said, squinting his eyes. "You're not a cop, are you? You're The Silencer."

Recker smiled. "You got me."

Recker immediately showed his gun and fired at the man in the passenger seat, hitting him three times in the chest. The driver reached for his gun but it was too late. By the time he put his hand on it, Recker had already hit him three times as well. Both men were killed instantly and Recker pushed the driver on his side across the middle console to prevent someone from seeing the dead man from a distance through the window. With those men taken care of, Recker turned around to head into the apartments. As he walked toward it, he reloaded his weapon in anticipation of the next round of action. Since the men inside the apartment didn't know what room Mia was in, Recker figured he'd run into them roaming around the hallways.

As soon as Recker entered the building, he saw one of them standing near the door, probably waiting for Mia to come out. The two men locked eyes and Recker instantly withdrew his gun and fired several shots at the unsuspecting man. Jeremiah's man was leaning against the wall, but slumped down to the ground as he held his midsection once the bullets entered his body. His shirt was soaked in blood as life quickly left his body. There was one man left. Recker didn't immediately see him and stood there silently, hoping to hear something to indicate where he was. Whether it was doors quickly opening and closing, or fast walking footsteps, anything that would give an indication of where the man was. Recker didn't hear anything though. Instead of standing there, or walking through the building to find the man, Recker instead went to room 108, just in the unlikely chance the man found where Mia was. Recker slowly opened the door and took a quick peek inside. He didn't see anybody at first glance. He stepped inside and closed the door behind him, still holding his gun, though he had it down by his leg.

"Mia," Recker whispered.

"Mike?" Mia asked, though Recker still couldn't see her.

Mia emerged from the kitchen where she'd been hiding. It wasn't much of a hiding spot, but in the event someone other than Recker came in, she didn't want to be standing in the middle of the room out in the open. She was relieved to see that it was him. She wasn't ecstatic to be there to begin with, but being there by herself in a strange room, in the middle of the night, had her terrified. Even though she knew Recker was in the vicinity, unlike the last time she was there, her nerves were still a wreck. Upon seeing him, Mia ran up to him and wrapped her arms around him, giving him a big hug.

"I'm so glad you're here," she said, holding him tight. "I'm not cut out for this type of stuff."

"Most people aren't," he said, enjoying holding her once again.

"I've been so scared waiting in here, thinking someone unpleasant was going to come in."

"I know. It's almost over."

"Almost? It's not done yet?" Mia asked, looking worried, as they released each other from their embrace.

"There were four men watching you. I've already taken out three."

"When you say taken out, you mean..."

"Killed. I told you I'd always protect you. No matter what you think of me."

"So, what about the last one?"

"I'll take care of him."

"How?"

"Well, he's somewhere inside the building. Probably checking the other floors. But he'll have to come out front at some point," Recker said.

Recker quickly tried to formulate a plan which wouldn't put Mia in any danger. Without knowing exactly where the other man was made things more difficult. There was a staircase at each end of the hall leading up to the higher floors, not to mention an elevator toward the middle of the building. It meant Recker couldn't stake out one spot, fearing the man could come out via another alternative.

"Why can't we just go now?" Mia asked. "Forget about the other guy."

"What if we start leaving and he sees us as we go out the door and pursues us? Or what if he sees us and don't know he's there and he takes a shot and hits one of us?"

"I just want this to be over."

"I know. And it will be... soon," Recker said.

The other thing complicating the situation for Recker was sure he'd be recognized as soon as the man saw him. Seeing as how Jeremiah's man in the car knew who he was, albeit a little late, it was a sign that Recker's picture had been distributed among the gang leader's men. Recker thought about just staying in the apartment with the door ajar slightly, so he could see anyone passing by, but there was a possibility the man might not come that way if he chose the elevator or other staircase. As he thought about how to move forward, Mia asked him what he was thinking, and Recker relayed the concerns running through his mind.

"Fine. Use me as bait," she said.

"What?" Recker asked, surprised at the request.

"Use me as bait."

"I'm not doing that."

"Mike, I trust you completely. I know you won't let anything happen to me. It doesn't mean I won't be scared out of my mind, but I know you'll protect me. You always have."

"I dunno."

"It's the best way, right?"

"I don't know. Maybe," Recker said, still not sold on the idea.

"Hurry up before I lose my nerve."

Recker sighed and looked away, not really wanting to agree to the plan, but not having any better options either.

"Would you do it if it was someone other than me?" Mia asked.

"Probably."

"Then treat me as if I was anybody else."

Recker nodded, reluctantly agreeing to her proposition. "But you're not anybody else."

She gave him a nervous smile as she waited for instructions. "So, what do you want me to do?"

"Well, seeing as it is you, I want you within arm's reach of me if something goes wrong," Recker said. "Stand just outside the door and keep your hand on the knob. You keep watching both directions, and as soon as you see someone coming, you duck inside. We'll keep the door open so it looks like you're just coming in."

"OK. What are you gonna do?"

"Well as soon as he sees it's you he's gonna follow you and see what number you ducked into. As soon I get sight of him, I'll start firing."

"This will work, right?" Mia asked nervously.

"It'll work. Promise."

Even though Mia had issues with Recker about how he viewed and handled their personal relationship, there was no doubt in her mind, nobody would be better to handle their current predicament than him. There was something soothing in his voice when he confidently said he'd handle something. Though there were never guarantees with anything, especially in volatile situations involving men with guns, but Recker's word was as close to one as humanly possible. Before she lost her nerve, Mia went over to the door and opened it, though Recker stopped her before she went into the hall. Recker wanted to make sure she didn't run into a surprise out there and stuck his head out the door first. With the coast clear, he signaled that she was good to go.

"How long do you think this will take?" Mia said.

"Not long. He should be here within a few minutes."

"What if he's already been by here and just goes outside instead?"

"Then he'll find his buddies and make his way back inside to find the person who did it," Recker said. "Either way, he'll be along soon. Remember, as soon as you see him, don't waste any time in getting in here."

"I'll remember."

Recker initially had thoughts about having her wait by the elevator. He could have probably covered her from the same door he was in, but he thought it was too risky. It was a longer shot to take, and he'd also risk the man taking Mia as hostage if Recker missed his first shot. In the end, Recker figured this was a much easier and less risky plan which didn't involve putting Mia in as much danger. He knew the man wouldn't come up shooting at Mia since Jeremiah needed her alive to keep Recker in line. Just as Recker suggested, it didn't take long to put the plan in action. Within three minutes of her standing in the hall, the man came pouncing down the stairs and threw open the door as he walked into the hallway. Mia immediately saw him enter and waited a split second until she was sure that the man locked eyes on her. As soon as he did, she pushed open the door and went into the apartment.

"He's coming," she said.

"Go in the kitchen and wait," Recker said. "Which way's he coming from."

"Your right."

Recker stood behind the door, still leaving it open a crack. He looked through the peephole until he saw the man approaching the door. The man cautiously approached the apartment and saw the door was not fully closed. He took a few steps toward the door and put his right hand on the front of his pants, presumably reaching for a weapon. Recker wasn't going to give him a chance to use it though. He violently flung the door open and stepped into the frame of the door in full view of the unsuspecting man. The dark-haired man tried to withdraw his gun from his pants but Recker was too quick for him. Recker started shooting, hitting the man in the chest and stomach at point blank range, continuing to fire until the man dropped to the ground. After the fifth bullet entered the man's body, Recker stopped the carnage and went into the hallway, looking around for onlookers. He quickly picked up the man's gun and grabbed his feet, dragging him into the apartment before the curious crowd showed up.

One of the perks of picking the Haddix building was the residents were used to gunfire, hearing it fairly frequently. Any other building probably would've brought out the apartment dwellers almost immediately. Here, though, most people weren't too keen on popping their head out of their door too quickly, for fear of catching a bullet after the fact. Plus, not very many people were very interested in being witnesses. The residents of the Haddix building mostly just wanted to be left alone and minded their own business. As Recker dragged the man's lifeless body into the living room, Mia showed herself from the kitchen, observing him leave the dead body as he went back to the door.

"All right, coast is clear," Recker said. "We've gotta hurry before the police show up."

Recker grabbed Mia's hand and led her down the hallway, leaving the building via a side exit located by the stairways at the end of the hall. As Recker led her away from the apartment building and through the trees and bushes on the side of the property, Mia was confused at where they were going.

"Where's your car? Where are we going?" she asked.

"This leads to the shopping center on the other side. My car's over there."

"Why?"

"That way nobody would see us leaving," Recker said. "Or if the police came before we left, we wouldn't have issues getting out of here."

"Oh."

Within minutes they were on the other side of the divider, quickly scurrying to Recker's car, though Mia was concerned about the fate of her own vehicle.

"What about my car?"

"We'll have to leave it for now," Recker said.

"Why couldn't I just follow you?"

"Because we can't risk it. Once Jeremiah realizes what happened, he'll put an alert out on your car. Every man he's got will be all over the city looking for it. And when they find it, they'll know where you are."

"I guess that makes sense. But doesn't he know your car? Won't he come looking for that instead?"

"Except I put on a different license plate every time I see him, just in case he's tagged it. That way I avoid that problem."

"Sounds like an awful lot of work," Mia said.

"Not as much work as doing this."

9

Just to make sure they weren't followed, Recker drove around for an extra thirty minutes, paying careful attention to any cars behind him. It would have had to be an excellent tail job to be able to follow him based on the circumstances, and since Recker was a master at this type of work. He hadn't met a tail yet he wasn't able to get rid of. Luckily, there was nothing he had to shake this night. When he pulled into the parking lot of the office shopping center, Mia was still confused at what they were doing.

"I thought we were going to the office," Mia said.

"We are."

"Uh, there's no offices here. Are there?"

Recker smiled. "The laundromat."

"Seriously?"

"What?"

"You two are running your entire operation out of a laundromat?"

"Of course not. There's an office over the top of it."

"Oh. Makes perfect sense," she said with an eye roll.

Recker led her around the back of the building and up the wooden steps to the office door. He could tell Jones was still awake since all the lights were still on.

"Home sweet home," Recker said, unlocking the door.

As they came into the office, Jones got up from his chair and walked over to the middle of the room to greet them. Seeing someone new come into their sanctuary was a nerve-wracking experience, even though it was a person they both knew well. It was still a day Jones had never anticipated having.

"Glad to see you both made it in one piece," Jones said, scanning the both of them for holes. "You are both in one piece, aren't you?"

"As far as we know," Recker said, patting his chest.

"Hi David," Mia said.

Jones gave her a smile, happy to see her in surprisingly good spirits. At least outwardly anyway. She didn't appear to be harmed or injured in any way, and her face didn't look all doom and gloom. But she stood by the door for a minute, like she was afraid or nervous to come in any further. Jones went over to her and gave her a hug, then took her arm to try to make her more comfortable.

"Wasn't sure if you'd still be awake," Recker said.

"You really thought I'd go to sleep before you came back or before I knew you escaped unharmed?" Jones asked.

"You really thought I might have problems?"

"Even you, Michael, can run into something you're not prepared to handle."

"So, this is where everything happens, huh?" Mia asked, looking around the room.

"This is it," Jones said.

"It's not quite what I expected," Mia said.

"It grows on you," Recker said.

"What were you expecting?" Jones asked.

"I don't know. Something a little fancier I guess."

"You mean marble floors, crystal chandeliers, tons of windows, things like that?"

"Uh, yeah, I guess."

Jones smiled, amused as he looked around the room himself. "Yes, it's not quite the Hilton, is it? But it works well and suits our purposes."

"Over a laundromat... not at all what I was expecting."

"All the five floor office buildings were taken," Recker said sarcastically.

"Don't you ever get any prying eyes or anything?" she asked.

"No. This is actually a perfect setup for us," Jones said.

"Am I the first person to ever be in here with you guys?"

"You're the first."

"I guess I should be honored you think so highly of me to allow me to be here," Mia said sheepishly.

"Did you bring some luggage or a bag of your things or anything?" Jones asked.

"Uh, well, I did. But I left the bag in my car. I didn't realize I'd be leaving it there."

"You left her car?"

"Figured it'd be better that way," Recker said. "If Jeremiah goes out looking for it, I didn't want it to be parked here. This way, he's got no way of knowing where she went."

Jones nodded, approving of his plan. "Good idea."

Mia walked over to the couch and plopped down in the middle of it, sizing it up. "Guess I'm sleeping on here tonight?"

"I'm sorry," Jones said. "It is quite comfortable though, I've spent many a night on there myself."

"It'll be fine," she said, faking a smile.

Jones told her where the bathroom was if she needed to use it, or if she wanted to take a shower in the morning. He also pointed out the Keurig machine, as well as the refrigerator, which was pretty well stocked with food at the moment, and told her to help herself to anything she wanted.

"What am I gonna do for clothes and necessities?" Mia said.

Recker and Jones looked dumbfounded as they stared at each other, neither of whom had thought much about her request prior to that.

"Drive back to her car and get her bag?" Jones asked. "Or stop by her apartment and grab a few things?"

"No, too risky for that," Recker said. "Just in case Jeremiah keeps a man on her car or her apartment in the event she comes back."

"I guess one of us can go to the store and pick out some things for her for the morning."

"One of us?"

"Well we certainly can't take her and parade her around in the store, can we?" Jones asked.

"I suppose not."

"You guys are gonna stay here tonight with me, right?" Mia asked. "I really don't wanna stay here by myself."

"Of course," Jones said, smiling, trying to put her mind at ease. "One of us often stays here, anyway. That's why there are two couches."

"So what are we gonna do?" Recker whispered in Jones' ear.

"Well, I suppose one of us stays here tonight and the other can go to the store and pick up what she needs."

"So who's doing what?"

"Well, considering your history with her, do you think it's wise if you stayed the night?"

Recker took a good long look at Mia and carefully considered the question, thinking about her attitude toward him lately, notwithstanding at the apartment, and also thinking about her current boyfriend. "No, I guess not."

"So I'll stay the night with her," Jones said. "Why don't you go to the store and pick up things she needs and come back in the morning with them?"

"What kind of things?"

"I don't know. Clothes and necessities are what she said."

"What kind of necessities?" Recker asked, fearful of what they might entail.

"I suppose we should ask her." Jones shrugged, turning back to their guest. "Mia, what exactly do you need?"

"Well how long do you think I'll be staying here?"

"A few days I suspect. A week at the most I would think."

"Pants, socks, a few shirts," she said. "You've seen the things I wear. You know what I like."

"I guess I can handle that," Recker said.

"I guess I also need a toothbrush, bras, and underwear," Mia said, not thinking much about it.

Recker, on the other hand, was not as comfortable with the request. He looked at Jones who was looking back at him just as uncomfortably, the professor glad he wasn't the one heading to the store to fulfill her shopping list.

"Uh... I'm not so sure I can handle that," Recker said.

"It's just clothes," Jones said nonchalantly, trying not to make a big deal of it.

"David, it's bras and underwear. I'm not equipped for that."

"Nonsense. Don't even think about it."

"Guns. I like guns. I'm familiar with guns. I know about guns. I can handle guns. I don't know about bras and underwear."

"Do you mean to tell me you can shoot five men point blank standing in front of you without a second thought and you're going to stand here freaking out about underwear?" Jones asked.

"Women's underwear. It means I have to go... look at them... touch them."

"You certainly have some strange views on things."

"How do I know what fits?"

"Umm...," Jones said, struggling to come up with an answer.

Seeing and overhearing Recker and Jones' conversation, Mia couldn't help but let out a laugh and shake her head at them. She thought it amusing how men like them, especially Recker, could have fears about picking out a lady's undergarments. After thinking about it for a minute, though, she figured it was understandable. It wasn't exactly their usual cup of tea.

"Would it be helpful if I wrote down my sizes?" Mia asked.

"Uh." Recker was lost for words, looking at Jones. "Yes?"

Mia smiled again. "Get me a piece of paper and pen and I'll write down what I need. I'll make it extremely easy for you."

Jones did as she asked and supplied her with a pen and paper. She immediately wrote down the items that she needed then walked over to Recker and handed it to him. She could see the fear was still ingrained in his face as he thought about getting the items.

"It's really not that bad," Mia said, trying to ease his fears. "Nobody will look at you funny for buying ladies bras and underwear. Men do it all the time."

"They do?" Recker asked.

"Sure. We're in the twenty-first century now, remember?"

"Oh. Well can't you just go without, um," Recker said, looking briefly at her chest. "Uh, no, never mind, I guess not."

Jones had sat back down at one of the computer terminals and put his hand over his mouth to prevent himself from laughing or smiling. He sympathized with Recker's fears as he wouldn't have been too keen on going to the store to pick up her things either. He was glad he chose to stay the night and convinced him it was the best option. Mia went into the bathroom for a minute to get ready for bed. While she was in there, Recker tried one last time to switch jobs.

"You sure you wouldn't rather change things?" Recker asked. "I mean, I'm out there far more than you are. It'd probably be good for you to get out for a little while. Smell the air."

"No, I'm quite content staying here for the night. Besides, I'm more used to staying the night here than you are."

"Oh. OK."

As soon as Mia came out of the bathroom, she went straight for Recker. He was standing near the door and ready to go. He just wanted to say goodnight to her before he left. She had a few things on her mind she wanted to talk to him about. Things that had been bothering her since their last conversation at the hospital. She looked at the floor, unsure where to begin.

"I guess, um, I need to apologize," Mia said.

"For?"

"You know, the things I told you in the cafeteria the other day."

Recker shook his head. "Mia, you don't have to do anything. It's fine. I'm not mad. I'm not upset. You had a right to say what you felt. It's no big deal. Apologies aren't necessary."

"No, they are. For me they are. In truth, I'm happy you're back."

"You are?"

Mia nodded, looking down again. "I was just hurt that you dropped off the grid like that. Especially at a time when I could've used a friend."

Recker squeezed his eyebrows together, unsure what she was referring to. "What are you talking about? Are you OK?"

"Yeah, pretty much. Remember you asked how things were with me and Josh?"

"Yeah. I think you said everything was fine."

"Yeah, I lied," she said, forcing a smile. "We, uh, broke up a couple months after you left. I think it was actually the week before I lost contact with you."

Recker looked away from her and glared at the wall, mad at himself for abandoning her. "I'm sorry."

"It's OK."

"Why didn't you say something the other day?" Recker said.

"I don't know. I guess I was just scared. I didn't want to admit how much pain I was in. And I guess when I saw you sitting there, it made me realize how much I actually missed you while you were gone. I guess it's why I snapped at you the way I did."

"He didn't... hurt you or anything, did he?"

"No, no, nothing like that. We just wanted different things. He was more interested in work and moving up the ladder. He's ambitious. And I'm just at the point where I want something more."

"Why didn't you tell me before?"

"I guess I didn't know what to say. I mean, what would you have done? Move back just to console my broken heart?"

"I dunno." Recker sighed. "Maybe I would've done things differently."

"You mean not dropped off the planet for three months?" Mia asked with a smile.

"Yeah, maybe."

"What I said, about leaving is what you know how to do best... I didn't mean it. It was someone else talking."

"No, it was you. It's probably something you've been wanting to say for a while, you just buried it down deep," Recker said. "The pain you were in just made it easier for it to come out."

"Maybe. Anyway, I hope you forgive me."

"Mia, there's nothing to forgive. I wasn't mad at you for what you said. In fact, most of it I probably agreed with."

"Do you think we can get back to the way we were before?" Mia asked, hoping to resume their friendship.

"I would like that."

Recker had serious thoughts about telling her he'd like to be more, but decided it wasn't the best time to drop news like that on her. Though he did miss Philadelphia while he was gone, and it really was like home to him, he realized what he missed most about the city was her. The memory of her soft green eyes, her silky black hair, her pretty face, remembering what her touch felt like, that's what kept drawing him back. Now the CIA wasn't on his tail, he began thinking maybe it was possible to do what he wanted to do with Carrie several years ago. He could actually move on. But those were thoughts he figured were better left to himself, at least for the time being. Maybe when the situation with Jeremiah was over, and they figured out where Bernal was, then he could figure out exactly what he wanted and with whom.

"Are you going to be OK with work?" Recker asked.

"Yeah, I'll be fine. I told them yesterday I had a family emergency, and I'd be away for a week."

"You're not going to get in trouble or anything?"

"No. I have five sick days I can use," Mia said. "If I need more, then I can use some of my vacation days. So, don't worry, everything's fine."

"Now I think of it, I guess it explains why you didn't put up any kind of a fight about leaving your boyfriend."

Mia let out a smile, "yeah, no use in fighting about leaving a boyfriend you don't have."

"Well, I should be going," Recker said. "You need anything?"

"Umm, a hug would be nice."

It was a request Recker couldn't, and wouldn't, deny. For the first time, his thoughts weren't to resist or hold back. He eagerly took her in his arms and tightly wrapped them around her as she embraced their closeness. She buried her head into his chest as she relished the affection he was showing. A few tears rolled down her face as she thought about the trouble she was in. Up until then, she'd put on a brave face and tried not to think about it too much. But she was only human, and a life of danger wasn't exactly something she was used to, or signed up for. She was usually a pretty strong person, but being targeted by a violent criminal gang was hard to deal with, even though she had someone like Recker looking after her. Recker could hear her sniffling and felt bad she had to go through this.

"It'll be over soon," he said softly.

Unlike previous times they'd embraced, Recker was in no hurry to let it end. He wasn't trying to pull back, or worrying about giving her false hope, or trying to convince himself it was a bad idea. He was just living in the moment. When they first began hugging, Jones looked away and started typing away on the computer, trying to keep himself busy during their moment of affection. He periodically looked back at them to see if they'd disengaged, but he was quite surprised to see how long their embrace was lasting. As Jones watched them, he figured it was the type of embrace which was probably a couple years overdue. For some time now, Jones assumed eventually the two of them would get to this point. They had a brief lapse of affection after he rescued her at the cemetery, but as they always did, managed to pull themselves apart after deciding it wasn't the right thing to do.

For Recker's sake, Jones hoped this time they had found each other for good. Even though in the beginning, Jones didn't think it was wise for him to get involved with Mia, or anybody else, he'd begun to realize Recker needed something else in his life. Maybe it was to replace the feeling of emptiness from losing Carrie, or maybe because Recker always seemed to long for something else, something to justify himself other than simply being known as a killer. With the CIA no longer following him, with Agent 17 no longer on his mind, Jones thought the time was finally right for Recker to lose the binds that tied up his soul. After a few more minutes, Recker and Mia finally were able to tear themselves away from each other.

"Well, I should be going," Recker said.

Mia laughed, wiping her eyes. "Yeah, I think you said so already."

Recker put his hand on her face and stared into Mia's eyes as they got lost in each other's gaze. He wiped some of the tears away with his thumb. She brought her hand up to her face and put it on top of his hand, gently rubbing his skin as she basked at his touch.

"When this is over, things will be different," Recker said. "For us."

Mia looked at him in amazement, not believing what just came out of his mouth. For so long she'd waited and hoped for him to say that he wanted her. It wasn't quite riding the white horse and sweeping her off her feet, but it was probably as close as he'd ever get. A smile came over her face as she thought about the possibility of them finally being together.

"But—" Mia said before being interrupted.

"No more buts, or ifs, or maybe's. No more games between us. I don't wanna deny what I feel for you anymore."

Tears started forming in Mia's eyes again as she realized what he was saying. Now she just had to hope he wasn't delirious or losing his mind in the excitement of the situation. Or that a good night's sleep wouldn't change his mind when he saw her again in the morning. On most nights, the implication of them being together would be enough to keep her up for hours in lieu of sleep, but with everything that had happened so far, even this news wouldn't cure her exhaustion.

"Get some sleep," Recker said, kissing her forehead. "I'll see you in the morning."

Once Recker left the office, Mia did an about face and turned toward Jones. "Did that just happen?" she asked, worried maybe she was hallucinating.

"It just happened," Jones said.

"I mean, I'm not dreaming, or seeing things, or talking to people who aren't there or anything, am I?"

Jones laughed, finding amusement in her fears. "No. He was really there."

"Good, 'cause I really thought maybe I'd lost my mind there for a second. I mean, he actually seemed like he wanted me for a second."

"Isn't it what you want?"

"Yes. I just hope he wasn't saying it to make me feel better or something and that he meant it."

"Have you ever known Michael to say something he didn't mean?" Jones asked.

"No."

"Then I'm sure he did."

"Would you be OK with it?" Mia asked, sensing he wasn't over-joyed by the prospect of them being together.

"Why wouldn't I be?"

"Well, I don't know, I just remember you saying something along the lines of like this wasn't possible for us."

"Circumstances change," Jones said. "At one time, I did believe him getting into a relationship with you would've been a mistake."

"But not now?"

"Now he's free from the CIA, he's avenged Carrie's death, there's nothing holding him back anymore. I think ever since I met him, there was something missing inside him. I thought for the longest time, it was just the pain of losing Carrie eating away at him, and once he killed the man responsible, that would have cured it."

"But it didn't?"

"No. I think what he's been looking for has been fulfillment. To feel whole again. It's what he had with Carrie. He felt complete. It's what he's been looking for, what he's needed."

"But why did it take so long for him to see I was standing right in front of him?"

Jones smiled at her. "I think he's always known. He could have never done this if the CIA was still looking for him. Because he was a target, you would be a target, and he would never allow you to end up harmed because of him. But once he knew he was free from them, he finally realized what would make him whole again. And it was you."

10

B y the time Recker showed up the following morning, both Jones and Mia were already awake. They'd show- ered and eaten something out of the fridge and were sitting at the table having some coffee when Recker walked in after ten.

"Thought maybe you'd forgotten about us," Mia said, smiling.

"Not likely," Recker said.

"A little later than usual," Jones said.

"Well I had to make pit stops," Recker said, holding up a shop- ping bag.

Recker walked over to the couch and plopped the bag on it as the others came over and joined him. He started to reach into the bag to take out what he'd bought but brought his hand back out of it as he thought better of it.

"Enjoy your trip?" Mia asked, a big smile on her face, enjoying watching Recker squirm.

"Yes, Mike, enjoy your trip?" Jones said, piling on.

"No and no, I did not enjoy my trip."

"Get everything?" Mia asked, looking into the bag.

"Everything you wrote down," Recker said.

"See, it wasn't so bad, was it?"

"It was terrifying."

"Really?" Mia asked, believing he was exaggerating.

"I was standing by the rack, looking at the, uh, the uh," Recker said, pointing at his chest. "The uh, you know."

"Bras?"

"Yeah, those. I know there were other women passing by giving me strange looks."

Mia laughed, amused at how traumatized he seemed to be. "I know it was hard for you, thank you," she said, giving Recker a hug. "I'll be back."

Mia took the bag into the bathroom to change as Recker and Jones watched her walk away. Once she closed the door, Recker could feel Jones' eyes beating down on him. He slowly moved his head and looked at his partner out of the corner of his eye.

"Can I help you?" Recker asked, turning his head fully.

"About last night."

"What about it?"

"Did you mean what you told her?" Jones asked.

"In regard to what? Were you eavesdropping?"

"It's not eavesdropping if you're talking loud enough for other people in the room to hear. And in regard to telling her things would be different between you."

"Fair point," Recker said. "And I did mean it. Every word."

"Why the sudden change of heart?"

"I don't know. I guess seeing her in danger just triggered something in me. It wasn't something I was planning on doing or saying. Seeing her crying on my shoulder, it just kind of came out. Think it was a mistake?"

"Not if it's what's in your heart."

"So, you approve?"

"I'm not your father or your keeper, Mike. If being with her makes you happy, if it's what makes you whole again, then you have my blessing. Not that you need it."

"It does make it easier knowing you're on board with it."

"I do have one question, though," Jones said. "Would you be proceeding with her if Ms. Lawson hadn't put you in the clear?"

"Unlikely. I lost one before because of the CIA. I wouldn't risk another, even if it meant me being miserable for the rest of my life."

"I want you to know I'm not trying to talk you out of this, but it seems to me you have another problem if you and her co-mingle."

"What's that?"

"It occurs to me, even if the CIA isn't after you, she still may be in danger. Look at what's happening now. Because of what you do, and your relationship with her, she's still a target," Jones said.

"So, what should I do? Never have a life outside of killing people?"

"That's not what I said. You just need to be cautious. If others with a similar mind to Jeremiah know of her... is all I'm saying."

"Once I get rid of Jeremiah, there will be no others," Recker said confidently.

"You're forgetting Vincent."

"I'm not forgetting him. I just don't think he'd ever stoop so low."

"You're putting a lot of faith in someone who is, let's just say, not on the side of the city," Jones said.

"He may not be. But I think, even at his lowest point, he still has some honor."

"Honor among thieves?"

"Something like that."

"And if he doesn't?" Jones asked.

"Then he'll fall like the others and I'll deal with it when the time comes."

Mia exited the bathroom, feeling refreshed from the change of clothes. She threw her arms out as if she was modeling her new wardrobe. She wasn't wearing anything fancy, just a t-shirt, jeans, and sneakers. But it fit nicely on her and was comfortable. Recker had good taste in women's clothes, she thought. She gave him a break and didn't tell him and tease him further.

"How do I look?" she asked.

"Great," Recker said.

"Well, with the pleasantries out of the way, I do believe it's time to get back to work," Jones said, sitting down at his computer. "In case anyone's forgotten, we do still have a cop hater on the loose."

"Oh, yeah, um, what do you want me to do?" Mia asked, drawing a look from both Recker and Jones.

"Do?" Jones asked.

"Yeah. I mean, I can help somehow," she said.

"Doing what?" Recker said.

"I dunno, beats me. But just point me in the right direction and let me do something."

"Mia, we have very complicated systems and software programs in place," Jones said.

"So, what do you want me to do? Just sit around and play solitaire all day and watch daytime soap operas while you two do all the work?"

Recker looked over at Jones and raised his eyebrows. "She's got a point."

"I'm not computer illiterate, you know," Mia said. "I may not be a wiz like you guys but I know how to move a mouse and type. You're looking for some guy, I can help. Four eyes are better than two."

"Fine," Jones said finally. "Pull up a chair."

Mia smiled and clapped her hands together as she rushed over to a chair and spun it around next to Jones. Though Recker was fairly good with computers himself, Jones was obviously the expert, and he'd be the one to show her what he needed and what she could do. As the day wore on, Mia actually handled herself pretty well and was more proficient than Jones assumed. Jones was impressed with what she was able to accomplish. She was no expert, but he didn't have to keep looking over her shoulder to make sure she was on task either. The situation with Bernal and Officer Perez was explained to her, and with Jones' guidance, they continued their search for the pardoned criminal.

While they were on the Bernal case, Recker started looking for ways to end the fight with Jeremiah. Though Recker had known the gang leader for several years, there was still so much Recker didn't know about him. Since they'd always had a good relationship, or at least cordial, and with all the other cases he had to work on, Recker never assembled as thorough a file on Jeremiah as he should have. Though he could try to pump Tyrell for more information, Recker wasn't sure how forthcoming he'd be. Both Recker and Jeremiah frequently paid Tyrell for his time and information on different projects, so it was unlikely he'd willingly offer to give up either of his payment distributors. Recker had heard of a few spots where Jeremiah liked to hang out or frequent over the years, but no place where he would definitely be at a specified time. Since Recker only met him at the boarded-up house for their meetings, and Jeremiah was unlikely to go back there until their business was concluded, he had to somehow figure out where he would be in order to take him out.

As the day grew longer, there didn't turn out to be much success on anybody's front. Recker exhausted his resources to find Jeremiah, but didn't get even one lead. He reached out to Tyrell as a last-ditch effort, but never got a return call from him. Jones and Mia also came up empty after trying to find Bernal. They tried everything they could think of, retraced their steps, but couldn't come up with a location. Seeing as it'd already been several days since they began their search, they assumed time was running short. Recker was ready to use desperate measures. He began pacing around the room, which was usually an indication to Jones that something was on his mind.

"I think it's time," Recker said.

"Time for what?" Jones asked.

"Time to get Vincent involved," Recker said as he stopped pacing to look at him. "I don't think we have another choice anymore."

"I thought you said you didn't want to get him involved?"

"I didn't. But what we're doing isn't working."

"Just to be clear, exactly which case are you interested in bringing him on board with?" Jones asked.

"Bernal."

"And why would he? What are we offering?"

"A deal," Recker said. "If he can find Bernal, I'll take out Jeremiah for him."

"What makes you think he'd agree?"

"You don't think he'd agree to a deal where his competition is eliminated?"

"Yes, I know it's enticing, but what makes us believe he can find Bernal either?"

"I don't know if he can," Recker said. "But it's more than we got now. How many more days can we go on with nothing?"

An agonized look came over Jones, knowing Recker was probably correct in his assessment. "I don't know. But I do know Bernal is unlikely to wait much longer to extract his own justice."

Recker grabbed his phone and called Jimmy Malloy, the usual protocol for getting in touch with Vincent. Even though Recker had a direct line to the crime boss, unless it was an immediate emergency, Vincent preferred Malloy being the principal contact. Within ten minutes, Recker got a call back from Malloy, telling him Vincent was willing to meet with him in one hour at the usual restaurant.

"That was fast," Jones said.

"Well I did say as quick as possible."

Recker wanted to be as prepared as possible for the meeting and printed out all the information they had on Bernal, so he had something to show Vincent, in the event he was willing to help. After taking a few minutes to print everything out, Recker put it in a file folder and got ready to leave. He touched Mia on the shoulder and told Jones he'd be back immediately after the meeting unless something else came up.

Once Recker got to the diner, he saw the same guard as usual at the door. Instead of going through the usual song and dance over his guns, he decided to just leave them in the car, only carrying the file folder with him. As he approached the entrance, the guard put his hand up as if to stop him from going any further. Recker simply opened his coat so he could see he wasn't armed.

"Figured I'd save us both the hassle and left them in the car," Recker said.

The guard shrugged. "I was gonna tell you not to worry about your guns today. You were getting a free pass."

"Are you serious?"

"Boss said you didn't need to be checked today. Guess you've graduated to trustworthy status."

"I should've graduated to sainthood status by now," Recker said, drawing a laugh from the guard. The guard opened the door for him, where he was immediately greeted by Malloy. "Don't you guys ever get tired of the same old thing?" Recker asked. "Maybe you should switch it up sometimes. Maybe every now and then have Vincent greet me at the door and you sit at the table."

Malloy grinned at the humor, though he didn't deem it worthy of a response. Instead, he did like he usually did, and led Recker to the back of the diner at the booth where Vincent was sitting. The boss was just about to cut into a steak dinner as Recker sat down across from him. Recker noticed he also had a plate in front of him.

"I took the liberty of ordering for you," Vincent said.

"Thanks."

"So, what do I owe the pleasure of this meeting?" Vincent chewed at his first forkful of steak, closing his eyes as he savored the flavor.

"Well, first, thanks for meeting me so soon. I was expecting to have to wait a little bit," Recker said.

"It's a good thing you contacted me before dinner."

"Anyway, I wanted to conduct some business with you."

"Oh?" Vincent asked, putting his fork in his mouth again.

"Well, first off, I have a few questions I'd like you to answer if you could."

"Depends what they are."

"Have you been having problems with Jeremiah lately?" Recker said.

"Problems? In what way?"

Recker shrugged. "In any way. Are you starting to jockey for position with him?"

Vincent put his fork down and sighed, pondering the question for a minute, and not looking too pleased at it even being presented. "In the past couple of months, I have transacted some business in what would be constituted as Jeremiah's territory. But it's not with the intent of beginning a war or playing any kind of game with him. I simply began doing some business with a new player and, much to my dismay, they only agreed to conduct it in Jeremiah's part of town."

"So, you're not actively trying to eliminate him?" Recker asked bluntly.

"Not at the present time. In another year or so, who knows? But right now, it's not on my plate so to speak. Why do you ask? Have you heard rumblings of a problem with him?"

Recker tilted his head and stretched his facial muscles, indicating he had. "Yeah, I guess you could say that."

"What have you heard?" Vincent asked.

"It goes a little deeper than just hearing a rumor."

"Considering I haven't heard anything, you seem to have me at a disadvantage."

"I actually had a meeting with Jeremiah yesterday," Recker said.

"I see," Vincent said, looking very concerned. "And the contents of the meeting."

"Largely you. He told me he thinks you're moving in on his territory and planning on eliminating him. He wants to hit you first before you get him."

"Hmm. That's an unfortunate turn of events," Vincent said, wiping his mouth with a napkin. "I appreciate you coming to me with this."

"There's more," Recker said.

"OK?"

"He wants me to kill you."

For the first time since Recker had known Vincent, he actually looked a little nervous. Sitting there across from him, seeing first-hand what Recker was capable of, knowing how dangerous he was, Vincent was worried about the revelation.

"And your reply?" Vincent asked.

"I'm not interested."

"Well I must say it's a relief to hear that, but why?"

"Because I have no quarrel with you," Recker said. "You and I have done business nicely together up until now. I've done things for you, you've done things for me. I see no reason why the situation can't continue."

"I would tend to agree," Vincent said, nodding. "I'll owe you for this."

"Don't mention it."

"I'll have to be cautious in the coming weeks and months."

"It actually brings me to why I'm here. I told you I had some business for you."

"That wasn't it?"

"No. There's more," Recker said.

"I'm listening."

"I'm willing to take Jeremiah out for you if you do me a favor."

"And the favor is?"

Recker slid the file folder across the table. Vincent looked at him briefly before opening the folder and scanning its contents. "Adrian Bernal. I'm looking for him and I can't find him."

"And you think he works for me?" Vincent asked.

Recker shook his head. "No. I just figured you might have better luck in finding him than I have."

"And your interest in him?"

"Case I'm working on."

Vincent threw his hands up, thinking there must've been more to it. "There must be something else at stake. You're willing to kill a powerful player in the underworld in order to find this hoodlum?"

"He's planning on killing a cop. Officer Perez," Recker said.

"And you know this officer?"

"Nope. Never laid eyes on him."

"Then what's the connection?"

"There isn't one. Bernal's a bad dude, looking to kill an innocent person. Perez is a good cop, trying to do his job the best he can. I'm just trying to prevent a bad thing happening to a good person. There's nothing more to it than that."

Vincent smiled, believing him totally. "It's one of the things I've always admired about you. Your sense of morality. You're like a light in a sea of darkness, just trying to break through. You're an honorable man, Mike. You live by a certain code, your own code. I've always respected you."

"So, we have a deal?"

"Perhaps. Far be it for me to assume there's more in play here, so you'll have to excuse my skepticism. But you're willing to kill a man like Jeremiah, which is no easy task by the way, just for help in a case you're working, albeit one of good intentions?"

"There may be more to it than I've laid out and it may not be as simple as I've made it out to be," Recker said. "But I've got my own reasons for wanting Jeremiah dead and they're kind of personal, so I'm not really too keen on sharing right now."

"Understood."

"So, do we have a deal?" Recker asked.

With a smug look on his face, Vincent nodded, moving his mouth around as he swallowed the last part of his food. He called Malloy down to their table and handed him the file folder.

"Adrian Bernal," Vincent said. "Find him."

"Right away," Malloy said.

"Enjoy the rest of your meal," Vincent said, smiling. "We'll find him."

"He's not as easy as you might think," Recker said. "I've tried all the spots."

"Well, we'll go over them again. Just in case."

"What makes you think you'll succeed in the spots I didn't?"

"Well, we may be a bit more persuasive than you were."

11

It'd been about fifteen hours since Recker had his dinner meeting with Vincent. Recker and his cohorts had been working since around seven, putting most of their resources into getting a fix on Jeremiah's trail. Jones, though, wasn't sure it was the best use of their time. He wanted to split their efforts and still focus on Bernal, not wanting to solely leave it up to Vincent to find him. As they were working, Recker periodically looked over at his partner, and could see by the pained expressions on his face that he was bothered by something.

"So? What's eating you?" Recker asked.

"Do you really think it's wise to just abandon our search for Bernal?" Jones said.

"We're not abandoning it. We're just enlisting other resources in our efforts."

"For the last few hours, all we've done is try to get a beat on Jeremiah. I'm not comfortable not seeing what's happening on the other fronts."

"David, what do you want to do? We tried our best. We tried everything we could. We came up empty. What else is there?"

"I don't know. I would just like to know and see what is being done instead of being left in the dark."

"When there's news to report I'm sure we'll hear something," Recker said.

"You're putting a lot of faith in Vincent to find him."

"Why shouldn't I? Has he ever not come through for us when we asked him for something?"

Jones sighed, agreeing with the sentiment, even though he still didn't like it much. "No, I suppose not."

"He did rescue us from that maniac," Mia said.

"Yes, I know," Jones said. "It doesn't mean I have to give him carte blanche over all our activities for the rest of our days though."

They continued working for a few more hours, still focusing on Jeremiah, much to Jones' chagrin. They tried to piece together news reports, public records, witness accounts and contacts in order to find where Jeremiah may have been hiding out. When Recker's phone rang, he and Jones eagerly looked at it, thinking Vincent had found their man. It wasn't what they were expecting though.

"Tyrell?" Recker said.

"Hey. Sorry I didn't get back to you sooner. Had a lot of things going on."

"It's not a problem. What's up?"

"I know you and Jeremiah got this thing going on right now and I'm getting caught up in the middle of it."

"Why, what's going on?"

"You're asking me to look for him. He's asking me to look for you. What the hell's going on with you guys?" Tyrell asked.

"He didn't tell you?"

"Nah, man, just said something about you double crossing him. I know that don't sound like you."

"He wanted me to kill Vincent," Recker said.

"Oh, wow. He didn't say nothing about that."

"I didn't figure he would."

"Did you say you would do it?"

"Yeah. Only because he was trying to blackmail me. Had to figure out a plan first."

"Blackmail you? How?"

"He was threatening to kill someone I know unless I did it. He had men following them."

"The prof?"

"No. Someone else."

Tyrell sighed, trying to figure out what he was going to do. "Listen, he wants me to try and draw you out somewhere."

"Why?"

"Why you think? To put a bullet in you, probably."

"Well that's not very nice," Recker said, joking.

"Yeah, it's all fun and games for you. I'm the one getting caught up in the middle here."

"Listen, Tyrell, I know you do business with both of us and you don't wanna sell either of us out. I'm not asking you to compromise yourself."

"Then what do you want me to do?"

"Give me something I can use. If he double crossed me, what makes you think he won't do the same to you sometime? You're not part of his crew either."

"I live out here, man. I deal with these guys every day, you don't," Tyrell said.

"I know. But I'll make it worth it for you if you give me something though. And I give you my word nothing will ever come back to you."

"You know sometimes I wish I never met you."

Recker laughed, thinking it wasn't the first time he'd heard that. "Congratulations. You just joined my fan club."

"What do you want?"

"Where can I find him? Where does he go? The only place I know is the house in Upper Darby where he meets me."

"Yeah, he won't show up there again for a while, probably. He's got places like that all over the city. Probably a dozen or so. He doesn't like to conduct business in the same place all the time in case someone plans to surprise him, know what I mean? Yeah. I can give you a few addresses but it probably won't do you any good."

"Gotta start somewhere."

"All right, I'll text you the places and you can do whatever you wanna do."

"Sounds good," Recker said.

"But listen, you better get him, you understand? Cause if you don't, and he kills you, and he finds out I was helping you, I'm probably gonna be joining you in whatever plot you wind up in."

"What? You wouldn't enjoy spending the rest of eternity together?"

"Hell no."

"Any other spots besides these meeting houses?"

"Uh, yeah, there's some nightclubs he likes to frequent some-times," Tyrell said. "Good luck if you wanna take him out in one of those though."

"Why? What's so special about it?"

"Well when he goes to those places he's got ten, sometimes twenty guys with him. Man, you'll never get near him. Especially if you're public enemy number one. As soon as you show up, you'll get bullets flying from every direction at you."

"You let me worry about that."

"I didn't say I was worried. I'm just telling you. Plus, those places are packed. You kill him in there and you'll be wanted all over town."

"Wanted by who? The police? They already want me. Nothing would change."

"I guess. If you take out Jeremiah, it's gonna leave a clear path for Vincent you know," Tyrell mentioned.

"I know."

"He's gonna have all the power."

"I know."

"I'm just saying."

"Would that bother you?" Recker asked. "You work for him sometimes."

"I dunno, I guess it'd be OK. I'd just have to pick up more work from him to compensate for Jeremiah."

"Don't worry about it. Like I said, I'll make sure you're taken care of."

As soon as Recker hung up, he put the phone down on the table as he waited for some of the addresses Tyrell had told him about. While waiting, he explained to Jones and Mia what his conversation with Tyrell was about.

"Were you on the debate team in high school?" Mia said. "Because you have a gift for getting people to change their mind on things."

"No, I was on the archery squad."

"No surprise there."

"And I don't think I really did much to change his mind," Recker said. "I think he knows if Jeremiah did it to me, he'd do it to him."

After a few more moments, Recker's phone started going off. It was texts from Tyrell listing some of the addresses Jeremiah used for meetings. He also listed a few of the nightclubs he knew Jeremiah liked to go to. Recker grabbed a piece of paper and started writing them down so they could put them through the computer and start analyzing the locations. As they started plugging the addresses in, Jones had one final thought about locating Bernal, not wanting to give up on it.

"Can we try one last thing with Bernal?" Jones asked.

"Are you still on that?" Recker said.

"Humor me for a second."

"If you want."

"Try having another talk with his girlfriend, Maria Guerrero."

"As me or as Detective Scarborough?"

"As your detective alter ego," Jones said.

"Why? What good would it do? She already blew me off once."

"She may be more willing to talk this time around."

"What makes you think that?" Recker asked, not seeing how the second time would be better than the first.

"If Maria Guerrero knows a man like Vincent is coming after her boyfriend, knowing his reputation, she may be more willing to help you out in finding him before Vincent does."

"David, I think it's a waste of time. Just let Vincent do what we agreed to let him do. Why are you so adamant about not giving Vincent the opportunity to do what we couldn't?"

"Because Officer Perez's life is at stake. And I'm still worried about whether Vincent will be able to find him either. Or whether he'll have the same sense of urgency we do. After all, how willing or eager is Vincent at saving the life of a police officer?" Jones said. "They're not exactly on the same side you know."

"Well, technically, neither are we."

"There is a fundamental difference between Vincent and us. I'm sure I don't need to explain it to you any further."

"Fine. If it'll make you happy, I'll go to Guerrero's house again, OK?" Recker said finally, seeing how important it seemed to be to Jones.

"That's all I ask."

"And if she gives me nothing again?"

"If she doesn't tell you anything, then I'll stop harping on it and leave it alone from now on."

"You will?" Recker asked, not sure he believed it.

"I give you my word. If you get nothing of value, then I promise

I won't say another word about it and let Vincent work his course, for better or for worse."

"All right. I'll give it one more shot with her. Then I'm checking a few of these houses that are on Jeremiah's list."

"Noted," Jones said.

Recker made sure he was loaded up, taking a few extra guns more than usual, just in case he ran into trouble at any of the addresses Tyrell had provided. He bid adieu to Jones and Mia and left the office, hopeful he'd come back with more information than he'd left with. After Recker was gone, Jones looked at Mia, thinking she was handling everything very well. She didn't seem to be fazed by any of the work they were doing, or how they talked, or what they planned on doing. She was much calmer about everything than Jones had expected.

"I must say you're doing a good job in handling your emotions," Jones said.

"Huh? What emotions?"

"Well, if you and Mike proceed with your relationship, then I have to say I admire how calm you seem. He goes out and meets crime bosses, and criminals, and dangerous people, men with guns who could try to kill him, but you don't outwardly show any worries."

"And you're surprised?" she asked.

"Truthfully, yes."

"Well I don't see how it'd do any good for me to be hanging all over him and telling him to be careful and all that. He already knows to be."

"I agree."

"I don't know. I guess I don't want to be one of those girlfr— well, whatever it is I am," Mia said, stopping short of labeling herself since she still wasn't positive yet what their relationship was. "I guess I figure if I keep harping on him to be careful, and worrying about him, and crying on his shoulder, then it gets his focus off what it should be on and onto me."

"I must say I admire your attitude," Jones said.

"I know how good he is, it's not like he's someone who's not experienced or something. If he's out there worrying about me and what I think, then I know that's probably when he'd end up getting hurt. I can't say I'm not worried or I never will be, but I can't let it show."

"Well, there's nothing wrong with showing worry and concern. As long as you don't let it become a sticking point. That's when it would become a problem," Jones said, offering some advice.

Recker's first stop after leaving the office was Maria Guerrero's home. Just as he did the first time he was there, he parked down the street and kept an eye out on the place. In the event Bernal doubled back to the comfort of his girlfriend's house, Recker didn't want to make the potential mistake of barging in and scaring his target away without knowing whether he was actually there or not. Recker sat there for two hours, just watching, and waiting and, without seeing a stitch of movement, decided he'd had enough of that. He got out of his car and walked to the Guerrero house and pounded on the door. Much to Recker's surprise, the door was answered much quicker this time. He only had to knock a couple of times before Guerrero came to the door.

"Hi, rememb...," Recker said, stopping when he saw the side of Guerrero's face.

Her face was swollen and bruised, and her eye was puffy. Gone was the overconfident and cocky person that he talked to before, and instead was replaced by a battered and beaten woman. She looked despondent in her current condition.

"Do you remember me?" Recker asked, concerned for her wellbeing.

"Yes," she said with a single nod of her head.

"Are you OK? Do you need help?"

Guerrero shook her head and shrugged, seeming indifferent. "What do you want?" she asked, holding her face, without a shred of the spirit she showed in their first encounter.

"Who did that to you?"

She shook her head again, not wanting to go into it. "Nobody."

"I know you didn't just run into a wall or something," Recker said.

"It doesn't matter. There's nothing you can do."

"Did Adrian do it?"

She shook her head once again, a painful expression overtaking her face. "No, it wasn't him."

"Then who?"

"Please, it doesn't matter."

Recker took her at her word it wasn't Bernal who had beaten her face to a pulp. But if it wasn't him, he wondered who else would have done it to her. It could've been one of his conspirators, but Recker figured it was a long shot, assuming whoever did it would've had to answer to Bernal for their misdeeds. Considering how she acted to him before, and she was most likely hiding the fugitive, even if she only knew where he was, he probably shouldn't have been as interested in her misfortunes as he was. But Recker ignored it all. What he saw right now was a beaten, humbled woman standing in front of him. After thinking about it, Recker thought he might have had the answer. He pulled out his phone and tapped into a computer database they used in the office Jones allowed him to be hooked up to. He scrolled through some pictures of the more well known, less than scrupulous, criminals the city had to offer. He stopped at the one he thought might have done this to Guerrero. Recker turned his phone around and showed her the picture.

"This didn't happen to be the guy, was it?" Recker asked.

Guerrero took a look at the picture but quickly looked away, not wanting to spend another second having to see the man's face again. The agonizing look on her face told Recker all he needed, without her having to say a word or confirm it really was him.

"Please go away," she said somberly.

"I can help you if you tell me where Adrian is now," Recker said.

"I... I don't know."

Recker couldn't tell anymore whether she was being truthful or not. Before it was easy to tell she was lying. Now, she just seemed like she wanted to curl up in a corner somewhere. "If you don't, some innocent people are going to wind up getting hurt."

"What's it look like to you right now?"

"I can help if you let me."

"If I knew anything, don't you think I would've already told the guy who did this?"

Recker wasn't sure how else, if at all, he could get through to her. He didn't have much more of a chance though. Before he could think of anything else, Guerrero ended the conversation by giving him a smile, then calmly closed the door on him. Recker walked back to his car, and though he wasn't happy the woman had been beaten, was content with his efforts. There wasn't much more he could do, especially if she wasn't willing to cooperate. Before Recker got going with his other business, he called Jones to let him know what happened and to inform him he was moving on.

"Looks like we close the books on Bernal," Recker said.

"The girlfriend still won't talk, huh?" Jones asked.

"No. She was much more pleasant about it this time, though."

"Oh?"

"I guess it's tough to be snarky when half your face is black and blue."

"Black and blue?"

"You didn't..."

"Of course *I* didn't," Recker said, anticipating where Jones was going with that.

"I should hope not."

"I didn't. But somebody sure did."

"One of Adrian Bernal's associates no doubt," Jones said.

"No, I don't think so."

"Why not?"

"I showed her a few pictures. A couple she had no reaction to. But one, one she could hardly look at. She turned away instead of looking at it."

"Whose picture was it?"

"Jimmy Malloy."

"I guess it means Vincent's making good on his promise," Jones said.

"He did say he could be more persuasive than us."

"I would've hoped it meant not beating up on women, though. I guess nothing's off limits to them."

"Not much," Recker said. "At least we know they're working the case though."

"What about Maria Guerrero?"

"What about her? I asked if she knew where Bernal was. I asked if I could help her. She still won't talk or accept help. There's nothing else we can do for her. You can only help people who'll let you."

"I know. I guess that's that then."

"Seems so."

"Are you satisfied now?" Recker asked. "Can you accept Vincent's on it? Can we move on?"

Jones sighed, still not liking it, but agreed anyway. "Yes. What are your plans now?"

"Stake out a couple houses on Tyrell's list."

"When you say stake out, you mean?"

"Well, we'll just see how it plays out."

12

Recker's first stop was an address on sixty-second Street. As he usually did, he parked down the street to survey the area for a while. The address actually wasn't a house and appeared to be a vacant building. It had two roll up bay doors, along with an entrance door, giving Recker the impression it was possibly an auto repair garage at one time, or maybe some type of shipping business. In any case, there was some graffiti on the bay doors and he didn't notice any kind of activity going on to indicate it was a thriving or active business.

Jones had gotten back to him with information on the building after digging into records and confirmed it did indeed used to be an auto garage. But it'd been closed for several years. The current owner of the building wasn't listed as Jeremiah, and the name on the lease didn't appear to have any connections to him, at least no obvious ones. It was possible one of Jeremiah's men had taken care of the contractual obligations to leave his name off it. Recker just sat and waited, hoping something would catch his eye at some point. If not, he'd eventually just break in somehow and see if there was anything inside which would give him some information into Jeremiah's business dealings. Luckily for him, he wouldn't have to resort to such dealings.

After a couple hours of waiting, he observed an expensive looking black SUV pull up, parking along the curb near the front of the building. Four men piled out of the car and milled around on the sidewalk by the door for a few minutes, seemingly joking around with each other. One of the men eventually pulled out a set of keys and unlocked the door, allowing the others with him to enter the facility. Recker gave them an hour to themselves before he decided to approach the building, just in case they had more visitors coming. He also wanted to make sure there was nobody else already inside the building, though he made what he thought was a safe assumption that there wasn't, considering they had to unlock the doors themselves. As he approached the building, Recker continuously looked around, just in case there were look-outs on the perimeter. Since there didn't appear to be any, he walked right up to the glass door and started pounding on it. Within a few seconds one of the men he recognized from the car came up to the door. He opened it just a little so he could see who the stranger was.

"What do you want, man?"

"Oh, I just came here to deliver a pizza," Recker said.

"What?"

"Pizza. Someone here order a pizza?"

The man looked at Recker like he was crazy. "No, no one here ordered a pizza!"

"Oh, my mistake. I must have the wrong address."

"You don't even have a pizza."

"Oh, I left it in the car till I made sure I had the right place."

"Well you got the wrong place. Hit the road, bud."

"Sure, no problem. Could you just look at this and let me know where this is before I go," Recker said, reaching into his coat for something.

The man didn't want to help him with anything and looked perturbed about Recker wasting his time and was about to shut the door in his face. Recker removed his gun from inside his coat and fired point blank at the man's chest, putting a couple holes in it. As the man fell backwards from the blast, Recker stepped over the man's dead body as he quickly identified where the other men were. There was a small folding card table in the middle of the room where the other three men were sitting. There were a few handguns on the table along with some sandwiches. As soon as the men heard the gunfire at the door and saw their friend fall, they jumped to their feet, grabbing their weapons. Recker fired a couple rounds, hitting two of them immediately, though not fatally. With bullets heading back in his direction, Recker took cover behind a small counter near the front door. It must have been a cashier station left over from its previous life.

The good news for Recker was, even though he was outnumbered, the other men didn't have much to take cover behind. There was actually nothing other than the small card table, which they flipped up on its side and crouched behind, though it didn't really offer much protection. It was tough for them to get any kind of shot off without exposing at least half their body. One of the men Recker shot in the thigh and the other got hit in the left arm. There was a brief lull in the action lasting about five seconds as the participants reloaded their weapons. Recker peeked over the counter and saw he had an opportunity to pick off the first person who showed their head. He pointed his gun, waiting for his next victim. The man to the far left of him was the first to raise up in anticipation of firing, though he never got the chance to. As soon as his body rose above the table, Recker blew a hole through the middle of his chest. Seeing their friend shot dead next to them angered the remaining two and spurred them into trying to avenge his death. They both fired furiously at the counter Recker was hiding behind, causing him to get down and take cover. He crawled to his left and the end of the counter, waiting for the right opportunity to strike. The last two of his targets continued firing at the counter, hoping the bullets would pierce through the wood and somehow find a way through and into Recker's body. They had no such luck, however.

Recker emerged from the side of the counter, firing away at the two men, catching them by surprise. The first man got hit in the shoulder and went down, then the man on the right got shot in the stomach and hunched over as blood started pouring out of his midsection. Recker got to his feet and quickly made his way over to the bodies of the remaining survivors. As the man in the middle, who was clutching his wounded shoulder saw his shooter standing over him, he reached for his gun. His weapon had dropped from his hand when he was shot and wound up laying only a few inches away from him. Recker noticed and kicked the gun away, the weapon sliding across the concrete floor until it hit the far wall. Recker pointed his gun at the man's head as he gave him a couple options.

"You got two choices," Recker said. "You can live or you can die. It's real simple."

"Screw you," the man whispered through gritted teeth against the pain, sweat beading on his face.

"Tell me where I can find Jeremiah and you'll be the only one that walks out of here. Or you can clam up like a good soldier and get buried with your buddies."

"Once Jeremiah finds out I sold him out I'll wind up next to them, anyway. That's no deal."

"Not if I kill him before he finds out."

"I ain't telling you nothing."

Recker straightened his arm out as he steadied the weapon, aiming at the man's chest. "Last chance."

The wounded man just looked away, not interested in the deal that Recker offered. A man of his word, Recker pulled the trigger and helped the man meet his dead friends. He heard the last survivor groaning, keeled over on his knees, and clutching his stomach, blood staining his hands and arms, not to mention the gray concrete underneath him. Though Recker assumed it would be a waste of time, he offered the guy the same deal as the last one.

"What about you?" Recker asked. "You feel like talking or you feel like dying?"

"I'm dead, anyway. I know I ain't gonna be able to make it to no hospital."

"I can call an ambulance real quick."

"Nah, I'm a loyal soldier. I'd rather die than betray my friends."

"Suit yourself."

Recker knew it was a lost cause trying to convince him otherwise and pointed his gun at the back of the man's head. He pulled the trigger, and the man slumped forward onto the ground. Recker took one last look at all the bodies just to make sure none of them were still breathing, and they couldn't give him a last second surprise. After confirming they were all dead, he took a look around the place to see if the thugs had any papers lying around which would give a clue as to where Jeremiah was now. The place was pretty scarce though, and there wasn't much to even check. There was a back office to the rear of the building with a desk and a filing cabinet Recker searched through, but the only things he found were meaningless papers. Nothing which would indicate where Jeremiah was or give away any of his business dealings. He took one last look around the building to make sure he didn't miss anything, then he also checked the dead bodies to see if they had any papers on them. Still nothing. He took a phone out of one of the dead men's pockets and scrolled through it, hoping he could get something from it. He saw a contact listing for Jeremiah and thought about calling it to let him know he was coming, but thought better of it. He figured once he took out some of his men, Jeremiah would get the word Recker was coming. There was no need to alert him beforehand and get his men hyped that Recker would be coming. With his work there finished, Recker started on his way to the next address on the list. As he walked out the door, he picked up his phone and called 911.

"What is your emergency?" the operator asked.

"Yeah, I'd like to report a shooting. There's four dead bodies inside a vacant building."

"What's the address?"

Recker gave the address then hung up. By contacting the police, he assumed Jeremiah would get the word that he hit his place rather quickly. He called Jones to let him know of the trouble he'd ran into at the first stop, and to let him know he was still alive and kicking.

"I'm heading to the second location now," Recker said.

"Anything of note at the first spot?" Jones asked.

"Uh, yeah, four dead bodies."

"Were they dead when you found them?"

"Nope."

Jones sighed, hoping he wasn't going to leave a trail of bodies everywhere he went. "Do you really think it's wise to be so public with this? Jeremiah will surely know it was you."

"That's what I'm counting on," Recker said.

"Why? Why do you want him to be ready for you?"

"Because I want him to know I'm coming. I want him to know I'm dismantling him and his crew one stop at a time. He threatened me, he threatened someone I care about. I'm not just gonna roll over and tickle him. I want him to know hell's coming."

"It surely is."

"Mike, just be careful," Mia said, listening on the speakerphone.

"Don't worry. It's not my time to go yet."

"Did you check if there was anything left behind we could use to get a fix on Jeremiah's location?" Jones asked.

"Yeah, there wasn't much there. It didn't look like a place they spent much time at. Probably just a spot to conduct business then leave immediately afterwards."

"I wouldn't be surprised if it's what all these addresses are," Jones said.

"Could be. It might be all Tyrell knows, the meeting places. He might not have been to any of Jeremiah's strongholds."

"Well, I've already pulled up your next stop," Jones said, looking at a picture of the house on the computer. "It's an end unit row home in West Philly."

"Is it boarded up?" Recker asked.

"It is."

Recker told his partner he'd let him know when his business was concluded after the next stop. He had a feeling it would be an almost identical situation as the first one. And Recker was just fine with that. In fact, as far as he was concerned, the more bodies piling up, the better he liked it. As long as his wasn't one of them. The more he thought about everything, the angrier he got about it. Now, he didn't want to just kill Jeremiah, he wanted to cripple his organization first, then kill him. He wanted Jeremiah to worry about him coming before he got there. Recker figured it would make killing Jeremiah much more satisfying. This was the side of Recker, Jones worried about. When this part of his personality emerged, the one that enjoyed being The Silencer, Jones knew there wasn't much he could do to stop it. All he could really do was get out of the way and hope nothing bad happened to Recker, because he knew plenty of bad things were going to happen to the people who happened to stand in his way.

When Recker got to the row home in West Philly, just like usual, he waited an hour or so to survey the area. Almost immediately, he saw a few men hanging around out front on the porch, alternating between there and inside the house. He saw three different guys go in and out of the house within the hour. Recker was assuming there was more. One thing he knew about Jeremiah was, he never seemed to travel light. In every situation Recker could think of where he interacted with Jeremiah, or members of his gang, there were always at least four of them. Whenever he met with Jeremiah, at the former auto garage, the men trailing Mia, there were always at least four. He figured this place would be no different.

Recker took a few minutes to think of his plan before he walked over to it. He assumed he'd have to improvise once the bullets started flying, but he wanted to at least have something to start with. Once he got out of his car and started walking toward the home, he noticed someone looking out through the upstairs window, which was not boarded-up. It was actually the only window of the house with open glass. Recker figured it must have been the lookout station, the guy who warned everyone inside if trouble was coming. If that was the case, then they'd all know he was coming well before he got to the front door. As he walked on the concrete sidewalk leading up by the house, nobody was on the porch. But as he started up the steps leading to the front door of the house, two men came out to see what he wanted.

"Far enough," one man said, with a gun firmly visible and planted in the front of his pants, inside the waistband. "What do you want?"

"I have a message from Jeremiah," Recker said. "He told me to bring it over right away."

The man looked at Recker eyebrows squeezing together, not knowing a thing about it. "He didn't say anything about you coming."

"Well, he was worried about phones being tapped. So he had me do it old school."

"OK. So, what's the message?"

"Well, he told me to only give it to the guy in charge."

"What's it about?"

"Something about the woman he was having tailed. You guys know about that?"

"Yeah, we know."

"The guys tailing her were killed, and she escaped. We think we got a location on her and I think he was giving you guys the assignment."

The man sighed and rolled his eyes, thinking he was being a pain. "Get Stash out here," he said to the other man out there with him.

Just a few seconds later, the man emerged with the third man of the group, a bald-headed man, tough looking, goatee, looked like a weightlifter. He also had a visible gun in the waistband of his pants. Seemed to be a staple of this crew. The leader looked the stranger up and down, giving Recker the impression maybe the man recognized him as The Silencer. If he did, Recker was going to have to come up shooting in a hurry.

"You got a message from Jeremiah?" the leader asked.

"Sure do."

"I don't recognize you."

"Oh, well, I'm kinda new. He just started using me last week," Recker said.

The man seemed satisfied enough, though he still didn't look that pleased. "All right, what do you got? Let's see it."

"OK, I'm, uh, gonna reach my hand in," Recker said, pointing to his coat, acting nervous so they wouldn't consider him a threat and he could get the jump on them. "I'm gonna reach in and get the message."

"Just do it."

Recker laughed, "OK. Just wanted to make sure you guys weren't trigger happy," he said, pretending to struggle in finding the note. "So how many guys you got in there, anyway?"

"None of your business. Jeremiah must be scraping the bottom of the barrel if he's hiring guys like you these days," the leader said sarcastically, growing impatient.

"Oh, here it is," Recker said, putting his fingers on the handle of his gun. "I got it."

Recker quickly pulled out his weapon, catching the three men off guard. His first shot hit the leader in the chest, then in a matter of seconds, turned toward the other two and hit the both of them before they were able to withdraw their guns. Without knowing how many were inside, Recker hurried to the door before he had company. Before going inside, he couldn't take the chance of any of the three men on the porch sneaking up on him inside. He had to make sure they'd all stay down permanently. Without a second thought, he delivered a headshot to each of the three gang members, though as it turned out, two of them were already dead so it didn't matter but, 'better be safe than sorry' as his old daddy used to say. It gave him peace of mind knowing he wouldn't have to worry about them again.

Recker returned to the screen door, throwing it open as he stood in the doorway, ready to fire. As soon as he showed himself, a bullet whizzed by him, ripping through the mesh screen in the door. Recker quickly identified where the shot came from, locating a man standing on the second floor, at the top of the steps. He returned fire, grazing the man in the leg, dropping him to his knees. The man cried out in pain and grabbed for his legs, though he knew he had to dispatch the dangerous man at the door before he came up and finished the job. As he brought his gun up and tried to aim at the man in the door, Recker took aim himself. He fired a couple more rounds, both of which found its intended target. The man at the top of the stairs lost his balance as the bullets ripped through his insides and proceeded to tumble violently down the steps. The man came to his final resting spot just in front of Recker. He was flat on his back with his arms outstretched, blood soaking through his white shirt. Recker gave him a nudge with his foot to make sure he was gone. He was.

All was quiet for a few moments. Recker wasn't quite sure which he preferred, the deathly silence or the action-fueled haze of gunfire and bullets flying all around him. At least when people were shooting at him he knew what to expect. He worried more when he wasn't sure what was around the corner or lurking in the shadows. As he stepped into the living room, he immediately noticed this house seemed to have more furnishings than the others he'd been in so far. There was actually a couch, some tables, and a few lamps. It actually looked like people spent time there instead of using it for a few minutes for a transaction then leaving for somewhere else. Recker cautiously and methodically went through every room on the first floor, ready for more shooting practice. Luckily for them, nobody else was present.

Recker then proceeded to go up the steps to the second floor. Once he reached the top step, he heard a noise coming from the first bedroom to his right. The door was closed, leading Recker to believe somebody was in there. The rest of the rooms on the floor, two other bedrooms, and a bathroom, had their doors open. Recker quickly swept his way through them to clear them before returning to the room with the closed door. He assumed he was going to be met with gunfire the moment he opened the door, maybe even once he jiggled the handle. Recker figured he'd bypass all that and quietly stepped toward the door then forcefully kicked it open. A gun fired, and a bullet lodged into the swinging door. Recker took a step inside the room and found his next target, ready to pounce on him. Just as he was about to squeeze the trigger, though, he let up and took his finger off it. The person who fired the shot at him looked awfully young. He looked like he was just a kid, couldn't have been more than sixteen years old. Seeing someone like Recker pointing a gun right at his head, the kid looked beyond terrified and dropped his own gun as he waited for the inevitable from the dangerous man.

"How old are you, son?" Recker asked.

"Sixteen."

"Your folks know you're here?"

The kid, still looking scared as could be, shook his head.

"What are you doing here with these people? How long you been here?"

"They were just initiating me this week."

"Is this really the kind of life you want?"

The kid just looked at the floor and shrugged. "What's your mom think about all this?"

"She's worried about me 'cause I dropped out of school."

"You know anything about the man you're working for, Jeremiah?" Recker asked.

"Not really. Just what they tell me."

"Well, I'll tell you now, there ain't no future in it. I'm putting him out of business."

The kid nodded, not sure what the man was going to do with him.

"You know who I am?" Recker asked.

"No, sir," the kid said.

"They call me The Silencer. You heard of me?"

Not knowing what to say, the kid nodded again.

"You wanna die before you hit seventeen?" Recker asked.

"No."

"Because if I was of that mind, you'd be joining your friends out there."

The kid nodded again, knowing the man could've killed him easily by now. "Are you gonna let me go?"

"It kind of depends on you," Recker said. "If you were two or three years older, you'd be dead already because I'd have killed you the minute I laid eyes on you."

"Yes, sir."

"I'm gonna give you a second chance, which I don't give many people."

"Thank you."

"I don't want thanks. I just don't wanna see you out on these streets again with a gun in your hands," Recker said. "You go home, hug your mom, get back in school, and do what she tells you. You do that, you'll be alright."

"I will," the kid said, running past him to get out of the house as quickly as possible.

Recker stopped him before he got out of sight though. "Hey," he said, stopping the kid in his tracks. "I mean what I said. I catch you next week or next year running with some thugs again, and you got a gun, next time I'm pulling the trigger. And you'll make your mom a very unhappy woman. You understand me?"

The kid nodded, "Yeah."

"Go on, get out of here."

Recker wasn't sure if his little talk would really do any good, or whether it would just fall on deaf ears, but at least he tried to help a young kid out. He showed a little compassion, which should've made Jones happy. He looked through the one open window and saw the kid fly out of the house and down the street. He wanted to make sure he didn't misjudge the kid and just send him downstairs and allow him to wait for Recker as he descended the stairs, giving him some free shots at him. Knowing there was nobody left in the house alive, Recker started looking around the house, going through each room for clues as to Jeremiah's whereabouts. He knew he didn't have a lot of time though, as he figured somebody would've reported the shots by now, and possibly the dead bodies if someone saw the activities on the front porch. He assumed the police would be there within a few minutes so he only quickly looked through each room in the obvious spots to see if something was lying around in plain sight. Once he was satisfied there wasn't anything to find, and as he thought he was running out of time, he started to leave. He walked out the front door and stood on the porch, looking up and down the street for signs of the police. Surprisingly, there was nothing coming yet. He stood between two of the dead bodies and looked down at them.

"I'm surprised you guys fell for that," Recker said, referring to the note trick they fell for.

As he walked down the steps, he heard sirens in the background. He assumed the police were on their way. Recker turned the corner at the front of the property and started walking down the sidewalk. Within another minute, a few police cruisers came driving by him. Recker turned his head away from the street and coughed to hide his face from the officers driving by. Once he got to his car, he sat there for a while and watched the police activity at the house. He also called Jones to let him know to scratch another one off the list.

"I take it there were no problems?" Jones asked.

"I guess it depends on what you define as a problem. It was nothing I couldn't handle."

"I almost hesitate to ask, but I guess I should, how many bodies should I be aware of?"

"Uh, let's see... uh, four."

"You can't remember? Do you need some extra time to think about it?"

"No, it was four," Recker said. "Well, it was actually five. But I only killed four."

"Oh, you let one get away. You must be losing your touch," Jones said sarcastically.

"No, I'm not losing my touch. One was a kid, probably fifteen or sixteen. I gave him a little speech, then sent him packing."

"Well, it was very sporting of you."

"I don't know about that. I just hope it did the kid some good and I never have to see him again. I let him off with a warning. Hopefully, it'll be enough."

"Well, you gave him a second chance. That's more than some people get. The rest will be on him. I hope he takes it."

"Yeah." Recker sighed. "I guess it's on to the next address."

"Why don't you come back to the office and recharge for a bit?" Jones asked, not wanting Recker to overexert himself.

"I'm OK."

"Mike, you can't wage a war and win it in one day. You've taken out eight of his men, stormed two of his meeting spots, you've sent him a message. If you keep going from house to house, eventually they'll be waiting for you. And they'll be shooting first."

Though Recker didn't want to admit it, he thought Jones might have had a point. "Yeah, maybe you're right."

"We've already crossed two off the list. Let's see how it shakes out before we make our next move," Jones said. "Maybe he'll do something crazy or desperate in response and make him play right into our hands."

"It might be wishful thinking, but OK, we'll give it a try."

13

By the time Recker had gotten back to the office, it was well after dinner. Though he agreed with Jones' premise of waiting to see if Jeremiah would make a move, he still was a little amped up and was ready for another battle immediately. He drove around for a while, hoping something else would come up he could deal with right away. Part of why he was so anxious to keep moving was that he knew what an inconvenience it was to Mia, having a death threat hanging over her head, and hiding out in a strange office indefinitely. He wanted to try to simplify her life as quickly as possible, even though he knew it wasn't likely to end this war right away. But Jones was right, he couldn't keep barging through every front door he came across. Eventually they'd be waiting for him and wouldn't fall for anything in his bag of tricks, they'd simply shoot first before he had a chance to open his mouth.

As soon as Recker entered the office, Mia ran over to him and hugged him. She wanted to give him a kiss, but figured she'd save it for another time, when there wasn't as much going on. She didn't want to overwhelm him with personal stuff when she knew he had other things on his mind.

"I'm glad you're back," Mia said.

"And in one piece," Jones said.

"Just another day at the office." Recker shrugged it off.

"Did you eat yet?" Mia asked.

"No. Haven't had time."

"We haven't either. I'll fix us some sandwiches."

Mia went to the refrigerator and got out the lunch meat to make the three of them dinner. Recker was starting to feel some exhaustion from the day's events. He sat down on the couch and looked up at the ceiling and tried to wind down a little. It was tough for him to block everything out of his mind, though, and replayed his last two stops in his head a few times. He looked over at Mia and was thinking about how well she seemed to be handling everything. She didn't give any outward signs of worry about herself. He admired her for how strong she seemed to be. Not a lot of people would act as calm as she was.

After they ate dinner, they sat around and started making plans for the following day. They still had a bunch of addresses for Recker to check out, though Jones wasn't sure it was such a good idea anymore. After what happened today, there was no way Jeremiah's men wouldn't be waiting for Recker to strike at any of the locations. Jones didn't feel it was even remotely possible Recker would have the same success as he did.

"After what happened today, do you really believe you're going to find anything at any of these locations?" Jones asked, holding the paper up that had the addresses on it.

"Maybe not. That doesn't mean it won't be worthwhile though."

"I guess it would depend on what we're talking about. Are we talking about trying to find Jeremiah and ending this as quickly as possible? Or are we talking about finding as many of his men as possible and killing all of them along the way? Which is it?"

"A little bit of both maybe," Recker said.

"Mike, this isn't a both situation. Finding and eliminating Jeremiah should be the only consideration. With him, it ends. It's not about killing his soldiers," Jones said. "Once he's gone, they will no longer be a threat. They won't go against you without his orders."

"That's kind of a big assumption, don't you think?"

"No, I don't. I think it's a reasonable assumption. You don't need to wage war against everybody. Just one man."

"That's what I'm doing."

"And what do you think will happen if you go to one of these houses and they are waiting for you? Instead of four or five guys, they lure you in, and inside they have twenty guys. What then?"

"Then I'll deal with it."

"You're not invincible. What do you think will happen if you get yourself killed?"

"I guess I'll be dead."

"And Mia? What do you think will happen to her if you're gone?"

Recker looked at her, getting a warm smile from her in return. "You sure like to hit below the belt."

"Sometimes it's what's necessary to bring people to their knees and make them realize what's at stake and what's important," Jones said.

"Can I put my two cents in?" Mia asked, putting her hand up.

"Of course," Recker said, although he had a pretty good idea which side of the fence she'd fall on.

"I agree with David. There's no way they won't have some type of trap set for you at these other places."

"And do you have another suggestion?"

"Didn't Tyrell mention something about Jeremiah going to nightclubs?" she asked.

"Yeah."

"Wouldn't it be a better plan to try and take him out there instead?"

"Do you realize how tall a task that will be?" Recker asked.

"How many nightclubs can there be?"

"In Philadelphia? Hundreds."

"Really?" Mia asked, obviously not a member of the nightclub scene. "I thought there were maybe twenty or so."

"No. There's no way of knowing right now what clubs he likes to go to or what night he goes," Recker said.

"But Mia may be on to something," Jones said. "Just hitting these houses on this list isn't going to accomplish anything, other than satisfying your thirst for blood. You're not going to find anything leading to Jeremiah in any of these places and the odds of you getting any of his men to talk or give him up are beyond... well, let's just say you'll have a better chance with a snowball you know where."

"OK. Even if I agree to forego the rest of this list, how are we gonna find out which nightclub he goes to?"

"Most nightclubs have security cameras, do they not?" Jones asked.

"Yeah."

Jones tilted his face and looked at him with his eyebrow raised. He waited for Recker to catch up.

"And you can hack into them," Recker said, finally getting up to speed.

"Once I get into their systems, I can start running facial recognition software over the past few weeks until we see which clubs he goes to. Maybe we can find a pattern. Maybe he rotates between a few clubs in particular."

"Plus, it'll keep him off balance," Mia said. "He'll be so worried and focused on you hitting these other houses that you'll throw him off when you don't show up."

Recker smiled at her, thinking she was a quick student. "You're learning quickly."

"I have the best teachers."

After they finished eating, Jones immediately got to work, trying to hack into every nightclub security system that he came across. He was sure he would be able to find Jeremiah somewhere. It just might take some time to comb through all that footage. Once he was able to pull up footage from the first club, Recker and Mia started looking through the videos.

"How easy is it going to be to spot him?" Mia asked, not quite sure how the system worked.

"Well, there's several different ways to program the software," Jones said, explaining the intricacies of his system. "We can program it to run itself completely in search of an exact match based on the information I give it. In that case, we simply sit back and wait for it to beep when it's finished."

"That's easy enough."

"But, considering the complexity and urgency of this situation, I've loosened the parameters somewhat."

"How so?"

"It's possible he knows how to avoid cameras, or block them out, or have them disabled. So in this case, I've programmed it to look for even partial matches, that way we can sort out one way or another whether it's him. So you may get several false positives," Jones said.

"It's also possible he has so many people around him that a camera doesn't get a good shot of his face," Recker said. "Maybe it only gets a partial look at his face."

"Yes. In any case, the software will beep and pull up the pictures of the subject in question. Then it's up to us to quantify whether it's really him or just a lookalike."

"Gotcha," Mia said. "How long will all this take?"

"With the amount of clubs in this city? Probably days, maybe a week. It really depends on how much footage we go through," Jones said. "It will go faster with all three of us looking. If it was just me, as it usually is, it would most likely take longer."

"How far back did you set it?" Recker asked.

"A month. I assume that will be more than enough time. If he hasn't been there in a month, then it's most likely not a regular stop for him."

They spent the rest of the night combing through security footage from a couple different nightclubs. There were a couple of partial matches that the system flagged, though after closer inspection, it was determined that it wasn't Jeremiah. After four hours of looking at a computer screen, Jones needed a break and got up to turn the TV on.

"Problem?" Recker asked.

"Just stretching my legs a little," Jones said.

"Two clubs down, two hundred more to go."

"I suppose we'll get there in time."

As Jones sat down on the couch, his eyes glued to the television screen, Recker could see that there was something playing he was interested in. Wondering what was fascinating him so much, Recker also stopped what he was doing so he could watch.

"Wanna clue me in as to what you're looking for?" Recker asked.

"News is coming on."

"So?"

"I want to see how your exploits from earlier are covered," Jones said.

"Oh," Recker said, not seeming the least bit interested.

Though Jones always seemed to care how the media painted The Silencer, or what they said about him, Recker never seemed to care one way or the other. He figured no matter what they said, it wouldn't change what he did or how he operated. Regardless of anything they ever said about him, it never bothered him if they said something bad, or made him feel better if they heaped praise, so what was the point in listening?

"Why do you bother with that stuff?" Recker asked.

"It never hurts to be informed."

"You already are. I informed you about it earlier."

Within a few minutes, the two scenes where Recker left the dead bodies flashed across the screen, drawing Jones' attention even closer. Mia also stopped what she was doing and got up, moving to the couch. Recker sighed, knowing no more work was getting done for the moment since everyone seemed to be more focused on the TV. Jones turned up the volume so they could hear the reporter speak.

"Earlier today, spurred on by a 911 call, police arrived at this scene," the reporter said, looking and pointing back to the former auto garage. "Inside, they found the bodies of four men, all of whom have direct gang ties, and were pronounced dead at the scene. It is not believed the 911 call came from any of the dead men, and may have been the shooter. Though the motive of the shooting remains unclear at this time, there is a report The Silencer may have been involved, though that is unsubstantiated at this time."

The reporter then turned it over to another reporter who was at the row home in West Philly. Jones looked over at Recker, who still seemed underwhelmed with everything and simply shrugged back at him.

"And we're here in West Philadelphia at this row home," the man said, turning toward the house. "The second major shooting of the day occurred here just a couple of hours after the one on sixty-second street, and also involved gang members. Police arrived at the boarded-up home, which appears to be a place where they conducted business activity inside, and found the bodies of four more gang related men, three of whom were found on the porch. There's no immediate word from the police on a possible motive, but nearby witnesses reported seeing a man walk out of the home immediately after the shooting. He was wearing a trench coat, and according to those witnesses, bore a striking resemblance to the man the media, and public, have affectionately called The Silencer. I should also point out another person was seen running from the house after the shooting, before The Silencer came out, if it was him, and witnesses have described this person as a kid, most likely a teenager. Theories abound within the neighborhood that The Silencer didn't want to shoot a kid and showed mercy on him by letting him leave unharmed."

"At least they threw in the good part," Recker said with a smile.

"So, to summarize, two crime scenes, a couple hours apart, eight men killed with gang ties, to the same gang it should be pointed out, and it appears... I stress appears, to be the work of The Silencer, though there is no official word that is the case," the reporter said, smiling, almost looking happy about it. "And we'll throw it back to you, Jim. The Silencer, he's out and about and looking like a one-man task force."

Nobody said another word as Jones got up and turned the TV off. For the amount of damage Recker inflicted, it was about as positive a news report as they could've made. It almost made him out to be a hero. No major surprise though, as the media and newspapers had usually talked about him in a positive way. There were only a few news anchors or reporters who talked of him as a negative for the city. Most seemed to enjoy covering stories The Silencer was reported to be involved in. He was kind of like a modern-day Robin Hood, only he wasn't stealing money for the poor. Instead, he was defending the innocent and killing the guilty.

"A one-man task force," Jones said, though not to anyone in particular as he walked back to the couch.

"You almost sound disappointed," Recker said. "Would you have rather they called me the face of evil? Or maybe the devil reincarnated?"

"On the contrary, it was a most enjoyable telecast of your exploits. Almost clapping at your daring escapades. Seemed the only thing missing was the standing ovation."

"Then why do you seem so annoyed by it? You almost seem like you would have wished they tore me apart or something."

"No, it's not that. I don't even know if I can quantify the meaning behind it. It just seems like they're beginning to glorify you. It's almost as if the reasons behind the killings don't matter, or the fact people are being hurt or killed, it's almost like it's the backstory. The headline is The Silencer strikes again."

"They're just doing what they have to do to sell newspapers, get subscribers, gain viewers," Recker said. "You know that as well as I do."

"I know. Is what you're doing important? Yes. Is killing sometimes necessary? Absolutely. It just seems wrong to glorify it."

Recker shrugged, thinking this was one of those times where Jones was taking it too far. "It is what it is. This is why I don't, and you shouldn't, care about listening to what others say. It makes no difference in the grand scheme of things."

"I guess you're right."

The trio went back to work for another hour before calling it a night. They had a lot of work to do and it'd already been a long day, especially for Recker. They figured getting some rest and coming back in the morning with a fresh pair of eyes and renewed energy would be just what the doctor ordered. They knew finding Jeremiah within any of the security footage they were going through was going to take some time. It was possible they could hit the mother lode quickly, but they all knew it wasn't the likely scenario. And it would turn out to be true.

A couple more days passed by without any new leads on Jeremiah's whereabouts. They got beeped a few times on the software program they were running, but every possibility the system brought up turned out to be a false hit. As another night wound down, Recker excused himself from the computer and went over to the coffee machine. He was quickly followed by Mia, who sensed Recker wasn't quite himself. She thought the lack of progress over finding Jeremiah might have been getting to him as he seemed more reserved than usual.

"You OK?" she asked, putting her hand on his back.

Recker looked at her and smiled, trying to put on a more positive face. "Yeah."

"You've been quieter today."

"Just tired I guess."

"You know you can talk to me if you need to."

"I know."

"So, what's bugging you?"

Recker looked down at his cup of coffee, stirring it around as he debated whether he wanted to pour out his feelings, which wasn't something he was fond of doing. "I guess I'm just a little mad at myself for allowing this to happen."

"Allow what to happen?"

"You being here."

"You don't want me here?" Mia asked, thinking he may have changed his mind about being with her.

"I want you to be able to enjoy your life. You've been here what, three or four days now?"

"I'm not complaining."

"That's because you're a good person. But the reality is, bad things have happened to you ever since you met me. You've been kidnapped twice, held hostage, almost killed, now there's another death threat on your head... and it's all because of me."

"Not entirely true."

"Which part?"

"Well, it's not all because of you," Mia said, trying to make light of things. "The one time was my fault for trying to be an investigator. You weren't even here for that one."

Recker looked at her and laughed, acknowledging her point. "Still, even so, you're here right now because you were seen sitting with me in a lunchroom."

"And I wouldn't change it. None of it. None of us know how things will turn out, Mike. We just make the best decisions we can and hope for the best. But it's not your fault."

"How you figure?"

"Because you told me numerous times how dangerous it was to be seen with you or be with you. I've always known that. Doing what you do, the people you know, I know sometimes there are risks, and I know sometimes there are consequences. It's not your fault. It's my choice. I understand as much. You never misled me, you never told me something just to keep me around, it was what I wanted to do. And if being here right now is a byproduct of that, then so be it. I wouldn't change it. As long as you're always here to protect me."

"You know I will," Recker whispered, leaning towards her

14

Six more days passed by, with still no sign of Jeremiah in any of the security camera footage they combed through. Frustrations were mounting, Recker the most, but even Jones and Mia were beginning to show signs of it. Though Mia tried to remain strong, as much as she could, being locked in an office for ten days without being able to go outside was starting to take a toll on her. She tried not to show it for Recker's sake, as she knew that him seeing her stressed would only serve to aggravate his own emotions further. He already blamed himself for most of what was happening, she didn't want to add fuel to his fire. After another unsuccessful day of searching, they were about to wrap things up for the night when Recker's phone rang. Whenever Vincent called personally, Recker knew it was something big.

"Hey," Recker said.

"It's a beautiful night out, isn't it?"

"I dunno. I haven't seen much of it. I'd say it's just fair."

"Well, the news I'm about to spring on you might brighten it for you," Vincent said.

"Which is?"

"First, I'd like to apologize for the length of time it's taken us to wrap up our end of the agreement. I must say he was quite elusive, much more than we initially gave him credit for. You were right, he was a slippery little guy."

"Bernal," Recker said.

"Yes. He's no longer a worry for anybody."

"You found him?"

"He's been... neutralized."

"You mean he's dead?"

"Well, I don't want to spoil things for you," Vincent said. "But I do believe if you catch the news in a few minutes, they may have something of interest for you."

"Oh? Like what?"

"As I said, I don't want to spoil things. I'll be in touch."

As Vincent hung up, Recker let the phone drop to his side, a look of confusion on his face. Jones could see whatever was said in the conversation was clearly perplexing to Recker. He just stood there for a minute, not moving in any way, deep in thought.

"Something troubling?" Jones asked.

"It was Vincent," Recker said.

"And?"

"And I don't know."

"Well what did he say?"

"Something about Bernal," Recker said, finally moving from his frozen stance.

"Is he dead?"

"I don't know. He wouldn't say. He just said he was neutralized."

"Well that could mean any number of things," Jones said.

"He said to turn on the news and there'd be something interesting on it."

"Well I guess we have to watch now."

Jones walked over to the TV and turned it on as the three of them sat down, greatly anticipating what was about to be shown. Even though Recker usually detested watching the news for his own exploits, he was eager to see what Vincent was talking about, especially since he wasn't involved in it. As the news telecast came on, nobody said a word as they all were focused on the contents of the show. After a few minutes, they came to what Vincent was referring to. A female reporter appeared on the screen with what was described as an explosive story.

"And it was a wild scene down here on North Eleventh Street as the body of a man who has since been identified as Adrian Bernal was found in the parking lot of the police department. The bullet-ridden body was discovered by officers of the sixth district several hours ago, and though the investigation into his death is still in its infancy, it's been learned Bernal was looking to kill one of the police officers in this district. We have also learned the police believe Bernal's killer to be The Silencer. Now, police are not divulging how or why they believe this is the work of The Silencer, but say they do have evidence suggesting it to be the case. We have talked to several officers off the record who have stated they believe The Silencer targeted Bernal in order to save one of their own, and for that, these officers expressed their gratitude to him."

As the reporter threw it back to the anchor desk, Jones turned off the TV after seeing all they needed to see. Recker continued staring at the television, even after it had been turned off. He was trying to think of why Vincent would want to prop him up like he just did. He could have gotten rid of Bernal easily and quietly, without any fanfare, but instead, Vincent chose to make Recker the hero of the story for some reason. Vincent definitely had a reason for doing so, he didn't do it out of the goodness of his heart, or because he felt like being a good guy. There was a business reason behind it. Something which would benefit him in the long run. Finally, after a few minutes, Mia spoke up to break the silence.

"Am I missing something?" she asked. "I don't get it. Why do they think it was you?"

"Because Vincent wanted it to be that way," Jones said.

"But why?"

"He's obviously after something."

Recker listened to them talking, while also trying to recollect every conversation he ever had with Vincent, before speaking up himself. "Before I took out Bellomi, Vincent told me he had people inside the police department on the payroll."

"So why not just give them the credit?" Mia said.

"Because he needs me to look good for something."

"For what purpose?" Jones said. "That's the question. And it's obviously something big."

Recker wasn't in the mood to debate it for the rest of the night, or spend the next few days wondering what Vincent had in mind. He already had enough on his mind. He didn't need more problems stirring around in his head. He immediately grabbed his phone and dialed Vincent's direct number. He didn't know if Vincent would pick up, but Recker wasn't going through Malloy for this one. He'd keep calling until Vincent answered. Somewhat surprisingly, Vincent answered after the first ring.

"I'm almost surprised it took this long for the phone to ring," Vincent said

"What was that about?"

"I figured you could use some goodwill amongst the police department."

"I don't need goodwill," Recker said.

"Well, maybe not, but you're the one who actually thwarted the plot Bernal was hatching. We were just the instrument that finished the job. But without your intel and guidance, it wouldn't have been possible. So, take the bow."

"I don't take bows. I don't do this for personal glory or headlines."

"Yes, I know. But having some friends within the police department can at times be a useful thing to have," Vincent said.

"I don't need friends."

"Oh, come now Mike, we all need friends. Sometimes it takes all kinds to be able to do the things that men like us do. Friends are willing to help you do things when a helping hand is needed."

Recker knew there was a hidden meaning behind that, though he wasn't sure what it was. "What exactly is that supposed to mean?"

Vincent didn't respond and moved on to the next subject. "So, how's your search for Jeremiah coming?"

"It's coming," Recker said.

"I couldn't help but notice his name hasn't emerged in any of the obituary columns. It's been ten days now. I have to say I expected you to have things wrapped up by now."

"Yeah, after our last meeting, he seems to have gone underground."

"I had a feeling he would."

"Getting anxious to move into your new territory?"

"Well, let's just say I expected our agreement to be over by now."

"Well if you can find him for me, you let me know so I can execute my end of it."

"Maybe I'll do that," Vincent said. "If we get anything, I'll contact you. Remember what I said about friends, though, Mike. Especially inside the police department. You did them a favor by taking out someone who came close to eliminating one of their own. There may be some who are willing to return the favor."

Before Recker was able to quiz him further on his statement, Vincent hung up. Now, instead of getting the answers he sought, Recker was only left with more questions. It was obvious Vincent had something specific on his mind, but he wasn't willing to share exactly what it was yet. Annoyed and frustrated at the events, Recker tossed the phone down in disgust, drawing a look from both Jones and Mia, who could tell he wasn't pleased.

"I take it you didn't get the answers you were looking for," Jones said.

"Not only did I not get the answers I was looking for, I didn't get any answers period. He gave me even more questions."

"What did he say?" Mia asked.

"He made a point to let me know how having friends in the police department was a good idea," Recker said, recalling the words vividly. "And he said by me doing a favor for them, maybe some of them would want to return the favor for me."

"What does that even mean?"

"Well, considering he has men inside the police, or at least on his payroll, he thinks somehow I can use them to my advantage in order to find Jeremiah."

"Even if that were true, finding the officer who was sympathetic to our cause and be willing to help, would not be an easy task in itself," Jones said.

"Unless we find the one who's on Vincent's payroll," Recker said.

They deliberated the merits of finding an ally on the police force, as Vincent seemed to suggest, for most of the rest of the night, eventually coming to the conclusion they weren't willing to go in that direction yet. They would rather keep on with what they were doing, going through the security footage, in the hopes of locating Jeremiah. At least for now. Recker was probably the one most interested in doing things Vincent's way. In his mind, it'd already taken longer than he wanted. He wanted it to be over now so Mia could get on with her life. And so could he. He was more willing to make a deal, if it meant getting rid of Jeremiah once and for all. Jones and Mia were the ones more interested in staying the course, even if it meant it took longer. But even though Recker was for it, he allowed the others to sway his opinion, at least for the time being.

Unfortunately, five more days passed, and they were no closer to finding Jeremiah than they were when they started. After Recker took out two of his properties and a bunch of his men, Jeremiah went completely into hiding. Though he usually visited one or two nightclubs a week over the past several years, he hadn't even done that. So even if Recker and Jones had found footage of him somewhere, it wouldn't have done them any good. Jeremiah wouldn't be showing up, anyway. By then, everyone was getting frustrated, and it was starting to show, though it showed the worst on Recker. With all of them working at a computer, Recker had enough. He thought it was getting them nowhere, and he'd had enough. He pounded his fist on the desk and angrily pushed his chair away, standing up and walking over to the window, looking down at the parking lot. Jones and Mia looked at each other, both of whom were leery of going over and talking to him. Eventually, Jones was the one who spoke up.

"Michael."

Recker spun around, anger seething off his tongue. "This isn't working, David. It's not working," he said loudly. "We've been at this for two weeks and we're still nowhere. We're not any closer to finding him."

"We knew it would take some time," Jones said. "To think we were going to get someone like Jeremiah in a matter of days was not a realistic time frame."

"OK. You're right. But we're not at a few days now. Yesterday was fourteen days. She can't sit in here forever," Recker said, pointing at Mia.

"Mike, I'm fine," Mia said, trying to diffuse his temper.

"But I'm not," he said, in a more soothing manner. "You can't live like this anymore."

"Honestly, I haven't really minded. I've been with you more these last couple weeks than in the past two years. I've enjoyed being close to you."

Recker tried to muster a smile, though he barely showed it. "I just want this to be over."

"We all do," Jones said. "But we can't force something which isn't there."

"But we can. And we both know what I'm talking about."

"Vincent."

Recker shrugged, "I'm ready."

"And what do you think will come out of this? Another deal with Vincent?"

"It's the same deal," Recker said. "I'm getting Jeremiah. I just need his help locating him."

"And you don't think it will come with an additional cost?"

"Does it matter at this point? Vincent will get what he wants, control of the city. That's all he needs."

Jones clasped his hands together and rested them against his forehead as he put his elbows on the desk, looking down as he collected his thoughts. Deep down, he knew Recker was probably right. They were having a tough time finding Jeremiah, much tougher than Jones thought they would. He just hated the idea of going to Vincent again. Though the two sides always seemed to align with each other up to then, Jones didn't like working so closely with them. After all, they were on different sides of the fence. Though Vincent sometimes helped them achieve their goals, at heart, he was still the boss of a major criminal organization which was slowly taking control of the city. That was always worrisome to Jones. But he looked over at Mia, thinking of her being cooped up in there for the last two weeks, and not making a sound. She never made one complaint, not one argument, and if she was ever frustrated, he never noticed it. No matter his feelings for Vincent or the situation, Jones felt they owed it to her to get it resolved. The quicker the better. He looked back at Recker and nodded, ready to give his blessing.

"You're right. It's time," Jones said.

Recker nodded back, taking a final look out the window before calling Vincent. "You know, I know we've talked before about this, but I can't help but think somehow, he's manipulated me this entire time."

"How so?"

"Taking out Bellomi. Now Jeremiah."

"We've been over this. You've done what was necessary."

"I know. But do you ever think he's orchestrated things, pushed things in a certain direction, to get things just right, to get things into a position where I'd have to respond the way I do?"

Jones shook his head, not having an answer. "Unfortunately, that's something I don't think we'll ever know. It's one of the reasons I hate being involved with him. Because we both know he's capable of things like that."

Recker then called Vincent, getting him immediately.

"Mike, what can I do for you?" he said.

Recker hesitated, almost afraid to say he needed help again. "I'm uh... I guess I'm ready to make some friends."

He could almost hear Vincent smiling through the phone. "Well, it's nice to hear it. Took a little longer than I anticipated, but nonetheless, still nice to hear."

"I can't find him." Recker sighed. "I've been looking nonstop and I just don't know where he is."

"I do."

"What?"

"I know where he is."

"You do? How?" Recker asked, surprised.

"I've always known. Don't forget, Mike, information is my business. I collect information like some people collect trading cards. It pours into me by the truckloads."

"Well if you've known, then why haven't you taken him out yourself?"

Vincent laughed, like he thought it was a ridiculous question. "Because it wasn't our deal, was it?"

"No."

"So, what do you need from me?"

"Just tell me where he's at. I'll get him," Recker said.

"Well, that's a little easier said than done. He's got at least ten to fifteen men with him."

"So, what do you propose then?"

"Remember what I said about friends, Mike. Let them help."

"And just what friends do you keep referring to?"

"It'll take some faith on your part," Vincent said.

"In what?"

"In me. Do you have it?"

"Yes."

"Good. Here is the plan then. Jeremiah has holed himself up in a house on the west side. As I mentioned, he's got men with him. At nine o'clock tonight, a small team of police officers will converge on the building. You will be among them."

"And do they know this?"

"Remember what I said about friends, Mike. You did them a favor by protecting one of their own. They would like to return the favor by helping you."

"And after it's done, they're just gonna let me walk out of there?" Recker asked.

"Faith, Mike, faith."

"OK. Even if I go along with this, if they converge on the building, why wouldn't they just kill Jeremiah themselves? What am I needed for?"

"Well, unfortunately in this day and age, the police aren't trusted as much as the olden days. Not with body cameras and the like," Vincent said.

"And? I know there's more."

"I want Jeremiah dead. Him in prison just means I'll have to deal with him again at some point, or men who are still loyal to him. But if he's dead, I don't have that problem."

"No argument from me there," Recker said.

"So, the officers converging on this building tonight may be on my payroll, but they're still police officers, not a death squad. If it turns out that Jeremiah is killed in a firefight as they storm the building, then there's no issue. They'd have done their job."

"And if Jeremiah doesn't put up a fight?"

"Well, that's something that we just can't have, can we?" Vincent asked.

"That's where I come in."

"Exactly. I can't have police officers executing an unarmed man, one who's given up, and have it on camera. That's an officer I'd end up losing."

"But I don't have a camera," Recker said, understanding the plan. "But aren't they gonna see me on camera?"

"Well, you know how technology is. It's a fickle thing. Two of the officers will have a problem with their cameras for a few minutes. They'll go offline long enough to do what needs to be done."

"So, I'm there as backup?"

"If they decide to fight and die, you can sit this one out. If they give up for another day, well, you'll be there to make sure that day never arrives," Vincent said.

"One more question, what do you need me for? You could have Malloy do that. He's just as willing and capable."

"Well, you know the old risk versus reward. If in the unlikely chance that something goes wrong, someone escapes, someone's identified, I can't have someone from my organization knowingly involved."

"But I'm a known independent."

"Exactly."

"So, who do I report to tonight?"

"Detective Nix. He's leading the team. He'll be apprised of the plan."

"And he'll be OK with it?"

"Faith, Mike, faith."

As they finished their talk, Recker put the phone back in his pocket and continued looking out the window. Jones was listening in to the conversation as much as possible, trying to piece together what he could from Recker's end of it. He didn't quite like what he heard.

"Would you like to fill us in?" Jones asked. "Because I'm pretty sure some of what you were saying sounded troubling."

Recker turned around and informed Jones and Mia of the plan. Mia seemed OK with it. She certainly wasn't going to go against Recker's wishes, and if he thought this was the best way to get it done, she'd go along with it. Jones, though, he wasn't so sure. Not only were they aligning with Vincent, but they had to put their faith in him, hoping the police officers wouldn't arrest Recker after he killed Jeremiah. Vincent could get rid of Jeremiah, and Recker, in a few short minutes.

"I'm aware of the risks, David," Recker said.

"But you're willing to take them, anyway?"

"I have to believe Vincent doesn't want to get rid of me right now."

"Why are you so willing to think that?" Jones asked.

"Because we're not enemies."

"It doesn't mean you're not a threat to him. All his enemies will be gone. He may think you're the next one."

Recker took a few minutes to think about it, but his mind was made up. It was something he couldn't pass up, regardless of the risks. "I have to do this."

Jones still had his reservations, but he knew he was unlikely to talk Recker out of it. Recker spent the rest of the night mentally preparing himself for what was about to happen, trying to go over all the possibilities he could face. He was texted the address, and while Jones had the idea of going there without help, Recker quickly shot the idea down. If Jeremiah had ten to fifteen men with him, even for a man like Recker, it'd be tough for him to get past everyone. Once eight o'clock hit, Recker started getting himself ready, checking his guns. Jones and Mia had walked closer to the door to see him off.

"Just be careful," Jones said, shaking Recker's hand.

"I will."

Mia reached up and kissed Recker passionately on the lips. "Just make sure you come back to me."

"Nothing will stop me from doing that," Recker said, giving her a smile.

Recker arrived at the house in question at 8:45. The police officers had already surrounded the end unit row home. Unlike the other properties that Jeremiah had, this one wasn't boarded-up. It looked like a perfectly normal home that any family would live in. Nothing to suggest that a dangerous criminal was inside with a bunch of his thugs. As Recker walked down the sidewalk, past the metal fence, a police officer was near the gate and looked back at him, seeing him approach.

"Are you him?" the officer asked. "You're The Silencer?"

Recker nodded. "That's me."

"I'm Detective Nix," he said, sticking his hand out.

Recker was a bit surprised, but he returned the handshake.

"We're just about ready to go in," Nix said.

"What do you need from me?"

"Nothing yet. The team will go in first. They'll clear everything. If you're needed, I'll let you know."

"And if I'm not, you're just gonna let me walk out of here?" Recker asked, still having doubts.

"Listen, some of us wanna lock you up. Some of us think you're doing good by the city and us."

"And where do you stand?"

"You saved one of us from biting the bullet," Nix said. "For me, you get a free ride. Even if you hadn't, every jerk you take out, is one more that I don't have to worry about. So, for me, as long as you're taking out the bad guys, we're on the same side as far as I'm concerned."

"Good to know."

"We're good to go," a voice said over the radio.

"All right, everyone go!" Nix commanded.

The officers went through both the front and back door, and within seconds, massive amounts of gunfire erupted. Recker and Nix stood there by the front gate, looking on and listening. It was an unusual stance for Recker, as he was usually the one doing the shooting. It felt weird that he was watching the activities unfold, waiting for someone else to do the dirty work. Felt even more strange that he was standing next to a police officer, who wasn't lifting a finger against him. Though it seemed like the battle was raging on forever, it was actually only about ten minutes. After that, voices started crackling over the radio.

"We'll be coming out in a minute," an officer said.

"What's everyone's status?" Nix asked.

"One officer wounded, shot in the arm, he'll be OK. No casualties on our end."

"Good. What about our targets?"

"Six dead. Four in custody. We'll be bringing them out."

"And the main one?" Nix asked, not wanting to mention his name over the air.

"He's locked in a room. I've got a man on it."

"All right, bring the others out. I'll send the package in."

"Ten-four."

Nix looked over at Recker and nodded. "Looks like you're up."

"OK."

Recker started to walk to the house but was interrupted by the detective. "Hey, when it's done, just slip out the back door."

"Thanks."

Nix nodded at him in appreciation. As Recker reached the front door, he was met by another officer. "Hey," the officer said. "My camera's gonna be out for about sixty seconds. I'll get you to the room then the rest is up to you."

"Got it."

The officer led Recker to the basement, which had been divided into a couple of rooms. There was another officer standing by the door to make sure Jeremiah didn't escape. He was given the nod to go away, which he complied with.

"Does he have a weapon in there?" Recker asked.

"Can't say for sure," the officer said. "He was seen retreating in there without anything in his hands. He locked the door once he got in there. Whether he's got anything stashed in there, we're not sure."

"OK."

"Thanks for all you do," the officer who led Recker there said, giving him a pat on the shoulder before leaving himself.

It all seemed very strange to Recker, getting what amounted to a police escort inside the building. He was getting patted on the back and words of appreciation, it almost seemed like a dream. He got out his gun and tried to think of how he'd handle it. He could just kick the door in and rush Jeremiah, but he didn't want to walk into a bullet either. He thought if Jeremiah knew it was him on the other side, maybe he'd react differently than if it was the police.

"Jeremiah," Recker yelled.

"Recker?" Jeremiah shouted back.

"Police are gone. It's just you and me."

"How'd you manage that one?"

"Guess it pays to know people."

"Yeah. Guess it does."

"You know why I'm here. Why don't you come out and get it over with?" Recker asked.

"Why don't you come in and get me?"

With his defiant tone, Recker got the feeling Jeremiah was armed in the room. Maybe he was just stalling the inevitable as long as possible, but Recker wouldn't take the chance of thinking he didn't have a gun and wind up taking a bullet himself. After looking around for a second, Recker didn't see anything else he could use. He also knew with the police in front, he didn't have a lot of time. Though they seemed to be giving him a pass out of there, he didn't want to take advantage for too long.

He took a few steps back, then violently kicked the door open, keeping mind to stay out of view. As soon as it flung open, bullets ripped into the door, as Recker took cover to the side of it. He peeked his head around to get a view of the layout. As he did, another shot rang out, a bullet whizzing past his head, just missing. There didn't appear to be much furniture in the room. It looked like just a couch and a table, along with a TV. Recker took another peek inside, and without any gunshots coming toward him, rushed inside. He dropped to the ground and waited for Jeremiah to emerge from behind the couch. As Jeremiah rose up to fire again, Recker unloaded four shots in quick succession, knocked his victim back against the wall, his gun flying out of his hand. After Jeremiah banged against the wall, he dropped to the floor. Recker quickly got up and rushed around the couch to his position, ready to finish him off if necessary. Jeremiah was just lying there, not moving, as blood poured out of his body from the four bullets lodged in his chest. Recker stood over him and shook his head, thinking it didn't have to end up that way. If Jeremiah hadn't taken the steps he did, they never would have had to become enemies. But it wasn't something Recker would worry over too much.

Just as Detective Nix suggested, Recker didn't waste any time stewing around, and took off through the back door. Though he didn't feel any uneasiness, he was still ready for anything, in the event he was double crossed. Luckily, everyone involved kept their word. Recker immediately went back to the office. Although he assumed Vincent would find out from his officers, Recker called him on the way back, just to let him know everything went according to plan. When he finally got back to the office, Jones and Mia were at one of the desks, looking like they were praying. They had their elbows on the table, and their hands folded together, resting against their faces. But once they heard the door jiggling, they rushed over to it, happy to see Recker returning. Mia almost knocked him over as she jumped into his arms, giving him a kiss and some much-needed affection. Jones shook his hand, also excited to see him return.

"Don't expect a kiss from me," Jones said.

"Don't worry, this is the only one I need," Recker said, wrapping his arms fully around Mia.

DOUBLE TAP

15

R ecker looked completely uncomfortable. There was no question he was out of his element. It was a day he knew was coming for weeks, and he wasn't looking forward to it at all. But he knew it was one of the give-and-takes that he had to do if he wanted Mia to remain part of his life. After three months of talking and deliberating, they finally decided on a place to live together. His apartment. His bare walls, his scant furniture, the barely livable arrangements, they were all about to go. Replaced by pictures, more comfortable surroundings, and things that smelled nice. And he wasn't all that warm and fuzzy about it.

"A little to the left," Mia said.

Recker closed his eyes and sighed, thinking if anyone saw him now, his reputation would take a severe hit. Well, maybe not severe, but he'd sure have to put up with a lot of ribbing and good-natured abuse. After all, hanging curtains wasn't exactly some-thing anyone would ever expect to see him doing. He certainly never thought so. But, it was the price he had to pay to be with the woman that he cared about. As long as nobody saw him do the homely duties.

"One day I'm shooting people and the next I'm hanging curtains," Recker mumbled to himself. "Unreal."

"What, honey?"

"Uh, nothing. Which way you want these?"

Though Jeremiah and his gang were now out of the picture, Recker didn't want Mia staying in her former apartment. He'd actually pleaded with her to quit her job and stay at home, that way he could be sure nobody would ever try taking advantage of her again. But that flew on deaf ears. Though Mia loved and wanted to be with him, she wasn't going to stash herself away and become a vegetable. She loved her job; she loved helping people, and she was determined to keep doing just that.

Recker still had concerns, but knew it was a lost cause in trying to change her mind. It just wouldn't happen. So he did the next best thing. He taught her how to be elusive. How to become invisible. And it wasn't just for her safety, but also for his. Nobody knew where he lived other than Jones. The last thing Recker needed was somebody following her and finding out where his home was. So they agreed that she would never drive straight home to the apartment after work. She would take a few extra turns to make sure there was nobody in her rear-view mirror. Recker taught her which ways to go, and also how to spot if someone was tailing her. Over the previous month, he rigged up some practice situations where he used a different car to teach her how to, not only spot someone following her, but also how to escape them. After a month of practice, Mia had gotten relatively good at the practice. She'd never be at a CIA level of elusiveness, but she wasn't half-bad. He figured if anyone ever attempted to follow her after that point, they'd most likely not be as good as he was. And if they were, they'd most likely find him eventually, anyway. She was at least good enough to satisfy Recker's worries for the time being. In any case, he'd continue working with her to sharpen her skills in the event she ever had to put them into use, which hopefully she wouldn't.

Once the curtains had been hung to Mia's satisfaction, Recker stared out the window for a few moments. As he was daydreaming, Mia continued unpacking some of her things, as well as some new things she'd bought for the apartment. Recker's gaze was interrupted as he noticed Mia putting some small, potted plants on the windowsill. He looked at her with a curious expression, almost like he wasn't sure what she was doing.

"What's that?" Recker said.

"Uh, plants."

"Why are you putting them there?"

"To decorate the apartment?" Mia replied, sensing that he was skeptical of her arrangements.

"Oh."

"Would you like me to take them down?"

"No. No. It's fine," Recker said, though he really did have some reservations about it.

"Are you sure?"

He tried to make a face to indicate he had no issues, though not very well. "Totally."

Mia smiled at him, thinking it was cute how he had hang-ups over a few small plants. "It'll be OK," she said, patting his shoulder reassuringly.

"I'm fine. It's just I've never actually had plants before."

"Don't worry about them. I'll take care of them."

"Good. Cause I'm good at killing things. Plants probably included."

Mia laughed and gave him a pat on the shoulder as she went back to some of the boxes that were littered along the floor. He turned around just in time to see the horror of her taking out a few pictures that were already in frames. He stood there dumbfounded, his mouth slightly open, as he watched her nail the

186

frames to the wall. There were some pictures of her, some of him, and some of them together.

"I need a case," Recker whispered. "I'm not made for this."

After putting a few pictures up, Mia turned around to grab another one when she noticed the blank expression on his face. Though she was amused at how uncomfortable the simplest of things seemed to make him, she tried to be understanding and not show it. She knew the barren landscape of the apartment before she got there was likely how his places had looked for the past ten years or so. It was probably all he ever knew. She walked over to him with a sad puppy dog kind of a smile and put her arms around him to give him a kiss, trying to be as sympathetic as possible. Though Mia was enjoying herself immensely, she knew it was hard for him. Change wasn't something that Recker was accustomed to or liked very much.

"It's going to be OK," she said. "I promise."

Her affection briefly helped to alleviate his anxiety over his changing life. A warm look into her eyes was enough to ease the fears of any man, Recker included. There was just something about the way she looked at him that made him feel more secure in his changing environment. At least when her arms were wrapped around him.

"When did you do all that?" Recker said, not aware that she ever had pictures of them made.

"Well, the pictures of us were the selfies I took of us. And the ones of just you were just pics that I took randomly. You've seen them before."

"I know. I just didn't realize that you printed them out."

"Is that a problem?" she said with a smile.

"No. It just makes things seem... permanent."

"I can take them down if it makes you uncomfortable."

"No, it's fine. I'm just... not used to looking at myself on the wall," Recker said.

Seeing the pictures of them together on the wall was a little jarring to him. In his mind, it was like a symbol of their relationship cementing. And though he still wasn't as comfortable with it as he tried to pretend he was, he knew Mia would be crushed if she had to take them down because of his uneasiness. It was just something he'd have to deal with.

Once Mia went back to hanging more pictures, Recker started feeling uneasy again. He started to think that maybe he just needed to get out of the apartment for a while. Maybe it was just the process of seeing all the changes unfold in front of his eyes that fueled his anxiety. Maybe if he went out and everything was done once he got back, he would feel much better about the situation. He thought maybe it wasn't the actual changes themselves that was causing his worries, and if everything was already done, it wouldn't bother him as much.

Recker pulled out his phone, praying that Jones had tried to call or text him. Even though he knew Jones hadn't, he hoped that somehow, he just missed the call. Maybe he didn't hear the ringer as Mia was talking to him about something. Or maybe he missed a text message when he was in a trance over what seemed like a strange apartment to him. But as Recker checked, his hopes were quickly dashed. There were no calls. No texts. But as he continued to watch Mia alter his apartment, or as he needed to get used to saying, their apartment, he knew he needed to escape for a while. Seeing he was supposed to have the day off, Mia was a little concerned when she noticed him looking at his phone.

"Everything OK?" Mia said.

"Oh. Uh, yeah. Yeah, everything's fine."

"Then why are you looking at your phone like that?"

"It's uh... it's David," Recker said, quickly thinking of something. "Yeah. He just texted me about something. I should probably call him back to see what's up."

"You were supposed to be with me all day," she said, disappointed about what she suspected was about to happen.

"Well, let me just see what he wants. Maybe it's not what you think."

Recker walked into the kitchen as he called Jones' number, hoping that the professor had somehow come up with a new case. The actual move-in day for Mia had already been postponed a couple of times when newer, more urgent types of cases had unexpectedly popped up at the last minute. Jones had personally assured her the previous day that nothing was on the horizon.

"David, I saw you called, what's up?"

"Um... what?" Jones said.

"So what's going on?"

"Nothing's going on. What call? I didn't call you."

"Oh. Well is it serious?"

"Serious? What are you talking about? Is everything all right there?"

"Yeah, everything's going fine here."

"I'm glad to hear it."

"So you really think you need me?" Recker said.

"Are we back to this again? What are you talking about?"

"Yeah, I suppose I can be down there in a while if you really think it's necessary."

"Michael, nothing is going on."

"She'll be disappointed, but she'll understand."

"Do we have a bad connection or something?" Jones said, looking at his phone in bewilderment.

"I can leave in about five minutes."

"Leave for what?"

"All right. I'll see you when I get there," Recker said, hanging up.

Jones sat there for a minute, trying to figure out what had just happened. He continued staring at his phone, lying on the desk. "I hope he hasn't gone crazy after less than one day of being domes-ticated."

Before going back into the living room, Recker looked at kitchen cabinets and let out a sigh. He wasn't that proud of himself for what he was about to do, deceiving Mia like he was. But he figured on the importance level as far as lies go, this one would rank on the bottom of the list. As he thought about it for a few more moments, he actually convinced himself it was better this way, anyway. Interior decorating wasn't his thing, and there wasn't much he could add. The only thing he could really do was get in the way. Mia would probably be better off, or at least faster, if she didn't have to stop every few minutes to massage his feelings over his changing apartment.

When Recker finally came back in, Mia didn't need him to say anything. She'd already overheard his conversation with Jones. Recker had made sure that he talked loud enough for her to hear. By the look on her face, he could tell that she wasn't pleased. She was just standing there looking at him, a picture frame in each hand, which were dropped down on each side of her by her knees. Recker started to open her mouth to explain before she stopped him. She lifted her left index finger off the frame and held it out in front of her, so he didn't say a word.

"I know," she sighed in frustration, yet still somehow mustering a smile. "You've gotta go."

"I'm sorry. It's just that something's come up."

"I know. I know. Something always comes up."

Recker walked over to her to try to smooth over her frustra-tions. He put his hands on her waist and brought her closer to him, giving her a gentle kiss on the lips.

"Bribery will not get you anywhere," Mia said, though the kiss wiped away the look of displeasure on her face.

"Are you sure?" Recker said, kissing her again.

"Well..."

"Besides, you'll get all this done a lot faster if I'm not here. You know I'm not really helping here."

"I just wanted this to be a special moment for us."

Recker knew it was important for her and took a moment to look around the room. "This isn't what's special. These things are just... things. The only special moment I need is when you're like this, when you're in my arms."

"You're lucky you're so good looking," Mia said, kissing him again, as all her displeasure faded away.

"I think it'll be better this way, anyway. You'll be able to do things the way you want without having to constantly look over at me to see if I'm hyperventilating."

"But what if I do something that you don't like?"

"I'm sure that everything you do will be perfect," Recker said. "Besides, the thing that matters to me most is that you're here. Everything else I can get used to. It might take some time, but I'll get used to it... eventually."

After a few more minutes of affection, Recker finally pulled himself away from Mia and went down to the office. And though she was initially disappointed at him leaving, she knew that everything would go by faster if he was gone. Not that her first priority was speed, but she didn't want to spend the whole day doing it either. When Recker got down to the office, about thirty minutes had elapsed since his phone call with Jones. Based on the strangeness of the conversation, the professor didn't know if Recker was actually coming or not. When he saw Recker enter the office, he stopped what he was doing and started peppering his partner with questions, wondering if he was losing his mind.

"Would you mind explaining what that phone call was about?" Jones said, getting up from his chair to greet his friend.

"Oh. I, uh, just needed to get away for awhile."

"Get away? Are you two already having compatibility problems on your first day of cohabitation?"

Recker thought for a moment. "What?"

Jones rolled his eyes, not believing that he didn't understand what he was talking about. "Are you two having issues already?"

"Oh. No. Nothing like that."

"Then why are you here? You both practically begged for a day off so you could fix up the apartment to suit both your tastes. And now you're saying you needed to get away?"

"Well, it's not a big deal," Recker said. "It's not like we're arguing or styles clashing or anything."

"Then what is it?"

"It's more or less me. I guess it's a little harder than I thought it'd be. Seeing everything transform from my way of doing things to a... more pleasant atmosphere will take some getting used to."

"Perhaps you're not as ready for this as you thought you were," Jones said.

"No, that's not it. I love her. I do. This is what I want. She's what I want. It's just... I've spent a lot of years doing things one way, my way. Not having to worry about what someone else would like or think."

"You'll adjust."

"I know. I just hope I don't drive her crazy in the process."

"Or me."

"So is there still nothing on the agenda?" Recker said.

"No. We're still clear."

Since he was there, and didn't have anywhere else to go, Recker sat down at the desk and went on the computer. He figured he'd just sit there for a couple hours doing busy work, trying to occupy some time before he went back home.

"So how long do you plan on continuing this little charade of yours and sitting here?" Jones said.

"I dunno. Two or three hours maybe. Why? Wanna get rid of me already?"

"No. Just wondering."

Jones also sat back down, though he had more definitive plans for his day. There were still a few cases that he was running down information on, but they were probably still a day or two away from acting on anything. His main goal for the day was finishing up on something that he'd been hiding from Recker. It was nothing like the last secret he was hiding from him, about Agent 17. This time, he assumed Recker would be pleased. At least he hoped so. After all, it was Recker's idea.

Finding another agent to work within their little group was something they'd discussed previously, and Recker knew Jones had started doing some work on it, Jones never divulged his progress or indicated how close he really was. Jones altered his search methods somewhat this time, though. If there was anything that he learned from Recker's situation, it was that he didn't want to get another former agent who was in hot water. This time, Jones focused his efforts on finding ex-CIA agents who were no longer employed with the agency, but were still in good standing. That way they would never have to worry about being tracked or worry about being found. After an exhaustive search over the past several months, Jones finally targeted someone, firmly believing that he found his man.

Jones hadn't made any plans on when or how he'd tell Recker though. He figured it would be more of a feeling out process. Recker obviously wasn't good with change, and even though he initially seemed on board with the idea, Jones wasn't sure it'd be good to spring it on him now with the changes he had going on with Mia. But it was also something that he needed Recker's approval on. If they brought in someone new, it had to be someone they could both work with. Someone they had chemistry with. Especially Recker. If they were out in the field, Recker had to feel comfortable that a new person would have his back. That he could trust him. That was no small feat. When it came time to calling on the new recruit, Jones wanted Recker to be there to get his thoughts. Recker was good with initial encounters, and getting a feel on how people were.

Jones decided he'd wait a few more days before talking to Recker about it. He just felt that now wasn't the best time to make Recker's life even more chaotic. He'd give Recker some time to adjust to living with Mia and being in what was basically a brand-new apartment. It was going to be tough for Jones, though, not to spill the beans on what he thought was an exciting development. The man that he tabbed for the next member of their crusade was someone that Jones felt would be a great addition to the team. Someone that wasn't all that different from Recker. Well, hopefully for Jones there'd be one small difference... that he didn't have the same appetite for violence.

16

Jones waited another week before talking to Recker about the prospective new member of the team. He assumed that was long enough for Recker to get used to his surroundings. And if it wasn't, well, that was as long as Jones was giving him, anyway. With each day that passed, Recker seemed a little more comfortable with how things were going. He didn't seem as anxious or nervous about what was happening at home. Then, one morning when Recker came into the office, Jones figured it was time to clue him in on his activities.

"Everything going well in your new man cave?" Jones couldn't keep a playful smile from playing across his face.

"Don't get cute."

"I'm sorry. I just couldn't resist the temptation."

"Yeah, yeah."

"Drapes fastened, pictures hung?"

"You don't fasten drapes," Recker said.

"Oh. Well I see we are learning new skills, aren't we?" Jones said, continuing the teasing. "Now you even know the correct procedures on curtains. My, my. If your enemies could only see you now."

Recker rolled his eyes, then looked up at the ceiling, contorting his face to make it seem like he was mad, though he really wasn't. "Are you done now?"

"Yes, I think so."

"Are you sure? Anymore quips or jokes? Might as well get them out now."

"No, I believe I'm done."

Recker sat down at the desk to start working as Jones walked over to him to spill the big news. Jones grabbed a file folder off the desk containing all his information before he approached his partner. He wanted to tell him early, before they got too knee-deep into anything.

"So, you remember what we talked about a few months ago?" Jones said, sitting on the edge of the desk. "About adding another person to the team?"

"Yeah." Recker wasn't paying Jones much attention as he typed away on the computer.

"Well, I've been thinking more about it."

"Oh? Finally come around on it?"

"Well, in a way. You're sure you're good with it?"

"Of course. It was my idea if you remember," Recker said, still not looking at him. "I mean, I don't want to add just anybody. As long as they got the skills and a personality that we'll both get along with, then yeah, I'm still good with it."

"Then perhaps you should look at this." Jones held out the folder.

Getting the clue that Jones had more on his mind than he was saying, Recker finally stopped typing and looked at the professor. He glanced at the file folder, then took it out of his hands. Recker opened it, immediately seeing a picture and bio sheet of Christopher Haley. He intently looked it over for a few minutes before looking back up at Jones.

"This is the guy?" Recker said.

"Unless you have objections."

Recker turned his attention back to the contents of the folder. He read the bio sheet a couple of times before moving on to the other information that Jones had compiled on him. Jones had printed out everything he could find on Haley. Every case he worked on in the CIA, his life before he joined the government agency, and every detail since he'd left.

"Well, I'll let you read that without me looking over your shoulder." Jones walked around Recker and back to his own workstation.

Jones had probably compiled at least a hundred pages of information and notes on Haley. Not only the facts and details of Haley's life, but he had also added his own notes and thoughts. It was a meticulously prepared folder, something one would expect coming from him, bringing someone in to an operation such as the one they were running, one that would take Recker several hours to go over. Though Jones wasn't going to bug Recker about his thoughts until he was completely done consuming the file, he did keep an ear out, hoping to hear any sounds that Recker might make as he was reading. Maybe some grumbles if he didn't like something he read, or maybe something more lighthearted if he approved. Something that would give Jones an indication on which way Recker was leaning before they discussed it after he was done.

Unfortunately for Jones, Recker never gave any clues or hints on his thoughts as he was reading. He was stone-cold silent. And on something like this, Recker wasn't going to rush his way through. He was going to sit, read, and analyze. Possibly several times over. Jones knew he was going to be in for a long day. It occurred to him that maybe he should've given Recker the file toward the end of the day. That way he could've taken it home with him. Now, it was unlikely they were going to get any further work done. Luckily there was nothing pressing. After five hours of silence, without either man saying a word, or asking Recker a thing about his thoughts up to that point, Jones couldn't stand being left in the dark anymore. He needed some clarification about Recker's thoughts.

"So, what do you think?" Jones finally said.

"I'm still reading."

"I can see that. But surely you must have some thoughts at this point. Either one way or the other."

"Not yet."

"Come on, Mike. You've been reading for five hours. You don't have any inclination on which way you're leaning after five hours?"

"There's a lot to think about."

"Yes, I understand that. Does he at least seem promising?" Jones said, hoping to get even the littlest nugget of positive emotion out of Recker's mouth.

"Uh... maybe."

Jones sighed and scratched behind his ear, frustrated that Recker wasn't going to humor him and tell him a thing. Recker wasn't going to do this on his own timeline.

"Do you think you'll have an answer today?" Jones said.

"Maybe."

"Oh, good lord. You're not going to give me the slightest of hints about anything, are you?"

"We'll see."

Jones knew it was a lost cause at that point. Recker wasn't going to tell him anything. And based upon the fact that Recker seemed to be reading the pages repeatedly, and he still had a few to go, Jones thought it possible that Recker might not even be ready to give an opinion before the day was over.

"Should I order a late-night snack?" Jones said, only partly kidding.

"Not something we should rush through."

"I'm aware of that."

"Maybe I should take this home with me tonight," Recker said. "That way I can have an answer for you in the morning."

"You're really going to put me through all that agony?"

"Why not? You're a patient person."

"In most cases. This doesn't happen to be one of those times."

"Why? What's so special about this? You seem very anxious for some reason."

"What's so special about this? We're talking about adding a number to our twosome. I've spent months working on this, finding candidates, discarding candidates, until I finally whittled it down to one. This one. So yes, I am a little anxious about this."

"Well I need time to analyze this. I can't give my thumbs up until I've fully vetted everything in here."

"Don't you think I've done that? Do you really believe I'd come to you with this unless I was absolutely sure on this?"

"What do you want? You want me to just rubber-stamp this?" Recker said.

"Of course not."

"Then let me dig into it on my own. I know you're anxious about it. Just relax."

Jones knew he wasn't going to speed up Recker's analysis, so he tried to block it out the best he could. He turned back toward his computer and started working again on some of the upcoming cases they had. He needed to do something engrossing, so he could forget about Recker reading the mountain of information next to him. The only thing he could think of was working on another case. And it worked. Jones completely blocked Recker out of his mind for the next hour until Recker finally made a noise.

"Crap," Recker said, drawing a concerned look from Jones, who thought he'd read something that he didn't like.

"What's the matter? What don't you like?"

"Nothing," Recker said, getting up from his chair.

"Then what are you doing?"

"It's past six o'clock. I'm supposed to be off today. Remember, I've got a girlfriend redecorating my apartment."

"Oh. I almost forgot about that."

"Yeah, well, I don't wanna be gone all day and night. She forgave me for coming. I don't know if she'll forgive me for staying indefinitely."

"What about Mr. Haley?" Jones said.

"I'll take his file with me and read it tonight."

"I was hoping I'd get a yay or nay from you tonight."

"Not likely. I'll have an answer in the morning," Recker said.

Though Jones wasn't especially pleased with waiting another day, he knew that was the best he was going to get. As Recker grabbed the file folder and walked toward the door, Jones tried one last time to get some information out of him.

"You're seriously going to just leave like that? You're not even going to give me a hint as to which way you're leaning?"

Without saying a word, Recker looked back and gave Jones a sinister smile, realizing he was torturing his partner without saying anything.

"You know, you have a mean streak in you," Jones said.

"Consider it payment for your needling about the curtains," Recker said, closing the door behind him.

In reality, Recker was very impressed with the file that Jones had accumulated on Haley. There were no obvious red flags that Recker could see. He spent eight years in the military, four of them in special forces, along with another eight years in the CIA doing clandestine operations. His assignments were for the most part carried out successfully, seemed to be highly thought of, and didn't seem to have any of the emotional baggage that Recker did. There really wasn't anything not to like. But Recker didn't like making decisions on the spot and wanted at least one night to stew it over. Plus, he knew that Jones wouldn't have recommended anyone unless he was certain it was the right pick. And there was a small piece inside him, enjoying making Jones squirm for the night as retaliation for teasing him the way he did.

When Recker got home, Mia had just finished the apartment. He walked in, hoping he wouldn't get the cold shoulder from her for being gone most of the day. As soon as he stepped inside, he was amazed at how different the place looked. It really did feel like he was in someone else's home. Pictures on the wall, flowers on the table, plants by the window, a couple extra lamps that he didn't recall having before. Mia really did do a wonderful job with it, he thought. And with everything finished, he hardly felt any anxiety over the latest changes.

He went over to the wall and stared at the pictures of them together. For the first time he could remember, at least since what happened in London, he finally felt at peace with himself. Looking at the two of them together, their cheeks pressed against each other, he felt like the emptiness he'd been carrying around for so long had gone away. He wasn't longing for Carrie anymore, wasn't wishing circumstances had been different, or that he'd acted in some other way. He was just relishing the fact he had found another woman who loved him unconditionally, much like Carrie did, and that he loved equally as well. For the longest time, he didn't think he'd ever find that feeling again. And for a while, he didn't think he even wanted it. But Mia changed all that.

As he was staring at the pictures on the wall, Mia snuck up behind him and wrapped her arms around his waist. Recker looked back at her and smiled. He turned around and kissed her, hoping she wasn't mad at him. By the warm smile she had planted on her face, he assumed that he wasn't going to get a tongue lashing, or the cold shoulder that he was worried about. As they stared into each other's eyes, Recker put his nose in the air, smelling something good coming from the kitchen.

"What smells so good?"

"Just figured I'd make a little celebration meal for our first night together in our new place," Mia said, her face beaming from ear to ear.

"Oh? What're we having?"

"Figured I'd go Italian tonight. Have some meatballs, spaghetti, lasagna, garlic bread."

"Wow. You're going all out. I don't know if I'll be able to eat all that."

"Smaller portions," she said gleefully, looking down at the folder that he was clutching in his hand. "What's that?"

Recker lifted it up as he explained what it was. "Just some work stuff."

"Oh. So how do you like the apartment?"

"It looks really nice," he said, looking around the room.

"Really? What bothers you about it?"

"Nothing."

"Really? There's nothing that's just eating away at you, nothing that's making you wanna just rip it down and throw it out?" Mia said, sure that there must've been something he didn't like.

"No, really. Everything's fine."

"OK. It's just, I know before you left you were a little uneasy about everything."

"Yeah, I know, that was just me being... stupid. Honestly, everything's fine. I wouldn't change anything. Especially the woman who made it all happen."

Mia couldn't resist planting another kiss on his lips, happy that he seemed to enjoy what she'd done to the place. "Dinner's just about ready," she said, taking him by the hand and leading him into the kitchen.

Recker sat down at the kitchen table as Mia went to the stove and started bringing the food over. She already had plates and utensils set up, along with a nice tablecloth and a candle in the middle. Once she was done putting all the food down, she sat down across from Recker. She couldn't help but notice he looked a little out of it.

"What's the matter? Doesn't it look good?" she said, her eyebrows scrunched down.

Recker shook his head and looked up at her. "No, no, everything looks great. It's just uh..."

"What?"

"I don't think I've ever had a tablecloth on here. Or a candle," Recker said, trying hard to remember. "Come to think of it, I'm not sure if I've ever even eaten on plates here. Except the paper ones."

Mia laughed. "You know, that really doesn't surprise me. You see these plates on the table? They're the only ones I found in the cabinets."

"Oh."

"I'm gonna have to go on a shopping trip. I've noticed you're a little sparse on a few things in here."

"That's the life of a bachelor."

"Well, that's over with now, right?"

"Looks that way," Recker said with a smile. "This might be your last chance to back out you know."

"Why would I want to do that?"

"Well, I'm not wanted by the CIA anymore, but it doesn't extend to the police department. Half of them anyway."

"I'm not really worried."

"You're not? If I'm caught, they could always arrest you as an accomplice or something," Recker said, warning her of the dangers, though it wasn't the first time they'd talked about it.

"And as I've told you before, you getting caught doesn't really worry me."

"It doesn't."

"No, you getting killed... that's what worries me. I mean, you're out there all alone most of the time, fighting against bad people," Mia said.

She was about to keep going but quickly thought better of it. The last thing she wanted to sound like was a worrywart of a girl-friend. Especially on a day like this, which was a big day for both of them. And she didn't want to be one of those girlfriends who was always nagging or crying about something. She knew Recker didn't need that either. She assumed that the quickest way her fears about Recker dying would come true, were if his mind was filled with drama at home. Worrying about her instead of focusing on whatever his assignment was. Mia was determined not to do that to him. At least as much as possible. She knew there would eventually be fights or disagreements, as in any relationship, but she was going to try her hardest to not let it be over silly stuff or things that could be avoided. If the unthinkable ever happened, and Recker died out there on the streets, it wouldn't be because of her.

"Well, we're taking some steps to make sure that doesn't happen," Recker said.

"What do you mean?"

"David and I are talking about bringing in another guy. Another Silencer."

Mia laughed at the way he referenced himself. "You just love calling yourself that, don't you?"

Recker smirked. "Yeah, a little bit."

"So, you're really thinking about bringing another person in?"

"That's what the folder's for. David's narrowed it down to one person."

"Why didn't you tell me about this before?" Mia said.

"I didn't know. David just gave it to me today. I didn't realize he was this close."

"So, what do you think?"

"His package looks good," Recker said, admitting to Mia what he wouldn't to Jones.

"You think you'll be able to get along with another guy?"

"Yeah, if he isn't a pompous jerk," Recker said with a laugh. "Besides, maybe that'll free me up at night for more time here with you."

"Well I'm definitely all for that."

"We'll see what happens. But having another person would definitely take some of the strain off."

"I'll be glad when or if it happens," Mia said. "I've always worried about you not having anyone out there watching your back. Especially with some of the situations you wind up getting yourself in."

"You mean the situations other people make me put myself in."

"So, when are you gonna make a decision on this guy?"

"I'll give David the go-ahead tomorrow morning when I go in. I just wanna reread everything to make sure it's the right call."

"Well you've always had great instincts on people. What's your gut say?"

"That he's the guy."

17

Just as Recker promised, when he came into the office the following morning, he was ready to give Jones his decision. The professor had a tough time sleeping and was awake before the sun came up. He was excited about possibly adding to the team, as well as anxious as he waited for Recker's answer. When Jones first started his search for a new member, he didn't anticipate he'd ever be that thrilled over it. He certainly wasn't that enraptured when the list of candidates first started appearing on his screen. He and Recker had developed a strong friendship and special chemistry. They couldn't do the work that they did without a powerful bond between them. He worried that a new person would possibly disrupt the dynamic that they'd built up. Jones' hopes weren't even that high at first. Finding someone like Recker, who would fit within their team, wouldn't be an easy task. He wasn't sure if it was even doable. It would be like catching lightning in a bottle twice, he thought. But as his search progressed, and he got further along and started diving into some of the candidates' backgrounds, Jones got a little more excited over the prospects of finding that elusive new member.

Jones had whittled the final list of candidates down to three before he selected Haley. In Jones' search parameters, he limited his search to men and women that were single. He assumed those that were married would have a more difficult time in making the move and doing the work that was required. Once the final three were chosen, it really didn't take Jones very long to narrow it down to Haley. As Jones made up the list of the desired attributes, Haley was the only one who checked off all the boxes. He was single, good with firearms, excellent at blending in, and willing to do the most difficult assignments. That was shown by his CIA case record. Haley had been stationed all over the world, Russia, China, North Korea, Africa, the Middle East, Europe, and South America, and spoke several languages. He'd been assigned at various points of his career to take out dictators, drug lords, firearm dealers, and corrupt politicians. His history was as promising as Recker's was when Jones first saw his file.

"You know, I miss the days when I used to beat you into the office," Recker said.

Jones was sitting at the computer typing away, but stopped at Recker's wisecrack. He turned to look at him. "By days, you mean one or two? Because I don't remember any more than that."

"Yeah, well, it's gonna be harder to do now you're living here. Now I won't even have a chance."

"Longing for nostalgia of our days of yesteryear already, are you?"

"What?"

"Nothing. Speaking of nostalgia and things that used to be and are no more, what is your opinion about Mr. Haley?" Jones said.

Recker tossed the folder down on the desk and sighed. Though he was still in favor of adding someone to the team, it was still a new wrinkle. It was another change that he'd have to get used to. Even though he wanted help, he still wondered how he'd react to another guy invading their space, especially when he had a bad enough time watching pictures get hung on the wall of his apartment. He wondered how he'd feel that first time he saw Haley do something that Recker was used to doing. Would he feel grateful, or thankful that he had help? Or would he feel jealous or threatened that someone else was doing his job for him? After a few more moments he came to his senses. He figured he probably wouldn't feel grateful or threatened. After all, there were plenty of bad guys to go around. Recker didn't have the market on them all to himself. There was more out there than he could deal with on his own. And that's what it was all about. Just getting the job done. By whatever means possible.

"I'm good with him." Recker said, finally admitting the truth.

"Hallelujah. I had ideas that you might not ever say what you really thought about him."

"I thought about it."

"I'm sure you did."

"Did you know all along, or did you just come to that conclusion overnight?" Jones said, wondering for his own amusement.

"I had a pretty good idea yesterday."

"Would it have killed you to at least say you were leaning in that direction, instead of making me wonder all day and night? And morning for that matter."

"It might have."

"Somehow I knew you would say that."

"So, what's your plan?" Recker said.

"With?"

"Haley. I mean, I assume you're not gonna just send him an email or a telegram and pitch him our little operation. Right?"

"Of course not. I was planning on seeing him in person and making him an offer."

"When will you be back?"

"When will we be back?"

"We? What do you need me for?"

"Because he's a highly dangerous man that I would like to have some backup on... just in case," Jones said.

"You recruited me alone."

"If you recall, there was some added muscle I hired at first to direct you from the airport. In case you weren't as cooperative as I'd hoped."

"Oh, yeah."

"So, are you ready?"

"For what?" Recker said.

"To go speak to Mr. Haley."

"Right now?"

"Do you have other plans?" Jones said.

"No."

"Well then there's no time like the present, is there?"

"A little notice would've been nice."

"Turnabout is fair play, is it not? You gave me no advanced notice on your thoughts last night. Therefore, I'm giving you none now." Jones flashed a devilish smile.

"You know, sometimes I think my personality may have rubbed off on you too much."

"I know, and it really gives me great pause for concern sometimes."

"How far is this excursion of ours gonna take us?" Recker said. "The one thing missing in his file was where he's at now."

"It's a short trip. He's in Baltimore."

"A nice, short drive."

"We'll be back before dinner. In time for you to hang more curtains tonight."

"Don't start that again. Besides, Mia's working the late shift."

They gathered up a few things from the office and began the drive down to Baltimore. It was only a two-hour drive so they would get there right around lunchtime. Haley was working for a home security systems company, so Jones knew they'd find him at his apartment. Thirty minutes into their drive, Recker had some questions about their upcoming encounter.

"What if he's got other things to do, and he's not there?" Recker said.

"Well then we'll wait until he gets there."

"Easy as that, huh?"

"Easy as that," Jones said.

"Nervous?"

"No. Why?"

"Just wondering. Isn't every day you try to recruit a new member for the squad."

"I've done it before."

"So, what's bothering you?"

"What makes you think something is bothering me?"

"Because I know you. You're not saying much, and you keep looking out the window like you're distracted by something. Unusual for you," Recker said.

"Just thinking about some things."

"You wanna spring it on me?"

"Just thinking about Haley."

"What about him? Having second thoughts already?"

"No. Just a few things I don't understand yet. There's a lot to be learned from his package. You can learn a man's history, his strengths, his weaknesses, but you can't learn everything. Some things you just can't tell until you meet someone and interact with them for a while," Jones said, still looking out the passenger side window.

"What are you getting at?"

"Haley left the CIA two years ago. And in that time, he's had four jobs. Worked in Virginia as a construction worker, in Pittsburgh at an industrial plant, in Delaware as a private security guard, now in Baltimore as a home security guard."

"Can't hold anything down," Recker said.

"I don't understand it. A man with his background, with his record, and he hasn't held onto any of those jobs for longer than six months. He's on his sixth month now with his current job. How do you figure it?"

"My guess? He's unsettled. He's looking for something. He's looking for a home, some sense of belonging. Something to hang his hat on. He's unsatisfied in his work, he's looking for more, and he hasn't found it yet."

"Well if that's true then that may work in our favor," Jones said. "That may make our offer more appealing."

"It probably happens to most guys who've done what we've done. You risk your life for your country and live in continuous danger and, then when it's all over, you find yourself schlepping around a broom somewhere. You feel like your work used to be important. You used to matter. Then you wind up a civilian and find out nobody gives two hoots about you anymore."

"It didn't happen to you."

"I guess I got lucky when I ran into you. Plus, I had something to keep me going. I didn't exactly go out on my own terms like most guys. It's probably also easier for those guys who have a wife or kids, some family to keep their spirits up. Haley doesn't seem to have that going for him."

"No, he doesn't. Never married. No kids. No immediate family to speak of. His father died when he was twelve, and his mother passed away three years ago to cancer. No siblings."

"Didn't he have a couple cousins or something?" Recker said, remembering the file. "Thought I read that in there somewhere."

"Yes, a few cousins down in North Carolina. As far as I can tell he hasn't spoken to them in some time. At least ten years that I could see. Has an aunt and uncle in Denver. Hasn't had contact with them in at least the same amount of time."

"Classic loner."

"I hope not. If he's too much of a loner, he may not be willing to join us," Jones said.

The two of them continued talking about Haley for the rest of the drive. They talked about his background, what would make him so useful to the team, and some of the records that Jones unearthed of him in the CIA. He posed some hypothetical questions to Recker to see how he would have handled some of the situations that Haley found himself in on certain assignments. Most of which Recker said he would have done the same way. They continued talking about Haley the rest of the way to Baltimore, rolling into the city at 11:30 and finding his apartment without much trouble. He had a third-floor unit in a decent area. It wasn't upscale, but it wasn't the bottom of the heap either. Once Recker and Jones got off the elevator on the third floor, they walked to Haley's unit, looking at each other as they stood at the door, making sure neither wanted to turn back before continuing. It was their last chance. Neither did, though. Jones knocked on the door. Haley answered almost at once.

"Can I help you?" Haley said.

"I certainly hope so," Jones replied. "I guess there's really no easy way to get into this, so I'll just get right to the point. We're here to offer you employment."

"Subtle," Recker said.

"I've already got a job."

"Yes, I know. I mean we're here to offer you something meaningful, something you can feel you belong to," Jones said.

"I'm not interested. Thanks."

Haley was about to close the door when Jones knew he had to think of something fast to keep the dialogue flowing. "I know you've been searching for something since you left the CIA," Jones said quickly. "We can help with that." He talked in his normal tone, and Haley stopped the door from closing.

"How do you know I worked for them?" Haley said, looking at

the two visitors more closely, thinking that Recker looked like an agent.

"We know everything about you," Jones said. "If we can come in, I can explain everything in greater detail."

"But first, if you could put the gun away that you have hiding behind the door we'd appreciate it," Recker said finally, with a smile.

Jones looked at Recker, then back at Haley, feeling a little uneasy that a gun was being pointed at them if he was correct, which he assumed he was.

"We're not here to hurt you," Jones said, hoping to ease the man's fears.

"If we were we probably wouldn't be standing here asking to come in," Recker said.

Haley knew they were right. If it was somebody gunning for him, they wouldn't give him the courtesy of knocking on the door. They'd shoot first, then exchange pleasantries after he was dead, though it would be one-sided at that point. He tucked the gun inside the belt of his pants and opened the door for his two visitors to enter. Recker and Jones walked into the living room and sat on opposite ends of a couch. Haley sat on a sofa across from them, ready to listen to what they had to say.

"So, are you guys with the agency?" Haley said.

"I used to be," Recker said.

"We're both currently in the public sector. We have nothing to do with any government agencies." Jones watched Haley carefully as he spoke.

"So, what's this offer you were talking about?" Haley said.

"We're here to offer you a job. I assume you're not satisfied with how your life is currently tracking considering you've had four jobs in four different cities in the last two years."

"How do you know all this?"

"Information is something that comes easily to me. Doing

something with that information, well, that's where you would come in."

Haley threw his hands up, not sure what his guest was saying to him. "What does all that mean exactly?"

"The short version is that we try to stop bad things happening to good people. We stop robberies, murders, assaults, kidnappings, all before the perpetrators have a chance to enact their crimes. Well, mostly anyway."

"How can you do that?"

"Like I said, information is something that comes easily."

"I don't understand what you need me for. If you get all this information, then why don't you just go to the police?"

"I suppose it's because, technically, my information is gathered through illegal means. Software programs that I've enacted that I learned from my time in the NSA."

"You were in the NSA?"

"At one time. A long time ago. And I learned that there's a lot of good people, innocent people that could be helped by us, that otherwise would just fall through the cracks," Jones said. "Unless we did something about it."

Jones had brought a small computer bag with him and opened it, removing some folders and a couple binders. He put them down on the table in front of Haley for him to look through. It was examples of some of the work he and Recker had done in Philadelphia. News reports, press clippings, the cases they'd worked on, Jones figured that would be more helpful in helping Haley make up his mind than just talking of their exploits. When he first contacted Recker, all he had to go on was faith that their mission could be successful. And all he had was hope that Recker would go along with it. Now, he didn't have to do that. He had real-life examples to show. There were noted cases where it was documented how much of a help they were. But Jones also wasn't going to shy away from admitting the pitfalls either. He was going to be upfront and honest in telling Haley that, though they'd be doing important work, he wouldn't be on the same side as the law. At least in the eyes of the police department.

Haley eagerly looked through the information that was presented to him. He'd already heard of The Silencer, as some of Recker's exploits had become known throughout the east coast. But to sit and have him sitting across from him, looking through some of their files, was something of a thrill for Haley. After hearing of some of their stories through newspaper or TV reports, Haley had always had thoughts of doing something similar. But he didn't know where to start or how to set up an operation like that, so it never got past the idea stage. He didn't have a Jones to oversee anything.

Jones and Recker were giving Haley all the time and space that he needed to go through the things they had provided for him, not eager to rush him into anything. They looked at each other a couple of times, both of them were confident that their approach was working. By the look on Haley's face as he consumed what he was reading, at the very least, seemed intrigued. Eventually, Haley picked his head up to look at his guests, plenty of questions going through his mind.

"I have to admit that I've heard of you guys before," Haley said. "You've kind of made a name for yourself."

"Sometimes too much," Jones said, giving Recker a glance.

"I guess I still have sorta the same question. What do you want with me?"

"Well, our reasons are many. First of which, I'm not that handy with a gun, I'm not a whizz at tailing people, I'm not somebody who excels at close-quarter combat. That's what Mike does. He's the one who's mentioned in all these stories."

"But none of that happens without David," Recker said, making sure Jones got his due and equal share of the credit.

"What I'm good at, is finding the information that these people need help. How I do that is a more complicated answer for another time. But what we're really looking for is another person out in the field, who can help in whatever situation is necessary. We've encountered several situations in the last year or so where another person would have been very useful."

"I'm good, but I can't be everywhere," Recker said.

"And you guys want me to join you?" Haley said, a little awestruck.

"That's why we're here," Jones said.

"I'm sure there are others who may have something better to offer than me."

"I analyzed thousands of files. I couldn't come up with anyone."

"My last couple of years haven't been filled with much to be proud of," Haley said.

"What you need is to be redirected," Jones said. "You need guidance, structure, something important to fight for. We can provide that."

"We can also provide the danger and getting shot at." Recker couldn't resist the quip.

Jones turned to look at his partner, giving him a disapproving look. "By the nature of our work, you will be placed in... difficult situations. That will be unavoidable."

"I'm not afraid to be in danger," Haley said quickly. "If you've seen my file, you know where I've been."

"We know. But I should also point out that even though you'll be doing the right thing, helping people, you will not be a friend to the police department. You will, at some point, become a wanted man. Unfortunately, there is no way around that. Your life as you know it will be over. You'll live and operate in secrecy."

"Living in secrecy's never been an issue for me. What about supplies, guns, stuff like that? Do I bring my own?"

"Whatever you wish. Bring whatever you like. Though I

should warn you and point out that Mike has an extensive collection of weapons. Guns will be the least of your worries. Guns, money, vehicles, nothing will be an issue. Everything you will need will be at your disposal."

"Sounds good."

"There's only three things you will need to worry about," Jones said.

"What's that?"

"Successfully completing your assignment, staying out of public view as much as possible, and staying alive."

"Three things that aren't an issue for me."

"Now, we have had our fair share of publicity for whatever reasons, but we try to avoid being put in the spotlight. The more media coverage we get, the more police attention we receive as well. We obviously would rather not have either."

"Works for me. I couldn't care less about attention," Haley said, seemingly on board with the proposal.

"So far, this has been a two-man operation. We have no egos, no ulterior motives, nothing else matters except helping those who need it."

"I don't have an ego to check. I'm all about doing whatever's needed. I've always been a team player."

"That's one of the reasons we're here," Jones said. "Your file indicates you'd fit in."

"Would we work as a pair or separately?"

"Sometimes both. It all depends on the type of case and how many we're working. Everything's on the table."

As Jones continued talking about their operation, Haley kept looking through the files and documents that were laid out on the table. He was trying to soak in as much as possible. Though he tried not to show it too much outwardly, Haley was ready to burst out of his seat to accept the proposal. He had nothing there that was holding him back. And it seemed like the perfect opportunity to get back in the game. This was the type of work he enjoyed, and he knew he was good at. Since leaving the CIA, he'd been searching for something to fill the void. This would be the chance he was looking for to feel like his work mattered again.

"What made you leave the agency?" Recker said. "I didn't see anything mentioned in your file. You could've stayed on a few more years if you wanted."

"Yeah. There was a woman. A girlfriend," Haley said, looking depressed the moment he thought about her.

"Well, that's eerily familiar," Jones said.

"What happened?" Recker said.

"Mike, that's not our business."

"No, it's fine," Haley said. "I'd rather have everything out on the table with you guys. I'm not hiding anything. I met a girl, and I fell in love with her. Was with her for a few years. But she got tired of the frequent missions which meant I was out of the country all the time. So, I agreed to leave the agency to preserve our relationship."

"I guess things went sideways?" Recker said.

"Yeah, you could say that. I was out of the country for about two months on my final assignment. When I came back, she was gone."

"She just left you?"

"Yeah. At first, I tried to look for her. Took a job down in Virginia to get by while I was searching. Then, after about six months, I found her. I used some contacts of mine from the CIA and found her living in Pittsburgh. So, I went there."

"And?" Jones said.

"She was with another man. She apparently met him even before I gave my notice," Haley said. "So, then I just kind of bounced around at a couple jobs till I wound up here."

"And you didn't kill either of them?" Recker said, half-jokingly.

Haley laughed. "No. Not that I didn't have thoughts about it.

But, no, they're both living, safe and sound, happy as can be I guess."

"Pity."

They talked for another couple of hours, Jones continuing to give Haley the rundown about how their operation worked, what would be expected, and what, if anything, Haley needed. Once they were finished, Jones started picking the papers off the table, and put them back in his computer bag. He looked at the time and figured they needed to be getting back to Philadelphia. It was already past three.

"Well, we should be heading home," Jones said, reaching into his bag for a business card and handing it to Haley. "Take a few days to make your decision. Think about it. I'd appreciate a phone call when you've made up your mind. Either way."

Haley took it and looked at it briefly, before handing it back to Jones. "I don't need this. And I don't need a few days to think about it. I'm in," Haley said happily.

"Are you sure?"

"Definitely. I've got nothing keeping me here. This is the type of work I'm made to do. This is what I'm good at."

"Just to be clear, we're looking for someone for the long term. We're not interested in someone who's only going to stick around a few months or so before looking for something else."

"That's not a problem. I'll be in it for the long haul. You don't have to worry about me," Haley said, knowing they had fears over his recent work history. "These last couple years with those other jobs, I was just trying to fit in somewhere. This is what I need."

Jones looked at Recker, who nodded his head in approval.

"Well then, it looks like we have a deal," Jones said.

"Welcome aboard," Recker said, shaking Haley's hand.

"What do you need me to do first?"

"Take care of whatever you need to do here. Pack up, quit your job, take care of any bills or anything else you have," Jones said.

"Make sure there's no outstanding issues that someone might track you down for."

"I can let my job know today. Won't take me long to pack. A day at the most. I can be up in Philly by tomorrow night."

"How's your car?"

"My car?"

"Yes, does it run OK?"

"Well, it's got about a hundred thousand miles on it, but I haven't really had many issues with it. Why?"

"Make sure you're still here tomorrow morning," Jones said. "You'll be getting a delivery."

18

_____

True to his word, after getting back to Philadelphia, Jones placed an order for a brand-new car to be delivered to Haley's address. To be specific, a silver Ford Explorer. It was just about noon when Haley heard the knock on the door. It was a salesman from the auto group who was dropping the car off. Prior to that, Haley really wasn't sure what kind of delivery he was getting. Jones didn't say anything definite and didn't mention a new car specifically. Since his car was still running reasonably well, without any major issues, Haley definitely didn't envision the delivery being a car. And a new one at that. As soon as Haley finished signing for it, he reached into his pocket for the card that Jones gave him with his phone number on it and dialed.

"Mr. Jones, I really don't know what to say about this new car."

"First off, you can dispense with the Mr. Jones. David will do fine."

"I really want to thank you for this."

"Don't mention it," Jones said. "It's just what I like to consider a signing bonus."

"It's tough for me to accept something like this. I mean, it's a lot of money."

"Money will be the least of your worries. Once you're three months on the job, you'll have earned that new car at least ten times over."

"OK. Well, I already had my car packed with my things, so I'll transfer everything over to the new SUV and then I'll be on my way," Haley said.

"Excellent."

"So, I should be there in about two or three hours I would think. Where should I go exactly?"

"Great. Once you get near the Philadelphia exit, send me a message, and I'll text you the address."

As soon as they finished their conversation, Jones continued his computer work, almost ready to assign a new case. Recker was due in the office any minute. He had stayed at home for the morning since there was nothing for him to work on just yet. Though he hadn't shunned any of his work duties since being with Mia, Jones had to admit that he missed Recker hanging around the office more. Now when there were lulls, Recker usually chose to stay home with Mia when she was off from work. Before they became an item, Recker usually just did some busy work in the office. Jones missed the banter and camaraderie that he often shared with his friend. Though he still had that relationship with Recker, it just wasn't as much as before.

Recker came in after one, looking as calm and refreshed as Jones had seen him in a long time. It'd been a few days between assignments, but it was something more than that. Jones assumed that his newfound home life was beginning to agree with him. For the last few days, Recker had no issues or anxieties over his changing apartment. After exchanging some brief pleasantries, Recker sat down at a computer next to Jones and started typing away. Jones turned toward his friend, unable to turn down what he thought was an easy target.

"You look very... relaxed," Jones said.

"Yeah, I guess I feel pretty good."

"I take it life at home with Mia is... soothing."

Sounding like Jones was hinting at something, Recker stopped typing and simply scrunched up his face as he looked at the screen, wondering what exactly his partner was trying to say. Recker started to say something but quickly thought better of it. If he was joking about his sex life, as Recker believed he was, he was just not going to get into it with him. Even in teasing, Recker was not comfortable in discussing that aspect of his life, no matter how close he and Jones were.

"Everything's good," Recker said, changing the tone of the conversation. "Apartment's set, curtains are hung, bedroom's squared away, it's all good. And I'm fine with all of it."

"I'm glad. I'm glad."

"Good," Recker said awkwardly, hoping Jones would talk about something other than his home life.

Like he was reading his mind, Jones did flip the discussion to other topics. "So, I just talked to Chris a little while ago. He's on his way."

"Great. When's he getting here?"

"Probably should be about an hour or two from now."

"Hopefully we can work him in slowly," Recker said. "Let him get a feel for the area before he gets thrown into the fire, let him get himself situated."

"Well, that's the hope. Unfortunately, we don't always get to pick the ideal scenario for things in our business."

"Speaking of which, what's up with that case you were telling me about? Ready yet?"

"Just about," Jones said. "I'm waiting on one more piece of information before letting you handle it."

"Which is?"

"A time."

"Already have the address and the perpetrators involved. Just need the date and time."

"What's the case?"

"Home invasion. Or it could just be a robbery. I'm still not sure about that."

"Oh good. Haven't had one of those lately," Recker said. "Who's the target?"

"Elderly couple in their seventies. Wealthy, no children in the house."

"Who are the suspects?"

Jones reached across the desk and shuffled a few papers around until he found the one he wanted. He looked it over briefly before sliding it over to Recker, who picked it up and analyzed it. He read the names and rap sheets of four individuals who appeared to be very violent in nature.

"How'd you get wind of this?" Recker said.

"Text messages between two of them. Seems one of them works as a handyman on the side and was in the house last week on a job. If only people knew how vulnerable texting is. People assume that their conversations are private, like they're just handing a letter to someone in person."

"Yeah, well, it's better for us that they don't."

"In any case, he apparently found the home to be extremely desirable when he was there and let a few of his friends know the same."

"It's just the three?"

"How many do you want?"

"Four's fine."

"Anyway, they've all got criminal records, they've all been noted to use firearms, and they've all done jail time. A very rough crew."

"You said home invasion or robbery," Recker said, knowing there was a massive difference between the two options. "That's kind of..."

Knowing what he was about to say, Jones put his hand up and nodded, acknowledging the difference. "I know. They apparently can't make up their mind about how they want to handle the situation. One wants to go in forcefully, regardless of who's there or not, and the other one wants to wait until the homeowners are gone to rob the place. The third one doesn't really care in either instance and the fourth one says he's only interested in doing a robbery, and if it's a home invasion, then he's out."

Recker continued reading the information about the crew, shaking his head. "Great crew. That actually makes them a little more dangerous."

Jones raised his eyebrows, not sure if he agreed. "Definitely more unstable."

"The more unstable they are, the more dangerous they become. More unpredictable."

"You'd prefer a more professional crew? One that was in unison?"

"Actually, yes. At least then you can kind of guess what they're gonna do and how they'll act. With these guys, if they can't even agree on how they'll hit, you can't really assume how they'll behave once they're inside."

"Well they all have violent histories, so I'd say they're capable of just about anything," Jones said.

Recker and Jones continued talking about the case for a few more minutes, before one of the computers started beeping. It was one of Jones' software programs sounding an alert that something was developing. Jones quickly swiveled his chair over to that workstation and eagerly read the screen to gauge the situation.

"Oh dear," Jones said.

"What is it?"

"It appears it's happening now."

"What is?"

"Our home invasion-cum-robbery. Apparently the top three have agreed. They just sent the fourth guy a message saying 'We're doing it now. Are you in?'"

Recker jumped out of his seat and rushed over to his gun cabinet. "The other guy reply yet?"

"He just replied back that he's in."

"How much time we got?" Recker said, closing the door after removing a couple of weapons.

"I would say an hour, tops."

"How long will it take me to get there?"

"If you leave now, you should be there in about twenty-five minutes."

Recker hurried out of the office and hopped in his SUV to get to the northeast home. The house in question was in a nice neighborhood of single family two-story homes, brick lined driveways, lush front lawns, full basements, and expensive looking cars. It was a wealthy area that looked more like the suburbs than the city. When Recker reached the development, thirty minutes had passed. Seeing a car in the driveway, Recker parked down the street until he was sure what he was dealing with.

"David, you need to tell me what kind of car the Tresselmans have."

Jones immediately pulled the information up on the computer. "It's a Cadillac. Why? Do you see something else?"

"No. Not yet."

"How do you propose to handle this?"

"Well, I got two choices."

"I don't believe I like either of them," Jones said.

"I haven't even said what they are yet."

"If I know you as well as I think I do, you're going to suggest you wait inside for our suspects to arrive and head them off at the pass, so to speak."

"And the other?"

"Does it really matter? We both know what you will wind up doing."

Recker let out a sigh that Jones knew him so well and that he'd become that predictable. "I'm really gonna have to start changing my tactics."

"Then I'll have to learn your tricks all over again. Just out of curiosity, what was your second option?"

"To jump them outside before they get inside."

"Too public."

"I know."

Their discussion was interrupted by the sound of Jones' phone going off. He quickly looked at it, seeing it was Haley.

"Hold on, Chris," Jones said, before going back to Recker. "Mike, Chris is on the other line. I'll get back to you in a second."

"Take your time," Recker said, as if nothing was happening.

"Chris, sorry, we just have something going on right now."

"Oh. I just wanted to let you know I'm about half an hour outside of the city," Haley said.

"Great. I'll give you the address of the office."

"Do you need me to help out with anything? I'm ready to go."

"I'm not sure it'd be fair to send you out on something blind, without getting a chance to settle in first," Jones said.

"Well, if you need something, just tell me what you want done, and I'll give it a shot."

"Quite literally, most likely," Jones whispered, taking a few moments to think it over.

Jones put Haley on hold as he went back to Recker to get his opinion. His first inclination was to send Haley to help, but didn't want to send him into something he wasn't prepared for. He also had hoped for Haley to get a little easier assignment at first.

"It's up to you, David," Recker said. "According to his records, the guy can handle himself fairly well."

"I just worry about sending him in without knowledge of the particulars."

"There's only one particular here, helping me stay alive and nailing these bozos."

"Very well," Jones said after more reflection. "I'm sending him in. I hope he'll get there in time to help."

"You and me both."

Jones hung up with Recker and went back to Haley. "Chris, I'm sending you to Michael's location. As soon as we hang up, I'll text you the address."

"Great. What's the situation?"

"Mike's at the house of an elderly couple which is about to be the subject of a home invasion. Four dangerous, violent men should be there within the hour."

"How should I handle it?" Haley said.

"However you and Mike deem necessary. Just remember, on any mission, you have two tasks, both of which are equally important. Protect those who need it and get back here in one piece."

"Ten-four."

As soon as he hung up, Jones texted Haley the location where Recker was. Haley was driving along the interstate at a nice, steady pace since leaving Baltimore, but now he pushed down on the gas pedal a little harder. He wanted to leave a lasting impression on his first assignment. He wanted them to know right away that they made the right choice in selecting him. In the day since he was offered the position, Haley felt rejuvenated, invigorated with life again. The last two years had been a drain on him, from having his girlfriend leave him, to going from job to job every six months. Now, he felt like he had a purpose again and he was excited to be doing something like he'd been doing for the government for so long. Though it wasn't the same thing, it was close enough for him.

Recker wasn't going to sit in his car and wait any longer for the crew to show up. He needed to get the Tresselmans out of danger before any bullets started flying. He got out of his truck and walked up the stone pathway to the front door, knocking on it as he looked around for any signs of trouble coming. After knocking a few times, Mrs. Tresselman eventually answered the door.

"Can I help you?" the elderly woman said.

"Yes," Recker said, still looking over his shoulder. He then pulled out a police badge and showed it to her. "I'm Detective Scarborough. I'm not sure how to put this exactly, but you and your husband are in a lot of trouble right now."

"Oh dear, we haven't done anything wrong."

"No, no, it's nothing you did. Did you have work done on your house last week?"

"Yes, we did."

"We got word from a confidential informant that one of those men was a very dangerous criminal."

"Oh, no."

"Yes, and we've since found out that he's recruited three of his buddies to come back to your house to rob you."

The old woman had a stunned look on her face, seeming to be in disbelief at what she'd just been told.

"I'm sorry to scare you, ma'am, but we have to hurry," Recker said. "We understand that they're going to hit this place any minute."

"What are we supposed to do?"

"Is your husband at home?"

"He's watching TV right now."

"OK. I need you and your husband to go somewhere safe for the time being until this is over. Do you have somewhere you can go?"

"Maybe we can go to a neighbor's house," she said.

"Perfect. Let's go get your husband and I'll take you over there."

Recker was let in by Mrs. Tresselman and walked behind her as they made their way into the living room where her husband was watching TV. She started to explain the situation to her husband, but started to get emotional and couldn't finish getting the words out, so Recker explained everything to him.

"I thought there was something funny about those guys last week," Mr. Tresselman said. "A couple of them seemed to keep wandering off like they were looking the place over. Kept mentioning how nice some of the things we had were. I told you something didn't seem right about them."

"I know," Mrs. Tresselman said.

"I'm not sure how long this will last," Recker interjected. "Do either of you two need any medication or anything? Something you might need while you're gone."

"Oh, I have some heart pills," Mr. Tresselman said.

"I'll go get them," his wife said.

After taking a few minutes to get the medication they needed, Recker led the elderly couple through the home and to the front door. Before exiting, Recker looked out the window next to the door, pulling the end of the curtain back with his finger. He saw a car turning onto the street and coming toward the house. It was moving fast. Recker could only assume that they were about to be hit. Knowing it was too late to get the Tresselmans out of the house and to safety, he had to improvise his plan, like he so often did. He turned to the married couple in the hope that they may have their own solution to the problem.

"It's too late," Recker said. "Looks like they're on the way."

"What do we do?" Mrs. Tresselman said.

"You have someplace in here you can hide till this is over?"

"Maybe the basement."

"All right. You guys head there now as quick as you can. No matter what happens up here, no matter what you hear, do not come up under any circumstances. When it's over, I will come get you."

"We got it," Mr. Tresselman said.

"OK. Go."

Recker watched the Tresselmans scurry off to the basement, then turned his attention toward the window, watching as the incoming car approached. He went back into the living room, standing near the hallway which gave a clear view of the front entrance. As he readied himself, Jones called.

"I'm about to be real busy, David," Recker hurriedly said.

"Just hold them off as long as you can. Chris is on the way."

"No problem. I'll just toy with them for a little while."

Sarcasm aside, Recker had no illusions about holding the gang off. If they came in hot and heavy and rushed in quickly, he would have his hands full. His best bet was to pick one or two of them off as they came through the door. Less than a minute later, the car pulled aggressively into the driveway, the inhabitants quickly piling out. They burst through the front door without much effort, and as soon as the first two intruders showed themselves, Recker opened fire. The leader of the group, the man who set everything up, the worker who'd been at the home the previous week, was the first one through the door. He was also the first one to hit the ground after getting a bullet in the chest courtesy of Recker.

The second man through the door dropped to a knee and started firing his AR-15 assault rifle. Recker took cover behind the wall as bullets ripped pieces of the wood off, crumbling to the floor. Recker peeked around the corner with one eye, stuck his hand out and returned fire, though none of his shots hit the intended target. He took cover once again as more rounds from the assault rifle came whizzing by him. Knowing he was unlikely to win the battle against his opponent from where he was, Recker retreated to a more advantageous spot for him in the living room. The other two members of the crew came in through the front door, following in their partner's footsteps. Ducking behind a sectional sofa, Recker waited until he could hear the gang come into the room before he made his next move. He heard a heavy footstep walk across a creaky wooden plank that sounded like it came from beyond the edge of the hallway.

Recker rose up from behind the sofa and quickly located the intruders. He fired off several rounds in their direction before ducking for cover once again as all three members fired their assault rifles, making the couch he was hiding behind look like Swiss cheese. Recker crawled along the floor to the edge of the couch and fired a few rounds from the side, hitting one of the men in the leg. As they returned fire, a bullet hit his weapon, knocking it away from his hand, flinging it across the room. He reached around his back and removed his backup weapon, trying to think of his next move.

"This is not how I hoped this was going to go," he said to himself.

Knowing he was both outnumbered and outgunned, Recker figured his best move might be to reason with his opponents. If he could talk some sense into them, he might just live to see another day. He couldn't stand there and have a shootout with them.

"Police will be here any minute," Recker shouted. "Get out of here now while you still have the chance."

The new leader of the group replied almost instantly. "You killed our friend. We're not going anywhere until you get what you deserve."

"Revenge ain't so sweet if you're locked up because of it."

The gang didn't bother to reply and simply lit up the couch again, Recker hugging the floor as much as humanly possible, hoping the bullets would fly over the top of him. Luckily for him, his backup was just about there. Though he used the GPS on his phone, Haley still had a tough time finding the place. With not being familiar with the area yet, there were a couple streets that came up on him a little faster than he anticipated. As he pulled onto the street, with his window open, he could now hear the distinct sounds of gunfire. Haley gunned his brand-new SUV toward the house in question, squealing his tires as the rubber burned along the pavement. He hopped out of his truck and withdrew his gun as he ran toward the opened front door. He quickly surveyed the situation, seeing a dead body lying just inside the door.

Though he couldn't see anybody yet, Haley could easily define there were at least three people around the corner. He could make out the sound of a Glock handgun along with at least two assault rifles. From experience, he guessed they were AR-15's, and the shots rang out too close together to only be fired from one weapon. Haley slid down the hallway slowly, careful so as not to give away the surprise of his presence. He held his gun in front of him and pointed it toward the ground as he inched closer to the combatants, gripping the handle of it with both hands. As he got to the end of the wall, he peered around the corner, easily making out two men with assault rifles who were standing near a couch and pelting the room with bullets. With a point-blank shot, and his presence undetected, Haley knew he could pick off one with no problem. He just had to hope he could also get the second one before the guy turned himself and fired. Haley pointed his gun at his first target, aiming for the side of his temple. He gently eased his finger on the trigger. His target dropped immediately from the impact of the bullet.

Haley didn't bother to wait to see the final impact. He knew he got him as soon as he pulled the trigger. Immediately after squeezing the trigger, he took aim at his second target. It was easier than Haley was anticipating. His second victim noticed his partner drop to the left of him and looked down at his lifeless body before realizing that a second shooter had snuck in behind them. Haley fired three shots at the man's chest, knocking him to the ground before he even realized what was happening. Though he didn't perish immediately, death overtook him only a few minutes later.

The room fell deathly silent as Haley waited to see if there was another shooter. He poked his head around the corner, and almost got his head blown off, as the remaining member of the gang clung to the wall and fired when he saw the strange head appear past the corner. Haley quickly emerged and fired off a couple of rounds before ducking for cover again. The last gang member took a step away from the wall to get a better angle on the new shooter, giving Recker the chance he needed to get back into the fight. Recker jumped up from behind the couch and saw the intruder with his back turned to him, giving him a perfect shot. And he took it.

Recker fired four rounds in quick succession, though the first two bullets were all that was needed to get the job done. The man fell forward with a massive thud as his head slammed into the laminate floor. Recker looked around, waiting for whoever else was in the house. He hoped it was Haley, though he couldn't be sure that it wasn't the police.

"Recker?" Haley shouted. "It's Haley."

"It's clear," Recker said calmly.

Once Haley showed himself, Recker put his gun away, then walked over to where his first weapon landed and picked it up. As he holstered his weapons, Haley checked on the pulses of the four men they'd just shot. All were dead.

"Figured you could use some help," Haley said, taking his first opportunity to joke with his new partner.

"Ahh, you know, I had it under control."

Haley nodded and looked at the dead bodies on the floor. "I can see that."

"Took you long enough," Recker said, firing back with a tease of his own. "I mean, I wanted to see what you could do, so I was toying with these guys for a while. I was doing my best to hold back as long as possible for you."

"Oh, is that what it was?" Haley asked with a smile.

"Well, I wanted you to make a good impression for David."

The two men shared a quick laugh before Recker came over to his new partner and shook his hand.

"Thanks for the assist," Recker said, returning to a serious mood.

"I'm glad I could help. What now?"

"Now we hurry up and get out of here before the police show up. The homeowners are in the basement. I'll let them know it's safe to come up and we'll be on our way."

"I'll wait outside for you."

Recker quickly scurried down the steps to the basement and let the Tresselmans know that everything had been taken care of. Trying to explain to them as quickly as possible to avoid any police entanglements, he told them who he really was. He didn't want to just leave four dead bodies in their house and just hope the police eventually arrived without giving them the satisfaction of knowing the truth about what happened. After they thanked him, Recker hurried out of the house before they had any more company that they'd have to deal with. Haley was sitting in his truck as Recker walked over to the driver side window.

"Everything's wrapped up here," Recker said. "We'll head back to the office and put a stamp on this. Ready?"

"Lead the way."

Recker got in his own car, leading Haley to the office. As they were driving, Haley felt pretty good about his first piece of action at his new job. It'd been a long time since he was involved in that type of altercation, but it felt good. Not the actual shooting or killing people, but feeling that what he did mattered, that it was important. He wasn't the only one thinking about what had just gone down. Recker was also thinking about Haley's first taste of action with them. For him, it couldn't have gone down any better. There was no doubt in his mind that Haley saved his bacon. It was a tough spot for Haley to be thrown into. He had no preparation, no heads-up, just tossed right into the thick of things. Sometimes it was better like that, Recker thought. But in any case, Haley proved right out of the gate he could be counted on as a pivotal member of the team. It'd still take some time to get used to each other, but Haley proved he could shoot, he wasn't afraid of close-quarter combat, and that he wasn't one who panics. Much like Recker, he dove right in and figured out the rest later. It was a good start to their relationship.

19

Recker had already called Jones on the way back to the office to let him know how everything went at the Tresselman home. Though Jones pressed for details, Recker didn't offer many. Jones was very curious about how Haley handled things on his first day, but Recker just told him that he was fine. No other remarks. Just fine. So, once the new Silencers returned, Jones was ready to pepper them with questions, excited to hear how things turned out.

"Mr. Haley, how did everything go?"

Haley took a quick look at Recker before answering. "It went good. Yeah, just showed up and did what I had to do," he said in an unassuming manner.

"I hated to drop you into a situation cold like that, right off the bat without a chance to get your bearings straight."

"Hey, it's the job. It's the way it was at the agency. I'm fine with it. Sometimes it's gonna happen like that. I'm just glad I got there in time."

"Mike?" Jones said, hoping to get his longtime friend's perspective.

Recker looked at Haley and nodded, giving him his seal of approval. "I can honestly say that things might have turned out differently if he wasn't there. He passes muster."

"What do you want me to do now? Another assignment?" Haley said, looking to Jones.

Jones smiled, appreciating his new hire's eagerness. "While I admire your zealousness, let's take a step back to breathe for a few minutes. Not to mention there's no other cases right now."

"Probably should start shopping around for an apartment," Recker said. "I can take you to a few spots if you want."

"No need, Michael. I've already taken the liberty of securing an apartment for Chris at Regal Apartments."

"Nice place."

Jones grabbed the brochure for the apartments off the desk and handed it to Haley. "I signed a six- month lease, but you're under no obligation to stay if you don't like it."

"I'm sure it'll be fine. I'm not picky," Haley said.

"Well, I just didn't want you to wander around aimlessly for a few days until you figured things out. I thought it'd be helpful if you at least had your lodgings figured out ahead of time. But like I said, if you don't like it after a few weeks, you're free to find something else."

"It really is a nice place," Recker said.

"I don't doubt it," Haley said. "If you've seen my last few apartments, you'll know I'm not very picky about where I live. As long as I don't need to booby trap the front door while I'm sleeping I'll be alright."

"I'm monitoring a few other situations as we speak, and though you never know when something will just pop up, it looks like it will be another day or two before the next case," Jones said, handing Haley the keys to his new home. "So, rest up, order some furniture, get yourself situated. Come back tomorrow morning and we'll start going over our operation in greater detail."

"Great. I'm ready to dive in."

Before he left, Recker stopped him with a few pertinent questions of his own. Well, he really only had one. "Chris, how much armor you got with you?"

"Armor?"

Recker walked over to his gun cabinet and opened it, letting Haley look over his arsenal. Haley studied its contents and picked up several of the weapons and accessories that were inside of it, looking thoroughly impressed by the collection.

"Wow, this is something," Haley said.

"You need me to make room?" Recker said.

"Nah. I only got two guns," Haley said, patting the handle of the gun inside his belt.

"Hmm. Not everybody shares your enthusiasm for firearms," Jones said with a snicker.

Recker gave Jones a disapproving glance, then looked at Haley, almost in disbelief that he didn't carry more weapons with him. Maybe Jones was right, maybe he did have an excessive love of things that caused massive amounts of destruction.

"Well, if you ever need anything, take whatever gets the job done," Recker said.

"Thanks."

"And if you wanna add to the collection, feel free."

Haley took a few more minutes to examine what Recker had collected up to that point, impressed with the amount and variety that he had stored. Though he was intrigued, and proficient in his own right, he didn't have the same love of weapons that Recker had. He knew how to use them, knew a lot about them, but they were just a means to an end for him. He didn't put much thought into it other than whatever he needed at the time. After Haley finished examining the gun collection, he bid his new friends adieu. Recker went over to a computer and started helping Jones decipher some information on a few upcoming assignments.

Before they got too deep into anything, though, Jones had some more questions about the Tresselmans. He worried about Haley being discovered already.

"I've already started monitoring police and media communications," Jones said. "How much attention will this get?"

"Well, you've got a home invasion in a wealthy neighborhood, with two elderly citizens, which were stopped by me, and you've got four dead bodies to go along with it. What do you think?"

"I was hoping Chris' involvement in our operation would not get out for a while. Element of surprise and all that."

Recker shook his head. "Should still be good with that. There were no witnesses, the Tresselmans never saw him. I already sent him outside when I talked to them."

"How about neighbors or people just happening to be walking by? Anything like that?"

"No, not that I saw. Should go down as just me being there."

Jones made a slight noise with his mouth as he thought of something. "That reminds me, I should talk to him about the notoriety he's likely to start receiving."

"What about it?" Recker said, not seeing what the concern was.

"Well, we both know that some people who start to read and believe their own press clippings... sometimes it goes to their head."

"I don't think that's something we have to worry about."

"I hope you're right."

"Nah, it won't be an issue. I think that's only a problem when you get someone who likes their work too much. He doesn't strike me as the type who gets caught up in the hype. I think he's pretty much like me. He's good at what he does, but he doesn't really get any pleasure or enjoyment out of it. Just do what you gotta do and move on. He'll be fine."

"Once again, you're probably right."

"Besides, how's anyone gonna know there's two of us?"

"You know as well as I do information spreads quickly. Take today, homeowner sees another man with you helping, sees you leave together, interacting with you, then tells police or the press there seemed to be another person with you. Boom, just like that, everyone knows there's two of you."

"Well you don't have to worry about that today."

"Good to know."

"You know it's going to happen eventually, though. And it'll probably happen sooner rather than later."

"I'm well aware it will happen eventually," Jones said.

"So why worry about it? It'll happen when it happens."

"Just because we know it will come to fruition at some point doesn't mean we shouldn't try to take advantage of the fact that we now have an extra person in play."

After a few more hours of work, Recker decided to kick back for the night. Mia worked until seven and Recker wanted to try to make it home around the same time she did. Part of him felt badly, though, as he knew he wasn't spending nearly as much time in the office as he used to. Not that he was shirking his duties at all, and whenever there was an assignment, he immediately responded whether he was at the office or at home. But after the last few years of him and Jones working hand in hand, often late into the night and at the expense of sleep, it seemed a little weird that he left a few hours sooner than he used to.

"Hey, you don't mind if I get out of here, do you?" Recker said.

"Not at all, why?"

"Just making sure you're good with it."

"Why wouldn't I be?" Jones said, not yet looking at him as he continued typing away at his computer.

"Well, it's sort of a new dynamic around here. Got a new guy coming in, I'm not here as much as I used to be, I have the stuff going on with Mia, you know."

Jones smirked and turned his head to look at his friend, hoping to ease his fears. "I started preparing myself for these days when I first realized that you and Mia were heading in this direction."

"So, you don't have a problem with it."

"Of course not. These last few months are the happiest I've seen you since I've known you. It's been a refreshing change."

"OK. I just wanted to make sure."

"Besides, you haven't missed anything. You've been as reliable as you've ever been."

Recker then thought of something that hadn't occurred to him until now. "That's not one of the reasons you decided to get Chris, is it? As an eventual replacement for me in case I started drifting away because of Mia."

"Don't be ridiculous," Jones said. "If the thought ever entered my mind, it was only for a fleeting second. The basis for getting Chris was exactly as we've talked about. Getting you the help you could use, and sometimes need, as well as having the chance to help more people."

"Good. Cause whatever happens with Mia, I'll still be the person that you need me to be. That won't change."

"I know that. Regardless, we both know the office is more my domain, anyway. As long as you're out there where you need to be, that's what matters most."

Once their discussion was finished, Recker left the office and headed home. Mia had already sent him a text message that she was on the way. When Recker got to their apartment, Mia had beaten him there.

"I was hoping to beat you here," Recker said.

Mia smiled, just happy to see him. She greeted him with a passionate kiss as soon as he stepped foot through the door. "I missed you."

Recker smiled back at her once their lips disengaged and put his hand on her cheek, gently rubbing her cheek. She put her hand on his, soaking in the moment. She then kissed his hand and took it in hers, leaning in for another kiss.

"I could do this all night," she said.

"Not a bad idea."

"I guess we should eat first, though."

"If you really want to."

"I stopped on the way for sandwiches," Mia said, somehow pushing herself away from him.

She grabbed his hands and put them on her waist as she led him into the kitchen. They sat down next to each other at the table as they started eating. Recker had told her in the morning about Haley coming, and she was wondering how it went. She was hopeful that with another guy there, Recker's time with the operation might soon be coming to an end. Or at the very least, drastically cut back. Though Mia had made several suggestive hints over the past several months they'd been together, most of them she disguised as part of a joke, or her comment was so brief that she quickly moved on to another topic. But much like how she didn't want him worrying about her when he was working, she didn't want to nag about him doing something else either. Though she'd be ecstatic if he eventually decided to live a quieter, more normal life with her, she wasn't going to beg or prod him to do it, or make him feel guilty about it. But upon hearing about the new guy in the fold, she couldn't help but think now would be the time to talk to him about her feelings. At least so they'd both know where each other stood.

"So, how'd things go today with the new guy?" Mia said.

"Good. I think it'll really work out well with him."

"How can you be so sure already?"

Recker finished chewing the piece of food in his mouth, then raised his eyebrows as he debated how much information he should divulge to her. If he told her the truth and said how much trouble he found himself in, he didn't want her to worry about it. Likewise, he also didn't want to blindly dismiss it, pretend it didn't happen, and lie to her. It didn't take him long to deliberate. He spent a long time being miserable after what happened to Carrie, and now he'd finally found himself happy again with Mia, he didn't want to jeopardize what they had by lying about anything. He figured there may be times when he had to shield her from the truth, whether it was for her own good or for whatever reason, but now wasn't one of those times.

"He really got me out of a tough spot today."

"What happened?" Mia said, putting her sandwich down to focus on him.

Recker explained the situation in detail, not leaving a single thing out. As he described everything, he could see the level of concern on her face as it contorted in different directions. After he finished, he waited for Mia to blurt something out that would indicate how troubled she was with everything. She didn't though. She tried to stay as calm as possible. She wasn't going to fly off the handle, or make a mountain out of a molehill, even though she was unsettled at the day's events.

"Well, it's good he showed up," Mia said, trying hard not to get emotional, though Recker could tell she was holding back.

"Yeah, seems like he'll be a good fit."

Mia wondered how far she should get into his profession with him, and calmly started asking some questions that she was thinking about earlier. "So... with a new partner, he should be able to take some of the strain off you, right?"

"In theory."

"That should mean you're able to take more time off, right?"

"That's the plan. To a point, anyway," Recker said, getting the feeling that she was working up to something bigger.

"Do you think there will ever come a time when you're no longer needed? Or maybe you won't want to do it anymore?"

There was the question that Recker was waiting for. He looked at her sympathetically for a moment, before letting his eyes fall to the table as he contemplated his answer. He didn't want to berate her for it, or dismiss her out of hand entirely. He knew she was trying not to sound like an overbearing girlfriend or try to influence his behavior. She wasn't trying to dominate him or make him submissive to her wants and desires. Recker wanted to answer tactfully and respective of her feelings.

"I don't know if there'll ever be a time when I'm not needed. I kind of doubt it. There's enough that needs to be done out there that we could hire five more people and it still probably wouldn't be enough."

"What about maybe walking away from it one day?" Mia said, finding it hard to look at him as she asked the question.

Recker's face looked strained as he tried to answer as delicately as possible. "I don't know what the future holds, Mia. Could there be a day somewhere down the line where I've had enough of this? I mean, maybe. I can't see that happening anytime soon, though. I like what I do, I'm good at it, and there's people out there who need me. People who could've gotten seriously hurt or killed if I wasn't around, including you."

"I know," she said, starting to backtrack so he didn't think she was trying to talk him into anything. "I'm not saying I think you should quit or anything. I was just wondering if you ever thought about it."

"I know. If that time ever did come, though, what would I do? I mean, this is basically, in one form or another, the only thing I've ever known in my adult life. I'm not really qualified to do anything else."

"Mike, you can do just about anything you want."

"Really? Because of that college degree I have? Or my design skills? Or because I have such talent in computer programming? Or... should I keep going?"

Mia sighed, understanding his point. "I know what you're saying. I'm just saying that I would hope at some point, even if it's the far distant future, that you would consider doing something else. Something less dangerous perhaps? Something where I wouldn't have to worry about whether you're coming home in one piece?"

Recker shrugged, not knowing what else he could tell her at that point.

"You could start your own business. Or just live a quiet life at home... with me of course," she said with a playful smile.

"That might not be so bad."

"You have enough money that you wouldn't have to do anything. You wouldn't have to reach for something."

"You know money is not something that motivates me."

"I know. I'm just saying that even if you eventually stopped doing this, you would never have to worry about a paycheck. You'd never have to worry about living week to week, or wondering how you're gonna pay for bills or repairs. You could wait until you found something else that you love."

"I already found something else that I love," Recker said.

Mia tilted her head and smiled, her heart almost melting, knowing that he was referencing her. The thought occurred to her though, that maybe he was saying it to get her to change the subject. If that was the case, she wasn't biting.

"Maybe start your own private security business," Mia said excitedly.

"Basically, the same thing I'm doing now."

"Except maybe not on the opposite side of the law."

"Technicality," Recker said, trying to lighten the mood.

Mia looked down at the table again, a somber look on her face. "I'm sorry," she said, thinking that she'd peppered him with too many questions.

"For what?"

"You probably think I'm nagging at you to quit or something."

Recker shook his head. "I don't think that."

"I told myself since that first night that we got together, that I wouldn't be one of those girlfriends that tried to change you or change who you are. And I won't."

"I know that."

"But sometimes it isn't easy knowing you're out there with guns pointed at you with men behind them that I know would like to kill you."

"That's why I try to avoid talking to you about things. It's probably easier for me to go through it than it is for you to wonder about how things are going," Recker said.

"I just hope I'm not going to be a sixty-year-old and still worrying about you doing the same thing out there," she said with a laugh.

Recker almost made a comment that he would regret, quickly stopping himself before the words left his mouth. He was about to tell her that he'd probably be long dead before sixty if he was still doing his current work, but realized that it would be an unthoughtful and unfunny comment. Luckily, he could see the foolishness of his words before he said them. He then thought of an alternative. Something that would probably be more soothing to her ears.

"I just hope if I make it to sixty that you're still with me," he said.

Mia shook her head. "It took me, us, several years to get to this point. I'm not gonna give it up now. If this is all you'll ever be, I'll be with you every step of the way. I'll never let you go. No matter what. I just hope you'll always feel the same."

Recker gave her a grin, then reached under the table to hold her hand. "I don't know how I'll feel in five or ten years. Maybe I'll still be doing what I do now. Maybe I'll still enjoy it. Maybe I won't, and I'll be ready to move on and try something else. I don't know.

What I do know is that my life is better because you're in it. You make me a stronger person and a better person. Whether I'm here, or I'm in Boston, or Seattle, or Texas, or even Japan, wherever I am, I can only hope that you'll be with me."

Mia looked at him endearingly and gave that sexy smile of hers that he loved so much. "You're never getting rid of me." She leaned over to him and sensually kissed him as they both got into the moment. After a few minutes of kissing, their appetites turned to each other, leaving their half-eaten sandwiches behind as Recker scooped her up in his arms and carried her into the bedroom.

20

I t'd been two days since the battle at the Tresselman home. A couple new cases appeared on the radar, and Jones split his new team up, much to Recker's displeasure. He wanted Haley to shadow him two or three times until he got the hang of things on his own. Jones, though, thought that would be a waste of time and manpower, not to mention unnecessary. Haley already proved on his first day that he could handle whatever was thrown his way. Jones didn't see the need to pair him up with Recker, unless the assignment called for it. But Jones also had another reason for keeping them apart at first. He wanted Haley to develop his own identity without any interference from Recker.

Recker was obviously a top-notch operator, and Jones couldn't ask for anyone better, but he didn't want Haley to be a carbon copy of him. He wanted Haley to have his own personality and his own way of doing things. Part of it was that he didn't want Recker molding Haley into that shoot first mentality that his partner sometimes had. Jones hoped that Haley would, when the situation called for it, find a more peaceful solution than Recker usually looked for.

Though Recker thought it would be better for Haley to follow him, it wasn't something he was going to quarrel over. Jones didn't think that was the best choice and Recker went along with it without much of an argument. Also, as Jones pointed out, Recker didn't have someone showing him the ropes when he first started. It was just a trial by fire. And he handled it just fine. Outside of a few extra dead bodies than Jones would have hoped for. He assumed that Haley would also handle things just fine. While Jones initially thought that it might take Haley some extra time to get back into the swing of things after basically sitting out the last two years on the sidelines, his work at the Tresselman home seemed to indicate it wouldn't take as long as he anticipated.

While Jones was pretty comfortable with Haley handling anything coming his way, he still gave him the lesser of the two cases they were working on. Recker was assigned a murder for hire case, while Haley was given another attempted robbery. Unlike the first one that Haley handled, this one shouldn't have been as interesting. For one thing, there was only one suspect. The second, the person in question did not have the same violent tendencies as the previous gang did. Whereas the first group that Haley encountered all had extensive histories with firearms, the new case involved someone who did not have that same love of guns.

Recker's case was a little more involved as an out-of-state gunman was hired and brought in by a husband to take care of his wife. The man was a very prominent businessman whose wife was close to filing for divorce. Rather than go through that, and have a very large alimony payment, the man decided that killing her was the better option. Through some less than scrupulous contacts that the man had with a local crime syndicate, the plan was put into action. At first, Recker tried to find the shooter. That proved to be more difficult than first imagined and they had to change tactics, instead, focusing on the wife. Recker's job was tailing her wherever she went. The information that Jones dug up indicated the hit was supposed to go down today, but they just didn't know the exact time, or where it was supposed to happen. So Recker waited, and waited, and waited some more.

He'd been tailing the woman since 7am, and he followed her to a salon, several clothes stores, two shoe stores, a restaurant, an antique store, and finally a gas station. He saw no abnormal signs that anything was about to happen. He didn't question the intel that they'd received, but these were the cases that he hated most. Following people around aimlessly. Especially when they spent the bulk of the day shopping. It wasn't as much the waiting as what he had to do while he was waiting. He would've preferred to just sit in his car. At least that way he'd have the radio. Tailing people as they shopped for clothes and shoes was almost nauseating. He couldn't even pretend to be interested in that. He probably wouldn't have minded so much if they went to a gun store or something, but fashion just wasn't his thing.

Recker hadn't checked in with Jones for several hours. The last time they talked was after Mrs. Tunsil visited her first shoe store. It was then that Recker figured it was going to be a long day. His hope was that whatever was on tap, that it'd happen quickly. Much to his chagrin, that didn't happen. Recker told the professor that he'd check later when something happened. Considering it'd been a while, Jones assumed nothing interesting had happened yet.

"Mike, are you there?"

"Where else would I be?"

"I take it there's been no sign of our shooter?"

Recker let out a rather loud sigh before answering. "Nope. No sign. Of anything."

Jones started to laugh, knowing how much Recker was bothered by his lack of inactivity, but quickly held it inside. "Well, something should be happening soon."

"Why? You get something?"

"No. But the initial contacts that we had indicated today was the day," Jones said. "Since it hasn't happened yet, that must mean it's getting close."

"Doesn't mean anything of the kind," Recker said in frustration. "Just means I've wasted half my day."

"We both know these situations are sometimes part of the job."

"Doesn't mean I have to like it."

"No, it doesn't. Where are you now?"

"Gas station. She's filling up. I assume she's heading home after this."

"Why would you assume that?"

"Because I think she already hit every shoe and clothing store in the area," Recker said, obviously irritated that he hadn't come into any action yet.

This time, Jones couldn't help but let out a laugh that Recker could hear, though he still tried to hide it by holding the phone away from him.

"Something you find amusing?"

"Oh no, no, nothing. So which part is giving you the most angst. The waiting? The shoe shopping? What?"

"I can sit in this car all day if I have to. But when I have to follow someone inside a store and find myself staring at dresses and shoes, my trigger finger starts getting itchy."

"Did you find any good deals or bargains?"

"David, don't start. Comedy is not your strong suit."

"Fair enough," Jones said with a laugh.

"You still keeping tabs on the husband?"

"Still at the golf course. Just took a call on his phone a few minutes ago."

"Get a fix on who it was? Shooter maybe?" Recker said, hoping.

"Unfortunately not. It was one of his assistants at the office. I already ran it down."

"Good alibi for him. Wife gets knocked off somewhere, and he's out at the golf course with his buddies. Out in the wide open."

"Indeed. He's playing in a foursome and they'll all obviously vouch for him being there. Makes it more difficult to implicate him."

"But not impossible," Recker said.

"No. There have been several murder-for-hire cases that have made the rounds in the last few years. If they leave a trail, they can be caught. But it is more difficult. And in this instance, they've covered their tracks extremely well."

"How long's Tunsil been at the golf course?"

"Well his tee time was 2:05. The average time for an amateur foursome to play a round of golf is about four hours, sometimes a little more."

"And how far away is the course?"

"About thirty minutes."

Recker looked at the time. "He's been playing for about two hours. Means he's got two hours left."

"At least. He also may spend some time in the clubhouse after they're done and kick a few back."

"Even if he goes straight home after playing, he probably won't get there until seven or so, wouldn't you say?"

"Most likely. And if he does decide to stay and spend time with the boys, so to speak, then you could be looking at another hour after that."

"In any case, I'd say it's likely that whatever goes down, it'll probably happen in the next two hours."

"Could be right, but why do you think so?" Jones said.

"I have a feeling that he wants it to be done while he's on the golf course. Like squarely in the middle of the round so there's no doubt about where he's at. If he waits until after he's done, then there could always be some doubt about his location. I'm willing to bet that he wants a positive ID that he's playing golf at the time his wife is killed."

"Well my own hunch says that you are probably correct. But even if we have the time nailed down, that still leaves how out of the equation."

Recker didn't respond for a minute as he thought about how Mrs. Tunsil's death might have been arranged. "Has to be at their house."

"What leads you to that?"

"She's been gone all day and not a peep. Not a strange look or an evil glance from anybody, no one following her... other than me. If it was going to happen out in public, they've had all day to make it happen. But they haven't."

"Did you consider the possibility that maybe someone was following her, and they spotted you doing the same, and that scared them off."

"Nope."

"Why not?" Jones said.

"Because I would've noticed if someone else was following her."

"Not if they were better at it than you are."

"Did you just insult me?"

"No. Just making a statement."

"Oh. Well, I doubt anybody they would've brought in would be better at following someone than me."

"Perhaps."

"Anyway, if they wanted it done in public, they've had plenty of chances," Recker said.

"Agreed."

"Maybe they wanna make it look like a robbery gone bad."

"Well, the Tunsil's do have home security."

"David, we both know that home security systems can be

easily bypassed if you know what you're doing."

"I'm well aware, Mike. But some systems do use anti-jamming countermeasures to prevent someone from blocking signals to the door and window sensors."

"And we both know that there are countermeasures to that too," Recker said.

"I know. But we don't know that the impending shooter knows them."

"We also don't know that he doesn't."

"So what do you propose?"

"If someone's at the house waiting for her, then I need to beat her there before she walks into something she can't handle. And that I can't stop."

"Where are you now? Still at the gas station?"

"Of course not. She's on the road. I'm a few cars behind her. She was filling up her car, not a tank. How long do you think it takes to gas the car up?"

Jones put his arm up in the air, waving it around as if Recker could see him flailing away. He thought about Recker's idea, that the shooter may have been at the Tunsil house, waiting for the wife to get home. It certainly made sense, though Jones wasn't that enthusiastic about Recker getting to the house ahead of time. He would have much preferred for him to wait until he got eyes on the shooter before making any kind of move. But he also knew that it might not be possible.

"So what do you want to do?" Jones finally said.

"I dunno. I'm thinking it might be best if I get to the house first and make sure nobody's there waiting for her."

"And if the place is empty?"

"Then I'll sneak my way back out. Don't act like it's my first time doing this sort of thing."

"The next question is going to be can you actually get to the house before Mrs. Tunsil does?"

"I'll be cutting it close," Recker said. "I think I can get in front of her from here. All I need is about a five-minute buffer."

"That would be great if she was still an hour away, giving you the time you need to get ahead of her. But she's only fifteen, twenty minutes away. That doesn't give you much time."

"I'll have to make it work."

Recker knew he'd have to take a shortcut if he was going to beat Mrs. Tunsil back to her home. At least what he hoped was a shortcut. As they drove through some of the one-lane streets of Philadelphia, there was no chance for Recker to speed around her. He'd have to take a turn somewhere and hope that did the trick. He took the next right, sped down the street, and turned left at the next light. He put his foot on the gas, but with traffic, he could only go so fast. After five minutes of stop and go traffic, it was clear to Recker that he wasn't going to beat Mrs. Tunsil home. He let Jones know he was going to have to scrap his plan.

"There's no way I'm going to get there first," Recker said. "Not with all this traffic. I can't even go fifty feet without stopping or slowing down."

"You're getting into rush hour traffic."

"I'm gonna have to improvise when I get there."

"What did you have in mind?"

"I'm not sure yet. This might be a time for Detective Scarborough to make an appearance."

"I've noticed you've been leaning on him more and more lately it seems," Jones said.

"Just when it seems like it's the best option. Have something better?"

Jones thought for a minute, though he couldn't think of anything else. "No."

Recker's new hope was that he'd at least get there around the same time as Mrs. Tunsil. If he got there even five minutes after her, it might be too late. That would potentially give the shooter all the time he needed to do the job and get away as Recker fought with traffic. When he got to Lombard Street, Recker could see that he was too late. Hopefully, not fatally so. He saw Mrs. Tunsil's car parked in front of the house, and saw her getting out of her black Mercedes. Recker quickly found a parking space and hurried over to her place, knocking hard on the front door, hoping she hadn't gotten too far inside yet. To his delight, Mrs. Tunsil answered almost immediately. As she opened the door, Recker could see that she hadn't settled in yet. She still had her purse in one hand and a stack full of mail in the other.

"Can I help you?"

As he so often had done before, Recker pulled out his badge and showed it to her. "Detective Scarborough, ma'am."

A concerned look fell over the woman's face, not thinking of any possible reason that the police would be there for. "What's this about?"

"I need to search inside your home."

"What for? Do you have a warrant? What are you looking for?"

"No, it's not for you. You're not in trouble with us. We're trying to help you. We have information that your life may be in danger."

"My life? What?"

"We've got information from a confidential source that your husband has hired a contract killer to take you out," Recker said, not beating around the bush.

"What? That's crazy."

"You and your husband are going through difficult times right now, correct?"

Mrs. Tunsil hesitated slightly before answering. "Yes."

"You're almost at the stage of filing for divorce, right?"

"Yes," she said again, wondering how he knew all this.

"Your husband is concerned that a divorce is going to be costlier than just taking you out. That's why he's out playing golf right now. To give himself an alibi."

Mrs. Tunsil didn't answer, looking like she was in shock. She was in her early forties and the Tunsils had been married for fifteen years. Though they'd had their ups and downs like any married couple would, she couldn't believe that her husband would go to this length to get rid of her, just to avoid divorce payments. Recker could see that she was having trouble processing what he just told her. It was understandable, he thought. If someone had told him that somebody was trying to kill him, he wouldn't bat an eyelash or even give it a second thought. This type of life was second nature for him. He was used to it. But nobody that was normal would hear that and immediately be OK with it.

"I know it's a little bit of a shock," Recker said. "We've been following you all day because we didn't know when the hit was supposed to happen."

"All day?"

"We got word that it was supposed to happen today. We just didn't know a time. With your husband playing golf, it makes sense that it'll happen now. I believe it might be possible that someone's waiting inside your home for you."

Mrs. Tunsil stepped to the side and turned her head around, looking at the inside of her home. She had that scary feeling that someone was behind her, the way someone does when they're watching a horror movie that frightens them into thinking someone else is next to them. Even though she initially had trouble fathoming that her husband would want her dead, after she took a minute to think about it, she realized it wasn't outside the realm of possibility. Their marriage had been careening down a dark path for a few years now. She long suspected that her husband had been having an affair for at least the last year and their arguments were getting longer and more spirited as time moved on. Now that she thought about it, a few things that Mr. Tunsil had previously told her, now made sense. An argument they had several weeks ago, the last time she mentioned the word divorce, her husband made a comment in passing that he'd kill her before he ever gave her any money in a settlement. At the time, she didn't pay much attention to it. She thought it was just one of those things that sometimes got said in a heated moment when people couldn't control their emotions. Up until now, she never even considered that he might have actually meant it. But now that there was a man at her door, telling her these unbelievable things, it would seem that it was believable indeed.

"What do you need me to do?" she solemnly said.

"Just step aside and let me comb through the house to make sure nobody else is here."

"We have a security system. Wouldn't that go off if someone was here?"

"If he's a professional then it's a good chance he knows how to bypass it," Recker said. "Pros know how to do it."

"Oh. Is it just you? Do you have a team with you?"

"No, just me for now. The rest of the squad will be on the way if I find something."

"OK. Umm, what should I do? Wait outside or something?"

"No. If he's not in here, then he could be out there waiting for you. I don't want to chance sending you out there. Do you have somewhere in here you can hide? A bathroom or closet or something?"

"There's a closet here in the hallway," she said, pointing to it.

Recker stepped inside and closed the door behind him. He took his gun out and walked over to the closet, opening the white bi-fold doors, and checking inside. With it being clear he motioned for Mrs. Tunsil to come over to him. It was a decent-sized closet, one that she wouldn't be cramped up in as she waited.

"I want you to get in there and wait for me."

"For how long?"

"Until I get you. No matter what you hear, do not come out under any circumstances, OK?"

Mrs. Tunsil nodded in agreement, though she was becoming more rattled by the second, evidenced by the fact that she now seemed to be shaking.

"Just try to take it easy," Recker said, seeing that she was more upset. "I won't let anything happen to you. Just sit in the corner there and wait until this is over. When I'm done, I'll tap on the door and call you, so you know it's me."

"OK."

With Mrs. Tunsil taken care of for the moment, Recker then started sweeping his way through the house. It was a three-story home, with the kitchen, living room and a bathroom on the main floor, bedrooms, and additional bathrooms on floors two and three. As Recker started searching through the house, he also looked for signs of entry from an intruder. An open or broken window, something that seemed out of place, anything that looked unusual. After clearing the first floor, Recker went up the spiral staircase to the second floor.

He looked in the bathroom first before moving on to the bedrooms. He searched through the first bedroom without any signs of an intruder. He then moved on to the second bedroom. He opened the door slowly, ready to fire quickly if the need arose. As he stepped inside the room, it seemed quiet. Recker looked over to the window and made an alarming discovery. The window was open. Only about a quarter of an inch. But it was enough to signal to Recker that perhaps someone recently made their way through it and was waiting in there somewhere. Of course, it didn't mean they were in that specific room. That could have just been the entry point, and they relocated to a more favorable spot. That window did overlook the back of the property, which obviously made it a more suitable place to enter the home.

Recker quickly scanned the room for where the shooter would

have likely been hiding. There were only two spots that he could have been. Either under the bed or inside the walk-in closet. The rest of the room was open. There was a chair, a desk, and a dresser, but they were all flush against the wall, giving no room for someone to be behind them. Recker dropped on all fours to the carpet as he looked under the bed. With that being clear, he cautiously walked over to the closet, clinging to the wall to try to remain out of sight and out of the line of fire if someone was in there.

Standing next to the closet, Recker let out a sigh as he readied himself. He gently put his left hand on the handle of the door and brought his right hand in front of his chest, ready to fire his gun if necessary. He quickly jolted it open and stepped in the frame of the door. Almost immediately, he was met with a fist that knocked him on his back as the gun slipped out of his fingers and onto the carpet a few feet away. As he shook off the blow, he saw a man standing in front of him, pointing a gun down on him. Moving fast, before the shooter had a chance to pull the trigger, Recker kicked the gun out of the man's hand. Recker got back to his feet before the shooter had a chance to pull out another weapon. The two then exchanged punches for several minutes, neither of whom seemed to be getting a clear upper hand.

The two men rolled around the floor, wrestling for superiority, though neither got it. Once they got back to their feet, they flung each other across the bed as they each tried to bludgeon the other one with punches. It was a give and take battle for a few more minutes. As they grappled with each other, the other man got the upper hand momentarily and got Recker on the ground. As he laid flat on his back, the man put his hands around Recker's neck, trying to choke the life out of him. Recker exerted a great deal of effort to break free of the man's grasp, but was having trouble doing so. As he struggled to breathe, he writhed around, knocking into an end table alongside the bed. A glass tumbled over and fell onto the floor. Recker alertly grabbed it and smashed it on the side of his attacker's face, successfully ending the man's hold over his neck, and sending him crashing onto the floor next to him.

Recker stumbled to his feet and delivered another punch to the side of the man's face, keeping him on the ground as he thought of his next maneuver. He looked around, seeing a lamp on the same table that the glass just fell from. He walked over to it and picked it up. Recker then went over to his opponent, who was starting to get to his feet, and took a healthy swing at the man's head with the lamp. The man instantly dropped to the ground once more, blood pouring down his face from a cut on his forehead. Somehow, he wasn't knocked out from the blow, though he was extremely dazed.

Recker tossed the lamp on the ground, then put his foot on it, as he grabbed hold of the cord, yanking it free from its former host. Recker wrapped the cord around the palms of his hand as he walked around his upcoming victim. As the man struggled to get to his feet, Recker put the cord over the man's face until it nestled against the skin of his neck. As the man put his hands up to his neck to try to wrestle himself free, Recker cinched back, strengthening his grip on it. As the man was severely battered and injured, he couldn't muster up the strength or energy to free himself from Recker's grasp. As Recker leaned back, both men fell hard on the floor, though Recker didn't let up on his stranglehold. The man frantically waved his arms around, trying desperately to get the cord away from his neck before he permanently passed out. Slowly, the man's efforts became less chaotic, and it was obvious that he was losing the battle. Soon after that he stopped struggling as his arms, along with the rest of his body, went limp.

Once he was sure that the man was definitely dead, Recker finally released his grip on the cord, letting the man's body slump onto the floor. He got to his feet and checked the man's pulse, making sure he was no longer a threat. He wasn't. He was a hundred percent dead. Still feeling the effects of the long, hard-fought struggle with the hit man, Recker stumbled across the room to pick up his gun. After putting it away, he pulled out his phone and walked over to the dead man, snapping a picture of his face. He sent the picture as an attachment to Jones, hoping he could identify who it was. Not that it really changed anything, but Recker would have liked to have known a name to attach to the body. Just to wrap things up completely.

"He lost," Recker said in the text, accompanying the picture. "Find a name to go with him."

"Will do," Jones replied. "Have Mrs. Tunsil check her email. The evidence will be there."

"Got it."

With his work there done, Recker exited the bedroom and walked down the steps to the main floor. He went into the hallway near the front door where the closet was and tapped on it, letting Mrs. Tunsil know it was him, just as he said he would. He opened the bi-fold doors and saw her sitting on the floor in the corner, a few clothes draped over her lap. She still appeared frightened and looked like she was fighting back tears. Recker reached his hand out to take hers, helping her to her feet. He led her out of the closet and into the hallway as he explained what happened.

"It's over," Recker said.

"It is? Like, for good?"

"So there was a man up there waiting."

Mrs. Tunsil gaped at him, then put her hand over her mouth to try to control her emotions. "Is he gone?"

"Uh, in a way. He's dead."

"Oh my."

"We had a bit of a struggle up there. Luckily, I wound up on top."

"Umm, where is he?"

"In one of the bedrooms on the second floor," Recker said.

"Don't go up and look. It's not a pretty sight."

"OK. So what now?"

"Police will be here soon."

"I thought you were the police," she said.

"No, more like a concerned third party. Stay clear of your husband until he's safely locked up."

"I don't understand..."

Recker interrupted before she could go further, seeing that she was having a hard time processing everything. "They call me The Silencer. I help people out of bad situations. As soon as I leave, log into your email. You'll find some evidence that implicates your husband in this. Show it to the police when they get here."

"I can't believe this is happening. Umm, OK, how long until they arrive?"

"Should be about five minutes."

Mrs. Tunsil rubbed her hands together as she tried to wipe the sweat off them. "I guess... thank you. For everything."

Recker grabbed her hands and held them together for a few seconds, helping them to stop from trembling. He tried to give her a reassuring smile, knowing it was a lot for her to take in. She closed her eyes and took a few deep breaths. She tried to smile to prevent some tears from flowing. After a minute, she nodded, letting him know that she was going to be OK.

"Well, I have to be going," Recker said. "The police don't usually like me interfering like this."

"Oh, um, do I tell them you were here? Or do I make something up?"

Recker smiled at her, appreciating the question. "No, just tell them everything exactly how it went down. Except me showing you the badge. That kind of helps me do these types of things."

"I'll leave that out," she said.

"You take care, all right? And the next time you get married... make sure you pick a better guy."

21

When Recker got back to the office, he looked like a tired man. Like a boxer who'd just gone twelve rounds and came out with a decision victory. But at least he was the last man standing. He was the one who could put his arm up in triumph. He took a little longer to get back than usual, taking some extra time to freshen up and mentally right himself after his long day and grueling battle. When he did show himself, Jones had some news for him.

"Well, I've seen you looking worse," Jones said, observing the cuts and bruises on his friend's face.

"Should've seen the other guy."

"I did. And I also identified him. His name was Marcel Lafleur, a Canadian citizen. He has quite the background."

"Professional?"

"To say the least. Former member of the Canadian Armed Forces. After that, started freelancing and hiring out his services to the highest bidder. He's thought to be connected to at least five murders, and probably more, though there's no concrete evidence that links him to them. He's very good at what he does."

"He was."

Jones continued typing away, moving his focus away from Lafleur and onto Jared Rizzo, the suspect that Haley was waiting on. Though Recker was beat up and tired, he still offered to help out on the other assignment. He wasn't yet used to slowing down and letting someone else take over.

"Sit down, take it easy," Jones said, insisting. "Remember, that's why we got him."

"Yeah, but why let him do something on his own if I can help?"

"Mike, relax. He helped you take down several violent and armed criminals. I think he can handle one man who isn't known to be as ruthless as the others."

"Kinda hard I guess," Recker said.

"What is?"

"Sitting on the sidelines and watching someone else do what you've been doing for the last few years."

"It's for your benefit," Jones said, still typing away. "Not only yours, but the city's, the people that need help. It also means you won't feel so stretched thin. You'll be able to stay fresher, do more things."

"I know all that. It's just... different. I'll adjust to it at some point. I've just never been someone who stands back and lets someone else do the dirty work."

Jones stopped typing and looked at his partner and nodded, knowing it was difficult for him to watch someone else do the things he used to do by himself. "So how do you propose explaining your face to Mia?"

"What do you mean? What's the matter with it?"

"Well you've got a cut above your eye, some bruising around it, a cut on the bridge of your nose, a bruise on your forehead, and a bruise on your cheek."

Recker looked at him dumbfounded, still not sure what he was getting at. "Why do I need to explain something?"

"You don't think she's going to see your face like that and expect you to explain what happened to it? That's what girl-friends, and wives do..."

Recker quickly and eagerly interrupted, wanting to make sure Jones didn't get out of hand with anything. "Wife? Hold on there, Skippy. Things are going good between us, but nobody's mentioned the m word yet."

"I realize it's a little bit of a sore spot with you and you don't want people thinking that you're going soft."

"I'm not going soft," Recker said.

"I know that. I didn't say that ..."

Recker interrupted again, wanting to make sure he got his point across. "Just because I may have hung a curtain or two in the past few months, or washed some dishes or something, doesn't mean I'm any different than I was before."

Jones could see that he hit a sore spot with him. It was obvious to him that it was something that Recker had thought of before he even brought it up. Perhaps it was a side conversation Recker had with Mia, or maybe it was just something that Recker thought of on his own, afraid that people would think his domestication would interfere with his profession. Jones, though, knew that wasn't the case. Though it was obvious that Recker had indeed changed, he was happier, not as brooding, but Jones did not notice any difference in his work habits. He was still the same guy that he'd always been.

"If you've calmed yourself down now, I can finish my thought," Jones said.

Recker sighed, thinking Jones was about to say something that would annoy him. Jones' only thoughts, though, were to reinforce to Recker that even though he seemed to be unchanged profes-sionally, he now had to be somewhat sympathetic and caring to Mia's thoughts and feelings. At least if he wanted the relationship to continue.

"What I was about to say is... that girlfriends tend to worry, especially when they see their boyfriend walking through the door with cuts and bruises on his face."

"I know that," Recker said.

"Well, how do you propose to handle that? Tell her the truth about what happened, or just ignore it completely? Or better yet, lie and tell her something else."

"What, like I fell down the steps from the office or something? Dropped my keys and the car door slammed in my face? Something like that?"

Jones raised his eyebrows, thinking those explanations were going a little toward the extreme side. Recker thought about it for another minute, wondering what Jones was getting at, still not sure what his point was. Silence filled the room, though it was not one of those uncomfortable silences. The two were close enough by that point that talking was sometimes an afterthought.

"So why do you wanna know what I'll tell Mia?"

"No specific reason," Jones said. "I was just curious."

"Oh. Well, I wasn't really planning on saying anything. Just one of those days."

"And you think that will go over well?"

"She's seen me with cuts and bruises before? Heck, she's seen me shot and bleeding."

"Yes, but that was well before you two were officially an item. Things are different when you're actually in the type of relationship you're now in. Things change."

"Why are you so interested?"

Jones snickered, not having any ulterior motive for his worries. "I'm just concerned about you as a friend, as a friend of Mia's, hoping you don't do something that would make things more difficult for you both."

"Such as?"

"Like not recognizing that telling her the truth is the best medicine you can give her, regardless of how hard it may be, or whether that truth would make her unhappy."

"So in your own sweet way, you're saying that I should tell her I was in close-quarter combat with a Canadian assassin, and that's where the cuts and bruises came from?"

"Yes."

"And you don't think that will provoke a longer discussion?"

"Mia's a very intelligent woman, Mike."

"I'm aware."

"And as such, whether you tell her the truth or not, she's likely to guess at what happened, anyway. And if she does, do you want to plant little seeds in her mind that you don't tell her the truth? When you plant a seed, it always grows into something bigger. If she assumes what happened, and you don't tell her, don't you think she will wonder what else you're not telling her?"

"Do I have to tell her every time I go to the bathroom too?" Recker said sarcastically.

Jones rolled his eyes. "Do as you wish. Girlfriends and significant others worry. It's just what they do. I like seeing you happy and hope that you can continue that way. Just some friendly advice."

Their friendly banter was interrupted by the sound of Jones' phone ringing. "It's Chris," Jones said. He answered it, putting it on speaker. "Everything OK?"

"Yeah, still no sign of Rizzo yet," Haley said. "I was just wondering how Mike made out? You told me earlier he was gonna try to find the shooter in the home."

"Oh. Yes. Mike is back, he's fine, a few bumps and bruises, but otherwise OK. The shooter's been terminated. All is good on that front. Mike will be back home tonight getting some TLC from his girlfriend, I'm sure."

Recker turned his head slowly to look at his partner, not believing what he just said. For the first few years that they'd known each other, Jones had a very dry personality, and hardly ever seemed to crack a joke. Now they seemed to come out of his mouth constantly. Especially when it concerned Recker's love life. It didn't really bother him, though sometimes he made it appear that it did, just to keep up his tough guy front. Jones looked up at Recker and grinned, shrugging his shoulders.

"Need some help out there, Chris?" Recker said.

"No, no, no. I'm good. Just gets a little boring out here, waiting."

"I know the feeling."

"Chris, anytime you feel the need to talk, I'm always here and available," Jones said.

"Good to know. Still no word on when Rizzo might hit?" Haley said.

"No, just said after dark. That could be 8pm or 5am. Just have to wait it out and see."

Though Haley wasn't ecstatic about waiting, it didn't bother him too much. He knew it was sometimes part of the deal. He was just happy to be back in the game. For him, waiting six hours in a car was better than working five minutes at a normal job. It was a good attitude for him to have, considering he'd have another four hours to go until his suspect showed up.

It was 11:30 and the homeowners, judging from when the lights went out, went to bed around nine. Haley saw a person walking down the street and immediately looked at his phone for Rizzo's picture to get a confirmation. As he walked under a streetlight, Rizzo's face was illuminated and Haley could definitely make him out despite his dark clothing. Haley didn't take his eyes off his target as Rizzo approached the house. Rizzo stopped and looked around, making sure nobody was watching. Haley was parked across the street, in the back seat of his new car, the tinted window disguising his presence.

Once Rizzo was sure that prying eyes weren't gazing down

upon him, he started to work. The row home had a walk-out basement, and Rizzo snuck up to the door that led inside. He quietly broke open the door within a minute and was inside the home. As soon as he vanished from sight, Haley exited his car and ran across the street, ready to do his business. He stood just beyond the door and peeked inside, not immediately seeing Rizzo. Haley withdrew his gun and stepped inside the house. He stood inside the frame of the door, looking around, trying to hear where the intruder might have been. After a few moments, he heard some rattling coming from the back of the house. The basement had been separated into two rooms. Where Haley was had been turned into a TV room, along with a computer, a couch, a chair, as well as a bathroom. The steps that led up to the main part of the house separated the two rooms. The part Rizzo was in had been converted into a toy room. It also led to the backyard as well as housing the washer and dryer.

Haley quietly walked to the middle of the room, near the steps, and waited for Rizzo to show himself. He figured it was safer for him to wait for Rizzo to come to him instead of him going into a room, not knowing exactly where he was. In what felt like an hour, though was actually only two minutes, Rizzo came out of the room, holding several items that he planned on stealing. Haley had his gun out, pointed at him as he came into view. As soon as Rizzo saw the outline of the gun-toting man in front of him, he knew he was in a lot of trouble. He just dropped the items in his hand without saying a word.

"I don't believe those are yours," Haley said.

"Umm," Rizzo said, throwing his arms in the air, not knowing what else to say. What else could he say? He'd been caught red-handed.

"C'mon."

With his gun, Haley pointed to the other room, having Rizzo follow him in there as he walked backward. He still wasn't sure exactly what he was going to do with the burglar. If Recker was there, it likely would have been over by now. There was a good chance he would have pumped a couple rounds into him and left to be done with it. But that wasn't Haley's style. While he obviously didn't have a problem firing away and killing someone if the situation warranted, as the Tresselman case showed, it never was his first option.

"You got any weapons on you?" Haley said. "Gun, knife, anything?"

"Nah," Rizzo said solemnly. He looked very worried about what the man with the gun was going to do with him.

Haley turned him around and had him face the wall and touch it, spreading out his hands and feet. Haley frisked him to make sure he had no weapons, but as Rizzo admitted, he was clean.

"Just stay there for a second," Haley said.

Haley took a few steps back and started looking around the room. He still kept his gun on Rizzo and looked back at him every few seconds, just to make sure he didn't make any sudden movements or try escaping somehow. There wasn't a lot that he could do with the burglar. He wasn't going to kill him or beat him up. Especially since the man had seemingly given up peacefully. Rizzo didn't make any attempts to get away or attack him. Haley could have tied him up, but he obviously didn't walk around with a string of rope hanging off him, and he didn't notice anything he could use in the basement. Haley noticed a closet and figured that would have to do. He directed Rizzo to move away from the wall and had him move closer to the door. Haley opened the closet, hoping it wasn't already filled with junk that would spill out as soon as he opened it. Luckily, there were only a few small things in there. Haley lifted his thumb and pointed at the closet with it.

"I gotta go in there?" Rizzo asked, hoping that wasn't the case.

"It's either that or I can shoot you."

Rizzo sighed in disgust, but complied with the request,

knowing there wasn't much he could do to stop it. As his record indicated, he wasn't a violent man by nature. Though he was a criminal, and burglary was one of his specialties, he wasn't prone to outbursts of violence. He'd never shot anyone before and he tried to shy away from physical confrontations whenever possible. He knew that once he stepped inside that closet that the next time it opened, there would probably be a police officer on the other side of it, ready to take him to jail.

"That thing even loaded?" Rizzo said.

"One good way to find out," Haley said with a certain vigor in his voice.

The manner in which he said it indicated to Rizzo that the man wasn't fooling around. He certainly looked like someone who knew his way around with a gun. Considering Rizzo wasn't exactly a gun aficionado, he wasn't the type to question anyone else's motives who was carrying one. Reluctantly, Rizzo finally stepped inside the closet. Haley immediately closed it and locked it. To make sure the burglar didn't escape once he left, Haley took hold of the computer desk and dragged it across the floor until it set in front of the door to prevent it from opening. Not completely satisfied with the setup, Haley looked around the floor for any other items he could use. He saw a milk crate on the floor that was packed with books and picked it up. He placed the heavy object under the desk, nestling it in front of the door. Once Haley was sure that Rizzo couldn't get away, even if he could unlock the door, he called Jones to let him know the job was done and seek further clarification on what to do from there.

"Everything's wrapped up here," Haley said. "Rizzo's under control."

"Great. What did you do with him?" Jones said, a slight hesitation in his voice. Usually when he asked that question of Recker it involved hearing about a dead body. Whether Jones thought it was warranted or not. He hoped that this wouldn't be another of those times. Especially with Haley.

"Right now he's locked in a closet in the basement."

"Oh."

"Is that wrong? Should I not have done that?" Haley said, noticing the apprehensiveness in Jones' voice.

"No. No. What you did was perfect. I take it he did not give you any trouble?"

"Nope. Easy as pie. As soon as he saw me he dropped the stuff and pretty much gave up. No struggle at all."

"Excellent. Great job."

"I didn't know exactly what else to do with him, so I figured stuffing him in the closet was the best option. I didn't have anything to tie him up with."

"Is the closet secured?" Jones said, hoping Rizzo wouldn't get loose once Haley left the premises.

"Yeah. I locked it and put a desk and a crate of heavy books in front of it. I mean, he may be able to pry himself out of there eventually, but it should take a while."

"I'll contact the police immediately. They should be there in a few minutes."

"Yeah, he won't be able to get out in that time."

"OK. After we hang up, wait approximately thirty seconds, then get out of there."

"Will do."

Haley did exactly as he was instructed and left thirty seconds after talking to Jones. Even though he was sure that Jones wanted him to leave the area right away, Haley stuck around for a little while. He wanted to make sure that Rizzo didn't somehow escape before the police got there. Haley did move his car to a new position, though, just to be out of the sight of any police personnel that would soon swamp the area. He moved a little farther down the street, but he still had a good sight line of the home and could see if Rizzo came out before the police came.

Jones, meanwhile, had already called the police anonymously to report seeing a burglar in the home. He made sure to tell them it was urgent, and the burglar was still in the house. He tried to monitor the situation remotely as he listened to police scanners. The police showed up within only a few minutes. Even after they arrived, Haley stayed until he saw them leading Rizzo out of the house in handcuffs. Once they did, he gave Jones the heads-up that the case was now closed. He was about to go back to the office to wrap things up, but Jones nixed that idea and told him to go home instead. With everything settled, Jones was about to call it a night himself.

Haley was just looking to learn as much as he could about the new operation he'd found himself in. There was still so much that he didn't know. Jones and Recker had given him bits and pieces of information and showed him a few things, but he didn't completely understand the nuts and bolts of the business. Wanting to get a head start, Haley showed up at the office at 8 a.m. the next morning, hoping he might be the first one there. He was a little taken aback, though not completely surprised, to find that he was actually the last one in the office. It didn't appear that they'd yet actually started working as they were both standing near the coffee machine. After a brief greeting from his new teammates, Haley got a cup of coffee himself.

"And here I thought I might actually beat everyone in," Haley said.

"Not likely," Recker said with a laugh. "Better get used to it. In the few years we've been doing this, I can count on one hand the amount of times I beat David into the office. It just isn't gonna happen."

"I pride myself on being first to distribute any information that may be necessary to start the day," Jones said.

"And it's gonna be even harder now that he's living here and doesn't have a separate place."

Jones took a sip of his coffee before asking Recker how his night went. "So how did you handle the topic of your battered and bruised face?"

Recker shrugged and shook his head like it was no big deal. "Just told her the truth. Told her exactly what happened."

"You left nothing out?"

"Not one detail."

"And how did she take it?" Jones said, though considering his friend didn't seem upset or troubled, he already assumed it went reasonably well.

"Fine. Like you said, she did the girlfriend worrying thing, but we talked about it."

"Who did most of the talking?"

"She did. But she knows this is what I do, and we've talked about it before. It isn't going to change anytime soon. She's dealing with it. She's a strong person though."

"Sounds like a great girl," Haley said.

"She is," Recker said. "I probably don't deserve her."

"Probably not," Jones said, getting an icy stare from Recker. "What? Well, I was only agreeing."

"So how's your apartment coming? All settled in?" Recker said.

Haley laughed as he thought about it. "Well, there's a TV, a couch, a bed, and a dining table. That's pretty much it."

"Sounds like you could use an interior decorator," Jones said. "Mike, you should help him with that. He knows all about hanging curtains, don't you?"

Recker looked up at the top of the wall and the ceiling, stroking his chin as he tried to figure out whether he should respond to the teasing. After a few moments of thought, he decided to just let it go. "If you want, one day Mia and I can come over and help you spruce the place up. Well, she'll most likely do most of the work. I just pretty much just stand back and do what she tells me."

"That would be great if you think she wouldn't mind," Haley said. "I wouldn't want to impose on her or anything."

"Nah, she'd love to do it. She loves doing that kind of stuff. Besides, she's already been asking me to meet you."

"Oh, really?"

"Yeah, she's hopeful that your being here is going to magically add years to my life."

22

R ecker and Haley had just come back from a rather
routine assignment, preventing a simple assault on a
man who was responsible for a couple of his ex-
coworkers being fired. The man was a retail store manager and
had recently fired two of his employees for stealing merchandise.
The employees had planned on getting back at the man by beating
him up one night as he closed the store and walked back to his car.
Recker and Haley easily stopped that, leaving the two assailants
down and out before they could get a hand on their intended
victim. They planned on keeping an eye on the situation in the
coming weeks, but after the beating that Recker and Haley dished
out, they suspected they would never hear from the pair again.

By coming back to the office later at night, Recker knew something was up. Usually when they had something go down past
nine o'clock, they just called it a night and reconvened the next
morning. Since Jones had asked them to come back after their
assignment was over, Recker assumed there was another case
coming. And probably coming immediately.

"Any issues?" Jones said.

"No, it's taken care of," Recker said. "I doubt we'll hear from either of them again. Couple of small-time punks who thought it'd be an easy thumping for them."

"They are still breathing, correct?"

"What do you take me for, an animal?"

"Just making sure."

"Alive, breathing, and going home to mama."

"Though they'll have some cuts and bruises to take care of," Haley said. "Maybe a few stitches too."

"So what's up?" Recker said. "I know you didn't call us back here just to chat about these two nitwits."

"I received a warning on the voicemail alert system," Jones said quickly.

"What's the target?"

"Liquor store. Store's open until ten. The message said they were going to hit it just before closing."

"How far away?"

"If you leave now, you'll get there about the same time they do."

"How many are we dealing with?"

"Four. And they're not afraid of using their weapons," Jones said, pulling up the gang's information on the screen.

It showed a picture of all four of the men along with their rap sheets. Recker and Haley both leaned forward, each standing on opposite sides of Jones, looking over his shoulders to read as much as they could before they got going.

"I believe this might be the same gang that hit that liquor store a few weeks ago that we rolled on late to," Jones said.

"What happened with that?" Haley said.

"Same thing. They walked into the store just before closing, then took everything out of the registers and the safe. Killed an employee and a customer on their way out," Recker said, remembering the details vividly.

"Was there provocation?" Haley asked, wondering what made the gang take the lives of two people.

"Not according to witnesses," Jones said. "Everyone was apparently complying to their wishes and demands without incident. The gang just seemed to open up on the victims for no reason at all."

"The same guy do the shooting?"

"No, it was two different shooters."

"I don't see a vehicle listed," Recker said.

"I'm still working on that," Jones replied. "If I get it before you arrive at the store I'll let you know."

"Forward it to our phones so we can look at it on the way."

"We both hitting this?" Haley said.

"You know it," Recker said, confirming the obvious.

Recker and Haley then rushed out of the office. Since Recker was more familiar with the area, he did the driving. They jumped into his SUV and Recker floored it to get to the liquor store on time. As they sped through the streets, Jones sent the information on the gang, complete with pictures, to the phones of both Recker and Haley. Haley immediately started studying their faces and looked at their histories and background info. Though he had no issue with taking on the gang themselves, he did have some questions on the assignment.

"Why not just call the police and let them know what's going on and let them roll on it?" Haley said.

Recker sighed, not annoyed with the question, but reliving what happened the last time this situation happened. "Because when this happened a few weeks ago, that's how we handled it."

"Police didn't help?"

"Not in time. We called in the tip and by the time they got there, the gang had already come and gone. We took too long on it. We debated back and forth on whether to get the police involved or just handle it ourselves. After we got the police involved I eventually rolled on it, but I didn't get there fast enough."

"That's rough."

"We should've just handled it ourselves," Recker said, shaking his head, still lamenting their lack of action at the time.

"No alarms went off?"

"No. That was one of the things we talked about. We assumed that one of the workers would hit the silent alarm when the robbery went down. We waffled on whether, if the alarm was sounded, if I would get caught up in between the gang and the police. If I kept them pinned down, or they kept me pinned down, could I slip away if the cops showed?"

"Reasonable worry," Haley said.

"Yeah, well, turns out the cops got there late, I got there late, the store got robbed, and two people got killed because of it."

"So how we gonna handle it?"

"I guess that will depend on if they're already there or not. Hopefully, we can get there before they do, and we can already be inside waiting on them. If not, we may have to shoot our way in. Or catch them as they're leaving."

"Might be too late, though. Especially if they shoot a couple people before they head out the door and we see them," Haley said.

Recker nodded, instead, only answering with a grimace. He was well aware that their best chance of stopping the gang was to get inside of the store before they did. If not, they'd most likely have to shoot their way in, and that would only endanger more innocent people's lives. The more Recker agonized over it, the more determined he was to not let the same thing happen again that happened a few weeks ago.

When they were about ten minutes away from their destination, Jones texted them with the make and model of the car that he suspected the gang was driving. It was a plain blue cargo van with a New Jersey license plate. Now it was always possible that they could be using a different car, or had stolen something new along the way, but according to what Jones could dig up, the cargo van was their likely choice of a getaway car. They kept a sharp lookout for the van when they finally arrived at the liquor store, which was in a small shopping center. There weren't a ton of parking spots and few places for it to hide if they were keeping it parked out of sight. Recker went through the lot, and even drove behind the buildings, in case they were waiting in back of the stores. Much to their delight, the van was nowhere in sight. But that still didn't mean that they weren't there. There were a few cars parked along the side of the building, and since the liquor store was an end unit, they assumed they were the cars of the store workers. They pulled up alongside them and shined their flashlight inside the cars one by one to make sure the gang wasn't inside one of them waiting to strike. Each of the four cars came up empty though. Not a single passenger in any of them.

Recker pulled the truck around to the front of the building again and parked. They made what they believed was a safe assumption that the gang wasn't there yet. If the car they were using wasn't to the side of the building, they figured it would've been parked near the front entrance along the curb. Parking in a regular spot would not have been conducive to a fast getaway should they need it. Recker and Haley waited a few seconds, looking into the store from the spot they were parked in. They could easily see a few workers walking around freely and two or three customers shopping.

"Time to head in?" Haley said.

"Yeah."

"How you wanna work it? Alert the workers that they're about to be hit?"

"Nah, I don't think that'd play well," Recker said, nixing the idea. "We go in there and start talking about getting robbed, talking crazy, they're likely to hit the panic button right away and not even let us finish a coherent thought. Next thing you know, instead of the gang showing up, we got a bunch of police officers waiting for us outside."

"All right, makes sense. Light these guys up as soon as they walk through the door?"

"I dunno. I think we gotta play it by ear. I wanna get all four of them. If only two enter and we kill them right away, the other two might rabbit."

"Might scare the rest of them off," Haley said.

"Or it might just make them come back in a week or two. Maybe even worse or more dangerous than before. A wounded animal is a dangerous animal. And I'd rather take out this entire crew now than worrying about having to deal with them again somewhere down the line."

Recker and Haley got out of the car and walked into the store. There was still ten minutes before closing. Plenty of time for the gang to storm in and do their business. Recker split from his partner as they both pretended to be customers, each walking a different aisle of the store, perusing the selection of alcohol. They both stayed within viewing range of the entrance, so they could be ready to strike quickly if needed. Five minutes passed, with still no sign of any activity from the gang. Two of the customers did leave, however, and no other shoppers entered, which pleased Recker. It meant two fewer people who would be in the line of fire.

With two minutes to go until the store closed, two rough looking characters calmly walked through the doors. Recker took a good long look at the pair, instantly recognizing them as part of the crew they were waiting for. A closing announcement boomed over the loudspeaker, trying to speed up the selection process of any remaining customers. The first two members of the crew split up, walking toward the back of the store. Then, the other two guys came strutting through the door. One of them stayed near the front door as the other one started waltzing through the aisles. The first two members that came in had grabbed something off the shelf and headed toward the registers.

To get their plan into action, one of the men pretended there was some type of problem at the register, bringing the store manager out. With the three employees from the store all hanging around near the registers, the crew knew there was nobody else to worry about. The gang had cased the store several times over the past two weeks and were aware how the establishment operated around closing time, and how many employees there were at nighttime. They often waited for a while after it closed to see how many store workers exited when they finally closed everything down, so they knew how many people they had to worry about.

Recker maneuvered his way to the front of the store, near the entrance, where the last member of the gang was waiting to make sure nobody else went in or out. He'd already communicated with Haley to not engage until he gave him the signal. As Recker walked to the front, the man withdrew his gun to keep what he assumed was a customer at bay. Haley, meanwhile, had walked to the back of the store to get within range of the man walking the aisles. Recker's signal was going to be his gun firing, and Haley wanted to be ready to extract some justice of his own before one of the robbers could get the drop on him first.

"Get down on the floor, buddy," the man said, pointing his gun at Recker.

"Oh, sure," Recker said nonchalantly, putting his hands in the air.

Recker got to one knee, putting his right one down, trying to lull the man to sleep by being as unthreatening as possible. As Recker put one of his hands on the floor, he noticed the guard took his eyes off him for a split second as he scanned the store for anybody else within his vicinity. That was just the opening that Recker needed to get the drop on him. He quickly withdrew his gun and opened fire at the man, unloading three shots that all lodged in the man's upper torso, dropping the guard immediately. Recker scurried along the floor to check on the man's condition, wanting to make sure he was dead, so he didn't have to worry about him coming back at him from behind.

Haley was standing near the end cap of one of the aisles, waiting for the sound he needed to hear. The crackling sounds of gunfire within the store was the signal that Haley needed to engage his own target. With the second member of the crew guarding the back, Haley had his gun drawn, and jumped from beyond the protection of the aisle. Catching the man by surprise, Haley immediately opened fire, firing two rounds, both of which connected with his target. One of the bullets penetrated the side of the man's head, causing him to perish before he even hit the ground.

After checking on the status of the man he shot, Recker hurried back to the security of one of the aisles to make sure he wasn't within easy range of the two remaining members of the gang. Haley also rushed back to the front of the store, spotting Recker and racing over to him. Seeing movement out of the corner of his eye, Recker turned toward his partner zooming toward him.

"You all right?" Recker said.

"Yep."

"You take the other guy out?"

"Yeah. Just the two left," Haley said, breathing a little heavy from the action. "How you wanna do this?"

"Looks like they got the three employees up there by the register. That means there should still be a customer floating around here somewhere. See if you can find them and get them out of here."

"OK. I'll have them go through the fire exit door in back."

"Sounds good. I'll start working these guys up here."

Haley immediately left and started combing through the aisles, keeping his head down in case of a random shot being fired in his direction. After a brief search, he found the last remaining customer, kneeling, and covering his head in the middle of one of the aisles. Haley sped over to him and tried to keep the middle-aged man as calm as possible.

"Hey," Haley said calmly, putting his hand on the man's shoulder.

The man withdrew his head from his arms, looking up at the armed man with a worried expression on his face.

"Listen, I'm gonna get you out of here, OK? I'm one of the good guys. Both of the robbers are up front with the employees. What I want you to do is keep your head down and go right down to the end of this aisle and make a left. There's a fire door there. I want you to go out the door and get to your car and get out of here."

"OK." The man nodded his agreement.

"Go. Keep your head down."

The customer did as he was directed and ran to the back of the store, hunched over the entire time. As he raced out the exit door, the alarm started blaring from the door opening. As the alarm went off, Recker looked to the ceiling. He knew that meant someone would be coming soon enough. Even if none of the workers hit the emergency button, someone would probably be coming soon since the alarm company would be calling momentarily about the unauthorized door opening. Recker knew they'd have to work fast to avoid any law enforcement that might be coming, but not so quickly that they'd rush something and get one of the innocent store workers hurt or killed. Up to that point, everything had happened so fast, that the gang hadn't even gotten any money yet. None of the cash register drawers had been emptied, and they hadn't got to the safe yet. But hearing the gunshots, and seeing their friend lying dead by the front door, they knew they had to scrap their plans and just figure out how to get out of there alive. What made things tougher for them at that stage was that they couldn't see who else was in the store with them or where they were.

Finally, the crew's leader spoke up in trying to get themselves out of there. "We got three people up here. If you don't let us out of here, they'll all wind up dead."

"I'm not the police," Recker shouted back. "I don't negotiate. Letting those people go is the only chance you have of getting out of here."

"Fat chance, man."

"Listen, it's just me. But you can see how dangerous I can be. I've taken out two of your guys already. I got no problem taking out two more."

Recker wanted to play coy with them, hoping that they didn't realize there was a second shooter, or that he was working with someone. If they believed it was just him, then they might get a free shot at the gang, or at least a better opportunity to take them out. Through the com device in his ear, Recker started talking with Haley to go over the plan.

"They didn't correct me or dispute it when I told them it was just me," Recker said. "Try to get to the far side of the store to see if you can get a better angle."

"Right."

"Try not to let them see you."

"If I can get a good vantage point, should I take the shot?" Haley said.

"As long as you're sure nobody's in the way. If you're positive you can take one out... do it."

Haley steadily went to the back of the store once more, moving slowly from aisle to aisle, making sure that he didn't make any noises to alert the gang of his presence. Recker was hopeful that Haley could make his way around to the other side of the gang undetected. It would definitely speed things up if he could. If the civilians weren't there, Recker would fire a few rounds in the gang's direction, just to get them distracted. But with the workers nearby, Recker couldn't take the chance of a bullet ricocheting off a wall and hitting them.

As he waited for word from Haley that he'd gotten himself into a better position, Recker took a moment to think about how nice it was to have some help in that situation. Before Haley was brought into the fold, Recker would've had to go about this in a completely different manner. Or in the event that he didn't, he would've had a much tougher time. If he would've had to worry about taking on all four men on his own, it was also likely that it would take a lot longer, possibly screwing up his probabilities of escaping before the police came. Even now, with Haley's help, it was a cause of concern for him.

After a couple minutes, Haley notified him that he was ready. "I'm in position."

"How's your view?"

"Uh, not as good as I'd like it to be. Looks like they're huddled down behind a couple of the registers."

"No clear shot?"

"No, not yet."

"We're gonna have to raise the target somehow," Recker said. "Gotta make them visible."

"Any ideas?"

Recker thought for a few moments before thinking he might've come up with something. "Yeah. I might."

Recker then explained his thoughts, not totally sure himself whether it was going to work. There was a risk involved. He thought they could probably take one of the men out easily, but he had no idea how the remaining member of the gang would react once they did. He could just give it up, or he could panic and start killing the civilians he had with him.

"You ready to surrender yet?" Recker yelled. "You know there's nowhere for you to go."

"We'll see about that."

Recker took a step to the side of the aisle that he was in, showing himself for a brief moment. Seeing only the tops of a couple people's heads, he took aim at the glass window that was in front of the register. Knowing that the glass would shatter, with minimal chance of injuring any of the civilians severely, Recker fired at it. He thought the people were far enough away from the glass that they shouldn't have to worry about pieces of glass raining down on top of them. But even if a few pieces did manage to strike one or two of them, they should've only produced a few minor cuts.

After the glass shattered, Recker was correct in that the people were far enough away that the pieces didn't reach them. But it did do as he hoped it would and spurred the two remaining gang members to start moving from their position. The man closest to Haley's spot rose up and started hurrying the store worker that he had with him, wanting him to move with him and use him as a hostage. The gang member grabbed the man by the back of his shirt collar, spurring him on to move along in front of him, shielding him from any bullets. They started to leave the comfort of the registers and move to the back of the store, though they only got about fifteen feet away. They passed right by Haley's position, giving the new Silencer a perfect view of his target.

Though the gang member and his hostage were relatively close to each other, there was enough separation for Haley to do what was needed. As soon as the store worker passed by, Haley had a clear shot of his target. Only a few feet away, Haley's shot penetrated the temple of the crew member, instantly knocking him onto his side. Upon hearing and seeing the carnage that was unleashed just inches behind him, the store worker froze in his position. Haley worried about him being exposed and quickly grabbed him by the arm and pulled him behind his location as they retreated back to Haley's former spot.

"You know the back exit, right?" Haley said.

"Yeah."

"All right, run, get out of here."

The worker ran as fast as he could down the aisle and swiftly made his way out the fire door in the back of the building. The last member of the gang had just risen above the confines of the register when he saw his partner start making his way to the back in the hopes of escaping. Once he saw his friend's head almost blown off his shoulders, he quickly retreated back to the register, still having the security of two hostages with him.

"Give it up," Recker shouted, hoping to bring the matter to a resolution quickly. "There's no way out for you."

"Now I know there's at least two of you," the man yelled in return. "I'm not making that mistake again."

"Doesn't really matter, does it? You know we're not letting you walk out of here with hostages."

"I'll blow their heads off right now if you don't let me out of here."

"And as I said earlier, I'm not the police. I don't negotiate."

"Well you better start, or these people are as good as dead."

Seeing as how they were at an impasse, Recker turned to Haley to see if he could sneak in behind the man. "Chris, you able to move closer?"

"Uh, maybe. Not sure."

"I think that's our best bet of ending this. He's not letting them go. We need to take him out now."

"What if he sees me coming?" Haley said.

"Do what you gotta do."

"No, I'm not concerned about me. I can handle that. I'm worried that if he sees me, he might kill one of those people he's got with him."

"Knowing what you did to his friend, I'm betting that if he sees you, he's gonna be more concerned about you than taking out one of them," Recker said.

"I can give it a shot."

"Even if you can't get to him. If we can get him to stand up, we can take him out. I can move a little closer. If you don't think you have a shot, if he stands up to face you, I can hit him from here."

The two Silencers both moved away from their current position, trying to get a little closer to the last remaining member of the gang. He still had two store workers huddled with him, crunching down beneath one of the registers. The man really didn't know what he was going to do. He had no plan at that point. All his buddies had been killed. It appeared that he was surrounded. It didn't seem like he could even leverage the store workers as hostages to buy his release. It really seemed hopeless for him. Beside that, he didn't even know who he was up against. If it was the police, he knew there was a certain guide that they followed in situations like these. But not having any idea who was on the other side, they didn't appear to be playing by any definite rules. They only seemed to be going by the idea that they had to take everyone out.

Haley dropped to the tile floor and started crawling along the side of the wall to make his way to the front register. As he was doing that, Recker also moved closer, crouching down as he maneuvered his way to the end register. The gang member was two registers away from him, and if he stood up, Recker had a clear shot at him. There was no way he'd miss at that range.

"I don't know if I can get in anymore," Haley whispered.

"It's all right. I can hit him from here," Recker said. "See if you can get him to stand up a little."

Haley thought for a moment about what he could do or say to get the man to reveal himself for Recker to finish him off. He was staring at a bottle of wine right in front of him and thought that might give them the diversion that they needed to finally end the conflict. He grabbed it off the shelf and tossed it toward the end of the register, shattering as it impacted against the ground. Thinking someone had snuck up behind him at the register, the man turned and instinctively started firing, his bullets hitting the front wall. As he did so, his head jumped up just slightly above the counter of the register, finally giving Recker a target to shoot at. Seizing the opportunity, Recker wasted no time in firing his weapon. He only needed one shot, and he didn't miss. Upon the bullet piercing through the side of his face, the man slumped over, dead as he hit the ground.

Recker got to his feet and walked over to his latest victim to make sure the situation was finally resolved. Seeing the blood pouring out of the hole in the side of his face, it was conclusive evidence that their work was now finished. Recker waved to the last two hostages to get on their feet, letting them know that the nightmare was over. As they ran to the front door to escape the carnage that was behind them, sirens blared in the background. The two workers ran right into the waiting arms of several police officers.

Recker looked out the front window and saw at least five police cars in front, the magnitude of their lights brightening up the entire area. Recker and Haley looked at each other, hoping they hadn't run out of time. Recker tapped Haley on the shoulder to get him to follow him as they raced toward the back door. Recker opened it just a bit, wanting to make sure they didn't run out into the flashing lights of police officers themselves. Unfortunately for them, there were already three cars stationed around the back. Recker looked at Haley and sighed, unsure how they were going to escape the predicament they were now in.

"What do we do?" Haley said, not seeming the least nervous about being surrounded.

"See if there's another way out. Go around the store and see if there's another exit somewhere."

"Even if there is, they're gonna be out there waiting."

Recker put his hand over his face and rubbed the sides of his mouth as he tried to think of another solution. For the first time that he could remember since starting this operation with Jones, he didn't see a way out. At least not one that left him alive. Shooting it out was not an option. His long standing policy was to never engage the police under any circumstances since they were on the same side, and he wasn't going to change that now, even if that was the only choice he had left. A few minutes later, Haley came back to let Recker know that he struck out. There were no other possibilities.

"What about a roof hatch?" Recker said, remembering he's used that several times to escape.

"Locked and deadbolted."

Since escape was no longer on the table, the grim reality set that Recker's final minutes as a free man were coming near. There was nothing else he could do but give himself up. The only question now was how to keep Haley in the clear. If Recker was out of the picture, he couldn't let Haley get dragged down with him. Jones would still need somebody out in the field to make things work. His thoughts turned to Mia briefly, thinking how disappointed and upset he was going to make her.

"Find the office and any surveillance equipment, tapes, anything," Recker said.

"And do what with them?" Haley replied, not getting what his partner was inferring.

"Make sure nobody can ever see what went down here tonight."

"Why?"

"Cause we're going down and I'm gonna make sure you don't go down with me."

"I'm not gonna leave you high and dry," Haley said, resisting the idea he'd escape the wrath of the law while his partner got hung up.

"It's not about that. People need to be protected... helped. They won't get that if we're both in the can. I'm already a known quantity. Nobody knows about you yet. And they don't have to. As far as anyone is concerned, everything that happened here tonight was me. I stopped the gang alone. You're just a customer. Wrong place, wrong time."

Haley sighed and made a grimace, not really liking the plan that Recker was offering. Though it obviously made sense to him, he wasn't keen on just leaving his new partner and friend in the clutches of the police.

"There is no other way," Recker insisted, seeing that Haley was having a hard time swallowing his proposition. "Go hit the office and get rid of those tapes so nobody can see what role you had here."

Haley sighed even louder as he looked down at the ground, not wanting to move an inch. He raised his head up and looked at Recker and nodded, finally agreeing to his plan, though he was still reluctant to do so. Recker moved the corner of his mouth to try to muster a smile, letting him know that it was OK. As Haley left, Recker watched him as he ran toward the front office. He knew that if he was now out of the game, that Jones would still have a good man out in the field. This was as bad as it got, and Haley showed no signs of panic or worry. Even looking at the loss of freedom, he wasn't about to abandon his partner, even though it would've been easier to do so. It was an admirable quality to have, and Haley had plenty. If there was any solace to be taken from this event, it was that the work that Jones and Recker had started would still go on. Haley was a capable replacement, and once he had a little more experience, it would probably be like Recker never even left.

Recker heard someone's voice blaring through a police radio, trying to make contact with him, though he didn't pay any attention to it. Haley came back and let him know that he destroyed the surveillance equipment, so there should've been no evidence of his presence once they were gone.

"What now?" Haley said.

"First, I'll call David and let him know what's happening."

Jones was already aware of some of the problems. He'd been monitoring police communications and knew that they were already on the premises. Though he worried about Recker and Haley getting caught up in things, he hoped that they were just getting a safe distance away before contacting him to let him know how the assignment went. When Recker called to let him know the situation, it was the call that Jones had dreaded for so long, the one he hoped would never come, though he always knew would happen at some point. He just hoped it wouldn't be for a long time in the future. Seeing Recker's call come in, Jones quickly answered on the first ring.

"The police just descended on the liquor store," Jones said, hoping he was informing Recker with new information.

"I know."

"Please tell me you and Chris are already long gone."

Recker made a noise that almost sounded like a laugh, but didn't reply back instantly. It was with that lack of an immediate confirmation that Jones knew his worst fears had come true. He closed his eyes and felt like his heart had sunk as he waited for Recker to acknowledge the fact.

"Can't," Recker said, unable to say anything more profound.

"You're still inside," Jones said, barely able to get the words out.

Recker sighed. "Yeah."

"Since that's the case, I assume that there's no possible way out."

"No."

"So what do you propose to do?" Jones solemnly said.

"There's only one thing to do."

"Which is?"

"Give myself up."

"No, there must be another way."

"David, if there was, I would've taken it by now."

"I can't believe that the only way out of this is to surrender," Jones said, trying to think of another solution.

"It doesn't have to be a total loss, though," Recker said, attempting to convey some sort of positive.

"And how do you compute that?"

"Chris doesn't have to go down with me."

"You'll have to explain this further."

"We've already destroyed all the security footage. They won't be able to connect the dots with him."

"And none of the customers or store employees saw him do any of the damage?" Jones said, unsure that the plan would actually work.

"Well, he helped usher a couple of them out the back door. I dunno, passing him off as a customer who just happened to be there seems to be the best way to get him out safely. I'm the only one they know about. He shouldn't get caught up in it."

"I just wish there was a better option."

"Believe me, so do I."

23

Recker and Haley tossed their guns on the ground to make sure there would be no battle once they exited the store. Recker looked at Haley and smiled, giving him a pat on the arm.

"Take care of things while I'm gone," Recker said.

"We'll figure out a way to get you out."

Recker nodded, appreciating the gesture, even if he thought it was an impossible task. "Stay back. I'll go out first. I'll tell them you're a customer and you're the last one inside. Just stick with the story. Don't act like you know me at all. No matter what happens."

"I will."

With Haley looking on, Recker finally opened the front door and walked outside. With the bright lights flashing, he squinted as his feet hit the pavement.

"Get down on the ground! Get down on the ground!" someone shouted.

Recker instantly complied with the orders, getting down to his knees and putting his hands behind his head.

"That's the Silencer! Go! Go!" a police lieutenant yelled.

Within a few seconds, a dozen police officers descended on Recker's position, surrounding him as they put his hands behind his back and handcuffed him. As they got him to his feet and started walking him to one of their cars, they read him his rights.

"Anybody else inside?" an officer asked.

"Just one customer," Recker said.

"All right. Watch your head," the officer said, putting his hand on Recker's head as he guided him into the back seat of a police cruiser.

With Recker secure, another squad of officers rushed into the liquor store to check the damage. They immediately ran into Haley before sweeping the rest of the store. As they brought him out to be questioned, he tried his hardest to get Recker off.

"The guy you have over there isn't the one who robbed the place," Haley said.

"Yeah, we know."

"There were four other guys and the guy you got is the one who stopped them. If it wasn't for him, who knows what would've happened?"

"We're not taking him in for this," an officer said. "He's wanted for other things."

"Oh."

"Just sit tight for a few minutes so we can get down your version of everything."

Haley kept his eyes glued on the police cruiser that Recker was sitting inside, hoping that somehow the doors would open, and he'd be released. It wouldn't happen, though. After a few more minutes, a few police cars left the scene, including the one that had Recker. As they started driving through the streets, the officer sitting next to Recker started talking to him.

"I know this don't mean much right now, but I wish I wasn't the one doing this."

"Why's that?" Recker said, looking out the window.

"Honestly? I was hoping you'd never get caught."

Recker stopped his gaze and looked over to the officer, realizing that he had a fan.

"My partner and I are both appreciative of the things you've done in this city. The more filth that you've taken out is less that we have to deal with."

"Well, hopefully I've never made things too tough for you guys," Recker said. "My intention has always been to help you."

"Wish we could just let you go."

"Don't worry about it. It was bound to happen sooner or later."

"Yeah, well, hope you have a good lawyer," the officer said. "Hey, you got any partners or anything that could bail you out?"

"No, I work alone. Besides, I'm pretty sure I'll be one of those guys held without bail."

"Too bad. For what it's worth, I hope you can figure a way out of this thing."

"Appreciate it."

As they drove, the officers seemed to be getting real chummy with their prisoner. It was obvious that they didn't enjoy taking Recker in, though it was kind of a thrill for them to be talking to him. Though the half of the police force that didn't want Recker around all hoped that they'd be the one to capture him, of the half that did appreciate having him around, most wished they could've bought him a beer or two to tell him they enjoyed his work. They were about ten minutes away from the police district they were taking him to. Stopped at a red light, there were no other vehicles behind them. As Recker sat there contemplating his future, he looked toward his left at the intersection and noticed a van speeding around the corner. It took a very wide turn and appeared to be gaining momentum, crossing over the yellow lines.

"Look out!" Recker yelled, trying to warn the officers of the impending danger.

There was nothing they could do to get out of the way. The unmarked van crashed into the front of the police car on the driver's side, spinning it around, facing the opposite direction as it came to a stop. Another car came zooming up the street, tires squealing, and smoke rising, as it halted just in front of the bumper of the police cruiser. Men jumped out of both the car, and the van, hoods over their faces and assault rifles in hand and pointed at the occupants. The two police officers, as well as Recker, were all temporarily stunned by the impact of the collision, though none of them were seriously hurt. The masked men opened the back door to the police cruiser, as the driver started regaining his senses. He reached for his gun, quickly sizing up the situation.

"Don't do it! Don't do it!" one of the hooded men told him, aiming his rifle at the cop's face. "Just sit tight and nobody will get hurt."

Though he wanted to engage their attackers, the officer thought better of it. He knew he couldn't outdraw them, and even if he somehow got the drop on one, the others would see to it that he never lived to see another day. There were at least six men that the officer could see, though there could've been a few more he didn't notice. In truth, there were eight. Four from the van and four from the car. Both of the officers had their guns taken from them and thrown onto the ground. With the door to the driver open, as well as the doors on both sides of the back seat, all the occupants had guns pointed directly at them. Both officers had now regained their senses completely, but were cooperating with the masked men's commands, not that they had much choice in the matter.

"All right, take him and let's go!" One of the men shouted.

The two officers were removed from the car and were ordered to throw their radios on the ground. The masked men stomped on them, smashing them into pieces and rendering them useless. Then, one of the hooded men stuck his rifle into the front seat of the police cruiser, aiming at the center console. He opened up and fired, completely ripping apart their computer and radio equipment as pieces of it flew into the air. Once the shooter was finished making their equipment inoperable, two of the men reached inside the back seat and put a hood on Recker's face, dragging him out of the car. With a man on each side of his arm, pulling him along the ground, they threw him into the opened van rear door. All eight of the hooded men hurried back into their vehicles and sped off, disappearing into the night. As they drove away, the police officers grabbed their guns off the ground, but with their radios and computers destroyed, they had no way of signaling for backup, or of letting anyone know where their attackers had gone.

The van was in the lead with Recker, the other car closely following as they headed to the meeting spot. After a few minutes of driving, they all removed their hoods. The leader of the crew, in the back of the van with Recker, removed his cell phone and called his boss to let him know how everything went.

"It's done, boss," the man said.

"Excellent. Any casualties?"

"Nope. It went off without a hitch."

"Are you being pursued?"

"No, we're good."

"And Mr. Recker?"

"Doesn't seem any worse for the wear. What do you want me to do with him?"

"Bring him to the warehouse as we planned."

"Got it. Should be there in about twenty minutes. Should we take off the hood?"

"Sure. Let's not keep him in suspense any longer. Let him relax a little bit. It's been a trying day for him."

The man did as he was directed and picked Recker up off the floor of the van, sitting him upright. He grabbed a piece of wire and placed it into the keyhole of his handcuffs, twisting it until the cuffs sprung open. He placed Recker against the side wall of the van as he sat back across from him.

"You can take the hood off," the man said.

Curious at who his captors were, and what they wanted, Recker placed his hand on the top of his head. He grabbed hold of the hood and slowly took it off. He squinted for a moment as his eyes readjusted. It didn't take too long since the hood hadn't been on him for too long. But it only took a few seconds for him to recognize the face of his captor. Recker didn't say a word as he contemplated what was happening. By the look on Recker's face, the other man could see that he was a little shocked.

"Surprised?" the man said.

Recker motioned with his face, indicating that he was. He couldn't figure out how Jimmy Malloy would've known where he was or that he was in trouble.

"Never thought I'd live to see the day that Mike Recker was stunned."

"First time for everything I guess," Recker said.

Malloy sat there, a confident look embedded on his face, content with the feat they just pulled off.

"So are you gonna tell me what this is all about?" Recker said.

"Looks like a rescue to me. Don't tell me you would've been more comfortable sitting inside a jail cell."

"But why? How?"

"You're asking questions that are way above my pay grade," Malloy said.

"Are they? We both know you're Vincent's right hand. You know everything he's planning. I assume this was done with his say so."

"Good assumption."

"How'd you know I was gonna be in that police car? How'd you know what was going down?"

"We got good intel."

"That's not something that was planned in advance. How could you have known so soon?" Recker said.

"Maybe we got an SOS."

"So you're not gonna tell me?"

Malloy shrugged. "Vincent can do that. My job was just to get you."

"So where we heading? We meeting him?"

"Yeah. You've been there before. Same place that you took out the Italian guy... the one that tried to kill you."

"That the new hot spot?" Recker said with a smile.

No matter what the deal was, or the reason behind his escape, at least Recker knew he wasn't getting killed. Well, it was unlikely anyway. It would have been an awful lot of trouble for Vincent to go to if he was just going to bury him later. But considering they had no bad blood, Recker was reasonably sure it wasn't the case. But he also doubted they broke him free just for friendship. Though they were on good terms, breaking him free from the police was a big move. A bold move that Vincent was unlikely to take unless he benefited from it somehow. He figured there must have been another shoe that was going to drop once he spoke to Vincent. He usually had something up his sleeve, or a long-term view on something he was worried about. Maybe he needed Recker for another job. Whatever it was, it wouldn't be long until Recker found out.

The rest of the car ride to the warehouse was quiet, barely a word being spoken by anyone. Recker had a lot of questions, but he knew they were unlikely to be answered by Malloy. He was a good soldier. Loyal. Maybe to a fault. He'd never spill any information that Vincent didn't want leaked out. Not even by accident. He knew his place; he knew his role, and he never overstepped any boundaries. Vincent could never have asked for a better second in command than him.

Once they got to the warehouse, the van parked right in front of the bay doors, followed closely by the car behind them. Malloy was the first to get out, then Recker. Though Recker knew which way to go, he let Malloy lead the way since he wasn't there of his own accord. As they walked up the metal steps, Recker tried to prepare himself for what might've been asked of him in return for the favor of freeing him from the police. He was sure it would be something he wouldn't like. He knew Vincent didn't do it out of the kindness of his heart. He just hoped it wouldn't be something that terrible. They walked across the warehouse floor until they got to the hallway that led to the room they conducted business in several times before. Malloy knocked on the closed door three times then opened it. Vincent was sitting behind the desk, waiting for them, looking relaxed.

"Mike, so nice of you to join us."

"Don't think I really had much choice in the matter."

Vincent smiled, knowing he was technically correct. "True. But you could have taken issue with coming."

"But then I wouldn't have found out what I owe you in return."

"You don't look too worse for wear," Vincent said, looking his visitor's face over closely. "A few bumps and bruises. Should go away in a few days."

Tired of standing, Recker sat down in the chair in front of the desk, across from Vincent.

"Quite a predicament you found yourself in," Vincent said.

"Yeah, sure was."

"So what led to that?"

"Was preventing a robbery," Recker said.

"You stop a robbery and yet you're the one led away in handcuffs," Vincent said with a smile, seeing humor in it. "The irony is unmistakable."

"I'm glad you see some levity in it."

"Maybe it's time you came over to my side of the fence. After all, if you're going to do good things and help people, and still wind up on the wrong side of the law, what's the point?"

Recker answered almost immediately, not even needing time to think of a reply. "The point is in helping the people that need it. Whatever happens after that is moot. It's not about me."

"Spoken like a true martyr." Vincent laughed. "I'll be sure to say those words over your funeral casket."

Recker also smiled, before getting back to wondering why he was there. "So are you going to clue me in to what favor I need to repay? I know you didn't rescue me for friendship or old time's sake."

"Tomorrow morning."

"Tomorrow morning? For what?"

"For your presence at the meeting. Usual place. Nine o'clock."

"You're gonna keep me guessing all night?" Recker said.

"I'll tell you this; I'm not going to ask you to do anything that would compromise your principles," Vincent said, trying to alleviate his fears without saying too much. "What I need you to do would greatly help me in a situation and would square us in any outstanding matters."

By the seriousness of Vincent's face, Recker could see that whatever it was, it was big. Maybe bigger than anything they've ever had to deal with when doing business together. But it was still worrisome nonetheless that he wouldn't divulge more details.

"Well, you've had a long day," Vincent said. "I just wanted to make sure you were safe and sound. You're free to go if you'd like to go home and relax."

"Well, I, uh, seem to have left my car somewhere. Probably not a good idea for me to be out walking around the streets on a day like this considering there's probably a manhunt going on. Not to mention this is probably the lead story on all the news outlets."

"Of course. Jimmy will take you wherever you'd like to go. Just say the word."

Recker stood up to leave, but quickly stopped himself, realizing that his host hadn't yet answered the biggest question that he had.

"So, uh, about how you found out I was in trouble or where I was?"

"Oh. I received a frantic phone call about your dire situation," Vincent said.

Recker squeezed his eyebrows together, not piecing together who could have possibly called him. "Who else knows the both of us and knew of my problem?"

Vincent grinned, knowing his dangerous friend probably already had the answer to his question if he just thought about it for a few moments. "I believe that is a question you probably already know. Search for the answer within and you shall find it."

Recker looked away for a few seconds, staring at the wall. There was only one answer that came to him, but he couldn't come to grips with it. There was no way that the professor would have called Vincent. There was just no way, he thought. Recker strained his brain to think of another solution, but he kept coming back to Jones. Haley didn't know Vincent. Mia didn't know where Recker was. It had to be Jones. But he still couldn't believe it. He looked back at Vincent, who was nodding at him. Seeing the shocked look on his face, he knew that Recker had come up with the answer.

"Yes, it's true," Vincent said, reading Recker's face.

"He called you?"

"I'm not sure which one of us was more surprised. You just now, or me when I took the call. I guess it just goes to show you the old adage is true."

"Which one is that?"

"About desperation. When a man is desperate enough, there are no lengths he won't go to in order to relieve the tension he feels. When backed into a corner, you'll do whatever it takes to crawl out of it. You, me, your partner, none of us are immune to it."

"I guess that's so."

Recker, still stunned, wasn't sure what else to say or what else he could reveal, without knowing exactly what was said between the two of them in their conversation.

"I know it comes as a surprise to you, but it really shouldn't," Vincent said. "I've always known you've had a partner of some sort. I knew this thing you do couldn't only be the work of one man. There always had to be another, lurking in the background. It's too big of an operation for only one man to take on."

"So what do you plan to do with this little nugget of information you now have?"

Vincent shook his head, not taking offense to any implications that may have been inferred. "Nothing. As I've said before, our relationship has been solid, benefiting the both of us numerous times. That doesn't have to change now. We've both basically left each other to our own devices. We haven't interfered in each other's business. Besides, as I've said, I need your help in a matter. It wouldn't behoove me to jeopardize our relationship over something like this."

Recker nodded, feeling a little better about the revelation, though it was still a little hard to believe. "So what exactly did he tell you about him, or us?"

"Not much actually. As you can imagine, our conversation did not last very long. There were other, more pressing matters that were extremely urgent, as I'm sure you're aware. We only talked of a few specifics before hatching the plan to spring your release."

"Who came up with that?"

"Well, your partner has his skills and I have mine," Vincent said, answering the question without actually confirming anything.

"OK, well, I guess I'll be seeing you in the morning."

"Yes, we will. Can't wait to see the both of you."

Recker had taken two steps, but then stopped dead in his tracks. "The both of us?"

"You and David," Vincent said with a smile.

"David?" Recker said, in shock that his name was actually being used and was now a known quantity.

"Yes. One of the conditions of our agreement was that the two of you would agree to a meeting tomorrow morning to discuss business."

"He agreed to that?"

"He did. You know how I feel about doing business with people. I like to know who I'm dealing with. Coming to agreements and arrangements with strangers is something that I abhor, as you know."

"Tomorrow morning it is, then," Recker said.

Recker followed Malloy out of the warehouse, neither of whom said another word until getting to a car. It was a different one than was used in the police hit-and-run. Those cars would be sitting idly by for a few more weeks until the heat died down. Malloy asked Recker where he was taking him, and even though the cat seemed to be out of the bag now with Jones revealing himself, the Silencer still couldn't let them see the location of their office. Or his home. He'd have to figure out another plan to get back. He quickly thought of Haley, since he was still an unknown. Then he reached down and felt his pocket, remembering that he no longer had his phone. What to do now?

He initially just told Malloy to drive, and after a few minutes, then he'd figure out where he was going. Since he no longer had a phone and couldn't communicate with anyone, he'd either have to walk his way back, or take the risk of being identified and step inside somewhere to use a phone. It was just about midnight, and Mia should be getting done soon. He figured the easiest thing to do would be getting dropped off at the hospital. At least some of the people there had already seen his face before, and nobody seemed to recognize him. Or if they did, they never notified the authorities.

Even though it was a hospital, and a public building, it was probably the safest place for him to go at the moment. Though he also knew that would require some explaining to Mia. Not that it really mattered, he thought. He was sure she'd see it plastered on the news, anyway. Malloy got to the hospital in about thirty minutes, a few minutes after midnight. Mia rarely went home on schedule, though, usually taking extra time to finish up her duties.

"Figuring on getting checked out?" Malloy asked, thinking a hospital was a strange place to go.

Recker faked a smile. "No, just figured I'd use a phone."

"Probably better places to do it. Might get recognized in there, what with you being a lead news story."

"Some of these people know me. I'll be fine."

"Oh yeah. Now I remember," Malloy said, taking the opportunity to needle him a little. "This is where that girl works, isn't it? You know, the one we rescued from Joe in that building a while back, isn't it?"

"Is it? I don't recall."

"Yeah, yeah, yeah, what was her name? Nancy, Mary... Mia," Malloy said, pretending to forget, though he remembered her name right away. "That was it. Mia."

"Oh, is this where she works?" Recker said, not giving in to the charade.

"You and her ever... you know."

Recker knew full well what he was hinting at, and he wasn't going to play the game with him. He wasn't going to admit that he knew Mia in any capacity, even though he knew it was likely by the way Malloy was talking, that they'd already done their background on her. Recker already knew that Vincent realized there was some connection between him and Mia after the Simmonds situation, but he'd hoped that he eventually let it go. By Malloy bringing it up, it was obvious that they hadn't. Maybe it meant nothing, but maybe it also meant they were still keeping tabs on her. Though it was an important question to consider, with the other things on Recker's plate, it was one that would best be left answered for another day.

"Thanks for the ride," Recker said, closing the car door.

Though he figured police would probably check out hospitals as a precaution, since this one was outside Philadelphia borders, he figured he was safe. Plus, he doubted they would check a pediatric wing for him. As Recker entered the hospital, he noticed a guard near the entrance that he was familiar with, and one that knew Mia.

"Hey, how you doing?" Recker asked. "Did Mia Hendricks happen to leave yet?"

"I don't recall seeing her. Did you check to see if her car was still here?"

"No, I didn't. I'll just go up and check."

With Malloy hanging around, checking for Mia's car was the last thing that Recker wanted to do. It was possible that they already knew which car was hers, but in case they didn't, he wasn't going to be the one that led them to it. Recker went up to the pediatric unit floor, immediately recognizing one of the nurses on the floor as he walked by in the hallway.

"Hey, nice to see you again," Recker said with a smile.

"Hey, you too," the nurse replied. "Come for Mia?"

"Yeah. She still here?"

"I think so. I think she was just about to leave. C'mon, I'll walk back with you and get her."

"Thanks so much."

The nurse led Recker past the locked doors and onto the baby unit, immediately paging for Mia to come to the front desk.

"Hey stranger," another nurse said, noticing Recker as she walked by.

"Hello," Recker replied, a little uncomfortable that so many people there seemed to know him by sight, even if they didn't know who he actually was.

"Hey sweetie, this is a nice surprise," Mia said as she approached him, shocked that he was there. She leaned in to give him a kiss, but quickly removed her lips from his as she noticed his face. "What are those bumps and bruises from?"

Mia put her hands on the side of his face as she inspected it more closely. She was still in her full nursing outfit, so she hadn't clocked out yet.

"You almost done? I'll tell you about it once we leave," Recker said.

"Yeah, give me five more minutes."

"OK. You have your phone on you? I need to call David."

Mia looked at him strangely, knowing something weird was going on. She took it out of her pocket and handed it to him, expecting an explanation as she did. By the look on her face, Recker could see that she was waiting for something.

"I'll tell you when we leave. Finish up," Recker said, dialing Jones' number.

Jones picked up after only one ring, assuming that Mia had seen something on the news and was calling in a panic over it.

"Mia, everything's fine," Jones said, hoping to quiet her fears quickly.

"It's me," Recker said.

"Oh, thank heavens. Are you alright?"

"Yeah, I'm at the hospital right now."

"What are you doing there? Are you hurt?"

"No, but I didn't have my car or my phone. Malloy dropped me off. Figured this was the best spot I could go. Can't exactly be walking the streets right now."

"No, understandable," Jones agreed.

"You heard from Chris? Where's he at now?"

"Chris is fine. He's actually here with me at the office right now. We were just going over the events from tonight."

"That's good. I was worried he might still be stuck with the police," Recker said.

"No, he's fine. They bought his story about being a customer."

"Good."

"So if Malloy already dropped you off, I assume you've already met with Vincent?" Jones asked, worried about how his partner would respond to the news.

"Yeah. He told me we're meeting with him tomorrow morning."

"And?"

"And what?"

"Are you going to blow up at me now or later for revealing myself to him?"

"Neither. You did what you felt you had to do. Nothing I haven't done a thousand times before."

"Yes, but after all the times I reprimanded you over having dealings with him to accomplish whatever task we were working on, and then I basically do the same thing, I figured I have a tongue-lashing coming," Jones said, a little mad at himself for allowing him to be found out.

"It's like I've told you before, sometimes you gotta align your-self with the lesser of two evils to get the job done. I'm sure if there was another option, you would've taken it."

"I know. It's just that there were no other options that I could see," Jones said, still trying to explain his decision making, trying to justify it in his own mind more than Recker's. "Chris was out of the picture, there was nothing Mia or I could do, once you were in the hands of the police, there was little I'd be able to do, outside of getting you a good lawyer."

"Just so you know, I wouldn't have given you up."

"Please, Michael, that was the last thing that ever entered my mind. I have no doubts you would rather spend forty years behind bars than give myself or the operation up. No, my only concern was getting you back, as safely as possible. I just had to hope that Vincent was both willing and able to help. Luckily he was."

"Do you know what this meeting's about tomorrow?" Recker asked, curious if he'd told Jones anything.

"No. I assumed it was a more formal introduction meeting, so he could pick my brain a little."

"I don't think it's that. It seemed more serious than something like that. Like something was really bothering him. I couldn't put my finger on it though."

"Well, whatever the case, we won't have to wait long to figure out what it is."

"I guess you wanna pick me up in the morning? My truck's still at the liquor store. At least I hope it is. Hope they didn't impound it."

"Should still be there. It's not registered in your name. If they run it, it'll come back to a valid citizen."

"You're saying I'm not valid?" Recker said, trying to crack a joke. "I'm hurt."

"You know what I meant."

As Recker hung up, Mia came back over with her jacket on, ready to go. As they walked down the hallways, she started peppering him with questions.

"Do you want to tell me what's going on now? Like where's your phone? Where's your car? Why do you have bruises on your face? I can go on and on."

"Something came up," Recker deadpanned.

"You really think that's gonna satisfy me?"

"No. Satisfies me though."

She gave him a look, indicating that she wasn't playing games. He tried not to look back at her, knowing that she was burning a hole through him with her stare. But eventually he gave in, as he usually did with her, since she was the one person he had a soft spot for.

"I take it you haven't seen any news reports tonight?"

"No, it's been a busy night. Why? What happened?" Mia asked, the concern in her voice elevating.

Recker then explained to her what went down at the liquor store. He started by saying why it was so important to stop the gang, letting her know how they killed a couple people on their previous job. He figured that would at least somewhat explain why he stayed as long as he did, even at the risk of being caught by the police. But no matter what he said, he knew she wouldn't like him putting himself in so much jeopardy.

"I thought bringing Chris in was supposed to put you in less danger," Mia said as they exited the hospital.

"Well, Chris being there is probably the only reason I'm still here. I might still be locked in a shootout with those guys. He took out two of them," Recker replied, keeping an eye out for Malloy as they walked through the parking lot.

"So now your face is plastered all over the place? Wonderful."

"Mia, nothing's really changed. I've always been wanted by the police. This doesn't change that."

"You know Vincent's gonna ask for something for this. He didn't just do it because he's got a heart of gold."

"I know. We're already scheduled to meet with him tomorrow."

Mia sighed, not liking anything she was hearing. "Great. Just promise me you won't do something bad in return. Don't just agree to anything he asks just because you feel you owe it to him."

"We'll see what he asks. I promise I won't kill a kid or the

314

mayor or anything," Recker agreed, getting in the driver seat of Mia's car.

As they were driving, Recker could see that she was still steamed. Not that he blamed her. He would've been more surprised if she wasn't. She worried about him. It was part of the deal. But he knew it was better coming from him now instead of her reading or hearing about it later. Satisfied that Malloy wasn't lurking around somewhere, Recker exited the parking lot, though he'd still do his usual zigzag pattern on the way home just to make sure. Even if Malloy was still around, Recker would make sure he'd lose him somewhere along the line. The entire drive home, Mia continued to express her concern over Recker's latest situation. Though she knew it wasn't his fault, and he wasn't being careless, she still couldn't help but worry about his well-being. After a few minutes of silence, Recker actually preferred the alternative. Though he didn't like to see her upset, he'd rather have her talking about what was bothering her instead of letting it sit and stew around inside her. Especially when he knew she was still thinking about it.

"I know you're not just gonna let it go at that," Recker said.

"Mike, I told you I don't wanna be one of those nagging girl-friends. I'm not gonna beat you over the head with the same stuff over and over again. You're obviously capable of doing what you do."

"But?"

"But nothing. There's no but. I just know that no matter what I say, it's not going to make a difference. It won't change anything. You're not going to do anything different, right?" she said with a shrug. "So I'm not gonna keep harping on it."

"OK."

Recker thought the issue was closed, but quickly was reminded otherwise. "I can't get the image out of my mind of you in handcuffs in the back of a police car."

"Wasn't that pleasant."

"And being rammed in broad daylight, sitting in a police car."

"It was actually nighttime," he said, trying to bring some levity to their discussion.

"I mean, what's gonna be next?"

"I'll probably find that out tomorrow."

24

Jones had gone to Recker's apartment a little early before heading to the meeting with Vincent. Mia invited him over, so they could all eat breakfast together. Though she liked it when they all shared some time together, part of it was her devious plan to know what the two partners had in mind for their meeting. She wanted to overhear their thoughts and also interject some of her own if the opportunity presented itself. She was a little disappointed that they didn't discuss nearly as much as she thought and hoped they would. Most of it was just general comments and ideas. Nothing specific.

"I must admit, I am a little nervous," Jones said, finishing his eggs.

"Why?" Recker asked. "You've met him before."

"Yes, but those were quite different circumstances. I was pretending to be someone else. Sometimes that's easier than playing yourself."

"I'm pretty sure he knew who you were the moment he met you. Or at least had an inkling."

"I don't doubt that. Still, a little unnerving to be meeting him officially for the first time. What if he asks personal questions?"

"Easy. Don't answer them."

"He won't be offended?"

"He respects people who stand firm in their beliefs," Recker said. "If you're unsure of anything, just look to me, I'll get you through it."

After Mia cleared away the dishes from the table, she sat back down and rejoined their conversation.

"Will you two please promise not to do anything out of the ordinary?" she said. "I know you'll both feel somewhat indebted to him for helping last night, but please don't compromise your principles out of some pride thing or feeling like you have to repay a debt."

"Well, I certainly don't feel the need to do anything of that nature," Jones said, much to Mia's delight. "But I do feel we owe it to him to see what he has to say."

"I agree," Recker added.

"But I won't be pushed into doing something that I will regret, either."

"That's all I ask," Mia said, feeling better about their meeting.

"What you got Chris working on today?" Recker said, wondering about their protege.

"Nothing yet," Jones replied. "I told him to take the morning off and not come into the office until noon. I said if he really wanted to do something productive, just take a drive around town, continue to get to know the city and the streets. He indicated he'd likely do that."

Once 8:15 hit, Recker and Jones finished up what they were doing and left for their rendezvous. Mia worked at noon, and probably wouldn't be home until midnight again, but expected a text or a voicemail letting her know how everything went. She was extremely worried about them agreeing to something they didn't want to do to repay Vincent for helping them out of a tight spot, caving into any pressure that he exuded.

They arrived at the diner a little before nine, but noticed the usual bodyguard standing outside the door, letting them know that Vincent was already waiting inside. Recker placed both of his guns in the glove compartment before getting out of the car. They began walking toward the front door of the restaurant, the guard spotting them as they approached. The guard made a face and tilted his head, putting his hand out toward Recker, both of whom knew the drill.

Recker opened his coat to indicate he was clean. "Didn't bother today."

The guard smiled, then turned his attention toward Jones. "Your turn. Need your iron."

"I beg your pardon," Jones said, insulted that the man thought he was carrying a weapon.

"He doesn't carry," Recker said.

"Still need to check," the guard said, shaking the professor up and down.

Seeing that they were both clean, the guard nodded for them to go inside.

"Well that was a little humiliating," Jones said.

"You get used to it," Recker replied.

As usual, Malloy was there inside the door to greet the pair.

"Nice to see... both of you," he said with a grin.

"I know the way," Recker said, putting his arm out to indicate that he didn't need to be walked to the table.

Jones followed Recker to find Vincent's table, who was sitting in the same spot he always was. Vincent was looking over a menu as his two visitors approached and sat down across from him. The waiter came over as soon as all the men were situated.

"Join me for breakfast?" Vincent said.

"We've already eaten," Recker said.

"Suit yourself. Pancakes for me," he said. "French toast. Orange juice. Bring an orange juice for everyone."

"Yes, sir," the waiter replied.

"David, nice to see you," Vincent said with a smile. "Much easier and more pleasant circumstances than the first time we met. Thank you for upholding your end of the bargain by coming here."

"I can't honestly say that I'm pleased, but a deal is a deal," Jones said.

"So I've always suspected that Mike had a man behind the scenes, getting him the information he needed. I can now safely assume that that's always been you."

"It has."

"So how do you do the things that you do? How do you anticipate where to be? How does that happen?"

"I'm afraid that the secrets of our operation must remain so. I'm very leery of details getting out," Jones said with a shake of his head.

"I understand."

"Should we get down to the nitty gritty?" Recker said, eschewing the small talk that he hated engaging in. "Though I know getting to meet the brains behind the operation was enticing, I'm sure that's not the only reason you wanted us here."

"Indeed not. As I mentioned to you last night, a very grave situation is encompassing me and my operation right now," Vincent said, a serious tone encompassing his face. "One that I'm at a loss for."

In all the dealings that Recker had with Vincent up to this point, he'd never seen him with a more serious expression. Not with Jeremiah, not with the Italians, and not with any of the cases Recker needed assistance on. This was on another level. After a brief pause, Vincent continued with his problem.

"Approximately two weeks ago, an attempt was made on my life," Vincent said, to the stunned ears of both Recker and Jones.

"Get the guy?" Recker said.

"No. Another attempt was made four days ago. Clearly both attempts failed or else I wouldn't be sitting here. It's obviously of great concern to me."

"When you say attempts were made, what exactly are we talking about? Guns, bombs, what?"

"In both cases it was a gun. The first time was from a rooftop. It narrowly missed me and hit one of my guards standing next to me. I had moved just in time. The second time was from a window across the street. Tried to pick me off just as I had gotten into my car. The bullet shattered one of the windows, but luckily missed any human targets."

"Know who's behind it?"

"We do not. That's one of the things that has me so concerned. Normally, things like this are to be expected from time to time. It wouldn't be the first time. But, I usually know where my enemies are coming from. I can prepare. Anticipate. This is a situation where I cannot do that."

"You have no idea whatsoever?" Jones interjected.

"I've used all the resources at my disposal. Contacts, sources, employees, police, everything has turned up dry. We don't have a single lead to go on."

"And you have no enemies that you're aware of?" Recker said.

"Well, we both know men of my power will attract those who wish to gain what I have. Overthrow me," Vincent said with a shrug. "But whoever it is, is operating completely in the shadows to this point. Nobody seems to have any answers as to their identity."

"Could be remnants of Jeremiah's gang. Or maybe even one of Bellomi's former employees."

"Naturally that's something we thought of as well. It's certainly plausible, and though there are some of both who are still roaming around, we haven't established a connection."

"I would lay odds that it's one of them."

Vincent threw his hands up off the table, neither agreeing nor disagreeing with Recker's statement. He just didn't know at this point.

"So what is it that you would like us to do?" Jones said, assuming there was a proposition coming.

"I've long been an admirer of your operation. And though I don't understand or comprehend much of it, I believe there are things that you can do that I can't."

"And you would like us to look into it for you?"

"I have nowhere else to turn at this point," Vincent said, sounding frustrated. "Though I'll obviously keep looking on my own, I'm not so powerful or oblivious that I can't admit that I could use some help."

"Did you check for any evidence left behind at either scene?" Recker asked.

"We did. There was nothing left at either location, however."

"If we agree to this search, what happens if we locate the person or persons behind it?" Jones said.

"All I ask for is the identity of whoever's behind this. Once that is learned, turn the information over to me and I will take care of the rest."

"And is it expected that we drop everything else we're doing to prioritize this for you?"

"Well, I'm a reasonable man, I know you gentlemen have other things going on. But if you could put a rush on it, I would surely appreciate it."

Jones looked at Recker, wondering what his take on the proposition was. But judging by the non-expressive look on his face, he didn't appear to have one. Recker's motto from the very first day he met Jones was that he wouldn't help criminals. He wouldn't save them, and he wouldn't stand in someone's way if they were in danger. Vincent, however, was a special and unusual case. Though he was a criminal, there was a certain degree of respect between him and Recker. Plus, Vincent had helped them numerous times before, not the least of which was the previous night.

"Do we have a deal?" Vincent asked, hopeful of their reply.

"We do," Recker said, not bothering to confer with Jones.

"Excellent. Thank you both."

"No need," Jones said, not upset about Recker agreeing to the deal. In fact, he was also leaning on agreeing to it. "After all, you did help us out of a sticky situation last night. I guess we owed you one."

Vincent waved his hand at him. "Ahh, I'm not keeping score. In fact, if you decided not to help in this instance, I'd never bring up what happened last night again."

"Well, we're still very thankful."

Vincent was being truthful when he said he wasn't keeping a tally on how many times they'd helped each other. And while he knew he'd helped Recker out more than the reverse, he never had any plans on using that against him, or as some sort of blackmail. At least not unless it was a situation that was beyond massive in scope. And he couldn't envision that day ever coming. Still, though, he took the opportunity to needle Recker a little.

"Though I do believe I've got the upper hand in favors," Vincent said in jest.

Recker knew his host was just teasing him, but wasn't about to back down to him either. "Maybe so. But I do believe the couple times I helped you were larger in scale than your side with me. I mean, two major mob bosses crippled allowing you to take over, that should have some more weight put behind it."

Vincent laughed, thinking it was probably true. "That's a fair point. Most likely accurate. Quality over quantity, is that how we're putting it?"

Recker didn't reply, instead giving a shrug. Vincent seemed amused by the exchange, while Jones didn't appear to be particularly enthused about the friendly banter.

"So is there anything you need from me to enact what you have to do on your end?" Vincent asked.

"All we need are the exact locations where these incidents took place," Jones told him.

Vincent immediately took out a pen and grabbed a napkin off the table. He wrote down the addresses of the two locations and also scribbled down some rough drawings of the buildings in the area. Once he was finished, he slid it across the table. Jones picked it up and looked at it, and though he recognized the streets, he wasn't overly familiar with it.

"Once we get a handle on what we're dealing with, one of us will contact you in the next few days," Jones said.

"I'll await your call," Vincent said

Though Recker and Jones were quick to leave, wanting to get started on the case right away, Vincent asked them to wait around until he finished breakfast. He wanted to talk about his problem in more detail. Once he finally finished, the three men got up at the same time and walked out of the diner, Malloy closely following. As they exited, the signal was given for Vincent's car to be brought up to the entrance. The driver got out and opened the back door for his boss as Vincent was giving Recker some last words before leaving. Jones was standing beside his partner as they conversed. A white car screeched into the parking lot, and as soon as Recker looked over at it, instantly recognized that it was trouble. As the white car sped toward the diner, Recker pushed Jones down on the ground to make sure he was out of the line of fire. He then quickly grabbed Vincent by his shirt collar and pulled him down behind the car. Just as they were getting down, gunfire started coming from the car. Malloy and the guard at the door returned fire as the car turned around and exited the parking lot.

Before letting either Jones or Vincent up, Recker took a peek over the hood of the car to make sure the danger was gone. Once he saw it was, he grabbed Jones by the back of his arms and helped him to his feet. As he was checking on his friend, Malloy had gotten his boss back to his feet as well.

"You all right?" Recker asked.

"I'm fine. Thank you," Jones said, brushing himself off.

"And you?" Recker said, turning his attention to Vincent.

"I'm good," Vincent said. "Though I'll be much better when you call and tell me you've figured out who's behind this. Do that and I give you my word that you will always have an ally in me, regardless of whether it suits my interests or not."

Recker nodded, appreciating the gesture. "We'll find him."

They then noticed that they did not escape unscathed. The driver of Vincent's vehicle had unfortunately been hit with one of the stray bullets and was on the ground holding his stomach. Recker and Malloy both went over to him to gauge the damage. Vincent stood there, looking on with interest.

"What's his prognosis?" Vincent asked.

"If he gets to a hospital soon, I think he'll live," Recker said.

Malloy looked at his boss, who simply gave him a nod, letting him know to call for an ambulance without even saying a word. Vincent then turned to his other employee, the man who always guarded the door for him.

"You stay with him until he reaches the hospital. Keep me updated on his progress," Vincent said.

"You got it, boss."

Vincent then turned to Recker to give him a few last words. "Thank you for dragging me down. I was a little slow in reacting."

Recker shrugged it off, not needing any thanks. "You'll be hearing from us soon."

"I look forward to it."

As Malloy passed Recker on the way to the car, he gave him a tap on the shoulder. A mutual respect had developed between the two over the years, though neither had trusted the other completely. But now, with this latest development, it seemed to bond them together. Though Vincent had always trusted Recker enough to let him do his own thing, Malloy had always assumed that at one point, he would have to take the Silencer out. It was nothing personal, he just figured he'd step on their toes eventually, and he'd have to be eliminated. Since he was Vincent's right hand, and most trusted soldier, the duty to eliminate Recker would fall upon him. Seeing Recker guard Vincent, and potentially save his life, helped Malloy to see that for the first time, they weren't really on opposite sides.

With their business concluded, Recker and Jones moved along. They got in Recker's truck and went back to the office, immediately starting on Vincent's problem. They were soon joined by Haley, who got in at noon as he was directed.

"Enjoy your driving?" Recker asked.

"Every little bit helps," Haley said. "Know the city better today than I did yesterday. Glad to see you're up and around after last night. Thought I might not see you again."

Recker let out a laugh. "You weren't the only one."

"I'm not ready to go solo yet."

"It should serve as a lesson to all of us how quickly things can go wrong out there," Jones said. "And perhaps should be a lesson that sometimes we need to change tactics."

"Implying that I stayed too long?" Recker asked, assuming he was referring to him.

"I'm not assigning blame, Michael."

"I didn't say you were. But you think I stayed too long?"

"Given the circumstances, yes. Yes, I do."

"Well how else do you think I should've handled it?" Recker calmly asked. If it was someone other than Jones asking, he might have taken offense to how he handled the situation. But seeing as how it was him, and Recker knew there was no malice in his words, he didn't get upset over being questioned.

Jones threw one of his hands up and shrugged, not sure he had a good answer. "I don't know. What I do know, is that if we overstay our welcome, things like last night will become more commonplace. And we will not always be able to get out of them."

"Should I just leave innocent people in danger to save my own skin?"

"The more ideal scenario might be to not let the situation get to the point it was. Maybe speed things along."

"Maybe we should've taken them out as they were walking through the door," Haley said, offering his own opinion, though he didn't know how welcome it would be.

"Yeah, but, if we didn't take them all out, we would risk having to deal with them again at some point," Recker replied.

"Wouldn't that be preferable than getting led out in handcuffs?" Jones asked.

The three men continued having a spirited discussion, each of them throwing out a few ideas and having them discussed and argued. But there was no bitterness or acrimony in their words. They were only interested in figuring out a better way to handle situations like that in the future, so they wouldn't have to take the chance on someone like Vincent having to bail them out. Because they knew that that would not always be available. It was also something they knew they wouldn't have to deal with often. Recker and Jones had been in business several years without ever getting into a situation like that before, even though there were some close calls at times. Maybe it was just luck that it never happened, or maybe it was because of their careful planning and great execution, but whatever the reason, they had to intensely scrutinize the liquor store event to make sure that it did not happen again.

They discussed the situation from the previous night for a

good hour or so, not really coming to a firm conclusion in any capacity. The general feeling after they exhausted all the possibilities was that Recker and Haley probably shouldn't have stayed as long as they did. Whether they took them out quicker, or waited outside, whatever it was, they couldn't engage in a long shootout or get into a hostage situation that would delay their escape. If it was a private residence, or business, maybe they could get away with it. But not in a liquor store in a shopping center that police could get to quickly. Once they had that squared away to everyone's satisfaction, Haley asked how their morning meeting went. Recker and Jones took turns in telling him how everything went down.

"Too bad I wasn't there to help. Maybe I could've got the guy."

"Went too fast," Recker said by way of explanation. "Nothing you would've been able to do. Not unless you were across the lot or something."

As Recker and Haley kept talking about the meeting, along with the attempted murder after it, Jones was already energetically working on leads. He pulled up camera feeds in the area and started combing through them, though he suspected it would be a waste of time and communicated as such to the team. Recker, being with Jones as long as he was, didn't need any more of an explanation. Haley, though, wasn't sure what the issue was.

"Why the negativity?" Haley asked. "Maybe we can get a license plate or something."

Recker smiled, thinking that was the logical conclusion. He let Jones do the explaining though.

"The reason it is likely a waste of time isn't that we won't find anything. There's a decent chance we will," Jones said.

"Then what's the issue? I don't get it."

"Well, Vincent already has men, or women, inside the police department, on his payroll. It stands to reason that he's already had them check nearby cameras."

"Sounds logical." Haley nodded.

"So if that's the case, and assuming it is, it's likely they've already run down a license plate if it was available."

"So it's probably a dead end."

"Presumably. We'll do our due diligence anyway, of course."

"So then what?"

"We dig deeper," Jones said.

"Well how much deeper can you go?"

"We're about to find out."

After letting their conversation finish, Recker had his own set of questions. Questions that may not be as easy for Jones to answer.

"Why is this the first time we're hearing about this?" Recker asked.

Jones stopped typing and turned to look at his friend, not sure he was getting his meaning. "What do you mean?"

"Well there've been two attempts made at Vincent's life and we've got nothing on it. Haven't heard rumors, nothing came through on the computer, nothing at all. Don't you think that's kind of strange?"

"I suppose so."

"I mean, why didn't we get wind of this?"

"If you're asking whether there's some kind of system glitch on our computers, then the answer would be no," Jones said.

"Sure about that?"

"I am very vigilant in making sure the computers and software are working appropriately and the way they should be."

"So there's no chance of it missing something like this?"

Jones turned away for a second, thinking intently about the question.

"When we started this, I told you I wouldn't help people who had a heavy criminal background," Recker said, remembering their initial conversations. "Did you program it in a way where any leads involving them would get wiped out or nestled away or something?"

"No. They still come in. If they do, and it turns out that the tip is something that involves such a person, I file it away and don't even mention it to you. But it still comes in."

Recker made a grimace, disappointed by the news. He hoped that it would be an easy enough way to check. All Jones would have to do is reset the parameters of the software program and they could work backward. But with Jones dousing Recker's hopes, they'd have to come up with another way.

"The more likely scenario is that we're working with one, possibly two suspects," Jones said, sharing his thoughts.

"And what makes you think that?" Recker said.

"Because I would assume that if it was a larger group, the software would have picked something up. Which leads me to believe that it's one or two people."

"So they don't need to text, call, or email to share their ideas or plans."

"Is there a way that it could be a larger group and the system's just not picking it up?" Haley asked, still not sure of everything the system was capable of catching.

"Of course. But that would mean that they're not using any of the usual code names or phrases that the system flags as a potential concern. And that would be very troubling."

"How many words exactly does the system pick up?"

"There are thousands of words and variations that the system looks for. Any type of threatening word or phrase that you can think of, the system will pick up. And it checks emails, voicemails, text messages."

"Maybe they're working old school," Recker said as a joke. "Maybe they're passing notes to each other in class."

25

With having the exact dates and times of the attempted murders of Vincent, it gave Jones a specific starting point to begin his search. His first move was to search through any area cameras, including street and traffic cams, as well as private security cameras that he could hack into. Since the computer program didn't have to comb through weeks and weeks of footage, the results came back quickly. It only took about two hours to get what they needed. Recker and Haley sat down next to Jones as they started looking through the pictures. Jones also began printing them out, so they could look at them more closely.

"You can make out the license plate on that one," Recker said, pointing at one of the pictures on the monitor.

Jones zoomed in on the photo, bringing the license plate number into full view as the letters and numbers grew bigger. He then brought up another screen, typing the number into it, quickly getting back a host of information.

"Well, the license plate number does not belong to that car, for one," Jones said, expecting that to be the case.

"Figures," Recker sighed. "Knew it wouldn't be that easy."

"Stolen?" Haley asked.

"The car in question looks like a Nissan Altima. That plate belongs to a 2013 Hyundai Elantra," Jones replied.

"What next?" Haley said, hoping there was more they could do.

"Now, we see if a camera happened to get a shot of any of the occupants," Jones said.

Jones continued his work, and based upon the locations of the photos they already had of the car, tried to project the path that it traveled. A few more pictures popped up from traffic cameras, but they didn't give them any more information. None of them gave a clear view inside the car. Jones pulled up a few camera feeds from private businesses. After another couple hours of combing through footage, they didn't appear to be any closer to finding their mysterious hit man. Jones was going to keep looking, but Recker and Haley weren't doing much good there. Recker figured they would be better served if they hit the streets to try to find some information.

"Even if we don't get any hits on the cameras that are worth anything, it's still possible we could get something on the email or text software, right?" Haley asked.

Jones stopped typing and turned toward him to answer the question. "It's not likely. Considering they've tried two hits already and we haven't picked up on anything I'd say the chances of us getting something at this point is a remote possibility."

"But still possible," Recker said. "I mean, they don't know we track this stuff. Just because they haven't done it yet, doesn't mean they won't."

"Yes, well, hold on to that thought."

"Well, you keep on with what you're doing, and we'll see what else we can learn."

"How do you propose to do that?" Jones asked, knowing that Vincent most likely already asked everyone that they would.

"Start with the first option as always."

Recker briefly explained to Haley their relationship with Tyrell and the history that they had with him. He then called him on the phone, hoping that he had some nugget of intelligence that he could share with them.

"Tyrell, hoping you can help me with something," Recker said.

"Depends on what you need."

"I don't know if you've heard, but Vincent's had a couple attempts on his life thwarted recently."

"Yeah, I know all about that. Vincent's been trying to pump me for answers. He called me at least five times the last couple weeks to see what I knew."

"Which is what?"

"I'll tell you what I told him," Tyrell said. "I don't know nothin'."

"You haven't heard anything?"

"Haven't heard rumblings, nobody bragging, nobody threatening to do anything. It's almost like he's getting hit by ghosts."

"Well we know that's not the case. Just off hand, do you know how many men from Jeremiah or Bellomi's former crews are still hanging around?"

"Why? You think one of them might be behind it?"

"It's a thought, isn't it?"

"Yeah. Well most of Bellomi's crew scattered after they got hit. A few stuck around and tried to start brand new again, but they just didn't have the same stones that their boss did. They didn't last too long. Most got picked up by the police, some got killed, but there might only be a handful left. And I don't think they harbor much animosity toward Vincent at this point. I don't think I'm tellin' you anything new, you know all that."

"And Jeremiah's crew?"

"That might be another story. Some of them mo-fo's are still hanging around, and they ain't too pleased about what happened to their boss."

"Stands to reason," Recker said.

"Yeah, well, they ain't too crazy about you either," Tyrell said with a laugh.

"Why? They know I'm the one that did it?"

"They know it was Vincent's doing. He was the one behind it. They don't really care who it was that pulled the final trigger. They know the man that ordered it."

"Then what's the issue with me?"

Tyrell laughed again, thinking some of the beatings he'd taken had taken a toll on his mental capabilities. "You, uh, forget about the two or three places that you took out before Jeremiah got offed?"

Recker thought for only a second, remembering the details vividly. "Oh. Yeah. I do recall something about that."

"Yeah, well, you put about, what, ten or twelve additional bodies in the ground?"

"Something like that," Recker replied, not remembering the final tally.

"And let me tell you, man, everyone knows that was you. Everybody," Tyrell said, his voice rising for emphasis.

"So in your grand opinion, is this the work of Jeremiah's crew, coming back for revenge? Or is it someone new in town looking to take some power for himself?"

"Gotta be one of Jeremiah's boys. At least to me. I got a hard time believing someone new could come in and do this without leaving some type of trace, know what I mean?"

"Yeah, that's what I figured too."

"You mean you and the prof can't figure this out yet? He can't work his magic on the laptop?" Tyrell sarcastically asked.

"Not so far."

"Wow. Never thought I'd see the day when you two were completely stumped like this."

"It's happened before."

"Oh, by the way, there was something else I wanted to talk to you about."

"Such as?"

"You know I opened that 529 account for my brother, Darnell, like you told me to."

"Good move."

"Yeah, well, I put about two thousand in there to start it out with."

"Strong start."

"That's the crazy part. I put that in there about six months ago, right?"

"Yeah."

"Well, I just checked yesterday and guess what? You know how much is in there?"

"Haven't the foggiest idea," Recker said, playing dumb.

"There was fifty thousand dollars in there, man. Fifty thousand. Five-O," Tyrell said, almost in disbelief of the amount.

"Wow. Looks like you made a good investment."

"Yeah, I don't think that was it."

"Hmm. Guess you got one of those mysterious benefactors," Recker said. "They seem generous. Hope you don't do anything to piss them off."

"Yeah, well, between you, me, and the wall I'm staring at right now, we all know who that person is."

"Now, now, Tyrell, don't snap to quick judgments that may not be correct."

"Are you gonna try to tell me it wasn't you?"

"Well, it may or may not be just me... or other people."

"Prof too?"

"I'll have to plead the fifth on the rest of this conversation," Recker said, not wanting to admit to his good deed.

"I hear ya on that. But seriously, I just wanted to tell you and the prof thanks," Tyrell said, starting to choke up on his words. Not being used to people offering such generous gifts, he usually had trouble articulating how thankful he was when it happened. But he didn't have to. Recker knew. So did Jones. And they knew the money was going to good use in Darnell's education. There was a kid with a good head on his shoulders. Recker and Jones periodically checked in on Darnell from a distance, making sure his grades were still good, making sure he was staying out of trouble, and just touching base with Tyrell about him. For Recker and Jones, money was not an issue. They had more than they knew what to do with and they certainly didn't mind spreading it around, especially when they were invested in the cause.

"Now that we're done with that, any ideas on which of Jeremiah's men might be behind this? A name? Anything?"

Tyrell sighed, trying desperately to think of a name. Unfortunately, he couldn't come up with one. None of Jeremiah's men, in his opinion, could've conducted such a stealthy operation on their own. Maybe with Jeremiah's guidance they could have, but not by themselves, not without him steering their direction. "No, I can't think of anyone offhand."

"And you haven't heard of a new player in town?"

"No."

"Well, I would think that if it was someone new, they would've announced their presence by now," Recker said.

"Maybe they figured Vincent's body would do the announcing for them."

"Yeah, maybe."

"I'll do you a solid though and keep my ear to the ground for you," Tyrell said. "If I pick up on anything I'll let you know."

"Appreciate it."

As Recker was talking, Jones kept working away, though he kept one ear somewhat listening to the conversation in the background.

"Judging by your side of it, I take it Tyrell wasn't much help," Jones said.

"No. Vincent already asked him anyway."

"Well we kind of figured that, didn't we? After all, Vincent already has him on the payroll, even if it's on a part time, or as needed basis. And considering Tyrell's closeness to Jeremiah as well, not to mention how connected he is on the streets, it's no surprise that he would have already reached out to him."

"The software that picks out these phrases, there's an area radius that it reaches, right?" Haley asked. "I mean, it's not picking up incidents in California or anything, right?"

"Yes, why?" Jones said.

"What if we expand the radius? Is it possible to do a search of the rest of the country and see if it can spot phrases that would indicate an outside person?"

Jones looked perplexed for a few seconds, not exactly sure what Haley was asking. After a little more thought, he got the gist of it. "If you're suggesting that I extend the parameters to include other parts of the country to see if we can find someone, say in San Jose, who's come into town for the purpose of eliminating Vincent, then yes, that is something I can do."

"How long would something like that take?"

Jones bulged his eyes out and blew his lips together, signaling it would be a tall task. "Something of that magnitude would take quite a while. Weeks at the earliest. But that is at a breakneck speed with everything falling our way. I suspect that it would probably take months to go through that amount of information. You're talking about the entire country instead of one city and millions upon millions of data that needs to be broken down. When I was at the NSA, the process could be streamlined much more quickly. But that's with dozens of analysts working on it nonstop. Not one person."

"What if you whittled it down?" Recker asked, thinking they could cut the process down. "Make it faster."

"In what way?"

"Only include phrases that would indicate Philadelphia. Airport, landmarks, the city itself, things like that."

"Well that would certainly speed things up a bit, but you're also taking the risk that they actually mentioned one of the things you're talking about. There's no guarantee they talked in any of those specifics."

"How about in subsequent messages? What if they mention killing in a text, then mention the airport in another?"

"Mike, that all can be done, and the system will pick those things up. But again, it takes time. The system analyzes millions of bits of data. Once it flags something, then it will have to be checked against whether the same user is a threat, whether that user actually has evil intentions, whether that user has said similar things, who they're talking to, and which means of communication they're using. It all can be done. But it will take time. Time that I'm not sure Vincent has. Or has the patience for."

"So what you're basically telling me is that we need to find someone out there on the street who knows what's going on," Recker said.

"It certainly would be helpful."

Recker wasn't really satisfied with the answer, but he accepted it for what it was. Jones would keep doing what he did best, but it was likely he wouldn't have an answer any time soon. And that was assuming that the shooter was from out of town, which was no guarantee. Jones could have been wasting his time in even looking in that direction. Recker took a step back and started thinking of other alternatives. He wasn't going to just sit there and wait for the system to come up with a match. Him and Haley needed to hit the street and see what they could shake loose. Somebody had to know something. It was just finding the person that did. After a few minutes of deep thinking, he thought he might have come up with something. At least something to start with.

"Hmm," Recker said, looking at Haley.

"What?" Haley replied, thinking he might have done something.

Recker shook his head. "Nothing. Just thinking."

"Would you like to share with the rest of us?" Jones asked, hurriedly typing away at his keyboard.

"Do we still have the list somewhere that Tyrell gave us a while back of Jeremiah's hot spots?"

The question made Jones stop typing as he turned and looked at his partner, unsure of his exact plans, though getting a general idea. "Why?"

"We need information. Maybe someone there has it. Simple as that."

"Assuming that one of Jeremiah's former soldiers is behind this. And assuming that those locations are still in business."

Recker shrugged. "Not really making any assumptions. Just a place to begin."

"But we don't know they're actually involved."

"Don't know they're not either. We know that some of Jeremiah's men are still out there. That's a fact. And we know that they're dangerous. Not on Jeremiah's level, but anyone who carries a gun has to be respected in some form."

"OK. I agree with all that so far."

"So it stands to reason that maybe they know what's going on. If they're behind it, maybe one of them let's something slip. Or, maybe they'll steer us in the right direction," Recker said.

"Considering what you've done to several of their locations

already, I believe the only place they'll steer you is over a bridge. A very high one."

"With your history, what makes you think they would tell you anything?"

"Probably not deliberately. But when the emotions start to get high, things sometimes come out that were not intended."

Jones looked at Recker for a few moments without responding, not liking his choice of words. It sounded to him like his partner was considering provoking a conflict in order to get a calculated response.

"You're not thinking about hitting one of these spots with guns blazing, are you?"

"No, not with guns blazing," Recker said with a laugh. "Maybe just on high alert though."

"Mike, we have other things going on right now. Getting into a war with the remnants of Jeremiah's gang doesn't exactly sound like the prudent thing to do at the moment."

"I don't have any intention of starting a war. Just want some information. But usually people whose emotions are running high or angry have a tendency to talk without thinking. That's what we need right now. People who say something without realizing what they're talking about."

"Again, you think they're going to say something useful to you?"

"Well, I have a way of drawing things out of people."

"Yes, usually their lifeline."

"No, well, yeah, but not in this case. If I can get them angry, they might say a thing or two we can use to our advantage."

"And just how do you plan on doing that?" Jones asked, still not on board with the idea.

"Just by showing up. People have a tendency to talk when I'm around. Usually out of fear, sometimes out of anger."

"I think you have officially lost your mind."

"Maybe. But if I show up at their door, they're gonna know something's up. If they don't wanna join their boss, they'll give me something."

"A gun in the ribs most likely."

"Don't be such a worrywart. It'll work. Usually when people see me, they either start to get worried or mad. Either should work for this."

26

After only a few minutes of searching, Jones found the list of Jeremiah's meeting spots in one of the desk drawers. He handed the paper over to Recker, who looked it over for a few moments.

"Where do you plan to start first?" Jones said.

"At the top," Recker replied. He then turned toward Haley to see if the newest member of the team wanted to join him in the festivities. "Feel like having some fun?"

"It'd be my pleasure," Haley said with a smile.

"Just remember to check in," Jones said, hoping that they wouldn't run into too much trouble.

"Would it be faster and easier if we split up? Each take a building?"

"Faster maybe," Jones replied. "Not easier. If you two are going to do this, I prefer you stick together. These aren't run-of-the-mill criminals we're dealing with. Even without Jeremiah's leadership, they're still dangerous. And likely heavily armed."

"David's right," Recker said.

"But after we hit the first couple, they're going to know we're coming," Haley said. "And they'll either scatter or they'll bunker down and be waiting for us. Might walk into something."

"Possible. But I'd rather hit them hard in the beginning and take our chances later. Strength in numbers and all that."

Haley nodded, OK with the plan no matter which direction they went. "Works for me."

Haley was an easy-going type of guy. He wasn't the kind of person who vigorously argued over much. He didn't have a problem voicing his opinion, or offering a different option, but once a decision on something was made, he usually went along with it without a problem. Unless he was extremely opposed to something, for the most part he just fell in line, and he did so gladly.

Recker and his partner left the office right away, hopeful that they would find some useful information somewhere along the way. In Recker's previous path of destruction when he was looking for Jeremiah, he'd only taken out three of his locations. There were still another seven on the list. Though it was possible that they no longer were doing business in any of them, Recker had a hunch that the places were still in operation. They knew some of Jeremiah's men were still kicking around so it seemed likely that they were staying in the locations that they knew so well. Plus, since Recker wasn't there the first time around, they had no reason to believe the addresses had been compromised.

Since they were going to the same place, Recker and Haley drove together. Recker thought about going separately, just in case they needed to split up for anything, or if they had to track down different leads if they learned anything after they hit Jeremiah's house, but he figured it was better if they just stayed together for the moment. As they were driving to the first location, an address in the western part of the city, Haley wondered what they were walking into. He wasn't around for their previous dealings with

Jeremiah and his crew and was curious about the type of people they were dealing with.

"So what are we likely walking into?"

"What do you mean?" Recker said.

"Well I wasn't here for all the fun you had with these guys before. I've only heard you and David talking about them. I haven't met any of them yet. What kind of people are they?"

"Dangerous," Recker said bluntly.

"I kind of figured that."

"They're of the talk less and shoot more variety."

"Oh good," Haley said, rolling his eyes.

"If we actually see someone and get to talk to them, keep your guard up at all times. Don't get complacent, even for a second. Don't trust any of them."

"Good to know. How many you figure are there?"

"Hard to say. Under Jeremiah, there seemed to be a different crew stationed at each location. I think usually between four and six people were there doing their thing," Recker said, remembering from his previous encounters. "Who knows if that's still accurate with Jeremiah gone."

"You think they have a new leader or you think they're all just scattered about, doing their own thing?"

Recker thought about it for a minute, not sure he had a good answer. "I dunno. Could be either I suppose. I guess it depends on whether the next highest in command had enough respect to get everyone else in line. Haven't heard much out of the gang since Jeremiah's death, and Vincent hasn't seemed very concerned with them, so maybe they have no leadership. I guess we'll find out soon enough."

Ten minutes away from their target location, Jones texted them some of the information he pulled up on the address. It was a row home in a rougher neighborhood, the owner of which he could not establish. Though there was a name of an owner listed, he couldn't find any additional information on the man. He assumed it was a fake identity. Jones tried to find out if the house was currently in use for anything, though he couldn't find anything that definitively proved whether it was or wasn't. They just couldn't tell if they were walking into anything or not. It could be a hot zone, or it could be completely abandoned.

As per his usual custom of not directly parking in front of where he was going, Recker parked down the street. Before getting out of the car, he and his partner put the com devices in their ears. In most cases, Recker would've preferred that they split up, with him taking the front while Haley covered the rear of the building. But the house was in the middle of a block with another house directly in back of it. Considering the neighborhood that they were in, Recker didn't want to take the chance of Haley getting in trouble. Especially if he was hopping fences, walking through other people's properties, and hanging out in their backyards. He didn't want him taking a stray bullet from a gun-happy home-owner who mistook him as an unscrupulous character. As they walked down the street, they kept their eyes peeled at their surroundings, while also periodically looking at the house to detect any movement coming in or around it. As they got closer, they could see most of the windows were boarded up with pieces of plywood. There was only one window on each of the second and third floors that were open.

There was a metal fence and gate at the end of the sidewalk that led up to the house. Recker stood on the opposite side of it for about thirty seconds, just staring at the house as he analyzed it before they approached. Sometimes before he got into a situation, he would get a feel for it first, like he would get a sense that something bad was inside. There'd be a feeling of danger. He wasn't getting that in this instance. It was just like a blank space. He wasn't getting any vibes at all. Haley hadn't been involved in this operation long enough to really get that same sense of things.

Even though he was an experienced operator in the CIA, it was still a new type of game for him.

"What do you think?" Haley said, not taking his eyes off the house.

"I don't know. I'm not getting anything right now."

"What do you wanna do?"

Recker made an agonizing face as he contemplated. "Move forward I guess."

Recker unlocked the gate from its latch as the two of them entered the property. Neither had their gun out yet, as they didn't want to give the impression that they were there for a battle if someone was watching. They both had their hands on the grip of their gun, though, just in case they had to react quickly. Their eyes were glued to the front door of the house, as well as the two opened windows, making sure that they weren't in the crosshairs of a shooter. They didn't notice a thing. Everything seemed quiet. But Recker also knew that sometimes meant the worst was about to happen.

As they stepped onto the porch, Recker and Haley looked at each other, both waiting for the other shoe to drop. They stopped and listened, hoping to hear a commotion on the inside, though all they heard was silence. Recker motioned for Haley to stand on the other side of the door. He was about to knock and didn't want Haley catching a gut-full of lead if the people on the other side of the door decided to open fire instead of answering. Considering nobody had come out to greet them yet, it was a distinct possibility. After Haley was in place, he finally removed his gun and readied himself to use it. Recker then stood on the other side of the door and huffed before knocking. He knocked loudly and made sure he was out of the line of fire as he awaited a response. A few seconds went by and Recker tried again. Still nothing. As Recker looked at Haley, he raised his eyebrows and shrugged, assuming that nobody was home. Trying to remain as silent as possible, Haley gave some hand signals, wondering if they should leave the premises. Recker returned the signals with a few of his own, pointing at the door, indicating that they should breach it. He then got out his weapon, which was a language that they all understood. Haley nodded in approval, waiting for Recker to take the next step.

Recker took a few steps back, then raised his leg and took a kick at the door. His first try at breaking it open was unsuccessful. He now hoped that the place was empty, because if it wasn't, anybody on the inside who didn't know he was there... well, they did now that they heard the door being kicked in. On his second try, Recker succeeded in kicking the door open. Recker, followed closely by Haley, rushed through the front door with their guns drawn, ready to fire. Silence still filled the air.

Recker motioned to Haley to check the upstairs while he checked the first floor. Though they suspected they were alone, they still kept alert in case they were being set up. Recker swept through the first floor, not finding anyone or anything out of the ordinary. After a few minutes, Haley came stomping down the stairs, also coming up empty. They met back up in the living room, Haley wondering what their next step was. Recker was casually walking around, trying to find anything that would be of interest to them. A piece of paper, a picture, anything at all.

"What are you looking for?" Haley asked.

"I dunno. Anything that would give us more than we got now."

The entire home was virtually empty. There were a few remaining pieces of furniture, but it didn't appear that anyone had been there for some time. The refrigerator was empty; the cupboards were bare, there were no clothes in any closets, nothing that appeared anyone was living there.

"Doesn't seem like anyone's been here for a while," Haley said.

"Yeah. I don't even think it's been used for business purposes either."

"What makes you think so?"

"A lot of dust."

"Maybe they forgot to bring the maid in."

"I don't see a table, chairs, nothing that would indicate some-body's been here," Recker said. "Even if you're just stopping here once in a while for business, you still gotta sit I would think. Unless they're doing it Indian style."

"What now? Next stop on the list?"

"Yeah. We'll send David a message and let him know we came up empty here."

They did as Recker suggested and sent Jones a text to let him know what they found on the first stop of their tour. The next stop was another house. Jones had already run the information on it, anticipating that the first stop was going to return no tangible results. Much like the previous house, Jones couldn't pull up the legit owner of the house, figuring it was also a fictitious name. When Recker and Haley got there, it proved to be a similar situa-tion to the one they just left. Right down to the dust. It didn't look like anybody had been at the second location for some time either.

"What now?" Haley asked, a little frustrated at coming up with nothing at the first two locations.

"We keep moving on."

Recker was determined to check out every single address on the list. There was a good possibility they'd all wind up being empty, but he still had to look and make sure. If there was even one single thing that they could find at any of these locations, it'd be a worthwhile effort. He wasn't discouraged yet or giving up hope that they'd find anything. Just like the first time, they called Jones to let him know their findings. He wasn't as convinced that moving forward with the list was as good of an idea.

"Mike, you know what they say about insanity," Jones said.

"That's only if you keep doing the same thing over and over again and expecting a different result."

"And what do you think you're doing?"

"I'm not expecting anything," Recker said. "We only have three more spots on the list. You never know what might turn up. If we stop now, how do you know we won't miss something? Might as well finish it off. Besides, what else we got right now?"

"Very well."

They finished their talk and Jones texted the information he had on the next location. Once they arrived, it was eerily similar to the last two stops. Quiet as could be. No signs of life. They moved on to the next address, not expecting anything different than they'd found up to that point. They were not surprised or disappointed at finding nothing once again. They moved on to the last spot on the list, assuming they would again find an empty house. The last location was a little different than the others though. Like the others, it was currently unoccupied. The biggest difference was that instead of a residential address, it was a business. It used to be a dry-cleaning business that closed up shop several years earlier. Recker and Haley sat in their car and watched the front of the store for half an hour, not seeing anyone go in or out.

"Figure it's vacant like the others?" Haley said.

"Well, chances are good. But maybe we'll get lucky."

"How soon you wanna hit it?"

Recker looked at the time. "Let's give it another thirty minutes."

Thirty minutes went by, still not a sign of life anywhere. Several people walked along the street, all of whom passed right by the store. They didn't think waiting any longer would make a difference, so the two men got out of the car.

"There's gotta be a back door," Recker said.

"I'm on it. I'll let you know when I'm in position," Haley replied.

Recker started walking on the street, browsing through some of the front windows of the stores that were open, waiting for a sign from Haley that he was ready. After a few minutes, he got it. The back alley of the stores was not especially big, just large enough to get a delivery truck in if needed. Haley was squatting next to a large, green trash dump as he watched the dry-cleaning business. He kept looking up and down the street to make sure there was nobody else back there who saw him. The back door to the business was a solid-colored door, so he couldn't look through it to see inside.

"Mike, I'm in position."

"Roger that. I'm about to enter through the front."

Haley started to move from his position but noticed a car zooming in from the far right end of the alley. He quickly scurried back to his position behind the trash container as he watched the car stop right in front of him. Four men exited the car and walked over to the back door of the dry-cleaning shop.

"Mike, hold up," Haley said, not wanting his partner to walk into something.

"What's up?"

"A car just pulled up back here. We got four men entering the store from the back."

Haley watched the group intently as they milled around the door, waiting for it to open. He noticed one of the men pull out a gun and hold it in his hand before putting it away again.

"They're armed," Haley said quietly.

"You gonna be able to get in back there?" Recker said.

"Uh, not sure. I don't think so."

"Meet back at the car."

As soon as the men had disappeared into the store, Haley moved from his position and went back to Recker's SUV. Recker lifted up the trunk door and started looking through some of the gadgets he had. Haley also started rummaging through some of the weapons his partner had come up with over the years. He pulled over a black bag and unzipped it, going through the contents. He pulled out something, almost in awe.

"Is this what I think it is?"

"Block of C4," Recker said. "Ever use it before?"

"Yeah."

Recker grabbed two assault rifles, throwing one over each shoulder as they got ready. Haley put down the explosives and did the same.

"How you figure on making entry?" Haley asked. "The only way I'm getting through that back door is if I blow it open."

Recker wasn't averse to the idea, but he was wary about an explosion. He only had a small amount, basically enough to blow open a fortified door, and it wasn't enough to damage anything in the surrounding area as long as nobody was within fifty feet of the explosion. But it would make a noise and there would be smoke. Considering they'd have to likely fight their way afterward, he didn't want to take the chance of police coming soon after that. He'd already had one run-in recently, and after having a close shave, didn't want to do it again so soon.

"Let's hold off on that for now," Recker said. "I don't wanna bring too much attention. Plus, we're still gonna have to look around after we're done in there. After the explosion, who knows how much time we'd get until the cops show?"

"So what's the plan?"

"Knock on the door and kill whoever gets in our way."

"Whatever happened to just talking?"

"OK. Knock first. If they look like they wanna talk, fine. If not, then shoot."

After Haley made sure his weapons were ready to go, he ran back to his former spot behind the trash container. The car was still parked in back of the building. Once he gave Recker the sign he was ready, both men approached their respective doors. Recker tapped on the glass door in front, while Haley knocked on the rear door with the muzzle of his rifle. Recker kept trying several times but got no response. Haley's endeavors were a little more successful. After only a couple of knocks, the back door opened just a hair. Haley made sure he was to the side of the door, so they couldn't look out and see who or where he was.

"What you want?" the man asked, seeming uneasy about the stranger.

Before Haley had a chance to answer, the man noticed the assault rifles on his shoulder and immediately felt threatened and tried to close the door. Haley rushed over to him, blocking the door closing with his shoulder. The man that answered ran back inside the building, screaming all the way.

"Cops!" the man shouted.

"Mike, they're on the run," Haley said.

Recker knew at that point that talking was unlikely and had to get inside quickly to help his partner. Though Haley saw four men enter, there was no telling how many were already in there. They knew there was at least one, since the other four men were let into the building, but they had no way of knowing how many more. They had to be ready for anything. Recker used his gun to break the glass and stepped inside the store, pieces of glass crunching underneath his footsteps. He was somewhat surprised that he wasn't met with a hail of bullets. A second later, he heard the sounds of what seemed to be some chaotic yelling coming from the back of the store.

"I'm in, Chris," Recker said.

As soon as the words left his lips, gunfire ripped through the air. "I'm engaged," Haley said, under fire.

"Coming your way."

As he waited for his reinforcement, Haley returned fire, hitting two of the men that he recognized from getting out of the car. Recker raced through the building to get to where the action was.

He still had to remain cognizant of any surprises coming his way as he did, though. Although the battle was in the back, he did pass a couple of doors that he had to clear. He couldn't take the chance of someone sneaking up on him from behind after passing them. The first door was closed, but he kicked it open and entered. It was a small room but appeared to be an office as there was a desk inside. There was a man sitting behind it who was feverishly trying to put stuff away after hearing the chaos coming from the back. He was the leader of the group, and since they all assumed it was cops hitting them, was trying to get rid of any incriminating evidence. As soon as Recker kicked the door open, the man stood up, surprised they got to him so quickly and before he finished what he was doing. Recker didn't wait and take the chance of the man drawing a gun on him and immediately opened fire, hitting him three times in the chest. Since he could tell there was no one else in the room, he left to clear the next one.

Recker exited the office and went a few feet down the hall to the next room. He kicked it open and immediately saw a couple guns pointing right at his face. Recker instantly dropped to his knees as the bullets flew over his head. From his new position on the ground, Recker returned fire, hitting both of his targets, causing them to fall over from the bullets that were now permanently a part of their bodies. He quickly got back to his feet and rushed inside the room, pointing his gun around in anticipation of using it again, though there were no more hostiles there. He went back to the two men he just put down to check on their status. They were both dead.

At that point, Haley wasn't too far removed from where he first entered the building. They had him pinned down to where he really couldn't move, though they couldn't get past him to get out of the building either. After a few more rounds of exchanging fire, Haley finally finished off the remaining two members of the group.

As Recker came out of the office and walked down the hallway, he noticed that the gunfire had stopped. Until he heard and saw Haley, though, he wasn't assuming that they were in the clear yet. With his gun in the air, he cautiously continued walking toward the back of the building. Once he got to the end of the hall, he noticed several bodies lying on the floor, blood pouring out of them.

"Chris?"

"Yo," Haley said, putting his rifles back on his shoulder as he walked over to him.

Recker looked him over, making sure he had no newfound holes in him. "You good?"

"A lot better than them, that's for sure."

"I think we got them all. I got three back there."

"I got five here. They yelled police when I got in, they thought we were cops. Well, there's no doubt they were up to no good. Were they the ones we were looking for, though?"

"They were Jeremiah's men all right. Now we just have to see if there's a connection to Vincent. There was an office back there that one of them was doing something in," Recker said. "Lot of papers and things. Looked like he was trying to pack up and move in a hurry. Maybe there's something there we could use."

"We're gonna have to move quick, though," Haley said, remembering their last outing together at the liquor store. "People are surely gonna report that gunfire. Police will be here soon enough."

"We'll just grab what's there and go. We'll look through it and sort it out later."

They went back to the office where Recker shot his first man and started rummaging through the papers on the desk. Most were already in folders or binders, making it a little easier to transport. Haley noticed a cardboard box in the corner of the room on the floor and picked it up. He brought it over to the desk and the two of them dumped every piece of paper they saw inside. After being satisfied they had everything, Recker carried the box through the back of the store. Haley led the way with his gun drawn, making sure everything was still clear for them. Seeing that the back alley was still clear, they went back to Recker's car and drove away, just as they heard police sirens in the background coming closer.

27

Before Recker and Haley made it back to the office, they let Jones know of the latest happenings. He was afraid of a shootout happening, though he wasn't surprised. But, at least they made it back. That was his main focus.

"Nice to see you made it back without handcuffs," Jones said.

"Get pinched one time in five years and you never hear the end of it," Recker said to Haley.

Recker put the box of papers down on the desk and, along with Haley, started to remove the contents. Jones swiveled his chair over and started digging into it immediately.

"We can handle going through this stuff if you got other things to do," Recker said.

"Well, the computer is already starting to go through the search guidelines, so I have some time to fill until we get any hits back. Do you think we will actually find anything in this mess?"

"Who knows? Can't hurt."

"Even if we don't find anything related to the Vincent case, we might find out something else," Haley said. "Maybe a different crime we can prevent."

Recker looked at him and nodded, thinking he got the idea. The new guy was fitting in nicely. He was not only an expert shot, and good in sticky situations, but he seemed to understand the long-range view of their operation.

There was a lot of information that they had to go through. There were at least a dozen binders and folders that were full of papers. Each one had a specific purpose that was useful to Jeremiah's operation. Notes, bills of sale, information on hundreds of people, assets, just about anything someone could think of, it was there. Almost immediately, they recognized that it was still Jeremiah's crew they were dealing with.

"I never realized just how in depth and organized Jeremiah's operation was," Jones said, shuffling papers around, somewhat impressed by the depths of the late leader's organization.

"Yeah, he really did keep tabs on just about everything." Recker nodded absentmindedly.

"What exactly are we looking for?" Haley asked.

"Anything that can be useful in any way," Jones said. "Either something that indicates a future problem that we need to stop, or something that indicates they're the ones behind Vincent's issues."

"You'll know it when you see it," Recker said.

The three men sat at the desk for a couple hours, reading every single piece of paper in detail, sometimes two or three times just to make sure they didn't miss anything. Each of them had a separate stack. When they were done with one paper, they put it in a pile for someone else to go through later. Just when they were beginning to think it was a useless endeavor, something caught their interest.

"Wait a minute," Recker said. "Here's something."

"What is it?" Jones asked.

Recker held up the paper in the air, reading parts of it. "Looks like a payroll sheet."

"How many names on it?" Haley asked.

Recker quickly counted the names. "Twenty."

"Well, fourteen now probably. I think you can cross six of those off."

"I can pull up information and photos of these twenty and see if any of them are the ones you just disposed of," Jones said.

While Jones started his task, Recker and Haley continued on with their reading. Thirty minutes later, they stopped once more, again finding something of interest.

"This is kind of weird," Haley said.

"Whatcha got?" Recker said, putting his paper down and looking at what his partner had.

"Looks like some kind of memo or email that they printed out," he said, reading it aloud.

"If you want me to do this job, you're gonna have to pony up a lot more. A million isn't enough."

"Any name on that?" Recker asked.

"No, lists the to and from emails though."

"Let me have that," Jones said, putting his hand out. "I'll see if I can cross reference the names from the email addresses."

Haley continued looking through a few more papers, but Recker sat still, not moving. He stared at the wall as he contemplated what the memo meant. A million dollars for a job. It had to be something big. Taking out the leader of a criminal organization would certainly qualify.

"That's gotta be it," Recker said, breaking free of his trance.

"What?" Haley asked.

"The needle we're looking for. A million dollars. That's gotta be for taking out Vincent."

"That's a big leap to make, Mike," Jones said. "It certainly is possible, but we need more solid evidence to be able to link the two together."

"You need evidence. I just need a hunch. A gut feeling."

"You could be right. I'm just saying it's a bit premature to say so at the moment."

"Would be nice to be able to get into their bank account records too. Seeing the flow of that million dollars would lead to a few answers."

"Assuming that it's already been paid. And assuming that it's going the way you think it is."

"What do you mean?"

"Well did you ever think that maybe it's someone offering Jeremiah's crew a million dollars to do something? Something completely unrelated to Vincent?"

"Of course it did," Recker said. "I just chose to dismiss it."

Jones rolled his eyes. "Oh. Sounds logical."

Recker went over to Jones' computer and bumped him off. "Let's make this go quicker. Me and Chris will work on getting these jokers names and photos. You get the names associated with those emails. And if you could get bank information, that would be real helpful too."

"If I could get bank information he says. Just like that," Jones whispered, mocking him. "As if it were that easy."

The three men then got to work on their respective assignments, none of which proved to be too difficult. Recker and Haley had the names and photos of all twenty men they were looking for within an hour. They got the pictures from DMV records, social media accounts, as well as police mug shots. Up to that point, they didn't look at the photos too closely, wanting to wait until they were completely finished before they started matching them up. Once they crossed the last name off the list, Recker and Haley started looking at the pictures more intently. They didn't recognize the first few pictures, but then, it started to look a little familiar.

"He was one of them," Haley said, pointing at the picture.

The next picture was another one from the battle. When they were done looking at all twenty photos, they had successfully matched all six of the men from the dry-cleaning store to the names on the payroll list. They let Jones know of their findings.

"Well, all six from the store were on the list," Recker said. "They're down to fourteen."

"Assuming that's everyone that's left in their organization," Jones replied, not sounding impressed. "It's a broad assumption to think that's it. There could still be more."

"Could be. But at least we've identified some of them."

After a little while, Jones started to unearth some interesting information on his end. He got names and addresses from both emails. He grabbed a piece of paper and started writing everything down that was on the screen. He then alerted his partners of his findings.

"I've got it," Jones said.

"What's the deal?" Recker said, him and Haley moving over.

"The email was sent from an address down in Atlanta. The receiving party was here in Philadelphia. I've already cross-referenced the name, and it was on the list that we discovered."

Recker looked at the paper then went back to grab the list of twenty names that he and Haley had just tracked down. The name was one of the ones that they crossed off after perishing in the battle at the dry-cleaning store.

"So they were trying to hire this guy for something," Haley said.

"It would appear so. I've been able to pull up a few additional emails between the two, including one that would indicate they finally came to an agreement."

Jones pulled up the extra emails on the screen so Recker and Haley could read them for themselves. It appeared that the two parties settled on a two-million-dollar payment. As they were reading, Jones continued working to find additional material.

"You were able to get all these just from an email address?" Haley asked.

"Well, it's a little more complicated than that. Email address, IP address, it all leads to something more substantial. I wasn't able to get into Jeremiah's computer system because they don't appear to be online at the moment. Our guy from Atlanta, Lee Tazlo, his computer was on. I was able to backdoor my way in and get the emails between the two parties."

"That's it," Recker said, getting an idea like a light bulb going off over his head.

"What?" Jones said.

"Can you definitely tell that Tazlo was hired to kill Vincent?"

"Not as of yet."

"Well, can you track him to see where he is?"

"I should be able to. Might take a day or two to track the bread crumbs. Why? What do you have in mind?"

"That we set a trap for him. Assuming he's here for Vincent."

"And what are you proposing?"

"If we do this right, we can get him before he makes another attempt."

"You still haven't said your plan," Jones replied.

"Well, can you send him an email, making it seem like it's coming from Jeremiah's computers?"

"Saying what?"

"Giving him bad information. Tell him you found out that Vincent's gonna be in a specific location on a certain day. If he replies in the affirmative, we know who's behind this. If he replies saying he doesn't know what you're talking about, then we got the wrong guy," Recker said.

"And what if he hears about what happened at the dry-cleaning store?"

"If you can send him something soon, he might respond by the time he hears something."

"Even if he does hear about it, he might not know it's Jeremiah's crew," Haley said. "He might not know where they're operating out of."

"That's true," Recker said. "If he's a hired gun, he probably doesn't know too much about their operation or where they're located. All he needs is the money and information on Vincent."

"What's the worst that could happen?" Haley asked.

"The worst is that he is indeed the guy we are looking for and he gets scared off thinking that we're on to him," Jones said. "Then he goes deeper into hiding and we have a tougher time locating him."

"It's worth the gamble," Recker said.

"And just how would we approach him?"

"I got something," Recker said, bumping Jones' chair over. "You set it up and I'll write down what to say."

Recker grabbed a pen and started writing down what he wanted Jones to say in the email. He wrote, "I heard from one of my sources that Vincent was shot. I haven't been able to confirm he's dead or not yet. What's the story?"

Jones read his note, not sure if it would work. "You think this will get it done?"

"One way to find out."

"Very well. I'll send the email, disguising it as coming from Jeremiah's crew."

"How complicated is that?" Haley asked.

"Child's play. Should only take me a few minutes."

"And then it's done?"

"Then it's done. And we pray that it works."

Jones sent the email only a few minutes later. They weren't going to just sit there and wait for a response, though. They couldn't be sure when one was coming, or if they'd be receiving one at all. Jones started retracing Tazlo's steps, trying to track his location from Atlanta to Philadelphia, if this was indeed where he was. As he dug into it deeper, he learned a little more about their suspected target. It appeared that he was working with someone.

"It seems that Mr. Tazlo has a partner," Jones said.

"How do you know?" Recker asked.

"From what I can gather, they bought two train tickets from Atlanta to Philadelphia about four weeks ago."

"Where'd they go from there?"

"Looks like a hotel. They checked out two weeks ago. I haven't been able to pinpoint exactly where they went from there."

"Timeline's matching up," Haley said. "They arrived four weeks ago. Then Vincent starts dodging bullets."

"Yeah. That's not a coincidence," Recker said.

They were hopeful that they'd get an email back from Tazlo, but it never came. They spent the rest of the night trying to determine his current location, though they couldn't. They called it a night and agreed to start up fresh again in the morning. Both Recker and Haley arrived back at the office early the next morning, about eight o'clock. Judging by the papers thrown about the desk, and the fact that Jones seemed like he was heavily into something, they surmised that he'd already been at it for a while.

"Did you even go to sleep?" Recker asked, knowing how his friend operated.

"Of course," Jones replied.

"Well, judging by how this place looks, you started a little before we did."

"Had a hard time sleeping. Got up early."

"How much early?"

"About two."

"What time'd you go to bed?"

"Midnight or so," Jones said, unconcerned.

"Hope it's been productive for you."

Jones got an uncomfortable smile on his face, probably due to the lack of sleep, and enthusiastically turned toward his partners as he delivered the news he was sure they'd like and appreciate.

"I've got them."

"Who?" Recker asked.

Jones' shoulders slumped, and the smile wiped away from his face. "What do you mean, who? The king and queen of England, who. Tazlo and his partner. I've got them."

"You're kidding."

"When was the last time I kidded about something like this?"

Recker tilted his head as he thought, looking up at the ceiling. "Never."

"Exactly."

"How?"

"Your plan worked. Our Mr. Tazlo responded to our email about five this morning," Jones said.

"What'd he say?"

"Here, read for yourself."

Jones pushed his chair away from the computer to let Recker and Haley have some room to look at the screen. Recker read the email aloud.

"Whoever told you that is blowing smoke up your ass. I'll let you know when he's dead."

"I guess that cinches it, doesn't it?" Recker said. "No doubt about it, he's our boy."

"So where's he at right now? We can surprise him and take him out," Haley said.

"He's staying at a small motel," Jones said. "But I don't think that would be our best move."

"Why not?" Recker asked.

"There's no doubt that he's got a partner for a reason."

"They're not staying together, are they?"

"No, they're not."

"Smart. If something goes wrong, something happens to one of them, the other completes the assignment."

"I think it will be better, easier, more convenient to take them both out at the same time," Jones said. "When they're making the hit."

"Yeah, but we don't know when that's gonna be."

Jones got another smile on his face. "We do now."

"When?"

"Noon today."

"Noon? That doesn't give us much time," Recker said.

"How'd you figure out the place?" Haley asked.

"After he replied to my initial email, I replied to his. I told him that we got an inside tip that Vincent was having a high-level emergency meeting at a place that would be perfect for a hit."

"You sly dog, you," Recker said, a grin on his face. "You set him up."

"Well, hopefully it will work."

"Where'd you tell him?"

"I made it for a restaurant in the northeast. Vincent's original home territory. There's a building directly across the street that's under construction. I told Tazlo that it would be a perfect spot to catch Vincent with a sniper rifle."

"We just need to get Vincent on board."

"Why? If we wait across the street, we can catch Tazlo and his partner as they start setting up."

"But what if they don't make themselves visible until Vincent arrives?" Jones asked.

"I'll call him and let him decide."

As Recker called Vincent, Jones and Haley started to go over plans, as well as pulling up pictures of the area. Jones was a little surprised that Recker joined them only a minute later.

"Did you call him?" Jones asked, looking for Recker's phone.

"Yep."

"That was a very short conversation."

"Wasn't much to talk about. I told him what the plan was, and he was in."

"Just like that?"

"Just like that. He wants to get this over with. He trusts us completely and is putting faith in us that we'll get the job done."

Recker leaned in and saw a few photos of the area and wanted to get down there as early as possible to go over where they could set up. The pictures were a good start, but there was only so much they could learn from the computer. They'd wind up getting there a couple of hours before the supposed assassination attempt, but Recker didn't mind waiting for a while if it meant finding their guy and eliminating him. Recker and Haley went over to the gun cabinet and grabbed some guns and ammo since they never reloaded after the dry-cleaning store battle. They left the office, threw their weapons in the back of Recker's SUV, and off they went.

"Hopefully Tazlo isn't setting up shop before we are," Haley said.

"The other issue is we still don't know what his partner looks like," Recker said.

They got to the restaurant in under half an hour and parked in the lot. They saw the building in construction across the street and walked over to it. It appeared to be a three-story office building, but the outsides weren't quite done yet as the windows hadn't been put in yet. They went around to the back of the building and slipped in through one of the windows. Recker motioned for Haley to check upstairs as he searched through the ground floor. After a few minutes, both reported the place was empty.

"Guess they don't work on the weekends," Haley said.

"I'll take the upstairs," Recker said, formulating the plan in his mind. "Why don't you go across the street and keep an eye on here and let me know when someone's coming."

"What about us both staying here?"

"Both of us looking out a window is dicey. They could spot us and scare them away. I'll stay tucked down out of sight. That way you can alert me when they're coming, and we can get the jump on them."

Recker stayed on the second floor, sitting underneath one of the open windows as Haley jogged back across the street, clinging to a building next to the restaurant.

"You think they'll come early and try to get him on the way in?" Haley asked. "Or will they come later and get him on the way out?"

"I would think the sooner the better. That way they'll get two cracks at it. If they couldn't line up a shot when he first arrives, they can get him on the way out."

They waited until 11:30, when Haley saw a couple of characters walk across the street toward the empty building. They each had a black duffel bag in hand.

"Mike, got two headed your way with black bags. These gotta be the guys."

"All right. Let me know when they enter the building and hightail it over here."

"You got it," Haley said, waiting a minute until the two guys reached the building. "They're walking around to the back of the building now. I'm on the move."

"Got it."

Recker stood up, and though he had an assault rifle on his shoulder, removed his Glock from its holster. He always preferred using the hand gun whenever possible. And with only two opponents, he figured that would do just fine. He thought about going down the steps to meet them, but quickly decided against it. If they were like him, they'd want to make sure the building was empty. Which meant they'd have to come to him. He could surprise them as they came up the steps. The only bad part was there was really no place to take cover since the building was still under construction. Recker thought he detected footsteps on the stairs, coming in his direction. He dropped to one knee to steady himself and raised his gun, aiming for the top of the stairs. A few seconds later, he saw the outline of a thinly built man reach the top of the stairs. Just as the man turned in Recker's direction, the Silencer surprised him by his presence and opened fire.

Recker dropped the man immediately, hitting him three times square in the chest. The man fell back, hitting the floor, the momentum of the fall causing him to fall back down the steps, rolling down until a loud thud was heard on the first floor. As soon as Recker heard the man's body hit the first floor, he heard more gunfire erupt. It sounded like Haley's gun. Recker started going down the stairs, then stopped about halfway as the gunfire stopped.

"Chris?"

"I'm here. We're all clear," Haley said.

Recker rushed down the steps and quickly located Haley, standing in the middle of the room. He was standing over top of the body of Tazlo.

"Looks like our work here is done," Recker said.

"Yeah. I noticed your guy had a... little bit of a fall," Haley said with a smile a mile wide.

"All right, no sense in wasting any more time here. Let's get out of here."

"Gonna stick around for Vincent?"

"Yeah. Might as well tell him in person that it's over. Do me a favor and pull the car out of the lot and down the street. No sense in letting him know about you before it's necessary."

"Will do."

The two of them went back across the street to the restaurant. Haley pulled the car out as Recker waited by the front door. As he stood there waiting, the clouds became darker and rain started drizzling down. A short time later, Vincent's car pulled into the parking lot, right at twelve o'clock. Malloy was the first to get out of the back seat, who came around the bumper of the car to open the door for his boss. Before he pulled on the handle, he looked at Recker, who simply nodded, indicating that the coast was clear. Malloy took a quick look around, then finally opened the door, with Vincent stepping out of the car. Vincent also glanced around, looking a little uneasy. Recker quickly put his mind at ease.

"It's done with," Recker said. "It's over. You don't have anything to worry about anymore."

A relieved look overcame Vincent's face. He reached out his hand to shake Recker's, appreciative of his efforts. As they shook hands, the rain started beating down harder as the sounds of thunder played in the background above them.

"If you're interested and wanna see for yourself, they're lying in that building across the street that's under construction," Recker said, looking over at it.

Though he trusted that Recker was being truthful, he still sent one of his guys over to check it out. A couple of minutes later, the man returned, indicating that he saw the two bodies lying on the floor.

"Who were they?" Vincent asked.

"Outside guns," Recker said matter-of-factly. "The remnants of Jeremiah's crew hired them to take you out in retaliation for you taking out their boss. They knew you were behind it."

"So is that it?"

Recker threw his hand up, not completely sure of his answer. "Well, we haven't come up with anything else. So, I don't know if you can be too comfortable. But, these are the ones that tried the previous two times."

Though Vincent was happy with the developments, he still seemed slightly displeased. "Well, we both know there are still more of Jeremiah's men out there. May not be the last we've seen of them."

"If it makes you feel any better, I raided one of their spots the other day and found a payroll sheet with twenty names on it. I then took out six of them. Assuming there's not more somewhere, their numbers are dwindling. But that doesn't mean they couldn't make life rough for you. But they may have other things on their plate, like reorganizing, or just surviving."

Vincent nodded, seeming a little more upbeat. "I can't thank you enough for the swiftness in your actions in concluding this matter."

"Well, I did owe you," Recker said. "I would say this squares us though."

"Indeed it does."

"I'll be seeing you."

Recker turned away from the group and walked past the restaurant, going down the street until he got to the car, where Haley was waiting for him. Vincent and Malloy watched him for a minute, before talking about their next course of business.

"What now, boss?" Malloy asked.

"Well, since we're already here at this fine establishment, we might as well have a celebratory luncheon."

"And after that?"

"One thing at a time, Jimmy. It's a beautiful day today, is it not?" Vincent asked, looking up at the sky and letting the rain splash down onto his face.

Malloy looked up and shrugged. "I guess so, sir."

"Remember when we first met Recker, I told you we'd give him a long leash, that one day he would prove useful to us."

"I was always doubtful. You turned out to be right, though."

"Yes. Our friend, Mr. Recker, has become a powerful ally for us," Vincent said, looking up at the rain again. "No doubt about it. It sure is a beautiful day."

HOLLOW POINT

28

ecker had just arrived at the favorite meeting spot of his and Vincent's. Though he was a few minutes early, he looked over at the door and saw the burly man at his usual spot, indicating his host for the meeting was already waiting inside. Recker got out of his car and walked over to the front entrance, opening his coat to remove his gun. The guard put his hand up to stop him.

"Boss says you can keep your guns from now on," the man said.

"Oh?"

"Guess he figured since you saved his life you get a free pass now."

"Well I suppose I'm entitled to some benefits from it," Recker said.

Recker walked through the door and was immediately greeted by Malloy. Though a mutual respect had grown between the two men over the years, they still weren't on handshake terms upon seeing each other. It was the same as always. They gave each other a slight nod, then moved on to their business. Recker went down to the usual table, sitting across from Vincent, who had just finished his breakfast.

"Mike, how are you?" Vincent asked.

"Fine."

Vincent pointed to his plate. "Can I offer you something?"

"No, I'm good."

"Had a feeling you would be. I know you usually don't join me in these little excursions, so I took the liberty of eating beforehand."

"My eating habits have changed a little bit lately. Eat more healthy, home cooked stuff."

"A wise decision on your part," Vincent said, patting his stomach. "I think I may have put on a few extra pounds from all these outside meals I've had."

The two men shared a laugh at his self-depreciation, though Recker was still in the dark as to what the meeting was about. When Malloy called him to request it, he didn't give any indications as to the topic they'd be discussing. And Recker couldn't figure out on his own what Vincent may have wanted. It'd been three months since Recker and Haley took out the assassin who was gunning for the crime boss. Since that violent day, they'd kept their distance from each other, though not necessarily on purpose. They just had no other business that required their cooperation in that time.

As far as Recker knew, nothing major had happened recently that would cause either of them to need assistance on anything, so he was at a loss as to what he was really doing there. And Vincent wasn't one to always get straight to the point. Sometimes he liked to run in circles for a little while until he reached his destination. Something Recker would just as soon avoid.

"So what's this about?" Recker said, hoping to speed things up a bit.

Vincent smiled, always appreciating how his guest liked to

skip the formalities and get down to business. "Always the straight shooter."

Recker shrugged. "I dunno, I just figure we're both busy people, have a lot on our plate, why prolong things? Plus, we're on good terms, no need to beat around the bush, right?"

"Indeed," Vincent said, wiping his mouth with a napkin. "I just thought we might chat about a few things that have happened over the last several months. Some things that I've been hearing."

"Such as?" Recker asked, not having the slightest idea about what he was inferring.

"Well, I've been hearing that business has picked up quite a bit on your end."

"It's been pretty steady. That's really nothing new."

"No, but you must be tired. You seem to be spreading yourself pretty thin lately."

Recker shook his head, knowing there was something else Vincent was leading up to. "I'm holding up just fine."

"I'm sure. You have broad shoulders, a passion for this line of work that never dies or wanes."

Recker grinned and scratched the back of his head, still waiting for the purpose of the meeting. He wasn't yet irritated by the runaround, but was growing a little impatient. He tossed his left hand in the air to indicate he didn't have any response.

"Very well, I'll stop this little charade that we're having," Vincent said, picking up on Recker's clue that he wasn't partaking in the game anymore.

"I'd appreciate it."

"There's been some rumors, some rumblings, that you've expanded your operation lately."

"There has?"

Vincent nodded. "It's been brought to my attention that there have been witnesses to you working with another man. Word seems to be getting around."

Recker looked stone-faced, as he knew Vincent usually picked up on visual clues to his questions as much as he listened to the actual responses. And this was a question he really had no interest in answering.

"You know you should never believe everything you hear," Recker said.

"A very good business practice."

"So, is that it? That's what this is about? The possibility of me having more assistants out there?"

Vincent nodded, and looked at the ceiling, measuring his words carefully. "We have a good relationship that we've built up over the years. Whether you have other people you're working with or not isn't really of my concern. You'll do your business in whatever way you see fit."

"Then what's the issue?"

"Well, as you know, a man in my position has to be well aware of what's going on around him. Has to know all the possible players in the field, who's on the same side, who are enemies, what might be some possible situations that could have to be dealt with at some later date in the future."

"Whether these so-called rumors are true or not isn't really something you need to be concerned with," Recker said, still not giving in.

"Well, that might be something that we disagree on," Vincent replied, motioning with his hands for emphasis before folding them together on the table.

"You should know that whether I do or do not have help out in the field isn't something you need to worry about. It has nothing to do with our arrangement."

Vincent nodded, knowing he was unlikely to pry out of his visitor the information he was seeking, though he still felt the need to ask the questions. "So, if these rumors turned out to be true..."

"Then, presumably, it might be something as simple as just having someone out there to watch my back. Hypothetically speaking," Recker said, sticking to his guns and not revealing what they both knew to be true.

It wasn't necessarily that he was trying to hide the information from Vincent. Recker always knew he'd probably be among the first to find out, especially with his contacts all over the city. It was more of a personal thing with Recker. He just didn't want to admit to anyone there was a new member of their operation before it was necessary. For Vincent's part, he wasn't going to continue to force the issue. He felt he had the answer to his question, whether Recker admitted it or not.

"I can see how, hypothetically, something like that might be a good idea," Vincent said. "Especially with some of the situations you wind up getting placed in."

"Yeah."

"I hope you don't mind the probing questions. I'm sure you understand my position, always having to be aware of any new players in town."

"No, I get it. But as far as you and I are concerned, nothing changes."

"Good to know. So how has David been these past few months?"

"Good. Busy."

"I can imagine. An operation such as yours must take a lot of time to maintain."

Recker shrugged. "We make do."

"I guess if you ever did take on another partner, it'd enable you to spend more time at home with your girlfriend."

Recker's eyes almost bulged out of his head hearing him talk about his girlfriend. It wasn't something he'd ever mentioned in any of their conversations. He hoped Vincent wasn't about to strong-arm him the way Jeremiah tried to, putting Mia in the middle of things. Vincent could see his guest looked a little unnerved with his statement and tried to put his mind at ease.

"Relax," Vincent said, putting his hand out. "I'm not trying to dig into your personal life, or create some type of friction or anything. I've already heard how that turns out."

Recker lifted his head up, not saying a word. But he didn't have to. His facial expressions did all the talking for him.

"Yes, I've heard about how Jeremiah tried to use her to get to me."

"How?" Recker asked.

"You forget, there are still a few of Jeremiah's men roaming around," Vincent said. "I've been able to have the pleasure of speaking with a few of them."

"And what'd they have to say?"

"Just how they tried to use the girl to persuade you to do their dirty work. Obviously, that was an epic fail on their part."

"It would be an epic fail on anyone's part," Recker said, trying to give a warning without making a direct threat. Nobody would ever use Mia to get to him again.

"I would agree. She was the, uh, the nurse that I helped to rescue, wasn't she?" Vincent asked with a smile.

Recker shuffled around in his seat, just about ready to light into his host with a bunch of words he probably shouldn't say. He somehow could put those thoughts aside for the moment and remain diplomatic.

"And just what do you plan to do with all this newfound knowledge of yours?"

"Nothing," Vincent answered. "We're just two friends sitting here, discussing our lives like regular people do."

"Except we're not regular people."

"True. But I think it only serves to strengthen the bond between us. There are rumors that there is another dangerous person in town, perhaps working with you, perhaps not. But I'm not worrying about it because you have told me there's nothing to worry about."

"Yeah?" Recker said, knowing he wasn't done with his speech.

"And I know you have a girlfriend who works at a hospital. A woman who has been caught up in a dangerous game before by a man who was obviously losing his grip. And it's not something you should worry about because I'm telling you there's nothing to worry about."

"I think I see where you're going with this."

"We've been through a lot together these past few years, haven't we?" Vincent asked, almost happily recalling memories most normal people would rather forget.

"Yeah, I guess we have. So, how's it felt being the only main player in town these past few months?"

"Well, there's always going to be minor nuisances here and there. People who want a bigger piece of the pie. Nothing that's really at a threatening level though."

"And are you satisfied with that? The power and territory that you have now. Or is there still more you'd like to accomplish?"

"Well, as you know, my enemies disappearing these past couple of years has happened at a surprising and breakneck speed. There's still much to do just maintaining and growing the business of what I now have. I'm quite comfortable with that for now."

The two men continued talking for another twenty minutes or so, neither saying anything of much significance. It was mostly just small talk, passing the time. As they both got ready to leave, though, Vincent dropped another little bomb in Recker's direction.

"Before we go, there was one more small thing I wanted to talk to you about," Vincent said.

"Which is?"

"As you know, I have several members of the police department at my disposal."

"Yeah?" Recker asked, not sure where this dialog was going.

"How would you feel about meeting one of them?"

"I've already had the pleasure. If you recall, that was one of the conditions of Jeremiah's demise."

Vincent feigned a look of ignorance. "Yes, of course. This would be someone different, though. Someone who is very interested in meeting you."

"I can't say I share the same viewpoint," Recker said, not sounding the slightest bit interested in the proposal.

"I'll pass it along."

"Just out of curiosity, who would this officer be?"

"A detective."

"And just why does he want to meet me?"

"He's a fan of your work," Vincent said.

"Excuse me if I'm not all warm and fuzzy about being someone's idol, but I don't think I mix particularly well with those on the other side of the line."

"Understood, but he's not looking to arrest you. I believe he has some business he's interested in discussing with you."

"So why can't you just tell me what it is?"

Vincent shrugged. "Because I don't know all the particulars. I believe it's a police matter."

"And he didn't share with you?"

"Well, just because he's on my payroll doesn't mean he isn't his own person. I don't get firsthand knowledge of everything that comes across his desk."

"Just the things that pertain to you?" Recker asked.

"Or things that I have a personal interest or stake in."

"I'm not sure that meeting with a detective is something I'm really interested in doing right now. I don't think it's too wise for me to play around too frequently with people who have the ability to lock me up."

"As you wish. I'll deliver the news if that's your final answer. I'm sure he could make it worth your while, though."

"No, it's OK. I still think I'll pass on the offer. The more I associate with the police, the surer I'd be that something would eventually go wrong."

"Always play things cautiously," Vincent said.

"No different than you, right?"

Vincent nodded. The two men only talked for a few minutes more before Recker excused himself and left the diner. He called Jones as soon as he left to let him know there wasn't anything that needed to be worked imminently. As he sat there in his truck, he looked over at the diner again, thinking about some of the things that were said. It was a strange request, he thought, Vincent asking him to meet with a police officer. Recker wasn't sure what to make of it. There was obviously a reason for it. And it was probably a big one. But whatever it was, if it was as big as he imagined it was, he assumed he'd be hearing from Vincent again on the subject.

When Recker got back to the office, Jones and Haley were sitting side by side, analyzing some information they'd been working on. Recker poured himself a cup of coffee and walked over to the window, not wanting to say anything to the pair and throw their concentration off.

"Are you just going to ignore us, Michael?" Jones asked.

Recker turned around to face them. "Looked like you were deep in thought there. Didn't want to disturb you two lovebirds."

Haley chuckled as he kept his eyes glued to the screen. Jones, though, pushed his chair away from the desk to further engage his friend. Recker's eyes danced around the room, like he was thinking about something. It was one of the clues Jones had picked up on in the time they'd been together. It usually was an indication something was bugging Recker. And usually, it wasn't a minor thing.

"So, what is it?" Jones asked.

"What's what?"

"You know. That thing you're thinking about."

"What makes you think I'm thinking about something?" Recker asked.

"Do we really have to play this game? Whenever you have a problem or something on your mind that you're not ready to discuss, you have that look on your face."

"What look?"

"The look you have right now," Jones said. "The one where you have trouble focusing on any one thing in particular. You look out the window, glance at the floor, sometimes the wall, perhaps the ceiling, or maybe a few other inanimate objects."

"Do you analyze me often, doctor?"

"Just when the situation calls for it."

"Oh. Very scholarly of you, professor."

"So, would you rather just get it out now or do you wanna have a song and dance for a couple of hours first?" Jones asked.

"Oh, I dunno. Who's gonna lead?" Recker said, continuing with the joke. "I mean, I forgot to bring my dancing shoes with me today."

While Jones didn't look very amused, Haley couldn't help but laugh again, overhearing their conversation, though he was still typing away on the computer.

"So, I take it you're insisting on the 'let's talk for a while until I pry it out of you' method?" Jones asked.

Recker tried to keep a straight face and continue with the charade, but just couldn't hold it in anymore and let out a laugh as well. Jones took a step back and took turns looking at his two Silencers and simply shook his head.

"I was hoping your sense of humor wouldn't emulate his," Jones said, looking at Haley.

Haley didn't reply. He just smiled and went back to what he was doing. Recker seemed to be enjoying the back-and-forth tug he and Jones were having. But, he figured enough was enough and finally came clean with what was on his mind.

"If you must know, I was thinking about Vincent," Recker said.

Jones scrunched his eyebrows together, wondering why the crime boss would be deep in his friend's thought process. "Why would you be thinking about him? You said nothing of much interest was said at the meeting. Was there more?"

Recker shrugged as his eyes shot past Jones, looking at different parts of the room. "Well, I dunno."

"What do you mean, you don't know? Either something was said, or it wasn't."

"Right before leaving, Vincent asked if I wanted to meet with a detective that was on his payroll."

Jones looked perplexed by the request. "For what purpose?"

"He wouldn't tell me."

"Seems a bit odd."

"I know. I can't figure out what it could have been about."

"Was it any of the ones that you met outside Jeremiah's house on that final day?"

Recker shook his head. "No. Said it was someone else. But, Vincent said it wasn't of his asking."

"What do you mean?"

"Vincent said this guy, this detective, asked to meet with me. Had nothing to do with Vincent. He was just acting as the intermediary."

"Well that is strange indeed."

"You don't think Vincent could be setting you up for something, do you?" Haley asked, finally interjecting himself into the conversation.

"No. I think we're still on as good a terms as we've always been," Recker replied.

"I wonder what it could be about?" Jones said.

"I dunno. I'm sure we'll find out soon enough, though."

"Were there any other interesting nuggets from the meeting you'd care to disclose?"

Recker shrugged. "Uh, he said he's heard rumors of another person being with me, so he asked if we had a new man in the operation."

"Oh?"

"I didn't confirm or deny anything."

"Well if you don't deny something, it's as much of a confirmation as actually confirming it," Jones said.

"Yeah, but I did it in a much more amusing way."

"Oh, well, as long as you had fun with it," Jones said, rolling his eyes.

"He knows we've got another man whether I actually admit it or not. The only thing he's really worried about is knowing who it is."

"Why?" Haley asked.

"You don't get to his level without knowing every person in the city who's capable of posing a threat to him at some point," Recker answered. "He just wants to make sure you're not someone he has to worry about in the future."

"So, will he?"

"No, I basically told him how it is. He's not gonna concern himself with it too much now."

"How can you be so sure?" Jones asked. "If you recall, he poked around quite a bit, asked several questions to try to get to the bottom of our operation initially. Unless of course you forget about Mia and I ducking out on Malloy down at the university."

"I haven't forgotten."

"Then how do you know he won't try to find out Chris' identity?"

"Because we came to an understanding," Recker said.

"An understanding? Care to expand on that?"

"He took me at my word that our new man has nothing to do with him and is nothing he needs to be concerned with."

"He did? Seems very unlike him to just accept something like that so easily."

"Well, it also might have something to do with me taking him at his word about something."

"Which is?"

"He knows about Mia," Recker said.

Jones just stared at him for a few moments. "You'll have to divulge a little more. He's always known about Mia."

"He knows she's my girlfriend."

As soon as he said the words, Jones stood there, stunned. Haley, too, stopped what he was doing and looked at Recker. It was a startling revelation for them.

"Seeing as how you don't seem too terribly upset, I take it you're satisfied with whatever it was that Vincent told you," Jones said.

"Well, he said he's heard about why that little beef with me and Jeremiah happened, with Mia being used as bait. And he knows where she's working."

"Well we've always suspected that."

"Yeah, but that's why he's not worried about Haley. He doesn't need to worry about our secret and I don't need to worry about his."

"So, he's basically letting you know he knows about Mia, but he'll never do anything to her, unless he's provoked," Haley said.

"That's basically the size of it."

"Is there anything else you'd like to share about this meeting?" Jones said in a huff.

"No, that was it."

"That was it. You initially told me nothing interesting happened, and yet, you just disclosed three different topics that were extremely noteworthy. Are you sure there's nothing else you'd like to share?"

"No, that's it."

"It seems as though we have different definitions of what's important."

Recker shrugged again, not giving it much more thought.

"Even if the other things can be shrugged off, I do wonder what that business with the police is about," Jones said.

"Well, if there's one thing I'm sure about when it comes to dealing with Vincent..."

"What?"

"We'll find out soon enough."

29

Without having a specific case to work on right then, Recker and Haley had gone out to lunch. Jones stayed behind to work on a few leads. He hoped to have a new case later that night or the following morning. They brought back a sandwich for their leader, who immediately started devouring it, holding it in one hand as he continued typing with his free hand.

"Take a break, David," Recker said. "It'll still be there in a few minutes."

Jones looked at his friend and nodded, pushing his chair away from the desk momentarily. "Did you two enjoy your lunch date?"

"Very nice. Food was great," Haley said.

"Hey, how's your apartment working out for you?" Recker asked.

"Oh, I love it. It looks so good. Mia did an unbelievable job with it. She really has a nice style and good taste. She could be an interior decorator or something if she ever decided to leave nursing."

"She likes helping people too much to do that. Maybe a side

386

gig or something."

"Well, tell her I can't thank her enough for making the place look so good. I never would've been able to do that."

Recker laughed. "She knows. That's why she did it. Probably didn't want it to look like an empty warehouse for a few years like mine did."

"Yeah, there are some days I wake up and I look around and don't even wanna leave the apartment."

"Hopefully that is only a fleeting thought," Jones said.

Mia had fixed up Haley's apartment the previous week after offering her services several times. She, Recker, and Haley had become good friends in the time since the new Silencer had arrived on the scene. The three of them sometimes had dinner together at one of their places at least once a week. Knowing how Recker treated his apartment before Mia moved in, she didn't want Haley's place to have that same devoid-of-life feeling to it. Even though they weren't in their apartments for most of the day, Mia thought they should still have a nice environment to come home and relax in. She figured it was good for their mental state to have pleasant surroundings at home, rather than blank walls to stare at.

After quickly eating his sandwich, Jones got back to work. Recker and Haley milled around the office for a little while, not having anything specific to do. Recker finally went to his gun cabinet and started cleaning some of his weapons, Haley giving him a hand.

"When's the next assignment coming?" Recker asked.

"Should be here shortly," Jones replied.

"What's the beef?"

"Possible murder."

"Oh good. Love those," Recker said sarcastically.

Recker instinctively looked over at Jones for a second, then went back to cleaning his guns. But something tugged at him that something was wrong. Jones had a concerned look on his face and seemed to be typing a little faster. He took turns working between two computers.

"Something up?" Recker asked.

Jones briefly looked at him before going back to his work. "A problem. Definitely a problem."

"Thought you said it wouldn't be ready until later?"

"No, not with that case. That's still on the same schedule."

"Then what is it?"

"A problem."

Recker looked at Haley and sighed. "Is this how I sound sometimes? Like, not giving direct answers."

Haley shrugged, not really wanting to admit it was true. They finished cleaning the guns and closed the cabinet, then walked over to the desk and sat next to Jones, waiting for him to tell them what the problem was.

"Would you like to expand on that now?" Recker asked. "You tell me I'm not very forthcoming sometimes, but you're not exactly Mr. Talkative yourself, you know."

Jones turned his head and looked at the pair and raised his eyebrows, not sure he agreed with the suggestion.

Seeing as how nothing else was working, Recker looked away and sighed in frustration. "Maybe we can help."

"Yeah, let us go out and work our magic," Haley said. "We got nothing else going on right now."

"I'm afraid this is nothing you two can work magic with. At least not yet," Jones replied.

"Jones, just spit it out. What's going on?" Recker finally asked, tired of the games.

"Well, it appears there was a shooting sometime this morning. I'm still trying to figure out the particulars."

"So, how's that pertain to us?"

"Yeah, unless they missed. If they didn't, should already be a police matter, shouldn't it?" Haley said.

Jones gave him a serious-looking face. "It is indeed a police matter. It seems as though the target was one of their own."

Recker took a few seconds to let what he said sink in. "What do you mean, one of their own? You mean somebody shot a cop?"

"That is exactly what I mean."

As Jones continued typing, Recker and Haley looked at each other, both understanding the seriousness of the situation. It was something none of them liked to hear. Recker put his hand over his mouth as he looked at the floor. His mind thought back to the situation involving Officer Perez and Adrian Bernal, causing Recker to make a deal with Vincent to find the would-be killer. After a few seconds, Recker broke free of his trance.

"Is the officer dead?"

The look Jones gave him told him all he needed, though Jones clarified it anyway. "Unfortunately, yes."

"What happened?" Haley asked.

"I'm still trying to piece things together."

"How'd you pick up on it?" Recker said.

"Only because the police have called a press conference for thirty minutes from now," Jones replied.

"So why didn't we pick up on it?"

"You know the reasons as much as I do. There's no crystal ball to pick up on these things. We can only pick up on what's planned... and shared. If it's not premeditated, or texted or called or emailed to an accomplice, you know we won't get wind of it. Not beforehand, anyway."

Recker sighed, already knowing as much, still frustrated nonetheless. "I know."

"If it's someone who just decided this morning to do something like that, then what can we do?" Jones asked.

"Nothing," Recker said, shaking his head.

"Believe me, Michael, I know it's unfortunate, and it bothers me as well, but sometimes we can't be there in advance."

"Especially with police officers," Haley said. "They get involved in so much stuff, a lot of it is just spur of the moment. Could've just been a routine call that escalated somehow."

Recker nodded, everything both men were saying making sense. It didn't make him feel better, though. Jones continued typing away, fiddling in his seat the way he often did when he found something that piqued his interest. When that happened, he tended to sit straighter as he looked at the screen. Recker noticed he was doing it now.

"You got something else?"

Jones gulped before answering, not liking what he was seeing. "It appears that there was another shooting of a police officer three days ago."

"What?" Recker incredulously asked.

"Three days ago, another police officer was shot. He was a little luckier, though, in that he survived."

"Did you already know about this?"

"It's the first I'm hearing about it."

"Why didn't we know about this already?"

"It wasn't publicly known until now."

"What?" Recker asked again, not believing it. "Since when has the shooting of a cop not been publicly known? That's usually a lead news story in any media outlet."

"I don't know, Mike, all I can tell you is what I'm seeing."

"There's gotta be more to it."

The three men didn't say another word for fifteen minutes, as Jones continued digging into the shootings. He finally found the reason they didn't hear of the first shooting.

"It appears that the police department kept the first shooting hush-hush," Jones said.

"Why would they do that?" Haley asked.

"It seems the first officer shot was actually on an undercover assignment."

"Which means they didn't want word leaking out that it was a cop," Recker said, understanding now why it was covered up.

"Makes sense," Haley said.

"Yeah, but how are you finding this out now?" Recker asked.

"In the wake of this latest shooting, that officer was pulled off that assignment this morning," Jones replied.

"Things are getting hot."

"So it would seem."

Jones continued sifting through the information at his disposal as Recker and Haley quietly and patiently waited nearby for any further bits of knowledge he could drop down on them.

"Well that's interesting," Jones said, his eyes glued to the screen.

"What's that?" Recker asked.

"It would appear that both officers were hit with the same kind of bullet."

"So? Doesn't necessarily mean there's a connection."

"Perhaps not. But it is interesting nonetheless."

"What kind of bullet?"

"Preliminary reports indicate both were fired from a .45 automatic. Both were hollow point bullets."

Recker leaned back in his chair, thinking about what might have been going on.

"Is that too much of a coincidence?" Jones said, saying what they all were thinking.

"Two shootings in three days against the same profession with the same type of bullet?" Recker said. "I guess anything's possible."

"One officer was undercover and another in uniform. Very well could be a coincidence."

"Like I said. I guess anything is possible."

"Should we start on it?" Haley asked.

Jones shook his head as he turned to face him. "The police have already started their own investigation on it. And believe me, with two of their own being shot, they will be completely thorough."

"David's right. As much as this crap bothers me, I don't think we need to roll on this one. They'll pull out all the stops on it," Recker said. "They'll find the guy, assuming it's just one. Even if it isn't, they'll find them."

Haley nodded, and even though he wanted to get in on it, understood the reasoning to stay away.

"Besides, we have another case to work on coming up," Jones said.

"Might be a good idea to keep an eye on the police investigation, though, just to see how it's going," Recker said.

"I will do that."

Jones went back to typing at his computer, as Recker rubbed both sides of his temple with his hand. Haley, though, wasn't ready to put the shootings to rest, thinking there may be something else involved.

"Hey, I just thought of something," Haley said. "Do you think that detective that Vincent was talking about might have something to do with this?"

Recker and Jones looked at each other, though neither said a word at first glance as they thought of the possibilities.

"Maybe the guy wanted to see if we'd heard anything about who it might have been," Haley continued.

"That's kind of a tall leap, wouldn't you say?" Jones asked. "Linking one to the other."

"Maybe. But that would classify as pulling out all the stops, wouldn't it?"

"A police detective asking help from us on a police investigation involving the shooting of one of their own wouldn't just be pulling out all the stops. It would be destroying all the stops."

Jones looked at Recker to see if he agreed with his assessment and mentioned something to him. But considering his friend totally ignored his comment, he assumed Recker was so deep in thought he just didn't hear him. Jones let him be for a moment until his lapse of concentration had gone then repeated his statement.

"Huh?" Recker said, though he did hear his friend talking. "Oh, well, I don't know. Like I've said twice already, I guess anything's possible. I guess it would depend on their leads, or lack of them, and how desperate they are."

"I couldn't see any scenario in which they asked for assistance from us."

They debated the pros and cons of such a scenario for a few minutes until Jones pulled up the press conference on one of the computers. The three men stayed glued in their seats as they watched the event unfold, none of them saying a word throughout the proceedings. Once it was over, Jones clicked off the website and switched the screen to something else.

"Well? What do you think?" Jones asked.

"Didn't really say anything we didn't already know," Recker said. "I think it's still too soon to know what's going on even for them."

With nothing more they could really say other than they'd keep monitoring the situation, the trio got back to working on their own business. After three solid hours of putting their nose to the grindstone, their concentration was finally broken by the sound of Recker's phone ringing. As it was after five, Recker thought maybe it was his better half calling. He got up to answer it, walking over to the counter where he'd left it the last time he'd gotten a drink.

"Probably Mia checking about dinner," Recker said.

He was surprised when he picked it up and looked at the screen, seeing it wasn't Mia. It was Vincent. Highly unusual, he thought, especially after just meeting with him that morning. He also thought it strange it wasn't Malloy calling. Usually Vincent's right-hand man made the initial contact when a meeting was arranged, or they started preliminary work on a problem. Vincent usually only called if it was something urgent that needed immediate attention. Recker picked up his phone and looked at his two partners and shook his head, letting them know it wasn't Mia.

"Surprised to hear from you again so soon," Recker said.

"Well, in situations like these, urgency is required."

"Just what situations like these are you talking about?"

"I suppose you've heard about the two police shootings by now?"

"Yeah, I watched the press conference they had earlier."

"Then by now I'm sure you know the severity that the department is dealing with right now."

"Yeah. I may be wrong, but I never figured you for someone who bled blue."

"We've known each other for a few years now, Mike, you know I'm a level-headed guy. I don't believe in chaos and letting the inmates run the asylum. Police are very much a necessity in our society today. Without them, who knows what kind of nonsense we'd be running into on the street every day."

"You don't want to return to the Wild West?" Recker asked.

"Ah, it was a glorified period of violence. Anyway, back to our topic, if you recall this morning, my police contact wanted to have a word with you."

"I don't think my answer has really changed since then. Still not all that interested."

"Well, I told him of your reluctance to meet."

"So, what's the issue?"

"He has asked me if I could try again to persuade you," Vincent said.

"Why all the interest on your part? You work for him or does he work for you?"

Vincent let out a small laugh. "You should know by now, Mike, that I don't work for anybody."

"You're just doing this guy a favor by talking to me?"

"I think there's a slight misconception when people think I have officers of the law on my payroll. I don't have them out there doing illegal things, killing guys, muscling people around, dealing drugs, things like that. They're good, hardworking officers. They just get paid to distribute certain information to me."

"Or bust up rival criminal enterprises," Recker said. "Or stand by and arrest lookouts of a city center gang while a third party goes inside a restaurant and eliminates the competition? Or surround a house that has a rival leader on the premises."

Vincent laughed again. "I guess you could look at it that way."

"What exactly does this guy want?"

"I believe it has something to do with the two police shootings. He knows you're someone I've done business with, I told him you have a way of finding out things that slip through the cracks, he asked me if I could reach out to you. It's as simple as that."

"You'll forgive me for my hesitancy, but it's not every day that a police officer asks to meet with me."

"You think I might be setting you up for something?"

"It's not so much that I don't trust you, I think we've always forged an understanding between us. But as much as I respect the boys in blue, that same trust doesn't go over the line for them."

"Mike, believe me, I didn't take the risk of rescuing you from the back seat of a police car, just to set you up a few months later. You have my word on that."

"Trust doesn't come that easily for me. I've gotten this far on my ability to read situations correctly, and being careful enough to avoid things that look a little shady," Recker said.

"And you have good instincts. But I'll tell you this, I guarantee this is not any type of setup. Not by me, not by them."

"I believe that it's not you. But what makes you think this guy's not looking for a promotion, trying to lure me out somewhere and get the drop on me? Or maybe even a guy who's got stars in his eyes and figures he can lay this whole mess at my feet."

"No, it wouldn't happen, and I'll tell you why. Because he came to me and asked me to set something up with you in good faith. Nobody uses me as an excuse to lay the hammer down. A man's only as good as his word. I know you feel the same way. How do I know it's not a trap? One simple reason, he knows I would not put up with it. If he uses my connections for a setup and makes a liar out of me, he knows, like everyone else, that after it was over, he'd be taking a swim in the river. And he wouldn't be coming back up for air."

The insinuation was clear for Recker. And though he believed every word Vincent had told him, he still wasn't sure about it. Though Recker always appreciated the work of the police, crossing lines, and interacting with them wasn't something he was fond of doing. Today's friendly cop could be tomorrow's enemy trying to lock him up. Still, there was something tugging at him that he should accept the meeting and find out what the detective wanted. Eventually, Recker relented.

"Fine. I'll meet with him."

"Great."

"But I'll do it on my terms. I'll name the place and time."

"Where and when?" Vincent asked.

"There's a little bar in the northeast on Grant called Gino's, you know it?"

"I do."

"I'll meet him there tonight at ten. I'll wait five minutes after. If he's not there by then, I won't be either."

"Understood. I'll convey your terms to him."

"Good. I hope they're acceptable because I won't alter them," Recker said.

"I'm sure they'll be fine. This might be a good time for your rumored friend to make an appearance."

"Well, if the rumor turned out to be true, I'm sure he would be. But he wouldn't be anywhere anyone would be able to see him."

Vincent chuckled to himself, admiring Recker's attention to detail. "I do wish you'd eventually come around and accept a position with me. We could do a lot of things together."

"Tempting offer, but I think I'll stick with the gig I got now for a while."

"I know. I've given up on possibly tempting you to the dark side for some time now. Anyway, how would you like to find out who the contact is? Want a secret handshake or something? Maybe one of you wears a certain color tie?" Vincent asked, joking. "Maybe one of you sits against the wall drinking a glass of milk through a straw?"

"That would be quite the sight, wouldn't it?"

"I would almost pay money to see it."

"I don't think we need to do anything that extravagant," Recker said. "Just tell me his name. I'll take it from there."

"Ah yes, you have your ways of finding things out, don't you? His name is Detective Tony Andrews. Been on the force about twenty years, black hair, has a wife, two kids."

"What district's he work out of?"

"Twenty-second. He's a good man, you have nothing to worry about with him. Some guys have shifty eyes, you know the ones I'm talking about. You can almost see the wheels spinning inside their heads, wondering how they're gonna try to pull one over on you. But not this guy. He's solid. You'll do good business with him. I'm sure of it."

"I guess we'll see."

Recker and Vincent exchanged a few more pleasantries, then hung up. Recker put his phone back on the counter and put his right hand on his hip, his left elbow leaning across the counter as he stood silently in thought. Though nobody else had said a word since the conversation ended, Recker could almost feel the tense stares of his two partners, beating down on him. He stood straight and looked over at them, a neutral expression on his face. Jones was the first to start hammering him with questions.

"Was that what it sounded like?" Jones asked.

"I dunno. What'd it sound like?"

"It sounded as if you agreed to make an appointment with the good detective that we were speaking of earlier."

"Well, I guess you heard correctly then."

"Weren't we talking about how it was not a good idea to do that?"

Recker looked at him strangely. "I don't recall any of us saying that."

"Oh. We didn't?" Jones asked, looking at Haley, who shook his head. "Hmm. Perhaps I was just thinking it in my head and didn't let the words pass my lips."

"I don't know, I look at it like this. We thought it was strange that an officer wanted to meet, we wondered what he wanted, now we'll know."

"Assuming it's not some type of trap set up to get you."

"You don't think it's a trick, do you?" Haley said.

"No, I don't think so," Recker answered.

"Why not?"

"Because I don't think that Vincent would allow it. It's like he told me, he didn't rescue me from a police car a few months ago, just to set me up, or let someone else set me up a few months later. It wouldn't make any sense."

"I somewhat hate to agree with the man, but that is a valid point," Jones said.

"You want me to tag along?" Haley asked.

"You know it," Recker said. "I may be trusting. But I'm not that trusting."

"Did you get a name of the guy?"

"Yeah. Vincent said his name is Tony Andrews, works out of the twenty-second."

"I'll pull his information up and see what we can find."

As Jones swiveled his chair around to work on the computer, trying to find out what he could about Detective Andrews, Recker and Haley began discussing the specifics of their upcoming late-night outing.

"What are you thinking?" Haley asked.

"Might be better to have you on the outside somewhere," Recker replied. "That way you can give me a little warning if you spot any trouble."

"How about if I sit in a car outside? If something comes up, you duck out the back and I'll fly around to the back door and speed out of there."

"Probably the best option. Either that, or you set up across the street with a rifle."

"Yeah, but if I do that, and trouble pops up, I might not be able to get to you in time. You might get surrounded."

Jones couldn't help but hear parts of the conversation and wanted to put his two cents in. "I think Chris' idea is better."

"Probably," Recker said.

"But neither strategy accounts for the possibility that the police could surround the building before he's able to get to the back door."

"Gino's Bar is at the end of a strip center."

"Yes, I'm aware of the location."

"He's got a roof hatch."

"If it gets too hot, you go up to the roof and make your way to the last building, then climb your way down," Haley said.

"Wouldn't be the first time I had to do that," Recker said.

Jones raised his eyebrows as he continued working. "Yes, but let's hope that it was the last."

30

I t wasn't long before Jones had pulled up a comprehensive file on Detective Andrews. The three men read over his information, but nothing stuck out that would make them apprehensive about the meeting. Other than being on Vincent's payroll, that is. But Andrews had a very good record, had been a detective for over ten years, and from what they could tell, wasn't a dirty cop. If they didn't already know he was in cahoots with Vincent, based on his record and file, they never would have looked twice at him.

"Seems like an upstanding cop," Haley said. "Nothing that would indicate he's not a trustworthy guy or anything."

"You mean, other than the fact he's a cop working with Vincent?" Recker asked.

Haley shook his head, agreeing with the point.

"Well, just because his record seems good, doesn't mean he's necessarily on the up and up," Jones said. "It could be he's just really good at covering his tracks and staying underneath the radar. We still must be cautious."

They continued preparing for the meeting, working right past dinner. Recker had forgotten he was supposed to go home for dinner with Mia. About six-thirty, Recker's phone started ringing again. When he went over to grab it, he made a grimacing face when he saw it was her.

"Hey."

"Hey, yourself," Mia said sternly, though she was just playing with him and wasn't really mad.

"So, how are you?"

"Good. You?"

"Good," Recker answered, thinking maybe she'd forgotten about dinner too. Or she just assumed something had come up and wasn't going to quiz him over it.

"Did you happen to forget something?" Mia asked, keeping up her angry front.

"Uh, yeah, I think so."

"You think? Or you know?"

Recker sighed, knowing he wasn't going to pull one over on her. "I'm sorry. I know I was supposed to come home for dinner. We just got caught up working on something."

"You know, I'm really getting tired of this," Mia said, still in full acting mode. "If you're gonna keep on doing this, I just... I don't know if I can continue."

"Continue?" Recker asked, starting to get worried about what she was going to say. "You mean us?"

"Well... I mean, continue... this charade," she said, unable to keep up the front anymore and letting out a laugh. "I really had you going there for a moment, didn't I?"

A look of relief swept over Recker's face as he wiped some sweat off his forehead. "Yeah, yeah, you did."

"I'm sorry, sweetie, you're not really angry with me, are you?" Mia asked.

Recker thought for a moment, thinking it sounded like he

might be getting off the hook for skipping dinner. "I guess that would depend on you."

"Me? Please don't be mad, honey, I was only joking with you."

"Well, how about we make a deal then?"

Mia wasn't sure she liked the sound of that. "What kind of deal?"

"I won't be mad at you for the kidding if you won't be mad at me for missing dinner," Recker said.

"I guess that's a deal I can live with."

Recker smiled. "OK, then."

"I get the better end of that deal."

"Oh yeah? How you figure?"

"Because I wasn't mad at you to begin with," Mia said.

"Oh," Recker replied, looking at the time. "I know I was supposed to be home around an hour ago. I hope you didn't have things waiting."

"No, actually I had to work a little late myself. I didn't get home until just a little while ago. Maybe ten or fifteen minutes."

"And you just felt the need to call and play a prank on me?"

Mia laughed. "It was kind of funny, don't you think?"

"Yeah, I almost fell on the floor laughing," Recker sarcastically said.

Mia figured they joked around long enough and changed the subject. "I take it you're not coming home anytime soon?"

"No, something really big came up."

"So, you're gonna make me eat alone again?"

"I'm sorry. I'll make it up to you."

"You better," Mia playfully said. "I miss you."

Recker looked over at his friends, not wanting to get too sappy and emotional in front of them and damage his dangerous reputation. He turned his head away from them and put his hand over his mouth as he talked more quietly.

"I miss you too."

Recker didn't talk quietly enough, though. Both Jones and Haley snapped their heads in his direction as he muttered the words, though they'd both heard him say such things before. Recker tried not to get overly sentimental in the work environment to keep his mind focused on business.

"Aww, I miss you too," Haley said, joking.

"Yes, we all miss you," Jones said, getting in on the gag.

Recker laughed to himself as he heard the pair behind him. He looked over at them, trying to give them a stern look to indicate his displeasure, but he couldn't pull it off. He waved his hand at them and turned his back to them again as he continued talking to his girlfriend.

"Was that David and Chris I heard?" Mia asked.

"Yeah, they apparently thought we needed an office clown or something."

"Tell them I said hi."

"I will."

"When will you be home?"

"Probably not till late," Recker answered. "Maybe eleven or twelve."

"That late?"

"I'm sorry. Something big came up."

"Such as?"

"Has to do with the police shootings."

"Shootings? I thought there was only one?" Mia asked.

"Another one happened this morning."

"Oh, no."

"Yeah, so we're gonna look into it."

"I don't get it. Why do you have to look into it? I'm sure the police are launching their own investigation into it, aren't they?"

"Yeah, they are," Recker said. "But somebody asked if I could meet to talk about it."

"If someone has information, why would they talk to you instead of just going to the police about it?"

Recker cleared his throat, not really wanting to tell her who the meeting was with because he knew she'd worry. But, since he was trying not to keep secrets from her, decided to just spit it out. "It's a contact of Vincent's."

"OK? Still seems kind of sketchy to me."

Recker sighed. "You know, you're too smart for your own good sometimes."

"I know. Maybe it's a byproduct of being around you so much. You've rubbed off on me. I hardly ever take anything at face value anymore. There's usually always something else beneath the surface."

"OK, the person I'm meeting is a cop on Vincent's payroll. He asked Vincent to contact me and set something up."

"You're meeting a cop?" Mia asked, astonished. "There's so many ways that can go bad."

"I know. And we've been over every one of them. Vincent has assured me this is on the level."

"I mean no disrespect when I say this, and I know he's saved you before, but you do realize he's a criminal, right? And they're not always trustworthy people?"

"I know. We've been over it," Recker said again.

"OK. Well as long as you know."

"Don't worry. I'll be fine. Nothing will happen."

There was silence for a second as Mia thought of her reply, trying not to sound like the worried girlfriend, even though she was. "Is Chris going out with you when you meet this guy?"

"Yes. He's gonna be on the outside keeping a lookout. First sign of trouble, he'll let me know, and we'll be out of there. Does that make you feel better?"

"I guess a little bit."

"I promise, everything will be fine. If I even had the slightest bit of hesitation about this, I wouldn't go."

"OK. I trust your judgment."

"I'll get home as soon as I can," Recker said.

"I know. I'll wait up for you."

"You don't have to do that. I know you had a long day."

"It's fine. I don't like going to bed without you. I always get this... never mind... I probably shouldn't say anything."

"No, what?"

"When I go to bed without you, I get this weird feeling that I'll wake up and you still won't be there, and you won't be coming home. I dunno, it's stupid. Just some dumb nightmare that I have, I guess."

"It's not stupid."

"Yeah, well, I think I'm becoming more of a worrywart as I'm getting older," Mia said.

"I wouldn't want you to be any different than you are."

Recker didn't realize he had been speaking louder, the other two in the room clearly hearing what he was saying. And they weren't going to miss the opportunity to tease him some more.

"I wouldn't want you to be any different either," Jones said.

Haley also chimed in. "I love you just the way you are too."

Recker slowly turned his head toward the pair and tried to give them an evil stare, though it didn't stop them from making a few more sarcastic responses. After a few more minutes, Recker and Mia finally hung up. Recker put his phone in his pocket and walked over to the desk to get back to the meeting preparations.

"I wasn't aware we had the goof troop come into the office," Recker said.

Haley snickered, trying not to look at him.

"Yes, well, it's not every day we hear someone with your talents talking sweet nothings into his girlfriend's ear," Jones said.

"Sweet nothings? Really?" Recker asked. "OK, how about we stop talking about my love life and get back to business?"

"I'll concur with that."

The three men continued going over and perfecting their plans for the meeting for the next couple of hours until they were all comfortable with it. Once nine o'clock rolled around, Recker and Haley left the office. It was a little under a half hour drive to the bar and Recker wanted to get there early to scope the place out first. Gino's was a place he'd been to a few times before, so he was already familiar with the layout, but wanted to make sure he didn't spot any unfriendly people staking up a spot on the outside waiting for him to arrive.

Recker drove through the shopping center parking lot several times, both him and Haley looking for undercover police in the area. Neither could spot any, though. After they made their fifth pass without noticing any signs of potential trouble, Recker finally pulled into a parking spot. Before getting out, Recker and Haley made sure their communication devices were working and placed them inside their ears.

"First sign of trouble, you let me know," Recker said. "Even if you're not quite sure."

"I'll keep an eye out."

Recker then got out of the car and walked into the bar. There was a good-sized crowd inside, but it wasn't jam-packed. Recker looked around the place, just to make sure Detective Andrews didn't beat him there, and to see if he recognized anybody else that might give him pause. Andrews wasn't there yet, and nobody else made him jumpy, so he found a table in the middle of the room against the wall. He ordered a beer while he was waiting.

"Hey, handsome," a woman said.

Recker's eyes had been focused toward the door and didn't even notice the attractive brown-haired woman standing just to his right. He was a little unnerved as he sensed the woman out of the corner of his eye, looking at him. He slowly turned his head to look at her and gave her a smile.

"Is this seat taken?" the woman asked.

"Uh, I'm actually waiting for someone."

"Your girlfriend?"

"No, just a, uh, just a friend," Recker replied.

"Oh. Well, in that case, mind if I sit down and join you for a while?"

Haley had been carefully listening and spoke into Recker's ear. "Think she might be a cop?"

"Uh, no," Recker whispered.

"What was that?" the woman asked.

"Oh, uh, I was just saying I don't think that'd be a good idea."

"Why not?"

"Well, I have a girlfriend. I wouldn't exactly be too comfortable."

"Why not? Don't trust yourself?"

Recker wasn't sure what to say and didn't really want to keep the conversation going too much longer. He hated awkward situations like these. Though he was good at coercing confessions out of people, or questioning them about their behavior, some things he wasn't as proficient at. Fending an interested and flirty woman away from him would definitely classify as something he wasn't entirely comfortable with. She wasn't an unattractive woman, but considering he already had the most amazing woman at home waiting for him, and he was there on business and waiting for his contact, it wasn't a proposition he was particularly interested in.

Recker looked up at her and smiled. "Maybe another time."

The woman shrugged and grabbed a napkin off the table. She pulled a pen out of the pocket of her jeans and leaned on the table, trying to give Recker an ample view of her cleavage through her low-cut top. Recker caught a quick glimpse of her chest before he realized what she was trying to do and cleared his throat and raised his eyebrows as he looked over toward the door, not wanting to view her assets. Out of the corner of his eye, he saw she was finished and standing straight again and he turned his head to look at her again.

"If you ever decide to change your mind, give me a call," the woman said, giving him a smile.

Recker nodded. "I'll do that."

The woman walked away, taking a quick peek back at him, hoping he'd be glancing at her in her tightly-worn jeans. He wasn't, though. If he was single, maybe he'd have given her a second look. But not with Mia. Recker thought it was inappropriate and disrespectful to be looking at other women, even if it was just in passing or for a quick second. He wasn't interested in playing around, or seeing what else was out there, or even just looking for fun.

"Did, uh, what I think happen... happen?" Haley asked, breaking up the silence.

Recker coughed, putting his hand over his mouth. "Yep. Sure did."

Haley laughed. "You sounded like a fish out of water."

"That type of stuff is definitely not my scene."

"You gonna call her later?"

"Are you crazy?" Recker asked. "I'd have to be an idiot to do that to Mia."

"I agree. Just checking."

"You want the number? You can have it. I'll save it for you."

"I think she might ask questions about how I'd have it," Haley said.

Recker looked over to see where the woman was, watching her standing by the bar, talking to another man. "Something tells me that I'm not the only one she's tried that with. She probably doesn't even remember everyone she's handed her number out to."

"Well, hopefully we can get you out of there soon to save yourself."

"You and me both. I think I'd rather have ten hit men walk through that door and attempt to kill me than have to deal with that type of conversation again," Recker said.

"I dunno, you seemed to have done all right with Mia. You can't be too bad."

"That was kind of an accident. And it happened naturally. If one of us went up to the other in a bar and started talking, who knows how it would have turned out? Maybe we would have never talked again."

"From the way I hear it, that's kind of how it happened, isn't it?" Haley asked.

"Not quite like that. It wasn't anything where one of us went up to the other and started flirting. She came up to me in a diner after spotting me tailing her. A slightly different circumstance."

"I don't know. You two seem perfect for each other. I'd like to think that somehow you two would have found each other no matter what."

"What? Like fate or something?"

"Yeah, something like that," Haley said. "Despite the business we're in, I'd like to think that not everything is left purely to chance. I'd like to think some things are just meant to be. Maybe I'm a hopeless romantic."

"Yeah, well, I'll leave all that kind of stuff to you," Recker said with a laugh. "How's everything looking out there?"

"Quiet. Not seeing anything out here unusual. The bar's open later than everything else in here and some cars are starting to leave, so most of the cars here are probably people inside the bar."

"That'll make it a little easier to identify trouble."

Five minutes to ten, Haley saw a white car pull into the shopping center and park in front of the bar. He kept his eyes glued to the car and a few seconds after the ignition shut off, a man got out from the driver side. Haley looked at the picture of Andrews on his phone and compared it to the driver. It was a match.

"Mike, Andrews just pulled in. He's walking in now."

"Got it. Any signs that he brought friends?"

"Negative."

"All right, keep a lookout."

Detective Andrews walked into the bar and looked around, not sure how he was going to recognize the man he was meeting. Vincent had assured him that Recker would find him once he entered the bar. He just stood there for a minute, trying to keep himself in plain sight to be recognized. Recker thought the detective looked a little nervous. It wasn't a particularly warm, muggy night, so he assumed the sweat on Andrews' forehead was due to his nerves. Recker then stood and waited for Andrews to lock eyes on him. Once their eyes focused on each other, Recker gave the detective a subtle nod. Andrews walked over to Recker's table and stood in front of him.

Andrews pointed at the chair, not wanting to assume anything with the famous vigilante. "You mind?"

Recker shook his head. "Go ahead."

Andrews pulled the chair out and sat across from him. He clasped his hands and fiddled with his fingers as he began speaking. "I guess I should say thanks for agreeing to do this. I know you must've had some reservations about it."

"I did."

"I figured as much. I just want you to know right off the bat there's no tricks involved or anything."

Recker nodded to let him know he understood. "So, what did you wanna talk about?"

Andrews looked around and wiped his forehead, still looking nervous.

"Looking for somebody?" Recker asked.

"No. Sorry. I guess I'm just a little nervous here."

"Why?"

"I'm a cop. You're a wanted man. We make strange bedfellows, no?"

"Is that any different than you working for Vincent?"

"That's a little different," Andrews answered.

"How you figure?"

"He flies a little bit underneath the radar more than you do. You've almost become a larger-than-life figure in this town. Seventy percent of the boys on the force wanna give you a medal and erect a statue in your honor."

"And the other thirty percent wanna lock me up?" Recker asked.

Andrews tilted his head and made a face.

"So which side do you fall on?"

"Listen, from what I can tell, you've never hurt an innocent person and only have targeted criminals. Plus, there was that business with Bernal a while back where you prevented a cop from getting shot. From where I stand, that puts us on the same side."

"Good to know."

"Hey, if I ever roll up on a crime scene and you're still there, you can keep on walking as far as I'm concerned," Andrews said.

"I'll keep that in mind."

"As far as working with Vincent, that's something that just kind of happened," Andrews said, looking away and making a face, indicating that he wasn't very proud of it. "My wife got really sick, had cancer, medical bills really started piling up, couldn't afford payments on the house, just got deeper and deeper in debt."

"And you reached out to him?"

Andrews laughed, almost not believing himself how it went down. "No, not quite. I was working a case that involved Jimmy Malloy, Vincent's right-hand man."

"I know him."

"One day, Vincent approached me as I was eating lunch at a diner, offered me a deal."

"What kind of deal?" Recker asked.

"To let another one of his boys take the rap instead of Malloy. In exchange for that, and for providing information that he might need periodically, he gives me a little something every month."

Recker nodded, sympathetic to the man's story. "Must come in handy."

"It does. I wanna make it clear, though, that I'm not a dirty cop. I don't do anything illegal, well, outside of that I guess. But I love my job, I love this city, and I love helping people. If it came down to helping Vincent or helping another cop, I'd choose the cop all day, every day. A hundred percent."

"What exactly do you do for him now?"

"He has certain business interests all over the place. If I ever get wind of anything that involves those interests, or any of his men, I let him know. That's all. I know, you're probably thinking I'm a hypocrite, but the reasoning is sound on my end."

Recker shrugged. "Who am I to say you're wrong? We all have to have a justification for what we do."

Andrews let out a laugh, agreeing with his point. "Yeah. I have to say, you're not quite what I was expecting."

"Oh? What were you expecting?"

"I dunno. I mean, I've seen your face before, you know, with it being plastered on the news and all. But you seem like a normal, regular guy just sitting here. You see and hear news stories about you and your work and I guess I kind of expected someone that's... I dunno, a lot different. Like one of those old-time movie gangsters that's just mean and nasty and wants to shoot someone on sight."

"Well, I guess people rarely live up to expectations," Recker said.

"Only personality wise. Your work still speaks for itself."

"Thanks. I guess we should stop talking about ourselves here and get down to business."

"Yeah. I guess you've heard about the two police shootings by now?" Andrews asked.

"I have."

"You don't happen to have any info on it, do you?"

"No. I didn't even find out about the first one until this morning," Recker answered.

"Yeah, they did a good job of keeping it out of the news."

"Is that what you wanted me for? To see if I knew of anything?"

"Well, partially. I'm actually one of the detectives who's been assigned to work the cases, along with four other guys."

"And you want me to help?" Recker asked.

"I know you got your own way of doing things. You've got some system perfected that you can find things out about people. In some ways, you're probably better at finding stuff than we are."

Recker smiled. "I won't argue there."

"Yeah, well, if you could keep an ear out and if you turn anything, maybe give me a shout?"

Though Recker wasn't against doing as the detective asked, something wasn't making sense to him. It was still very early in the investigation period. The fact Andrews was already asking for help seemed a little strange. If it had been a few weeks or a month, and the police weren't making any headway, Recker might have understood reaching out to him. But the second shooting just occurred that morning. It was way too soon in his mind to be asking for help from someone who wasn't considered on the same side of the law. It reeked of being a desperation move. One that didn't need to occur just yet.

"You'll have to forgive me for being a little skeptical, but isn't a little soon to be asking for help from me?" Recker asked.

"What do you mean?"

"The first shooting just happened a couple days ago. The

413

second this morning. I mean, that's hardly enough time to just get the facts of what happened written in your notebook, isn't it?"

Andrews moved his head around and sighed, looking at various people in the bar. Recker could tell by his face he was holding something back. Andrews then ordered a beer, figuring he could use a little something extra in his system to help explain things.

"I guess that's why you're as good as you are, huh?" Andrews asked.

"I'm good at reading people."

"So I see. All right, so look, these aren't the first two shootings that we've attributed to this guy."

"How many more?"

"The first one that we think he did was a couple weeks ago. The victim was a low-level drug dealer."

Recker looked at him strangely, not seeing the connection to a minor drug player and two police officers. "So how you figure they're related?"

Andrews took a sip of his beer. "Well, it gets a little more complicated than just that. First, he was killed with a forty-five hollow-point bullet."

"Not really what you would call conclusive evidence."

"No, but there's more. Then last week, another guy dropped dead, courtesy of a forty-five hollow-point bullet."

"What was his line of work?" Recker asked, assuming it was something illegal.

"That's just it. He wasn't a criminal. He was just a regular guy."

"Then how does it fit?"

"Apparently, this guy rode his bike to and from work every night. Same route every time. About five days after the drug dealer went down. And the path that he rode every night, was the very same area that the drug dealer frequented. Matter of fact, they were killed one street apart from each other," Andrews said.

"That is a pretty big coincidence."

"Yeah. So, we're figuring that maybe the guy saw a transaction go down, something he wasn't supposed to see, and he got taken out for it."

"Question the guy's family or anything? Maybe he told someone what he saw," Recker said.

"Ahh, we checked. He was a young kid, about twenty-two, still lived with his mother and younger sister. They didn't know anything about it. I doubt he would've told them anything and bogged them down with that kind of stuff."

"That's fine, but I still don't see how that relates to the two officers getting shot."

"The first officer that got shot was Anthony Rios. He's a seven-year veteran on an undercover assignment. Guess how he figures into this?"

"He was buying off the drug dealer?"

Andrews nodded. "Bingo. Guess where he was shot?"

"Same area."

"Same street as the drug dealer."

"What was his name?" Recker asked.

"Kevin Maldonado."

"What was Rios' assignment?"

"To get in close with Maldonado and figure out where he's getting his stash from. He was a name we started hearing more from, moving up the ladder, you know what I mean?"

"I think so."

"We think there might be an emerging drug player in the city and we believed Maldonado had ties to him."

"What about the cop this morning?"

Andrews threw his hand up and looked disgusted as his eyes glanced around the room. "That we don't know. We haven't figured out yet how that comes into play."

"No ties to any of them?" Recker asked.

"Not that we've uncovered so far. Rios was in a narcotics unit. The officer that got shot this morning was Peter Kirby. He works in a patrol unit. As far as we can tell, he hasn't had any interaction with Rios or Maldonado."

"And you're sure it's the same shooter?"

"Same type of bullet, same markings. We're pretty sure it's the same guy."

"And you don't have any other leads or suspects?"

"Not yet, no," Andrews answered, shaking his head.

"How about something in their personal life? Maybe the answer lies there, and they killed the drug dealer and other guy to make it look like it's something else."

"Well, we obviously haven't been able to check out everything with Kirby yet since it's still fresh. Rios, though, nothing turned up adversarial."

"And nobody on the street knows anything?" Recker asked.

"Not so far."

"Did you check with Vincent to see if he knows anything?"

"No."

"Why not?"

"You may not believe this, but I try to keep my conversations with him limited. I don't want to ask him favors that I might have to repay later," Andrews said.

"What is it that you're actually asking me to do?"

"Poke around a little, see what you can dig up. I dunno, maybe we're missing something, maybe something got overlooked."

"Seems a little weird that you're here asking this of me," Recker said. "Seems like you'd have the whole department and then some at your disposal for this."

"Well, you're right there, but when you don't have any leads or suspects to work off, you get desperate pretty quick. Especially when it's cops that start falling. And believe me, they're the only reason I'm even here. If it was just a bunch of criminals getting whacked, I wouldn't be here either."

"You think there might be more to come?"

Andrews sighed. "I don't know. I hope not. But, something's telling me there's gonna be more if we don't wrap this up quick. And I'd make a deal with just about anyone to make sure no other cops get it."

"Rios is still alive, though, right?"

"Yeah, was released yesterday and pulled off the undercover assignment this morning."

"He doesn't have any ideas?"

"None. He's as in the dark as the rest of us."

"And if I actually make headway on this?" Recker asked. "What is it that you want me to do? Wrap him up in a bow for you?"

"I guess that depends on what the situation calls for. If there's any way that you can let me know so I can take him in, I'd appreciate getting a heads up on it. If it's a situation where your life is on the line and you gotta take him down, then you gotta do what you gotta do. If that's the case, I'd still appreciate it if you could let me know so I can wrap the case up."

Recker had all the information he needed at that point and wanted to start winding things down. He didn't want to sit there too long and make himself a target, just in case. He was pretty sure Andrews was leveling with him about everything. He didn't get any sense the detective was trying to mislead him or manipulate him in any way.

"All right, I think I've got enough to start with," Recker said.

"Does that mean you're on it?"

"I'll see what I can find out."

A relieved look came across Andrews' face and he broke out a smile. "Just so we're clear on everything, I can't offer you money or anything for this."

"It's fine. I'm not interested in money."

"OK, well, if there's anything I can ever do for you, just name it. Within reason. I can't get you out of jail or anything if you ever get brought in. Maybe I can help you avoid that if I ever hear someone's on the verge of nailing you, though."

"I'll remember that."

"Well, thanks a lot. Really appreciate this," Andrews said.

He hesitated for a second, not sure whether he should put his hand out and offer to shake Recker's. He didn't know if the man known as The Silencer would be all that interested in shaking the hand of a police officer. Andrews finally stuck his hand out, nervous about the response, hoping he wouldn't just get blown off. Recker, after a brief hesitation himself, put his hand out to finish the handshake. Andrews got up to leave, before remembering a few final questions.

"Oh, uh, do you have a name or something to call you?" Andrews asked. "Kind of weird just calling you Silencer, you know?"

Recker wasn't sure it was in his best interests to reveal any part of his name, but then figured why not? It was an alias, anyway, and even if Andrews decided to run it through his computers, it wouldn't come back with anything. There was really no harm in him knowing his name.

"Mike."

"One final thing," Andrews said. "How can I reach you or get in touch if I have something else for you or if you find out anything?"

"I got your number."

"You do? How?"

"Like you said earlier... I've got my ways."

31

Recker stayed seated as Andrews left the bar. He alerted Haley the detective was on his way out and for him to keep an eye on him. Andrews immediately got in his car and pulled out of the parking lot. As soon as he did, Haley let Recker know.

"Mike, Andrews is gone."

"See anything out there?"

"No, quiet as it was before."

"Did he get on his phone or anything as he walked to the car?" Recker asked.

"No. Didn't do anything suspicious. Went right to his car and left right away."

"All right, good. Pull around to the back door and pick me up."

"You got it. On my way."

Recker got up from his table and walked over to the bar. The bartender on duty that night was also the owner of the place.

"Charlie, you mind if I go out the back?" Recker asked.

"Yeah, no problem, let me just open it up for you."

Two years earlier, Recker saved Charlie from getting robbed.

From that night on, Charlie let Recker know if he ever needed anything, to let him know. Recker took him up on that and used his bar a few times for meeting purposes. Charlie was always very grateful for The Silencer in helping and saving him that he never breathed a word about him occasionally showing up. He always felt better, and safer, when Recker stopped by periodically and he was happy to help him out in whatever way he needed. Even if it was just the use of a table for an hour or two.

"How was your meeting?" Charlie asked, as the two walked to the back door.

"Went fine, thanks."

"Good. Glad to hear it."

"Thanks for letting me use your place," Recker said, patting him on the shoulder.

"Oh, no problem, champ. Anytime you ever need it, just say the word, you know that."

Charlie unlocked the back door and opened it a sliver before closing it quickly.

"You want me to peek out there just to make sure there's no shenanigans out there?"

Recker smiled, appreciating the gesture. "No, I think it's OK."

"Well OK, if you say so."

Charlie opened the door again, and the two shook hands before Recker walked out. Haley had the SUV parked only a few feet away so Recker hopped in the passenger seat. As the car started to drive away, Charlie gave the pair a wave goodbye, though he didn't know who the driver was.

"You know that guy?" Haley asked.

"Yeah. He owns the bar."

"I think he recognized me."

"No, you're good."

"You trust him?"

"Hmm?" Recker asked, staring out the window. "Oh, yeah. He's fine. I stopped a robbery here last year. He told me if I ever needed to use his place for anything to just say the word."

"Oh. Good deal."

"Yeah, I've used the place a few times. He's trustworthy. Even if he sees you, he won't say anything."

As they drove back to the office, they talked about the specifics of the meeting.

"What'd you think?" Haley asked. "Think he's on the level?"

Recker nodded. "Yeah. I think he is."

"Still seems weird to me."

"Certainly isn't normal," Recker said.

"You think he was holding something else back?"

"Why? You think so?"

"I dunno. I guess I'm just having a hard time getting a grasp on this."

"I think he's afraid more bodies are gonna drop before they find out who it is and is just trying to prevent it as much as possible."

"Yeah, I guess so."

They continued tossing questions back and forth with each other as they discussed the situation, each coming up with some ideas as to what might have been going on. Once they got back to the office, all the lights were still on as Jones was banging away at the computer keyboard. As soon as he heard the two of them enter, he swiveled his chair around to greet them. He looked the two of them over as they walked closer to him.

"I don't see any holes," Jones quipped.

"They had bad aim," Recker shot back.

Jones looked to Haley for the straight story. Though they hadn't reported running into any trouble, Jones couldn't always tell when Recker was joking. Even when he was in a gunfight, he sometimes played it off as if it was no big deal. So the times he said he wasn't, but made a joke referencing it, Jones sometimes looked at him cross-eyed.

Haley shook his head. "There was no trouble."

"Let's keep this short," Recker said, grabbing a chair, and sitting. "Mia's waiting up for me."

"Let's get to the gist of things then, shall we?" Jones asked. "Your thoughts from the meeting?"

"He seemed like he was legit. I didn't get any bad vibes or think he was trying to pull the rug out from under me."

"What exactly did he want?"

Recker shrugged. "Seemed like he just wanted help if we could give it."

"And that's all there was to it?"

"Well, not quite. He did reveal that there have been more than two shootings that they attribute to this shooter."

"Oh?" Jones said, looking confused. "I didn't hear of anything else."

"The other two victims weren't cops. One was a drug dealer, and the other was an innocent person who they think may have been a witness to something."

"Witness to what?"

"Don't know. But the undercover cop, the drug dealer, and the witness, were all shot in the same area. Two on the same street, the other on the next street over."

Jones ran his fingers over his mouth, deep in thought. "Now that is interesting, isn't it?"

"The police don't seem to have any leads or suspects," Recker said. "I think they're just worried, at least Andrews is, that more bodies are gonna drop soon before they get a beat on whoever it is."

"I guess they're just trying to throw their nets out as wide as possible in hopes of catching something."

Recker threw his hands up. "Guess so."

"Did he give you any other details, files, anything we can use to start looking into it?"

"No. What do we need that for? Since when couldn't we find out whatever we needed on our own?"

"Good point. I just thought it might be a little quicker," Jones replied.

Recker stood, ready to call it a night. "Well, I guess we can get started on it in the morning."

"Well, at some point tomorrow, anyway."

"What do you mean?"

"Have you forgotten we have other things to attend to?" Jones asked. "We're not here to serve at the whim of the police department. I told you earlier that we were close to working on another case of our own."

"Guess we'll be pulling down double duty."

"Is it something that requires both of us?" Haley asked. "Maybe I can take the case and Mike sticks on the police thing?"

"We'll discuss it more tomorrow," Jones said. "As I said, we'll handle our own business first. As much as I respect the police and don't wish any harm to come to them, they do have their own investigation capabilities."

Recker seemed indifferent. He certainly wasn't against helping the police out, but understood Jones' point of view.

"How bad is this upcoming case?" Recker asked.

"It looks as though it could be quite severe," Jones answered.

"How soon is the threat level?"

"Could be tomorrow. Possibly the day after. I have not nailed down a definitive time frame yet."

"You haven't nailed it down or they haven't figured it out yet?"

"They have not said specifically yet."

"All right. Well, I guess we'll figure all that out tomorrow."

The three men then went their separate ways for the night. Jones stayed up for another hour to work some more, while

Recker and Haley went to their respective apartments. Just as she promised, Mia was up and watching TV to pass the time as she waited for Recker to get home. As soon as he did, she rushed over to him and threw her arms around him as they passionately embraced for a minute or two.

"I take it everything went well tonight?" Mia asked.

"Just like I told you it would."

"I know. I'm sorry for worrying."

"It's fine," Recker replied with a kiss.

Mia helped him take his coat off and walked over to the closet to hang it up. As soon as she put it on the hanger, she put her hands inside the pockets to make sure there was nothing in there Recker might need. She pulled out a piece of paper and saw a woman's name and phone number written on it. Slightly alarmed, though not terribly so, as she was sure he had a good explanation for it, Mia closed the closet door and started walking toward the couch where Recker was now sitting.

"Would you like to explain what this is?" Mia asked, holding the napkin up in the air between two of her fingers.

Recker squinted for a second, not sure what it was. He quickly realized what it was and batted his eyes. He was a little mad at himself for not ditching it or giving it to Haley. He had completely forgotten about the woman who gave him her phone number. As she waited for an explanation, Mia put her hands on her hips, giving off a vibe that she was either annoyed, jealous, or both. In reality, she was sure there was a logical reason behind it. She trusted him completely and didn't give the tiniest thought to him ever cheating on her. But she liked to have a little fun with him sometimes.

"Oh, that," Recker said.

"Yeah, this."

"Well, there's a funny story behind that."

Mia made a huge fake smile. "I'll bet."

Recker laughed. "No, really. I was sitting at a table in the bar waiting for my contact to show up and this woman walked up to me and gave it to me."

"And you just conveniently put it in your pocket?" Mia asked.

Recker faked a cough as he cleared his throat. "Well, I was actually going to give it to Chris to see if he wanted to call the girl up or something."

"Oh. Because you just love to play Suzy Matchmaker now? You're just an old-fashioned romantic at heart and want all your friends to be healthy and happily in love for the rest of their lives?"

Recker couldn't help but let out a smile at the reference. He was sure he'd never be called Suzy Matchmaker again. But it was kind of amusing. "Uh, yeah, something like that. I figured if I'm gonna be lucky enough to find the woman I'd like to spend the rest of my life with, why shouldn't everyone else?"

This time, it was Mia with the smile. "Good save. You know, you're becoming much more of a smooth talker."

Recker didn't really have a comeback and just shrugged. "Honest. It's exactly the way it happened."

Mia slowly marched over to him, trying to keep her mad face plastered on, though she was having a tough time accomplishing it. Once she reached the couch, she leaned over and planted a kiss on Recker's lips.

"Of course I believe you. Looked like you were starting to sweat there for a second, though," she said with a smile.

"Eh, not really. I would hope that you know it would take a lot more than some girl in a bar to take me away from you."

Mia faked another offended look. "A lot more? It better be darn near impossible."

"Well, I don't want you to get too comfortable," Recker joked.

Mia raised her eyebrows and looked at him sternly, still playing around with him. "You wanna say that again?"

"Maybe I should just quit while I'm ahead."

Mia nodded. "That might be a good idea."

Mia leaned in and put her hands on the back of Recker's head, giving him a kiss on the forehead, then another kiss on the lips. "I love you," she said.

"I love you too," Recker replied.

Mia then stood straight and looked at the napkin for a moment. "So, what should I do with this? Put it back in your pocket? Give it to Chris? Throw it out?"

"Might as well just throw it out."

"Why? Don't you think Chris will want it?"

"Well, considering that woman seemed to be going to just about every guy there who looked like he was alone, I don't think she'd be his type."

Mia gave him a disappointed look. "Mike, don't assume she's that type of girl. Maybe she was just lonely and looking for someone. Doesn't mean she was ready to go home with every man she came into contact with."

"You're right. I shouldn't assume."

"Was she pushy or anything?"

Recker shook his head. "No, not really. Ahh, just throw it out. Chris can get his own girls. I did."

Mia walked into the kitchen and tossed the napkin into the trash can.

"I think I'll just get ready for bed," she said, walking past him and into their bedroom.

Recker sighed. "Yeah, probably a good idea."

After just a couple minutes, she opened the door and stood within the framework, wearing nothing but a baseball jersey that just barely covered all her essentials.

"Would you care to join me?" she seductively asked.

"Yeah, I think I would."

"Unless you're too tired or something."

Recker got up and hurried into the bedroom. "Not that tired."

32

Recker, Jones, and Haley met up in the office just after eight. They had a quick breakfast before they started discussing business and making plans for the day. They all sat at the desk as Jones started going over their next case.

"You have things nailed down yet?" Recker asked.

Jones sighed and looked at the computer screen, usually a sign there was something he didn't like in what he was about to say. "Not totally. And unfortunately, we're going to have to roll without having the full plan in play."

"What do you mean?"

"Well, I know the players involved. I know the general basics of the scheme. I just don't know how it will all unfold."

"What's going on?" Haley asked.

Jones gave each of the Silencers a folder with all the particulars, each getting the same exact information. It was easier that way, instead of them passing papers around back and forth.

"As you can see, this may get very deeply involved," Jones said.

As Recker looked at the information, his eyes shifted around, and a deeply concerned look fell over his face. "The victim's a six-month-old baby girl?"

"Well, Kathrynn Rocco is the target. I believe she is not what this group of kidnappers is really after though."

"Not a ransom attempt?"

"Hardly."

"Her mother is Judge Sandra Rocco?" Haley said.

"Yes," Jones said, pointing at him. "And that's where it gets interesting. Judge Rocco is about to preside over a high-profile trial involving a criminal defense attorney who was arrested over some shady dealings he had."

"When's this trial start?" Recker asked.

"Three days from now."

"So, they're gonna kidnap the child in hopes of swaying her decisions?"

"I would think that's the play."

"So, they're just gonna hold this kid until the trial's over?" Haley asked.

"It looks like that's the plan," Jones replied.

"So how are they gonna do it?"

"Well, Judge Rocco has a nanny that cares for the child during the day. From what I can gather, she takes the baby for a walk every day unless it rains."

"And on a set schedule," Recker said, looking disturbed.

"Almost like clockwork. She takes the baby to Rittenhouse Square Park at one o'clock every day."

"Why not just put a sign on the kid that says kidnap me?"

Jones could understand his friend's frustration, though he tried to limit it. "Mike, not everyone is as alert to these things as we are. You can't always blame people for not thinking like us."

Recker nodded. "I know. I just... it just bothers me when a kid is involved."

"I know. And we'll do everything we can to protect her."

"The nanny isn't in on it, is she?"

"No. She's a twenty-five-year-old that's apparently known the judge for six years, since she was in college. There doesn't appear to be any connection."

Haley scratched the top of his head as he read the information in the folder. "If there's been any threats, why isn't the judge and her family under protection? U.S. Marshals should be involved, shouldn't they?"

"They would be if there was a threat levied," Jones replied. "The problem is, there hasn't been any."

"They haven't made any threats against the judge?"

"None whatsoever. The good judge has no idea what they're planning or even that there's any kind of threat at all."

"So how many people are involved in this?" Recker asked.

"That's a little tougher to determine right now. I know three definitely, but I suspect there's more."

"Why do you think that?"

"Some of the messages they've sent each other indicated there was at least one or two more," Jones said. "Now, perhaps they were speaking in code, or just being cautious, but several emails I intercepted seemed to suggest another man that they reported to."

"So, what exactly is their plan?" Haley asked. "I mean, they have to have something other than just snatching the kid in broad daylight."

"Chris is right," Recker said. "Rittenhouse Park isn't exactly an off the beaten path area. There's a good number of people there. If they just take the kid out in the open, they're gonna draw a lot of attention to themselves."

"Unfortunately, that's all the information I have right now. I don't yet know how they're going to do it. I just know that they will," Jones said.

The trio fell silent for a minute, all of whom were thinking about the situation. "They're going to need an elaborate setup," Recker said.

"They're probably gonna have a car already running nearby that they can jump into," Haley said.

"So, assuming they're not just gonna walk up to the nanny and take the kid from her and run, they're going to have some sort of distraction."

"That would seem to be the most likely scenario," Jones said. "But that also leads us up to problem number two."

"Which is?"

"I still haven't pinned down the date this is happening."

"You mean you still don't know?" Recker asked. "I was under the impression this was going down today."

"It very well could be today."

"Or not?"

"Or not," Jones replied. "Either they're using code phrases to disguise the date, or they just have not set a timetable yet."

"Or there's a third option."

"Which is?"

"That they have set a date and you just haven't gotten it yet," Recker said.

"Yes, it is possible that they may have met off channel."

"So, what are we gonna do?" Haley asked.

Recker sighed, not really liking the only choice available, though he knew there was nothing else they could do. "Looks like we're gonna be taking a walk in the park."

"For how long?"

"Until someone shows up," Recker replied.

"How positive are we that it's actually gonna go down in the park?"

"I'm quite certain, why do you ask? Do you have another idea?" Jones said.

"Well, knowing that it might be busy in the park, could it

happen somewhere else? Maybe on the street walking to the park or on the way back?"

"The judge lives within walking distance of the park so I guess it is theoretically possible it could happen on the way there. But all the information that I could piece together indicated that it would be done in the park."

"Probably would be a good idea if one of us had eyes on the kid as soon as they leave the judge's house," Recker said.

"As long as you keep your distance."

"Why?"

"If you're too close, and the kidnappers also have their eyes on the nanny from the moment she leaves the house, then it's quite possible they'll spot and notice you," Jones said. "Could blow your cover sky-high."

"Might be a chance we have to take. Even if we're spotted, might be enough to scare them off."

"I don't think so."

"Why not?"

"Because we now know that these people are targeting the judge," Jones said. "We know what they're planning and can act accordingly. If we play this right, we can foil the plot, and disable the perpetrators."

"Alive?"

"That is my hope. If they're alive and arrested, they can be questioned, then perhaps it will be learned how far up the chain it goes and whether it was in fact ordered by our shady lawyer friend. But if we spoil the plan too soon, then there's no telling whether they'll try to strike again, whether they'll abandon this plan and try something different, or whether we'll even learn of the new plan at all. That is a lot to leave up to chance, don't you think?"

Recker nodded, agreeing with the professor's thoughts. "That is a lot to leave up to chance. All right, we'll just have to stake the park out every day until the thing goes down."

"What about the police problem?" Haley asked.

Recker looked at Jones, deferring the question to him.

"I will begin to look into it today," Jones said. "I don't know how much I'll be able to uncover, though. I'm much better at discovering problems before they happen than after the fact. Besides that, it's not like we have much to work with. We don't really have much in the way of information or evidence that would point us in any specific direction."

"Maybe we need some extra eyes and ears in the field," Recker said.

"And by that you mean?"

"Tyrell."

"Mike, as good as Tyrell is, and he is quite good at finding and getting information, don't you think the police have their own contacts on the street? I mean, I'm sure they have their own Tyrell's."

"Maybe so. But I would put money on ours over theirs."

"As you wish."

Recker took out his phone and called Tyrell's number. In the time since Jeremiah was killed, Tyrell had not been as active on the streets. He still did some occasional jobs for Vincent, as well as whenever Recker needed something, but his other activities had been cut down. He was still making as much money, if not more, than he was with Jeremiah. Recker usually had a need for him at least a couple of times every month and he always made sure Tyrell was well compensated.

Recker probably gave Tyrell more money than was necessary, but he wanted to make sure Tyrell wasn't short on what he needed. Mostly because he didn't want Tyrell branching off and trying other things that were more dangerous and risk the possibility of getting arrested. Part of it was because they were friends. The other part was because they'd spent the last several years cultivating a relationship that ran like a finely tuned vintage car. If Tyrell got himself jammed up, then Recker would be left without a guy on the street who could get the information that he did. Either that, or he'd have to try to find someone new. And Recker wasn't much interested in that scenario. It took time for Recker to trust new people. He already knew what Tyrell could do, he knew he could be trusted.

"Yo, what's up?" Tyrell greeted.

"Hey, have some work for you."

"Whatcha got?"

"You know anything about those police shootings?" Recker asked.

"Nah, not really."

"Do you know about them though?"

"I heard a cop got shot this morning. That's about it though."

"Well, it goes a little deeper than that."

"Usually does."

"I want you to start digging your nose into it and see what you can find out. There's been one uniformed officer shot, one undercover cop, a drug dealer, and what appears to be a possible witness."

"All right, I'll see what I can do," Tyrell said. "What kind of time frame are you looking at?"

"As soon as possible. No telling when the shooter will strike again."

"OK, no sweat. Why you involved with this, though? Not really your MO."

"Let's just say someone on the inside is concerned and wants as much help as possible to put an end to this quickly."

"All right, you got it, man. I'll start now. Send me an email with as much as you got on it."

"I will. I'll have David do it in a few minutes. I'm on my way to something else right now."

After they hung up, Recker instructed Jones to send the email to Tyrell as he asked. They still had some time before they had to go to the park, so they spent every bit of it going over the layout of the park and where each of them would be.

"Let's go over the people we know are involved in this," Recker said.

They started studying the sheets of information that Jones had compiled on the people he had identified as being a part of the caper. As they began going over it, Recker's phone rang.

"You sure are popular this morning," Jones said.

Recker pulled out his phone again, surprised that Malloy would be calling him.

"Yeah?" Recker answered.

"You free to talk for a few minutes?" Malloy asked.

"Yeah, I guess so."

"Good. Boss wants to talk to you, hold on."

"Mike, how are you?" Vincent asked.

"OK. You?"

"Not too bad considering."

"So, what's up?" Recker asked.

"Just wondering how your meeting with our mutual friend went last night?"

"It went fine."

"Good. I take it everything was on the up and up like I said. That's part of why I called, just wanted to make sure I wasn't made a liar out of."

"No, everything went down without a hitch."

"Glad to hear it."

"Do you plan on giving our friend a hand?" Vincent asked.

"I'll see what I can do. I'm not making any promises. I've got other stuff I need to work on, but if I learn anything, I'll pass it along."

"That's fine. It helps you in the long run, anyway."

"How's that?" Recker asked.

"The more people you know in places of authority, the more chances are that you'll get help when you need it the most."

"I don't do things with the expectation of someone owing me a favor later."

"Of course not," Vincent said. "But it doesn't hurt to know people. Especially people such as us who aren't exactly known for being on the right side of the law."

"I suppose not. I take it that since he came to me for assistance that you don't have any ideas yourself as to who's behind it?"

"I do not. If I did, I'd serve the shooter up on a silver platter myself. This kind of behavior is bad for business."

"I guess this type of stuff is bad for everyone, huh?"

"Yes, it is. Brings too much heat, too much scrutiny, too much publicity and public pressure. Bad for all of us."

"I guess that means it's fairly safe to assume that it's nobody involved in your organization?" Recker said.

"Nobody involved in my organization would dare do something like that. Even if they're only occasionally employed by me. Something like that would have to be authorized by me personally. If someone did that without my knowledge and consent, they would be dealt with severely."

The two men continued talking for a few more minutes, neither saying anything more than what was already said. As far as Recker could tell, Vincent's main concern seemed to be that no nefarious behavior went down. Though many people had differing opinions of the crime boss, and most of them would probably be accurate, Vincent did strive to be a man of his word, especially to those people he respected or worked with. And Recker qualified on both counts.

435

"Anything we need to be concerned about?" Jones asked, since he knew Vincent usually didn't call just to shoot the breeze.

"No. I think he just wanted to make sure I wasn't in jail."

"Huh?"

"From last night. Meeting the detective. I think he just wanted to make sure I wasn't set up," Recker said.

"Oh. Well how nice of him to be concerned about your welfare."

"Yeah. Enough about him. Let's get back to business."

33

It was eleven o'clock, and Recker and Haley were getting ready to leave. Before they left, they all went over the information and plan one more time with Jones. There were three men they knew were involved. All of whom had criminal records. Recker was almost positive there would be more, though. The three men they were aware of had all worked together previously. They weren't known to work with anyone else, but something was gnawing at him that there had to be more. He figured if they were to pull something like this off, they had to at least have six or eight people working it. Of course, he hoped he was wrong, and there were only the three. The fewer people he had to deal with, the better he liked it. As Recker and Haley were about to leave the office, Jones had some last-minute advice for them.

"Can we please avoid a firefight in the middle of the park?" Jones politely asked.

"What? You wanna take away all our fun?" Recker replied.

"I wouldn't dream of it."

When Recker and Haley got to the park, they spread out as they planned. Recker started walking to the vicinity of Judge

Rocco's house, while Haley meandered through the park, looking for signs of anything that might look peculiar. As Recker walked along the street, he also kept his eyes peeled for any signs of trouble. Since he knew there might be someone already watching the Rocco house, Recker made sure he kept moving. He didn't want it to look like he was also watching the house in case he was spotted too.

Being alert as he usually was, Recker didn't see anything that looked suspicious. He walked around the block then stopped at the end of the street and leaned up against the side of a building. He was curious if Haley saw anything yet.

"Chris, you got anything on your end?"

"No. Not that I can see, anyway. I don't even know what I'm looking for, though."

"Well, you see the three guys we're looking for?"

"No. But I kind of doubt they're just gonna walk past me either," Haley said.

"Never know. Remember, they don't know we're here. So, they're not looking for us like we are for them."

"Yeah, I guess. Would be easier if we knew what they were gonna do."

"At least we have the time it's gonna go down," Recker said. "Other than that, we're just gonna have to wing it."

"You're right, it could be worse if we didn't know what time it was happening. Around the clock surveillance would be rough."

"Just keep your eyes peeled."

Recker looked at the time. It was twelve-thirty. A half hour until the nanny took the Rocco child for her afternoon walk in the stroller. Recker anxiously watched every person who walked by, every car that drove by, hoping he'd spot one of the men he was looking for. He didn't, though. At least not yet. Once one o'clock hit, he looked down at the Rocco house and noticed the front door swing open. He noticed the nanny coming out with the baby in her arms.

Recker let Haley know. "Chris, they're coming out of the house now."

"Roger that."

Recker got ready to move and started walking toward the park. He was walking slow enough that, eventually, the nanny and baby would walk past him. He thought it would look much more natural than if he tailed them the entire way there. He periodically stopped and looked at the scenery, pretending to take pictures of the nature around him to give them a chance to catch up to him.

"Anything yet on your end?" Haley asked.

"All clear so far."

Recker looked back to make sure he didn't see anyone else tailing the nanny. He didn't notice anything suspicious though. But it didn't mean they weren't there. He kept walking to the park then pretended he had a phone call. He stopped and made some hand gestures as he blurted some words out to keep up the ruse in case anyone was watching him. After a few more minutes, the nanny walked past him. Recker gave her a smile as she did, still pretending to be on the phone. He gave her a head start on him before he started walking behind her. The entire way to the park, Recker was waiting for the sound of screeching tires against the asphalt, or frantic screams of someone about to make the child heist, something chaotic that would indicate what was about to happen. A warning. But there was none. As they got to the park entry, Recker let his partner know where they were.

"We're making our way into the park now," Recker said. "Where you at?"

"I'm right smack in the middle."

"OK. We're coming in by 19th street. Come this way and then we'll switch off."

"On my way."

Recker followed the nanny into the park, keeping a safe distance between them. After a few minutes, he saw Haley walking in their direction. Once Recker saw him, he peeled off and took a different path. He still stayed in the area and kept an eye on their subject as Haley moved in closer. Once the nanny took a seat on one of the benches, Haley did the same, not too far from her position. After a few minutes, another young woman came along, also with a stroller. As far as Recker and Haley knew, she wasn't supposed to be meeting anyone. Recker quickly contacted Jones to see if he had an idea of what was going on.

"David, the nanny's meeting another woman," Recker said. "You know who it is?"

"Hold on, I'm checking."

Haley stealthily took a picture of the two women and sent it to Jones. "David, just sent you a picture of them."

Jones looked at his phone as soon as it alerted him of the message. He quickly looked at the photo as he started comparing it to people he had on his screen.

"Anything yet?" Recker asked, getting impatient.

"I'm still checking," Jones replied.

"Soon would be nice. I guess it's not necessary, though, it's not like we're trying to prevent a kidnapping or anything."

"Sarcasm will get you nowhere, Michael, and it won't help me get the information faster either."

"I know, I know."

Jones was typing away speedily, swiveling his chair between two computers. On one, he was comparing pictures of who he suspected the woman might be, as well as checking phone records on the other computer. He was trying to go as fast as he could, knowing what was at stake. Recker knew Jones was trying to get the information as quickly as possible and it wasn't so easy to get it within a few minutes.

"They're talking and laughing," Recker said. "I see a lot of smiles so maybe they already know each other."

As they waited for Jones to give them something, Recker's eyes scanned the area, though he still didn't see anything out of the ordinary. The park seemed like it was hustling with people and Recker just couldn't see how they were going to kidnap the child with all these people around. Of course, then he thought maybe that's what the kidnappers were counting on. Maybe they were going to use the crowd to blend in to disguise their movements. After five more minutes, Jones finally came up with something.

"I've got her," Jones said.

"Who is she?" Recker asked.

"Her name is Jordan. Her and the nanny are good friends it appears. Seems they meet at the park three or four days a week. I hacked into their text messages. They plan these outings in advance, agreeing to meet each other the night before or that morning."

"She have a criminal record? Maybe she's just setting her up."

"No. Seems as though they went to college together. Nothing in her background would suggest she would be mixed up in something like this either."

"Are they both nannies?"

"No, the baby Jordan has is actually hers. It's an eight-month-old boy," Jones said.

"All right, thanks. We'll keep our eyes open."

Recker and Haley did just that for the next hour as the two women sat on the bench and talked with their babies in their strollers. The girls did get up and walk around for a bit, followed closely by Haley. Recker took an alternate path and tried to get out ahead of them. They walked around the park until two-thirty, eventually saying goodbye and going their separate ways. The nanny immediately started walking back to the Rocco house, with

Recker and Haley still on her tail. They staggered their positions, so they weren't seen walking together.

The two Silencers were on high alert, expecting something to happen. It didn't happen in the park, so they figured it would happen on the way back. Every car that drove by, every person they passed, Recker was ready to pounce and unleash his fury on the kidnappers. They were slightly surprised that once the nanny got back to the house, nothing had happened. Since Recker walked by the house earlier, he didn't want to do it again and get made. This time, Haley walked past the home to see if he could make out something Recker couldn't. But just like his partner, Haley didn't find anything unusual either. After Haley walked around the block, he met back up with Recker near the park entrance to figure out their next move. Before they did anything, Recker let Jones know everything seemed clear.

"David, the nanny's back in the house with the baby. Nobody made a move toward them."

"Well, we did say that we did not know the date that this was supposed to happen," Jones replied. "Perhaps tomorrow will be the day."

"Yeah, maybe. We're gonna stay here for a little while and see if we spot anything."

"You don't think the kidnappers are there, do you?"

"I dunno. Probably not. But you never know. Maybe they were here watching too, trying to make sure their plan was good," Recker said.

Once Recker hung up, he and Haley walked back into the park, with a careful eye out on spotting any of the men they saw in the photos.

"You really think they might be here?" Haley asked.

Recker shrugged. "I don't know. Usually something like this needs precision planning, right?"

"Yeah."

"Well, you gotta go out and scout the location and predict any issues that might pop up. Can't do that behind a computer screen or in a dark, dingy room. Gotta go to the spot it's gonna go down and get your eyes on everything directly. If you were kidnapping somebody here, what would you do?"

"I'd probably spend a week or two in the spot it was going to happen and observe everything, try to pick up on any patterns," Haley answered.

"Same as I would do."

"You don't think maybe we got spotted, do you? Maybe today was the day, and they made us, and it spooked them."

Recker made a face and shook his head, not sure he could really answer his question. "Tough to say. On one hand, I kind of hope that's the case. Maybe that would mean they change tactics and leave the child out of this."

"But it could also mean they do something completely different or out of left field," Haley said. "Something we don't see coming."

Recker sighed, readily acknowledging it as the truth. "I know."

They walked through the park for another hour, trying to find any of their potential suspects, or see if anything seemed odd to them. Still nothing seemed unusual. Then they walked along the perimeter of the park, observing buildings across the street to see if one of them could be used in the caper. They also looked for cars, specifically vans, or trucks that could be used for a getaway. Recker assumed the kidnappers would not use a car that could be easily identifiable and would choose an unmarked van so the inside couldn't be seen through a back window.

After they spent a considerable amount of time walking around the area, they concluded there was nothing else they could do there. They weren't frustrated, but they were a little dismayed they didn't see or hear anything that would get them closer to figuring out the kidnapping plan. Though they didn't feel like they wasted their day, they sure didn't feel like it was productive either.

"Let's head back to the office and see if we can find something else out on this," Recker said, tapping Haley on the arm.

They went back to the office, hoping Jones had found something else, anything at all, that would help them. Recker would settle for the tiniest of details right then. When they walked in, Jones didn't bother to turn around and greet them. Instead, he was hard at work trying to come up with the little nugget they needed to get ahead of the situation.

"Please tell me you've come up with something," Recker said, walking past the desk on his way to the refrigerator. He grabbed two twenty-ounce soda bottles and tossed one of them over to Haley.

The look on Jones' face, along with his sigh and the shaking of his head, basically answered his question for him. Jones was trying to find that small kernel of information they could use, but it just wasn't happening. Nothing he did or tried provided anything more than they already knew.

"What about these guys' addresses?" Haley asked. "Why don't we just find where they live and go take them out?"

"That would certainly be one way to do it if I was able to find out that piece of information," Jones replied.

"You can't locate them?" Recker asked, taking a sip of his soda.

"I cannot. Wherever they are, they are not using credit cards, so I can't tell if they're in a hotel or what."

"What about using their phones to get a trace?" Haley asked.

"I've tried. The signals bounce around several locations."

"So, they're either using some type of blocker or maybe they're moving around a lot," Recker said.

"What's even more disturbing is that I haven't gotten any trace on their phones since late last night."

"What's so disturbing about that?"

"I've gone through their phone records for the past month and they communicate with each other quite often. Daily. Now, just before they're supposed to do a big job, they've suddenly gone silent?"

Recker nodded, trying to wrap his head around it. "Usually it's the reverse. Usually you start talking more as the job gets closer, wanting to make sure all the details are accounted for, making sure there's no slip-ups."

"So maybe they're not as close to pulling the job as we thought they were," Haley said.

Jones threw his hands up, exasperated. "I just don't know. All indications from the conversations I saw and heard was that the job was going to be done soon."

"There's another possibility," Recker said.

"Which is?" Jones asked.

"That they switched phones."

Jones titled his head and raised his eyebrows, intrigued by the suggestion, realizing that he may have been on to something. "Yes, I guess that is possible."

"Most crews wouldn't go to that level, but some might. Especially those who are concerned about their communications being tapped or that they're being followed. They either switch to another line of communication or they might have just swapped phones entirely."

"If they did, then that would likely mean that the job is in fact imminent."

"Probably," Recker said. "Any way you can tell if they got new phones?"

The painful expression on Jones' face indicated that it would be unlikely. "I very seriously doubt it. If they're smart enough to know to switch phones, they're equally likely to be smart enough to know to get burner phones that they'll pay for with cash."

"And avoid cameras," Haley said.

"That too. It is also likely that as soon as the job is over that they would toss those new phones away somewhere."

"I guess the only thing we can do is keep showing up at the park and hope we nail them."

Recker sighed, knowing that was the only thing they could do. "Yep, that's about it. There's always tomorrow."

34

The rest of the threesome's day was spent working on the kidnapping case, trying to get any type of lead, since all they had for sure was the place and time. But at least it was better than nothing. They couldn't find any other information on the group than they already had. They had names, pictures, phone numbers, but they didn't have their current location. And their phones had been silent for much of the day except for two or three incoming phone calls from outside sources that went unanswered. They were coming up on seven o'clock and were close to calling it a day.

"We're pretty sure the Jordan girl isn't involved somehow?" Recker asked.

"I would stake my five-hundred-thousand-dollar pension on it," Jones remarked, getting an unusual stare from both Recker and Haley, knowing full well he didn't have any such pension.

"Always nice to bet with something you don't have."

Jones almost chuckled, but instead just gave a wry smile. "Indeed. No, but really, there's nothing that I can tell that she is even remotely involved."

"Check her phone records?" Haley asked.

"I have. Hasn't matched up to any of the kidnappers."

"You check into our police problem at all?" Recker said.

"I've dipped my toes into the water, so to speak."

"And?"

"It's still very early, but no promising leads to start with," Jones said. "But as I mentioned this morning, we don't have much to work with."

"Well, we know the type of bullet for all four shootings," Haley said. "That's something."

"Yes, it's something. But not much. From the reports I've seen, markings on the bullets indicate they were all fired from the same weapon. But connecting that to anybody right now is going to be tricky."

"We're gonna have to figure out how the four victims all knew each other. There has to be a connection between them," Recker said.

"We say victims, but in actuality, there were only three. Don't forget, the undercover officer did survive."

"Then the question will be, was he targeted specifically, or was he targeted because of something he was doing at that particular time and spot?"

"And we just simply do not have enough information to be able to tell right now," Jones replied.

"I hope somebody finds out something before another body drops."

"You keep saying that as if it's a forgone conclusion. You don't know that to be the case. It could be that perhaps those four were involved in something that we haven't yet discovered and that will be the end of it."

"You're thinking the cops were into something dirty?" Haley asked, assuming that was what Jones was referencing.

"I'm not thinking or saying anything of the kind. Perhaps it was something illegal, perhaps it was not. I don't know. And neither does anyone else. And it is way too soon to tell whether this is part of a larger scale plan that will end up with more victims or whether this was a more narrow-minded event."

"I like to prepare for the worst," Recker said.

"Yes, I know. And I'm not saying you won't be proven correct, eventually. I'm just saying right now, we don't have enough information to head in any specific direction."

"Well, hopefully there won't be anything else. But I have a feeling we won't be that lucky."

Recker stood, ready to call it a night. Jones and Haley were going to keep working, since they didn't have anyone at home waiting for them.

"Sure you guys don't mind me taking off?" Recker asked, feeling bad about leaving them.

"Not at all, Michael," Jones answered. "Not much else for you to do here, anyway. Go home, take care of your beautiful and better other half."

"I'll stay if you really want me to."

"We got it, Mike," Haley said. "No biggie."

"It always feels like I'm abandoning you guys when I leave before you do."

"Well, I never leave so that's a moot point for me," Jones replied.

"True."

"Yeah, and I don't have much else to do anyway," Haley said. "If I had a girlfriend, maybe I'd be joining you in walking out the door."

Jones shuffled his shoulders around like he got some chills. "I shudder at the thought."

"What? Don't want me to ever have one?"

Jones stopped typing and turned to look at him. "It's not that I don't wish you to ever have a woman, if that is what you desire. My only hope is that if that does become the case, that you don't engage in a five-year back-and-forth battle with yourself in whether you actually want one."

Recker squinted as he stared at Jones. "You're referring to me, aren't you?"

Jones threw his arms up. "I'm not mentioning any names. I'm just saying, to know what you want and not waffle back and forth for five years on the subject."

"Hey, it was not five years. You're exaggerating."

"Am I?" Jones asked. "OK, maybe the five years is a bit much of a reach. But you have to admit that your feelings for Mia sometimes changed with the weather."

"They did not. I always cared for Mia. I just wasn't sure if it was the best idea to get involved."

"Yes, I know, every other day."

Recker gave his friend a bit of a nasty face, though it was only in joking. He realized it took him longer than it probably should have to truly embrace the feelings he had for his now-girlfriend. Jones then turned back to Haley to continue the conversation.

"All I can say is, be glad that you weren't here to live through the torture of him sorting out his feelings," Jones said, continuing the tease. "It was almost like he was back in high school trying to figure out whether he should ask out a girl in his class for a date or something."

Recker couldn't help but let out a laugh at the reference. "It was not. Now you're being overly dramatic."

Haley also started laughing at the friendly banter between the two partners. "Well, I promise if it ever happens that I'll try not to act like I'm in high school again."

"All I ask is that if it does happen, make sure it's someone who's as reliable and trustworthy as Mia," Jones said. "God forbid you get involved with someone and break up with them after a month and then we get police knocking down the office door."

"Did you guys ever have any hesitancy about that with Mia? I mean, any doubt at all?"

Jones shook his head. "Not one. But she proved her worth and loyalty very early on before they even dated so it was not so much of an issue."

"I would trust her with anything," Recker said.

"Speaking of your beautiful girlfriend, I take it that she's home tonight?"

"Yeah, why?"

Jones shrugged. "No reason. Just asking. That's usually the only time you leave, when she's home."

"Is that a problem?"

"No, not at all. I told you, you've never shirked your duties here. You just proved it last night by meeting the detective after hours. So, go home, spend time with your girlfriend, and give her some extra kisses from me."

"Yeah, me too," Haley said.

"I'm sure that won't be too much of a problem. The extra kisses that is," Jones said with a smirk.

Recker feigned being mad and stormed toward the door. "I'm not sitting here and taking this ribbing from you guys."

Jones and Haley couldn't help but laugh. "We'll see you in the morning," Jones said.

"Assuming you're still able to stand up after...," Haley said.

"Not listening to it," Recker playfully said, closing the door behind him before Haley could finish the joke.

After Recker left, Jones and Haley continued with their work.

"You don't have to stay here, you know," Jones said. "You can take the rest of the night if you want."

"Eh, it's like I told Mike, I don't really have much else to do, anyway."

"As you prefer."

"Besides, I still feel like I have more to learn. I'm a few years behind you guys at deciphering all this stuff," Haley said. "I think the more time I spend in here, the better off I'll be."

"I wouldn't think too much about that. You've done a very good job at assimilating into everything these past few months."

"You or Mike haven't had any regrets about bringing me in or anything, have you?"

Jones stopped working and looked at him. "Not for a second. Why, do you get that impression?"

Haley shook his head. "No, not at all. I just wanted to make sure I've been doing all right and that I haven't made any stupid mistakes."

"No need to fret about that. You're exactly what Mike and I were hoping for. We couldn't have asked for or expected to get a better candidate than you."

"Good."

Jones continued looking at him, trying to analyze Haley's face, hoping there wasn't more to it than what they just said. "You're not feeling dissatisfied, are you? Or regret coming aboard?"

Haley put his hand up and smiled, trying hard to reassure his boss it wasn't the case. "No, really. I love being here. I like being around you guys. I like doing the work. It's a lot better than what I was doing before. So, no, everything's fine, really."

"OK. I was starting to think maybe you were looking to get out or resign or something," Jones said.

Haley shook his head. "Wouldn't dream of it. That's why I was asking if you guys were pleased with me so far. I just... I really like and enjoy being here and being part of the team."

After they finished their little exchange, they kept working straight up until nine. It didn't seem like it did much good, though, as they didn't find out anything new about the Rocco case. It was at that point Jones felt the need to call it a night as well and told Haley to go home and rest up.

"Well, there's not much else we can do tonight," Jones said. "Hopefully tomorrow is a more fruitful day for us."

"You think it'll go down tomorrow?"

"One thing's for sure, it's going to be soon."

"We'll be ready," Haley said.

After eating dinner with Mia, they both tried to relax on the couch for a while and watched TV. Mia had previously asked what case they were working on, so she was already aware of the situation with the judge. As they were watching a movie, she suddenly sat up, Recker's arm sliding from her shoulders. Mia turned to face him with a look on her face like she was about to surprise him with something.

"I've got it," she said.

Recker looked at her curiously, not sure what she was referring to. "You've got what?"

"Your problem."

Recker let out a laugh. "Which one? I've got several."

"Your judge problem. You know, with the baby."

"What about it?"

"You said you guys couldn't figure out how they were going to take the baby in the middle of a big park with a lot of people around."

"Yeah?"

"Well, I figured it out," Mia said.

"You have?"

"Don't you see? It's so obvious."

Recker wasn't sure if she really had a satisfactory answer or not, but wasn't going to dismiss it yet either. "Well then, please tell."

"They would have to create some type of diversion," Mia said, getting up from the couch. She started walking around the room, getting into the moment like she was an old-time movie detective as she thought about the crime.

But Recker wasn't impressed just yet. "We've already figured that part."

Mia stopped and pointed her finger at him. "Yes, but how are they going to do it?"

"Uh, we still don't know yet."

A huge smile came over Mia's face as she started to relay her thoughts. "They'll have to need the help of a woman."

Recker immediately knocked the idea. "There's no woman in the group. It's a three-man team."

"That you know of. Listen, they'll need the help of a woman to pull this off."

"And just how do you figure that?"

"They'll obviously need to get up close to get her, right?" Mia asked.

"Yeah."

"If I'm out walking a baby, and a strange man, or men, coming walking up to me, I'm gonna feel a little taken aback. The threat level's gonna go up a little. Even if they look completely nice and normal."

"It's not normal for men to gawk at other peoples' babies," Recker said, catching her point.

"Right. But if a woman does that, it's not so unnatural. I wouldn't necessarily think twice if another woman came up to me and did it."

Recker lifted his head up and looked at the ceiling as he thought about what she was saying. It certainly made sense, but it didn't really give them much else to work with.

"I mean, I can go along with all that, but it doesn't get us any closer," Recker said. "There's no woman that we know of on the crew. It's possible they could bring someone in, or have someone that they know, but we still don't know who that would be. Doesn't really tell us how either. I'm sure, even if it's a woman, they're not just gonna walk up to the nanny, snatch the baby out of the stroller, and run out of the park."

"Probably not."

"As soon as the nanny realizes the baby's been taken, she's gonna start screaming her head off and alert everyone in the area. There's no guarantee that woman's gonna make it out of the park at that point."

A confident look came over Mia's face, thinking she came up with the answer. "But not if she doesn't know the baby has been taken."

"Well, yeah, that's the issue. How are they gonna do that?"

"It's simple."

"How's that?" Recker asked.

"They won't wait until they get too deep into the park. It'll be right when she goes in, or right when she leaves."

"And just what are they gonna do?"

"The old switcheroo," Mia answered.

"The what?"

"They'll switch babies."

"And just how do you think they're going to do that?" Recker asked.

"I've got it. I've got it."

"OK?"

"Right when she enters the park, there'll be a woman," Mia said, then slapped her hands together as she changed course. "No, make that a man and a woman."

"Why?"

"For a diversion. I bet they'll pretend to be a couple, and they'll approach her as she walks into the park. Maybe they'll pretend to bump into her or maybe they'll just start talking about the baby or something."

Though it was beginning to make some amount of sense to

Recker, he still wasn't convinced that would be the actual plan. "And how will they take the child?"

"While the woman is conversing with the nanny, the guy will take off with the baby."

"And she'll just be OK with him taking off with the kid?"

"Of course not. They'll do something to distract her," Mia answered.

"Oh, of course," Recker said in a mocking manner.

Mia paced around the room for another minute as she continued to think of the plot. She then got another look on her face like she just figured something out, then walked over to the couch and stood in front of her boyfriend as she explained.

"What if they have the same exact stroller?" she asked.

"Did they get a buy one, get one free deal?" Recker sarcastically said.

Not amused, Mia rolled her eyes. "Don't be silly. You said there's probably a good chance they've been staking her out, right?"

"Yeah."

"Then they probably took pictures of her with the stroller, then bought the same one."

Recker raised his eyebrows, curled his lip, and tilted his head, thinking maybe she was onto something. "Possible."

"I will bet you anything that's how it's gonna go down."

"Anything, huh?"

"Well, almost anything," she seductively said. "What? You think I'm wrong or I'm completely out of my mind?"

"No, I can't deny it makes some sense."

"I'll bet that the nanny enters the park, and another couple walks over to her and starts talking. They'll have the same stroller. The woman will distract her somehow, then the man will switch strollers and quickly head back out of the park while the women are still talking. The nanny won't even know what's going on until it's too late."

"Which means it's likely they'd have a getaway car nearby," Recker said.

"So? Did I solve your problem for you?" Mia happily asked, holding her arms out wide.

"Well, I guess you will have if that's actually how it happens."

"Think about it."

"Uh, I am."

"No, I mean, there's a three-man crew you said, right?"

"Yeah."

"So, there's one man waiting in the car, one man in the park with the stroller who's the getaway man or whatever you call him, and the third guy is milling around, ready to run interference if needed," Mia explained.

Recker folded his arms and put his left hand over his mouth as he looked at his girlfriend and thought about her idea. He couldn't readily discount it as he believed it was a credible and thought out plan. Whether it was what the kidnappers would do was another story. But it was something to think about. They talked about it for a few more minutes and Recker thought he should call Jones and see what he thought of the plan. Just before he did, though, Mia stopped him, having a few more ideas to run past him.

"You know what else I was thinking?" she asked.

Recker couldn't believe she had more to add. "What, did you just watch the mystery movie of the week or something?"

Mia waved her hand at him. "Oh, stop. You know, I'm off tomorrow."

Recker didn't pick up on the hint. "Yeah? I know you are."

"So. I was thinking, maybe I could go with you and help."

Recker immediately put his hands up to stop her from going any further. "No, no, no, no, no. Absolutely not."

"Why not? I can help."

"Didn't we decide a long time ago that you weren't going to do that type of stuff anymore?" Recker asked. "You remember what happened when you tried to do that?"

"You always bring that up."

"To make sure you remember it."

"I didn't know what I was doing then," Mia said.

"And you do now?"

"It's not like I'd be going out on my own. You'd be there, Chris would be there, I'd only be going to help."

Recker shook his head several times. "No. Not gonna happen."

"Don't be stubborn. You could use the help."

"I've got help."

"Mike, why won't you let me help you?"

"One, because it's not necessary. Two, because you're not trained for it," Recker answered. "Why are you so interested in it, anyway?"

Mia shrugged, not wanting her reasons to sound stupid. "I just want to be important to you."

Recker quickly stood and put his arms around her. "Of course you're important to me. Why would you even say that?"

"I dunno."

"Listen, you've done more for me than you even know, or that I could ever say. You're the most important thing in my life."

She put her head on his chest. "I know. I just... I wanna feel like I can help you."

"You know you've helped me. In more ways than I can count."

They sat back down on the couch as they continued their conversation.

"But if I'm right, then you might need another person," Mia said.

"And how do you figure that?"

"There'd be three people there. The two guys, plus the girl, not even counting the driver. Now, what if you and Chris get caught up in a fight with the two guys and the woman decides to take things into her own hands and grabs the baby herself?"

"That's a lot of if's and maybe's, don't you think?" Recker asked. "I mean, you're acting like all this is guaranteed to happen. This isn't like a definite, you know."

"But what if it does?"

"Why are you so hell-bent on coming along? You've never been like this before."

Mia shrugged. "I don't know. Maybe it's because I'm off tomorrow and have nothing else to do. Maybe it's because I just want to spend more time with you. I don't know. Why are you so against it?"

"Because I don't want you to get hurt."

"You and Chris will be there. What's the worst that could happen to me?"

"Uh, you want me to go down the list? How about if we get in their way and they come up shooting? Ever think of that?"

Mia rolled her eyes, knowing he had a point, though she didn't want to acknowledge it. "How about if I ask David?"

"You're gonna ask David?"

"Why not? If he's OK with it, would you agree?"

"No!"

"Why not?" Mia asked.

"Because he's not your boyfriend, and he's not the one who'd be out there with you."

"You are a stubborn man; do you know that?"

"So I've been told."

Recker then walked into the kitchen and called Jones to see what he thought of Mia's idea.

"And I wanna talk to him before you hang up," Mia said. "And don't tell him to say no before you hand me the phone."

Recker rolled his eyes and sighed, but agreed anyway. As soon as Jones answered, Recker started to tell him Mia's plan in detail, remembering everything she said without leaving a single thing out.

"So, what do you think?" Recker asked.

"I would say that it certainly seems plausible."

"What about a woman? Can you filter out who that might be?"

"Well I've already compiled a list of known associates," Jones said.

"Are there any women on it?"

"Yes, there are several."

"Any way to narrow it down?"

"I guess I could work on it a little bit for the rest of the night. I can't say I will definitely be able to pinpoint one woman, though. But I'll see what I can do."

"So, you think it could go down that way?" Recker asked.

"I definitely do. I could see that scenario happening. I can also say that I can envision just about any other scenario happening as well, considering we don't have any leads on how it's going to go down."

"All right, I guess we can talk about it more in the morning."

Mia cleared her throat, making sure Recker heard her before he hung up. He looked over at her, and though he didn't really want to hand the phone over, did so anyway.

"David?" Mia said.

"Hello."

"Mike didn't mention it to you, but what would you think about me going out with them tomorrow?"

Jones was silent for a while, not sure how to respond. He was almost positive it was a trick question.

"David?"

"Oh, I'm... honestly not sure what to say."

"Well, would you have a problem with me going out with Mike and Chris to help out?"

Jones hesitated again, though for not quite as long. "And what did Mike say?" he asked, finding it hard to believe that Recker would have approved it.

"Well he said no. But I think I can help and I think I can be useful."

"I'm going to go along with him."

"But why?"

"Because I'm not getting in the middle of any of your spats," Jones said.

"We're not having a spat."

"Why are you getting me in the middle of this?"

"Aren't you technically in charge?" Mia asked.

"Well..."

"David, if there turns out to be a woman there, don't you think I could help if Mike and Chris are busy?"

"Umm, possibly. Didn't you swear off doing this type of stuff a long time ago?"

"Why does everyone keep saying that? I can handle it. Besides, it's not like I'd be by myself. Mike and Chris will be there."

Jones didn't want to get into an argument, or a long drawn out conversation about the subject, and just hoped to end the discussion as quickly as possible. "Well, let me think on it for the night and I'll talk to Mike about it in the morning."

"You're just trying to get rid of me."

"I would never."

"Yeah right. You have no intention of saying yes or going against Mike."

"I have gone against Mike many times," Jones said.

"Yeah, but not when it comes to me."

"Well there are boundaries."

Mia sighed, resigning herself to the fact that nobody was going to say yes to her proposal. "Fine. I know when I'm not wanted."

"Mia, it's not that. We just want to keep you safe."

"I know, I know. I know the line. Well would you mind if I at least came into the office tomorrow? At least let me do something."

"Are you off tomorrow?"

"Yes."

"I don't see the harm in that if Mike is willing."

"I'll probably have to beg, crawl, and pray for him to approve."

35

The team was all set up in their respective positions. Recker was down the street from the Rocco house, waiting for the nanny to step outside with the baby. Haley was wandering through the park, looking for a sign of potential trouble. He was particularly keeping an eye out for a man and a woman with the same kind of stroller the Rocco baby had. He'd been walking around for a half hour without any luck. Jones was in the office, still typing away, hoping to find some last-minute solution that would let the secret out of the bag. As they were waiting for the action to begin, Jones couldn't resist a last-minute shot across Recker's bow.

"Mike, how is the third wheel doing?" Jones asked.

Recker gritted his teeth as he thought of a reply. "Just fine."

"Hey, I object to being called a third wheel!" Mia said.

Jones chuckled. "Sorry, it wasn't intended as an insult toward you."

"Uh, huh."

"Hey, you're the one that let her come along," Recker said.

"Don't lay this at my feet. She's your girlfriend," Jones replied.

"Are you guys seriously gonna do this?" Mia asked. "You're gonna argue about me knowing full well I can hear you?"

Recker let out a sigh that was clearly audible in everyone's earpiece.

"Something upsetting you, Mike?" Jones asked.

"No. Nothing at all."

"Don't get upset, Mike, you know I can be helpful here," Mia said.

Recker still wasn't that pleased that she was there. "How'd I let you talk me into this?"

"Because deep down you knew I was right."

"No, I don't think that was it. I think you did some trickery on me or something."

"Don't be ridiculous. I merely pointed out the facts, which were accurate, and you came around to my line of thinking, as you should have."

"I must've been out of my mind."

"Oh stop. I'll be fine. This will work."

"It working isn't what I'm worried about," Recker said.

"Mike, cool your jets."

Haley, who'd been carefully listening to the playful exchange, couldn't hold back any longer and let out an audible laugh.

"At least you're amusing to somebody," Jones said.

"You planned this all along, didn't you?" Recker asked.

"Planned what?" Mia sweetly replied, acting like she didn't know what he was talking about.

"Don't pretend like you're oblivious. You know darn well what I'm talking about."

Though Mia really did know, she wasn't going to give in. "I really don't know."

"You played it off like you wanted to go to the office this morning and help out with logistics and stuff. But you were really planning this all along, weren't you?"

Mia replied, trying to talk and sound as sweet and innocent as possible. "Honestly, Mike, I just wanted to help in the office. That's all."

Recker scoffed, letting out a laugh, knowing full well he was right. "That cute and innocent act isn't gonna work with me. You know I know."

"Excuse me, but did we just stumble into an old Abbott and Costello routine or something?" Jones asked.

"Maybe I should be glad I'm single," Haley said.

"Indeed."

"Really, Mike, if you didn't want me here then you should've just said so," Mia said.

"I did. Several times."

"Well, obviously you weren't persistent enough."

"Or some people are just hard headed and stubborn," Recker replied.

"Mike, don't self-deprecate yourself like that over the air in public."

Jones and Haley both laughed at the same time.

"Mike, you seem to have met your match," Jones said.

Recker opened his mouth to reply, but honestly couldn't come up with a reply and just waved his hand in the air a couple of times before letting it settle on his face. He shook his head and rubbed the sides of both temples and let his hand slide down his face and onto his neck as he looked up at the sky.

"What, nothing else to add?" Mia asked.

"Nope. Nothing."

As much as the team, maybe except Recker, seemed to be enjoying the playful banter amongst the couple, Jones looked at the time and knew they had to get down to business. It was only a few minutes before the nanny was due to leave the house.

"OK. It looks like playtime is over," Jones said. "We've only got five minutes to go on the countdown. Is everyone in place?"

Recker, Haley, and Mia all confirmed they were. They stationed Mia on a bench inside the park, near the entrance the nanny usually came in at. They figured if something did go down there, like she thought it might, she'd be right on top of it. And if it didn't, she could easily follow the nanny through the park without attracting anyone's suspicions. Mia fought hard to get to that point. She spent the entire night before trying to wear down Recker to let her come along. She talked the entire morning, first to Recker, then to Jones and Haley, about letting her tag with the group. Her and Recker got to the office a little after eight, and almost immediately, Mia started working on the team in the effort to let her get in on the park detail. After over three hours of her constant badgering, she finally got the blessing of Haley first. Once the first domino fell, she got Jones to see the light. Her boyfriend was the toughest case, as she knew it would be, and with the other two giving her the green light, Recker finally got worn down to the point where he saw the benefit in her joining the plan in the field. At least until she was out there. Once she was in place, Recker doubted why he let himself get talked into it. But Mia always was a special case with him. She had the ability to change his mind or persuade him to do something he really didn't want to like nobody else could.

Within a few minutes, the nanny came out of the house right on time. Recker was at his spot at the end of the street waiting for her. Just as he had the day before, he walked around the block to see if he noticed anyone else waiting for her. But just like before, he noticed nothing unusual.

"She's on the move," Recker said.

"Let's hope today's the day and we nip this thing in the bud," Jones replied.

Recker walked away from the park and down the street as the nanny walked closer, just to avoid the possibility of being spotted. Once she got near the intersection of 19th and Rittenhouse,

466

Recker made a sharp turn and quickly walked back toward her, in anticipation of something happening soon.

"Hey, I just saw a man and a woman with the same type of stroller," Haley reported.

"Where at?" Recker replied.

"Uh, should be walking to you now."

"It's going down like Mia said."

"I'm on them."

"Mia, get ready," Jones said.

"I don't see anyone yet," she replied.

"You will. Just sit tight for now."

"We're entering the park," Recker said, walking briskly. "I'm only a few feet behind her."

"Mike, give her some space and just stand by the exit path for now," Jones said.

Recker complied with Jones' wishes and stood by the small iron gate and tried to look inconspicuous. There were several benches up ahead and a couple of paths leading away from his direction, but nothing was blocking his way so he couldn't catch up to them if they went in another direction. Plus, he figured Haley might get to them before he did, anyway. Recker continued looking around, hoping to see the couple his partner described. After a few minutes, he did.

"I see them," Recker said. "The nanny just sat down on a bench across from Mia."

"What do I do?" Mia asked.

"Nothing yet. Just relax. You only need to focus on the woman. Don't worry about anything else."

After five more minutes elapsed, the couple Haley reported were now within view. They were walking toward the nanny's position.

"I think we're about to get action," Recker said, looking around for other members of the crew.

"The guy is definitely one of them. Spot on image from his picture," Haley replied.

"I don't see the other two anywhere."

"I'm sure they're nearby," Jones said. "Stay alert."

Recker and Haley watched intently as the couple approached the nanny. They seemed friendly enough, striking up a conversation with her. They watched the three of them laughing about something, and the two women seemed to be getting along very well, almost looking like old friends. Recker's eyes then were diverted to another couple who were walking toward the same bench as the others.

"I don't believe it," he said with a whisper.

"What?" Jones asked.

"There's another couple with the same stroller."

"You're kidding."

"I wish I was."

"I see it," Haley said. "I recognize the guy. Same crew again."

The third couple arrived near the same bench as the others and also struck up a conversation with the group. After a minute, they were all talking, smiling, and laughing. Recker was as sure as ever they were going to pull a switch any minute, as soon as they found the right moment.

"Be on your toes," Recker said, getting ready to pounce.

A few more minutes went by and Recker observed one of the men getting ready to leave. One of the women was distracting the nanny, and the man switched strollers, taking the one with the Rocco baby in it. He bid the others goodbye and started walking away from the group as the rest of them continued chatting away. With the nanny being distracted by the women, and not looking at the strollers at that moment, she didn't have any clue the baby she was in charge of was being taken away.

"They just did it," Recker said. "They just pulled the switch."

"I saw it," Haley replied.

"Mia, you go toward the stroller for the baby."

"What about the woman?" Mia asked.

"Forget the woman. I'm going after that guy. If I take him out, I wanna make sure nobody else is around to snatch the kid while I'm busy."

"OK."

Mia did as Recker wanted and got up from her seat and started following the man who just left with the wrong stroller. Recker started running toward the man to cut him off from escaping. As he did, Haley moved into position between the group and the path the man just walked down. That way, if anyone saw Recker interfering, Haley would be ready to block them, giving his partner enough time to subdue the man and take control of the situation.

The plan seemed to work perfectly. Mia was right behind the man, ready to take control of the stroller once he lost his grip of it. She looked at Recker coming out of the corner of her eye. Recker ran across a patch of grass and past a couple of trees as he ran full force at the unsuspecting man. Wanting to catch him off-guard, Recker jumped at him as soon as he was within range. Recker gave him a flying cross body tackle, knocking them both to the ground. As soon as they wrestled on the concrete, Mia grabbed the stroller to make sure it didn't roll away, or fall into the wrong hands.

Recker had quickly straddled the man on the ground and gave him several punches to the face. The man was so stunned at what happened he didn't have much of a chance to fight back. As people started to look at the commotion, one of the other men ran toward them. Haley quickly put a stop to that though, spearing the man in the gut with his shoulder, knocking them onto the ground as well. Much like his partner, Haley also began delivering shots to the man's face.

The two women who had accompanied the crew members looked on in horror, realizing the plan was falling apart. Seeing the two men seemed to be subdued, the women quickly scurried out of the area. The nanny looked at them strangely and wasn't sure what was going on, wondering why they just ran off and left their babies and strollers behind. She looked in what she thought was her stroller and was horrified to discover it wasn't hers at all. Inside was only a child's doll. Quickly being taken over by panic, she reached into the other stroller and discovered there was only a doll inside that one as well. She backed up, a look of pure fear taking over her face. She then looked over and saw Mia standing there with what she hoped was her stroller and ran over to her. Mia saw her running over to her and smiled. She put her hand out to try to get the woman to calm down.

"It's OK," Mia said. "She's fine. She's fine."

"Oh my God, I can't believe this," the nanny said, picking the baby up out of the stroller. She held her tightly in her arms and hugged the child, thankful she was all right.

Mia rubbed the woman's back for a second and patted her on the shoulders to calm her down. "It's all over."

"Thank you so much. I don't even... I mean... what... what were they trying to do?"

"It was an..."

Before Mia could say too much, and more than she should have, Recker and Haley interrupted her. In anticipation of running into trouble, and trying to abide by Jones' wishes that they didn't use their guns, they brought zip ties with them to bind the suspect's hands together. Once they did that, Recker and Haley dragged their victims over to one of the benches and tied them to the bench until a police officer arrived and took them into custody. Once they approached the two women, a car hastily pulled out of a nearby parking spot and sped off. Recker could only assume it might have been the getaway car.

"Thanks for your help in watching the stroller, ma'am," Recker said, putting his hand out to shake Mia's hand, pretending as if he didn't know her.

Mia quickly picked up on the charade and shook his hand. "Oh, yes, no problem. Just glad I could help."

"I was just telling her, I don't know what happened," the nanny said. "I mean, what were they doing? Were they trying to take the baby?"

Recker nodded. "Unfortunately, they were. The two men are part of a criminal gang."

"But why did they come after us?"

"The baby is the daughter of a judge, correct?"

"Yeah. Were they trying to get back at her for something? Were they gonna hurt the baby?"

"We don't think so. We think it was part of a plan about an upcoming trial the judge has."

Recker was getting antsy still standing in the area and realized they had probably been there too long already and looked around for a police car.

"Well, we're gonna have to go. Just stay here until the police arrive and tell them what happened so these guys get put away," Recker said.

The nanny looked confused as she thought the two men standing in front of her were police. "Wait, you're not the police?"

Haley shook his head. "No, we're not."

"I just thought you were like undercover or detectives or something."

"Nope."

"Then how do you know all this?"

"That's not important. What is important is that the judge takes the necessary steps in protecting you and the baby. At least for the next couple of months," Recker said. "Police should be here soon, so you shouldn't have to wait long."

The nanny rubbed her head, feeling a little overwhelmed with it all. Recker noticed she wasn't looking so good.

"Perhaps this nice lady here would be willing to wait with you until the cops get here," Recker said.

"Yeah, I could do that," Mia replied.

"You guys can't stick around?" the nanny asked.

"No, I'm afraid not. Cops aren't exactly pleased with us either."

"What do I tell them about you?"

"Just tell them exactly what went down. If they ask who we were, just tell them The Silencer was here."

The nanny's eyes opened wide, almost in shock with what she just heard. "The Silencer? You're him?"

"In the flesh."

"I've heard so much about you."

Recker smiled. "Yeah. Well, I gotta go. You take care."

Recker and Haley then quickly walked away. As they left the park and crossed the street, they saw two police cars rolling into the area. As they walked away, he wanted to let his girlfriend know what they were doing.

"We'll be waiting in a restaurant over on Locust," Recker said. "Soon as you're done, walk over there."

"OK," Mia replied.

Recker then let Jones know the mission was over. "David, everything's done here."

"Excellent. Everything went off without issue then?" Jones asked.

"Well, all things considering. The two guys are apprehended, police should be taking them in soon. The nanny and baby are fine. The two women that were helping them got away. Not much we could do about that, though."

"They were the least that we should be concerned about. Like you said, all things considered, it was a good day's work."

"There was a car that I saw peel off after everything went down. Might've been the third guy," Recker said. "Looked like a black SUV. Couldn't make anything out."

"I'll check nearby cameras and see if I can get a make on anything."

Recker hung up and continued walking toward Locust Street to wait until Mia finished up with the police.

"Mia should be alright back there, right?" Haley asked.

"Yeah, why?"

"I dunno. With the police and all."

"They don't know she's with us. I figured it might look more suspicious if she left with us. I didn't want anybody to connect her with me. It's better if it's thought she was just a passerby and happened to be in the area."

"Speaking of connecting people to you, you sure it was a wise idea to let that woman know who you were?" Haley asked.

Recker shrugged. "I don't know if it really matters at this point. Everyone knows who I am."

"She didn't until you told her."

"If they ask questions and show her a few pictures, she'll recognize it's me, anyway. Besides, I figure it's better if I identify myself to the public, let them know I'm there to help them, put a face to the name and the stories they've heard of me. That way, if they ever see me and recognize me, they'll know I'm there to help and won't call the police."

"I guess that makes sense. Kind of like preventive medicine."

"In any case, of all the people I've helped over the years I've been here, none of them have said a bad word to the police about me, or tried to give me up or something. Even ones who were just bystanders, or witnessed me doing something. I think the public knows I'm here to help them and accept it."

"Wish the police felt the same way," Haley said.

"Well, they gotta do what they gotta do. We both know that."

"Speaking of which, I guess we got some time to work on their problem now."

"Maybe, maybe not."

"Why not?"

"Well, this was a three-man crew, right?" Recker asked.

"Yeah."

"Well we only got two of them. And we don't know who those two women were with them. Are they part of their gang now, or were they just two girls they plucked off the street and promised a lot of money to if they helped them?"

"True."

"One thing's for sure, if one of these guys are still out there, this might not be over."

36

Three days had passed since the incident at the park. Recker and Haley had successfully stopped several other criminal acts since then. They had just finished an assignment and got back to the office after lunchtime. They brought back a sandwich for Jones, and after he finished it, they got down to work again. Jones informed them of an impending situation that was all too familiar to them. As Recker and Haley sat, Jones swiveled his chair around to talk about it.

"It looks as if we've got another problem with Judge Rocco."

"They going after the baby again?" Recker asked.

"Not at all. Now it seems as though they're going to go after the judge directly."

Recker looked confused. "You mean they're gonna try to kill her? What sense would that make?"

Haley agreed with the assessment. "Yeah, even if they kill this judge, another one will still be assigned. It's not like they can just kill every judge they come across."

"It's not quite that dire," Jones said. "I don't believe they plan on killing her. They know that would be a stupid move. I do believe, though, that they plan on making decisions, and life in general, very rough for her."

"In what way?" Recker asked.

"I believe they're going to try to scare and intimidate her."

"How are they going to do that?"

"That I'm not yet sure."

"What'd you pick up on?"

"Text message from the last remaining member of the gang," Jones answered.

"I thought that was silent for the last few days?"

"It was. Until this morning. I picked up on a message between him and another number which I have not yet identified."

"Get a location at least?" Recker said.

"Yes. It's not much help, however. Whoever is on the other end of the line, they're not in this city."

"Where are they?"

"I've got it narrowed down to a location in Boston."

"Boston?"

"I can only assume it's either a superior or possibly whoever hired him," Jones said.

"What did the message say?" Haley asked.

"It was from Ross asking how they wanted him to get to her."

"Vague wording," Recker replied. "Could be just about anything."

"They indicate a time frame?" Haley asked.

Jones shook his head. "No."

"Gonna be the same deal again. We're gonna have to stake out her house again."

"Maybe," Recker said.

Just as the threesome was about to delve into things further, Recker's phone rang. It was Malloy. Curious as to what he wanted, Recker quickly answered.

"Hey."

"Just wanted to pass something along to you," Malloy said.

"OK?"

"Our mutual friend wanted to have another conversation with you."

"Our mutual friend? Are we talking about the one who has a shiny badge and lots of cool little gadgets at their disposal?" Recker asked, trying to make light of it.

"That's the one."

"It's not necessary. I'll call him directly."

"Fine with me. I'm just passing it along. By the way, how you doing on that?"

"Who's asking? You or Vincent?"

"Uh, I guess you could say both," Malloy answered.

"I didn't know you cared so much about police problems."

"I don't. Just a passing interest."

"Well just so you know, and you can tell Vincent, that we haven't made much progress on it yet."

"Shame."

"Yeah, I can tell you're heartbroken," Recker said.

As soon as Recker hung up, he let the others know what the conversation was about. "I'm already tired of going through third parties for this."

"Why not just give Andrews a phone number to reach us?" Haley asked.

Recker gave Jones a look to see if he agreed with the idea. While Recker was fine with it, he knew Jones was a little apprehensive about mingling with the police department.

"What do you think?" Recker asked.

"I suppose it can do no real harm," Jones said, opening one of the drawers, revealing a bunch of prepaid phones. "None of them can be traced back to us."

"Which one?"

"Take your pick. As I said, it doesn't matter."

"And when this is over, if he decides to be a big man and take us on, you're sure none of these can come back to here?"

"No, they've all been reprogrammed to bounce off towers far away from here," Jones replied.

Recker picked up one of the phones then closed the drawer. As he deliberated calling the detective, he wondered what else the officer wanted. They hadn't heard of any other incidents going down. Maybe he was just wondering if Recker made any progress. After a few more minutes, Jones found Andrews' phone number and wrote it down on the desk. Recker then wasted no more time in calling. The detective picked up after the second ring.

"This is Detective Andrews."

"I hear you wanted to meet," Recker said.

Andrews had just gotten into his car and was about to head back to his office, but put his car back in park as he took the phone call. He looked out both front windows as well as the rear-view mirror to make sure no one was around listening, not that they really could with the windows up and the air conditioning on. But he was a little paranoid about someone overhearing him talking to the wanted man.

"Uh, yeah, yeah, I did," Andrews said.

"I'm a little busy right now, can't really get away. Talking on here will have to suffice."

"No, that's fine. I've heard about how busy you are."

"You have?" Recker asked, not knowing what he was referring to.

"Yeah. Heard about that stuff that went down at Rittenhouse Park the other day."

"How you know that was me?"

"Oh, uh, the girl identified you. Said you told her who you were."

"Oh."

478

"Yeah. Good stuff. Believe it or not, you have more friends in the department than you might think," Andrews said.

Recker was sure he wasn't calling just to talk about his exploits and quickly shifted the conversation around. "So, what else is up?"

"Oh, yeah, I was just wondering if you'd come up with anything on our little problem?"

"Not yet. We don't really have a whole lot to go on," Recker said.

"Yeah, I know. Well, we might have a little more now."

"Why's that?"

"We've got another body," Andrews answered.

"Damn."

"It's actually the first cop that got shot. That undercover officer I told you about. Shot dead walking out of his house this morning."

As he was speaking, Recker put his hand over the phone and snapped his fingers at Jones with his other hand to get his attention. As Recker put the phone back to his ear, he made a circling motion to Jones to let him know something was going on.

"Killed this morning?" Recker asked, loud enough for Jones to hear.

Taking his cue, Jones immediately started typing away to pull up whatever snippets of information he could find. It wasn't long before he found a few online articles from some of the local newspaper and television websites.

"I guess it's the same shooter?" Recker asked.

"Well, we can't definitely say for sure right now. The bullet's still inside him and there was no other evidence at the scene. From the size of the hole in his chest, it looked pretty close to the same as what we've been dealing with."

"He was definitely targeted then."

"I know."

"There's gotta be a common link between the two cops and

that dealer," Recker said. "The other guy probably happened like you said, saw something he wasn't supposed to."

"As far as we can tell, there's no links between the two officers. They're from different districts."

"I'm sure you've gone deep into their packets, is there any chance they're dirty or involved in something?"

Sometimes officers took offense when someone mentioned one of them being dirty, but Andrews didn't even give it a second thought. He quickly responded. "I dunno. Everyone we've talked to, friends, partners, relatives, other cops, nobody's said a bad word about them."

"That doesn't mean they weren't into something," Recker said.

"I know. But from what we can gather, they were just hard-working cops. Nothing more. Now, if you were to ask me to put money on the line and say that, I wouldn't do it. But we haven't uncovered anything that would lead us in that direction."

"What about former partners? Other districts they've worked in? Any commonalities there?"

Once again, Andrews rebuffed the point. "No. Neither one of them have ever worked in the same district at any point in time."

"Ever investigated the same people?" Recker asked.

"Nope. We've checked. I mean, if you think it'll help, I can give you copies of their records."

"It's not necessary. I can get them on my own."

"You can? How?" Andrews asked.

"Not important. What is important is if you've identified any other officers that you think may be in danger? Any partners, former partners, other cops they've been in contact with, anything like that?"

"No. Another dead end."

"You don't have a whole lot going for you right now, do you?"

"Now you see why I reached out to you when I did," Andrews answered.

"All right, well, we'll dig into their files further and see if we can find some common links."

"Thanks. I appreciate that."

"In the meantime, take this number down," Recker said, giving the detective the number to the prepaid phone. "If you need anything else, get in touch with me there. I don't like going through Vincent for things."

"Yeah, no problem."

"Just a warning, if you try to trace it, it's gonna lead you nowhere, so save yourself a lot of time and aggravation by not even bothering."

"I figured as much. Didn't think you'd give me anything that would lead straight to you," Andrews said. "Not that it would matter. Remember, I'm one of the cops that thinks you're doing good for this city."

"Well, feelings sometimes have a habit of changing. I just wanted to let you know in advance."

"Understood."

"Oh, and I don't want you giving that number out to anyone, even other cops who may be fans of mine," Recker said. "If someone else in the department calls me other than you, that phone's gonna be in the river the next day."

"No problem again. I figure the less I say about you the better it is for everyone."

"All right. Assuming there's no other problems, I'll probably call you again in a few days to let you know if I've come up with anything."

"Sounds good."

As soon as Recker hung up, he put the phone in his pocket and leaned forward on the desk to get a better view of the computer screen. He read each news story Jones found on the killing. After the fourth and final article, he took a seat next to Jones and Haley and began discussing the case, as well as their options.

"Why didn't you see this earlier?" Recker asked. His tone was not accusing in nature or suggesting Jones wasn't on top of things, but just a simple question. "You're usually right on this type of stuff."

"Because quite honestly I wasn't looking for it. So far, my entire morning was spent digging into any further action against Judge Rocco."

Recker nodded. "Well, I guess me and Chris can dig through the police records of the two officers and see what we can find if you wanna stay on top of the Rocco stuff."

"Maybe one of us should sit on her home for a while," Haley said, mindful of the latest threat against the judge and wary of leaving her without the protection of one of them.

Recker agreed, though he wasn't sure they needed to sit on it all day. He looked at the time before replying. "Well if she's in court all day, she's not likely to get home until what? Six, seven, eight, something like that?"

Jones looked at him, unsure who he was asking the question to. It didn't sound like Recker was talking to anyone in particular. "Are you by chance asking me to check on her itinerary?"

Recker smiled. "Crossed my mind."

Jones rolled his eyes before swiveling back to the computer. "Very well. Since you asked so nicely."

Recker laughed to himself as Jones began checking Judge Rocco's court log. While he was doing that, Haley was still a bit uncomfortable with the situation. He thought they should have been on the judge more. Maybe even tail her as she left the courtroom.

"What if they try to knock her off or something on her way home?" Haley asked.

Recker shook his head, sure of his answer before he even said it. "They're not gonna try to kill her. Like we said, killing her does them no good. They'll just assign another judge. Can't kill all of them."

Jones was still listening even as he was doing his computer work. "Besides that, U.S. Marshals are providing protection for her on the way home."

"No, they don't want to hurt her," Recker said. "They wanna scare her, intimidate her. That's what they wanted to do by kidnapping her child. Let her know they could get to her, get to her family."

"So maybe they'll go after the kid again," Haley said.

"No, the messages I intercepted specifically made mention to the judge," Jones replied. "Nothing was said about the child. I believe the incident at the park has made them wary of that again. They probably believe the child already has security nearby when they go outside. It'd be a worthless effort to try that again."

"Well if the Marshals are going to be outside her house, what else could they try?" Haley asked. "And if they're stationed there, what good would we do? They've already got it staked out."

"No, they are not being stationed there. The judge has only requested security to and from the courtroom. They will not be outside her door all night."

"I'm assuming she has some type of alarm system?"

Jones nodded. "That would be correct. But we all know that's no real deterrent to a professional who knows what he's doing."

Recker sought to put his friend's mind at ease. He knew how frustrating these things could be at times. He felt it too from time to time and probably more often. "Don't worry. Whatever they're planning, we'll put a stop to it," he said, nodding at Haley. "We'll be there."

37

Recker and Haley had been watching Judge Rocco's house for over an hour. They weren't only waiting for the judge to get home, but also to see if she had any strange visitors come to the house. Haley was stationed near the front of the house, while Recker was in the back. Since the backyard of the house backed up to the property of a house behind it, there weren't many places for Recker to hide out and wait. He had to get into the backyard. There was a very small storage shed he had broken into as he watched the house.

"Getting anything out there yet?" Recker asked.

"No, all clear. You know, why doesn't she just invest in a personal bodyguard? Seems like it'd be a good idea."

"I don't know. I guess some people just feel like it's an intrusion or they don't need it."

"Well, after what happened the other day with her daughter I'd say it's necessary," Haley said.

"Well she's got protection now, and she's using it. That's why I think whatever's going down is gonna happen inside that house.

They've gotta know she's got marshals protecting her now on the outside."

About ten minutes later, the judge arrived at her home, escorted by members of the U.S. Marshal's service. Haley alerted Recker to their presence so he'd know. They accompanied her to the door, and one man went inside the house with her. Once she was safely inside, the rest of the men went back to their car. They waited a few minutes just to make sure there were no problems then left once the coast seemed clear.

Haley immediately notified Recker, letting him know a man went inside with her. "Who do you think it is?"

"I dunno. Either one of the marshals or she's now got a personal security guard," Recker answered.

"I thought she thought it wasn't necessary."

"Maybe she changed her mind."

"Well it seems she's got things covered now."

"We'll see."

"Seeing as she's got someone in there with her, think we should pull out?" Haley asked.

"Nah. We're already here. Might as well see it through."

A little over a half hour after Judge Rocco returned home, the nanny then left. Once again, Haley gave his partner the heads up. Recker figured whatever might happen would take a while. He assumed it would be pitch black out before someone tried to sneak into the house. He periodically checked in with Jones to keep him informed of what was happening on their end, as well as seeing if he had learned anything new. Even as the two Silencers were outside the house, Jones was still feverishly checking to gain any new knowledge of the plot he'd uncovered.

As the night wore on, they didn't see any signs of danger. Nobody even came close to approaching the house, in either the front or the back. But there was a nagging feeling that kept tugging at Recker as he watched the house. There were still several lights on in the house, which seemed unusual to him. He knew from what Jones told him she had a full court schedule tomorrow. Recker figured she would have gone to bed as soon as possible with that schedule in mind. He watched the house for another half hour before calling Jones to tell him of his suspicions.

"David, what time did you say the judge usually leaves in the morning?"

"From what I can gather she is usually out of the house by seven-thirty," Jones answered. "Why do you ask?"

Recker hesitated for a moment, not even sure in his own mind what was bothering him. "I don't know. Something seems weird here."

"Such as?"

Recker let out a deep and audible sigh, indicating his uncertainty. "I don't know. I can't put my finger on it. Something just seems off."

Jones stopped what he was doing to fully concentrate on Recker's issue. "You are going to have to expand on that slightly, Mike. What exactly are you seeing or hearing?"

"Well, there's still several lights on in the house."

Jones didn't immediately reply, taking a few seconds to think. "And why is that a problem?"

"I dunno. Just seems like a judge who's got a full schedule tomorrow, with a baby in tow, would be going to sleep by now. But there's still at least three lights on that I can see."

Jones took a few more seconds to think, trying to analyze what he'd just been told. "Well let's look at it logically. She has a six-month-old baby. It could be that she's not asleep because the baby's not asleep."

"Possibly," Recker said.

"And she is a judge with a full plate tomorrow, as you said. It could be that she's staying up late to review the upcoming cases she has. Perhaps she is just studying. I know you always try to find the darker side of everything, but sometimes things are exactly what they appear to be."

"Yeah, maybe."

Jones then remembered that a man went inside with the judge when she came home. "Didn't you also state that a guard was with her?"

"Well, I didn't state it, but yeah."

"Maybe he's making his rounds," Jones said. "Maybe he doesn't want the house to be dark. Maybe he's just being extra cautious."

"Or maybe something's wrong."

This time it was Jones' turn to sigh. He knew no matter what he said, or could say, nothing was going to satisfy his friend. He was always going to think the worst. It was just Recker's nature.

"Can I just ask why you assume none of what I said is the case?" Jones asked. "Why does your mind automatically turn to the worst-case scenario?"

"Because it usually is."

"What do you propose to do?"

"I dunno. You know what else is bothering me?"

"I'm sure you'll explain."

"With some of those lights being on, I haven't seen anyone pass by," Recker said. "Not even a shadow."

"And so, I'll ask again, what do you propose to do?"

"I think I wanna go in."

Jones squirmed in his seat, envisioning a whole lot of ways that could go wrong. Dozens of thoughts went through his mind, all of which ended up badly for his team. Though he was hesitant to agree right away with Recker and give his blessing for them to enter the house, Jones did trust his instincts. No matter what the situation, Recker wasn't often wrong. Even when he didn't have much to go on, Recker's intuition was usually right on the money. Especially when he was the one in the field. It was tough for Jones to gauge sometimes how bad a situation was sitting from his chair.

He wanted to get Haley's opinion before anything was officially decided, not that it necessarily guaranteed anything, as Recker could decide to go in no matter what anyone else said. Even so, Jones liked to gather all the facts from as many sources as possible before anything happened.

"Chris, have you been listening to what Mike and I have been discussing?"

"Yep."

"And what is your take on it? Have you noticed anything suspicious on your end?" Jones asked.

"Uh, I dunno. I mean, what Mike says makes sense. But then again, what you say makes sense too."

"What're you, playing Switzerland?" Recker asked.

Haley laughed. "I could see both scenarios being right."

"And how do you plan on getting in there?" Jones asked, expecting some type of elaborate plan.

Recker had a much simpler answer, though. "There's a back door."

"Oh, yes, how foolish of me to expect something else."

Just as they were about to agree on Recker and Haley moving in to check out the house, Jones thought of a different plan. He thought it was a much easier and simpler idea.

"Hold up on storming the house," Jones said.

"Why?" Recker asked.

"I've got a better way. I've got the judge's phone number right here. I'll just give her a call. If she answers, we'll know she's fine. If not, then maybe something's up."

Recker wasn't as impressed with the idea. "I've got a couple of comebacks on that."

"Go on."

"What if she is one of those people who doesn't answer the phone if she doesn't know the number calling?"

"I guess that's a thought."

"Or what if she answers and somebody actually is there and makes her answer in a way that makes it seem as though everything is fine?"

Jones could see that his simpler and easier idea was about to go by the wayside. "You've made your point."

"Or what if she actually is sleeping and just forgot to turn out the lights?"

"I said you made your point."

"I was just throwing out a few retorts," Recker said.

"Yes, yes, I get the gist of it."

"So, no matter what happens with that phone call of yours, it might not really mean or change anything."

"I understand that. I hear what you're saying."

"If someone is in there, though, it might give them a warning. They might think she was expecting a call and put them on high alert."

"I'm taking it that you think we should just bypass the phone call?"

"I think we'd be better off."

After a few more minutes of discussion, it was agreed upon that Recker and Haley would stay put for a little while longer to see if anything changed. Once midnight struck, they were given the go-ahead to move in. The time moved by quickly, and without seeing any type of movement inside the house, Recker was ready to go. Before moving, he coordinated plans with Haley.

"I'll go in first through the back," Recker said.

"Where do you want me to go?"

"Just sit tight for a minute until I give you the word. If there's nothing wrong, then I don't want both of us struggling to get out of there. If I come across anything, I'll let you know and you come in."

"Right," Haley replied.

Recker exited the small shed he was stationed in and

approached the back door of the house, running over to it as fast as he could. Once there, he picked the lock and had the door open in under a minute. As he walked inside the house, he withdrew his gun, ready to fire if necessary. He walked through a dark area which appeared to be some type of storage room. He cleared a couple other rooms, letting Jones and Haley know his findings up to that point. Recker then found some steps that led up to a door and what he assumed was the main part of the house.

Recker gently turned the knob on the door and slowly opened it, peeking at what was on the other side. One of the lights was on and as Recker closed the door behind him, observed that it was the main living area. To the left of him was the kitchen, and Recker retreated to it to make sure nobody could come up behind him. Once he knew it to be empty, he went back to the living room, keeping his guard up the entire time. He peeked into the room to make sure no one was around the corner then cautiously walked into the middle of the room. To his far right were steps that led up to the bedrooms. He didn't need to see anything else, though, to know that something was definitely wrong.

At the bottom of the steps was a man lying on the floor face down, his wrists tied together against the staircase. Recker assumed he wasn't dead, or he wouldn't have needed to be tied up, but went over to him just to make sure. The man was still breathing, but he had a nasty bump on his head, and some blood on the back of his skull thanks to a nice-sized gash. Recker looked up the stairs but didn't see or hear anything coming from that direction. Still, he knew something had to be up there. They had both entrances covered, and nobody had left. Before going ahead, he let the others know what he encountered.

"Is it the security guard?" Jones asked.

"I don't know. I didn't see him. I'll take a picture of his face and send it to Chris."

Recker quickly pulled out his phone and snapped a picture of the man's face and sent it to Haley for confirmation. If it was the security guard, it was a clear sign the judge was in trouble. If it turned out not to be the guard, then it led to the possibility it was an intruder the guard took care of and had the judge in a more secure location. If that was the case, they didn't have long to wait as it was likely the police would have been notified by now. If that was true, they risked staying there, and getting trapped.

Luckily, Haley recognized the face instantly. "That's the guard," he said.

"All right, get in here," Recker replied.

Haley got out of his car and ran across the street. Like Recker, he got through the door in less than a minute. He quickly found Recker in the living room. They agreed that once they got up the stairs, they'd split up and take different rooms. When they got to the top of the steps, Recker went to his left as Haley took the right. Recker's first room was what looked like a spare bedroom. It was very neat and orderly, and looked like it hadn't been used much. As he was checking, Haley's door opened into the baby's room. He quickly cleared it, then walked over to the crib to see if the baby was inside. She was sleeping.

"Baby's in her crib," Haley said.

"She OK?" Recker asked.

"Yep. Sleeping like a baby."

"Ha," Jones said, appreciating the humor. "How à propos."

After exiting his room, Recker went down the hall to the next door. He thought he heard something and put his ear against the door to listen. He heard a man talking. It didn't sound like a pleasant conversation, as the man's voice kept raising; he wasn't happy about something. As Haley was checking out another room, Recker started turning the handle on the door, ready to burst in on the discussion.

Recker forcefully pushed the door open and immediately saw the judge sitting in a chair tied up with a gag in her mouth. He then noticed a man standing to her right with a gun in his hand. As soon as the man saw the stranger come into the room, he pulled his gun up to fire. Recker, though, beat him to the punch and raised his own weapon. Recker pointed at the man and immediately fired, pulling the trigger twice. Both shots lodged into the man's chest, knocking him onto the floor. Recker quickly scanned the rest of the room to see if the man had a partner, but there was no one else in sight.

"I got one down," Recker said. "Keep checking the rest of the house."

"I'm on it," Haley replied.

Recker walked over to the fallen man and stood over top of his lifeless body. With the amount of blood coming out of his shirt, and the range he was shot at, Recker figured he was dead. He reached down to check his pulse just to make sure. The man was dead. Recker took a careful look at his face and recognized him as the third member of the gang they were looking for. Then Recker looked back at the judge and walked over to her, removing her restraints. After she was untied, and the gag removed from her mouth, she felt and rubbed her wrists.

The judge looked up at the man who she assumed was a police officer, appreciative of his efforts. "Thank you."

"Glad I could help."

She then remembered her protection and stood. "My security guard, he got hit in the head."

Recker put his hand out to let her know to relax. "He's fine. He's got a nasty bump, but he'll be OK."

"Oh, thank God."

"My baby…"

"You're baby's fine. Still in her crib sleeping, not a care in the world," Recker said with a smile.

A look of relief swept across Rocco's face as she sat back down. "I don't know what happened. It all happened so fast."

"Well, we've been watching your house for a while and didn't see him come in, so he must've already been here waiting for you when you got home."

Rocco looked puzzled. "You've been watching my house? Why?"

"We got word that something might happen."

"Word? Why wasn't I notified?"

Recker shrugged, drawing another curious look from the judge. "We don't usually do that."

"What district are you with?" Rocco asked.

Recker shook his head. "I'm not with the police."

"What? Who are you, then? What are you doing here?"

"Just helping where I'm needed," Recker answered.

Rocco looked at his face a little closer, studying it. It was a face that looked familiar to her somehow, though she couldn't place it at first. "Have you been in my courtroom before?"

Recker smiled, thankful he couldn't say he had. "No."

"I've seen you somewhere before."

"I get that a lot."

Haley then reported back after checking the rest of the rooms. "Rest of the house is clear."

"All right, I'll meet you back outside," Recker replied.

"Who are you talking to?" Rocco asked.

"I have friends."

Rocco continued studying his face. She knew she'd seen it before. She was positive of it. After another minute, she snapped her fingers as it came to her. "I've got it."

"You do?"

"You're him."

Recker knew what she was referring to, but chose to make light out of it instead, not wanting to make a big deal of it. "Well I've never been called a her so that's a good start."

Rocco smiled. "You're the Silencer, aren't you?"

Recker looked away for a second, not really giving any type of confirmation or denial. He didn't need to give one in either direction, though. The judge already knew it was true.

"Why the special interest in me?" she asked.

Recker looked perplexed, not sure of her meaning. "Special interest?"

"I was told you also intervened at the park the other day. I guess I also have you to thank for that."

Recker shrugged, not looking for thanks. "Just glad I was able to get there in time to stop it."

Rocco looked at him and smiled again. "So, you're the famous vigilante. You know, I've always thought we might meet one day."

"Oh?"

"Yes, but I always assumed it'd be while I was wearing my robe and you'd be in handcuffs."

Recker let out a slight laugh. "Sorry to disappoint you."

"Well, as thankful as I am for helping me and my daughter, I have to say it wouldn't help you if you do find yourself in that situation."

"Didn't think it would."

"I mean, if you ever do wind up in my courtroom, I'd have to throw the book at you."

Recker smiled, not at all bothered by the warning. "I'd hope for and expect nothing less."

Rocco then gave him a wink. "But let's hope it never comes to that."

Recker nodded. "I can agree with that."

"How do you do what you do?"

"Trade secrets."

The judge nodded, not wanting to pry too much into his affairs. Though they were technically on opposite sides, and due to her profession, she was officially against what he did, Rocco was grateful for his assistance in helping her family. But she was a

494

person of integrity, and if Recker ever did show up in her court, she couldn't do much for him. As much as Recker was enjoying the conversation, he knew he had to be going. Sticking around any longer would be risky.

"Well, I'll let you get back to your business," Recker said. "I'll have the police called in a few minutes."

Rocco blinked and nodded. "Thank you. I certainly hope I never have to see you again. In any setting."

"That makes two of us."

"Before you go, can I ask you a personal question?"

"Sure."

"Why do you do it? All this. You know it will probably end badly for you. Do you do it for kicks? Notoriety? Money? What?"

"Honestly, I just do it 'cause I wanna help people. Don't give a damn about money, fame, or anything else. The only thing I get out of it is the satisfaction of helping people and making sure they're safe. That's all."

"So that's really all there is to it?"

"That's really it."

"What'd you do before this?"

"Why the third degree?" Recker asked.

Rocco shrugged. "Just curious. You're a polarizing figure. Just wondering what makes you tick."

"Before this I worked for the government in various situations overseas. Didn't end so well for me. But don't go looking me up. You won't find anything."

The judge just nodded and gave a faint smile. "I kind of figured that would be the case."

"You stay safe."

"You figure this is the last of this type of stuff against me?"

"Well, there was a three-person crew contracted to work against you," Recker said. "Two are locked up, and this one's killed, so I think that should be the end of it. We'll keep an ear out just in case they come up with something new, but I've got a feeling they'll get the hint that this isn't gonna work."

"You said we, there's more of you?"

Recker smiled, but wasn't about to divulge anything else. "Let's just say that I'm not alone."

38

It'd been a week since Recker and company saved Judge Rocco from the break-in of the last remaining crew member they had been watching. Jones had kept tabs on the judge, typing in a few extra parameters into his search engine to see if he could uncover any further heinous attempts to sidetrack her in an upcoming trial. As far as he could tell, she was in the clear. After two failed attempts, the powers that be behind the attacks had nothing else they were working on.

With the judge no longer an issue, Recker and Haley focused on other cases, neither of them working together on any assignment since then. They were both busy, though, each having at least one assignment a day, and on a couple of occasions, two or three. There were several robbery attempts, kidnappings, a few planned murders, as well as an arson attempt, and a couple of planned assaults. After the busy week, and with their slate of cases currently empty, Recker had planned to sleep late one morning. He took turns with Haley, who slept in the day before. He didn't come in until twelve, which was around the time Recker was planning on coming in. Mia had a late shift that day and Recker was planning on spending the morning with her. Unfortunately, as it often did, his plans didn't work out the way he intended.

Though Recker got to sleep in a little, waking up at nine, the rest of the morning was not as quiet as he was hoping. He'd just finished eating breakfast with Mia when his phone started ringing. When he got to the table and saw who it was, he looked up at the ceiling and let out a deep sigh, knowing his morning was about to be cut short. Whenever Jones was calling at a time when Recker was supposed to be off, if there ever was such a thing, it meant something major had just happened and his private time was coming to an end. Before answering, he looked over at Mia, who gave him a faint smile, also recognizing what the call would probably mean.

"Hey, what's up?"

"Sorry to do this to you," Jones said. "I know you were looking forward to having the morning to yourselves."

"It's fine. What's going on?"

"Bad news I'm afraid. It appears that another police officer has been shot and killed."

"How?" Recker asked.

"Walking out of his house last night on the way to begin his shift. He did the overnight watch."

"It's been what, week and a half, two weeks since the last one?"

"Yes. And our special phone rang this morning and has a voicemail on it from our detective friend," Jones said.

"You didn't answer it?"

"I think the less he knows about our business the better. He only knows you, only has dealt with you, I think we should keep it that way."

"Yeah, probably right about that. You listen to the message?" Recker asked.

"I did. It was basically just going over a few details of this shooting and asking you to call him back when you could."

"Have you been able to look into it yet?"

"Well, thankfully we've got a little lull in our case log right now, so I was able to check a few things out so far. Haven't got too deep into it yet, but it's still early."

"Any connections to the other victims?"

"No," Jones said. "Once again, he worked in a different district, no obvious relationship to the other officers."

Recker stayed silent for a few moments, the phone still pressed to his ear, as he tried to think of their next move.

Jones hoped his silence meant he thought of something. "Come up with anything?"

Recker let out a sigh, not sure if he did or not. He had something, whether it was any good or not, was still to be decided. "I don't know yet. Cops are going down every week. I think it's time we stepped things up a notch."

"What do you mean?"

"We need to get active about this. We've been pretty passive over it."

"Well, to be fair, it is a police matter and they've been investigating it themselves," Jones said.

"Obviously hasn't meant much."

"We have also had our own things to work on."

"I know, I know. I'm just saying, now, we need to ramp it up."

"And what do you have in mind?"

"Tyrell hasn't reported back with anything. How about if we give him pictures of the three cops that were killed, not in uniform, and see if he can start knocking some doors down?" Recker answered.

"I suppose we could do that."

"And I wanna have another chat with Vincent."

"Can I ask what for?" Jones asked, not seeing what good that would do.

"He might know something."

"Excuse me for being argumentative, but he already inquired about it once before, did he not? When he first introduced you to Detective Andrews?"

"Yeah."

"I guess I don't understand what the point of it would be."

"He didn't know at the time who was behind it," Recker said. "That doesn't mean he might not know what the connection is."

Jones hesitated before replying. "I guess I can see what you mean. But that is also supposing that there is a connection to be found."

"Yeah, it is."

"It might just be some random lunatic."

"I'm guessing no," Recker said.

"Why?"

"I dunno. The more I think about it, the more it seems like something that's planned."

"Even lunatics have moments of clarity, Mike."

"I know. But when cops are shot walking out of their house, to me, that shows they were targeted. Those people specifically. Not cops in general. If it was just some random person going on a rampage, I don't think he'd be sitting and waiting outside their house, assuming he even knew where they lived. He would just wait for a parked patrol car or something, create a false call they'd have to roll on, something like that."

"I might be able to go along with that," Jones replied.

"Start working on those pictures and I'll call Vincent to set something up."

"OK. If I can't find anything, then I'll just digitally alter their police profile pictures and make it look like they're not wearing a uniform."

"Whatever's faster for you."

As soon as Recker hung up, he glanced at Mia, who was sitting on the couch. She had the TV on, but she wasn't paying much attention to it. But she was listening to what her boyfriend was saying. And she didn't like it very much. Recker could tell by the scowl on her face and the unfriendly stare she was giving him, that something wasn't sitting well with her.

"What's that look for?"

"Hmm? Oh, nothing."

"Mia? I know that look. Something's bothering you, just tell me what it is."

She quickly relented, not wanting to get into a long, drawn out give-and-take with him. Especially since he always found out what was bothering her, anyway. "It's just I heard you say you were going to meet with Vincent."

Recker batted his eyes for a moment, not understanding what the issue was. "So?"

"You know I hate it when you meet with him."

Recker sat next to her and put his arms around her. "You know sometimes I have to."

"I just don't trust him. I'm always afraid he's going to double-cross you somehow."

Recker smiled, then planted a kiss on her cheek. "Believe me, he's not gonna double-cross me. If he was going to, he'd have done it long before now."

"You're acting like he's a moral person or something. He is a criminal you know."

"I know that. Trust me. I'll be fine."

"You'll take Chris along as backup?"

Recker rolled his eyes, but agreed with her request, even if he wasn't positive the other Silencer would be tagging along. "Yes, I'll take Chris along."

He took a few more minutes to put Mia's mind at ease, then called Malloy to set up a meeting with Vincent. Luckily, the crime boss was willing to meet with him in about an hour. He had to go to the office first before the meeting, so he couldn't hang out with Mia much longer.

"Make it up to you later," Recker said.

"It's OK," she replied, after getting a kiss on the cheek. "Want me to bring dinner home?"

"You're working late."

"Well, something tells me you'll be working late too."

Recker smiled. "You know me too well."

Recker took a few minutes to get himself together, then gave Mia a goodbye kiss before heading to the office. When he got there, Jones and Haley were both sitting at the desk working. Recker walked around to the front of the desk, facing them.

"You print out those pictures yet?" Recker asked.

Jones nodded, then reached for a folder on the desk and handed it to him. Recker opened the folder and saw five four by six pictures, three of the cops, one of the drug dealer, and the one they assumed to be the innocent victim.

"Meeting at the restaurant?" Jones asked.

"No, at the trucking place," Recker replied.

"Are you really hoping he will tell you something?"

"Not hoping for anything. Just ticking off the boxes. Maybe something will come of it."

"Want me to go along?" Haley asked.

Recker briefly thought of Mia when he asked the question, but he knew there was no reason for backup. He and Vincent were on good enough terms where he didn't even have to entertain the thought of something going wrong. Plus, saving Vincent's life should have been enough to earn Recker a lifetime pass from him. Though he knew he was technically breaking his promise, he knew it just wasn't necessary. If there was even a one percent chance, Recker would've agreed to let Haley come along as backup. But with things as they were, he felt Haley was better off working on other things.

"No, I'll be fine," Recker said. "We got anything else in the hopper?"

"Yes, but nothing that's critical enough to warrant both of you being on it," Jones answered. "Chris can take care of it."

"What is it?"

"There's a man threatening his ex-girlfriend."

"How bad?"

Jones shrugged, not knowing how to answer. "How bad are these things usually? There's a threat that's severe enough for us to act on. Don't worry about it. I'll put Chris on it. Concentrate on your business with Vincent."

Recker agreed and looked at the photos in the folder again. It also had information about each of the victims. As he glanced at the contents, Jones wondered about a few things Recker mentioned to him previously.

"What about Tyrell? When was the last time you heard from him?"

"Five or six days I guess," Recker answered.

"Are you still sending him the pictures?"

"Oh, yeah, I almost forgot about that. I'll give him a call now and see what's up."

Recker immediately called Tyrell, who answered on the second ring.

"Hey, what's up?"

"Just wondering if you've made any progress on that police thing we talked about?" Recker asked.

"Nah, not so far. Nobody seems like they're that interested in talking."

"Kinda figured that'd be the case. I'm gonna email you some pictures. Flash them around, see if anybody recognizes them."

"Will do."

After his conversation with Tyrell ended, Recker took a few more minutes to read some of the files on the fallen police officers.

He got so caught up in what he was looking at he almost forgot the time. Once he looked at the clock on the wall, he quickly shuffled the papers back into the folder.

"I need to get going," Recker said.

Recker walked out of the office and headed for Vincent's trucking business. When he got there, the front gates were already open, with a few trucks pulling in and out of the premises. Recker usually was only there at nighttime, when most of the business was done for the day. He had almost forgotten there was an actual business in operation. The security guard was already given instructions to clear Recker when he got there. Recker pulled into a parking spot and headed into the facilities. It was only a minute or two until Malloy greeted him.

"Does he ever go anywhere without you?" Recker asked.

Malloy just smiled. "Not usually."

Recker looked out the window at several trucks coming in and out. "Bustling place."

"It has its moments."

"Almost forgot that this place had an actual business purpose during the daytime."

Malloy led Recker through the warehouse, and down the hallway, until they reached the office door. Malloy opened the door and let Recker in, revealing Vincent sitting at the desk. Recker glanced at the décor, but it looked the same as it always did. Vincent was writing something in a notebook, then stopped and tossed the pen down on the desk as he put eyes on his visitor. He closed the book as Recker sat across from him. Malloy closed the door behind him and leaned up against the wall to the side of the two men. Vincent leaned back and put his elbows on the arm of the chair and clasped his hands together.

"Jimmy told me there was something you wanted to talk about."

"Yeah. Thanks for agreeing to meet so soon," Recker said.

"No problem. The least I could do for you. Usually when you request something, there's a certain urgency involved."

"I wanted to talk about the problem you got me involved in."

"The problem I got you involved in?" Vincent asked, not sure where he was going with the question.

"Meeting your law enforcement friend, getting caught up in his situation."

"Well that was hardly my problem. I was simply the middle-man. You were free to help or not help as you saw fit."

By the face that Recker replied with, Vincent could tell that he wasn't making much progress on the case.

"I take it that it's been giving you fits," Vincent said.

"I guess that's one way of putting it. You still don't have any information on it?"

Vincent shook his head. "If I knew of anything, you wouldn't even be here right now. I would've given that information to Detective Andrews already. That would've eliminated the need for you."

"You know all the people killed so far, right?"

"Yes, three officers and two civilians if I'm not mistaken."

"One of them was a low-level drug dealer," Recker said.

"I'm sure you have a point with that."

"Well, you have control over this entire city now. I would think that you would have information on anybody active in this town. No matter how small."

Vincent made a face and shrugged. "And you think I know of every single person who's doing something illegal?"

"I would be surprised if you didn't."

"Well then I guess you will be surprised to know that I don't lay the hammer down a hundred percent. I don't concern myself with small-time dealers and criminals. They're small time for a reason."

"You just let anyone operate on your turf without being checked?" Recker asked.

"I'm more concerned with the bigger picture. I don't need to know every single detail that's going on out there. I think that's where men in power get tripped up sometimes. They worry about things that aren't especially meaningful. If there's a few hoods out there dealing drugs or weapons, I'm fine with it. If they stay small and are only putting money in their own pocket; food on their table. It's when they have bigger ambitions and start taking it out of my pocket that I'll have an issue with it."

"And everybody knows that?"

"Most do. If they don't, then someone will put them in line."

Recker pulled out his folder and put it on the desk, sliding it over to Vincent.

"What's this?"

"Pictures, names, information of the deceased," Recker replied. "I know you said you don't know anything, but I thought maybe if you saw the names, looked at the faces, maybe something would ring a bell."

Vincent grabbed the folder and held it above the desk and opened it. "Fair enough."

Recker silently looked on as Vincent looked through the contents of the folder. The boss took several minutes, giving it an honest effort. With almost anyone else who might have been there, Vincent likely would have just given it a cursory look and not put much effort into it. But to continue the goodwill they had with each other, Vincent genuinely tried to recall seeing any of the names or faces. Before Recker slid the folder to him, he hadn't seen either. He only knew the situation based on news reports and what he'd been told. He didn't concern himself with the names at that point. After several minutes, Vincent shook his head and closed the folder.

"Afraid I can't help you. None of the faces look familiar. I haven't come across any of these names before either."

Recker could see he was being given an honest answer. Vincent wasn't giving him some fluff or anything. There was another question on his mind, and he hoped Vincent wouldn't take umbrage at it.

"None of these officers were on your payroll, were they? No offense meant."

Vincent smiled. "No, they were not. And no offense taken."

"Just figured I'd ask."

"If they were on my payroll, don't you think I'd have some knowledge of what was going on?"

"Maybe. Or maybe they weren't paid well enough for you to care."

"Fair enough. In any case it's a moot point since they're not."

"I guess there's one more question that has to be asked," Recker said.

"Well, I think I might be able to anticipate what that question is, but you go ahead anyway."

"You're not behind this, are you?"

"What do you think?"

"I'd say it was unlikely, but like I said, the question has to be asked."

"Then my answer would be no, I'm not. If I was, do you really think I would reach out to get you involved to investigate? That would be a pretty stupid thing to do on my part considering how well you do your job."

"Not talking of you specifically, but, generally speaking, people do stupid things all the time."

"Agreed. But I am not one of those people," Vincent said.

"No doubt about it. Well, you made an effort," Recker said. "That's all I could ask."

Vincent, trying to help him and offer something useful, slid the folder to the side of the desk, pointed in Malloy's direction.

"Jimmy? Take a look if you will."

"Sure," Malloy said, moving toward the desk.

Malloy did as his boss did and looked at the pictures carefully. Once he was done with them, he moved on to the names and information of the victims. After he gave it a few minutes, he had the same response as Vincent. He put everything back in the folder and handed it to Recker.

"Don't know any of them either."

Recker sighed in frustration, though he wasn't too surprised. "I won't take up any more of your time."

"Sorry we couldn't be of help," Vincent said.

"Figured it was worth a shot."

"Just out of curiosity, what do your instincts tell you?"

"My instincts?"

"Yes. Surely you have some thoughts or theories about what's going on, whether you can prove them or actually have any proof to lead you to it."

Recker's eyes darted around the room for a few seconds as he pondered the question. Vincent was right. He did have some thoughts he really hadn't shared until now. He tried not to offer any ideas about anything he at least didn't have some evidence that would lead him in the right direction.

"So far there's no link that connects any of these people together."

"But you feel there is one?" Vincent asked.

"I do. I kind of doubt five people being shot in a matter of weeks is random. Could it be? Sure. I just have a tough time believing it."

"What would the connection be?"

"I don't know. The dealer, the innocent victim, and the undercover officer were all shot in proximity to one another. That leads me to believe something happened that wasn't supposed to be seen. Or something happened that wasn't supposed to."

"And the other officers?"

"Cops being shot outside their houses indicates a personal connection," Recker said.

"And what does that lead you to?"

"It leads me to believe that maybe they were involved in something they shouldn't have been."

Vincent nodded, having the same feeling. "Perhaps you're right."

Recker left the office and drove out of the lot. He let Jones know nothing came of the meeting. Even though he believed Vincent didn't know anything, something was tugging at Recker that he knew more. Maybe it was just his cynical nature. But it almost seemed to him Vincent was trying to lead him down the path that Recker eventually stumbled upon without saying anything. But like most things with Vincent, Recker could never be completely sure of anything. He would just have to hope Tyrell would have better luck.

39

Another week went by with two more shootings of police officers. Both officers were killed walking out of their houses. With not having anything new to work with, Recker was willing to do just about anything to get the crucial piece of evidence they needed to find out who the shooter was. Right now, he'd settle for just knowing what the connection to all the officers was. And he knew there had to be one. The growing sentiment amongst the police, according to Andrews, was the attacks were random, and there was no link between any of them. It was a belief shared by Jones, and even Haley was starting to come around to that line of thinking. Recker seemed to be the last holdout. It was possible he'd eventually be proven wrong, but he just couldn't make himself think some crazy person was going around shooting cops. He knew there had to be more to it than that.

With that desperation in mind, Recker called for a meeting with Tyrell at Charlie's Bar. The place didn't open until four, but Recker had called and asked him if he could use a table. As Charlie always got there at one to start setting up for the night, and that Recker was always welcome anytime, he had no problem in letting the Silencer use his establishment. It was two o'clock, and Recker and Haley had arrived right on schedule. While they were waiting, Charlie brought a couple of drinks over for the two men.

"Here's a couple of sodas for you gents," Charlie said, putting the two glasses down.

"Thanks, Charlie," Recker replied.

"Ah, no sweat, boys."

As soon as Charlie walked away, Haley took a sip of his drink. "Wonder what's keeping him."

"I dunno. He's usually not late."

A few more minutes went by before they heard a tap on the wood of the front door. Charlie walked over to it, and after quizzing the visitor, let him in. Tyrell walked over to the table and sat across from his friends.

"Took you long enough," Recker said, not letting go of the opportunity to kid him.

"Hey man, I hit traffic."

A minute later, Charlie came by with another drink, putting in front of Tyrell. "I'll leave you boys to your discussion. If you need anything else, just give me a holler. I'll be in the back."

"Thanks, Charlie," Recker said.

Tyrell took a drink, then stood and removed his jacket. Recker looked at it closely as Tyrell slung it over the back of his chair.

"That new?" Recker asked.

Tyrell took a look behind him at the jacket before answering. "Yeah. Just got it a couple days ago."

"Nice. Looks shiny."

"Genuine leather."

Recker looked at the jacket again, then Tyrell. He opened his mouth and was about to make a joke, but Tyrell put his hand up to stop him from going any further.

"Listen, man, I like the jacket. It's comfortable. I can do without any of your sarcastic responses."

Recker smiled and let out a laugh, unable to contain himself. "All right, let's get down to business then."

"Before we start that, can I just say how weird it is that there's two of you now?"

Recker and Haley looked at each other, neither of whom thought there was anything weird about it.

"Why?" Recker asked.

"I dunno. For so long I was just dealing with one of you running around, saving the city. Now there's two of you. I dunno. Just don't seem natural."

"This isn't the first time you two have met."

"I know. I was just sayin'. I just can't believe there's two of you crazy mo-fo's running around the city now, playing superhero, stalking around in the middle of the night."

"We don't stalk around," Haley said, joking.

"And it's not always the middle of the night," Recker said.

"Yeah, yeah. So, what'd you want to meet about?"

"We wanna get more proactive about this police thing," Recker said. "Cops are dropping like crazy around here and we need to put a stop to it now."

Tyrell made a face, making Recker think he wasn't on board with the idea.

"What, you don't think so?"

Tyrell shrugged. "Nah, it's not that. But, I mean, I don't know what else we can do. You know I've checked around. Nobody's got nothin' to say. You know the cops have put everything they got on this. And Vincent, you checked with Vincent. Even he don't know what's going on. Now if I don't know, Vincent don't know, and the cops don't know... maybe there ain't nothin' to know."

Recker shook his head. "I just can't believe that. There's always somebody that knows something. There's always a piece of evidence out there somewhere. We just have to find it."

"I dunno, man. I don't know where it is."

"Maybe it's like fishing. Maybe we just haven't used the right kind of bait."

"You know I don't fish," Tyrell said.

"If you wanna catch a different kind of fish, sometimes you gotta put a different kind of bait on the hook to reel them in."

"And what would that bait be?"

"Money," Recker answered.

"Money?"

"Yeah. So far, it hasn't been offered. You were just using your connections, Vincent wasn't really looking, and the cops don't bribe for information."

"Maybe not the ones you know," Tyrell said, scoffing at his suggestion. "I know a few who do."

"Regardless, the ones who are investigating this, don't."

"So whatcha you got in mind?"

Recker reached into his pocket and removed an envelope. He set it down and slid it across the table. Tyrell picked it up and looked inside. As he was holding the envelope, looking at the money that was inside, he peeked up at Recker.

"How much is in here?" Tyrell asked.

"Couple thousand."

"And I'm supposed to use this to get the answers we're looking for?"

Recker nodded. "That's the plan."

Tyrell folded the flap of the envelope back down and put it in the pocket of his jacket. "And you think this is the right kind of bait?"

"You don't?"

"I dunno. Beats me. I'm just asking."

"Can't hurt."

"How much of this am I supposed to use?"

"As much as you need," Recker answered.

"What makes you think this is gonna give you the answers you're looking for?"

"We all know money talks. Maybe people just haven't been motivated enough to give us what we need."

Tyrell slouched down in his chair and put his elbow on the arm of it and balled his hand into a fist as he rested it against the side of his mouth. He was contemplating the situation, and what he was being asked to do.

"Can I just ask why you're so dead set on thinking that this isn't the work of some whack job out there? Why does everything gotta be some conspiracy theory or something?"

Recker leaned over and made a grimace as he itched his side as he contemplated the question. "I dunno. I guess I just have a hard time believing this is the work of a crazy person."

"Why?"

"Just doesn't feel like it."

"Seriously? That's all you got? It just doesn't feel like it? Nothing specific to go on?"

Recker shook his head. "Nope. Just a hunch."

Tyrell rubbed his mouth with the palm of his hand. "And what are you gonna do if this doesn't pan out?"

"I don't know. Haven't thought about it. Guess we'll cross that bridge when we come to it."

Tyrell sighed, thinking this was gonna be a waste of time. He was willing to do it since he got paid for it no matter what, but based on his conversations with some of his contacts previously, he just didn't think they'd have anything more to share, even with money being thrown in their faces. But he was known to be wrong before with some of the people he dealt with, and Recker was right because money had a way of loosening lips sometimes.

"All right, I'll give it a shot," Tyrell said. "Hope we can turn something for you. I'll start working on it right away."

"Appreciate it."

Tyrell took one last sip of his drink then stood and put his new jacket on.

"Snazzy," Recker said.

"Hey, what'd I tell you about that?"

Recker laughed again. "Just couldn't resist a parting shot."

"Yeah, I bet. So, what do I do in the event I do find someone willing to talk, assuming there is such a person, and this ain't enough?" Tyrell said, tapping the envelope in his pocket.

"There's three thousand dollars in there. I think that should be plenty."

"Never know. I'm just asking."

"If you find someone who's looking for more, you let me know."

"I'll do that."

Tyrell started to leave but was interrupted by Recker, who had some last-minute instructions for him.

"Tyrell?"

"Yeah."

"Just don't be giving that money to anybody who might have information," Recker said. "They better have something, and it better be right, and it better be good."

Tyrell looked at him strangely, like he was talking to someone else. "What do you think I am? A rookie or something?"

Recker smiled at him. "I'm just saying."

Tyrell waved at him then left the bar. Recker and Haley stayed a few minutes longer to finish their drinks and discuss things a little more.

"You really think he's gonna come up with something?" Haley asked.

"I do. Wouldn't have done it if I didn't think it'd work."

"Well, sometimes people throw crap at the wall and hope that something sticks. Doesn't mean they believe that it will."

"I think Tyrell will find out something," Recker said. "He knows enough people that he'll find someone who'll start talking. I believe that someone knows something. Somebody has to."

They stayed another five minutes, then when their drinks were finished, started leaving. Recker went to the back office to let Charlie know they were going and to thank him for letting them use his place. When the two Silencers got back to the office, Jones had some news for them.

"Well, Tyrell's gonna hit the streets again," Recker said. "Armed with some extra funding, of course."

"We may not even need it," Jones said, typing away, not even bothering to look at them entering the office.

Recker's mood quickly perked up, thinking, and hoping his partner had found something. "Why? What's up?"

"I'm not sure but I may have found a common link. Nothing concrete yet, but it's a start."

"What'd you come up with?" Recker asked, sitting at the desk next to him, eagerly looking at the screen.

Haley also pulled up a chair, sitting just behind the two men, looking between their shoulders.

Jones finished up what he was typing before explaining. "Three months ago, Officer Jennings opened up a new bank account with a five-thousand-dollar deposit."

"OK?" Recker asked, not seeing a connection so far.

"Officer Bridges did the same thing three months ago."

"Nothing we can really pin down," Haley said.

Jones put his finger in the air, indicating he wasn't done yet. "Officer Wheaton opened up a new bank account six months ago."

"That's three," Recker said.

Jones still wasn't done. "And five months ago, Officer Clemont did the same."

"All with the same amount?" Haley asked.

Jones nodded. "All with the same amount. Five-thousand-dollar deposits."

"That is a pretty big coincidence."

"I'm still not done. None of these new accounts were opened up in those officer's names."

"Then whose were they?" Recker asked.

"Names of relatives. Mothers and wives mostly."

"How'd you pick up on it?"

Jones gave an unassuming shrug. "Well, nothing came up in their personnel packages or their records, so I just figured I would try to dig a little deeper. Jennings was the only one who did not open up an account in someone else's name."

"I wonder why?" Haley asked.

"Jennings was not married, and his parents were already deceased. He also was an only child, and he did not have any children of his own either."

"Oh."

"Figure out where that money came from?" Recker said.

"Unfortunately, no. They all deposited checks from a newly established security company. They all had the words 'Consulting' written in the memo line."

"Trying to make it look legitimate."

"Indeed," Jones replied. "But, I've checked the company's history and they are as phony as a three-dollar bill."

"Not a real company?"

"Fake name, fake owner, fake business account, all come back with dead ends."

"How about trying to get into the bank account footage?" Recker asked. "If we can get a picture of the guy opening the account, maybe we can hone in on him."

"Unfortunately, that is no longer possible."

"Why's that?" Haley asked.

"Because the bank only keeps their security footage for six months. There is nothing left to check."

"Figures."

"What about the bank account itself?" Recker said. "Can you get into it? Find any other transactions that might go somewhere."

"I've already been ahead of you. There are no other transactions, and while the account is still technically open, there is no longer any money in it."

"Damn."

"The account was opened a year ago with a small deposit of a thousand dollars. It was built up over the next three months until it reached a total of thirty thousand."

Recker didn't need any further explaining to know what that meant. Thirty thousand dollars, six officers, five thousand each. The account was opened specifically to pay them in a manner which would not draw suspicion. If it was investigated, it would seem they were being paid consulting work by a security firm, which was not unusual work or behavior for cops who were looking for a part-time or side gig.

"Seems pretty clear that something's going on here," Haley said.

Recker and Jones both agreed with the assessment, though neither voiced it right away. Recker always had that hunch anyway, so it wasn't exactly a surprise for him. But it was the link, the one piece of evidence they'd been looking for that confirmed his suspicion. After a few minutes of silence, Recker looked over at the computer genius.

"Well? What do you think now?"

"I would say that you were right," Jones answered, shuffling a few papers around. "I would say that is definitely a link."

"And a shady one at that."

"What now?" Haley asked.

"We keep digging until we hit gold."

"Perhaps it would be wise to let our detective friend know about this," Jones said. "Assuming he doesn't already. Maybe he could shed more light on it."

Though Recker wasn't sure Andrews could tell them more than they already knew, he agreed to call him anyway, just to cover all the bases. After a few rings, Andrews picked up, sounding like he was out of breath.

"Hey, hey," Andrews said, sitting in the chair at his desk.

"Just run a marathon?"

Andrews took a few more seconds to collect his breath. "No, no, I was just on the other side of the office. Wanted to make sure I wasn't in earshot of anyone."

"Oh. Well, I got some news," Recker said. "Not sure if you already know it or not."

"Go ahead."

"Jennings deposited five thousand dollars in a new bank account a few months ago."

"Uh, yeah," Andrews said, shuffling folders around on his desk until he found the right one. He opened it up and started looking at it. "Yeah, it was some consulting work he did on the side or something for some security firm."

"I take it you didn't look too deep into that."

"No, just a cursory look. Everything seemed on the up and up, why?"

"It's a fake company."

"What?" Andrews asked, not believing it.

"There's nothing real about it."

"We ran the basics, everything seemed to come back fine."

"Should've dug deeper," Recker replied.

"Even if that's true, though, that doesn't prove anything."

"It does when you look at the other officers who also opened up false bank accounts with a five-thousand-dollar deposit."

"We didn't find any evidence of that."

"Should've looked harder. One was opened in the name of his wife, the other three in the names of their mothers."

Andrews sighed loudly into the phone, clearly frustrated. "All six got checks from the same security company?"

"You got it."

"Do I need to check this place out?"

"No, don't bother, it'll be a waste of time," Recker answered. "It's a dead end, I've already checked it."

"We still haven't gotten any leads that suggest any of them were anything but clean."

"Well, six officers who are now dead and all opened up bank accounts with a five-thousand-dollar check from a false business sure does raise a lot of red flags, doesn't it?"

"It does. But where do we go from here?"

Recker thought for a few seconds before replying. "Maybe we need to dig into bank accounts for everyone on the force."

Andrews' eyes almost bulged out of his head. "Everyone on the force? You know how long that would take?"

"Plus, wives, spouses, parents, kids, uncles."

"That's a massive undertaking. That'll take months, maybe years, if it can be done at all. You need court orders to check the bank account of everyone on the job."

"You need court orders," Recker said. "I don't play by the same rules, remember."

"But if we're gonna catch the guy behind this, I need solid evidence that I can take into court and put him away with. If they put me on the stand, I very well can't just say The Silencer gave it to me, can I?"

"I suppose not. I'll get back to you when I have more."

"Wait a minute, wait a minute," Andrews said hurriedly.

"What?"

"You have anything else you need me to run down?"

"No, that was it."

"You don't happen to have the bank statements with those deposits, do you?"

"Why?"

"If you do, send them to me, maybe I can use them and talk with their relatives and figure out what's going on. Maybe one of them can tell me something."

Recker didn't reply immediately, but thought it wasn't a bad idea. He wasn't sure how likely it was that one of the cops told anyone in their family what they were doing, especially if it was illegal, but he figured it was probably worth a shot.

"All right, you'll get an email within the hour with what you need."

"Thanks. If any of them say anything interesting, I'll let you know," Andrews said.

The two then hung up, though their conversation gave Recker an idea. He didn't know how workable it was, or how long it would take, but he thought it might just work. But it would depend on Jones' ability. Before telling the others what he was thinking, Recker put his hands in his pocket and paced around the room for a few minutes, trying to get it straight in his own mind. Jones didn't want to wait any longer before finding out what was on his mind, though.

Typing on the keyboard, Jones looked up over his laptop. "Mind sharing what's going through your mind?"

Recker stopped upon hearing his voice, though he didn't hear the entire question. "Huh?"

"You're pacing. Something's going on in that head of yours."

"Oh. Well, I've got an idea."

"Splendid. What is it?"

"Not so sure you'll think it's splendid when I finish saying what it is," Recker said.

"Why is that?"

"Because you'll be doing all the work."

"Oh. If I know you as well as I think I do, I'm going to say this is going to require quite a bit of computer skill."

"More than me and Chris got for sure."

Jones looked a little beleaguered, knowing his workload was likely going to increase dramatically sometime in the next few minutes. "Might as well just say it."

"I have an idea about how to identify who else might be involved in this."

"Let me stop you right there," Jones said. "Now you're assuming there is someone else involved. Maybe all the work has been done."

"I'm guessing not. I have a feeling the net is gonna catch a lot more fish before this expedition is over."

Jones still looked troubled, but wanted Recker to get on with it. "Well, continue."

"We know six officers got a five-thousand-dollar payment. What if we check into the backgrounds of everyone else to see who else got a five-thousand-dollar payment?"

Jones sat there motionless, batting his eyes for a few moments as he stared at Recker. He couldn't believe what he was saying. "Correct me if I'm wrong, but are you actually suggesting we check into the bank accounts of every single member of the police force?"

Recker made a face as if he'd just been hit with a sharp object, knowing how intensive it sounded. "Yes?"

"Do you know how massive an undertaking that would be?"

"Uh, yes?"

It was one of the few times Jones seemed dumbfounded and at a loss for words. "I, uh, I don't even know where I would start."

"Well you dug up these guys."

"These guys as you put it, I was looking at specifically. Do you know how many officers there are in this city?"

Recker looked at Haley for backup. "What was it at last count, over six thousand? Something like that?"

"I believe so," Haley replied.

"And you want me to check every single one of them?" Jones asked. "And by this question, I'm assuming you don't mean just the officers themselves, but their extended family as well?"

Recker knew how tall a task he was asking and just smiled widely. Jones wasn't ready to give up on telling him just how big it was, though.

"Six thousand officers," Jones said. "Then if you get into spouses, kids, parents, siblings, I mean, the results could be staggering. We could easily reach thirty to forty thousand names before we are done."

Recker tilted his head. "Possible."

Silence filled the room for a minute as Jones thought about how massive a request he was being asked. He had no doubts he could do it, but he knew he couldn't do it quickly. Certainly not fast enough for their purposes. There was just no way it could be done by himself in a fair amount of time. Probably not for months. And that would be with him working basically around the clock and not devoting any time or resources to any of their other cases. It was a thought that didn't hold a lot of value to him.

"I just don't think it would be the best use of our time... my time. Could it be done? Yes. But the time involved," Jones said, shaking his head. "How many other people will not get helped because we've gotten sidetracked on this one issue. A big issue to be sure, no doubt about it, but still... one case as opposed to hundreds of others. And with the evidence starting to point toward criminal circumstances, I'm not sure it's a time investment that's worth making."

Recker listened intently to what Jones was saying and sighed, knowing he was right. The plan could work, but it would just take too long. He nodded in agreement to forget about it. Then Haley snapped his fingers, not ready to let it go so quickly.

"I got it," Haley said.

"What?" Recker asked.

"Something similar. But maybe better. And maybe faster."

Jones was equally intrigued and sat up straighter in his chair to listen. "Well let's hear it."

"Same thing basically, but instead of checking each individual name, we check the bank instead."

Jones' heart sank again, once more realizing how much work that entailed for him. "Do you know how many banks are in the Philadelphia region?"

Haley shrugged, not having any idea. "Gotta be what, a thousand?"

"Maybe two," Recker said.

"That's infinitely better than checking thirty thousand names."

Jones was still not impressed. "Do you know how long and difficult it is to hack into a bank's system?"

Haley threw his hands up to answer the question. Recker, putting some serious thought into it, thought it could really work though. It was much more practical than his previous plan, he thought.

"I've got a better way to make it go more smoothly," Recker said.

Jones didn't seem so convinced. "I would love to hear about it."

"Can you devise a program to only look for certain things in a bank's system?"

"It can be done."

"Every officer's payment has been a flat five thousand dollars. Once you're into the bank's system, have it only look through deposits of exactly five thousand dollars over the past six months. There can't be that many. I mean, how many people will put in a five-thousand-dollar check?"

Jones slouched down a little and leaned back in his chair, putting his index finger on his lips as he thought about it.

Haley tried to make it sound a little easier of a task. "And it's not really even a few thousand banks. Some branches have dozens or a hundred. That'll make it go by a little easier."

Jones looked over at him. "Don't try to sugarcoat it."

"So, what do you think?" Recker asked.

Jones sighed, not really wanting to take on such a task, but reluctantly agreed. "I suppose I can give it a shot. I love how you two make it sound so easy for me."

"Hey, we're willing to help. But like you always say, you got your skills, and we got ours."

"Now you're using my own words against me."

Recker laughed, but then got more serious. "Hey, if it gets to be too much or is more difficult than we thought, then we'll try something else."

"Agreed. I'll do my best. But in the meantime, I'll hope like heck Tyrell finds something before I do. And that's the first time I've ever hoped that someone else found information before me."

"It certainly would make things easier, wouldn't it?"

40

As Jones started hacking his way into different banking institutions, the team still hoped Tyrell would be the one to come up with the missing piece. They all felt like they were close, closer than it appeared they were. Recker thought with the right piece, everything would fall together. Jones figured he could start with the smaller banks and eliminate them a little more quickly, or he could start with the bigger banks, the ones with multiple branches, that way he could eliminate a bunch at one time. He figured it was better to get rid of the most amount possible and started with some of the bigger ones.

Recker was in contact with Tyrell every day, keeping up to date with his progress. Five days had passed since Recker had given him the envelope stuffed with money and he was hoping they'd have a little more to show for it by now. Unfortunately, just as Tyrell had suggested it might go, it seemed to be no different than the first go-round. Nobody seemed to have anything to say. He wasn't through with all his contacts yet, but he wasn't expecting much to change. Tyrell had just left the apartment of one of those contacts when Recker called.

"Yo, what's up?" Tyrell asked.

"Just seeing how you were making out."

"Same as before, man. Whole lotta nothin'."

Recker sighed loudly into the phone to signal his displeasure.

"I feel ya, man, but I don't know what else I can do. I can't make people talk."

"I know," Recker said. "It's not you. I'm just ready to be done with this thing."

"Why you even getting all worked up about it? It's not even your thing, right? I mean, that cop came to you. This ain't on your feet."

"I dunno. Doesn't really matter who came up with it. Fact is, I was asked to help. When I do something, and I can't figure out what's going on or get to the bottom of it, it pisses me off."

"I hear you, man, I hear you."

"Have you talked to everybody again?"

Tyrell took a moment to think and rubbed the back of his head. "Uh, lemme see... uh, no, there's a few more."

"Any chance any of them are promising?"

"Man, I don't wanna even give you the slightest bit of false hope. The chances of one of these cats telling me something is next to nothing."

"All right, I'll talk to you later."

Tyrell kept going, talking to anyone he thought might have had some knowledge of what was going on. One by one, though, he struck out. It'd been several hours since he last spoke to Recker and he thought he should update him on his lack of progress. He pulled his phone out of his pocket and looked at the screen in anticipation of dialing, then just happened to look across the street. He thought he caught a glimpse of a man walking into the neighborhood pharmacy. The man went by the nickname of Bones because he was tall and thin. He had a similar background to Tyrell and was someone who usually knew what was going on in the streets. Tyrell hadn't talked to him previously because Bones had been out of town for the past two weeks. Tyrell crossed the street and ran into the pharmacy to catch up with the man. Once they saw each other, they slapped hands and gave each other a hug.

"Man, where you been keepin' yourself?" Tyrell asked.

"Been spending time with my family over in Jersey for a couple weeks. Going through a rough patch right now?"

"Oh really? What's been going on? Everything all right?"

"Nah, not really. My brother died, and I was over at his house for a spell, trying to help keep his wife and kids together. It's been rough, man, been real rough."

"Aww, sorry to hear that, bro. They gonna be able to pull through?"

"I dunno. He didn't really have no savings, so it's gonna be hard for them. Gonna be a single woman raising a couple kids. You know how hard that is."

"Yeah."

"I mean, I'll do what I can, send them a few dollars here and there. Just hope I can do enough. It's hard enough making money for my own family, know what I mean?"

"Yeah, definitely do," Tyrell said, hoping they could help each other. "Hey, you think you could help me find some people that I'm looking for?"

"Maybe. Got some names?"

"Man, I got names, pictures, everything."

Tyrell then pulled out the pictures from his new leather jacket and handed them to his friend. Bones took a minute to study them. Tyrell kept a close eye on his friend's face as he looked at the pictures, hoping he'd give off a clue. And he did. Bones made a couple of expressions that showed he might have known them, or at least know something about them. He then passed the pictures back to Tyrell.

Bones shook his head. "Sorry, man, don't know these fellas."

"You sure?"

"Yeah. Can't help you with that."

Tyrell didn't believe him. The clues Bones made with his face told him he did know them. Tyrell moved in closer to him to make sure nobody else in the store could overhear them. "Listen, there could be a lot of money involved in this for you if you know these bulls. All I'm asking is for you to tell me what you know or what they're caught up in. Could really help your family out."

Bones gulped as he nervously looked around the store. Tyrell could see he looked anxious for some reason. He tried to spur Bones on to tell him what he knew.

"Nothing will come back to you. You got my word on that," Tyrell said. "You know I wouldn't put you in a position like that."

"These are some dangerous cats you're playing with, man."

"So, you do know something."

"I know you're messing with some bad people. You'd be best to leave this alone. This is out of your league. Mine too."

"Listen, I'm not asking for me. I'm just working. I've been asked to find the information and pass it along. Whatever happens after this ain't on me or you."

"I dunno, man," Bones said, wiping the sweat off his forehead with the sleeve of his shirt.

Tyrell knew he needed to convince the man a little more. They'd known each other a long time and knew each other's reputations. Like Tyrell, Bones was highly regarded by all who did business with him. He had a reputation of being trustworthy and reliable. Tyrell was about to use that trust.

"Bones, man, this is big. Bigger than the both of us. There's some big-time players involved in this. They're looking for information, and they ain't gonna stop until they get it. Who knows how many people are gonna get hit before this is over?"

"Hit? Whatcha talkin' about?"

Tyrell had forgotten that since Bones was gone for a couple weeks, he probably wasn't as up to speed on what was going on. Tyrell then spent a few minutes explaining the situation.

"So, all those people are dead now?"

"Yeah. You know The Silencer, right?" Tyrell asked.

"Yeah, man, who don't?"

"Well he's in on this."

Bones nodded and took a product off the shelf and went over to the cash register to pay for it. Tyrell walked over to the door and waited for him to finish. After he was done, Bones came over to the door and motioned with his hand for Tyrell to follow him. Bones opened up and started talking as the two walked along the sidewalk.

"How you know The Silencer?" Bones asked.

"Straight up? I do some work for him from time to time."

"Seriously? Wow, that's some shit right there."

"Make sure you keep that on the down low," Tyrell said.

"You ain't gotta worry about that with me, you know that."

"Well, he's looking for these guys. He knows something's going on. And believe me, he ain't gonna stop looking."

Bones seemed to be more willing to talk about the subject knowing Recker was in on it, though he appeared to be more interested in finding out more about The Silencer. "What kind of guy is he, man? What's he like?"

"Who? The Silencer?"

"Yeah."

"He's a good dude, man. A really good dude. Got good intentions, wants to do right by people. It don't matter if you're black, white, Asian, catholic, protestant, Muslim, he don't care about none of that. To him, you're either good or bad."

Bones let out a laugh. "What's he working with you for then? You know, me and you, we're not exactly classified as great citizens."

"Nah, it's not like that with him. He's after the real bad dudes. He's not after guys like you and me just trying to survive. We don't really hurt nobody. He's after the people who got black hearts, who don't give a crap about who they hurt as long as they benefit from it."

Tyrell could tell Bones was still wrestling with whether he should tell what he knew. Though he thought his friend would eventually get there, Tyrell figured he'd sweeten the pot to get there sooner. He pulled out the white envelope from his pocket and waved it in front of him, making sure Bones saw it.

"There's three thousand in here," Tyrell said. "He authorized me to give it to whoever gave me the information he's looking for."

"Three thousand?"

"Yeah, as long as the information checks out. Think about it, man. That's three thousand you could give to your brother's family, help them out. Do some good by them. You ain't mixed up in any of this, are you?"

"Nah, it's not like that. I just don't want it to get back to me."

"You got my word on that, bro. I don't need to tell anyone where the info came from."

Bones stared at the envelope, enticed by what was inside. "When would I get that?"

"Probably a day or two. I'll relay the information, he'll check it out. If everything comes back good, I'll swing by you and hand it off."

"Then that's it?"

"That's the end of it."

Bones nodded, agreeing to the terms of the deal. They stopped walking and scurried over against the wall of the storefront they were in front of. Bones took another look around just to make sure nobody was nearby listening.

"OK, I don't know all the details of what's going on and all."

"Just tell me what you know," Tyrell said.

"All right. I don't know all the people in those pictures you showed me. But I recognized two of them."

Tyrell quickly dug the photos out of his jacket and showed them again, so Bones could point them out. "Which ones?"

Bones pointed to the two that he knew, then Tyrell shoved them back in his pocket.

"You know those guys were cops, right?" Tyrell asked.

"Yeah. There's a few more of them too."

"There are? You know their names?"

Bones made a face and shook his head. "Nah, not their real names. Know a few nicknames though if that helps."

"Yeah, that'll help a lot."

"The other two guys I know, one guy is nicknamed Siv, the other was nicknamed Butch."

"Siv and Butch?" Tyrell asked. "They variations of their names or something?"

Bones shrugged. "No idea, man. Just know that's what they were called."

"You actually seen this Siv and Butch?"

"Yeah, a couple times. They're cops too from what I understand."

"You know what all this stuff's about?"

"I can't say for sure about the shootings or anything like that," Bones answered. "But the two I pointed out, and the two names I gave you, they were dealing. They were into some heavy stuff."

"The cops were dealing?"

"Yeah. It goes like this. Ever since Jeremiah got taken out, everything in this town goes through Vincent. At least the main stuff. There's some little dealers here and there that either Vincent don't know about or he just don't care because they ain't that big yet. I mean, you know all this, I ain't gotta tell you that."

"What about these guys?"

"They see an opportunity to pick up where Jeremiah fell. They think they can make a lot of bread and Vincent won't be able to touch them because they're cops. Either that or they'll make a deal with Vincent where they'll scratch each other's backs or something."

Tyrell thought it sounded good, but there were still a few things that didn't make sense to him. "So, who's killing these guys then? Is it Vincent? He knows there's a new group coming up, and he's putting them down. Or are the cops taking out their own? Fighting with each other or something?"

Bones shrugged, not having any idea. "I don't know. What I do know, is these guys were starting to make some deals, make contacts, putting stuff together. All the other stuff that's been going on, I can't speak to that."

Tyrell nodded, taking it all in. Once they were finished, and Bones gave him all the information he had, Tyrell handed him the envelope. Bones looked a little surprised that he was giving it to him already.

"What's this?" Bones asked. "I thought you had to check out what I was saying first."

"I believe you. I don't think you'd make all that up."

"Never know, man. I could be lying to you."

Tyrell smiled. "Hey, it's no skin off my nose. Don't mean nothin' to me. The Silencer, though? That's another story. Trust me, if you're lying, he will find you."

"I got nothing to worry about. It'll check out."

"I know it will."

"Hey, are you like, real tight with him?" Bones asked.

"Why?"

"I dunno. You said you do some work for him from time to time."

"Yeah."

"Maybe you could put in a word for me if he ever needs some-thing. You know, look me up. You know I know things out here. Maybe I could help him out if the price is right."

The two men shook hands as they finished their talk. "I'll put the word in."

41

After Tyrell was done with his questioning, he went back to his house before calling Recker to let him know what he found out. Though he did trust what Bones had told him, Tyrell liked being extra cautious whenever he found out interesting information. He didn't like to blab about it in public places, just in case there were wandering ears around. Plus, if someone was watching or following him, he didn't want to make it seem like he got something so good he had to call someone about it right away. That would immediately make Bones look bad and put him in danger if those cops happened to be watching him. Tyrell just didn't take those kinds of chances. He wanted to make it look like they were just having a normal conversation between friends.

Once Tyrell did call Recker, he recalled his entire conversation with Bones, not leaving any details out. He even went over it two times to make sure he didn't forget anything. Recker was happy they finally had a lead to work on, though he still had questions and reservations about it. He was taking information from someone he didn't know. He always was hesitant to do that, even though he trusted Tyrell's judgment completely.

"How solid do you think this information is?" Recker asked.

"I think it's good. Real good."

"You trust this guy?"

"I do. I think he was straight up leveling. I don't have any doubts about that."

"All right. Good job with everything."

"Thank you, thank you. Just my normal excellent work," Tyrell said with a laugh.

"OK, we'll take it from here."

"You got it. You need something else, just let me know."

"We will."

After hanging up, Recker then let Jones know what Tyrell found out. Haley was working on a case and wasn't scheduled to be back until later that night. Before doing anything, they discussed it amongst each other for a few minutes.

"What do you think? Call Detective Andrews and give him the names?" Jones asked.

Recker shook his head. "No, I don't think so. I don't think we should tell anyone about this until we're certain what's going on."

"Well, let's find out who this Siv and Butch are first."

Jones immediately went to work on his computer, pulling up police personnel files. He typed in the names to see if anything popped up automatically, not that he was expecting it to. They didn't sound like last names to him. Nothing came up instantly. Recker pulled up a chair next to him and started looking through the files on another computer, seeing if any names looked similar. He was quickly halted by Jones, who had started another search already.

"Hold on, hold on," Jones said, tapping Recker on the shoulder.

"What's up? Find something?"

"Possibly."

With Jones' first search, he was looking for those two names specifically. He then performed a search for any names that included Siv or Butch, even a partial name. He got a hit on one of them.

"There's a few possibles," Jones said, reading the screen, then pointing to some names. "Here, you take these three, see if there's any connection to our list of fallen officers. I'll take the other three."

After both men looked at their respective lists, Recker couldn't see any connection to the officers who were killed. Jones, though, thought he found the missing link.

"I've got it," Jones said. "Detective Jay Sivelski."

Recker eagerly moved his chair over to see the screen and started to read it. "He knew Jennings."

"Indeed, he did. It appears he also knew Bridges. I can link him to those two. He recently worked cases involving both officers."

They spent a few more hours trying to learn the identity of the man they knew as Butch. But it was to no avail. They couldn't find any evidence of someone named Butch. But it didn't mean he wasn't there. They knew he had to be. Once they found the first name, they knew the other one wasn't far behind. After exhaustively searching, both Recker and Jones leaned back in their chairs to decide their next move in finding out the man's real name.

"I think we should contact Andrews," Jones said.

Recker looked at him, not sure he wanted to go in that direction yet. "I dunno. If they're guys he knows, friends with, it might complicate things."

"But won't it eventually get to that point, anyway? I mean, what difference does it make if you talk to him about it now or you wait a week or two until we have all the evidence and lay it out for him? The circumstances will still be the same."

Recker nodded. "Yeah, I guess you're right about that."

"And whatever happens as a result of it, we will get there sooner. Besides, aren't you the one who said we should trust him?"

"Don't go using my own words against me."

Recker concluded that calling Andrews was the right move. Hopefully, he could figure out who the other guy they were looking for was. The detective didn't pick up until after the fifth ring.

"Hope this isn't a bad time," Recker said.

"Uh, no, no. I was just at home. Had the phone in a different room."

"Day off?"

"Yeah. Yeah, I get them occasionally."

"Must be nice."

"So, what can I do for you?" Andrews asked.

"I'm getting closer to figuring out what this is all about. I need your help to connect some missing pieces though."

"OK. What do you need?"

"First of all, you're probably not gonna like some of what I've learned. I need to know whether I should push on with this or just cut bait now."

"Why? What's the difference?"

"Well, if you're on board with what I tell you, then I can proceed," Recker said. "But if you're one of those cops who doesn't want to bring any dirt on fellow cops, then I'm wasting my time and I'm not gonna want to go any further."

Andrews already knew what that meant without having to be told. "They're dirty, aren't they?"

"Yeah. Yeah, they are."

"What difference does my opinion make to you? Wouldn't you do the same thing, regardless?"

"No. I'm not waging a war against cops, dirty or not," Recker answered. "I know some in the department have a high opinion of me. Maybe that gets me extra leeway in terms of people looking for me, maybe not, I don't know. But I do know I'm not jeopardizing that reputation over something that may get swept under the rug, anyway. Only time I would go after a cop is if an innocent person's life was at stake. Cops engaged in criminal activities with other criminals isn't something that really bothers me to be honest."

"OK. I hear what you're saying. And I'm on board. I'm not a saint. You know I've done things for Vincent. But cops are being killed out there. And if other cops did it, then that's something that we need to do something about. Everyone in the department will be on board for that. So, whatever you got, just lay it out there."

"OK. I've got two names for you. Do you know a Detective Jay Sivelski?"

Andrews thought for a second, but that was all he needed. "Uh, yeah, Sivelski? Yeah, I know Siv."

"Well he's involved. There's another name, but it's only a nick-name, that's all I've got."

"What is it?"

"Guy's name is Butch."

"Butch. Butch," Andrews said, taking a minute to think about it.

"Anything?"

"Uh, yeah, maybe. There's a guy in patrol, Barry Orwell, he's a sergeant, his nickname is Butch."

"You know him?" Recker asked.

"I mean, I've bumped into him a few times, but I don't know him that well or anything."

"But you know Sivelski?"

"Yeah, I've worked with him a few times. How are these guys involved?"

"That I don't know," Recker said. "I don't know if they're gonna wind up like the others, or whether they're at the top of the food chain, but I know one thing, somebody's gotta be running this thing."

"Well if you're looking for leaders, Siv would be at the top of my list."

"Why's that?"

"He's a go-getter," Andrews said. "He's a take charge kind of guy. Orwell too. Big, muscular type of guy. Doesn't mind giving orders. Wouldn't be surprised if they were the ones giving directions."

"Well, we need to find out who else is in their little group, exactly what they got going on, and why some of them are getting knocked off."

Before finishing their conversation, Recker agreed to send Andrews via email some of the things they'd uncovered. After putting his phone away, Recker sat on the desk with his back to Jones and looked out the window. Something still didn't seem right to him.

"What is it now?" Jones asked.

"What?"

"What else are you concerned about?"

"Something doesn't feel right," Recker answered.

"How so?"

"We're now going by the assumption that for some reason these cops are knocking each other off, right?"

"Yes, I suppose so."

"That's what's bothering me," Recker said.

"What? You don't think they would turn on each other? They're as much criminals as they are police officers. That's what criminals do."

"Yeah, but I dunno, it's just... it's not making sense to me. If you're gonna knock off fellow cops that have been in your little group that've been doing not so nice things, then that means you either don't trust them, or they're making a lot of mistakes."

"Or perhaps they changed their mind and don't want to continue those pursuits," Jones said.

"Maybe. But that still baffles me. If I'm a cop and I wanna do something like this, don't you think I would make damn sure that whoever I pick to join me, is in it for life? That in six months or a year they're not gonna change their mind and put everything I was working for in jeopardy? I'm having a tough time wrapping my head around that."

Jones nodded. "I see what you mean. Perhaps you're right about that. Maybe they are not picking themselves off."

"If that's the case, then we're back to where we started. If it's not them, then cops are getting killed and we don't still don't know by who."

Jones put his index finger in the air to counter the point. "Not necessarily. Whichever way it leans, we're still closer than we were in the beginning. We now have a pretty good idea why this is happening. We just need to narrow it down a bit further."

Recker got off the desk and started walking around the room, still deep in thought. If they went with the theory that the police officers weren't killing their own, which was viable conjecture, then they had to figure out who would have wanted them dead. And he kept coming back to the same conclusion, even if he didn't want it to be so. He went back to the desk and sat next to Jones as he sought confirmation of his opinion.

"So, if it seems unlikely that the cops are killing each other, and I'm not saying that it is yet, who would stand to benefit by that?"

Jones' eyes danced around the room as he thought about it, though he was unable to come up with an answer. "I don't know."

"Think about it. There's one major criminal organization in town and we both know who runs it."

"Vincent."

"He told me himself he doesn't worry about small players," Recker said. "That he doesn't worry about anyone until they start trying to grow bigger."

"And you think he may have viewed this upstart crew as a threat?"

"He said he didn't know anything about this crew. We know they've been in operation for at least six months, and probably up to a year. You think Vincent would be in the dark about a bunch of rogue cops going into business for themselves? In territory that he supposedly owns?"

"It does seem somewhat peculiar that he would not know," Jones answered.

"And, considering he's got cops on his payroll, don't you think one or two of them may have gotten wind about something like that and let him know what was going on? Even if they didn't know exact specifics. Even if they only had suspicions of something or heard whispers that someone was looking to take a percentage of his operation. Don't you think they would've told him about it?"

"It does seem likely. But then again, he came to you to help investigate this matter. Why would he do that if he was involved? Surely, he knew you would eventually get to the bottom of it and figure out the details. He knows you well enough by now to know you would. But even if he only knew you by reputation, it would seem like a gamble that doesn't need to be taken. He's smarter than that."

"Unless he figured that I'd somehow get swept up in it anyway and tried to manipulate how things went from the beginning of it."

"I'm not sure I can picture Vincent killing cops, regardless of whether they were involved in illegal activities or branching out and taking a piece of his profits."

"Well, I don't think it's something he'd prefer to do if there were other options available," Recker said. "But maybe he didn't think there were other options."

42

Three days after the investigation into Detective Sivelski and Sergeant Orwell began, another police officer was killed. Unlike the others, it didn't take long for Recker and Jones to link this one together. This time, they connected the officer to Orwell and Wheaton immediately, and also found a five-thousand-dollar bank deposit in the officer's name. Recker was beginning to get impatient as he sought to conclude the case. When he started this endeavor with Jones, he swore he'd never get between criminals who were looking to knock each other off. And now, it seemed as if that's what he was doing.

Though the victims were cops, they were obviously into some bad stuff, and whoever was knocking them off, Recker wasn't sure if he should be getting involved in it. That's why he came up with the idea to get right to the heart of the matter. Jones thought it was very risky and something they didn't need to chance right then. But as usual, Recker won out.

Recker and Haley were waiting inside the home of Detective Sivelski. It was a little after eleven, and his wife and kids were upstairs sleeping. They'd only been waiting for about twenty minutes. They had Tyrell watching the district Sivelski was working out of and let them know when he left to go home. Detective Andrews had told Recker what shifts Sivelski was working so they could coordinate the best time to talk with him.

Recker was waiting in the living room, off to the side of the house. Haley was stationed near the back door. When the headlights from the driveway flashed through the windows, they knew the detective was home. With the living room pitch black, Sivelski wouldn't see Recker until it was too late. Within a few minutes, the door started wiggling with the sound of clanging keys just outside it. Recker was sitting on a chair in the corner of the room, waiting for a light to turn on. Once the door closed, Sivelski walked over to a lamp and turned it on. He immediately jumped back when he saw the strange man sitting in his living room. He reached for his gun inside his jacket.

"I wouldn't do that," Recker said.

Sivelski, noticing how calm the man was, and that he didn't have a gun in his hands, stopped his movements. "What do you want?"

"Just to chat."

"Who are you?" Sivelski asked. He then looked at the stairs, thinking of his wife and children.

"They're fine. Sleeping. I'm not here to hurt anybody."

"Then what do you want?"

"Answers."

"To what?"

"Sit down," Recker said. "And before you get any sparkling ideas of doing anything other than exactly what I say, know there's another man in the next room over."

"You're bluffing."

Recker smiled. "I don't bluff. Ever."

By the serious look on the man's face, Sivelski took him at his word and sat. "So, what's this about?"

"I know the things you've been doing outside your police duties."

Sivelski put a strange look on his face and shrugged, pretending to have no idea what was being referred to. Recker knew that pulling the truth out of the detective's mouth wasn't going to be easy, so he looked to speed the process up. He reached into his pocket and pulled out a bunch of folded up pieces of paper. He then just tossed the papers onto the floor, one by one.

"Bank statements for you and your buddies," Recker said. "Including the five-thousand-dollar deposits. The fake security company you set up to try to disguise it. Statements from people who say you're trying to move into Vincent's territory. How long do you wanna try to keep up this charade?"

"What's it to you?"

"People have asked me to look into it."

Sivelski scrunched his eyebrows together as he looked at the man more closely. After scrutinizing him further, he recognized the face, and a wry smile developed across his lips. "Ah, I know you who are now. You're the city savior, the crusader that's helping little old ladies cross the street and saving cats stuck up in trees."

Recker took no offense to his obvious insult. Instead of getting angry, he replied with his usual sense of humor. "I don't know where you get your information, but I haven't saved any cats in trees."

"My mistake."

"I take it you're not one of my biggest fans."

"I can take you or leave you, man. Are you expecting me to confess to something? Kill me? What's your play here?"

Recker shook his head. "There's no play. And if I wanted you dead, you would be already. I just want to have an honest conversation with you and then I'll be on my way."

"Then I'm on my way to jail, is that it?" Sivelski asked.

"Listen, I'm not really interested in seeing you go anywhere."

"Then what are you doing here?"

"I'll be honest with you if you agree to do the same."

Sivelski shrugged, waiting to see what he had to say first. "We'll see."

"A member of your department reached out to a mutual contact of ours to see if I'd look in on the case."

"Why would they do that?"

"Apparently, they had no leads," Recker said. "I guess when cops start going down and there are no suspects, you tend to get desperate and look for help in unorthodox places."

"And you think that leads to me?"

"Unless you're telling me you're not responsible for it."

"I don't really need to tell you anything."

Recker was starting to get aggravated at the lack of cooperation. "Listen, I don't really wanna play this game with you all night. I've got other things to do and I wanna move on from this case. If you are involved in killing other cops, then it doesn't really concern me. If it's someone else, then I'd like to find out who it is."

Sivelski moved his head around as he thought of what to do. "You really think I would have killed other cops?"

"I have no idea."

"And if I admit to anything here? What then?"

Recker could sense the man's wall was starting to break down. "Whatever's said here stays between you and me."

Sivelski rubbed his mouth and nose before replying. "All right. Honestly, I had nothing to do with those guys being killed. I have no reason to do that."

"So you guys were starting your own little operation on the side?"

Sivelski hesitated before answering. "Yes. There's a lot of money to be made out there. We sure ain't gonna get rich being on the job. Why not? There's not a lot of competition out there."

"Except for Vincent."

"We figured we could handle him. Besides, he'd have to be crazy to think he could take us on."

"Have you butted heads with him yet?" Recker asked.

"Yeah, we've had some words."

"He definitely knows about you guys?"

"Oh, yeah. I talked to him myself."

"I talked to him a few days ago. He said he didn't know anything about you guys."

Sivelski made a displeased face. "He's lying out his ass."

"Do you have any idea who's been killing these guys?"

Sivelski shook his head and shrugged. "If I did, don't you think I'd have taken care of it already?"

"Not necessarily. It'd be hard for you to do that and explain how you know that. I would think you'd have to explain how your relationship with those other officers works."

"Really not as difficult as you make it sound."

"You think it's Vincent taking you guys out?" Recker asked.

"I don't know. Maybe. I don't know if he's dumb enough to do that though. He'd know how much heat that'd bring down on him."

"Who's in charge of this operation? You? Or Butch?"

Sivelski looked surprised that he knew the sergeant's name.

"Yeah, I know."

"It's my deal. They all take orders from me."

"So how many more you got on this gig?" Recker asked. He could see that Sivelski was hesitant in answering the question by how he was shifting in his seat and stalling. "Might as well tell me. I'm gonna find out on my own anyway."

"Three more."

"Any of you worried about being the next one with a hollow-point bullet buried inside you?"

"We're working on it."

"Hope you make it fast or else this case will be over for me before we know it."

"I'm touched by your caring philosophy about our well-being," Sivelski said.

"Well, before any more of you wind up in the cemetery, maybe you should try to put out the word to save yourselves."

"The word? What word?"

"That you're leaving the business. You obviously stepped on the wrong toes of somebody," Recker answered. "And they're letting you know it. One dead body at a time. If you don't let them know quickly, that wife of yours upstairs is gonna be planning your funeral."

"I'll keep that in mind."

Recker was satisfied with the question-and-answer session and believed he was getting the truth out of the detective. He didn't have anything else that needed to be said. He got up and walked across the room to the front door. Just as he opened it, he turned back to look at the detective, who was still sitting in the same spot. "Maybe you should stick with what you're supposed to do best. Protecting the people out there."

Recker didn't wait for a response before leaving and just walked out the door. But there wasn't one coming, anyway. Sivelski had nothing else to say. All he could do from that point was think about their discussion and figure out what he wanted to do from there. After leaving the house, Recker let Haley know he was gone so he could slip out the back. They both walked around the block to get back to their car, getting there at the same time.

"Get what you wanted?" Haley asked.

"Yeah, I think so."

They went straight back to the office so Haley could pick up his car as both went home for the night after that. Along with Jones, they'd already agreed that whatever was learned, they'd reconvene in the morning to go over it, as well as discuss their next options moving forward.

Feeling like they were at the cusp of figuring the entire plot out, Recker got to the office earlier than normal the next morning to get a jump on things. As usual, Jones had already beaten him to the punch.

"How long you been going at it?" Recker asked.

"Oh, about since six."

"Heard from Chris yet?"

"Yes, he just texted me a few minutes ago," Jones said. "He's picking up breakfast on the way in. Should be here in a half hour or so."

"Good. We have a lot to discuss."

Recker then told Jones about his conversation with Sivelski, letting him know everything that was said, as well as his own suspicions. After he was finished, Jones had a hard time believing it.

"You really believe Vincent is behind this?"

Recker nodded. "I do. No one else could pull this off. No one else would have the stones to do this."

"But why?"

"I think he got wind of a growing threat and put an end to it quickly."

"But why play the game like he has no idea what's going on?" Jones asked.

"I've been thinking about that. Put yourself in his shoes. If it gets out that he's the one behind the killings, how much heat will that bring him?"

"A considerable amount."

"More than he wants. He's not stupid. He's got cops on his payroll. If they find out that he's taking out cops, even ones that are dirty, who's to say whether they'll turn on him? Even the dirty ones tend to stick together. But just the same, he wants to take out anyone who's competing against him. Just makes it trickier when they're wearing badges."

"Makes it trickier to determine what we should do too," Jones said.

"From what I can tell, we have a couple options."

"Which are?"

"We forget about this entire thing and let whatever happens happen. Or we barrel into it head on and go wherever it takes us."

"Meaning we take on Vincent."

"And probably throw away all the goodwill we've built up with him along the way in the process," Recker said.

"Or? Maybe we tell him what we know and see if he comes clean."

Recker didn't think that was a wise idea though. "No. That would just put us on a collision course again. But there is another solution."

"And that is?"

"That Sivelski and his bunch admit that they're in over their heads and admit defeat."

"And just how likely do you think that is?" Jones asked.

"I guess that depends."

"On what?"

"On how much they want to live."

Recker asked for an emergency meeting with Vincent based on his conversation with Detective Sivelski. He didn't let the crime boss know what the meeting was about in advance. Luckily, based on their past relationship, Vincent always made time for him. Since it was mid-afternoon, Vincent told him to meet him at his trucking business where they'd conducted so many meetings before. Once Recker arrived, Malloy led him to the same office as usual. Like usual, Vincent was sitting behind his desk as Recker walked in. He took a seat, not wanting to waste any time on the subject.

"So, what's this about?" Vincent asked. "Seemed pretty urgent based on your call."

"I would just like to know from you where things stand."

"From me? In regard to?"

"This whole cop thing," Recker answered.

"I thought we'd been over that."

"And I talked to a certain detective who's involved in a group of cops who started going into business for themselves who told me that you've talked to them about their business."

Vincent stared at Recker for a few moments, taken slightly off guard. But he remained cool and calm like he usually did. "If you're referring to a Detective Sivelski, then yes, I know all about him and his little operation."

"You told me before you didn't."

"You showed me pictures and names of men who'd been killed. You asked me if I knew them. I did not."

"So, you didn't know they were part of Sivelski's crew?"

"I did not."

"You know how it looks, right?" Recker asked. "You told me yourself that you don't pay attention to people until they start getting bigger. Then suddenly, this crew, who looks like they could be a threat due to their positions, and they start dropping like flies."

Vincent grinned, knowing how it appeared, but not ready to admit any involvement. "I can see how it might look to some. I can't really help outside appearances though, can I?"

"So, you're saying that you're not responsible for taking these people out?"

Vincent leaned forward and put his hands on the desk. "Even if I said I did have a hand in it, and to be clear, I'm not saying I did, where would that put us?"

Recker shrugged. "Same place as before. I don't think it would change our deal at all. I'm just looking for answers."

Vincent smiled again. "Well that's good to know. But in saying that, my answer still hasn't changed. Whatever is happening to these officers is not my doing."

Recker nodded, feeling like they didn't have much else to discuss. He still couldn't be sure whether Vincent was actually being truthful with him, but even if he wasn't, it was obvious that he wasn't going to admit to anything. Before he left, though, Vincent had some parting words for him.

"I'll tell you, Mike, since this is starting to look like I have a hand in it, that's very concerning to me. Makes me look guilty."

"So?"

"So, I'm going to start putting my people on it."

"To do what?"

"To find who *is* responsible for this. Jimmy," Vincent said, pointing toward the door. "Start making the arrangements."

"You got it, boss," Malloy replied.

Recker looked at him, not sure of his motives. But whatever they were, hopefully it would help resolve the situation sooner.

"I guarantee you that we'll find this person by the end of the week," Vincent said.

Recker went back to the office to talk to Jones and Haley about the meeting. Though he was initially convinced Vincent was the mastermind behind what was going on, now, he just wasn't sure. Jones and Haley were equally as perplexed. They had their theories, several different versions of them, and they all made sense, but they couldn't prove any of them. Not yet. And they weren't sure they could. Unless more bodies dropped.

43

Recker was having another conversation with Vincent. This time it was on the phone, even though it wasn't Vincent's preferred method of contact. Recker was pacing around the office as he talked, with Jones and Haley working on computers, though both were keeping an ear out to try to get some inclination of what they were discussing. Even if they couldn't hear any specifics, they had a good idea of what was being talked about.

It'd been five days since Recker's emergency meeting with Vincent. In that time, Recker tasked Tyrell with keeping an ear out on the street to see if he got wind of Sivelski throwing in the white towel. Tyrell reported back after a couple of days that he heard no such development. And they'd soon learn the consequences of that. Two days ago, news broke out Sergeant Barry Orwell had been killed on duty after responding to what was supposed to be a domestic disturbance. But when he arrived at the house in question, there was no disturbance. In walking back to his car, a shot rang out across the street, killing him instantly.

Last night, they were greeted with the news Detective Sivelski had been murdered, only a few steps from his front door. Recker and company were reasonably confident that was the last of the police shootings. Though there were three other members of the police crew still at large, they weren't the brains of the outfit. With the two leaders, Sivelski and Orwell, being killed, it was believed the others would cease operations. But it still left questions unanswered, such as, who was behind it. Most people didn't know the reasonings behind the killings, and for them, it was still an uncomfortable time. For all they knew, some nut job was targeting police officers. Most people would still need closure. That's basically all Recker was still looking for to provide.

Once Recker got off the phone, he kept walking around the office for a minute. Eventually, he came back over to the desk and tossed his phone on it. He stood there, not saying a word, leaning on the desk. Both Jones and Haley looked up at him, and both read him the same way. He didn't look particularly pleased.

"Would you care to tell us what that look on your face is for?" Jones asked.

"He says they're close."

"Close to what?"

"Finding the person responsible," Recker answered.

"Well that's good news."

"Yeah, so why don't you look happy about it?" Haley asked.

"I dunno. I guess because I just find it hard to believe."

"Why?" Jones said. "You know Vincent has plenty of contacts on the street, more than we do. What's hard to believe about it?"

"Just doesn't feel right. This whole thing hasn't felt right for a while."

"Well, regardless of that, it seems as though it might be coming to a head. And that's what we want, isn't it?"

"I guess so."

"I'll be glad when it is," Jones said. "I'm ready to put all of this behind us. You know I wasn't exactly thrilled about taking this case on to start with. I'll be happy to not have to put any more time and resources into it."

"Do we even need to keep looking into it?" Haley asked. "I mean, if Vincent's close, then it seems like he's further ahead of things than we are right now. Maybe we shouldn't even bother checking anymore."

Recker wasn't too keen on that idea. "Well, let's keep on it a few more days, just in case Vincent isn't as close as he thinks he is."

Jones was only too happy to oblige Haley's suggestion and started shifting some of his time to other things, though he still kept an eye on things. But from his vantage point, there wasn't much else he could do. It seemed as though all the computer work that was necessary had already been done. While Jones started looking into other upcoming cases, Recker and Haley stayed on their current assignments. They were still working on those assignments when Tyrell called about six hours later.

"What's up, Tyrell?"

"Hey, got something big for you."

"What is it?"

"Might have a name for you," Tyrell said.

"Name of who?"

"Of the guy who's been shooting cops."

"What?" Recker said, almost in complete disbelief.

"I think I got the guy."

"What's his name?"

"Jeffrey Flowers."

Recker snapped his fingers to get his partner's attention. Once he did, he repeated the name to them, so they could start digging up his background information.

"How'd you get this?" Recker asked.

"Well you said to keep digging, keep pressing. That's what I've been doing."

As was his nature, Recker was still skeptical. "And someone just finally came to you and volunteered the information?"

"I dunno, man. I've just been continuing to work it."

"The guy who told you, you know him?"

"Yeah, I've dealt with him a time or two over the years."

"You trust him?"

"Yeah, you know, as much as you trust anybody out here," Tyrell answered.

"What's your take on it?"

"I think it's good."

"All right, we'll start checking it out," Recker said.

"It is kind of strange now that I think about it."

"What's that?"

"Well, this dude does a lot of work for Vincent. Even more than I have. Kind of weird that he'd come to me with the info instead of just giving it to him."

"Vincent told me he was getting close. Maybe this is what he meant."

"No, I don't think so."

"Why not?" Recker asked.

"Because he told me he didn't mention it to him."

"How much did you have to give him for it?"

"Only five hundred," Tyrell said.

"Five hundred? That's it?"

"That's it."

"A tip like that is worth a ton more than that. Why would he just give it to you for such a low amount?"

"Beats me. People out here do some strange things from time to time. Can't always figure out someone's motivations."

"I'll go along with that."

As soon as Recker was done on the phone, he checked out the computer to see what Jones had on Flowers. As they ran down his list of prior criminal offenses, the red flags in Recker's mind were going off. It didn't seem to match up with the type of person he was expecting to be behind the killings.

"There's nothing on there that indicates he's the guy we're looking for," Recker said. "I mean, there's not a violent crime on there."

"That does not mean he hasn't upped his game," Jones said.

"David."

"I know it does not seem likely. But nevertheless, it needs to be checked out, does it not?"

"Yeah."

"Well then, let's see if I can pin down an address for him and investigate. Then we can come up with our own conclusion."

"Kind of funny, guy with the last name of Flowers doing stuff like this," Haley said, appreciating the irony.

"Yeah. A lot of funny things seem to be going on here," Recker replied.

"Besides his history, what else is bothering you about him?" Jones asked. "Or is that it?"

"A guy who's known to associate with Vincent, one of his contacts on the street, and he doesn't go straight to him with it? Instead, he comes to us? And for only five hundred dollars? That just screams all kinds of nonsense to me."

"As I said, let's just check it out and see what comes of it."

Recker agreed, and even if he thought it was a false lead, it was still a lead that needed to be run down. Jones spent roughly thirty minutes on the computer before he came up with something. He printed it out and handed it to Recker.

"Lives in an apartment off the boulevard," Jones said.

Recker looked at the time and figured it was best to wait another hour or two for darkness to really set in before heading over there. He went over to his cabinet and pulled out a couple weapons for his next rendezvous, then looked at Haley.

"Feel like having some fun tonight?"

"I think I could be persuaded to join the party," Haley replied.

"Please, just exercise some caution when you get there," Jones said. "I realize he doesn't have a violent past on paper, but that doesn't mean he hasn't graduated, or that he isn't dangerous."

"Don't worry. I won't be taking anyone for granted on this case," Recker said.

Once ten o'clock rolled around, Recker and Haley left the office on the way to Flowers' apartment. It was a modest apartment in a decent area, not some run-down place off the grid or an apartment people tried to hide out in. They staked it out for an hour or so, trying to work out if he was there or not. Flowers had an apartment with a balcony on the third floor, so Haley waited by the outside, looking up at it, waiting for signs of movement. It was dark the entire time they were there, leading them to believe the man they were looking for may not have been home.

Recker didn't want to wait any longer and went up to the third floor and stood outside Flowers' apartment. He stationed himself there for a few minutes, keeping his ear pressed to the door as he struggled to hear any type of noise coming from inside. After five more minutes of inactivity, believing the apartment was empty, Recker let Haley know he was going in. Haley moved from the back of the apartment to join his friend inside.

Recker picked the lock and opened the door. He had his gun out, ready for a battle if one presented itself. It was dark and not a single sound was heard. Hesitant to go any further for fear something was waiting for him, he put his hand on the wall to feel for a light switch. After a few seconds of searching, he found it and flicked it on. As soon as the lights went on, Recker's eyes were immediately drawn to the middle of the floor in the living room area. There was a man's body, lying face down. Blood was starting to seep out from the outline of his body and staining the carpet.

"We got one down," Recker said.

"There in thirty," Haley replied.

Recker started checking the other rooms. There were two bedrooms, a bathroom, and a kitchen. He cleared the kitchen first before starting on the others. He stepped over the dead body as he walked to the other rooms. As he was in the first bedroom, Haley announced his presence to make sure Recker knew it was him if he heard noises.

"I'm in," Haley said, closing the door behind him so nobody could sneak up on him.

"Check the bedroom on the left. I got the other one and the bathroom."

"Got it."

After the two searched the other rooms, the place was empty. They met back up in the living room to go over the situation. Recker knelt beside the body to get a better look at his face.

"That Flowers?" Haley asked.

"Yep. Spitting image. Looks just like his picture."

"What do you think happened?"

"I dunno," Recker said, pushing the body off the floor just enough to see the blood coming out of two holes in his chest. "I'd say from the amount of blood he's lost that he got shot."

Haley looked around the room, noticing two shell casings on the floor and pointed them out. "There's the evidence."

Recker stood and looked around the room. He then started searching through it as Haley looked through the bedrooms. They were looking for anything that would tie him to the case. It didn't take long for them to find it.

"In here," Haley shouted.

Recker quickly came in, seeing Haley rummage around through a dresser drawer.

"Whatcha got?" Recker asked.

Haley was careful not to touch anything with his hands so as not to leave fingerprints and used a shirt to pick up the evidence.

"Gun," he said, picking it up and holding it high for his

partner to see. He then set it back down in the drawer and picked up a box. "Ammunition."

"Hollow-point bullets," Recker said.

By the look on Recker's face, Haley could see he still didn't look pleased.

"Hoping this stuff wouldn't be there?" Haley asked.

"I dunno. Maybe. Just seems like everything's been tied up neatly."

"Well, I think our work here is done. Should probably get out of here soon before the police come. Someone might have called them already."

"Yeah. Let's go," Recker said.

They left the apartment and called Jones to let him know Flowers was dead, and not of their doing. It was a good thing they decided to leave when they did, or they would have had to deal with a police presence, as they showed up only five minutes later. They agreed to go home for the night and meet up again in the morning to go over their next steps. Recker was the last one to arrive in the office the following morning.

"Everyone see this?" Recker asked, tossing the newspaper down on the desk, which indicated the cop killer had been killed himself.

"Yes," Jones said.

"Seems as though it's wrapped up."

"So why do you still sound unhappy?"

Recker shook his head and sighed. "Because it all just seems so neat and tidy. I mean, c'mon, you guys don't really think Flowers did this, do you?"

"Even if he was set up to be the patsy, there's not much else we can do at this point," Haley replied. "He's been made to look guilty, the rest of the crew is going to scatter, there's not going to be any more bodies, it all ends here."

"And we are not going to pursue it any further," Jones said.

"We're not?" Recker asked.

"No. We're not. I know what's going on in that head of yours."

"Oh yeah?"

"Yes. You're thinking Vincent is behind it and you're thinking about confronting him about it."

"And I shouldn't do that?"

"No. Why put the relationship you've built up with him in jeopardy over something we don't know whether we should even be involved in to begin with? Let's move on."

"What do you think actually happened?" Haley asked.

"I think Vincent found someone he could pin this whole mess on. Then he made sure it somehow got back to me about Flowers, which is why Tyrell got the info so cheap. Then I'm thinking he sent his right-hand man over there to finish the job, plant some evidence, tie it off."

"Malloy."

"Yeah. Now, everyone sleeps easier, his competition's eliminated, nobody suspects him, like I said... all neat and tidy."

"Like David said, there's nothing else we can really do at this point."

"I know. Doesn't mean I have to like it, though."

Recker's phone then rang.

"What can I help you with, Detective?"

"Just wanted to say thanks for helping out with this," Andrews answered. "Don't know if we would've gotten to this point without you."

"Just glad I could help."

"Well, a lot of the boys down here wish they could thank you."

"Not sure I really deserve any thanks," Recker said.

"I know I said I hoped to have him alive and take him in, but there's quite a few of us who wanted to do what you did, anyway."

"What makes you think it was me?"

"Who else would it have been?" Andrews asked. "I know you

like to play it coy and all and can't admit to anything. But just to let you know, I think you've got a few extra converts to your fan club down here."

"Always nice to know."

"Anyway, just wanted to say thanks. I don't suppose we'll continue to get a chance to work on any things together?"

"Not likely," Recker said. "You can probably toss that phone now. It'll go off the grid in a few days."

"Well, good luck to you. If you ever wind up at my desk, I'll conveniently forget to lock your cuffs or something."

Recker laughed. "I appreciate that."

After hanging up, Recker, though disappointed with the conclusion of the case, seemed to be ready to move on.

"I guess it's on to bigger and better things?"

"Yes," Jones answered. "I have several things going on now. Should have another case to work on by tomorrow."

"Great."

"The detective say anything interesting?"

"Ah, usual. Everyone thinks it was me that did it. Seems it's bought me a few extra friends on the force should I ever need them."

"Well, I guess that is a perk should it ever be needed."

"Yeah. Seems as though everyone thinks I'm a hero. Even when I'm not."

HIGH VELOCITY

44

Recker and Haley had just made it to the large, glitzy hotel. The man they were looking for, Darren Harmon, wasn't that far ahead of them. They tried to head him off at the club he visited first, but they were just a hair too late. Harmon first popped up on their radar after texting a buddy that he was going out that night to some bars and clubs to find some women he could have his way with. He mentioned in the text he had something extra to help him in that regard, leading Jones to believe he was going to drug someone.

Jones found out Harmon booked a room at the hotel, though he didn't have enough time to find out the room number. It took him a little time to find out which bars Harmon liked to frequent. Since the information came in so late, the team didn't even have time to stake out Harmon's home address. When they got the alert from Jones' program, they immediately started hitting bars and clubs in the area to try to find the suspect. Once Jones finally found the bar Harmon was likely to be at and when Recker and Haley arrived, they learned from the bartender Harmon had just left with a woman on his arm.

Upon arriving at the hotel, Recker and Haley showed Harmon's picture to a few people and asked if they'd seen the man, hoping they'd get lucky. Unfortunately, no one did. After asking around, Recker and Haley looked around the lobby, trying to figure out their next move.

Recker touched the com device in his ear to get in contact with Jones. "David, we're striking out here. You getting anything?"

Jones was feverishly typing away, trying desperately to come up with a room number. "I'm working on it."

"We don't have much time. It's not gonna take this guy too long to do what he came here for."

"I know. I'm just about there."

Haley then tapped Recker on the arm. "We might as well start walking the halls. It'll give us a head start. Maybe one of us will be nearby when he finally gets it. Or maybe one of us will hear something walking by."

Recker nodded. "If this girl's been drugged, we're not likely to hear anything. But it's a good idea, anyway. I'll do the even floors, you do the odd. Let me know if you find anything."

Recker let Jones know what they were doing as the two silencers broke up and started roaming the halls. The two men quickly walked down their respective floors, looking and listening for any potential signs of the man they were looking for. Even though they knew it was unlikely they were going to find anything, that was all they could do. They had to hope the woman would be able to scream, leading them to the room, or, if she had enough energy, run out of the room if the drugs hadn't taken full effect yet. But they still knew their best chance at finding them was Jones. It was a twenty-floor hotel with almost a thousand rooms. Without some type of fluke occurrence, Recker and Haley knew they were basically looking for a needle in a haystack.

As Recker walked through the first floor, Haley was done on

the second at basically the same time. They each walked up their respective stairs to start searching the next floors.

"Chris, anything?"

"Negative."

They continued the pattern for a few more floors until Recker and Haley were on the fifth and sixth floors. By that point their hope was about to evaporate, even though they had a good chunk of the hotel still left. They knew there was nothing else they could do on their end. As they reached the end of their floors, Jones lifted their moods.

"Got it. Twelfth floor. Room 1226."

"On the way," Recker said.

Recker and Haley immediately raced up the stairs to get to the twelfth floor, though Haley was closer and would get there first. Upon getting to the twelfth floor, Haley threw open the door and ran down the hallway until he reached the room in question. He took a quick listen at the door but didn't hear anything. He had to take it on faith that Jones was right. If not, it would be quite embarrassing to walk in on someone who did not have ulterior motives at hand. He also didn't have time to wait for Recker, even though he wasn't too far behind.

Haley slowly jiggled the handle to see if they had the good fortune of it being unlocked, but they weren't that lucky. Haley took a few steps back and was about to kick it in before he remembered it wouldn't work. Jones had already told them the hotel doors were much stronger than residential doors due to having to meet a high fire rating, and being lined with steel, it was likely security would be there long before Haley was able to kick it in. He took a few steps toward the door again and knocked loudly.

"Room service!"

Haley shook his head, figuring this had no chance of working. He figured he must have seen at least a hundred movies where something like this happened and he always thought it was ridiculous. It would never work. He knocked loudly again and looked down the hall to see if Recker was in sight yet. He wasn't. Haley put his fist on the door and was ready to pounce on it again. Before he could, though, the door swung open. The man on the inside seemed quite displeased he had to answer the door for something he didn't ask for.

"I didn't ask for any room service," the man angrily said.

Haley immediately recognized Harmon from his picture and pushed the door open further.

"What are you doing?!" Harmon asked, backing up.

Haley didn't bother to respond. Instead, he let his fists do the talking for him. He reached back, curled up his fist, and unleashed a right hand that struck Harmon's jaw, sending the stunned man down to his knees. With the man not being a threat for the moment, Haley took a quick look around the room and saw a woman on the bed who was only wearing a bra and underwear. She wasn't moving and at first glance appeared to be sleeping, though Haley suspected she was knocked out with the help of a drug.

Haley turned back around to face Harmon, who had gotten back to his feet, and now also had a weapon in his hand. Harmon had removed a pocket knife and was holding it in his right hand as he faced his intruder.

"I don't know who you are, but you made the wrong move coming in here," Harmon said, trying to sound tough.

Considering Haley was an inch or two taller and about twenty pounds heavier, he didn't feel much of a threat from the man. Seeing as how all he had was a small pocket knife, and Haley had a gun he hadn't pulled out yet, it was all the more unconcerning to him. Even without weapons, with all the hand-to-hand combat training he'd received over the years, there weren't many men Haley would feel uncomfortable facing.

"Is this the part where I'm supposed to wet myself?" Haley asked. "Tremble in fear for what you might do to me?"

"You have no idea who you're messing with."

Haley smiled, seeing Recker standing in the doorway behind Harmon. "Well, considering there's two of us, I'd say you better stand down."

Harmon shook his head. "That's the oldest trick in the book. I'm not falling for that one."

Recker didn't say a word. He brought his gun out and took a good, hard blow to the back of Harmon's head with his weapon, knocking the suspect to the floor. Harmon was out cold. With the situation in hand, Recker took a step inside and closed the door behind him. He then stood over Harmon's body for a few seconds.

"Sometimes the oldest tricks are the best," Recker said.

"Girl's over here," Haley said, pointing to the bedroom.

"She all right?"

"Don't know. Didn't get a chance to check yet. Looks like she's knocked out. Either that or she's a heavy sleeper."

Recker knelt beside Harmon and checked his pulse. "He'll be all right in a few hours."

"Besides the lemon on his head."

"He's lucky that's all he got."

After kicking the knife to the other side of the room, Recker and Haley went into the bedroom to check on the woman on the bed. As they did, Recker let Jones know Harmon was subdued.

"David, we're in the room. Looks like we got here a little too late."

"Oh no," Jones said. "Is she dead?"

Haley stood next to the woman and checked her pulse. "She's alive. Gonna wake up with a headache though."

"Let's be thankful that's all she'll have."

"How you wanna do this?" Recker asked. "The woman's knocked out. Harmon's knocked out."

As they were talking, Haley started moving throughout the room, looking for some evidence. He was hoping Harmon didn't use his entire stash and that he still had more drugs out in the open somewhere.

"I'll call the police and tell them there's a disturbance in that room," Jones said.

"What good will that do?"

"They'll see an unconscious woman on the bed and do testing on her and hopefully discover some illegal substances in her system. I'll make sure I tell them I think the woman was taken against her will or something. Don't worry, she will be in the clear."

"This might help," Haley said, standing by the dresser and holding up a clear bag. It had a dozen small, round, white pills inside. Haley put his nose by the opening and took a whiff, but the pills had no odor.

"Hold on, looks like Chris might have found his stash," Recker said.

"Excellent," Jones replied. "I'll put the call in to the police now."

"What if she wakes up disoriented before they get here?"

"Can you tell how many pills she's taken?"

Recker looked over at Haley, who shook his head. "No, there's no telling how many were in here to begin with or how much is in her system," Haley said.

"Considering they didn't have that big of a head start on us and the fact she's already knocked out so quickly, I would say it's safe to assume she's got quite a bit in her."

"Then I'd say it's not likely she'll wake up before they arrive," Jones said. "The police should get there within five minutes."

"What about Harmon?" Haley asked.

"How incapacitated is he at the moment?"

"Very," Recker answered.

"Then leave him and get out of there."

"Roger that."

Recker and Haley looked at each other. "Time to hit the road?" Haley asked.

"I'd feel better if we tied this idiot up first."

Recker looked around but didn't have anything to bind Harmon's hands together. Recker did the next best thing and dragged his lifeless body over to the closet. Haley opened the door for him and Recker stuffed Harmon into the closet. Once they closed the door, they brought a chair over and nuzzled it just underneath the knob. It was unlikely Harmon would wake before the police arrived, but Recker wanted to be certain the criminal wouldn't make a surprise escape. With Harmon safely tucked away, Recker and Haley quickly left, scurrying out of the hotel before the police arrived. Just as Recker and Haley had gotten to their car, they noticed the police cruiser pulling into the parking lot.

"Looks like things are good here," Recker said.

After letting Jones know the police were there, Recker dropped Haley off at his apartment before going home for the night himself. They both came back into the office early the next morning since Jones said it looked like they were beginning to get a heavy workload with some new cases coming in. Recker was the last to get there, as usually seemed to be the case lately. It wasn't that he was late, as it was only eight o'clock, but the others didn't have a pretty girlfriend that prevented them from getting in earlier. But he usually made up for it by stopping for breakfast for the three of them.

As Recker made it into the office, though, he could tell right away something was going on. Haley was being still and silent, a telltale sign Jones was working on something and nobody wanted to disturb or distract him. Jones was sitting at his computer, flailing away at the keyboard at an unusually fast rate. Unusual in how he worked in an everyday manner. It was quite normal for him to act that way when there was something important and urgent going on.

"Should I ask?" Recker said.

Haley looked at him, his hand covering half his face. "You shouldn't."

"Well, he did say we had a heavy workload coming up this week."

"No, this is not that," Jones said.

"Oh. He is here," Recker said with a fake smile.

Recker put the bag of breakfast sandwiches down on the table as he maneuvered his way behind Jones to see if he could tell what he was working on.

"You know I don't like you sneaking up behind me when I'm trying to ascertain something," Jones said.

"Well, I'm sorry, professor, but you know you would make things easier on us all if you just came out and told us what the issue was."

Jones stopped typing for a second and turned his head to look at Recker as he made his way to a chair next to him. "There's been a killing."

Recker didn't sound impressed. "There's always a killing."

"Two of them to be precise."

Recker looked at Haley, still not seeming concerned about the matter. "OK. Would you now like to tell us what makes these two killings so important?"

"They're people we know."

The look on Recker's face turned more serious. Now he was concerned. He knew it wasn't Mia since he'd just left her at the apartment and she wasn't going in to work today. He quickly ran through the list of all the other people he knew, though there was one name that quickly jumped into his mind. "Tyrell?"

Jones stopped typing again to look at him, though this time he had a quizzical look on his face. "No. Why would you think such a thing?"

"Uh, because he's the closest person I know, and you haven't told me anything else. How about you ending our misery and telling us who's dead?"

"Oh," Jones said, almost seeming unaware he was keeping them in suspense. "Well it's two members of Vincent's crew."

A look of relief swept across Recker's face. "Is that all? You shouldn't do that, you know."

"Is that all? That's all the emotions you can muster?"

"Uh," Recker said, looking over to Haley for guidance, though none was coming. He then shrugged. "Sorry?"

"Do you not see the significance of this?"

Recker looked up to the ceiling, hoping the answer would somehow fall to him. "Uh, nope, I guess not. What's the significance?"

"The significance is the undisputed mob boss of this city, a man you know, a man we've worked with and have a business relationship with, has lost two members of his team."

"And?" Recker said, seeming very unconcerned. "To be honest, I'm still kind of ticked off at him for that whole police thing he got us involved with, so excuse me if I'm not exactly shedding a tear for him in this trying time."

"Regardless of that, you don't just go around killing members of his squad without expecting some kind of blowback," Jones said.

"And you think what? It's gonna come back on us? He's gonna think I did it?"

"Perhaps."

"Won't happen."

"Or that we'll know something about it."

"Doubt it."

"Or that he might expand on our business arrangement and try to get us involved in his business," Jones said, fearful of getting into a larger conflict they had no business of being involved in.

"That could be possible."

"Even if none of that's the case, that still brings up a bigger issue," Haley said.

"I think I can anticipate what you are about to say, but go ahead anyway," Jones said.

"Who's dumb enough to take out a couple of Vincent's men?"

"There's a couple more questions to add to that," Recker said.

"Which are?" Jones asked.

"Did someone take those guys out knowing they're Vincent's men? Or was it just dumb luck they didn't know what they were getting themselves into?"

"I wouldn't call taking out Vincent's men any kind of luck," Haley said. "Bad luck, maybe."

"I have one more to question to add to that," Jones said.

"Which is?" Recker asked.

"Do we have a new player in town?"

Recker and Haley looked at each other, wondering if that was the case. "Heck of a way to state your arrival," Haley said.

"Can you think of a better one?" Recker said. "If you're gonna come in here and challenge Vincent and try to take a piece of the city away from him, you better do it in full force. And you better announce yourself and your intentions early. Cause if you come in here and try to dance around, he'll chew you up and spit you out."

"So, how we gonna find out? Or are we?"

"I think we'll know the answer to that if any more of Vincent's men drop in the next week," Jones said. "Or if he retaliates, assuming he knows who did it."

"Or we could put some ears on the street," Recker said.

"What do you have in mind?"

"Who's the best guy we know at that?"

"Tyrell."

"If something's going on, he'll find it."

45

Recker was already in the diner, waiting for Vincent to arrive. It was the first time Recker could remember actually beating Vincent to a meeting. It'd been two days since Jones learned of Vincent's men being killed and Recker could only imagine the crime boss was a little unnerved the last few days. Recker took the liberty of ordering a coffee and a bagel while he waited. As he dug into his food, his phone rang. It was Tyrell.

"How's it going?" Recker asked.

"Can't complain."

"How you making out with that assignment?"

"Not too good, man. Listen, from the people I've talked to, nobody knows anything about them guys getting knocked off."

"Don't know, or just too afraid to say something?"

"Nah, they don't know nothing," Tyrell said. "But there's a lot of theories floating around."

"Which are?"

"Most people think there's a new player in town."

"Why?"

"Has to be. Nobody's gonna knock off Vincent's crew unless you want a war. And the only way you're doing this is if you're fighting for territory."

"Maybe it was an accident or some guys who didn't know who they were," Recker said.

"No, those guys were ambushed, man. Whoever took them out knew full well what they were doing."

"All right, well keep your ears to the ground and let me know if you hear anything else, huh?"

"You got it."

Recker went back to his food as he contemplated what he'd just heard. If it was true there was another player in town fighting with Vincent, Recker wasn't sure if that was actually good or bad. On the plus side, maybe it was someone that could keep Vincent in check in case he roamed a little farther with his ideas and priorities. On the negative side, it was one more person Recker would have to worry about. And it was possible that whoever it was might not be as easy to deal with as Vincent. Recker had just finished his food when he looked through the window and noticed Vincent's entourage coming. The men took their usual positions outside, while a couple others cleared the inside to make sure there were no hostile people waiting for the boss. Those men took another table further down as Vincent and Malloy walked in. Malloy stood near the door as he usually did while Vincent sat down at Recker's table.

"Even got our usual table," Vincent said with a smile. He seemed rather upbeat for a man who'd just lost a couple of men.

"I almost wasn't sure what to do with myself. First time you weren't already here waiting for me."

"Yes, I'm sorry about that. Had a few other important matters to attend to first."

"Funeral arrangements, maybe?" Recker asked.

Vincent glared at him for a moment, the pleasant look on his face evaporating due to the subject matter.

"I assumed that's what we came to talk about," Recker said.

"Since you've brought it up, what have you heard?"

Recker shook his head. "Nothing."

Vincent gave him a cross-eyed look, thinking that surely couldn't be true. "Come now, Mike, with all the information you and David are able to glean from a stroke of the keyboard, I'm sure something must have come across your desks."

"Well, I hate to disappoint you, but that's exactly what I'm telling you. Didn't find out about it until David saw it on the news. Put some feelers out on the street that came back empty. I'm afraid I got nothing to tell you."

Vincent seemed content with the answer, taking Recker at his word. "It's of no matter. I will find out who it is and crush them."

"Do you have any leads?" Recker asked.

Vincent stirred his coffee as he debated how much information to share. In the end, he figured there was no use hiding anything. "We had a few, unfortunately none of them panned out."

"You think it's a new gang looking to take over?"

"I do."

"Why?"

"How much do you know?" Vincent asked.

"Not a whole lot. Just that two of your men were killed by some factory or something."

"Well they weren't just killed by a glancing bullet or some type of skirmish in a deal gone sour. My men were ambushed. There were entrance wounds in their chests and their backs."

"So, they were set up."

"They were lured there. Then executed."

"What were they there for to begin with?"

"We'd gotten a call from someone looking to sell some

weapons," Vincent answered. "They went there to look over the merchandise."

"For your own purposes?"

Vincent smiled, unusually forthcoming in describing his business dealings. "No, I've got agreements with various factions up and down the east coast for redistributing weapons. I get a shipment then pass them along for a higher price."

"What about the guy that made the initial contact with you about this?"

"A small-time guy we've done business with before."

"Think it was him?"

"No, he's not someone who has higher aspirations," Vincent replied. "He's quite content in his current rank in the food chain."

"Then someone got to him."

"We've already questioned him. He doesn't know anything."

Recker knew there had to be more to it than that. "Well if he set up the meeting, and you think he wasn't involved, then it came from someone else he's done business with."

"Trust me, he's already been dealt with in a sufficient manner. He's given us everything he knows. He gave us a name and phone number of the man he was working with. We've checked both out. They came back empty. A fake name and a phone number that leads to nowhere."

"Even trails that wind up empty start with something. Maybe you took the wrong path."

"Perhaps so. But we've taken that avenue as far as we can go for the moment." Vincent reached into his pocket and pulled out what looked like a business card. He put it down on the table and slid it over to Recker. There was a name and number scribbled on the back of it.

"What's this?" Recker asked.

"The name and number of the man we used to facilitate this deal."

"And why are you giving it to me?"

"Maybe you could put your resources to work on it?" Vincent said. "I can promise you, I will make it worth your while if you can provide me with any further leads."

"I'm not looking for money."

"I know you're not. That's why I'm not offering it. But I'm hoping the promise of further considerations in the future on my part will be enough to entice you."

Recker smiled. "Don't you still owe me for saving your life?"

"Do I? I thought that had been repaid by you escaping from that police car."

"Hmm. Forgot about that."

"Are we still keeping score?"

"Never was to begin with."

"I've lost count how many times we've done things for each other," Vincent said. "I'd prefer to think of it as continuing to strengthen our already strong business relationship."

"That's a very lawyer-ish, CEO way of looking at things."

"It fits, does it not?"

Recker couldn't dispute it. The moment he heard the news of Vincent's men being killed, he knew he'd somehow get roped into it. But he also couldn't deny Vincent had been a strong ally of theirs. The times they needed help, and there'd been more than a few, Vincent was always there to lend a hand or bail them out of trouble. Recker picked the card up and studied the name on it for a few seconds before putting it in his pocket.

"I can't guarantee anything," Recker said.

"Of course. I understand."

As Recker put the card away, he stared at Vincent for a few moments, wondering if he should bring up the last case they were involved with. He still wasn't happy about feeling like he was used for Vincent's gain. Part of him felt like he should let it go since it was over and done with. But part of him wanted Vincent to know he knew what he did. Recker didn't like feeling he was being played for a patsy. In the end, he chose to speak out. Even if doing so in some way damaged their relationship, Recker wasn't keen on keeping secrets, especially when it made him look like an idiot. At least that's how it seemed in his mind.

"I'll give this a look for you, under one condition."

"Name it," Vincent said, not yet realizing what was about to come.

"I want the truth about that police thing you got me involved with."

"The truth?"

"You played a lot of games with me on that one and I can't say I'm particularly pleased about it."

"Such as?"

"Such as telling me you knew nothing about what was going on when you really did," Recker said. "I got credit for killing someone taking down police officers when I didn't have a thing to do with it."

"You didn't?" Vincent asked, still not willing to admit any involvement. "Who did then?"

"You wanna hear what I think went down?"

"Sure. Why not?"

"I think you either heard about, or dealt with directly, a rogue faction of cops who were starting their own little organization that was moving in on your territory. But you couldn't go around killing police officers, could you?"

Vincent smiled, already knowing Recker had all the pieces of the puzzle figured out. "I'm intrigued with what happens next."

"Now, I'm not sure whether that's because you just didn't want the heat of killing cops, or because you've got men in the department on your payroll and didn't want to risk them turning on you."

"I guess it doesn't really matter in either case, does it? All amounts to the same thing."

"Yeah, I guess so," Recker said. "So, to keep up your charade, you play it like nothing happened on your end. You get me involved, get me in touch with a detective that's in your pocket, all in the hopes of distancing yourself from everything."

"Sounds ingenious," Vincent said with a smile.

"Almost. So, what else happens? You find some sucker you could pin everything on, send Malloy over there to take care of him, and conveniently let me find him a hair too late. Evidence is planted in his room, he's dead, I get the credit, your competition's eliminated, a cop killer's gone, everything's tied off so neat in a tiny little bow."

"So, what's the problem?"

"The problem is I don't like being played for a fool."

Vincent nodded, understanding his position. In truth, if he was on the other side of the table, he probably wouldn't have liked it much himself. "So, what do you want from me? An apology?"

"Just an acknowledgment that everything I said is correct and how it went down. And that it won't happen again."

It didn't take Vincent long to think about the proposition. Especially now he was asking for Recker's help again. He knew admitting his involvement in the matter wouldn't somehow come back to him or be held against him. "I bet you're a real good card player too."

Recker smiled. "I don't play cards."

"Maybe you should. Could probably win a lot of money."

"If I was interested in that."

Vincent nodded again, finally willing to admit it. "Fine. You win. Everything you said is a hundred percent true and accurate. You nailed it. There's nothing I can or will deny. So, what do we do from here?"

Recker shook his head. "Nothing. I just want assurances from you it won't happen again. I don't like working in the dark."

"You've got it. You've also got my apologies. I give you my word it won't happen again."

"I would hope not. I would like to think our relationship wouldn't be severed by something so trivial."

"I cannot argue there." Vincent then pushed his coffee away from him and clasped his hands together. "I hope that's now been settled to your satisfaction."

"For the moment. I'll see what I can find out with this," Recker said, taking the card out of his pocket again and holding it in the air.

A devilish grin came over Vincent's face. "I'll anxiously be waiting."

Recker immediately went back to the office, where he found Jones and Haley hard at work, both banging away at their respective keyboards.

"Hey, look, you two almost look like the nerd twins."

Haley let out a laugh, while Jones kept plugging away, not even breaking stride. "Flattery will get you nowhere," the professor said.

"Takes a lot to insult you," Recker said.

Jones finally looked up at him and smiled. "Complaining?"

"No. Just stating facts."

"Now that we're done with the comedy improv; can we get down to business?"

"Everything's fine. Finally got a confession."

Jones scrunched his eyebrows together and contorted his face. "Over?"

"That whole police scandal he got us involved in."

Jones looked disappointed. "Are you still harping on that? I thought we agreed to put that to rest. It's done and over with."

Recker looked over at the wall and sighed. "Yeah, well, it wasn't for me."

"What good did it do?"

"Got me the answers I was looking for. Relax, David, everything's fine. He acknowledged his role in everything."

The look on Jones' face suddenly changed to a surprised one. "He did?"

Recker nodded. "Absolutely. I told him exactly what I thought and what I suspected him of and he came clean."

"To everything?"

"One hundred percent. As a matter of fact, he even offered an apology," Recker proudly stated.

"He did?"

"Gave me his word he would never do it again."

"Now there's a man who's looking for something," Haley said.

Jones sharply turned his head. "Such as?"

"Man like that doesn't go around apologizing for his actions, or even admitting them for that matter, unless there's something bigger at play. There's something else he wants for his admittance of guilt."

Recker pointed at his partner as if he had just gotten a prize for getting the correct answer to a puzzle. "You got it."

"He wants something?" Jones asked.

"That he does."

Jones' shoulders slumped, and he closed his eyes, getting a sinking feeling they were about to be dragged into something. "What is it?"

Recker reached into his pocket and grabbed the business card Vincent gave him. He held it in the air for a few seconds for everyone to see, then tossed it down on the desk. Jones picked it up off the desk and looked at it for a few moments.

"Should I ask what this is?" Jones said.

"You shouldn't," Recker answered. "But I'll tell you, anyway."

As he waited for the answer, Jones passed it to Haley. "I can hardly wait."

"The name and number of the guy Vincent used to facilitate a gun transaction."

"And that interests us how?"

"Because Vincent believes that guy holds the key to finding out who ambushed his men."

"And he'd like our help in finding out?" Haley said.

"You got it."

"Wonderful," Jones said.

"Hey, I told you we were gonna get roped into this."

"Doesn't mean you had to agree to it."

"Well, what if this is a new arrival of someone in town and we don't like them as much as Vincent?" Recker asked.

"Whatever happened to not helping known criminals?"

"I amended that policy."

"To what?"

"Unless it somehow helps us."

Jones rolled his eyes and turned back to his computer to start working again. Haley handed the card back to him. "I guess we better get started then."

"Never know, maybe this'll be fun."

46

Recker and Mia were sitting down at the table having breakfast before they went their separate ways for the day. Mia was doing a double shift today and wouldn't have another opportunity to discuss with him what was burning in her mind for the last week. And she didn't want to keep thinking about it for a few more days before talking to him about it. Though she knew what his likely reply would be, she still held out a faint hope she could somehow convince him.

"So, does it look like you guys are going to be busy in the next few weeks?"

Recker stopped chewing his food for a second as he pondered the question, thinking it was a strange one to ask. He shrugged it off though as he finished chewing. "About average I guess. Tough to say sometimes. You know how it is, sometimes things pop up at the last minute."

"That's what I figured."

"Why do you ask?"

"Oh, I don't know," Mia said, flashing him one of her smiles. "Just asking."

Recker wasn't convinced though. He knew what that face meant. Behind that sweet, innocent, sexy looking smile of hers was a devious plot in her mind. He was just waiting for her to spill it. But after a few more minutes of silence and sensing that the other shoe was ready to drop, Recker couldn't hold back his curiosity any more.

"So, uh, did you have something in mind that you wanted?"

"For what?" Mia asked, pretending to be clueless.

Recker cleared his throat before continuing. "Well, it kind of sounded like you had, you know, something in mind when you asked that question."

"What question?"

"About how busy we were."

"Oh, that question."

Recker faked a smile of his own. "Yeah. That one."

"No, not particularly. What makes you think I had something in mind?"

"Umm, I dunno, maybe because you never really ask that since you know how quickly things can change."

"Oh, don't I?"

"No, you don't."

"Oh. Well, I guess I was just making conversation."

Recker finished his food then pushed his plate away. "No. You don't just make conversation like that about my work. You always have specific things in mind if you do inquire about it. So, I know it's not just making conversation. You don't do that. So, go ahead and spill it. What's on your mind?"

Mia wiggled her mouth around and scrunched her nose at him, not liking that he figured her out. "So, do you think you know me so well because of what you do or because we've been living together for a while now?"

Recker smiled. "Probably a bit of both."

Mia grinned at him again, not knowing exactly how to say

what was on her mind. She was almost sure he'd rebuff everything she'd say, anyway. But she held out hope if she phrased it just right, that maybe, just maybe, he might consider it. "So, um, you know, I was thinking…"

Recker thought it was funny how she was stumbling over her words and having trouble getting started. He figured it wasn't too serious or else she would have just come out and say it. "Thinking's usually a good start."

The comment drew one of Mia's playful stares. "Funny."

Recker laughed. "Just come out with it. Whatever's on your mind, just say it."

"OK. Well you know I have some vacation time coming up I need to use."

"Yeah?"

"Well, I was thinking about using some of it soon."

Recker shrugged, still not seeing what she was getting at. "OK. Yeah, sounds like a good idea. You could use the time off."

Mia smiled again, thinking it was cute how he was a world-class CIA operator and could track down any criminal he set out to get, but he couldn't figure out what she was hinting at. "Well, I was kind of hoping to get away somewhere. You know, like get out of the area for a week, actually go somewhere, like a beach or something. Some place like that."

"Oh," Recker said, not sure how he felt about it. He was a little surprised she wanted to go away by herself, but he didn't want to stand in her way either if she felt she needed some alone time.

Mia could see by the look in his face that he didn't exactly approve of the idea. "What? What is it?"

"Nothing."

"Yes, it's something. I can tell. I can always tell."

"Well, I don't want to sound like a jealous, obsessive boyfriend or anything."

Mia scrunched her eyebrows together, having no idea where his line of thinking was going. "But?"

"No but," Recker said. "You should if that's what you want."

"What I want?"

"Yeah. I mean, I'd obviously miss you and wouldn't want to be away from you, but if you feel you need to go away for a week or so, then I think it's a good idea and you should."

Mia closed her eyes and sighed. She put her hand up to her face and rubbed her forehead, thinking this was not how she pictured it going in her mind when she initially thought of this conversation.

"Uh, no, no, you don't understand. I wasn't planning on going by myself."

"Oh?" Recker asked, thinking he'd seen this scene play out in several movies. It was usually right about now the bombshell was dropped on an unsuspecting partner, having to pick up the pieces after being dumped for someone else. Mia could see in his eyes he was starting to have questions, other things going through his mind.

"No, no, nothing like that," she quickly reassured him. "I love you. I would never dream of doing something like that."

A sense of relief lifted off Recker's shoulders. "Then what are you saying?"

"I'm trying to say I want to go on vacation... with you. Us. You and me."

"Us?"

"Yeah."

"Oh." Recker turned his head away slightly and looked toward the floor.

That wasn't quite the response Mia had counted on. It wasn't even an objection. "What? What does that mean?"

"What's what mean?" Recker said, turning his head back to her.

"Oh. You said 'oh.' What does that mean?"

Recker shrugged. "I don't know. Just an oh."

"You don't just say oh."

"I don't?"

Mia shook her head. "No."

"Oh."

They stayed silent for a minute as Mia waited for a response. But as Recker's eyes danced around the room, she wasn't sure if he was thinking about it or not. She even suspected he might have even forgotten the question.

"Mike?"

"Hmm?"

"What do you think?"

"About what?" Recker asked.

At this point, Mia wasn't sure if he was actually being this absent minded or if he was purposely trying to avoid answering the question. It wouldn't have been the first time he completely tried to push a subject to the side he didn't want to talk about. It was sometimes his way of trying to let someone down easy, by not talking about whatever the subject was.

Mia then laughed, believing that's exactly what he was doing. "No, you're not gonna play that game with me this time."

"What? What game?"

"The avoid answering a question game, then talk about something else in the hopes I'll eventually move on to something else. That way you don't actually have to talk about what you don't wanna talk about."

Recker tried not to crack a smile. "Is that what I'm doing?"

Mia put her finger in the air. "That's exactly what you're doing and I'm not letting you get away with it. Not this time."

Recker shrugged. "OK."

"So, can we talk about what I said?"

"Which was?"

Mia rolled her eyes and took a deep breath. "The part where I asked about us going on vacation... together."

"Oh... that."

"Yes... that."

"I don't think I've ever been on a vacation," Recker said.

"That doesn't surprise me."

"I wouldn't know what to do?"

Mia looked at him in a disbelieving fashion. "You're not a robot, Mike. You just go somewhere, have a good time, relax, leave your worries behind, that's pretty much it. I think you can handle it. And, oh yeah... you don't have to shoot anybody."

"Not shoot anyone? That sounds depressing. Sure you're not sending me to some hospital or something?"

"Really?"

Recker laughed. "I dunno. Did you have some place specific in mind?"

"Not really. I just would really like for us to get away somewhere and have a romantic week together. Where we don't have to worry about hospitals, or guns, or cases, or work, or anything. Just the two of us. We could go to the shore or the mountains. Anywhere's really fine with me."

Even though Mia was excited by the proposition of them going away, she could tell her partner was not quite as enthused. He didn't have the same glow on his face as she did.

"Isn't that one of the reasons you guys brought Chris on?" Mia asked. "So he could take some of the pressure and responsibilities off you, so you had a little more time to relax. I mean, if you work every day, eventually you're gonna explode. Everyone needs some downtime. You gotta unwind every now and then."

"Yeah, I guess."

"What's the matter? Don't you wanna go somewhere with me?"

Recker gave her a face. "You know it's not that."

"Then, what is it? What are you hesitating about?"

"I don't know. I guess I hate change. Anything out of the routine makes me feel out of my element."

"I'm not asking you to go away forever," Mia said. "Just for a week. And it doesn't even have to be right now. Maybe in a few weeks, next month, the month after. I would just like to know we have something together that's outside of all this."

Recker got up and walked around the table. He took Mia's hand as he brought her up to her feet and put his arms around her. "We do have something outside all this."

Mia couldn't help but look somewhat disappointed, figuring her vacation idea was never going to happen. Recker gently caressed her chin, then tilted her head up so she'd look at him. He then kissed her lips and scooped her up in his arms, her legs straddling around his midsection and crossing together around his back.

"I'll talk to David about it," Recker said, finally getting a smile across his girlfriend's face.

"Promise?"

"I promise."

Recker then walked into the living room, Mia still glued to his arms. He reached into his pocket and pulled out his phone.

"What are you doing?" Mia asked.

Recker gave her a flirty stare and smile. "Telling him I'm gonna be late."

47

ecker sauntered into the office, ready to get down to work after taking some extra time with Mia. He drew a crooked look from Jones as he did.

"So glad you could make it and join us this morning," Jones sarcastically said, eyeing him up and down.

"Well, I know how much you struggle to keep things together without me being here, so I figured I owed it to you and the team to show up."

Though Recker was smiling after his quip, Jones simply rolled his eyes, not wanting to admit he found it humorous. "Well, you look... refreshed."

"Oh, don't start this again."

A wry smile came across Jones' face as he turned back to his computer, figuring he wouldn't tease his partner too much this time. Sensing their bantering was done, Recker looked around the office and wondered where Haley was.

"Where's Chris?"

"While you were home in bed getting your groove on, we had

something come up," Jones said, still not able to resist jabbing at him again. "He's out taking care of it right now."

"Anything serious?"

"Nothing too bad."

"Should I roll on it as backup?" Recker asked.

"I do not believe that will be necessary. It's a simple robbery attempt. One or two guys max. Chris should be able to handle it relatively easily. Neither guy has an extensive criminal history or are particularly violent."

"Newbies, huh?"

"I suppose one could say that," Jones replied. "Besides, you have something else you need to deal with."

"I do?"

Jones wrote some things down on a piece of paper, copying them from the screen, then turned and handed it to Recker. "Yes, you do."

"What's this?" Recker asked as he read it.

"What does it look like? A name and an address."

"But for what?"

"I have tracked down the man Vincent's supplier dealt with."

"Huh? Vincent said he'd already dealt with him and was convinced he knew nothing more about it."

"Yes, the supplier," Jones said. "But his supplier gave him a name and phone number of someone who didn't exist, remember?"

"Yeah, Vincent said it was a dead end."

"Yes, for him, it was a dead end. For me, it was not."

"What'd you get?"

"Well I've traced that fake name and number to another fake name and number, which led to another fake name and another..."

"I kind of get the point," Recker said, not really wanting to listen to the same thing repeatedly.

"Oh, well, anyway, everything led me to that name and number there," Jones replied, pointing to the paper.

"Donald Little. What do you know about him?"

"From what I can gather, he's a rather shrewd businessman. And while I have not had the chance to delve too deep into his background, I can say he has several questionable things on his record. And I don't mean record as in criminal, of which he has none."

"He's just into some shady stuff."

"Precisely. But he does have some rather loose connections to several criminal organizations, as well as individuals with no organization ties, which leads me to believe he is someone who may play on the outskirts of the enterprises themselves."

"He's a guy who sets things up," Recker said. "But doesn't get his hands dirty himself."

"From the looks of it."

"So, what does this guy do for a living? On paper, anyway."

"Private consulting."

Recker couldn't help but laugh. "If that isn't cover for doing shady stuff and screaming you're involved in illegal stuff, then I don't know what is."

"Yes, well, the odds are good. But we won't know unless you pay him a visit and talk to him."

"And what if he doesn't feel like talking?"

"We both know you can be... persuasive."

"You think this guy is directly involved in this?" Recker asked.

"I don't know. I can't say he definitely knows the parameters of what's going on, but I think it's safe to assume he knows the players in the game."

"This his house or his office?"

"As far as I can make out, he doesn't have an office."

"This guy's as dirty as it gets. I don't even need to see anything else."

"Well if this is his home, does he have protection?"

"Tough to say," Jones answered. "I have not uncovered definitive proof in either direction as to whether that is the case. To err on the side of caution, I would suggest assuming there are one or two."

"When you want me to head out?"

"No time like the present."

Recker went to his cabinet and removed a couple of weapons for his chat with Little, expecting it wouldn't be quite so pleasant of a time. After grabbing his guns, he started to leave the office, walking past Jones. Just as Recker got to the door, his mind turned to Mia for some reason. He started thinking of what they had talked about that morning. He kept staring at the door, wondering if he should mention something to Jones.

Though Jones wasn't specifically watching what Recker was doing, he did notice he walked past his desk after grabbing his guns. Without saying another word or having any more questions, Jones assumed he was leaving. With not hearing the door close, Jones stopped working and turned around, observing Recker standing there. It appeared to him Recker was just looking at the door. Thinking it was strange, Jones watched him for a minute, wondering what he was up to. After a couple minutes, Jones couldn't take the suspense anymore.

"Is there something wrong with the door?"

"No, looks all right," Recker answered.

"Then why have you been staring at it for five minutes?"

"It hasn't been five minutes."

"OK. Let's call it three and a half. Are you OK?"

"Yeah, fine."

"Then why are you inspecting the door?"

"I'm not inspecting it," Recker replied. "Just thinking."

"Perhaps you would like to share?"

Recker sighed, not really wanting to come out with it, but also didn't want to keep it bottled up inside for a while. He figured it was best to just say it and get it over with. He turned around and walked back over to the desk. Jones studied his face and automatically knew what it entailed. While he didn't know the specifics, he knew that face. He'd seen it before. It was that face Recker had when Mia said something that was troubling him. Something he didn't want to think about but was now forced to. Jones didn't even wait for Recker to begin.

"So, what was it Mia said that is bothering you?"

Recker looked puzzled as he sat on the corner of the desk. "What makes you think she said something that's bothering me?"

"Please, Mike, I've seen that look from you before. It's obviously not something work related. Whenever you have a problem with Mia, you get a particular kind of look on your face."

"I do?"

"It's unmistakable."

"I'm gonna have to work on that."

"I'm quite certain whatever you do won't have the desired effect that you are looking for," Jones said.

"Thanks for the vote of confidence."

Jones smiled, but then turned his attention back to the issue at hand. "Anyway, enough kidding around, what is it you are having a problem with."

Recker rubbed the back of his head as he thought of how best to say it. "Mia sprung something on me this morning."

Jones' eyes almost bulged out of its sockets as he imagined what it could have been. He was already fearing the worst. "She's not, um, you know..."

Recker leaned in closer to him to try to figure out what he was trying to say. "What?"

"You know," Jones said, putting his hand on his stomach and making a circular motion.

Recker quickly denied the assumption. "Oh, no, no, no... no, nothing like that."

Jones looked relieved and wiped his forehead, even though there was no perspiration on it. "Thank heavens."

"Why would you even think such a thing?"

"Well, you were being somewhat secretive. Seemed like the thing to think."

"Oh," Recker said, then pretended to be offended. "What would be so bad about that?"

"Well, nothing..."

"What, you don't think I could be a father?"

"It's not that..."

"You think I'm not capable of having a child?"

"No, that's not what..."

"What, because we're not married yet?"

"Yet?" Jones said.

"You don't think I could handle a kid?"

"That's not..."

"You think I'd be a bad father?"

"No..."

"So, what is it?"

Jones figured there was nothing he could say at that moment that would satisfy him or end the conversation, so he thought it best to move on. Jones closed his eyes and scratched the side of his face as he collected himself. He tried to get their discussion back on track to what Recker's original problem was.

Jones clasped his hands together. "Can we get back to what we were originally talking about?"

Recker stared at him for a few seconds. "Which was?"

Jones put his hand on his head, almost sorry he asked to begin with. "Something in regard to Mia."

"Oh. Yeah. So, we were talking this morning at breakfast..."

"Is this before or after your little escapade?"

"Can you just let me get back to telling my own story without interrupting with questions pertaining to my love life?"

Jones couldn't help but chuckle. "By all means. Proceed."

"And it was before."

"How enlightening."

"Anyway, Mia was talking about taking a... vacation."

"And she wants you to take some time off to go with her."

"How'd you know?" Recker asked. "Did she already call you or something?"

"No, Mike, she hasn't called. But it doesn't take a genius to figure that out."

"Oh."

"So, what was your reply?" Jones asked.

Recker threw his hands up. "I don't know, what was I supposed to say?"

"Did you say anything?"

"I just said I couldn't make any promises, and I'd talk to you about it."

"Oh, great, so now if you go back to her and say no, she's going to think I put the kibosh on it and she'll be mad at me for you not going."

"I said I'd talk to you about it," Recker said. "I didn't say it was up to you."

"Well that's basically what you're implying."

Recker sighed. "Yeah, I know."

"So, what is it that's bothering you about this? You don't want to go?"

"No, that's not it."

"You think if you go you will be escaping from here and running out on your responsibilities? Or is it you think if you go you will somehow be letting us down or we'll think less of you? Like you are not doing your job anymore."

Recker made an expression that indicated his friend hit the nail on the head. "Yeah, I guess that's probably it."

Jones immediately tried to quell his fears. "Mike, when you took this job, when we started this, I never said it had to be a twenty-four-hour a day, three hundred and sixty-five days a year job. Now, I know we haven't taken much time off in the last few years, but I don't think that's been out of necessity. I believe it's been more because our life mostly revolved around here. That is no longer the case. At least not for you."

Recker's shoulder slumped as he thought of his situation even more. "I guess part of it is I feel like I'm being pulled in two different directions. On the one hand, I love Mia, I wanna spend more time with her. I wanna be the man she sees and deserves."

"And the other hand?" Jones asked.

"Part of me gets pulled to here even if I don't need to be. I feel like if I'm not here at least ten hours a day that I'm shirking my duties."

"Mike, that's never been an issue. You have always put in your time."

"I guess I don't want to disappoint you guys. You especially."

"That's something you never have to worry about. This operation we've got going on has far surpassed my expectations when I first had thoughts of it. And you're a big reason why."

"I guess maybe it's just that things are different now," Recker said. "Things have changed. Change is hard for me. It's never been something I've accepted very well. I've always struggled with it."

"Change is inevitable. In our professional lives, in our personal relationships, nothing ever stays the same. We are always in a constant state of flux. The world spins around and we have to try to adapt to whatever is thrown our way. You either accept it and change with it or you reject it and wither away and die. That's the decision we all face."

"You always have a way with words."

"I think you should go," Jones said. "Not right this minute, but when this thing with Vincent is settled, when things die down a little, maybe a few weeks or a month, I think you should take her and go away for a week."

"You really think so?"

"I do. I think it would be good for you. Clear your mind, rejuvenate a little. There's more to the world than this little office and those streets out there. It won't blow up because you leave for a week."

"I would hope not."

"And if there's one thing I know about women, which albeit is not much, is you have to make them feel wanted and important. Or someone else will."

Recker nodded, feeling like his mind was made up on the matter.

"Besides, that is one of the reasons we brought Chris on, to take some of the load off your shoulders. Right?"

"Well, yeah, but not so I could see the world and leave you two guys behind."

"Mike, it's for a week. You don't have to feel like you're abandoning anybody. It's really OK."

"Yeah, this time it's for a week," Recker replied. "But what about after this? What about a few months from now or next year when she wants to keep taking things further?"

Jones smiled, thinking his friend was completely overthinking and reacting to this. "Such as?"

"This time it's a vacation. But next time might be wanting me to do something else, change jobs, move away, start a family, take things to another level."

"It's like I said about change, it's always happening. Emotions change, feelings change, what we think today might be different tomorrow. When I first asked you to get involved in this, nobody said it had to be forever. We were taking things one day at a time.

We never said we had to do this until we're eighty and they're putting us in the ground. Even me, who knows, maybe one day I'll decide I'd like to try my hand at something else."

"You really believe that?"

"Who's to say? Maybe one day I won't get the same level of satisfaction or I'll feel differently about what we're doing. It could happen. But I'm willing to roll with the punches as they come. I think you need to be more willing to do the same."

Recker nodded, sliding off the desk and onto his feet. "Good talk, Dad, thanks," he said, tapping Jones on the arm.

Jones shook his head, trying not to show even the slightest bit of a smile as he watched Recker walk out of the office. "My pleasure, son."

48

Recker had been sitting outside Donald Little's house for nearly an hour, as he usually did when staking out someone new for the first time. He'd seen a few people come in and out, none of whom looked to be of the friendly variety. There also didn't seem to be any great security detail either. Though Recker did notice a man at the top of the long circular driveway, it seemed as though anybody could go in. There wasn't a gate at the end of the property to keep anyone out. Little's house wouldn't be considered a mansion, but it was a large house with five bedrooms, four bathrooms, three-car garage, swimming pool, and all the extra amenities one would expect in a house like that.

After sitting a little while longer, Recker figured he'd seen all he needed to make a move. Watching the house for two hours gave him enough perspective to know how to handle the situation. He got out of his car and walked across the street to Little's property, walking up the long driveway. The guard, dressed in an expensive-looking suit, saw him coming but did nothing to stop his approach. Once Recker got relatively close, the man put his hand up to stop him from coming any closer.

"What kind of business you got here, bud?" the man asked.

"Oh, just wanted to talk to Little."

"Yeah, you and a bunch of other people. Nobody gets in without an appointment though."

"Oh, you need an appointment."

The man nodded. "Yep."

"Oh. Well how do I go about getting one of those?" Recker pleasantly asked.

"Let me put it this way. If you don't know, you ain't getting one."

"Oh, so it's like that, huh?"

"It's like that."

"I don't suppose if I slipped you a few bucks under the table you could amend that policy, could you?"

The man didn't reply, and instead, just stared at Recker with a menacing scowl on his face. That was all the answer Recker needed, not that he seriously expected his offer to work.

"No, I guess not," Recker said.

"Take a hike, man, and go through the proper channels."

"Well, how am I supposed to go through the proper channels if you won't tell me what they are?"

"Figure it out. If you don't know, you don't know the right people."

"And here I thought I knew pretty much everybody."

"Guess not," the man replied.

"Sure you won't change your mind?" Recker asked, getting ready to take matters into his own hands. "This is your last chance."

"Last chance for what?"

"To not have to go to the hospital."

The guard laughed, finding Recker more comical than an actual threat. He put his hand on Recker's shoulder and gave him a push to spur him on to leave the property. Recker immediately grabbed the man's wrist and twisted it around, causing the guard to moan as the pain radiated through his arm and shoulder. Recker then stepped under the twisted arm and delivered a hard kick to the man's gut. With the guard hunched over, Recker unleashed several overhand punches to the side of the man's head, causing him to fall over. Though the man was hurt, he wasn't yet incapacitated, which Recker needed to happen. Recker took out his gun and walloped the man over the back of his head, knocking him out cold. Recker felt the man's pulse, to make sure he wasn't more seriously hurt. Though he was sure the man probably wasn't on the proper side of the law, he didn't have any motive to kill him, yet.

Recker didn't want to leave the guard lying on the ground in full view of anyone who might be going by so he grabbed the man underneath his arms and dragged him over to the front door. He figured he could stash him inside once he got in. Recker rang the doorbell and patiently waited for someone to answer. He didn't even seem concerned he had a knocked-out guard lying next to him. It was almost like an afterthought.

Recker rang the doorbell two times as he waited for the door to open. Finally, it did. Another rougher-looking gentleman appeared, also dressed in a nice suit. He immediately saw the body of the other guard and got on high alert.

"What happened here?" the man asked, putting his hand on the front of his jacket. Recker assumed the man had a gun inside it and was ready to pull it if necessary.

"Oh, I dunno, man, I happened to be walking by and saw this man passed out in front of the driveway there," Recker said, pointing to the area the man used to be standing. "I figured I should bring him up to the house so whoever was here could take care of him."

"Oh. Thanks. Did you see anyone else near him?"

"No, man, didn't see a thing. It was just him. If you want, I'll give you a hand getting him inside."

"Thanks."

The guard removed his hand from his jacket, seemingly no longer feeling a threat from the stranger. He stepped outside and walked around the passed-out guard's body, ready to pick him up. Recker quietly moved in back of the man and withdrew his weapon again. And once again, he batted the back of the man's head with his gun. The man immediately slumped to the ground, partially on top of the first guard. Recker also checked his pulse and was satisfied with his work thus far. He was two for two.

With the door open, Recker quickly took a peek inside the house. With no one else coming, he looked back to the fallen guards, wondering if he should drag them in or leave them where they were lying. They were on a small covered porch, hardly noticeable from the street, if at all, leaving Recker to figure they were OK staying where they were. Recker then went inside the house and locked the door, wanting to make sure nobody else came in. If the men woke up, he didn't want to be surprised by them. By locking them out, he assumed he would hear them making a ruckus to get back in the house or if they improvised trying to get in somewhere else.

Recker hadn't been in the house for more than thirty seconds before he saw another man approaching him. By the man's appearance, and considering he was dressed like the others, Recker assumed he was another guard. The man seemed to make a beeline for Recker.

"Can I help you?" the man asked, seeming like he was a little taken aback at seeing the stranger's presence.

"No, I'm good."

As soon as Recker uttered the words, he uncorked a right hand that landed flush on the man's nose, stunning him and knocking him back against the wall. With the man glued to the wall, Recker took advantage of his position and kneed him in the stomach, then delivered a few more punches to the man's face. Then Recker took the back of his head and repeatedly threw it against the wall behind them, creating a hole in the wall as a remembrance of the activity. Somewhere amongst the head bashings, the man passed out and slipped out of Recker's grasp, sliding down to the ground. With the man out of commission, Recker took a look around, hoping that was the last of the guards.

"Hope there aren't too many more of these," Recker whispered to himself.

Recker quietly walked through the hall and into a few rooms, finding the place eerily quiet. It was one of those times when it felt like somewhere along the way, someone was going to jump out on him and try to get the drop on him. It wouldn't have been the first time. But this was not going to be one of them. After he went through each room on the first floor, he found the house empty. He was starting to worry Little wasn't even there at the moment.

"Hope I didn't do all this for nothing," Recker said.

Recker walked through the kitchen until he came to a sliding glass door that led to a patio area. He stood there looking through it, seeing a man sitting at a round glass table, reading a newspaper. His back was to the door Recker was looking through. Recker, still feeling a bit uneasy thinking he may not have found the last of his trouble, took one last look around before heading out to join the man. Recker slid the door open and stepped outside, beginning to walk toward the seated man he assumed to be Little.

Once Recker got to the table, he stopped next to the man, pretending nothing was out of the ordinary. He saw some caviar on the table and helped himself to a spoonful. Never having the chance to have any before, Recker eagerly tried it, always wanting to see what it tasted like. Once the spoon left his mouth, he made an agonizing face as he licked his lips.

"What'd I tell you about eating that stuff?" Little asked, not bothering to look up at his visitor as he continued reading the paper. "You know, I was just reading about this guy...," Little said, suddenly looking up. The newspaper fell out of his hands as he jumped in his seat a little as he wondered who was standing next to him.

Recker still had a nasty look upon his face from the caviar. "Too salty."

"Who the hell are you?"

"How does anyone eat that stuff?" Recker asked, walking around the table and sitting down across from his host. "I mean, do you actually like that?"

"It's an acquired taste," Little answered, taking a look back to the house, wondering where his guards were.

"Oh, if you're looking for your goons, they're all taking a nap right now. They'll be fine in a little while except for the bumps on their heads."

"Who are you, and what do you want?"

"Just wanna have a nice little chat with you," Recker said, taking a look around. "Nice place you got here."

"Cost a fortune."

"I bet. You have maid service?"

"Of course."

"I figured you were the kind of guy who had people come in."

Little smiled, assuming the man had some type of business proposition to make to him. "Are we going to just talk about my comfortable lifestyle or are you going to tell me who you are and what you're doing here?"

"I'm getting to it."

"The suspense is killing me," Little said.

"Better hope that's the only thing killing you."

Little took a sip of his drink as he impatiently waited for his visitor to proceed. He looked up at the bright blue sky. "Sun only has a few hours left in it today. I certainly hope we have a resolution to whatever this is by then."

Recker smiled at him. He seemed cool and collected. Here was a stranger in his house and he didn't seem the least bit bothered by it. He had to know Recker was dangerous by now seeing as how he took out all the guards along the way. But Little wasn't rattled or nervous. Recker could tell this wasn't the man's first meeting in dangerous circumstances. He knew how to handle himself. Little was a middle-aged man, in his late thirties or early forties, but had a youthful appearance. Most people would have figured he was ten years younger than he actually was. He was of average height and weight with a full head of hair that looked like he just came out of a nineteen-eighties television show. He didn't have a particularly gruff appearance, and most wouldn't have assumed him to be in this line of work. But it usually served to his advantage as he stayed out of the limelight as was his preference. He didn't seek attention but loved the money and lifestyle the business afforded him.

"Let's talk about Vincent," Recker said.

"Who?"

"Maybe you've heard of him. Powerful mob boss, connections everywhere, head of the major criminal element of this city. You recently sold guns to his enemies which helped kill several of his men."

Little put his hands up to dispute the facts. "Whoa, whoa, whoa, I haven't sold guns to anyone. And I don't know who this Vincent fellow you're talking about is."

Recker could appreciate the fact he wasn't willing to spill the beans just yet. He didn't figure Little would at first. He assumed he'd have to break the man down to get there. But Recker really didn't want to take too long to do it. Recker reached into his pocket and pulled out the paper with Vincent's contact and slid it across the table.

Little picked it up and read it. "Am I supposed to know this man too?"

"Yep. He's the guy Vincent had a deal with. He brought some people to Vincent with a weapons deal and the thing went sideways. Vincent's men were killed in the process."

"Don't know anything about that."

"Well, I think you do."

"Guess we have a fundamental difference of opinion then."

Recker looked unconcerned. "Guess we do. Maybe I should bring Vincent here to include him in this chat of ours. He might be interested in what's said."

Little's confident look slowly eroded. Up to now he assumed the man in front of him wasn't any kind of major player since he didn't recognize him. Recker took out his phone and scrolled through the numbers until he came to Vincent's. He slid his phone across the table, so Little could see he wasn't bluffing. He figured that once Little saw he really did know Vincent personally, maybe his tone would change, and he would be more receptive to answering questions.

Little looked at the phone without picking it up. "Am I supposed to call someone."

"No. Just pick it up. You might be interested in what's on it."

Little was a little hesitant to do so but did comply with the request. He picked the phone up and saw Vincent's name and phone number. He recognized the number. He also knew it wasn't something Vincent handed out readily. He knew if this man in front of him had it, he was a much bigger player in the game than he assumed him to be.

"So, who might you be?" Little asked.

"Let's just call me a concerned third party."

"If you want answers, then I need to know who I'm dealing with."

"I'm known on the street as The Silencer."

Little's face was now one of curiosity and caution. He obviously had heard of Recker's reputation as most in his line of work had.

"So, what role do you have in this turn of events?" Little asked.

"Vincent's lost a couple of his men. He wants to know who's responsible for it and he's run into dead ends. So, he's asked me to help him look into it."

"Interesting. I didn't know The Silencer got involved with those who fly under the respectability of the law."

"Vincent and I have helped each other over the years," Recker replied. "We have a respect for each other and basically avoid each other's interests."

"I see. So, what do you want with me?"

"My investigation has led me to you."

"I didn't have anything to do with that situation," Little said.

"I beg to differ. Now, you can either tell me and be done with it or I can call Vincent to include him in this little discussion we're having."

"He doesn't know you're here?"

"Not as of yet," Recker answered. "That can change rather quickly though."

Little stared at his visitor for a few moments as he considered his options. Though he really did not want to admit his role in anything, the last thing he wanted, or needed, was Vincent showing up at his house asking the same questions.

"So, what is it you would like to know?" Little asked.

"Just your role in what happened?"

Little sighed, not happy about coming clean. "If I admit to anything, I would like your word it doesn't leave this table."

Recker grinned. "Don't want it getting back to Vincent I take it."

"Something like that."

"As long as you weren't the one that killed his men, I don't think he needs to know every little detail," Recker said. "At least he won't hear it from me."

A slightly relieved look came over Little's face. "You must understand that I do business with Vincent. If he knows I'm also doing business with other people who might be looking to take him out that would look very bad upon me."

"Probably wouldn't do much for your future either."

"Yes, well, I guess you can understand my concern."

"I'm not interested in your business dealings other than the situation we're talking about," Recker said.

Little threw one of his arms up, resigned to the fact he might as well tell the truth. "Why not? As long as what I tell you stays between us."

Recker nodded, indicating it would.

"Very well. A group of men approached me several weeks ago about procuring weapons," Little said, remembering their initial meeting. "They said they were looking to start up operations around here."

"Did you know they were looking to challenge Vincent?"

"They didn't mention him by name, but it didn't take a genius to figure out what they were up to. I mean, if you wanna start making a name for yourself in this city, odds are you're going to be going up against Vincent at some point."

"So, how does that lead up to what happened with Vincent's men?"

"Well, I got them an initial shipment to start them out with. Everything went very smoothly. Then they started inquiring about Vincent and asked if I could set up a meeting."

"So, you did?"

"They paid me very handsomely to do so. Double my normal fee."

"And you didn't think that was strange?" Recker asked.

Little shrugged. "I am not paid to think. I am paid to facilitate transactions and bring parties together. That is all that concerns me. What happens with those parties after that is not of my concern."

"Well if all the parties wind up dead that will bring your little empire to a screeching halt, won't it?"

"Maybe, if they were the only warring parties in the universe," Little replied. "But we all know no matter what happens, no matter who dies, there will always be someone to replace them. Always. That's the way the world works. There will always be someone who is looking to take more... and do so in a forceful and violent manner."

"So, if what happens in these deals doesn't concern you then why did you use several fake names to make sure it didn't come back to you?"

"Because we both know Vincent's reputation."

"I think you're lying out your ass," Recker said. "You know what they were planning or else you wouldn't have bothered using other names. All you cared about was the money. I'm good with it. It don't bother me. Just say so."

Little sighed again. "Fine. I had a pretty good idea they were planning on using the meeting to ambush some of Vincent's men. I didn't really like it..."

"But the money was too good to pass up."

"Yes. OK? Is that what you wanted to hear?"

"Yeah, pretty much," Recker answered.

"If you wanna keep this out of Vincent's lap, then I need to know names, places, phone numbers, the works."

"You're asking me to betray a client's confidence," Little said.

"I don't care what you call it. You give me what I want, and I guarantee your name will never cross Vincent's ears. He is a rather big client of yours, is he not?"

"Yes. And if these other people find out I led them to you, what then?"

"They'll most likely be dead before they find out it was you and have a chance to seek revenge against you," Recker said.

Little was still apprehensive about handing over his information but knew he really didn't have other options. The man in front of him was in complete control of the situation. Little wasn't the violent type, that's why he employed guards, or else he would consider trying to take matters into his own hands. There was a small black bag sitting on the table which contained many of his secrets. He started to reach for it but was interrupted by Recker before he actually got to it.

"Before you pull anything out of that bag, I would hope you'd understand I'm probably a much better shot than you."

Little looked at him and gave him a wry smile. "It never even entered my mind."

"I know it didn't. You're much too smart to do something that stupid. I mean, why get yourself killed over something I could just take, anyway?"

"Exactly."

Little pulled the bag closer to him and unzipped it. He looked inside and saw his notebooks, a phone, and a gun. He took another glance at Recker, who by reputation, and by his own observations, didn't appear to be a man anyone wanted to mess with. Little bypassed the gun and gently removed the notebooks and phone so as not to make Recker nervous. Once they were plainly seen on the table, Little pushed the bag away. He started rooting through one of his books, getting to the page that had the information of the guys Recker was looking for. Little tore the page out, handed it to Recker, then closed his book. Recker eagerly read what was on the page. It was the name and phone numbers of three men.

"These it?" Recker asked.

"Those are the only three who I talked to."

"Do you know how many men are in this operation they got going on?"

"That, I couldn't say," Little answered. "They were understandably tight-lipped about their organization activities. And as far as my business was concerned, it wasn't on my need-to-know list."

"Are these three the top dogs or are they messenger boys?"

Little shrugged. "Who knows? They spoke like they had decision-making authority. They talked in a forceful manner. My impression was they were high up in the food chain. How high? Anyone's guess I suppose."

"Is this it?" Recker asked, holding the paper up.

"That's all I know. Don't know exactly who did the killings, don't know anything about how this group operates."

"You have any other business with them lined up at the moment?"

"Haven't heard from them since that day."

"Possible they don't wanna lean on you and rely on you too much, knowing the relationship you have with Vincent. Might think you'll have second thoughts and turn them over to him."

"Possible," Little replied.

"All right, thanks." Recker pushed his chair away and stood up.

"I don't suppose you hire out, do you? I could use you in certain situations."

Recker smiled. "Not to the likes of you."

"Fair enough. I don't suppose we'll be seeing each other again."

"I dunno. Knowing what you do, I wouldn't bet against it. Oh, and uh, just in case this is a load of crap..."

"It's not."

"Well, a word of warning, if it is... you'll be seeing me again."

"I'm not worried about it." Recker started walking past the man, but Little sought further and final reassurance on their agreement. "Remember, not a word to Vincent as per our deal?"

"Not a word."

Little smiled as Recker walked back into the house, closing the sliding door behind him. Little went back to reading his newspaper as if nothing happened. He didn't seem the least bit concerned about Recker being in his house unsupervised. He assumed Recker would be leaving as quickly as possible before anyone else showed up. Recker didn't bother looking for anything else in the house. He had everything he needed. He didn't get the sense Little was lying to him or fed him bogus information. As Recker walked to the front door, he saw the man lying on the floor against the wall. He was starting to move around again. Recker wanted to leave something to remember him by and forcefully kicked him in the head, knocking him out again.

"Oh, sorry about that," Recker sarcastically said.

Recker then reached the front door and unlocked it, stepping outside onto the porch. Both men were still out cold. Recker stepped over them.

"You guys really need to stop laying down on the job."

49

After visiting Little, Recker went straight back to the office. He wasn't about to tell Vincent anything yet until they'd thoroughly checked out the names on the list and knew what they were dealing with. Telling Vincent the names without them checking them first was a dangerous proposition he thought. When Recker got back to the office, Haley was back from his assignment and talking to Jones about it. They broke off their discussion when they saw Recker walk in.

"How was your conversation with Mr. Little?" Jones asked.

"Went about as well as it could go, I guess," Recker replied.

"What did you learn?"

Recker took the paper Little gave him out of his pocket and handed it to Jones. "I imagine this might help."

"What is this?"

"Names and numbers for the guys Little dealt with."

"Anything else?" Haley asked.

Recker shook his head. "No, that's all the information Little had. He said they weren't very willing to go into details on whatever enterprise they got going on."

"Stands to reason," Jones said. "Nevertheless, this should do nicely. It should at least give us a launching point."

"Let Vincent know yet?" Haley said.

"No, I don't figure he needs to know anything until we've got something worth sharing," Recker answered.

"Before I start working on these, should I ask if we're going to be in the news for anything?" Jones asked.

"Such as?"

"Oh, I don't know, dead bodies or anything?"

"What do you think I am, a haphazard violent person who goes around shooting everyone in my way?"

Jones looked at Recker and batted his eyes, thinking it was as loaded a question as he'd heard. He then looked at Haley, then around the room as he thought of how to answer. "I'm not sure I am the best person to answer that question."

Recker laughed, knowing he set one up on a tee for him. He was actually a little surprised Jones decided to strike out on the opportunity. "No, there are no dead bodies. Some injured ones, but not dead."

"He have guards?" Haley asked.

"Three. Not much of a problem, really."

As Recker and Haley talked about their latest assignments, going over strategy details, Jones started plugging the names into the computer. Gabriel Hernandez, James Milton, and Jamar Teasley. It didn't take long for the hits to come back on the computer. They all had lengthy and violent criminal histories, though none of them were originally from the Philadelphia area. Hernandez was from the Baltimore area, Milton from New York, and Teasley from Boston. There was no immediate connection on why they were now seemingly working together. And there was nothing in their pasts at this point to indicate they had crossed paths with Vincent at any time. As the team read their histories, they started throwing some theories around.

"Just because it's not obvious what the connection is to Vincent does not mean they don't have one," Jones said, cautioning them to not abandon that idea yet.

"It also doesn't mean they're the brains behind this operation either," Recker said. "Could be someone higher up the food chain who was aware of these three and brought them into the fold."

"Or it could be these three have a connection to each other and saw an opportunity here to take some territory for themselves," Haley said. "Start up their own gang with them at the top."

"Simply too soon to tell right now," Jones replied. "Any of the aforementioned scenarios could be realistically possible."

"How about we tap into their phone records and see exactly when they hit town?" Recker asked. "Then we can start piecing things together from there. Maybe see some common denominators. Work backwards."

"Sound idea. Why don't you guys go take a break for a couple of hours while I get started?"

"You trying to get rid of us?"

"Not at all. But you both have lives outside of here."

"I do?" Haley asked, not knowing what other life was being referred to.

"I think he's trying to give you a hint," Recker said.

"Oh."

"I'm not doing anything of the sort," Jones replied. "I'm just saying I don't need help with this and I can do it quite capably on my own. And probably faster."

"Well, I don't know about you, but I can take the hint," Recker said.

"Why don't you go have dinner with your better half or something? I'm sure she would love to see you."

"She's working a double."

"Maybe I should go out and get a girlfriend," Haley said.

"Please, no," Jones replied. "I'm not sure I can take both of you having a girlfriend at the same time. Do me a favor and wait a couple years first."

Recker and Haley laughed and joked around for a few more minutes before finally leaving the office and allowing Jones the solitude he was requesting. Haley decided to go home and relax for a couple hours, while Recker went straight to the hospital to see Mia. Though he knew she probably wouldn't be on break for another hour or two, he figured he'd wait, like old times before they actually got together. He went right to the cafeteria and found the table they used to always sit at as he waited. As Recker sat down, he sent Mia a text message to let her know he was in the building. He didn't wait as long as he expected, as Mia's pretty face showed up only an hour later. She was surprised he was there but very happy to see him. She grabbed a few things to eat on a tray then joined him at the table, giving him a big hug and kiss.

"So, what do I owe this big surprise?" she asked, sitting next to him.

"Had some time to kill. Figured I'd spend it with the most beautiful girl I know."

A wide smile overtook Mia's face, happy to hear the sweet words. She leaned over and gave him another kiss, a little longer than the first one. "You sure know how to melt a girl's heart."

"Guess I've had a lot of practice."

Mia shot him a look causing Recker to start laughing. "You better not," she said.

"I'm just joking. I couldn't resist."

"Yeah, yeah." Mia started eating her food and couldn't help but think there was something else on his mind. Something important. "So, you gonna tell me the real reason you're here or are you gonna make me guess?"

"There's no other reason. Why do you think there is? Can't I just stop by and have dinner with you?"

"No, you can, and I love it when you do. It's just... not the normal."

"Well maybe we should make it normal."

"So, there's nothing else on your mind?"

Recker thought back to their earlier conversation at the apartment. "Well, maybe there is something."

"See, I knew it."

"No, nothing bad," Recker said. "I was thinking about what we were talking about earlier. You know, the vacation."

"Oh." Mia didn't sound very excited, mostly because she already had it in her mind they wouldn't go. She didn't want to get her hopes up only to have them dashed.

Recker could tell she thought she was about to get disappointed. "So, I already talked to David about it."

"Oh? And?" Mia asked, still not even the faintest bit of hope in her voice.

"He said he didn't see any problems with it."

"Really?" There was finally a hint of excitement heard in her voice, thinking they might actually have a shot at it.

"Yeah. So... I think maybe we should go."

Mia's face lit up and her eyes almost popped out of their sockets as she stared at her boyfriend. "Really?"

"Yeah."

"You really mean it?"

"Yeah, I think we should go," Recker said.

Mia lunged over and hugged Recker so hard he almost fell out of his seat. "Oh, I'm so happy."

Recker smiled, feeling good she was as happy as she was. She deserved to be, he thought. "You're sure you wanna take me on vacation?"

"There's nothing else I'd rather have."

"Not even a few diamonds or something?"

"Not even diamonds," Mia answered. "You're the only thing I want or need. I knew it from the moment I met you."

She planted another kiss on his lips as they embraced for a few more moments. After letting each other go, they went back to their respective seats and continued eating their food. They also started discussing vacation plans.

"So where should we go?" Mia excitedly asked. "The beach? The mountains? Somewhere warm?"

"Honestly, I don't care. It's up to you. As long as we're together and you're happy, that's all that matters to me."

"Well, I don't want it to be me making all the decisions. I want it to be the both of us."

"OK, OK. How about we talk about it over the next few days, then make a decision."

"OK. So, when can we go?"

"Well, we've got some things going on right now with Vincent, and possibly a new gang in town, so that might take some time. Let's wait a few weeks or maybe a month or so. Is that OK?"

Mia leaned in and put another kiss on his cheek. She was just so happy to hear him say he was going; she didn't even care about the date. "As long as we're going, any date is fine. I'll need about two weeks to put my notice for a vacation in here."

They continued to talk about their vacation plans for the rest of Mia's break period. Once it was over and she had to go back to work, all she wanted to do was throw herself into Recker's arms and go home with him. But since she had to work again, she settled for a hug and a kiss. As Recker left the hospital, he felt good he made Mia happy. She was really the only personal satisfaction he had outside of work. Nothing else mattered to him other than trying to make the city a safer place and trying to be the man that deserved her love.

Since Mia was working and he didn't have much else to do, and he didn't want to hang around at home, Recker went back to the office. He hoped Jones would have had, at least, something by now. It'd been about two hours. As Recker walked in, Jones was at his usual position, doing what he normally did. Working frantically between two computers, sliding his chair back and forth until he got the information he needed. Well, it always seemed a little frantic to Recker, but for Jones, who handled computers so easily, it really wasn't much effort as far as he was concerned. Recker sat down next to him and turned a computer on.

"Come up with anything yet?" Recker asked.

Jones turned his head and looked at him with a blank expression on his face. It was almost like Jones wasn't sure who he was. "How long have you been here?"

"Oh, about two hours."

Jones turned his head back to his computer as he stared at it, deep in thought it seemed. "Really?"

Recker scratched the back of his head, in disbelief of how absent-minded Jones could be at times. "Uh, no, not really. I just got back. Remember, you sent us away for a couple hours while you did your research?"

"Oh. Yes. Of course."

"You have no clue, do you?"

"Of course I do," Jones answered. "I remember perfectly. I'm not senile yet, you know."

"Good to know. So, do you have anything yet?"

"What would you classify as anything?"

Recker looked perplexed then put his hand up to his ear and started tapping it the way someone does after swimming when they're trying to get water out of his ear. "We must have a bad connection here or something."

Now it was Jones' turn to look confused. "What?"

Recker put his hand up, wanting to restart the entire conversation. "You know what? Let's just start over. Have you uncovered any other information about the three men you started digging into?"

"Oh. Yes. Why didn't you just come out and say so from the beginning?"

Recker rolled his eyes and looked at the ceiling, not even wanting to deal with it anymore. "So, what'd you find out?"

"First of all, Hernandez, Milton, and Teasley, have all been in other crime organizations, but none of them have ever been in charge of one, or even in the hierarchy of one."

"So, they're likely working for someone else."

"Correct. Furthermore, they all received and made calls to the same phone number in the week before Vincent's issue popped up."

"Someone brought them here," Recker said.

"Correct again. Now to this point, I have not yet pinpointed a name to go along with that number."

"Someone's trying hard to conceal their identity."

"Correct... again."

Jones went back to typing, leaving Recker alone with his thoughts. He sat there staring at the floor, rubbing his chin, thinking. Jones tried to ignore him and keep working, but he kept looking at his friend out of the corner of his eye. It always unnerved him when Recker was sitting there in thought, not doing anything. Almost as much as when Recker was out in the field looking to shoot people. Almost. Mostly because he knew when Recker got like that, in his thinking mode, he had a specific thought in mind that usually proved to be right. Finally, Jones couldn't take it anymore and stopped typing, swiveling his chair back around to face his partner.

"So, what are you thinking about?" Jones asked.

"Just getting things straight in my mind."

"Like what? What specifically is bothering you?"

"What makes you think something is bothering me?"

"Because I know that look."

"I'll have to learn to become less predictable," Recker said.

"Not likely."

"Yeah. Anyway, sounds to me like someone's building up an organization from the ground floor."

"For what purpose? To rival Vincent?"

Recker nodded. "Yeah. And it has to be someone high up, who's used to this type of thing, who has connections. Because these three guys are from three different areas. Only someone high up would know who they are and where to look."

"A mobster from another city, perhaps?"

Recker shook his head and continued thinking. "Not likely. Tough enough getting two factions to cooperate, let alone three." After another minute, Recker snapped his fingers, thinking he finally got it.

"What?" Jones asked.

"I think it's fair to say whoever's behind this isn't some run-of-the-mill thug, right?"

"I would assume so."

"I mean, this has involved planning, secrecy, involving other people while remaining in the background. That requires a certain level of sophistication."

"I would say as much."

"Someone who's done this type of stuff before," Recker said.

Jones shrugged, still not getting his point. "But all Vincent's enemies have been killed off, the other gangs destroyed, and any remnants still alive have been driven off long ago."

"Maybe we're not looking for an enemy."

"Well I certainly hope we're not looking for a friend," Jones replied. "With friends like that..."

"What if it's someone from another city who's retired, or was run off, or replaced, or relocated, something along those lines? They already know how to run organizations like this, they already know how to operate, and they know how to get things done."

"But for what purpose?"

"Maybe they see an opportunity. They see only one man in town and figure they can move in and take part of it. Or maybe they think they can take it all. If it's someone like I said, who was forced out somewhere, but still thinks they can be in charge, maybe they're looking at this as a new opportunity. They're aware of these other gangs and start recruiting from them, promising them higher positions, more money, more everything if they join him in this upstart group."

Jones took it all in, thinking it sounded plausible. Whether it was likely, he wasn't sure. But it was as good a theory as any of them had at that point. A few minutes later, Haley came back. Recker started talking to him about his latest idea and Haley bought in. While Jones continued running down the leads he had on the other three characters, Recker and Haley started researching displaced mob bosses who'd lost their power in the previous couple of years. As Recker started pulling things up on the screen, he sighed, thinking it was going to be more work than he thought it would be by the number of names he was seeing.

"This might take a while," Recker whispered.

Haley then tapped Recker on the arm. "Hey, I just had a thought that might make it a little easier."

"I'm all for that."

"What if we ask Vincent? I'm sure he would know far sooner and easier than we would. He's probably got all this information at his fingertips."

Jones couldn't help hear them talking and put his two cents into the conversation. "I would caution against that."

"Why?" Haley asked.

"Because we don't have proof of that being the case yet and we don't want Vincent going off half-cocked with information we don't yet have any validity of."

"David's probably right," Recker said. "Besides, if we tell Vincent what we're thinking, he might go off on it alone and not tell us anything, thinking it's mob business."

"So? If they wanna duke it out, let them," Haley said.

"Problem is they might duke it out without it being the right move. And, in a situation like this, Vincent might try to cut the problem off head-on. I'm not sure that's the best move here."

"I would agree," Jones said. "I think our best course of action is working quietly, not letting those people know we're on to them and springing ourselves on them when they least expect it."

"Besides, we've built up goodwill with Vincent," Recker said. "I'd hate to throw it all away now for someone else."

50

Recker, Jones, and Haley had been working all night to try to figure out what they were dealing with. Since Mia was at work, Recker didn't have the inclination to go home and stare at the walls. It actually felt like old times, with him and Jones working all day and night, trying to get to the bottom of something. The three hadn't spoken in a while as they were all entranced in their own work and the room was deathly silent. The silence was broken when Recker's phone rang, startling them since they were not expecting a call. Recker grabbed his phone and looked at it.

"Who is it?" Jones asked.

"It's Tyrell."

"Wonder what he wants?"

"Maybe I'll answer it and find out," Recker sarcastically replied.

Jones rolled his eyes. "Indeed."

"Tyrell, what's up?"

"Yo, man, what's happening?"

"Nothing. Just working some things," Recker said.

"One of those things got to do with that Vincent mess?"

"Yeah, it would. Why? You got something?"

"Well you told me to keep my ears open, so that's what I've been doing."

"Whatcha got?" Recker asked.

"Ain't much, man, just a time and a place."

"Time and place for what?"

"I'm not even sure," Gibson answered. "All I know is something's supposed to go down at some abandoned building near center city."

"Center city's a big place."

"Well, yeah, I know, I got the address, it was just a figure of speech."

"Oh." Tyrell then gave Recker the address of the building. "So, what'd you learn?"

"Just that some deal's supposed to be going down there around ten o'clock tonight."

Recker looked at the time and saw it was just after eight. "Doesn't leave us much time."

"No, it don't."

"What kind of meeting?" Recker asked. "Who's involved?"

"That I can't tell you. All I know is it's some new group. Everything's very hush-hush. Might be those guys that hit Vincent last week. Can't say for sure but that's kind of the indication I was getting."

"Where'd you get this from?"

"Friend of a friend of a friend of a friend of a... girlfriend. Or something like that."

"Sounds reliable."

"Yeah, well, I didn't say it was. I'm just telling you what I hear. Up to you to figure out how reliable it is."

"What's your gut say?" Recker asked, trusting Tyrell's opinion, knowing he wouldn't intentionally pass on bad information.

Gibson paused for a second. "I dunno, man. Something doesn't feel right about it."

"Such as?"

"I dunno. I can't really put my finger on it."

"You don't think there's gonna be a meeting?"

"No, it's not that. I think there will be."

"Then what's the issue?" Recker asked.

"It's just... I don't know. I got a bad feeling about it for some reason."

"Well something's gotta be making you feel that way."

"Yeah, but I don't know what. Maybe it's just that it seemed like it came too easy. It almost feels like the information was supposed to get out and be passed on. Know what I mean?"

"I think I do."

"It almost feels like someone's being set up."

"I guess the next logical question would be who?"

"That I don't know, man."

"No ideas on who might be involved?" Recker asked.

"I mean, no, not really."

Recker then picked up a paper off the desk and started reading the names. "Hey, did you ever hear of a Jamar Teasley, James Milton, or Gabriel Hernandez?"

"No, who they?"

"We think they might be involved in the Vincent thing."

"Oh. Well, no, I never heard of them before."

"All right, thanks. We'll check on the meeting."

"OK... wait a minute, hold up."

"What?"

"Now I'm thinking of it, I think I did hear one of those names before," Gibson said.

"Which one?"

"The first one you said. What was his name, Tease... Teasley?"

"Yeah, Jamar Teasley."

"When I heard about this meeting going down tonight. Someone said something about Tease is gonna handle it or something like that. I really didn't think nothing of it at first. Sounded like a nickname or something. Maybe they just shorted the guy's name or something."

"Yeah, could be. Thanks Tyrell, we'll check it out."

After getting off the phone, Recker immediately passed on the information to his colleagues, so they could start discussing its merits. They started checking other sources, looking on the computer, calling people on the phone, all in the hopes of somehow verifying the upcoming event. And they didn't have much time. Once Recker saw it was eight-thirty, he called off any further attempts to learn what was going on.

"All right, there's no use in going any farther with this thing," Recker said.

"What?" Jones asked.

"If this thing's going down at ten, it's already eight-thirty, we don't have time to keep going. We gotta move now."

Jones sighed, not liking the idea, but agreeing there wasn't much else they could do with such a short time frame. "I wish we had a few extra hours."

"But we don't. And we have to roll with the information we got."

"Do we? It's not necessarily something we have to do. We do not know for sure this is related to anything. In fact, it could turn out to be a complete waste of time. Or it could be something we don't even have to involve ourselves with."

"But, if it is?" Haley asked. "I don't think we can afford not to check it out. If it's a waste of time all we lose is an hour or two."

"I agree," Recker said. "We can't afford not to. Could be the big break we're looking for."

"And if it's a trap?" Jones asked.

"For who? It's not for us."

"One can never be too sure of anything in this line of work. You, above everyone, should know that. Everything is not what it appears."

"I'm well aware. I didn't say we should just roll in there in our tuxedos and plop ourselves down in the middle of the room and wait to be served. But if there's a remote chance this is somehow connected to Vincent's issue, then we need to check it out."

"It appears I'm being outvoted."

"We should probably get going if we're gonna scout the place out ahead of time," Haley said, mindful of the time.

"Yeah," Recker said, grabbing his weapons. "We'll call you with the details."

"I'll be anxiously awaiting your call," Jones replied.

Recker and Haley rushed out the door and into a car, traveling down to the abandoned building together. They got there with about half an hour to go before the meeting was supposed to take place. They drove by the building a couple of times to see if they could spot any activity going on or anyone else who happened to be waiting outside. They didn't notice anything out of the ordinary, however. Nothing other than it appeared to be an abandoned building. Judging by the heavy-duty equipment stationed all around it, along with the barriers that were set up everywhere, it looked like it was about to be demolished. It was a perfect spot for a meeting. Nobody around.

"Definitely looks like a good place," Haley said.

Recker drove around for a few minutes until he found a good place to park, eventually settling for a nearby parking lot. It was a couple blocks away and the pair quickly got to the abandoned building, trying to keep out of sight at the same time. They stuck to the sides of buildings, staying out of the light as much as possible. They snuck over a barrier in the back of the building, getting into the building through an opened window that had previously been knocked out. Once inside, Recker gave Jones a quick text letting him know they were there. After that, Recker and Haley worked up a plan. It was a large ten-story building they had to go through. They didn't know if anyone was there yet and they didn't know exactly where the meeting was supposed to take place. They wanted to clear the building first to make sure they weren't surprised by anyone already inside, but they also didn't want to be checking the building and have someone enter without them knowing.

"If we're both up there on different floors and someone comes through here without us knowing about it, we're gonna be on the outside looking in," Recker said.

Haley hesitated in replying, thinking about the situation before he offered up his own solution. "How about if one of us stays down here out of sight to keep an eye on anyone coming in? The other one checks the other floors."

Recker thought about it for a minute, eventually coming around to the idea, figuring it was probably their best option. "All right, who's gonna stay down here?"

"I'll take down here. If something comes up, I'll shoot you a message."

Recker nodded and took a deep breath before taking off, running through the first floor to look for the stairs. As he finally found them, Haley took another look out the window for visitors. After seeing the streets empty, he went around to check the other openings. Considering there were at least five or six doors, along with tons of windows, someone could have slipped in almost anywhere. Haley wouldn't be able to stay in one place and keep his eyes open on one spot. He'd have to keep moving around and checking them all. It was a tall task.

In only a few minutes, Recker was moving at a frenetic pace. He had already cleared both the second and third floors. With the building having seen better days, not all the walls were still standing, and most of the fixtures were no longer intact. But there were also no lights working, so it was tough to see in the dark. Recker thought about attaching a small flashlight to his gun to help him see better but decided not to use it as he didn't want to risk giving his position away by someone seeing the light before he got there. As he got to the fifth floor, Haley was starting to get anxious, wondering if they had company yet.

"How you making out up there?"

"No action yet," Recker answered. "Anything your end?"

"Quiet as can be."

"If this meeting's legit, we should be seeing something pretty soon."

Recker was more right than he knew. Almost immediately after saying the words, he thought he detected movement not too far from him. It sounded like someone stepping on some of the debris that littered the ground, mostly pieces of the walls and ceilings that had started crumbling down. Recker stopped dead in his tracks and listened for a minute, hoping to hear the sound again. And he did. He thought it sounded like too heavy of a step to be any kind of animal that would be up there on the fifth floor. He assumed birds, mice, or other smaller types of animals could have been up there, but none of them would have created heavy footsteps as they walked or scurried along. Only a person would have made the sounds he was hearing. As Recker listened, it sounded like the steps were moving away from him. He wasn't sure if he'd been made or if someone was doing the same thing he was doing, only doing it first.

Recker quickly moved in the direction he heard the footsteps moving to, hoping to catch up to whoever it was. Though he wanted to catch up to the person quickly, Recker didn't want to move so fast that he gave his own position away. He still tried to move as quietly as possible. He followed the sounds for several minutes until he reached the stairs. He let Haley know as he threw open the door.

"Chris, think I got someone up here. Going up to the sixth floor now."

Recker ran up the steps to the next floor, expecting to get a reply from his partner. He never did though. Now alarm bells were starting to sound in his head. There was no reason Haley wouldn't respond unless he had found himself in trouble. But if he was in a jam, Recker figured Haley would have let him know something came up. Or he assumed he would have heard shots. It was strange. Recker tried one more time.

"Chris, you there?"

Again, he got no reply. Now Recker had two choices. Continue after the man he heard or go back down to the first floor and check on Haley. In the end, Recker figured it was better to keep moving. Maybe it was just a bad connection preventing him from communicating with his partner. Or maybe Haley was seeing something but was trying to keep silent to keep himself hidden. And just maybe the man Recker was after could give him more answers than if he had gone back down to the first floor.

Recker threw open the door and slowly stepped out of the stairwell. Once he was completely inside, he was stunned and jolted to feel the cold steel of a gun pressed against the side of his neck. He closed his eyes, incredulous that he let himself walk right into it. His mind was preoccupied with what was happening with Haley that he didn't concentrate fully on his own actions.

"Turn around slowly," the voice told him.

Though Recker hadn't yet complied with the directive, he knew that voice. It was one he heard before. He slowly turned his head to the right as the gun was taken away from his head. While at first, his eyes gravitated toward the gun pointing at him, they eventually looked past it and at the man that was holding it. Recker was more than a little surprised at the face he was seeing. When he and Haley were en route to the building, Recker envisioned a lot of scenarios unfolding, but none of them included Jimmy Malloy holding a gun to his head.

"What the hell are you doing here?" Recker asked.

Malloy took his finger off the trigger of his gun and slowly brought it down to his side, eventually putting it back inside his jacket, letting Recker know he wasn't there for trouble. At least not with him. "Probably the same thing you are. Got wind of some type of meeting going down with possibly the people that hit us before. Boss sent me to investigate."

"Where'd you get wind of that?"

"On the street. One of our informants."

"What are you doing up here?" Recker asked.

"Didn't know where the meeting was taking place. Wanted to clear all the floors to make sure it wasn't going down up there. You?"

"Same thing."

"Hope it's not going on downstairs while we're up here."

"I got someone down there keeping a lookout."

Malloy smiled. "Ahh, the ever elusive partner we've been hearing about. Finally bringing him out of the shadows, are you?"

"Have to unleash him sometime, I guess, huh?"

They continued discussing what they knew of this meeting, wondering if either of them had heard anything different than the other. They hadn't though. In fact, they'd both heard the same story. Almost word for word. Not one different detail.

"Almost like someone wanted us to know," Recker said.

"Oh, you get that feeling too?"

Recker's head turned to look at their surroundings. "Got a bad feeling about this."

"Yeah, I hear ya," Malloy said. "You wanna soldier on and clear the rest of the floors together?"

"Yeah, I guess. I'm not sure we're gonna find anything to our liking though."

"Or maybe we just won't like what we find."

They took separate paths as they cleared the rest of the floor, Recker still trying to contact Haley. After determining the floor was empty of other visitors, Recker and Malloy spent the next few minutes clearing the rest of the floors. Once they finished up with the tenth floor, they stood in the middle of the room to discuss their options. Their next move was to descend to the main floor and figure out why Haley wasn't answering. If there was a crowd of people there, they'd have to be careful how they entered.

"Ready to go?" Recker asked.

"Let's do it."

Before they could enact their plan, though, the door to the stairs swung open, several men rushing through it. Gunfire erupted before Recker and Malloy even knew what was happening and could respond. Bullets were flying everywhere. Recker and Malloy dropped to the ground and removed their weapons to return fire.

"Looks like we got ambushed," Malloy said.

"Yeah, we were set up all right. Question is which one of us is the target?"

"Maybe both of us."

The sound of bullets ripping through the air and glancing off concrete was all that could be heard for several minutes as the battle ensued. Recker and Malloy were pinned down with what appeared to be five or six men attacking them.

"How we getting out of this one?" Malloy asked.

"Not sure yet," Recker replied, reloading his gun.

As the back and forth continued, no one appeared to be gaining the upper hand. Considering they were outnumbered, they thought it was strange their attackers weren't trying to get closer. They seemed to be content in how things were going.

"A little strange they're not being more aggressive, don't you think?" Malloy asked.

"Maybe they don't have to be."

"What do you mean?"

"I don't know. Maybe this is the plan," Recker answered. "Maybe they just wanna keep us busy for a while. Or maybe they got more people coming. Maybe they don't need to take any risks at the moment. Maybe they just figure on waiting us out."

"That's a lot of maybes."

"Sure is."

"I got one more," Malloy said.

"Yeah?"

"Maybe if we don't move soon, we're gonna get so up against it we're not gonna be able to get out."

Recker couldn't help let out a small laugh. "Maybe."

"So, what do you wanna do? Go out like gangbusters? Rush them?"

"Eh, I dunno."

Their plans were soon made for them as the door to the stairs swung open again. This time, it was Haley coming through it. He heard the ruckus and immediately rushed up the stairs. As soon as he came through, he got the jump on the other guys, immediately taking out three guys on his right. As he did, the three guys on his left jumped up and started firing at him. As they did, Recker and Haley saw their attackers making themselves visible, and the two men jumped up to fire at them as well. With everyone out in the open, bullets started flying in every direction. Men were dropping everywhere.

After taking out his initial three guys, Haley was shot by the others and immediately went down. Recker and Malloy unleashed their barrage at the three men, who had a little time to shoot back before they perished. Malloy also went down in the fray. Once the dust had settled, the only man left standing was Recker. He looked down at Malloy, who was holding his stomach and bleeding. He then rushed over to the men who had ambushed them to see if any of them were still alive. They were dead though. With not having to worry about anybody jumping up and shooting at him, Recker turned his attention to Haley.

"You all right?" Recker asked, looking at his wounds.

Haley coughed and smiled. "I've been better."

Recker looked at Haley's leg, which looked like it had several entrance wounds in it. He then put his hands on Haley's chest and arms, feeling for any other bullet holes. "You're not hit anywhere else?"

Haley laughed. "Isn't this enough for you?"

"Well, could be worse I suppose. You able to put pressure on it?"

Haley stuck his hand out for Recker to help pull him up. Once he got to his feet, Haley took a step, but the pain was unbearable, and his leg couldn't support his weight, causing him to crumple down to the ground again, though Recker caught him as he fell to cushion the blow.

"Looks like we got a problem," Haley said, trying to make light of the situation.

"Yeah, and you're not the only one."

"What do you mean?"

"Well I ran into Jimmy Malloy up here," Recker said. "Turns out he was here doing the same thing we were."

"Guess he knows about me now, huh?"

"That's the last thing I'm worried about right now." Recker turned his head to look in Malloy's direction, but he was still down on the ground, hardly moving. "He got hit too. I'm gonna go check on him."

"Go ahead. I won't move. I'll stay right here."

Recker smiled, then hurried over to Malloy's position. He could tell right away that his wounds were a little more serious than his partner's were. It looked like he was bleeding heavily from his midsection, but he was still alert as he held his stomach.

"Guess that was your partner saving the day?" Malloy asked.

"Yeah."

"Good deal."

"Yeah, well, not so good," Recker said.

"Why not?"

"Because now he's down too. All the bad guys are gone, but both of you have been shot, and looks like neither of you can move very well."

"Guess that is a predicament," Malloy said.

"And it's not my only one. Not only can I not carry both of you at the same time, I don't know if there's any more of them down there waiting for us?"

"I've heard you can do just about anything."

Recker smiled. "Just a rumor."

"You tried calling for help?"

Recker pulled out his phone and dialed Jones' number, but it kept saying he had no service. Whoever it was must have been jamming the signal. He had a look of disgust on his face, giving Malloy all the answer he needed.

"Guess that's a no, huh?"

Recker let out a deep sigh as he looked around the room. "I'll figure something out."

51

Before doing anything about trying to escape, Recker's first order of business was to tend to the two wounded men. He tore some clothing off the dead men to use on Haley and Malloy to close off their wounds and try to prevent any more blood loss. Haley couldn't put pressure on his leg which meant he needed to be carried out. Recker didn't even want to attempt moving Malloy out of fear he might kill him by moving him. Recker went back over to Haley to brainstorm.

"So, what's the plan?" Haley asked.

"Don't have a good one yet."

"I suppose calling for help's no good?"

Recker shook his head. "Afraid not. Think they're using a cell jammer to block the signals."

"Figures. They sure set this up good."

"The way I figure it, we got two choices," Recker said, not really liking any of them himself. "One, I leave both of you here until I can bring in the cavalry."

"Which is? We don't exactly have the police on our side you know."

"Probably Vincent. His guy's here too. He'd bring the rest of his crew and descend on this building like there's no tomorrow."

"And option two?"

"I put your arm around me and help carry you out of here as you're hopping on one leg."

"It'll take you forever to get out of here doing that," Haley said. "And if there's more down there waiting, it's not gonna be easy."

"I know it."

"What about Malloy under that scenario?"

"I'd have to come back for him. I can't carry two people out of here and he's too banged up to try."

"There's a third option," Haley said. "We all just stay here until help arrives. You know once Jones doesn't hear from us he's gonna get antsy. Once he tries to contact us and figures out he can't, he's gonna be worried."

"Who knows how long that'll be? The downside to that is we didn't come here loaded for bear. If they brought a lot more people to the fight, we're gonna be low on ammunition pretty quick. I don't know how long we'd be able to hold them off."

"So, what do you think the play is?"

Recker sighed and looked around the room. "I dunno. I don't really wanna leave you here."

"But it's probably the best move," Haley said, finally saying what Recker wouldn't. "You'll move faster without someone weighing you down. Besides, I can stay here and protect him while you're gone. He'd be a sitting duck if we're both gone."

Recker reluctantly agreed and helped Haley get back to his feet, putting his arm around him so Haley didn't have to put pressure on his injured leg. Recker helped him hop over to Malloy's location, setting Haley back down beside him.

"So, you're the new guy, huh?" Malloy asked with a smile.

"So they tell me," Haley replied.

"At least we met with a bang."

Recker thought about leaving the two without much ammunition, then looked over at the dead men. He rushed over to them and pilfered their guns, as well as any ammunition he could find. He brought the weapons over to Haley, setting them down in front of him.

"It's not a lot but you're better off than you were," Recker said.

"It'll do."

Recker then looked at Malloy, who was in quite a bit of discomfort. "When were you supposed to check in with Vincent?"

"No set time. It'll probably be another hour before he starts getting fidgety if that's what you're thinking."

"Well, I'm gonna have to try to get a hold of him, anyway. I don't know how far they're jamming the signal for."

"Might not be that far," Haley said. "They jam it too far away from this building, where other people are having problems, it might lead to complaints and someone looking into it. Probably something they don't want."

"Could be."

"If someone heard the shots, police might be on the way too."

"I kind of doubt it," Recker replied. "I think you'd be hearing sirens by now if they were. This isn't a residential neighborhood. It's late at night, business area that's mostly deserted, I don't think there's many people around to report it. Probably why they picked this spot."

"You should probably get going."

"Sure you'll be alright?"

"As sure as I can be."

"I'll be back as soon as I can."

Haley was positioned so he had a good angle to see the door, so he could see whoever was coming in. As he watched Recker leave, he hoped he wasn't seeing him for the last time.

"You know, if he gets shot or doesn't make it out of this building, we're as good as dead," Malloy said.

"Figured that was the case, anyway."

"So, how'd you get dragged into this thing, anyway?"

"I don't see how that's really a concern right now considering our predicament," Haley said.

"What difference does it make? You guys were former CIA, weren't you?"

"Even if we were I couldn't confirm it."

"I always had a feeling that was it. Either that or you were former military. Or even both."

"Hate to disappoint you, but we're not gonna sit here discussing my past."

"As mysterious as your friend," Malloy said with a cough.

"Just the way it is."

"So, did you know Recker from your previous life or did you get recruited blind?"

Haley kept his eyes and guns focused on the door, ready for another round of action. "Already told you, I'm not gonna talk about it."

Recker slowed down as he got to each level, almost expecting someone to jump out at him as he passed the door to each floor. As he passed a couple of floors, he worried about getting trapped. He envisioned a scenario where he passed a floor, only to have someone come out behind him, while at the same time, someone else jumping out from a floor he'd yet gotten to. That way they'd corner him in the stairway. He hurriedly ran down the steps hoping to avoid further conflict, even though he figured that was unlikely to happen. As soon as he passed the sixth floor level, the door swung open, revealing a figure in the doorway. Recker jumped back, startled, and immediately began firing. The man getting shot at instantly dropped to the ground, the bullets flying over his head as he covered up. Recker took a few more steps toward the man, a little puzzled he wasn't being shot at himself.

When the bullets stopped coming at him, the man uncovered his head and looked at Recker.

"What the hell, man?" Tyrell asked. "You always shoot at your friends?"

A look of relief and horror came over Recker's face at the same time. He was relieved it wasn't an unfriendly person trying to kill him, but he was upset he almost killed his friend. He was a little quick on the trigger expecting someone else. Recker rushed over to him and helped him to his feet.

"What the hell are you doing here?" Recker asked.

"Well I thought I'd come over and give you a hand. Had I known you'd almost kill me I would've stayed snug in my bed."

Recker tapped him on the arm. "Sorry about that. I assumed you were someone else."

"Obviously," Tyrell replied, brushing himself off. "Who'd you think I was?"

"Well there's six dead bodies up on the tenth floor that tried to ambush us. I kind of assumed you were one of them."

"Well I'm not."

"So I see."

"Where's your partner? Leave him behind?"

"Kind of. He's still up there. Took a couple in the leg and had trouble walking," Recker answered. "Malloy's up there too. Took one in the stomach. He's bad and needs help soon or he won't make it."

"Man, that's rough. I had a feeling something wasn't right here. That's why I came over. The more I thought about it, it just didn't seem right to me. Thought I'd come here and give you a hand if you needed it."

"I could use all the help I can get right now. How'd you get in here? Anyone else downstairs?"

"Nah, man, I just came through a back window and started looking around."

"And you didn't see anyone else?"

"Only some mice."

"So that means there isn't anyone else or they let you come up so as not to tip me off."

With Tyrell now there, Recker hesitated for a minute before pushing on. Now there were two of them, he wondered if they should go back up and get the others. One could help Haley while the other helped Malloy. At least now he knew there was nobody else between the sixth and tenth floors. He knew he could get them at least that far without any further battles.

"If we go back and get them, Malloy might not make it if we're not careful," Recker said.

"Last I checked the elevator ain't working," Tyrell replied. "Even if Vincent's men come, it's gonna be awhile and they're gonna have to carry him down these same stairs, anyway."

"But at least they could try to get him out on a stretcher to minimize the damage."

"Six of one, half dozen of the other. When you get Vincent here, who's to say he won't bleed out? Which means all your planning goes to waste, anyway. And who knows, maybe we get out of here safely and they storm the building and take out Haley. Just my opinion, man, but I think you're taking a greater chance leaving them up there. But like I said, just my opinion. I'll go with whatever you decide."

Recker thought about it a few more seconds and wound up coming to the same conclusion. He couldn't escape the nagging feeling something bad was going to happen to his partner and Vincent's right-hand man if he left the building with the two of them up on the tenth floor by themselves. Now with Tyrell there, he didn't have to leave one of them behind.

"Let's go get them," Recker said.

They rushed back up the steps until they came to the tenth

floor. Recker slowly opened the door, knowing Haley was going to have a gun pointed at him.

"Chris, it's me," Recker said, hoping to avoid having to duck a bullet.

"Come on in."

Recker and Tyrell walked through the door, stepping over the dead bodies. Haley immediately noticed Tyrell walking behind Recker, surprised he was there. It was even more of a surprise Recker had returned so soon. Haley assumed that meant there was a bigger problem somewhere downstairs.

"Fancy meeting you here," Haley told Tyrell. "Welcome to the party."

"Well I didn't get an invitation, so I just figured I'd crash it."

"So, what's going on?"

"We're clear down to the sixth floor," Recker said. "So, we can at least get you to that point without a problem. Well, other than you guys moving around."

"I've been meaning to work on my hopping skills anyway," Haley replied.

"We don't know if there's anyone else here so keep your gun available in case we get jumped somewhere along the line."

"Ready, willing, and able."

Recker and Tyrell then went over to Malloy. They both reached down and gently picked him up and got him to his feet.

"You gonna be able to make it?" Recker asked.

"Won't be winning any races but I'll make it," Malloy replied.

Tyrell helped Malloy walk over to the door, though very slowly, as Recker went over to Haley and put his arm around him. They hobbled out the door, making sure they didn't go too far ahead and leave Tyrell and Malloy behind without being able to protect them. Both injured men grimaced and groaned as they went down the steps, the pain radiating throughout their bodies.

"Just be ready as we pass by these floors in case somebody jumps out at us," Recker said.

"I hate surprises," Tyrell replied.

They continued moving slowly, taking a lot of time to go down the steps. After they got to each floor, they paused for a few seconds to give the injured men a little time to catch their breath. As they continued descending the steps, they were about halfway between the sixth and seventh floors when Recker suddenly stopped.

"What's wrong?" Haley asked.

"I heard something."

"What was it?"

"Sounded like someone walking up the steps," Recker said, looking over the railing as far down as he could see.

"Anything?"

"No."

"Sure you heard it?"

"Positive," Recker answered.

"Maybe it's friendly," Tyrell said.

"Only problem with that is the only friendly people we know are right here."

"Unless it's Jones or Vincent," Haley said.

"I think that's wishful thinking. Kind of soon for either of them to show up."

"What do you wanna do?"

"Keep going. No point in stopping now."

They passed the sixth floor without incident and stopped again once they got to the fifth. They had concerns about going any further.

"One thing's for sure, they gotta know we're here," Haley said. "Moving quietly, we're not. Not with me hopping all the way."

Recker knew he was right but wasn't sure how they could

combat that. After a minute, he thought he'd come up with something. He had to hope that it would work.

"All right, if someone else is here, let's make them think we ducked out somewhere," Recker said.

"How we gonna make them think that?" Tyrell asked.

"By making a lot of noise."

Recker banged his gun against the metal railing so the clanging noise would be heard echoing down the stairwell several levels below them.

"Let's get in! Let's get in!" Recker shouted, making sure his voice was loud enough to be heard by anyone else.

Recker put his finger up to his mouth to make sure the others didn't say a word. He pointed back to the stairs they came from as he and Tyrell sat Haley and Malloy down, away from the door that led into the fifth floor. They stayed in position, almost paralyzed, waiting for someone else to come. They stayed silent as Recker stuck his head out, listening for the slightest of sounds to indicate someone was coming. A few seconds later he heard what sounded like footsteps shuffling up the stairs. He turned his head around to look at the others and stuck two fingers in the air to indicate two men were coming.

Recker then opened the door, making sure it hit the wall to give off another noise that could be heard. He wanted the men to have no questions about which door they ducked into. Recker then readied himself and stuck his gun out in front of him, ready to fire. He took a few steps back up the steps to give himself a higher vantage point once he saw the two men come into view. The sounds of the footsteps were growing louder and closer. Within a few seconds, it seemed as if the men approaching were almost on top of them. Recker tightened his grip on his gun, then loosened it as he relaxed his fingers.

A few seconds later the two men arrived, each holding a gun. Recker stayed back for a moment, silent and out of sight. He didn't recognize either of them. He knew they weren't Vincent's men. Recker was familiar with the faces of everyone in Vincent's organization, at least the ones Vincent didn't mind being identified. Vincent always figured it was best if Recker knew the names and faces of most of the men he employed, outside of his informants and contacts, that way, if Recker ever ran into one of them on a job, he would be less likely to kill them. One of the men slowly opened the door and took a peek inside, without going in yet. Recker stepped fully out into the stairway to greet them.

"Looking for me?" Recker asked.

The two men turned their heads and instantly swung around, guns pointed at him. Recker already had the drop on them though and beat them to the punch. He hit them with one shot each, then tagged them with another as they both dropped to the ground. Not sure if they were dead, Recker hurried down the steps and grabbed their guns. One of them was dead, but Recker could see the other was still breathing, though he wasn't moving very much. It didn't look like the man was very alert so Recker tapped his cheek a few times to wake him up more.

"Hey, who hired you?" Recker asked. "Why are you here?"

The man mustered up enough energy to spit some saliva out of his mouth. "Screw you."

Recker didn't take offense and didn't even get mad at the man's belligerence. He simply tapped his face a couple more times. "Who sent you? Who'd you come here for?"

"You're not getting out of this building, man."

Recker was starting to lose his patience, knowing he didn't have a lot of time to sit there and play games and dance around the truth. "Looks like you're bleeding pretty bad there. But it's possible you might be able to make it. I can give you two options. You can give me some answers and I'll leave you here breathing and maybe you can make it to a doctor in time. If continuing to live doesn't interest you, then I can put a few more bullets in you and put you out of your misery."

The man puffed out his lips, not believing anything he was hearing. "Don't be stupid. I'm not an idiot. We both know you're gonna kill me no matter what. You're not letting me leave here."

"Listen, I don't know you from a hole in the ground. I got nothing against you. Other than the fact you're here trying to kill me. But men like us, we should have some type of honesty amongst each other, don't you think? I give you my word."

The man took a deep breath, though it hurt to do so. He still wasn't sure he could believe Recker, but he figured he might as well choose the alternative where he at least had a shot at living.

"Who's the head man?" Recker asked.

"Don't know. All I know's who hired me."

"Who was that?"

"Guy named Hernandez."

"Gabriel Hernandez?"

The man nodded, trying to conserve his energy by not talking when he didn't have to.

"Why? What were you here to do?" Recker asked.

"They let word slip out on the street about some meeting here tonight. They wanted Vincent's crew to get word about it and come down here."

"So they could be ambushed?"

The man nodded again. "Yeah."

"How many men are here with you?"

"Uh, I dunno, about fifteen I think."

Recker immediately looked at Haley. "Eight more to go." Recker then turned his attention back to the injured man. "Where are the rest of the men waiting?"

"I'm not sure. Different spots."

"So why this play against Vincent?" Recker asked. "What do they want out of it?"

"Gabe said they were looking to take some territory off him. Let him know that a new power was in town."

"They wanna take him out completely?"

"Not sure. I don't know all the details. I'm not that high on the totem pole. I think they just wanna get their foot in the door to start with and go from there."

"And you don't know who's looking to take it over?"

"I've only dealt with Hernandez so far."

"Maybe he's the head guy."

The man shook his head. "No. He mentioned something about getting orders from someone. Never mentioned who though."

"Why aren't cell phones working?"

"They got a jammer down on the first floor."

Recker had all the information he needed. Staying any longer was risking someone else coming up on them before they were ready. "All right. Thanks."

"You gonna kill me now?"

"A deal's a deal. Hope you never come into my sights again though."

The man laughed. "Yeah. Me too."

Recker went back to Haley and put his arm around him as they started descending the steps again. Tyrell was right behind them with Malloy. Suddenly, another shot rang out. Recker swiftly turned, ready to fire, assuming it was the injured man with a concealed weapon or something. But he was wrong. Malloy still had a gun in his hand, and as he passed the injured man's body, unloaded a couple of shots into him, finally finishing the man off. Though he was badly injured himself, Malloy was never out of a fight, even if he could barely walk. Recker locked eyes on him and gave him a puzzled look, wondering what he was doing. Malloy wasn't going to feel badly about it though, no matter what kind of looks Recker threw his way. Malloy had a different code of ethics.

"What? I didn't promise him anything," Malloy said. "Besides, he just tried to kill us. He don't deserve to leave this building alive. We'd wind up seeing him again. If not today, then tomorrow, or next month. I just made things easier for later."

Recker wasn't really pleased about Malloy shooting him, mostly because Recker gave the man his word. But he really couldn't dispute Malloy's logic about possibly seeing the man again if he left the building. There was a good chance of it. So, with that being said, and with other things more pressing, Recker wasn't going to harp on it. They kept moving. Once they got to the fourth floor, they stopped, expecting to run into some more company. They stayed still for a few minutes as they waited, but eventually moved on after nobody appeared.

"Maybe they're saving everyone for the main floor," Tyrell said. "Have one big, huge firefight."

"Maybe," Recker replied, thinking it was entirely possible.

Once they got to the third floor, they stopped again for a minute as they waited for another visitor. This time it proved to be the right decision. Recker and Haley stayed put as Tyrell moved ahead of them with Malloy.

"Using us as bait?" Malloy asked.

"Got a problem with it?" Recker said.

Malloy laughed, though he coughed at the same time. "No, not really. I'd probably do the same to you."

Once Tyrell and Malloy passed the door and started going down the steps, the door flew open. Two more men appeared in the doorway, guns in their hands as they took aim at Tyrell and Malloy. They didn't even take notice of Recker and Haley to the left of them, waiting higher up on the stairs. As the men showed themselves, Recker and Haley instantly fired on them before the men were able to do the same to their friends. Both intruders went down immediately with head shots, dead long before they even hit the ground. After hearing the shots, Tyrell and Malloy turned around to see the damage that had been done.

"Guess we should say thanks?" Malloy asked.

"Save it for when we get out of here," Recker answered.

Recker and Haley then took the lead again, doing the same waiting game on the second floor. There wasn't any activity this time. They waited a few more minutes before traveling down to the first floor. They stood just behind the door that opened up to the first floor.

"By my count there should be six left," Recker said.

"Assuming that guy was telling you the truth," Malloy replied.

"I got a feeling as soon as we open that door we're gonna be ducking," Haley said.

"Good possibility," Recker said.

Recker knew there was a good chance that as soon as the door opened, a barrage of bullets would be heading in their direction. With two men having a hard time moving, he wasn't sure they'd be able to maneuver out of the way in time. Then he figured out another plan.

"You guys stay out of the way and against the wall," Recker said.

"What are you gonna do?" Tyrell asked.

"Experiment."

"This ain't science class you know."

"If they're out there waiting for us, as we assume they are, there's no way we're all gonna get through that door without getting hit."

"So, what do you have in mind?" Malloy asked.

"You guys stay here. Cover my tail. If anyone comes down that stairway to sneak up behind me, you know what to do."

"You're gonna take out the rest of them?" Tyrell asked.

Recker smiled. "Why not? There's only six of them. The odds are in my favor."

Tyrell started laughing. "That's what I love about you, man, never a doubt in your mind who's coming out on top."

After putting Haley against the wall, Recker got down and swung the door wide open. As soon as it opened, several rounds of automatic gunfire were heard. All four men inside the stairwell ducked down as the bullets glanced off the walls around them. Recker started making his way to the door again when he was stopped by Haley grabbing his arm.

"I can go out there with you," Haley said.

"What are you gonna do?" Recker asked. "Hop over the bullets."

"I can still crawl. I'm not out of the fight."

Recker thought for a minute before realizing he could probably use the help. Crawling out the door was probably the only way they were making their way inside unscathed, anyway.

"All right. You take the left and I'll take the right," Recker said.

Recker and Haley got down on the ground and opened the door, hearing another round of gunfire headed for them. They crawled out the door, each of them going in a different direction. As the door closed behind them, Tyrell wondered if he'd wind up seeing them alive again.

"Think I should go out there and help them?"

"Tyrell, gunplay has never exactly been your specialty."

"Yeah, well, desperate times call for desperate measures. Isn't that how the saying goes?"

"If I were you I'd stay right here," Malloy said. "Besides, they're not expecting you out there. They might shoot you by accident."

Tyrell then thought back to earlier in the night when Recker almost shot him coming out of the fifth floor door. "Yeah. You might be right about that."

It was dark inside the building, but there were pockets of light coming in through the windows, thanks to a bright full moon. Recker was crawling along the floor as quietly as possible, trying not to give his position away. He came across some small, broken pieces of concrete and took a handful of it. He then turned on his side and threw it across the room, hoping for a reaction from their opponents. He got the desired result. Upon hearing the noise of the concrete hitting the floor, the men opened fire at that spot, giving their position away. Recker then jumped to his knees and fired at what he could make out as faint outlines of the men's bodies. Within a few seconds, he heard the sounds of bodies violently thumping down on the ground.

As Recker hurriedly scurried along the floor to get out of the line of fire, since he blew his own cover, the men turned in his direction to fire. As they started firing, Haley crawled along the other side and had a few of them in his sights. With his wound, he wasn't as quick to get to his feet or knees, so he continued to lay on his stomach as he took aim. He fired several rounds at the outline of the men, getting the same result Recker did. Within a few seconds, they heard the bodies of two more men hitting the ground.

As Recker continued crawling, he suddenly saw the leg of a man in black pants almost directly beside his head. He knew he was in a lot of trouble and quickly turned over and fired up at the man, just as the other man fired at him. The bullets fired at Recker hit the ground in the spot he was before he rolled over. Recker's shots landed in the man's midsection, causing the man to fall on top of Recker. Another man came racing over to the shots and started shooting at Recker, though the bullets wound up lodging into the body of his dead friend that shielded Recker from the lead. Recker then aimed his gun up at the man, though it was hard to do so with the weight of a two-hundred-pound man on top of him. Suddenly, though, a few more shots rang out, and the man fell to his knees, blood pouring out the holes in his chest. That gave Recker a much easier target as he fired a few more rounds, finishing the man off. Once the man slumped to the ground, Recker looked past him and saw Haley slithering on the ground. They gave each other a salute as Recker got to his feet.

Recker took a quick look around and saw no one else hiding in the shadows. He then walked around the floor to make sure there was nobody else there. Once he knew they were alone, he went back to Haley and got him on his feet again. He then went to the stairway and knocked on the door to let them know it was him, that way nobody had an itchy trigger finger and shot him by accident. Once he got a confirmation, he opened the door.

"We're good to go," Recker said.

"Good thing you announced yourself," Tyrell said. "I was about to return the favor for that little incident you pulled upstairs."

"You'll have to wait for your revenge another time."

"I guess I can let it go this time."

"So, you guys wanna get out of here or are you starting to feel at home?" Recker asked.

"It is starting to grow on me a little."

"As much as I like the banter, you think we can do it after I get these slugs out of me?" Malloy asked.

"You wanna go to the hospital or does Vincent have a guy?"

"Just call Vincent. He'll set it up. Might as well take your guy there too."

Tyrell picked Malloy up and the four of them headed out of the building.

"You guys sure know how to party," Tyrell said.

"What do you mean?" Recker asked. "This was just a regular night for us."

52

R ecker and Vincent were sitting in the waiting room as they waited for the doctor to come out. After leaving the abandoned building, Recker called Vincent and explained the situation. Vincent had him go to a doctor that was on his payroll. Tyrell helped get the wounded men there, then took off as soon as the doctor started checking them out. While they were waiting, Recker called Jones and explained everything that happened up to that point. Dr. Luke was a licensed doctor and had his own practice, but he also did some work off the books and behind closed doors for extra money. He was a very skilled doctor and had done work for Vincent's organization many times over the years. As long as the money was there, Dr. Luke could be trusted to keep whatever private work he was doing silent.

"Seems like a pretty good setup for an underground doctor," Recker said, looking around the room. "Not the usual stuff you'd find like no lighting and bars on the windows and things like that."

Vincent laughed. "That's because he's not some hack who

happens to hatchet people up on the side. This is his work. He's a good doctor. We've used him many times over the years."

"Saves on your insurance deductibles I'm sure."

Vincent smiled. "Not really my main objective in coming here. Secrecy is a much more valuable commodity."

"So, what are you gonna do if you lose your right-hand man in there?" Recker asked.

"It's not something I have to worry about right now. Jimmy will pull through. Thank you for helping him through it. We're lucky you were there."

"Why did you only send him? Kind of dicey, don't you think?"

"At the time we thought stealth was the best option. Figured with a meeting like that, it was better to send one man. We weren't looking to get into a gunfight. Our only goal was getting as much information as possible."

"How'd that work out for you?"

"Well, we did get some information out of it. We know the meeting was a sham and there is a specific new threat trying to take over the city," Vincent said. "It must be someone with a high profile who has experience in these types of things."

"What makes you say that?"

"Only someone who knows what he's doing and done this type of stuff before would have the patience to sit back and wait, operate in the shadows. People who are new at this overstep their boundaries, they get too eager, make mistakes. They can't wait to project themselves and show everyone who they are. Can't wait to make a name for themselves. That's how I know this person, whoever he is, has power behind them."

"You're worried about him," Recker said. "I can tell."

"I worry about things I cannot see. That's why I need to get to the bottom of this quickly, so I can prepare countermeasures."

"Out of curiosity, would you be willing to concede control over certain parts of the city to prevent a large scale conflict?"

"You mean would I give up part of my territory and hand it over to whoever this person is? To avoid a war?"

"Yeah."

"An interesting question to ponder to be sure," Vincent replied. "One I couldn't possibly answer at this time. Not until all the particulars are known."

"Just a thought."

"Well since we're dealing in hypotheticals, I'm sure this isn't the scenario you had in mind for me meeting the new member of your squad."

Recker shrugged. "I knew it would happen at some point. I didn't have any preconceived ideas about how. With what we do, I figured it would probably be some time that wasn't very convenient."

After being in the doctor's care for a couple of hours, he finally came out of his little operating room, which was divided into a couple sections in case he had several patients. As he walked out, Recker and Vincent both rose from their chairs, anxious to hear the news about their friends.

"So, what's the prognosis?" Recker asked.

"Well, I'll start with your guy first," the doctor replied. "He's in relatively good shape. Bullet didn't hit any major organs or anything, just muscle tissue. He won't be able to walk around on his own yet, so he'll probably have to use some crutches for a week or two."

"And after that? Long ranging effects?"

"Will probably take around six weeks to heal, I would say. He'll still have to do some physical rehab for a while to get his strength back. Probably won't be able to run any marathons and walk uphill or things like that, but he should get back to almost where he was before. Might have some numbness occasionally, but if he does some rehab, shouldn't have too bad of a long-term issue."

"Good to know. Thanks."

"Just keep him out of firefights for a little while."

"Do my best."

Dr. Luke then turned his attention to Vincent. "As for Malloy, it looks like he'll pull through. The bleeding's stopped, he's stable, he'll have to stay here a few more days though so I can keep an eye on him, just in case."

"OK. Long-term prognosis?" Vincent asked.

"We're probably looking at a few months' worth of recovery time. He's not getting back in the saddle in a few weeks. It'll take some time."

"But he should get back to where he was?"

"In time, yes. But he can't push it too soon or he'll rip everything open again. I know he's your go-to guy, but if you want him to get back to a hundred percent, he needs time."

"Well then, we'll have to give it to him." Vincent put his hand on Dr. Luke's arm. "Thank you, Doctor. You'll receive a payment in the next few days."

"No rush," Luke replied. "I know you're good for it. I better get back in there."

"When will they be able to leave?" Recker asked.

"Haley should be able to leave tomorrow. I want him to stay overnight for observation, make sure infection doesn't set in. As for Malloy, he'll have to stay a few days since his injury was a little more severe."

Dr. Luke then left the room to tend to his patients again, leaving Recker and Vincent alone.

"You gonna be able to survive a few months without your top guy by your side?" Recker asked.

Vincent smiled, realizing the question was somewhat tongue in cheek. "He's not the only member of my organization I trust or employ you know."

"But he does draw the top assignments. Especially with an emerging threat on your hands. You gonna be able to handle it?"

"Why such concern?" Vincent asked. "Are you throwing your hat in the ring to replace him? Finally taking my employment offer? If so, I might be able to arrange it."

"No, I think I'm still good."

"No need to worry about me. I'll make do with what I have."

Recker smiled. "I wasn't worried."

"Do you need a lift out of here?"

"No, Tyrell walked and took a bus after he left so I still have the car."

The two men parted company, with Recker going straight back to the office, where Jones was nervously waiting. Even though Recker had previously told him Haley's wound wasn't life threatening, Jones was still anxious to hear the results. Having any of them shot was an altering dynamic that would affect them all. Jones was waiting by the window when he saw Recker pull in then went to the door to let him inside.

"Not used to having a doorman," Recker said as he walked in.

"How's Chris?"

"He'll be fine. On crutches for a week or so, then rehab after that. It'll probably be a good four to six weeks until he's fully healed again."

"No lingering issues?" Jones asked.

"Probably not. Nothing serious, anyway. Maybe some numbness or weakness every now and then, but he should be able to make a full recovery."

Jones closed his eyes and sighed, pleased to hear the news. "Thank heavens for that." Recker went over to the counter to get a cup of coffee as Jones walked around him and sat down at the desk. "Certainly was a hairy situation we got involved in."

Recker took a sip of his coffee, not seeming too bothered or affected by the events. In fact, he seemed rather calm to Jones considering Haley was being tended to by a doctor at the moment. "Sure was."

"You don't seem very upset about what happened."

"What's to get upset about? It's the work we do, the risks we take. If it turned out differently, my mood would probably be dramatically different. But Chris will be fine. Malloy made it. The only people who turned up dead was the other guys. No use in getting all choked up over it."

"I think perhaps we should excuse ourselves from this arrangement we have with Vincent," Jones said. "At least over this issue he currently is involved in."

"Why?"

"Because there is no doubt this is becoming a turf war. Something we do not need to concern ourselves with. This person challenging Vincent appears to be very dangerous and I highly doubt will be going away soon. We must be cautious. And, if I might add, if it becomes known you're helping Vincent, and killing them, it will put you directly in their crosshairs. I'm not sure that is an additional enemy we need to make at the current time."

"Maybe. But we're already involved. We already gave Vincent our word."

Jones had thoughts about giving more of an argument against continuing to help, but then thought better of it. He knew he would only be wasting his breath. Recker would never go for pulling out of the deal at this point, especially after what happened to Haley. Instead of talking about the case, Jones diverted the discussion elsewhere.

"I suppose this will affect your vacation plans now."

"Huh?" Recker said.

"Well, if Chris is on the shelf for six weeks, then you'll have to postpone your plans with Mia."

"Oh great. I hadn't even thought of that. Now she's gonna think I'm getting cold feet about it or something."

"I'm sure if you tell her what happened she'll understand."

"We'll see."

"I think I might be getting closer to finding out who's responsible for all this," Jones said.

"You've got him?"

"Not yet. But I think by tomorrow I might have the answer."

"How?"

"Do you forget the parameters by which we were working with before you did this old west shootout?"

"Oh. Yeah, I guess I did a little," Recker said.

"Speaking of the shootout, I suppose this will garner headlines and front page news."

"Yeah, but it won't come back to us."

"You're sure about that, are you?" Jones asked.

"Don't see how it could. The only people involved are either dead, wounded, or hiding from the police, anyway. Who's talking?"

"You're positive there were no other witnesses?"

"I can't guarantee anything, but I don't see who else would be there."

"Let's hope you're right."

"Should we get down to work?" Recker asked, ready to get to the next chapter of this incident.

"I think you've been through enough in one night. Take the rest of the night off. We're not burning the midnight oil here. Mia's probably at home waiting for you by now, anyway."

Recker looked at the time and saw it was approaching one in the morning. "She was covering part of someone else's shift, so she got done at midnight."

"Haven't told her about any of this yet I take it?"

"No, not yet."

"Well, go home, get a good night's sleep," Jones said. "Don't worry about getting back here until ten-ish."

"Why so late?"

"Because if I am correct in thinking I can locate the mysterious person we're looking for then tomorrow might be another long day. Get the rest while you can."

"Gee, can't wait. Maybe we can end the day with another bang."

53

Once Recker got home, Mia was already curled up in bed sleeping. Recker joined her and went right to sleep. When she finally did get up, it was after eight, and she was a little surprised to see her boyfriend still sleeping next to her. It was very unusual for him to still be in bed at that time, though she didn't know exactly what time he came home. She got out of bed and made breakfast, finally waking him up at nine o'clock.

"Wake up, sleepy," she said, playfully tapping him on the shoulder.

Recker laid there for a few minutes, looking like he was having a hard time moving.

"Have a rough night?"

"Yeah."

Mia's playful expression slowly turned to one of concern as she pulled the covers off him and started inspecting his body for bruises, cuts, or bullet holes. She ran her hands up and down his body, thankfully not finding anything.

"Looking for something in particular?" Recker asked.

"Signs of injury."

"Can I ask why?"

"Well you tell me you had a rough night, you're still in bed at nine o'clock, and you seem to be having a tough time moving. All very obvious signs of serious injury," Mia answered.

"I'm fine. I'm not the one who needs worrying."

"What's that supposed to mean?"

"Chris got hit last night."

"Oh no. Is he OK?"

"Got it in the leg. Should be back to normal in about six weeks or so."

"Oh, thank God."

"May throw a wrench into your vacation plans," Recker said.

"I don't even care about that right now. What happened?"

Recker spent the next few minutes explaining what happened the night before in detail, not forgetting even the tiniest of details. After he was finished, Mia let out a rather loud sigh and leaned back against the headboard.

"What?" Recker asked, knowing something was bothering her.

"Just... I dunno, seems like you're getting put into tougher situations all the time."

"I've always been in tough situations. That's the job."

Mia shook her head. "I know. But it seems like you've gotten away from helping the people that need it most. Now you're getting mixed up in a turf war between criminals you always said you wouldn't get involved with. You're not helping anyone innocent."

Recker stared straight ahead for a minute, knowing she was technically correct, things had gotten more complicated over the years since they started their operation. Things weren't as clear cut as they were in the beginning.

"It's not as easy as that," Recker said. "Things happen, relationships evolve. To do some of the things we do, sometimes we need help from people who don't always have the best of intentions. And that comes at a cost. And that cost is, sometimes, I need to get involved in situations that, on the surface, I probably should be staying clear of. Some of the happy endings we've had wouldn't have been so happy without Vincent's help."

Mia sighed again, already knowing everything he said was true, though it didn't make her feel much better about it. "I know. I just hate it when you get involved with him. I guess it's because I know whenever he's in the picture it seems like the danger factor goes up like a thousand percent. Especially when someone's after him."

Recker couldn't dispute the fact things seemed to ratchet up a notch when Vincent was involved. And he wasn't going to try to give her a bunch of fluff they both knew wasn't true to make her feel better. So, he didn't even try. He took her in his arms and hugged her for a few minutes. They spoke no more and simply let their embrace do their talking for them.

It wasn't until ten-thirty Recker finally made it into the office. Before getting there, he called Haley to make sure he was doing all right. Jones was in one of his fierce typing moments as Recker walked in, not even paying attention to his presence.

"You're late," Jones said, not even breaking stride with his typing, or looking his partner's way.

"You said after ten. You didn't say how far after. Besides, I had to check in with Chris first."

Jones stopped typing instantly and swiveled his chair around. "I called him about two hours ago and everything seemed fine. Nothing has changed I hope?"

"Nope. Still fine. Should be leaving in a couple hours."

"Great news," Jones said. "He mentioned coming back to the office after he left, but I told him to go home and relax for a bit."

"He's not gonna want to sit home and vegetate for the next six weeks."

"I'm well aware. I'm not grounding him permanently. Just for today. Then if he's up to it tomorrow, he can come into the office."

Recker then sat down at a computer and started fiddling around. "So, what can you tell me about our mysterious friend? Narrowed it down yet?"

"I've got it narrowed down to two people I believe."

"OK," Recker said. "How did you arrive at that conclusion?"

"I followed the clues."

"But there are no clues."

"You would be incorrect with that assessment," Jones said. "Remember what we were thinking. Displaced crime bosses who have migrated in this direction."

"And how many have there been?"

"None."

Recker scrunched his eyebrows together as he lowered his head, scratching the back of it. He wasn't quite following yet. "Umm, maybe it's just me, but if there haven't been any, then how have you been able to trace someone here?"

"Relatives."

"Relatives? What's that supposed to mean?"

"While there haven't been any former bosses relocated to our area, there are two relatives of former bosses I have traced to the area."

"And they are?"

"I'd rather not say until I have pinpointed the exact person," Jones said.

"And when will that be?"

"Perhaps an hour or two."

"Want me to help?"

"No, I think I can manage on my own."

Recker threw his hands up. "So, what do you want me to do? Sit here and look pretty?"

"If you're capable of doing that."

Recker rolled his eyes but didn't say another word. As Jones went back to his work, Recker shuffled around the office, trying to keep busy. He eventually did what he normally did when he wasn't sure what else to do. He went to his gun cabinet and started cleaning his weapons. He was taking a little longer than he normally would have, finishing up in about two hours. The entire time, Recker was keeping an eye on Jones to see if he could tell when he was finished. After closing the cabinet, Recker got a drink before heading back over to the desk. He sat down next to Jones without saying anything, waiting for the professor to finish. As they were going on the third hour, Recker was starting to get impatient. He cleared his throat before talking, making sure he was loud enough for Jones to hear.

"I don't know if you know this, but we're on hour number three now," Recker said. "You're a little behind schedule."

"Better to be slow, late, and correct instead of fast, early, and wrong."

"So it is." Recker went back on the computer to keep himself busy. "But my patience is starting to wear thin."

"Patience is a virtue as they say."

"Yeah, but it's not one of mine."

Jones chuckled, though he still didn't break stride in his typing.

"How much longer?" Recker asked.

"About ten or twenty minutes."

Recker immediately looked at the time. "I'm gonna hold you to that."

"I have no doubts of that."

Only a minute later, Recker's phone rang.

"Saved by the bell," Jones said.

"It's Chris," Recker said, putting the phone next to his ear. "Yo, bud, what's up?"

671

"Hey, I'm good to go, so I was looking to leave in a few minutes."

"That's great."

"Yeah, but I don't have a way of getting out of here unless I hobble to a bus stop," Haley said.

"Oh, yeah, I forgot I took the car. Stay put and I'll be right there. Give me about twenty minutes."

As soon as Recker hung up, he started moving around, looking like he was about to go somewhere. Jones wasn't sure what was going on.

"Is there an issue?" Jones asked.

"What? Oh, no. Chris is ready to leave, and he's got no transport, so I'm gonna go pick him up."

"Excellent news. Just to be clear, no matter what he says, no matter how good he says he is, do not bring him back here. Take him to his apartment."

"Yes, sir. Guess that gives you some extra time and lets you off the hook too."

"Lucky me."

"I'll be back in an hour and I better get some answers by then," Recker said.

"I guess I should speed it up then."

Recker headed straight for Dr. Luke's underground offices, which weren't actually underground, but in a rather remote location. The front entrance to the facility was always closed, with bars on the windows and doors, along with blinds so no one could see inside. Anyone coming and going had to do so through the back entrance, which could only be opened from the inside. Once Recker got there, Haley was already standing outside, leaning up against the side of the building. Recker got out of the car to give his partner a hand.

"I hear you need a lift."

"Just rumors," Haley said, walking to the car with the help of crutches. Once they started driving away, Haley inquired as to their plans for the rest of the day. "So, where we heading?"

"We're heading to your apartment."

Haley sighed, not wanting to go home and rest. "I know David wants me to take the rest of the day off, but I'd rather get right back into things. I don't need to be set on the sidelines."

"It's not a punishment. You've had a rough night. He wants to make sure you don't push yourself before you're ready."

"I don't wanna sit around my apartment and stare out the window for a few weeks and do nothing."

"It won't be that long. If you're up for it, he'll probably let you back in the office tomorrow. Like I said, he doesn't want you to push it. Just relax, do what you can in the office, and do your rehab."

"I know one thing," Haley said. "I can guarantee it's not gonna take me six weeks to come back."

"Oh yeah?"

"Four at the most. A few weeks ago, I ordered one of those home gyms."

"Just don't overdo it."

After taking Haley to his apartment, Recker stayed with him for an hour or so, to make sure he was in a good frame of mind. Recker wouldn't have left him if he thought Haley was down in the dumps. Recker continued talking to him about coming back to work the next day as long as he was feeling up to it, making sure his head was still in the game. Once Recker left Haley's apartment, he immediately called Jones to let him know he was headed back to the office.

"How's Chris?" Jones asked.

"He'll be fine. Wants to come back now and get into it but I convinced him to take the day. Told him if he feels up to it tomorrow, I'll pick him up in the morning and bring him in."

"You're sure that's not too fast?"

"He wants to feel like he can still contribute and not be useless," Recker answered. "He'll be fine. I can tell you something else, he'll be back in four weeks, ready to go."

"As long as he's healthy enough."

"Speaking of ready to go, are you?"

"Am I what?"

"Ready to go. You know, with the thing you were working on you promised me would be ready by now."

"Oh, that," Jones said.

"Yeah, that." Recker got the feeling he was about to be stalled again.

"Well..."

"Jones... you told me it'd be ready."

"And it is."

"It is?"

"Yes, it is."

"Well?" Recker asked, anxious to hear the person's name.

"I think it would be better if I told you when you get back."

"You're really gonna do that to me?"

"Yes."

"Gonna keep me in suspense the entire way over there, huh?"

"If you want, I can tease you even more with it," Jones replied.

"How's that?"

"It's probably not anyone you would think of."

54

Recker almost flew into the office once he got there. He immediately took a seat next to Jones and stared at him until he was acknowledged, not saying a word. Jones slowly turned his head, a little uneasy with the icy stare being thrown his way. He turned back to his computer and tried to finish what he was working on but couldn't shake Recker's eyes burning a hole through him. Jones looked at him out of the corner of his eye, trying not to turn his head in his partner's direction.

"Yes?" Jones asked. "Something on your mind?"

"We really gonna do this again?"

Jones finally turned his head completely toward him. "Oh. The, uh, the mysterious person."

Recker gave half a smile. "Yeah. That one."

Jones picked up a file folder on the desk and handed it over to him. "Oh. Well it's all right there."

Recker looked at him like he thought he was being kidded again. "In here?"

"Promise, it's all there."

Recker still wasn't sure he was being told the truth but eagerly opened the folder and started devouring its contents. Almost immediately, his eyes bulged out, not believing what he was seeing. He brought his head up and looked at Jones, who simply nodded.

"That's correct," Jones said.

"It's a woman?"

Jones knew Recker would be a little shocked at the revelation, even though they'd run into women criminals before. "Yes. Women do commit crimes you know."

"Yes, I know, but..."

"You weren't expecting one in this instance?"

Recker shook his head. "No, not at all."

Recker continued reading the file, which was a comprehensive bio Jones had compiled on the woman. He was still a little stunned, though he knew he shouldn't have been. He'd certainly been around long enough to expect the unexpected.

"You're sure it's her?" Recker asked.

"There is no doubt. I have traced her to here. She's definitely in the city."

"You know where she is?"

"Surprisingly... yes," Jones answered. "If she's trying to conceal her current whereabouts, she's doing it badly. In saying that, my suspicion is she's not trying."

"Where is she?"

"Currently staying in a very luxurious hotel, as she has been doing for the last several weeks."

Recker took his eyes off the folder again to look at Jones. "A hotel?"

"Again, not what you were expecting?"

"No." Recker sighed, not understanding what was happening here. He didn't get why this woman would be trying to conceal her identity in trying to knock off Vincent's crew, but then stay out in the open in a hotel, which was not the actions of someone trying to hide.

Jones studied Recker's face as he read the material in the folder. He could tell Recker seemed to be having trouble digesting some of it. "What is it in particular that's giving you trouble?"

"I don't know. Nothing I guess."

"Stefania Nowak, thirty-six-years old, wife of Paul Nowak, who is now deceased as of one year ago," Jones said. "If you've gotten that far, she's made calls to Boston, New York, and Baltimore in the past six months. And who do we know from those places?"

"And the hits on Vincent's crew happens to coincide with her arrival," Recker said. "I dunno, maybe I'm just having a hard time seeing her as the head person in this. Says here her husband was in charge of an organization in Boston. With his death, she faded into the background. If this is what she wanted, why not continue with what her husband started?"

"You're assuming she, in fact, had that chance. And, according to my research, she did not. Immediately after Paul Nowak's death, the leadership changed hands to one of his captains, and that is why she faded into the background. Not any grand design by her, but because she was forced to."

"She mustn't have been that involved with the business if that's the case. Otherwise they would have kept her on in some capacity."

"Be that as it may, she may have had more of an influence in her husband's organization than anyone knew. Either she was secretly involved in the day-to-day operations, or she was taking a lot of notes, studying her husband's business in anticipation of one day taking over."

"I still don't get it, though. If that's the case, and that's her ambition, why not stay and fight for control over the business your husband started?" Recker asked.

"Perhaps she was more interested in starting something from

the ground floor. Something she could put her own stamp on. Or maybe she felt like she was continuing his legacy instead of starting her own. It's impossible, at this point, to know her true motivations. Whatever they are, though, I think it's safe to say she does have some skills at this. To pull off the hit on Vincent's men, then the attempted hit last night, does require some abilities."

"So, now the question becomes; what do we do about it?"

Jones tilted his head, a little perplexed, not sure there even was a question. "To my knowledge, our little part in this is over. Complete. We were tasked with finding out who this was. We have done that."

"So, you're saying just hand everything over to Vincent and take a step back and let whatever happens happen?" Recker asked.

"What other option is there?"

"We become proactive in this and drive her out of the city before she gets a stronghold in it." Jones made a face, obvious to Recker he didn't agree with the proposition. "You don't agree?"

"If we're talking honestly, then no, I don't."

"Our mission here is to take on the bad guys."

"No, our mission here is to help the innocent," Jones replied. "Saving one bad guy from another does not qualify."

"But if we let another criminal element into this city, more innocent people will get hurt. It's inevitable."

"Are you sure you're worried about that or is it you don't want to see Vincent replaced?"

Recker glared at him, not really liking the question, no matter how valid it was. He thought for a minute before replying. "Even if I were to admit that... it's not a case of saving him, per se. It's more the fact that in the world we live in, there's bad people in it. You're never going to have a crime-free city or society. There's going to be people who try to capitalize on the hurting of others. That's just the way it is."

"I agree with that."

"So, in admitting there will always be a criminal element, I'd rather try to keep the one that most aligns with our own interests."

"But how do you know Ms. Nowak would not?" Jones asked.

"I don't. But it's like they always say, dance with the girl that brought you. The grass ain't always greener on the other side."

"They also say don't cut off your nose to spite your face."

"How's that apply here?"

"I don't know. I figured if you could throw out a saying so could I."

"Anyway, we know we can coexist with Vincent. There's a healthy respect between us. He's largely stayed out of our way. We know we can trust him to a certain degree. He mostly stays to his own dealings and doesn't bother with business that involves us. There's no guarantee that same deal will apply to Nowak."

"Again, you're assuming a lot of things about someone we don't know," Jones said.

"Vincent also has a lot of contacts in this city, some of which have helped us. We've been able to lean on that knowledge at times. If Nowak takes over, that eliminates a source of information to us. She's not gonna have that same level of contacts and sources he does."

"But you're also assuming she and her organization will survive against Vincent. If we turn the information over to him, let him deal with it. My instincts tell me if the two factions come to battle, he will, in fact, come out on top. All without us having to get involved in it further or lift a finger in either direction."

"Guess we're in a tie here," Recker said. "Maybe we should duel it out in a cage fight or something."

"Don't be ridiculous. We'll simply talk it out like we always do until we come to a satisfactory conclusion."

"Satisfactory for who?"

"For both of us."

"There's a third member of this team now, you know."

"Of course there is," Jones said. "Don't talk to me like I'm slighting him. He's simply not here right now."

"There's one way to solve this if you're up for it."

"I'm not donning boxing gloves."

Recker laughed. "No, something much easier than that."

"I'm listening."

"Let's put it up to a three-person vote. Those in favor of staying involved and those in favor of handing it off to Vincent and stepping aside."

Jones hesitated for a second, thinking whether he was OK with however the vote turned out. He concluded he was. "Fine. If you are really on board with it."

"I am."

"No matter which way it goes?"

Recker shrugged. "No matter which way it falls, I'll hop on board."

"And we're not to tell him which way our votes fall."

"Agreed. Besides, it'll make him feel better, like he's still part of things."

Recker immediately got Haley on the line, who picked up after only one ring. Recker put the phone on speaker so Jones could hear.

"Need me back already, huh?" Haley joked.

"Well, kinda, we do have a question for you."

"OK, shoot."

"Interesting way of putting things considering your current predicament," Recker said.

"So, what's the question?"

"Well, we've found out who our mysterious player is and you're going to be the deciding factor in what we do with that information."

"How's that?" Haley asked.

"Not telling you who's voting which way, but one of us wants to stay involved in the situation to get rid of the new threat, and one of us wants to hand the information over to Vincent and let him deal with it, then walk away."

"So, whichever way I swing, one of you is gonna be mad at me, is that it?"

"Nope. David and I both agreed to let you be the swing vote. Whichever way you decide will be fine for both of us. There'll be no hard feelings or anything either way."

"A lot of pressure here."

"Don't look at it like that," Recker said. "We're all friends, nobody's gonna be mad, anything like that. We're all a team here and you get a vote in what we do since we're split."

"Sounds good."

"You wanna know the details of who this person is?"

"No."

"You don't?"

"No. Doesn't really make a difference as far as I'm concerned," Haley answered.

Though Recker didn't know for sure, he believed he was about to be disappointed with his other partner's answer. From the sounds of it, he thought Haley was about to side with Jones.

"You're sure nobody's gonna be mad at me for my answer?" Haley asked again.

"We're all friends here, Chris," Recker replied. "We're a team here and we're gonna stay that way. This isn't big enough to change any of that."

"OK. Well then my vote is to hand the information over to Vincent and step away from it."

Recker looked over at Jones, who had a slight grin on his face, happy with how the vote turned out.

"Sorry for whoever I voted against, though I have a pretty good idea who's who," Haley said.

"Out of curiosity, who do you think was which?" Jones asked.

"I'd say David voted to step away and Mike voted to keep after it. Am I right?"

"Right on the button."

"You know, I'm not sure I like how well everyone knows me," Recker said, choosing to make a joke instead of getting mad he didn't get his way.

After a few more minutes of conversation about Haley's health, Recker let him get back to resting. He immediately looked back at Jones, who seemed to be very pleased at the turn of events.

"You look pretty satisfied," Recker said.

"I must admit I am."

"You knew all along he was gonna side with you, didn't you?"

Jones put a couple fingers in the air. "Scout's honor, I had no idea."

"Scout's honor, huh?" Recker said with a laugh. "I think you did. That's why you went along with it so easily. Going to him for the tiebreaker."

Jones shook his head, still admitting to nothing. "Honestly, I had no idea. I think by now, just like I do with you, I have a pretty good idea of how Chris' mind works. He's much more level headed in his thinking than you are. No offense."

Recker smiled. "None taken."

"While he doesn't take things to the extreme that I do, he still looks at things more analytically than you do. He sees more of the big picture. My only concern was that with getting shot last night, his emotions would cloud his judgment and he would want to get back into things and hope to get some revenge."

"You know I would."

"Yes, I know. Like I said, he does not get as emotionally involved and looks at things with a more level head."

"Guess he's been everything you hoped he would be, huh?" Recker said.

"And more. I think it's fair to say he's worked out even better than we could have hoped. But in getting back to our situation, how are we going to handle it?"

Recker shrugged, thinking it was already resolved. "I thought we just voted on it."

"We did. And I guess my real question isn't how, but when?"

"Well, guess there's no time like the present. Might as well do it now. How much should I give him?"

"Give it all to him," Jones answered. "We have no more need of it or any reason to conceal any of it for our own purposes. He should be happy with it."

"I don't think happy is quite a strong enough word for how he'll feel about getting this. It'll be more like the fourth of July with fireworks going off."

"I'm sure it will be once he actually comes face-to-face with Ms. Nowak."

55

R ecker called Vincent and let him know they had the
name of who they believed was behind everything.
Though Vincent pushed to learn the identity of the
person right away, Recker was able to convince him to wait a day,
until the following morning. They agreed to meet at their usual
place, where Recker could turn over the contents of the folder
they'd compiled on Nowak. Recker didn't want to give Vincent a
name and let him go off half-cocked without having all the information at his fingertips. He wanted to deliver it in person, so
Vincent knew everything he was up against.

When Recker arrived at the diner, he saw the usual guard was
standing by the entrance, so he knew Vincent was already there.
As Recker walked up to the door, the guard gave him a head nod.

"Ever miss the old days when we used to argue back and forth
about how many weapons I had?" Recker asked.

The guard laughed. "Not really."

The two shot the breeze for a minute before he went inside.
For the first time, there was nobody there to greet him. With
Malloy currently out of the picture, it was a weird feeling for

Recker to not see him there. He looked down to the usual table and saw Vincent sitting there. Recker walked down to it and hopped in the booth across from him.

"A little weird not seeing Malloy there," Recker said.

"Not so easy for me either."

"How's he doing by the way?"

"He's going to pull through," Vincent said. "Dr. Luke's keeping him another couple of days, then he'll be released."

"Good to hear. Why take him there, by the way? Why not a regular hospital?"

"I'm sure you of all people should understand the answer to that. People who go to medical facilities with gunshot wounds invariably invite questions. Questions I don't want answered. And law enforcement personnel I may not want to deal with. It's simpler this way. Wouldn't you say?"

"Oh, yeah, I agree. I wanted to see if your reasoning would be any different than mine."

"You said you had something for me?"

Recker plopped the file folder down and slid it across the table. "Should be everything you're looking for."

A pleased look came across Vincent's face, hoping he was finally about to learn the truth about who was coming after him. He opened the folder and eagerly started reading. It wasn't long before he perked his head back up and looked at Recker, surprised at the name.

"Stefania Nowak?"

Recker nodded. "Surprised to us too."

"Without trying to sound disbelieving, how accurate do you believe this information to be?"

"We put it at about ninety-nine percent," Recker answered.

"That's about as near a guarantee as you can get."

"It's her. Well, you'll see as you keep reading and get to the details. Ever had business with her or her husband before? Something that went sideways?"

Vincent shook his head. He periodically looked up at Recker to talk as he continued reading, soaking it all in. "No. I knew of her husband though, Paul Nowak. He was killed about a year ago."

"Why would she be targeting you? Ever take business away from them somehow?"

Vincent tossed one of his hands in the air, unsure about any past dealings. "Not to my knowledge. It's sometimes difficult to gauge how your actions will affect others. But, considering she's from a different area, I don't think our paths would have crossed very often."

"Yeah, we really couldn't find any kind of connection either. Maybe there isn't one. Could be she's just targeting you because this is a big city and you're the only major player left in it. She might think there's room for one more. Or she could think it's an easier path since there's only you, instead of going to another city where she might have to deal with multiple people."

Vincent didn't reply for a couple minutes as he stared at the information at his fingertips. His eyes couldn't read fast enough for his liking as he wanted to devour everything in an instant.

"So, what do you think you're gonna do?" Recker asked, even though he knew it was unlikely Vincent would reveal any of his plans to him.

"Tough to say right now. These things require a great deal of thought and planning. As you remember, I'm not an impetuous man. I won't rush into something that won't be to my advantage."

"Maybe she's not looking to take you out. Maybe she just wants a little piece for herself."

"There's only one problem with that," Vincent said.

"What's that?"

"As you quite honestly told me several years ago, no one is satisfied with having a little piece. Everyone eventually wants more. And if it's not dealt with appropriately at the beginning, then it becomes a bigger issue."

"So, you don't think you could possibly coexist?"

"Why would I want to coexist?" Vincent asked. "I have prevailed over the leaders of three other factions that loomed over this city for several years. Why would I want to go back in time and have to give up what I was working towards for so long?"

Recker nodded, understanding his concerns and reasons. "Makes sense. Just figured I'd ask."

"Now in saying that, it doesn't mean I will hit her immediately. It doesn't mean I will hit her at all. Perhaps I'll set up a meeting first and discuss her intentions with her. Maybe we're all worrying about nothing."

"Sounds like a good idea."

"With Jimmy out of commission for a while, maybe you could even join me for this meeting."

Recker smiled, having a feeling something like that was coming. "Yeah, I don't think that'd be possible."

"David won't allow it, huh?" Vincent said with a smile.

"Our deal was to find out who was behind this and we've done that. Our arrangement wasn't to get involved in the fight."

"Just figured I'd ask. Speaking of partners, it was nice to finally see the new one of yours. What was his name? Chris?"

Recker nodded. "Haley."

"Old friend of yours?"

"Nope. Never met him before he came here."

"He must be very highly regarded then for him to join your operation."

"He is. He's every bit as good as I am."

Vincent grinned, thinking of some unlikely possibilities regarding the new man. Recker could tell by his smile he had some thoughts in his mind.

"He's not gonna join you either," Recker said.

"Well, it was just a thought."

~

Stefania Nowak was in her luxurious hotel room, conducting business and making plans for her upstart organization. She knew it was likely it would eventually be discovered she was the brains behind what was happening thus far. She also knew it was likely someone would find out where she was staying. Though she was checked in under a false name, she was aware that would only provide cover for so long. In anticipation of someone coming, Nowak always had a couple of guards stationed outside the door. Nobody got in unless they were expected. She was in the middle of deciding their next route in her little crusade against Vincent. Knowing she had already bested him twice, getting one over on him both times, she knew it would only get harder from there to continue doing that. She knew by Vincent's reputation he would be more cautious from that point on.

Nowak's planning with a couple of her underlings was interrupted by a small commotion outside. It sounded like her guards were raising their voices. It could only mean they had an unexpected visitor. She started going to the door to see what was happening, but was stopped by Milton and Teasley, who didn't want her to expose herself in case something violent went down.

"We'll check it out," Milton said.

Nowak stayed in the background as Milton and Teasley went out the door. There was a man trying to approach the room, who was now face-planted on the ground, courtesy of the guards.

"What are you doing here?" Milton asked.

"Like I was trying to tell these thugs, I got a message for your boss."

"Which is who?" Teasley asked, not wanting to give away her name in case it was a trick.

"Stefania Nowak."

Milton nodded toward the two guards, one of whom had his knee on the back of the man's head. They got the man to his feet and patted him down to check for weapons.

"He's clean," a guard said.

The man, who was dressed in a suit, readjusted his clothes as he gave a nasty look to the guards who had tackled him.

"So, what are you doing here?" Milton asked.

"Like I said, I got a message for your boss."

"What is it?"

"I was told to give it to her."

"Nothing gets to her until it goes through me first."

The man shrugged, being told in advance it was likely to go down this exact way. The man then reached inside his suit jacket and removed a note, handing it over to Milton. As Milton went to grab it, the man pulled it back.

"I was told this was only to be read by Ms. Nowak."

Milton looked at Teasley, then back at the man, skeptical of what was happening. "This note isn't getting to her unless I know who it's from."

The man smiled. "It's from Vincent. He sends his regards."

Milton's face took a more concerned tone to it. "Agreed," he finally said.

The man then handed the note over again, this time letting Milton take it from him. "Be seein' ya soon." The man put his hands up to the top of his head as if he was tipping his hat, even though he wasn't wearing one, then turned around and started leaving. Milton and company stayed there for a minute and watched the man as he got on the elevator.

"A little strange," Teasley said.

"Strange ain't the word for it," Milton replied. "Well, might as well let her see whatever this is."

"Can't be good."

"We'll see."

The guards retook their stations by the door as Milton and Teasley went inside. They saw Nowak coming out her bedroom, not seemingly concerned about what was happening outside. When she saw the looks on their faces though, she had a feeling something was up.

"What was all that about?" Nowak asked.

Milton walked over to her and handed her the note. "Looks like business is about to pick up faster than we expected."

A great deal of concern overtook Nowak's face as she looked at Milton and took the note from him. "What's this?"

Milton didn't respond except for a head shake and a shrug. Nowak eagerly unfolded the paper and her eyes were immediately drawn to who the note was from rather than its contents. Once she saw it was from Vincent, the hairs on her arms stood out of nervousness as she wondered what he wanted, alarmed he already knew where she was.

Ms. Nowak,

I believe it is time for us to meet. We have a great many things to discuss. As soon as you are ready, I am at your service. At first, I thought it would be wise to have an introductory meeting at a neutral site, but then I thought, it would be better if I just came to you. Therefore, you may simply walk down to the lobby. I am waiting in the hotel restaurant.

Regards,

Vincent

Nowak's eyes widened, and, for the first time since she arrived in Philadelphia, looked nervous. This was completely unexpected and out of the blue.

"Are you OK?" Milton asked, noticing his boss' expression.

Nowak handed him the note. "He's here."

Milton read the note, looking as nervous as his boss. "What do you think he wants?"

"I don't know. It seems unlikely he would choose here as a place to hit us if that's what he had in mind. If that were the case, I'm sure he'd pick a neutral place."

"What would he have to talk about?"

"Maybe he's just here to give you a warning or threaten you," Teasley said.

"Could be," Nowak said.

"You know, you don't have to go down there," Milton said. "You're under no obligation to meet him right now. We can wait until you're ready, under your terms. This is too soon. We can sneak you out the back."

"He's sure to have men in the lobby as well as in the back. Don't believe for a second he hasn't planned for every possible reaction on our part."

"We can wait awhile. Let me call the rest of the boys and have them come over."

"And turn this hotel into a bloodbath? That doesn't help us a bit if we're all led away in handcuffs."

"So, what's the play?"

"We'll go down and meet him," Nowak answered.

"You sure? What if he tries something down there? He could have us outnumbered. Or he could try to surprise us with something."

"Maybe. But, like I said, I don't think this would be the ideal time for him to do that. If that was his goal, I doubt he'd give us the courtesy of announcing his visit first. He could have just stormed this room if that was his intent, don't you think?"

"Yeah, I guess so."

"Let's think positively for a moment," Nowak said. "Maybe he's terrified of what we're doing and wants to join forces."

"I think that's wishful thinking."

56

W ithin five minutes, Nowak was ready to meet her opponent. But she wasn't going alone. Milton and Teasley would accompany her, at least into the restaurant, until she saw what the setup was. Once they were all ready, they stepped out of the room into the hallway. Before leaving, she had last-minute instructions for the guards at the door, in case someone tried to sneak into the room while she was gone.

"We'll be in the restaurant," Nowak said. "Nobody is allowed to be up here."

"Right."

Nowak, along with her assistants, went to the elevator and down to the first floor. They slowly walked through the lobby, carefully looking at their surroundings to see if they thought any of Vincent's men were staked out there. They couldn't be sure, though. It was a busy night and there seemed to be a lot of people coming and going. A few people looked like they might have been lookouts, but nothing they could definitely determine.

Other than the uncertainty of the meeting, Nowak was relatively sure it would be a peaceful gathering. Going on that assumption, taking her subordinate's suggestion of leaving was not a preferable option. She knew Vincent would have people watching in back of the building. Because that's what she would do if the roles were reversed. The best option they had was listening to what he had to say.

When they finally got to the hotel restaurant, Nowak stopped in the entrance area and looked around for her host. The restaurant was packed with customers, but she found him without too much trouble. She then made a beeline for the table, her second-in-commands closely following her along the way. Vincent did have people watching in the lobby and they had already given him the heads-up Nowak was on the way, so he was aware she was coming. He kept his eyes focused on her as she approached the table.

"May I sit?" Nowak asked, almost a glow on her face as if she was meeting a date.

"Please do," Vincent replied with a smile, also sounding pleasantly happy with her presence. Based on their initial encounter, one would never know they were enemies.

After helping their boss with her seat, Milton and Teasley began to sit down. Before they reached their seats though, Vincent made sure to let them know they weren't welcome.

"This is a private meeting," Vincent told them. "There are other tables available."

They didn't really like it and looked to Nowak for guidance, who nodded at them, so they knew it was OK to leave. Once they were out of listening range, Vincent spoke.

"Thank you for meeting me on such short notice."

"I didn't think I really had much choice considering you probably have the building surrounded with your people," Nowak said.

Vincent knew that was an accurate statement, but didn't want to throw it in her face that he had the upper hand. "Well, you still could have chosen an alternate path than this one." He pointed at the glass in front of her. "I took the liberty of ordering a glass of wine for us. I hope it's an acceptable choice."

Nowak smiled, a little surprised at how gracious her host was being. She took a sip of the wine. "Not too bad."

"I'm sure I took you a little off-guard with me coming here."

"Just a little. I did not anticipate being found out so quickly. You must have good sources."

"You cannot get to the top and stay there without having good intelligence. If you're here much longer, you'll find out mine is second to none."

"I'll remember that."

"Before we get down to any business discussion, I'd like to pay my respects on the loss of your husband last year. I was sorry to hear that."

"Thank you."

"Now that's out of the way, I'd like to get down to why you're here in this city and why you've attacked me specifically."

"You certainly don't beat around the bush, do you?" Nowak asked. "Right to the point."

"It depends on the circumstances."

"As for why I'm here, it's strictly business. You're the only game in town and I believe there is a financial opportunity here."

"And it's as simple as that?" Vincent asked.

"Yes, it is."

"Then why have you attacked my men on two different occasions lately?"

"Well, if you're going to move into a new city, what better way to establish yourself than by taking on the biggest and the baddest to let everyone know who you are?"

"And you think you can just come in here, try to take me on, and bully me, and think there won't be repercussions? That I'll just take it lying down and let you operate?"

"Well I don't see any guns pointed at me," Nowak said with a smile, feeling very sure of herself.

"I think you're playing a very dangerous game here. One which you may not understand the full value of what you're up against."

"That's very disappointing."

"What is?"

"That you think of me as an ordinary woman who's in over her head," Nowak answered. "That I'm someone who couldn't possibly understand the inner workings of business. You see, I was very much involved with my husband's dealings. I watched, I learned, I listened, I attended meetings, I asked questions... I wasn't the trophy wife who was only there to brighten up the room."

"My intention was not to downgrade your capabilities, but to emphasize I am not a man to play games with."

"Oh, I'm fully aware of your reputation, Vincent. Everyone on the east coast knows who you are and recognizes your achievements. Especially how you've managed to rid this city of your enemies in the last few years. Very impressive."

"But not impressive enough to scare you away."

"Not when there's an opportunity such as this one," Nowak said.

"And you think you'll fare differently than my past enemies?"

"Well, I think I might if that's the route I chose to go. But I don't. We can work equally with one another, you know."

"You mean a partnership?" Vincent asked.

"No, nothing that extreme. Something where we acknowledge each other and peacefully coexist."

Vincent put his hand over his face and rubbed his chin as he looked at her. "Perhaps you could tell me why I'd be willing to hand over part of what I've worked so hard to achieve?"

"Because I've already shown you what I'm capable of. If it's a war you want, you can have it."

"It seems to me you've already made the first volley in that direction," Vincent said.

"Oh, come now, that was just merely me announcing my arrival," she said, flashing an innocent smile at him. "There was no harm meant to you behind it. I figured you could lose a few insignificant men at some low-level business dealings. I mean, how much could that cost you?"

Vincent had moved his hand up to his lips as his finger moved back and forth across them. He intently listened and hung on every word his guest was saying. And with each passing sentence that came out of her mouth, the more he found himself disliking her. Nowak could tell Vincent seemed to be having problems with her story and sought to help him understand.

"Listen, I don't want to have a war with you," Nowak said. "I believe it's unnecessary and wouldn't be good for either of us. My intention was not to shoot the opening salvo in a conflict with you. My only intention for this whole charade was to prove to you I am your equal."

"Then why not set up some type of meeting with me and explain your intentions?"

Nowak laughed, thinking how ridiculous it sounded. "Oh, please. Like you would have even given me the time of day if I walked into your office and we had this conversation. You would have waved me off, thinking I couldn't possibly do some of the things I say I can."

"Perhaps."

"There is enough room in this city for the two of us. For both of us to make money. That is the end goal, is it not?"

"Money is only a small part of it," Vincent answered.

"How about you tell me what you're into and I'll make sure I stay out of it? I'll only operate in things that you're not."

"Very gracious of you."

"Like I said, there's enough here for the both of us to work with; we don't have to be enemies."

"You and I both know the only way to truly operate in cities like this is to have power. And I have it. Drugs, guns, blackmail, laundering, counterfeiting, extortion, you name it; it all runs through me."

Nowak smiled, thinking he still didn't see the big picture. "There are other things to get involved in, you know."

"Even if there were, there's only so long you can operate without wanting a bigger slice of the pie. Eventually, you want more. It's human nature. I once operated in this city with two others, not because of choice, but because that's what I came into. Then there were two. Then there was one. No one is satisfied in sharing with others."

"I get the feeling you're not interested in my proposal."

"Nothing personal," Vincent said. "You seem like a very charming woman. And in another city, I'd wish you much success."

"But not this one?"

To diffuse the tension, Vincent sat for a moment, thinking of other options at their disposal. "I'll tell you what I can do for you. I'll overlook the two occasions you threw down on me."

"Very generous of you," Nowak said.

"You pack up and move to another city, start up your operations elsewhere, and I'll even give you a hand. Give you a loan, with a nice interest rate on my end, loan you men, information, resources, whatever you need to successfully get off the ground."

"Well, that is a kind offer. I'm kind of partial to mine though."

"You see, that's where you have to learn your place in the pecking order. I'm on top here. And I'm not about to let someone come in here and blast away at me then dictate terms to me with the hopes I'll just lie down and take it."

"So, my plan is being rejected?" Nowak asked, still a pleasant look on her face, not really expecting him to throw in with her.

"Rejected, torn up, and stomped on. But I do hope you'll take my offer under consideration. And because I'm a generous man, I'll give you three days to accept my terms."

"And if I choose to stay?"

"Then I'll make you wish you hadn't."

"Is that a threat?"

"Let's just call it a very stern warning," Vincent replied. He then looked at the time and excused himself. "I'm sorry for leaving so quickly, but I have other matters to attend to."

"I understand. So, how will I get in touch with you in the next few days if I decide to accept your offer?"

"Just put the word out on the street like you did your last trick. I'll hear it."

"And if you don't hear from me?"

"Then I would suggest you start traveling with more than two guards."

Vincent then stood and walked away from the table. As he walked away, about ten other men placed at various spots throughout the room also stood and soon joined him. Nowak watched as he exited the room, followed by his group of men. Milton and Teasley then joined her table.

"How'd it go?" Milton asked.

"About how we expected," Nowak answered.

"What'd he have to say?"

"Gave us a deadline of three days to get out of here. He's even willing to help us set up in another city."

"Kind of him," Teasley said.

"More than generous."

"Are we taking it?" Milton asked.

"Of course not. We're staying here. Mr. Vincent will just have to deal with it."

"Should I get Gabe to bring up the rest of the men?"

"Yes," Nowak said. "We will be needing them in short order."

"What about that other thing?"

"What other thing?"

"You know, that other guy you were talking about. That Silencer guy."

"Oh yes. He's got a big reputation around here and I wanna meet with him."

"How are we supposed to find him?" Milton asked.

"How do you find anybody? Put the word out. Talk to the right people. Do that and we'll find him."

"And what if he doesn't want to meet?"

"Then you make him want to," Nowak answered.

"Got it."

"He's a man that could help us in this upcoming war."

"And what makes you think he'll be willing to help us?"

"Money. That's what makes the world go round. Give him enough money and I'm sure he'll be willing to help us do anything."

57

Recker arrived at the office, finding both Jones and Haley banging away at the keyboard. After grabbing some coffee, he joined them at the desk.

"What's the good word, people?" Recker asked. "Find our next case yet?"

"We are working on it," Jones replied.

"How long?"

"Oh, a day or so probably. Enjoy the break."

"Who said I wasn't?"

"We know how you get when you have too much time between things," Jones said. "You start to go stir-crazy."

"How you feeling, Chris?"

"Hanging in there," Haley answered. "Better than yesterday. Oh, David told me about your vacation plans. Sorry about ruining them for you."

Recker gave him a pat on the back. "Don't worry about it."

"Is Mia mad?"

"Nah. She's more concerned that you're OK. Besides, I told her we weren't canceling plans, just pushing them back two or three weeks. She's good with that. As long as I'm not canceling them permanently. Then we might have an issue."

"Have you heard anything regarding the Vincent, Ms. Nowak issue?" Jones asked.

"I heard they had a meeting at her hotel in the restaurant two nights ago."

"Any idea how that went or what was discussed?"

"Haven't a clue. Somebody told somebody, who told Tyrell, who then told me."

"Interesting development. That's something I wasn't predicting would happen. A meeting between the two."

"What'd you think would happen?" Recker asked. "That Vincent would just go in there blasting away?"

"As a matter of fact... yes."

"You know as well as I do that's not how he operates. He waits for the right opportunity."

"Nothing like surprising your opponent when they are least expecting it," Jones said.

"Too public. Vincent will wait for the perfect time to strike. And he'll do it with a vengeance."

"Well, I hope nobody innocent gets caught up in the conflict between the two of them."

"Guess we'll see how it all shakes out."

The three of them continued working on some preliminary information on upcoming cases for a few hours until Recker's phone broke the silence and their concentration. It was Tyrell again.

"What's up?" Recker asked. "Got more on that meeting the other night?"

"Uh, no, not quite. Got something just as interesting though. Maybe even more."

"More? Well that's quite a lead-in."

"Yeah, I figured you would think so."

"So, what's up?"

"Got word on the street somebody's looking to talk to you," Tyrell said.

"Somebody's always looking to talk to me."

"Yeah, not new female crime bosses though."

"Nowak?"

"Yes, sir."

"She wants to talk to me?" Recker asked.

"That's the word."

"Who says?"

"Got it from the same source who told me about that abandoned building thing the other night."

"So, it's pretty solid."

"I'd say so."

"Any idea what it's about?" Recker asked.

"Don't know. But what does anyone want to talk to you about? Help. They all recognize who you are and your place here, and they all want you on their side of things. Just the way it works."

"So, she wants to recruit me against Vincent?"

"That'd be my guess. You want me to get word back to her somehow?"

"No, I don't think that's necessary."

"What're you gonna do?" Tyrell asked.

"Maybe I'll pay her a surprise visit."

Tyrell laughed. "How did I know you were gonna say something like that? You would."

"No use in changing how I operate, right?"

"Yeah, if you say so."

"Got anything else for me?" Recker asked.

"You need more?"

"I'm always looking for more."

"Yeah, well, you're gonna have to look on another day."

After Recker finished his conversation with Tyrell, he put the phone back in his pocket. Though he didn't immediately look at his partners, he could almost feel the heat of their eyes staring at him. He slowly turned his head and saw both Jones and Haley with their eyes glued on him.

"Something I can do for you two?" Recker said.

"For starters, you can tell me why you feel the urgent need to meet with Stefania Nowak," Jones replied.

"Who said I was doing that?"

"You did."

"I did?"

"You said her name, then you said something about her wanting to meet with you."

"Oh."

"Doesn't take a genius to figure it out," Jones said.

"Tyrell said she's looking to talk to me."

"Why?" Haley asked.

"He thinks she's probably looking to recruit me somehow in her war against Vincent," Recker answered.

"Sounds about right."

"I thought we came to an agreement the other day about us staying out of this thing," Jones said.

"We are. I'm not getting involved."

"Well if you're planning on meeting with her, then I would say that is getting involved. Tell me why you're seriously considering this? What purpose does it serve?"

"There's a new player in town, possibly a major and dangerous one, and I think it would behoove us in our business to see what she's all about," Recker said.

Jones put his elbow on the table, then dropped his head into his hand and shook his head, knowing Recker was going to meet with the woman anyway, no matter how many objections he had.

"Why do I even bother?" Jones said to himself.

"What's that?" Recker asked.

"Oh, nothing. Can I ask another question even though I realize it will probably fall on deaf ears?"

"Never stopped you before."

"What happens if she is looking to take you out for whatever reason?"

"Why would she do that?"

"I don't know. Maybe because she's heard you help Vincent from time to time," Jones said. "Or maybe because she knows you were at that building the other night and is angry you got in her way and disrupted her plans. Could be any number of reasons."

"All valid reasons not to go."

"But you will anyway."

"Curiosity usually gets the better of me," Recker said.

"I'm painfully aware."

Recker then grabbed his gun and held it in the air. "Don't worry, I won't go in empty-handed. I'll be ready if something goes down."

"You don't think they're actually going to let you meet her armed, do you? They will surely pat you down first."

"Surely."

"Well then?"

"I'm not giving up my weapons."

"Oh, that should go down well," Jones said.

"We'll see."

Recker then looked at Haley. "Feel like getting out of the office for a bit?"

"What'd you have in mind?" Haley replied.

Recker grinned. "I got a little something."

Upon hearing that, Jones moved his hand over his eyes, really not liking where this was heading. "You're not seriously contemplating taking him back out into the field already, are you? I mean, he can't move quickly enough if something happens."

704

"For what I have in mind, moving won't be necessary. He'll be safe and stationary the entire time."

"Why do you do this to me?" Jones asked.

"Do what?"

Jones started patting his pockets as if he was looking for something. "Give me heartburn, headaches, high blood pressure." After a minute, he found some aspirin.

"Relax. It'll work out."

Recker went over to his gun cabinet and opened it, looking for a specific weapon. He pulled out a rifle with a laser scope on it. He then walked over to Haley and handed it to him.

"You'll need this," Recker said.

Haley smiled, thinking he understood what his partner had in mind. "When you wanna do this?"

"No time like the present."

Jones knew it was going to happen and didn't see the point in arguing against it any further. Now he could only hope nothing went awry.

"Let me know when it's over so I know you're both not dead in a ditch or a gutter somewhere," Jones said.

"You always have such an eloquent way of phrasing things," Recker replied.

"As do you."

Recker and Haley left the office to go to Nowak's hotel. Along the way, Recker explained his plan in detail so Haley would know what he had in mind.

"You sure that room will be available?" Haley asked. "How do you know there's a spot there?"

Recker smiled. "I've actually been to that hotel before, so I already know the layout."

"What'd you go there for?"

"A couple years ago, a businessman who had some questionable business practices was on the wrong side of a hit for hire."

"You stop it?"

"Yeah."

When they finally got to the hotel, they immediately went to the floor Nowak was staying. Once they stepped off the elevator, Recker and Haley went their separate ways. All the rooms faced each other, as there was a big balcony that encompassed the inside part of the hotel. They immediately knew which door was Nowak's, as the guards standing in front of it gave it away. With Recker approaching them, nobody paid much attention to the guy on crutches who was walking on the far side of the floor, directly across from them. As Recker got within a few feet of them, one of the guards put his hands up to prevent him from coming closer.

"Hold up, man, that's as far as you get here."

"I think I'm expected," Recker said.

"I wasn't informed of that."

"Well, tell them I'm here."

"And who are you supposed to be?"

"I'm told I'm The Silencer. I'm also told your boss was looking to meet me."

"Oh," the guard said, his face looking a little awestruck, clearly hearing of Recker's reputation beforehand.

The two guards looked at each other for a moment, neither of whom seemed to be sure what to do next.

"How about one of you go in there and tell someone I'm here?" Recker said. "That way we're not standing out here all day."

"Wait here," the guard said, ducking inside the room.

"I'll wait here."

The guard looked back at Recker, giving him a glance that indicated he wasn't amused by the quip. As he waited, he put his finger on his ear, pretending to be cleaning it out to not give away Haley's voice was coming through on the com.

"I'm in position," Haley said.

As soon as he said that, Recker quickly twirled around to look at where he was, giving the illusion he was looking at the features of the hotel. Haley had taken up residence in a maintenance room located across from Nowak's room. The room was always locked, but with the guards paying more attention to Recker, no one noticed Haley was picking the lock. He left the door open a crack to give his rifle enough room to point at the guards. He stayed just inside the door, making sure the rifle didn't stick out of the door to not give himself away if anybody was walking nearby.

A minute later, the guard finally emerged from the room again, this time with Milton behind him. As Milton closed the door behind him, he looked Recker up and down to see if the description he'd heard matched the man in person. It did.

"You look about the same as I pictured you would," Milton said.

Recker smiled, not able to resist taking a small shot at the man. "Can't say the same for you. Thought you'd be bigger."

Milton also didn't look amused. "I'm sure."

"So, we gonna stand out here jabbering all day or am I gonna talk to your boss?"

"Ms. Nowak is currently in conference."

"So, are you saying she can't see me?" Recker asked.

"Maybe come back later today or tomorrow. Or leave your number and we'll contact you when she's available."

"Listen, pal, I'm busy, this is a one time offer. I didn't come here to be poo-pooed and given the runaround by the neighborhood lackey. If she doesn't see me now, I won't be back. I heard she was looking for me. I don't really give a damn if I talk to her or not."

Milton sighed and looked somewhat disgusted. "Wait here."

"I'll wait here."

Milton gave him a second look before going back inside the room again. Recker then looked at the guards and started some small talk to pass the time.

"I like the system you guys got going on here. You try to bore people to death before they get to go inside?"

Neither of the guards replied. They actually hoped he'd be out of their hair soon as they weren't particularly impressed with his personality. A couple minutes later, Milton came out of the room again.

"You're in luck, Ms. Nowak is ready to see you now."

Recker laughed. "I'm in luck? Like how you phrase things bud. You're a real charmer."

Recker started moving toward the door but was stopped by Milton, who put his hand on Recker's chest to prevent him from going in.

"No guns," Milton said.

"Excuse me?"

"You heard me. No weapons are allowed inside. We'll need to frisk you."

Recker took a step back as he balked at the request. "You don't need to check me. I'll tell you right now; I'm carrying."

"Boss' orders. Nobody gets inside who's packing."

"Well then, that presents a bit of a problem, doesn't it? I don't meet new people I don't trust without packing."

The guards, along with Milton, stood in front of the door to block Recker's path.

"Listen, does she wanna talk to me or not?" Recker asked.

"With no guns," Milton replied.

"Well here's the deal. I either go in, guns in my possession, or I walk away never to return."

Recker could see on Milton's face he was uncomfortable sending him away. It was obvious his boss really wanted to meet him and talk to him. If not, he figured Milton would have already told him to take a hike after balking at surrendering his weapons.

"If you want, I can make this easier for you," Recker said.

"How's that?"

"You see that red dot on your shirt?"

Milton scrunched his eyebrows together, not sure what he was talking about. He looked down at his shirt, but there was no red dot. "What are you talking about?"

Right on cue, Haley aimed his rifle at Milton's chest.

"You might wanna check again," Recker said.

Milton looked down again, this time seeing the red dot. He immediately knew what it was. A nervous look came over his face as he realized he was in the crosshairs of a sniper.

"Nobody takes my guns," Recker said. "I either go in with them or I leave. I don't really have a preference which way this goes so I'll leave the decision up to you."

Milton took a deep breath, finally ready to concede his position. Nowak really wanted to talk to him, and he was under orders to make it happen, so he relented. "Fine. You can keep your guns. Just realize if something happens..."

"Then what? I'll never make it out? Somehow, I think I would. I'll give you my word, though, nothing will happen unless someone tries to kill me. Fair enough?"

Milton nodded. "Oh, uh, and can you do something about this?" Milton asked, pointing to the red dot on his chest.

Recker put his hand on his ear. "Stand down." Within a few seconds, the dot disappeared. Recker then smiled at Milton and slapped him hard on the shoulder. "Let's get this party started, huh?"

58

ecker walked into the room, Milton closely behind him. Recker looked around and saw Teasley standing watching him but didn't see Nowak. He stood in the middle of the room for about a minute, with nobody saying a word. Recker was starting to get a bad feeling about being there. In case he badly misjudged what was about to happen, he stuck his hand inside his jacket, ready to pull out his gun if the situation called for it.

It turned out to be a false alarm for him, though, as Nowak showed up only a few seconds later. But it wasn't quite the initial appearance he imagined it would be. She came out of the bathroom, her body wrapped in a thick white towel that went from her chest to her mid-thigh. She walked right up to Recker and looked him over, in a much more lustful way than Milton had done earlier. She stuck her hand out to shake hands, which Recker reciprocated.

"So, you're the famous Silencer."

"That's the rumor," Recker replied.

"A little more good-looking than I was anticipating."

"Scars are coming next week."

"And a sarcastic sense of humor. I like it."

"It's just for you."

Nowak turned to her underlings to shoo them out of the room. "Leave us. Wait outside."

Milton and Teasley looked at each other, both surprised by their boss' wishes. It was highly unusual for them to leave her alone, as they hadn't done so in any other meeting she had up to that point. And it wasn't something she previously indicated she would do when she told them about meeting Recker.

"But... he's still armed," Milton said, not comfortable leaving her alone with such a dangerous man, who still had guns on him.

"Oh, is he?" Nowak asked, looking back at Recker seductively. "Well... everyone should live dangerously at some point."

"Ms. Nowak, I don't feel..."

"I don't pay you to feel anything. I pay you to do what I tell you."

Milton didn't look pleased at following her orders but eventually did as she asked. He looked at Teasley and nodded toward the door for him to follow him out. Once the two of them were outside, Nowak looked at Recker and touched him on the chest.

"Thanks for coming."

"Curiosity gets the best of me sometimes," Recker said.

"Follow me, so we can talk. I can change at the same time."

"I can wait out here for you. If it won't be too long."

"Oh nonsense," Nowak said, grabbing his hand. "Come into the bedroom with me. I won't bite. At least, not where it shows."

Though it was against his better judgment, Recker let her lead him into the bedroom. Once in, she directed him to a chair in the corner of the room. He sat down, expecting Nowak to duck behind a screen or into the bathroom off the bedroom. He was a little stunned she dropped her towel right in front of him, exposing her plentiful assets. She was thirty-seven, but still had the appearance of a woman who might have been ten years younger. She swore it was due to all the spa treatments, creams, and lotions she religiously used. With her youthful face and good body, she hardly looked the part of an organized crime boss. And she wasn't shy about using it if it helped her get what she wanted.

Standing there in front of Recker in all her glory, Nowak sure didn't rush to put any clothes on. She put on an act of not being able to find what she wanted to wear, all in the hopes of maybe seducing the mysterious man. Recker put his elbow on the arm of the chair and put his hand up to his face as he continued looking at the naked woman in front of him, studying her every movement. But Recker wasn't watching her with a lustful eye as most men in that situation might have done. With a beautiful woman of his own waiting for him, he had no interest in desiring somebody else, no matter how good they might have looked. No, he kept his eyes on Nowak because he knew the tactic she was trying for. It must have been something she'd tried, and succeeded with, on other men. He kept watching to see if she was planning on some type of diversion. The old watch her body while she pulls a gun, or somebody comes from a different room he's not watching trick. Nowak continually looked over at her visitor, and after a few minutes, realized her plan wasn't going quite the way she hoped. She slowly started putting her clothes on, not getting any reaction out of Recker.

"So, do you have a first name or does everyone call you The?" Nowak asked.

Recker laughed, finding some amusement in the question. "My friends call me Mike. My enemies call me Mr. Silencer."

This time it was Nowak's turn to laugh. She really enjoyed his sense of humor. Standing there in black lingerie, she hoped Recker was beginning to change his opinion on what might happen, though she had a feeling she was failing with her objective.

"So, before I get fully dressed is there anything you'd care to do or discuss before we get down to business?" Nowak asked, a slight seduction in her voice.

"I can't think of a thing, can you?"

Nowak looked extremely disappointed in his lack of interest and continued dressing, which consisted of pants, heels, and a revealing blouse. Once she was done, she walked over to the bedroom door.

"Well, if there's nothing else you can think of doing in here, would you follow me out to the main room?"

"I'd be delighted," Recker said.

Nowak stopped in the middle of the room and turned around to face him. "Well, if I can't interest you in anything spicier, can I offer you a drink?"

Recker put his hand up. "No, thank you."

"Do you always play everything straight down the line?"

"Only in the presence of strangers."

"I was hoping we could get to know each other more deeply and in more detail."

"Why?"

"I'm told you have a large, looming presence in this city," Nowak answered. "And considering I'm planning on being here a while, I figured you and I should get to know each other more intimately. You wouldn't have a problem with that, would you?"

"Some people might."

Nowak rubbed her finger across Recker's chin briefly before making her way to the bar area. "So, you have a girlfriend, do you?"

"A good man doesn't kiss and tell."

Nowak smiled. "Fair enough. You're obviously devoted to her. Like a good man should be."

"I don't mean to rush things along here, but I really didn't come here for you to analyze me. I heard you were looking for me, so here I am. How about we just stick to the business aspect of this?"

"Well if you would rather be boring about it," Nowak said, walking from behind the bar to a chair. "I always like to mix business with pleasure."

"Not me."

"So I'm gathering." Nowak pointed to a big white chair across from her. "Come sit, so we can discuss... business."

Recker complied with her wishes and sat. Up to this point, he wasn't very intrigued and was beginning to think he'd made a mistake in coming. He wasn't sure there was anything she could tell him that would have made him think otherwise.

Nowak took a sip of her drink. "So, why do you think I asked you to come here?"

"I assume you want me to help you get rid of Vincent."

Nowak smiled, not very surprised at how perceptive her guest was. "I can offer you a great deal."

"I'm sure you can. Is that it?"

"Of course not. As I'm sure you know, I have not been in town very long and I'm still figuring out the game here. Now, I already know pretty much all I need to know about Vincent. I know what he's into, the people in his pocket, and the things he does."

"You sure about that?" Recker asked, not believing she did, knowing Vincent as well as he did. "I've found he's a man you really can't count on for knowing anything about."

"Well, I may not know every single little detail about everything he does, but I know what I need to know. What I don't know is how you fit into it?"

"I don't."

"Oh, well that's fantastic, because I've heard from some of my moles on the street that you and he have a very close relationship."

"In a few instances our business interests have aligned,"

Recker replied. "We're not friends, we're not partners, we are not anything together. I do my own thing."

"I'm delighted to hear it."

"Why? Planning on making me an offer?"

Nowak grinned. "You are well-versed in the game, aren't you?"

"I didn't just graduate hitman school yesterday."

"So, since you two aren't intertwined at the hip, as they say, would you be interested in a proposition?"

Recker smiled. "Never on the first date."

"I'm sure if we were to come to some type of agreement, I could make it extremely worth your while."

"Why does that not surprise me? And just what type of agreement are you looking to make?"

"Well..."

Recker didn't mind engaging in an evasive question-and-answer session from time to time, especially since he was used to it in talking to Vincent, but he wasn't interested in continuing it this time. "Instead of this runaround conversation we're having, why don't you tell me what you really want?"

"Tell me, is it all business with you all the time?"

"Mostly."

"Your reputation paints you as one of the best," Nowak said. "Somebody who's not to be messed with. They say if there's a fight on your hands, you want The Silencer guarding your back."

"Well I don't know who 'they' are, but my cooperation in any matter depends on a variety of factors."

"Which are?"

"I have my own criteria which I choose not to divulge," Recker answered. "I also don't get involved in disputes between rival crime families."

"Well, that's disappointing to hear. May I ask why?"

"Because I'm not interested in choosing sides. I'm not here to help you or him exert your power or influence or help you make money. I'm here to help prevent innocent people from getting hurt by people like you."

"What are you? A saint or an angel or something?"

"Hardly. Just someone who tries to do the right thing."

"Sometimes the right thing can be influenced by a sizable check," Nowak said.

"Not with me. Don't give a hoot about money."

The two talked for a few more minutes, Nowak continually trying to break him down into at least considering joining her side. The more they talked though, the more she began to realize it was a worthless pursuit. Nothing she did or said seemed to interest him. She couldn't interest him with her body or her money. He was quite the unusual man in her estimation. Since he had shot down everything she had to offer so far, and since she badly desired his help, Nowak figured she'd basically let him write his own check.

"How about we do this? You tell me what you want or what interests you, and I'll see what I can do?"

"Just like that, huh?" Recker replied.

"Why not?"

Recker was silent for a few moments, trying to think of an answer for her. There was nothing he could come up with though. "I'm afraid that's a question I can't really answer."

"You can take a few days to think about it if you wish. I aim to please."

"No, it's not that. It's just there's nothing you could offer me that would persuade me to join your side or get involved in this conflict at all."

Nowak flashed a smile, though underneath it was a temper she was beginning to lose. She was able to control it though. "So, tell me, if you're not interested in anything I have to offer, or anything I have to say, why did you agree to come here?"

"I'm always interested in meeting new people I might come across one day."

"So, you're leaving the door open to us working together at some point?" Nowak asked.

"Nope. I'd say it's unlikely. I'll just give it to you straight. After today, I hope I never run into you again. And whatever your plans are for being in this city, I'd like to stay out of them. I'm here for one reason and one reason only and that's to protect the innocent. Whatever game you have going on with Vincent or any other criminal doesn't really concern me."

"Straight down the line."

"If we ever see each other again, it's likely because you knocked over the neighborhood grocery store or worked over an old man walking down the street or trying to intimidate a law-abiding person into doing something illegal that benefits you. If any of those are the case, then we'll be seeing each other again real soon."

Nowak nodded, finally seeing the man in front of her couldn't be bought with anything she was trying to sell. "So, you're trying to tell me you and Vincent have come to that same understanding?"

"Vincent and I have learned to stay out of each other's way. I don't get involved in any of his dealings as long as innocent people aren't caught up in it, and he doesn't do anything that might cause me to stop it."

"A nice, neat arrangement."

"Has been so far."

"So, maybe you and I could come to that same arrangement," Nowak said.

"I don't see why not. I'm not looking to make enemies, just telling you how things are here."

"I understand. I only hope my relationship with you will eventually be a little closer than the one you have with Vincent."

Recker looked at her with a sharp eye and grinned, wondering if she ever stopped with the double entendres. In his view, she was obviously a woman who wasn't used to hearing the word no. He figured she was used to men doing whatever she wanted, for whatever the reason, and jumping at the chance to please her... in any situation. But she was learning he was someone who stood with his own convictions. In analyzing him, Nowak assumed he was someone who would rather go down with the ship than to do something against his own principles. Those were the types of people that usually gave her trouble. She knew she would have to keep her eyes on him and stay guarded.

They conversed for another twenty minutes, Nowak continually probing him on more personal questions he kept evading. Recker knew her game. She was trying to find out everything she could about him in the hopes of using something to her advantage against him. Anything she could find that she could potentially use in the hopes of luring him to her side of the equation. But with his background of working in the city the last few years, plus his time in the CIA, he was well-versed in this kind of information gathering. He was easily able to brush her inquisitions aside.

"You know, I get the impression there's more to you than meets the eye," Nowak said.

"Now what gives you that idea?"

"You're a mysterious man. You stick to a certain set of ideals and don't deviate from them. You have a demeanor about you that suggests there's something else that lies beneath that rugged exterior."

"Everyone has a past and skeletons in the closet."

"Indeed, we do. But some are more interesting than others. What did you do before coming here?"

"What makes you think I did anything?" Recker asked.

"Because everybody was something else once."

"It's nothing worth mentioning in my case."

"I can't believe that to be true."

"Well, I guess we'll just have to leave it at something that's for me to know and you to find out. You seem to like playing games enough to do that."

Nowak smiled. "I think we've got a good understanding of each other. At least to start with."

"I would say so."

"Perhaps we could meet again under less formal circumstances," Nowak said, sticking her chest out to give Recker a better view of it.

Recker wouldn't take the bait though. "No, I don't think we could."

59

It'd been several days since Recker's meeting with Stefania Nowak. The city was a relatively quiet place since then, at least as far as gangland business went, as nobody had turned up dead yet. That was about to change, though, and in a big way. It was release day for Jimmy Malloy. He was finally being let go from Dr. Luke's care, and since he was the number one man, Vincent was showing up personally to welcome him back. Unbeknownst to him, Malloy was going to get another welcoming party, a larger and more unfriendly one.

Dr. Luke helped walk Malloy out of the back of the building, with Vincent on the other side of him. There was a black Cadillac parked only a few feet away, and the driver got out the car to assist Malloy into it. As the driver scurried around the back of the car, another car zoomed in, screeching to a sudden stop. Vincent looked wild-eyed as he suspected what was going on. Only a second later, the windows of the car went down and guns appeared in its place. The automatic rifles opened fire at the bunch, not seemingly aiming at a specific target. Vincent pushed Malloy down to the ground and stayed on top of him as the driver began to return fire. Dr. Luke started to run back toward his office but was hit in the back with several shots, dropping him to the ground long before he got there. Vincent's driver was able to hit the car with a couple of shots, though he did no real damage, and he didn't hit any of the occupants either. As the exchange of gunfire continued, the driver suddenly went down, a barrage of bullets entering his body. Once he was out of the way, the mysterious car squealed its wheels and turned around, going out the same way they came in. Vincent saw their attackers leave by observing the vehicle underneath his own car. When he knew they were out of the picture, he finally got back to his feet, and helped Malloy up to his.

"You OK?"

Malloy brushed himself off and checked for new holes in him. "I think I'm good."

"You sure? Anything hurt or anything?"

Malloy held his rib cage area, but mostly because it was still sore from the previous slugs taken out. "No, just a little sore. I'll be alright."

With him taken care of, Vincent then turned and saw his driver lying on the ground, in a pool of his own blood. Vincent knelt, not seemingly caring about getting blood on his pants, and touched the head of his former employee. The man had been with Vincent for almost ten years and was a valued member of his organization. He would be missed. Malloy then tapped his boss on the arm and pointed at Dr. Luke. Vincent was saddened at the sight of the fallen doctor. Vincent got up and walked over to him, hoping by some miracle he was still alive. Vincent observed three bullet holes in the doctor's back and knew no miracle would be arriving on this day.

"What do you wanna do?" Malloy asked.

Vincent got on his phone and made a call to the police department and one of the detectives on his payroll. He wanted to make sure it was one of them who rolled on the call. He didn't want to be dealing with a lot of unnecessary questions that would accompany a detective who didn't have that relationship with him. He was sure somebody probably heard the shots and called it in to the cops already, and though he didn't plan on sticking around at the scene, as soon as the driver was identified, somebody in uniform would be showing up at his door. He hoped to avoid that whole predicament.

Once he was done with his phone call, Vincent helped Malloy into the passenger seat of the car. Vincent then hopped into the driver's side and left the area, only a few minutes before a patrol car showed up. Silence filled the car for several minutes as the two men steamed over the loss of the two men they left behind. Both were valued and trusted men. It was something Vincent would not let pass as easily as he did the first hit against him.

"Who do you think it was?" Malloy asked.

"I don't think it's something we really have to guess on. We know who it is. We know who's behind it. A very unfortunate and misguided woman."

Recker arrived in the office, still talking on the phone. His phone had been blowing up all day from sources he had on the street, including Tyrell. But the topic of conversation was all the same. They were all telling him about the attempted attack on Vincent at Dr. Luke's office. As he reached the desk, he hung up, ready to talk about the events with the team. Jones wasn't sure if his partner had heard the news yet and was eager to discuss it. Jones dropped what he was doing as he turned toward Recker.

"It appears we have a delicate situation on our hands."

"Murder and attempted murder are usually not all that delicate," Recker said.

"So, you've heard the news, I take it?"

"I've heard about it so often already my ears are ringing."

"What're we gonna do?" Haley asked.

Recker looked away as he shrugged, not really having an answer. "I didn't know we were gonna do anything. I thought we had a vote a few days ago to stay out of this thing."

"I guess it seems more real now."

"Well, we all knew that, barring an agreement between those two, this day was coming."

"It would appear that agreement did not materialize," Jones said.

"Understatement of the year."

"I would say the only thing for us to do is continue to monitor things, make sure it doesn't spill out into unintended places."

"If it does, then we'll intervene," Recker said. "But not before."

Nowak was pacing around in her hotel room, acting somewhat nervously, which was uncharacteristic for her. She usually seemed much more confident. But it'd been a week since the attempted hit on Vincent and Malloy and there'd been no response in the form of retaliation. It was not what they had counted on or planned when dreaming up this scenario. Nowak and her cohorts were counting on them fighting back and exposing themselves even further, opening themselves up for bigger hits and damage upon their organization.

"I don't understand what's happening," Nowak anxiously said, smoking a cigarette. "Why is he staying silent?"

"Maybe he's just waiting," Milton replied.

"Waiting for what? To get picked to pieces? To die slowly? Our contacts haven't dug up a single thing about them planning anything? What are they doing, just crawling into a hole some-where hoping this will blow over?"

"He does have a reputation for not rushing into things," Teasley answered. "Could be he's planning something big. Some-thing that would take a while to plan."

"Such as what? Blowing up the hotel with me in it? He wouldn't dare be so bold."

"Speaking of which, when do you plan on moving opera-tions?" Milton asked. "Can't stay in this hotel forever."

"I'm comfortable here. I also know Vincent is not going to be so daring as to try to take me out here. There's safety out in the open. It's when you cross into the shadows that things happen. He's not going to try something in full view of everybody and draw attention to himself. Me moving is probably exactly what he's hoping for."

"I dunno. People get murdered in hotels all the time. I don't think it's above him to try it."

"Well that is why I pay for security, is it not?" Nowak asked.

"I say we keep on hitting him while we got him reeling," Teasley said. "Let's keep up the pressure."

"And what exactly do you have in mind?"

"Let's attack every building he owns. Businesses, warehouses, facilities, men, everything. Let's hit him a couple times a day until he's extinct or so scared he never shows his face above ground again."

Nowak paced around the room for a minute as she thought about it. She started moving her head around, indicating that she was in support of the action. She then stopped her pacing and sat down, eventually agreeing with the move.

"Start making preparations," Nowak said. "Draw up a plan of which buildings to hit and when. I want a precise plan. Dates, times, people involved, everything. And I want it by tomorrow."

"I'll get on it right away," Teasley replied. "I'll leave now and do some scouting. I'll have something for you tomorrow."

"Good."

Teasley left the room as he embarked on his mission to scout some of Vincent's known business locations. After he left, Nowak and Milton continued talking about the plan.

"What do you think?" Nowak asked. "Will it work?"

"I think it's good. I know you originally wanted to try to draw him out and get him that way, but I don't think that's gonna fly. He's too smart for that. He knows you'd be expecting him to retaliate. That's why he's not. He's trying to wait you out. Let you get impatient and make a mistake."

"Well then we'll just have to make sure his mistake is in not trying."

When Teasley made it down to the lobby, he kept his head on a swivel, as all Nowak's men did nowadays, since they were on the lookout for any of Vincent's faction. As he stepped through the main doors, he waited outside for a few seconds, cognizant of any cars that might be in the area. He almost expected a car to drive by, roll down its windows, and start blasting away at him. He put his hand inside his jacket and placed his fingers on his gun, thinking he may have cause to use it as he walked to his car. He was a little surprised, though not disappointed, he got to his car without incident.

Before starting his car, he pulled up the maps on his phone and plugged it into the car charger. He pulled out a small book and plugged in a couple addresses into the map app for directions. He then reached into his pocket and pulled out his keys and put them into the ignition. Teasley took a quick look out the window to make sure nobody else was around then started the car. Almost instantly after the engine turned on, the car exploded, resulting in a massive fireball shooting up into the air. The windows on each of the cars next to it shattered from the impact. Pieces of Teasley's car were torn off the vehicle and landed all over the parking lot. There wasn't much left of either the car or Teasley. What was left of the car was still on fire. There were more explosives used than were actually needed, but Vincent wanted to make a powerful statement.

The blast could be heard by everyone within the hotel and probably a couple miles beyond it. As soon as they heard the massive explosion, Nowak and Milton ran to the window. They opened the blinds completely and stared out the window, their eyes instantly drawn to the burning car they immediately knew was Teasley's. Nowak's jaws tightened as anger started boiling inside her.

"You were wondering why there was no response yet?" Milton said. "I'd say he's answered with a certain kind of flare."

"I would say the game is now in full force."

"Should we go down there and check it out?"

"Why?" Nowak asked. "There's nothing we can do down there."

"What do you wanna do now?"

"We'll do as we just discussed. We'll start hitting Vincent in spots all across the city. We'll do it in random areas, so he won't be able to pick out a pattern and be ready for us. We'll have his head spinning so fast he won't know what's happening or where we'll be next."

"I'll start working on it tonight."

They continued staring out the window at the wreckage as they talked of their plans, observing a burgeoning crowd down below. A little to the left of the blast, Nowak saw a couple men just standing there, looking up at the hotel. Though she couldn't see their eyes at that distance, by the positioning of their heads, she knew they were looking at her. She was a little shocked at their appearance, even though she probably shouldn't have been. She kept her eyes fixed on the pair, wondering if there were about to be any other fireworks soon to be set off.

"They're here," Nowak said.

"What?"

"Vincent and his goon. They're here."

Milton put his hand on the window. "What? Where?"

"To the left of the car. Just standing there. Looking at us."

"I'll get the boys ready," Milton said, about ready to rush off and tell some of the others.

Nowak put her hand on his forearm to prevent him from leaving. "Don't bother."

"What if that was just for starters? Maybe they have more planned."

"It's not."

"How do you know?"

"Because they wouldn't still be standing there if there was more to come," Nowak answered.

"What do you suppose they're doing there? Just standing."

Nowak sighed. "Sending me a message."

"Maybe we should send one back."

"We will. In time."

All parties concerned stood in their respective spots for a few more minutes, continuing their staring contest. It was almost as if each side was waiting for the other to blink and step away first. With Vincent still staring up at the window, Malloy started tugging at his boss to leave the scene, figuring someone would start connecting them to the blast.

"We should probably get going," Malloy said, grabbing his boss' arm.

"Yeah, you're right. I just wanted to make sure she got the message."

"I think it'd be pretty hard to ignore."

"Yeah, I guess you're right."

With his underling tugging at him, Vincent finally capitulated and stopped staring at the hotel and walked back toward their own car. Just before getting in, they stopped, Malloy wanting to get Vincent's thoughts on what happened.

"What do you think they'll do in response?" Malloy asked. "I'm sure they'll have one."

"Oh yes. They'll have a response. You can count on that."

"What do you think it'll be?"

"I would suspect they'll try to hit us again," Vincent replied. "Make sure you put everyone on high alert."

"Will do."

"Every man, every building, every car, everything. Might be tomorrow. Might be in a week. But you can be sure it'll be coming."

"With all due respect, sir, I think you're being too generous."

"In what way?" Vincent asked.

"Giving them a chance like this. Instead of letting them get a chance to regroup and hit us again, we should keep after them. Take it to them while they're on their heels."

"A sound strategy Jimmy. We'll take it under advisement."

"A beautiful day, sir?"

Vincent smiled and looked up at the sky. Even though there was no sun and it was a bit of an overcast day, it didn't much matter to him. It was perfect as far as he was concerned. "Yes, Jimmy, I'd say it was a beautiful day indeed. A very beautiful day."

60

A few more weeks passed, with both Vincent's and Nowak's organizations taking shots at each other. Several men on both sides were killed, though neither launched a full-out war on the other. They were both being cautious in how they approached the situation. From Nowak's perspective, she never wanted a full-scale battle with Vincent, anyway. Her approach was more one of respect. She wanted Vincent's respect that they could share the city without him losing much, if anything. At this point, she wasn't interested in taking him out. Nowak wanted him to know she was as tough as he was and she wasn't leaving without a fight. That was why she held back a little. She didn't think an all-out war with Vincent would be good for anybody. And she wasn't certain it was one she could win. At least, not yet. Not until she had some time to build up her organization, both in terms of men and money.

For Vincent, he didn't consider Nowak's organization to be much of a threat. At least not a major one. Though she showed some guts up to that point and wasn't backing down yet, he still believed the waiting game would pay off, as it usually did. He knew she didn't have as much power within the city as he did and couldn't afford a long engagement. He figured time was on his side. Rushing was where men made mistakes. And he figured that would be his undoing. He also wanted to avoid a full-out war as he knew that meant he would probably lose a good amount of men and resources. War between two factions was rarely good for anybody. Everyone took casualties. Vincent was trying to avoid that if possible. He hoped that eventually Nowak would see that he wasn't relinquishing any control or letting her set up shop within his territory and she'd pack up and leave. It would be a standstill.

For Recker and the team, not much had changed since the war between Vincent and Nowak started. They hadn't been dragged into anything, and, so far, nobody innocent had gotten caught up in their entanglements. But they had a feeling that wouldn't last forever. Eventually, someone who wasn't involved in the deal would get hurt.

They'd been working on a case involving an investment banker who looked to be engaging in some fraudulent activity and Recker was ready to make his move on the guy. Jones intercepted some text messages indicating the banker, Todd Brinson, was meeting with a contact at an outdoor restaurant in the downtown area. Recker was already at the restaurant sitting by himself and eating his meal when he saw Brinson arrive.

"Looks like our guy is here," Recker said into his com.

"Is there anyone with him yet?" Jones asked.

"Not yet."

Jones looked at the time and saw it was five minutes to one, the scheduled meeting time. "We still have a few minutes."

Recker kept his eyes fixed on Brinson, who took up a seat several tables in front of Recker, watching his every movement. The banker looked a bit nervous, looking in every direction. Recker assumed he was looking for his visitor. Five minutes passed and there was still no sign of anyone. It appeared to Recker that Brinson was starting to sweat as he was dabbing his cheeks and forehead with a napkin.

"This guy's looking really nervous," Recker said.

"Still no sign of anyone?" Jones asked.

"Not yet." Recker looked across the street and saw a familiar face walking across it. He kept his eyes fixed on the man as he came over to the restaurant and sat down across from Brinson. "Guys, we have an interesting situation here."

"What's happening? Have we finally identified the person he's meeting? Is the other party there yet?"

"Oh yeah. He's here."

"Well who is it? Do we know him?"

"Gabriel Hernandez," Recker replied.

Jones was very surprised to hear the name. "Hernandez? What is he doing there?"

"Without knowing details, and if I had to guess, I'd say maybe we know how Stefania Nowak is funding her operation."

"Now the question is whether Mr. Brinson is a willing participant or if he's being blackmailed or coerced somehow."

"I'll find that out real quick."

"How do you plan to do that?"

"Ask him," Recker said.

"I'm not sure that's wise. If he is a willing participant in this endeavor, then introducing yourself and talking about it could blow the case sky high. He might clam up and we'll never know where it leads."

"Oh, I think we do."

"Just because Hernandez is there does not necessarily mean it's tied to Nowak. He could be operating independently of her on this deal."

"With people like Vincent and Nowak, they don't employ people who act independently of them," Recker said. "They want people to fall in line. They won't do something unless they're told to."

"Perhaps you're right, but I'm still not sure showing yourself is the right move."

"Guess we'll find out."

Jones sighed and rolled his eyes as he turned to Haley, who was sitting beside him. "Why do I even bother?"

Haley laughed. "He's usually right."

"Yes, but let's not admit that too often. He'll be even harder to live with than he is now."

Since they were at an outdoor restaurant, Recker brought a book with him that way he could pretend to bury his head in it and partially conceal his face. He wasn't sure if Hernandez would recognize him so Recker lifted the book up in front of his face, with his eyes just barely able to see over the edge of the book. It was enough to see what was going on, while at the same time, hoping he wouldn't be recognized.

It wasn't a particularly long meeting between Hernandez and Brinson. It seemed as though it was only a verbal type of meeting as Recker didn't observe anything being passed between them. One thing he did notice was Hernandez appeared to be doing most of the talking. And it didn't always seem that friendly, as Hernandez talked somewhat animatedly at times to explain whatever his point was. After about fifteen minutes, they seemed to be done. Hernandez pushed his chair out and stood, giving a few last words to the banker, none of which appeared to be that pleasant either, judging from the veins popping out of the side of his neck.

"Hernandez is leaving," Recker said.

"I urge you to proceed with caution," Jones replied.

"Don't I always?"

"Do I really need to respond to that?"

Recker laughed, knowing how preposterous it sounded. "Gotta hurry before Brinson leaves."

"If you intend to do this, it might be better if you let him leave," Haley said.

"Why?"

"What if someone still has eyes on him?"

"That's a good point, Mike," Jones said, hoping that would persuade him not to meet him yet. "If he is not there of his own free will, they very well could be watching him. And if they see you sitting with him, who knows what would happen after that?"

"All right, you convinced me," Recker said.

"So, you'll come back here to the office?"

"No, I'll just follow Brinson as he leaves and pull him over somewhere."

"How did I know that's where this was headed?"

"Lucky guess?"

"Hardly."

A few minutes later, Brinson finally got up from his table and started walking along the street. Recker quickly paid for his meal and took off after him, staying far enough behind at first to see what the man was up to. As he walked, Recker kept looking all around to see if he could spot another tail on Brinson, but he didn't notice anything. After another ten minutes of walking, Recker finally sped up, ready to pull him to the side. Recker waited until they got to the right building until he finally caught up with him, wanting to make sure they went into a building where they could have some privacy to talk. Once they finally passed in front of the bookstore, Recker nudged Brinson to the side with his shoulder. Recker kept pushing him to the door with his body without much of a problem. When Brinson turned around to object to how he was being treated, Recker threw open the door and shoved him inside.

"What is going on?" Brinson asked.

Recker didn't answer and instead looked back toward the street through the window. "You know if anybody's watching you?"

"Excuse me?"

"Anyone following you?"

"I'm not in the habit of being followed."

"Yeah, well, there's a first time for everything, isn't there?" Recker said.

"What is this all about?"

Recker looked around the bookstore and saw a couple of chairs by a shelf in the corner of the store. "That'll work well. Over there." He pointed.

"I'm not going anywhere until you tell me what this is all about."

Recker grabbed him by the arm and forcefully shoved him to the spot he wanted him to go. Luckily Brinson was not as big or as strong as Recker, so he wasn't able to put up much opposition to his demands. When they finally got to the corner, Recker pushed him toward one of the chairs.

"Here. Sit down."

"I'm not..."

Recker interrupted him before he could object. "I said sit," he forcefully said. "Then I'll tell you what this is all about."

Brinson took a deep breath, then figured he should comply with the man's wishes. Since he wasn't hurt yet, he could only assume the man didn't have intentions of harming him somehow. Especially in a bookstore. Brinson didn't know where he went wrong, but somewhere along the way, he figured he must have taken a wrong turn in his life. First dealing with Nowak and Hernandez, now with this guy in front of him, who he also assumed wanted him for some illegal or immoral reason. Brinson sat, waiting for the other shoe to drop, waiting for the man to tell him what he wanted, which was sure to be something he didn't want to do.

"Well?" Brinson asked.

"Well, what?"

"Well, what do you want? Let's get on with it."

"I'd like to know what you were doing with Gabriel Hernandez back there at the restaurant?" Recker asked.

"Having lunch. That's what most people do at a restaurant, right?"

"Most people. Except I noticed neither of you had any."

"Decided we weren't hungry," Brinson said.

"Listen, if you're in trouble, maybe I can help you. If you're knee deep in something you shouldn't be of your own accord, then maybe I can help soften the blow, so you don't get hurt as bad. Either way, it's your choice. But either way, you're gonna tell me what I wanna know."

"Why should I tell you anything?"

Recker reached inside his jacket and pulled out a wallet with a badge and ID card. "Detective Mike Scarborough."

Brinson got a weird look on his face. He looked both scared and relieved at the same time. Recker had trouble reading him. He couldn't be sure what Brinson was feeling at the moment.

"I really wanted to go to the police, but I just couldn't," Brinson said.

Recker was a little surprised he just blurted it out but was happy considering it saved them both a lot of time and aggravation of him trying to coerce the information out of him. "What's going on?"

"Couple weeks ago, I got a call out of the blue from some woman named Stephanie. She said she was interested in trying to raise some capital for a new business she was starting and asked for a meeting with me."

"And you did?"

"Yeah. Everything seemed fine. Met one or two times after that, then I learned what she was really after. She wanted me to falsify records and documents from some of my other clients and siphon the funds into an offshore account in her name."

"And you agreed?" Recker asked, sure there must have been more to the story.

"I had to. She..."

"She's got something on you, doesn't she?"

Brinson looked down and shamefully nodded. "Yes."

"What?"

"I had an indiscretion a couple weeks ago."

"What kind of indiscretion?" Recker asked.

"Look, I'm married. I have a beautiful wife, a son, a daughter, and I love them very much."

Recker closed his eyes and sighed, knowing full well where this was going. "And?"

"One night I stopped at the bar for some drinks with a couple buddies of mine. Towards the end when everyone started leaving, this woman approached me and started talking. At first, I didn't think much of it but after a while, and a few more drinks, she started really coming on to me, like really aggressive."

"And you couldn't say no?"

Brinson looked like he was fighting back tears as he shook his head, not able to say anything at first. "I swear I didn't want to, but she was just..."

"Yeah, I know, it was all her," Recker said, not really finding much sympathy for the man. Though he was reasonably sure Nowak had set the meeting up and planted the woman, it still took two to tango.

"I just... wasn't strong enough to say no."

"And you two went to some shady motel or something?"

"Yeah, something like that."

"Let me guess, a couple days after that meeting with this Stephanie woman, you started getting some compromising photos?" Recker said.

"How'd you know?"

"You're not the first sucker to fall for that trick."

"They said if I didn't help them they'd send the pictures to my wife and ruin me," Brinson replied. "She'd divorce me, take the kids, the house, everything. I couldn't let that happen."

"Ever think of just being honest and telling your wife everything that happened?"

Brinson just shrugged, not sure what else to say.

"Never know. She might've just surprised you and believed your story. Maybe she would've hung with you. You know that whole marriage thing, for better or worse, in tough times and all that jazz."

"I didn't want to take chances."

"So, what have you done with them so far?" Recker asked.

"Well, not much really. I told them it would take some time for all that. If I rushed things and made mistakes, somebody would catch on fast."

"So, you haven't actually sent any money to them?"

"Not yet, no," Brinson answered. "That's what the meeting at the restaurant was about. He was upset it was taking this long and wanted me to hurry it up. Said if I hadn't sent the first payment through within the next five days, then my wife would get the first set of pictures."

Recker sat there for a minute, thinking of their next move.

"What do I do?" Brinson asked.

"You'll go back to your office and undo everything you've done so far."

"But the pictures."

"Unless you want a long prison sentence, that's exactly what you're gonna do. I'll take care of Hernandez and his boss."

"But, my wife?"

"I'll visit your wife and tell her someone's trying to blackmail you with fake pictures," Recker said. "I'll tell her you're cooperating with us and that as a result of that, someone may try to get back at you with photoshopped pictures. That should satisfy her."

Brinson took a huge sigh of relief. "Thank you."

"Don't thank me yet. You just make sure you undo everything."

"What do you want me to do after that?"

"Nothing. After that, you keep going on with your job like nothing else is happening."

"But Hernandez... he's gonna contact me again," Brinson said. "What am I gonna tell him?"

"You tell him it'll be a couple days. That should be enough time for us to get to work on them. I'll be in touch with you to see if there's any further contact."

"OK. Thank you. I really appreciate it."

Recker nodded at him as Brinson got up and left. Recker continued sitting there for a few minutes, trying to take everything in. He had the com on the whole time, so Jones and Haley could hear everything said.

"Well, what do you guys think?" Recker asked.

"I would say Nowak is going to give us problems," Haley replied.

Jones was silent for a moment, trying to collect his own thoughts. "I would tend to agree."

"I think we can all agree on one thing," Recker said. "If she sticks around, she's definitely gonna wind up giving us more problems than Vincent."

"I'm afraid you might be right about that."

"What do you wanna do now?" Haley asked.

"Right now, I'll go talk to Brinson's wife like I said I would. After that, I dunno. Try to stop this mess somehow."

"Might be a taller order than it seems."

"I know. I've also got a feeling it won't be so easy."

61

Recker had just finished talking to Mrs. Brinson and was walking back to his car, as he reached the door and was about to unlock it, he felt an object jam into the small of his back.

"I wouldn't reach for anything if I was you," a voice said. "In case you were wondering, I'm not using my finger."

Recker slowly raised his arms into the air. "I know the barrel of a gun when I feel it."

"Good. Do as you're told and maybe you'll live through this."

"Maybe?"

The man took a few steps back so Recker could turn around and face him. As he did, the man smiled at him. "Maybe not."

"Can I put my hands down now, Mr. Hernandez?"

"Just so you know, I don't have the only gun pointed at you, in case you had some funny ideas."

"I never have funny ideas," Recker said. "Cute ones sometimes, but never funny."

"Smart guy."

"Mildly intelligent."

"All right, you can cut the jokes now," Hernandez said. He then did a pat down on Recker and removed both his guns, sticking them in his own belt. "OK. You can put your arms down now."

Before doing so, Recker stuck his finger in his ear, pretending to scratch it. He was actually turning his com on to let the others know what was happening. Then he put his hands down and looked around to see who else was out there. He couldn't see anyone at first, but that didn't mean nobody was there. He could've tried to give Hernandez a problem right then and there but decided to let it play out and see where the situation was headed.

"Your boss know you're out here on the street playing with guns?" Recker asked.

"There you go with the jokes again."

"Want me to keep going?"

"No, I want you to shut your mouth."

A few seconds later, another car pulled up alongside them, ready to take them away. Recker resisted getting in at first. Hernandez pushed his gun further into Recker's back to give him some encouragement.

"I really shouldn't leave my car behind," Recker said.

"In."

"You do realize if my car's left here, eventually somebody's gonna come looking for it."

"So what? We'll be long gone by then. Get in."

Recker complied with the man's orders and got into the back seat, Hernandez sitting next to him, continuing to jab his gun into Recker's ribs. Just to make sure he didn't try anything funny, there was another man on the opposite side of Recker, along with a man in the front passenger seat.

"Looks like we got a full house in here," Recker said. "Where we heading?"

"You'll know when we get there," Hernandez replied.

"Well, can you at least tell me what this is about?"

"You know."

"I do? See that's the thing, I really don't. Maybe you could explain it to me?"

"You just had to go meddling into the Brinson thing, didn't you?" Hernandez asked.

"Well that's kind of my nature."

"I saw you talking to him in the bookstore. Considering you're now talking to his wife, we can only assume you somehow put the brakes on our deal."

"You know what they say about assuming."

"You know what they also say about meddling in someone else's business. It can get you killed."

"That a fact?"

"So is that where we're going?" Recker asked. "Dumping me in a river? Concrete slab? In a ditch?"

"Not just yet. Ms. Nowak would like to have another chat with you first."

"Oh, I look forward to it."

Once Recker had pushed his comm on, Jones and Haley had been listening to everything in the office. Their cars had tracking devices on them, in case of a situation where it wasn't known where they were so they could be located, which was why Recker was pushing to use his car. But it really didn't matter. Their com devices were also equipped with a GPS chip inside, so Jones was able to pull up his location on the computer. Now the only question was how to get him out.

"I'm gonna have to go," Haley said.

He was eager to get back out in the field. It'd been four weeks since he'd been shot in the leg and he was no longer on crutches. He actually felt pretty good. He was only walking with a slight limp at this point, hardly even noticeable. The biggest question was how he'd move if he got into a jam. If he had to twist, turn, and run, would his injury worsen? But Haley wasn't thinking about that now. His only concern was helping his friend out of a tough spot. Judging by Jones' lack of response, he could tell he wasn't that keen on the idea.

"There's no one else," Haley said.

"We could call Vincent."

"Malloy's still out of action. He's the only one in his bunch I know is tough enough to handle this. And with Vincent still looking to take Nowak out, he may say it's worth getting Mike caught in the crossfire if it means taking out the rest of her group at the same time."

Jones looked at him and nodded, reluctantly agreeing with his view. "I suppose that is true."

"Look, I know you don't wanna put me out there again before I'm ready... but I am. They said six weeks, and it's only been four, but I feel fine. I've been working out extra, I'm moving OK, there's nothing to hold me back. It's not like I'm going out there on crutches again. It's gotta be me."

Jones nodded again, knowing they didn't have much time to debate it. "You should get going. I'll let you know which way they go."

Haley rushed out the door and got into his car, driving towards Recker's last known position. As he was driving, Jones contacted him to tell him if the car that had Recker turned on a different street. Only a few minutes after Haley had left, the dot signifying Recker's position had stopped.

"Oh dear," Jones mumbled, knowing it was a bad sign they stopped already. He was hoping it wouldn't be for a little while to give Haley a chance to catch up to them. Jones hopped onto another computer to plug the coordinates in then called Haley to let him know.

"Chris, looks like Mike's now stationary."

"Where?" Haley asked.

"Address comes back to a factory on the outskirts of the city. I'm looking up now whether it's still in use."

"How far away?"

"You've probably got another twenty minutes or so to go."

"I'll step on it."

Hernandez had just gotten Recker out of the car and they approached the abandoned food factory. It had only recently gone out of business, with Nowak acquiring the property only two months ago.

"Oh, no thanks fellas, I'm pretty full. I ate earlier," Recker said.

"Let's go," Hernandez said, giving him a push in the back.

Recker and his four bodyguards went inside as they waited for Nowak to show up. Once inside, one of the men found a chair for Recker to sit in. Then they tied him to it with a rope.

"Not very hospitable of you guys," Recker said.

Hernandez sighed, getting tired of Recker's smart aleck mouth. He wanted this assignment to be done with. "Do you ever get tired of the jokes?"

"No, not really. Why? Do you?" Recker could tell he was getting on the man's nerves and only hoped he could keep it up. He figured the more annoyed he got, the less focused he would be when the time came to kill him, which would make it an easier task.

About five minutes passed before Nowak finally appeared, surrounded by three more of her men. Absent was Milton. Hernandez came over to the door to greet her before she got within range of Recker.

"He give you any trouble?" Nowak asked.

"None at all."

"Strange. What about his partner?"

"No sign of him," Hernandez answered.

Nowak instructed the three men she came in with to wait outside, just in case Recker's partner showed up. She remembered what she was told from the hotel, about someone having a laser pointed at Milton, so she knew Recker had one. The fact he came so easily was another thing that alarmed her. Nowak then walked over to him, standing just in front of him.

"You look a little overdressed for a place like this," Recker said, observing her expensive-looking black dress. It looked like she was dressed for a gala or a fancy dinner party.

"I like to dress up for important people."

"Let me know when he gets here."

Nowak smiled. "You know it doesn't have to be like this."

"Like what?"

Nowak pointed at him. "Like this. You sitting in a chair tied up. Adversaries with me. Enemies."

"I hadn't thought of us as enemies."

"But you're stepping in between my business dealings, costing me money."

"Told you I would," Recker said. "You wanna do illegal stuff with other illegal people, that's on you and I really don't care. When you bring innocent people into things, that's when I get involved."

"I'd hardly call Mr. Brinson an innocent party."

"Oh, come on, hooking him up with a woman so he'd cheat on his wife and help you embezzle funds isn't exactly the same as comparing him to a thief or a murderer who does it because he enjoys it."

Nowak walked around Recker's chair, putting her hand on his shoulder and running it across his back. "You know something? I really like you. I really do. I'm not sure what it is about you, but I find you have a magnetic personality that draws me closer to you."

"If only I had a dollar for every time I heard that."

"But there's one thing that really irritates me about you and it's that high moral compass you walk around with."

"I'm surprised there's only one."

"You see, you're already proving to be a pain."

"Not the first time I've heard that either," Recker said.

"And I can't have you going around, continuing to interfere in my business. Especially as I'm going up against Vincent."

"Is this where you and I part company?"

Nowak put her hand on his face and rubbed his cheek. "It doesn't have to be that way. Not if we come to an understanding."

"Such as?"

"Well, let's look at your options here. I will offer you a deal because I like you and I really value what you could bring to the table."

"Encouraging."

"Agree to help me, not interfere in my business again, and you can walk out of here with all your body parts still attached as God has given you."

"And if I don't agree?" Recker asked.

"Well, I'm afraid you're kind of a loose cannon. And as much as I like you, I can't afford to have you running around the city getting in my way again. So, as a consequence, you'd have to be buried here." Since Recker was tied up and couldn't reject her advances, Nowak sat on his lap then kissed him on the lips. "Or you could join me." Nowak then kissed him again, hoping to weaken his defenses and bring him to his senses.

Recker still wasn't the least bit interested in joining her but knew he had to do something quickly. Though he assumed somebody was coming, thanks to leaving his com on, he couldn't be sure when that help was arriving. The only thing he could do was stall.

"So, what's it gonna be?" Nowak asked.

Recker softened his stance, trying to make it seem like he was interested in her. "Doesn't seem like it's much of a choice, does it?"

"I don't think so."

"I guess my mind's made up then."

Nowak then planted another kiss on him, Recker pretending that he enjoyed this one. "I promise you won't regret it."

"So, what do we do first?" Recker asked.

"I have plans. We'll discuss them later."

Though Nowak was enjoying sitting on his lap, she finally got off him, though she couldn't resist touching him some more. She eventually was able to break her hand away from him and walked back over to Hernandez.

"Untie him," Nowak said.

Hernandez looked at Recker, not really sure about doing what he was told. He didn't trust him as much as his boss seemed to. "You sure that's a good idea?"

"Yes. He'll play ball with us."

"How can you be so sure?"

"He'll do what he's told."

"But what if he takes off after we leave here and we don't see him again?" Hernandez asked.

"We don't have to worry about that. Because he won't be on his own from here on out. We will always have a few people with him to make sure he complies with what we want."

"But we can't have someone with him twenty-four, seven, can we?"

Nowak smiled. "Why not? If he's not with you guys, then he'll be with me."

"OK, if you say so."

"Untie him and bring him to the new place," Nowak said, walking toward the door.

"Where are you going?"

"I have something else to deal with right now. Take him to the new place and wait until I get there."

"As you say."

Nowak left the building, taking with her the three men who she left waiting outside. Once she was gone, Hernandez went back over to Recker. He still didn't have a good feeling about untying him and letting him loose. He wasn't as confident as his boss he was going to join their team. Hernandez took a deep breath, then walked around the back of Recker and started cutting loose the rope. Recker stretched his arms around, then got up from the chair.

"Boss seems to put a lot of faith in you," Hernandez said. "Me... not so much. You do anything other than what she tells you and I'll put a bullet in you myself."

"I'll remember that."

"See that you do."

Recker put his hand out, hoping to get what belonged to him. "Can I have my guns back now?"

Hernandez smiled and shook his head. "Not just yet. Not until we actually see you're upholding your end of things."

"Well how am I gonna do that if I don't have my stuff?"

"When the time comes."

Then, Recker heard Jones' voice in his ear. "Mike, Chris will be there momentarily." Recker tilted his head and moved it around so it wasn't obvious someone was in his ear. It was a good thing his com device was so small it wasn't noticeable unless someone really was looking for it.

"All right, let's go," Hernandez said, pointing to the door with his gun. Recker walked in front of everyone. Once he got to the door and opened it, he stopped. "Why are you stopping?"

"Sorry," Recker replied. "Habit. I never go through a door without knowing what's on the other side. Something I picked up over the years."

Hernandez wasn't impressed and didn't want to hear it. "Keep going."

Recker did as he was told and stepped outside, looking around to see if he could see Haley. He couldn't, but he sure hoped he was there. He was only a couple of feet from the car when another voice boomed in his ear.

"Hernandez is to your left," Haley said. "You take him, I'll take out the others. I'll shoot on your move."

Seeing as how he was almost at the car, Recker wasted no time in following Haley's directions. Almost immediately, he twirled around and rushed Hernandez, spearing him in the gut with his shoulder, knocking them both to the ground. The blow from Recker knocked the gun from Hernandez' hand. As they wrestled on the ground, the other three removed their guns to help their teammate. Haley was on a rooftop on the building directly facing the food factory entrance. As soon as the other three removed their guns, Haley opened fire with his sniper rifle. Within the span of a few seconds, he had successfully taken out the other three men without much of a struggle. The men didn't know where the shots were coming from and didn't have a chance to make it back inside the building for cover.

After a couple minutes of wrestling, Recker got the upper hand after delivering a few punches to the side of Hernandez' face. Recker reached for the gun lying on the ground and grabbed hold of it. Just as he did, Hernandez hurriedly removed one of his other guns to try to stop Recker's progress. Recker quickly spun around on the ground and fired three shots rapidly in succession, all of which lodged into Hernandez' midsection. The man instantly dropped to his knees, then face down on the ground as the blood he was losing quickly soaked the rest of his body, as well as the concrete underneath him.

Recker got up and checked each of the men to see if any were still breathing, though none of them were. He then looked for

Haley but didn't see where he was. A few seconds later, he noticed Haley's car zooming in. Recker quickly hopped in as they sped out of the area.

"A little close for comfort," Recker said.

Haley smiled. "Had it all the way. Where to?"

"Let's head to that hotel Nowak's staying."

"Why?"

"Because I don't like her."

"Fair enough."

Recker let Jones know he was OK and where they were heading. Though Jones objected to their destination, Recker didn't pay much mind to him and went, anyway. When they got to the hotel, they cautiously moved through it, not sure if Nowak's men would be waiting for them. Recker thought it unlikely since he didn't think word would get back to her so soon, but he couldn't say for sure. They eschewed the elevator and went up the stairs.

"What's the plan?" Haley asked, trying to keep up with his partner, though he was falling a little behind due to his leg.

"Shoot whoever gets in our way."

"Oh. Good plan."

"You all right?" Recker asked.

"A little sore. No big deal."

"I can take care of it on my own."

"Don't worry about it. I'm fine. Do it like last time?"

"No, I think they're on to that trick by now. Let's just rush them."

Once they finally got to Nowak's floor, they could immediately tell something was different. They looked toward her room and didn't see the guards. That was a red flag right away. She wouldn't have left herself unprotected like that.

"Maybe they're all inside having a powwow," Haley said.

"I kind of doubt it."

The two men hurried over to the door. Recker took a quick

jiggle of the handle to see if it was open, but it was locked. Recker then bent down to pick the lock as Haley stood guard and watched for any unwelcome visitors passing by. After a minute, Recker had the door unlocked. He slowly opened it as the two men stepped inside. Once in, they split off to check the room. But there was no one there. After a few minutes, the two met back up in the main room.

"Empty," Haley said.

Recker sighed, wishing Nowak was there. If she was, he could've ended her entire organization then and there. Now, they'd probably have to start over.

They stayed a few minutes to search the drawers, cabinets, and closets to see if any information had been left behind, but there was nothing of value. They let Jones know their findings then went straight back to the office. Jones was already hard at work trying to find out Nowak's new location when the boys got back there.

"Anything?" Recker asked.

Jones voiced a loud sigh, which was all the response that Recker needed. "I'm afraid not."

"She just up and vanished?"

"She checked out of her room yesterday."

"And you can't get a fix on her now?"

"Unfortunately, not," Jones answered. "Everything I used to track her before has been no help. Phone, cards, everything's been silent the last few days."

"Most likely she's switched everything," Haley said.

"Undoubtedly so."

"Damn," Recker said. "If she had stayed one more day, we could've ended things." He was more than a little disappointed in the developments, as he knew that meant Nowak would be around a lot longer, since she'd now have some time to regroup. He viewed Nowak as a much more dangerous threat than Vincent as she didn't seem like she was as interested as Vincent was in having a business arrangement that benefited both of them. She was only out for herself.

"The only thing we can do right now is put her to the side and work on other things," Jones said. "At some point I'm sure she'll turn up and we'll run into her again."

"Sooner rather than later, probably."

"Yes, well, in the meantime, we can start working again on our own things."

Recker then looked at Haley. "Assuming you're well enough to keep things going for a week, you can do it without me, if that's all right."

"Works for me," Haley said.

"Why?" Jones asked. "Where do you intend on going?"

"You forget that Mia thing?"

"Oh yes. I had forgotten for a moment."

"She hasn't."

"You'd like to go now?"

"No time like the present," Recker answered.

"Well, since it's relatively slow at the moment, I see no harm in it," Jones said.

"Good, because I never thought I'd say this."

"What?"

"I think I need a vacation."

ALSO BY MIKE RYAN

ABOUT THE AUTHOR

Mike Ryan is a USA Today Bestselling Author. He lives in Pennsylvania with his wife, and four children. He's the author of the bestselling Silencer Series. Visit his website at www.mikeryanbooks.com to find out more about his books, and sign up for his newsletter. You can also interact with Mike via Facebook, and Instagram.

facebook.com/mikeryanauthor
instagram.com/mikeryanauthor

Printed in Great Britain
by Amazon

26280900R00423